TRAGIC - MANIC - PANIC

ROOK AND RONIN

NEW YORK TIMES BESTSELLING AUTHOR

JA HUSS

ISBN: 978-1-950232-34-5

Edited by RJ Locksley
Cover Design by JA Huss

Tragic

Rook & Ronin Book One

J. A. HUSS

CHAPTER ONE

Rook

Life. Sucks.

I step off the curb, dodge a few cars, and head straight for the Starbucks. I can't even remember the last time I had Starbucks, but today, with only ten dollars to my name, I'm getting a ten-freaking-dollar coffee. Quality Cleaning can kiss my ass—I might be poor and I might not have a whole lot going for me right now, but I've never been a thief and I've never been a liar. If they want to try and charge me for stealing a ring I never took, they'll get a fight.

I know it was that stupid Delores who stole that ring. I know it. She blamed it on me and now I'm fired, still living out of a homeless shelter, and on the completely wrong side of town.

I take a deep breath and smell the coffee.

Coffee.

I haven't had a decent coffee in like… well, maybe ever. Even in my other life I wasn't the kind of girl who hung out on the trendy side of town. And this place is definitely trendy, lots of bars—and not the kind that have strippers or that look like they only serve old men at eight in the morning. The kind that serve young people who are out looking to get laid on Friday nights. And men who like sports. The baseball stadium is very close, so there are lots of sports bars.

All the people who are going in and out of this Starbucks look like they work around here, like they belong. I look down at my clothes and wonder if I fit in. My jeans are not designer, shit, they're not even Levis. And my hoodie is from the thrift store near the shelter.

Who gives a crap?

I let a young hipster couple exit and then push my way into the crowded shop. The line is long, but I've got time, so I stand there with more patience than pretty much everyone else in that place, and wait my turn. The barista is patient as I ask questions and I order the biggest latte size they have, ask for real cream and hazelnut syrup, and top it off with whip cream instead of foam.

It takes another ten minutes for them to make my frothy drink and then finally, I take a look around for a place to sit. I have to stand for a few minutes but eventually a man leaves a table and I swoop in, sit with my back to the wall, facing the door, and try to pretend I'm just another girl on a break, getting her usual drink before going back to her trendy job.

That I have a job, period. That I'm not out on the streets, that I'm not a victim, that I'm not scared shitless that Jon will somehow find me.

I take a deep breath and let it out like the counselors at the shelter taught me. This fear of Jon is not rational. I realize this. I mean, I've been gone two months now and no one has even come looking. I gave them a fake name at the shelter, but the maid service needed a real name, and I've worked there for six weeks and no one came looking.

And that sorta bugs me because I pretty much disappeared off the face of the Earth and no one even noticed.

It makes me feel small and inconsequential.

I sip my drink as I look around, the hot liquid soothing me and making my day special. I wonder what Charles is doing these days? He's been gone from the shelter for a few weeks now. Had to go back to jail for a week to serve out some sentence for… something. I never asked. Never wanted to know to be honest. And then he just never came back.

It's that way with pretty much everyone at the shelter. They come and they go. Everything is transient. Just like Starbucks. The people come in, get what they need to get through their day, and then they leave.

A four-seater table opens up next to me and a swarm of tall, thin girls sneak in and claim it, sighing in relief that they found a place to sit and chat, tossing their well-conditioned hair, and clasping their well-manicured hands around tall expensive cardboard cups of coffee.

My hair is a dull dark brown. If I take really good care of it, it's shiny and near-black. But it's barely getting minimal care right now, let alone good.

And I just spent my last ten dollars on a coffee so this hair has no hope. I laugh a little under my breath. As if hair was my biggest problem. *You have no money for* food, *Rook.*

Man, I am so stupid.

The beautiful girls, I learn though eavesdropping, are all models. It figures, right? The select few in the world get everything, while the rest of us poor jerks get to scrub toilets for a living just to make enough to buy food and sleep in a homeless shelter at night.

One girl, a red-head with skin as fair and smooth as ivory, complains loudly about the last photographer who refused to let her even do a test shoot, whatever that means. Another girl passes around a business card, all the others talking about how he's an asshole and they've all been turned away. The red-head who was complaining, thinking she is someone special, realizes to my satisfaction that she's as plain and unwanted as the rest.

The blonde with glossy pink lips grabs the card from the other girl's hand and flicks it in the air. I watch as it sails across the table and plunks me in the head. All the girls start laughing in a fit, grab their coffees, and make a quick escape.

I pick up the card and study it. It's thick and white and says:

Antoine Chaput—Photographer of Artful Beings

That's all. No number, no contact information at all. I flip it over and there's some very messy handwriting in blue ink. An address and the words—*Test shoot, 1 PM, May 17.*

Under the address are the words that make my mouth

drop open. *$100 per hour if booked.* The *if booked* is underlined, like whoever wrote it was trying to make a point.

I fish out my phone to check the time. Just short of twelve thirty.

Even though the data plan I purchased months ago for emergencies is almost maxed out, I plug the address into the GPS app on my phone and bite my lip as it pulls up the map. It's only a few blocks over and suddenly my sucky day is getting a little brighter. I shrug on my pack and rush out the door, half running with excitement, half with desperation, towards a job I have no chance of ever getting, especially dressed like this.

But for the first time in a very long time, I feel something besides anger and hopelessness and shame.

I feel a spark and I don't get many of those, so no matter what happens, I'm gonna see where it takes me.

It's windy for mid-May and by the time I make the old warehouse building containing the photographer's studio my hair is a freaking mess. I try to smooth it down a little after the heavy lobby door swishes closed behind me, but it's pretty useless.

I climb the stairs to the fourth floor and arrive at Antoine Chaput's translucent glass door very winded and in complete disarray. There are two names on the door. *Antoine Chaput, Photographer*, of course. But underneath it says *Elise Flynn, Stylist.*

I can hear yelling inside.

And crying.

And then things are breaking and I sink to the floor in fear as Jon's fists come into my mind. But it's like a bad car accident on the freeway—something terrible is happening. I refuse to move my feet, I refuse to plug my ears, and despite the fact that I'm scared shitless by whatever is happening behind that door, I can't turn away from my stolen appointment with Antoine Chaput.

A half-naked young girl bursts through the door, wearing only a pair of pretty panties and matching bra, pulling on her expensive designer jeans as she hops down the hallway, and then before she even buttons them up, she tugs a sweatshirt over her head and spies me on the floor in the corner.

"I'd hide from him too! He's such an asshole! I hate you, Antoine!" she screams. "And I will never," she picks up some anger here, "*never* let you photograph me again, even if you beg me!" She slips on some cute ballet flats, hopping once again to maintain balance, and is about to leave when she has a thought. I can see her thinking because her eyes roll up a little and her head tilts—like she's a cartoon character with a comment bubble coming out of her mouth. "And I'm keeping the lingerie. Asshole!"

She already said he was an asshole, but I suppose when you're that angry a varied vocabulary isn't the first thing on your mind. The irate girl turns back to me then. "You better be ready. He's in a fit today and I'll never work for him again!"

And then she storms down the stairs, dragging her large bag behind her, still swearing and punctuating her one-sided conversation with the occasional, "Ha!" as she descends.

I stare dumbfounded at the empty stairwell wondering what the hell I'm doing here.

"She's overreacting. Don't let her get to you."

I look over at the man with the deep voice and my mouth drops open a little. He is even more beautiful than the girl who just left. To call him well-built doesn't do his body justice and I can see quite a bit of it because he's only half-dressed. In fact, he's still buttoning up his jeans, tucking in his pockets as he stands there next to me.

He catches me eyeing his fingers and laughs. "Sorry, today was supposed to be a sexy shoot." He shrugs it off like he comes out in the hallway buttoning up his pants all the time.

"Uh"—I clear my throat a little—"yeah."

Oh my God, I am so dumb. Uh, yeah? That's all I can think of to say?

He raises one eyebrow at me and reveals a slow smile that climbs up his face. His eyes are an electric blue and they remind me of my own. I've never seen anyone who had blue eyes like mine—I'm not bragging or anything, it's just a feature that I was born with, something that sets me apart. One of the few things actually.

He notices me studying his eyes and then he bends down to me. I instinctively scoot away from him, pushing myself back into the corner as my heart starts to race. He takes the hint and stands back up. "Sorry, didn't mean to invade your space or anything."

Another voice snaps my attention back to what I'm doing. "OK, let's go, girl. Get in here, you heard Clare, he's in a fit. So let's just humor him and maybe we can all go home early, what do you say?"

I nod, still cowering on the floor.

"Oh, come now." A petite woman with short-cropped blonde hair pushes the half-naked guy out of the way and continues talking. "He's already cooling off. Clare pushes his buttons, everyone knows she's difficult. Do you have your invitation?"

She's looking at the card in my hand so I stand and thrust it at her. Half-naked guy is still watching me and just as I'm about to brush past his bare chest, he stops me with a hand on my arm. I pull it away quickly. "Don't."

"Sweetheart, you won't get far here if we can't touch you."

I scowl at him and swallow hard.

"It's a test shoot, Ronin, don't get her worked up." And then the woman takes my hand and leads me inside.

Ronin mumbles out a response as he follows and then the door closes behind me and I expect all manner of terrible things to start happening, but all the woman does is push me over to what looks like a shampoo station. She takes my bag, tucks it into a corner, and then motions me into a changing area and tells me to take off my hoodie.

I look around for Ronin, but he's disappeared. "But I don't have anything on underneath."

"Nothing?"

I shake my head.

"Well, that's not very smart." She rummages through a drawer and throws a tank top at me. "Put that on."

I do and before I can even turn the corner of the little screened-in changing area, she's pushing me back into the chair. "I don't know who your stylist is—what did you say your name was?"

"Rook Walsh," I say weakly.

"Oh, yes. I remember now," she says as she picks up the ends of my very long hair, "*Rook*. You need to tell that stylist of yours that these ends need a touch-up. Antoine prefers *au naturel*, but it must be healthy—so trim these ends if he invites you back. Today is just a test shoot, but we've got good light coming in the afternoon and you know how Antoine loves *au naturel* light." She winks at me and I laugh.

"I'm Elise, by the way. Antoine's lover."

She says it so casually, this word. *Lover*. It implies so much more than girlfriend. *Lover*. It drips with sex. I smile at her. "Nice to meet you—"

But she's dousing me with water and my words get lost in the feeling of having my hair washed by a professional again. In the shelter I'm lucky if I get a shower twice a week. You have to work in the kitchen for three days to get one shower. But I had one last night, so I'm not too dirty.

Elise's fingertips start massaging my head and then she squirts some tropical-smelling shampoo on it. She lathers it up, starting at the bottom and then working the thick froth into my scalp. It feels so good I almost moan with pleasure.

Then the rinse again. The water trickles down my scalp, sometimes a stray stream will slide down the edge of my cheek and it sends a shiver up my whole body. I feel myself relax just as Elise wrings out the excess water and then very carefully works the conditioner in.

"Long day, Rook?" she asks me.

"Yeah," I reply, sedated and warm. "I got fired today."

"Oh, I'm sorry. It's hard to make it as a model, I know. When I was just starting out I had to work all sorts of odd jobs. Waitressing, bartender, I was even a tow truck dispatcher at night. Whatever it took to keep my nail appointments and have a nice wardrobe. I suppose it's that way for you now, huh?"

I open my eyes. "Sorta."

"What kind of job was it?"

"Cleaning houses."

"Oh, yeah, I've done that too, those were the worst. I got accused of stealing once, and I never even took anything."

I try to sit up but she pushes me back down. "Me too! I didn't take that ring, Delores did, and they fired me."

She clicks her tongue at me and shakes her head. "Well, you're pretty enough and skinny enough and your legs and hair are long. Antoine likes all these features you have—so if you just do exactly what he tells you, maybe you'll find a better job today. Right?"

"I'd like that," I whisper.

Elise smiles. "You're not like the others, Rook. You're calm and quiet, and a bit tragic, if you don't mind me saying."

"I don't mind it." *Because it's true*, I don't add.

"Antoine is hard to work for, I won't lie. But you might do, so just keep your mouth shut and do everything he asks."

I nod as the water sprays down my face again and keep my mouth shut for the rest of the time. I catch that Ronin guy walking around a little in the part of the studio I can see. He looks over at me each time, almost stopping to take a second look as Elise pulls and tugs my hair through her various brushes.

He's watching me.

CHAPTER TWO

Ronin

I leave Elise with the new girl and join Antoine in his office. As older sisters go I could do a lot worse than Elise, and since she raised me since I was ten, I am eternally grateful and only want her to be happy. But honestly, Antoine drives me up a wall. She's been dating him forever, so he practically raised me as well, but a father figure he is *not.*

Describing him as an artist should really do the trick—he's got all the stereotypical attributes like selfish, asshole, romantic, asshole, creative, asshole, temperamental, asshole. I could go on and on, but what's the point. He's an asshole.

And since he refused to speak to me and Elise in anything but French for the first five years we all lived together, we're both now fluent.

So I guess I can thank him for that.

But French is a pretty stupid language to know when you live in Denver. Maybe if I move to Quebec or Paris it might come in handy. And actually, we did go to Paris with him last year to do a show, but he hates it there just as much we did, so I doubt we'll be going back.

He speaks more English now, but that's only because he has to talk to more people than just Elise and me. Back when he was just starting out it was just us, so he could get by without speaking English if he wanted. But now, Antoine Chaput is big time and he's got a lot of people keeping this place going.

And none of them speak French.

"She'll get over it, Antoine," I tell him as I take a seat across from his desk. "Just let her walk out."

Antoine is running his hands through his hair, messing it all up and making himself look ridiculous, but he is about to flip out over this Clare shit, I can tell, so I run interference. "She's on the rag today, she told me. And you know how bitchy she is on the rag."

She doesn't have her period today, she's just a raging bitch and not in her right mind every day, but this puts the blame on her instead of him, and that's what he wants—so fuck it. I give him what he wants to keep the peace.

"She's done. I don't want to see her again! No more!"

I shrug. He says this at least once a month. Clare walks out pissed off all the time when we let her work, it's nothing new or extraordinary. They do this dance so often, it's like a couple of dorky kids doing the box-step at senior prom.

I reach over and grab an apple off the perpetual fruit basket Antoine has on his desk and take a seat in the deep leather couch that gives me a full view of the studio so I can watch for the new girl. Antoine is still mumbling about Clare.

"English, Antoine," I say as I chew.

"Ne pas parler la bouche pleine!"

"Clare's only purpose in life right now is to drive you crazy, let her go." I swallow so he'll stop concentrating on the food in my talking mouth and listen to my words instead. "Fuck her. There's a new girl out there, did you see her?"

He perks up at this, but then he sighs and collapses into his desk chair. "No. She's probably no good. I have no one for this campaign. No one."

"She'll work, Antoine. She's tall, thin, black hair, blue eyes—like mine," I add, because my eyes look like someone got carried away with the special effects in a sci-fi movie. My peepers have made me quite a bit of cash over the past few years and the fact that this girl has eyes like mine is pretty interesting. "If ever there was a girl who is crying out that she's TRAGIC, it's this one. Just wait until you see her."

I take another bite of apple and he sighs, trying to peek out the door and see something, but not be noticed for noticing. I can hear them talking, just faintly, but I'm intrigued. "Want me to go spy?" I ask, smiling.

"*Oui*," he grins back.

That grin says we have to stick together or they will overpower us. They being woman, us being men. He's forever on this guy thing with me, like we are in some secret fraternal society—sometimes these secret plans even come with a wink. I let him have his fun and get up to go spy. I want to see her again anyway. Before she comes out and has to pretend to be someone else.

"I want a full report, and don't let Ellie see you, or she'll complain to me later."

"*Oui*," I reply.

CHAPTER THREE

I sit on a stool near the entrance to Elise's studio and eat my apple, chewing casually as I watch Ed and Alex mess with some sets. They have a whole team of people to handle the lights and move shit around, but this is all for the TRAGIC campaign, not this girl's test shoot.

If you're lucky enough to get an invitation from Antoine to come sit for him, you get one shot to make him fall in love. If he does, you might get another invitation, but only if he has an immediate need for you. If he doesn't love you at first sight, i.e. if he needs Elise to make you pretty or alluring, or sexy, or tragic—whatever—he won't ever ask you back. Elise is here to bring out the mood he wants, like a make-up artist in the movies. She's not here to make you into the thing Antoine is looking for. Either you are that thing, or you're not.

And I know this girl is tragic. He's gonna love her because I've watched Antoine choose hundreds of girls over the past twelve years and I love her.

Her look, I clarify to myself. I love *her look*.

I toss my apple core into a nearby wastebasket and listen in as the girls talk on the other side of the partitioned wall. Elise will have to fill me in later because I can't really make out what they're saying.

Test shoots last for about an hour or so, sometimes less. Sometimes more, but if Antoine goes over an hour with you on a test shoot, he's definitely in love with you.

When Elise went for her test shoot he took pictures of her

for five hours. Then he made us move in with him so she'd never leave. He fell hard for her even though she's nothing like any of the models that come through the studio. She's small, tiny really, she has the most severe pixie haircut to match her fairy frame, and she's quiet and graceful. She's like a little dancer, not a bitchy model like Clare.

And that's how I know Antoine is a good guy, even if he does act like an asshole most of the time.

He loves my sister. And my sister is good people.

I get up and walk casually towards the front door, which is located just a few steps away from Elise's station, and peek in as I walk by. Elise starts shaking her head at me as I watch the girl hide under her long hair. Elise has it all combed over her head in different ways, trying to partition it off for blow-drying. They don't talk now, the dryer is too loud, but I'm pretty sure the girl is watching me from under her hair. I can see the brightness of her eyes.

I continue walking and go through the door, then jog down the stairs and go out to the street. It's just a way to pass time and it will give me another excuse to walk past again in a few minutes when I go back up.

Downstairs it's busy because there's a baseball game today. We rent out our parking lot on game days since we're practically across the street from the stadium. Our lot is already full, the attendants standing guard to prevent anyone else from coming in. The streets are packed with people and there are lots of bars and restaurants to make the place look safe and trendy. And for the most part, it is. But at night, you do not want to be a girl alone in this neighborhood.

I wave to a couple of guys I recognize from elementary school standing on a corner handing out flyers. Probably for a party this weekend.

Our building is an old factory that Antoine bought back when the property values in Five Points were shit. It's six stories tall, but we gutted the top three floors to create the massive windows that allow for natural light to pour into the studio. It's all about the light with Antoine. One half of the sixth floor contains our apartments. I have one and Elise and Antoine have one. There's a large open terrace off the studio where we do most of our outside shots. Most of the other floors are either empty or used for artistic shoots.

The neighborhood has grown up with the new stadium. It used to be pretty bad, but after living here in Antoine's studio for the past twelve years, this building and neighborhood, crime statistics and all, is the only place I'd ever call home. I people-watch for a few more minutes, then head back up and enter the studio just as Elise is tugging the girl across the room. I want to talk to her so bad, but I catch Antoine in the doorway to his office and Elise jerks her head at me as she tells the girl to wait near the window.

I watch her walk and look over at Antoine again. He's smiling, but he's talking in French about Clare. She called him and gave him an earful and I know from the tone of his voice that Clare is wearing him down, weaseling her way back into another job. I sigh and follow Elise to try and calm Antoine's nerves.

The new girl will have to wait a little longer because no matter how many times I tell myself I don't give one fucking shit about Clare, I can't help myself. I still do.

CHAPTER FOUR

Rook

Elise walks towards Antoine, but turns back when I start to follow. "Go over to the window, he wants to shoot by the window today. And just do what you're told, OK?"

I nod and she walks away with a brisk pace as I make my way to the window, looking up and gawking at how magnificent this place is.

Studio is not really the right word for it, it's several stories tall, and now that I think about it, it's the top floor of the building, even though we're only on the fourth floor of what appears to be a six-story building on the outside. There's a long modern staircase made up of concrete stairs and metal railings that leads up the far side of the room near Antoine's office, and the second story is loft-like with a set of double doors in the middle of the open hallway.

When I turn to the windows, I can totally see why Antoine would want to shoot pictures over here. They are massive. Two stories tall, each ten feet wide and the golden sunshine pouring through them lights the whole place up like heaven. Like angels with trumpets are about to fly in and celebrate the beauty that is this room.

The floors are a polished warm oak, and the whole place is filled with different set-ups. Like sets or something for photographers. Ladders and those umbrella things that you see in photo shoots to reflect light this way and that.

Antoine, Ronin, and Elise are arguing in the back room, but I can't understand them because they are all speaking

French. Suddenly the door slams and I jump a little at the noise, but then enjoy the silence as they finish their argument in private. I'm sure Antoine took one look at me and refused to even bother getting out his camera.

I peer through the window and enjoy the view. It's spectacular and looks out onto a busy street. There are a few tall buildings nearby, but it's mostly small businesses contained within old historic buildings—various stores, restaurants, and bars. I watch the people below, going about their lives. I watch the women in particular. How many of them have lived with abuse? I try not to think about it really. It's over now. It's behind me and I'm sorta moving on. There have been a few incidents at the shelter with some of the druggie men, but I have a knife. I cut one guy across the arm when he touched me in my sleep. Since then they've left me alone.

I hate that place though. And all these women over on this side of town seem happy. I'm sure there are plenty of them who suffer abuse and are good at hiding it like I was, but from this vantage point, it seems unlikely that they are anywhere near the type of situation I was in back in Chicago.

Jon and I met in high school. Well, I was in high school, and that's only on a technicality because I never actually *went* to school. He was five years older. I realize now that lots of abusers look for young girls because they are easier to control and scare into silence, but at the time I just thought it was cool that an older guy liked me. He thought I was sexy, he told me things no boy ever told me. He treated me like a woman even though I was a girl.

I liked it at first. That he was tall and strong. He had his own place, a car, a job, a brand new college degree. It seemed like a perfect opportunity for me. A way to escape my stressful life and let someone else think about all these things people require for survival for once. No teenager should have to worry about living day to day the way I did.

So I let him take care of me. And maybe for a little while I could fool myself into thinking his strange obsession with controlling everything about me was normal, or a way to express his love.

But then his fists got involved, and by that time I was so dependent on him there wasn't a chance in hell I could make it on my own any more. He never lifted a hand to me at first, but slowly, over the course of several months, he alienated me from the few friends I had, asked me to quit my job, and moved us out to the country where he had access to a small family home that was sitting unoccupied.

And that's when it all changed. He spied on me, he monitored things like gas and groceries. Weird shit. And I was just too stupid to figure it out. Or just too young maybe.

Life in Chicago was the only life I knew before coming to Denver. It started out better than it ended up, that's for sure. I used to have a family. A mom at least. But she's been gone for a while now. I have nothing left of her, not even a picture. So the image of her burned into my memory is all that I have.

I'm pretty sure that memory is a bit skewed. For example, I picture her in a dress with an apron, but I'm almost positive that I'm thinking of one of the moms on RetroTube at night, and not my mother.

My mother didn't bake pies, she smoked crack.

But that's what happens when all you have left is a memory. Things change over time, other memories and images invade and reshape it.

You forget things.

And mostly you tend to forget bad things and I find that to be dangerous. Because if you forget the bad things, chances are those bad things will come back to get you again.

I try really hard to keep my memories of living with Jon fresh so I don't forget.

And I don't even care if this is healthy or whatever. The counselors at the shelter hinted that it's best to let the past go, but I don't agree and it's my life, my death. So I'm the one who gets to make the final decision.

I feel satisfied at that because I love making my own

decisions.

Like today, for instance. I walked out of that job after they accused me of stealing. They did fire me first, and I could've stayed and groveled, but I didn't. I walked away.

Now I'm homeless, jobless, and broke. But at least I'm not scared and at least I'm not broken and at least I'm not letting people who know nothing about me dictate who and what I am. Even though I spend my nights with drug addicts and criminals, and probably rapists and maybe even murderers—I am less afraid in that shelter than I was at home with my ex-boyfriend.

The noise of a camera shutter snaps me back to reality. "No, don't move, Rook. You're perfect right there."

I take my attention back to the window and the memories, ignoring Antoine. If that's what he wants, then fuck it. What do I care? This whole thing is probably a set-up anyway, to get me to do porn movies or something.

The shutter continues to snap, but Antoine becomes more and more chatty. Directing me to move my arm, or tilt my head, or close my eyes, or frown.

I do it all just like he asks. Just like Elise told me to.

And I never once smile.

And he never once asks me to.

"What are you thinking about, Rook?" Antoine says later, when he's fussing with his camera and everyone else except that Ronin guy has left.

I look over at Antoine. He's tall and thick. Not fat by any means, just thick. His hair is dark and his eyes are blue, like mine, like that Ronin guy. He's wearing dark jeans and a black t-shirt, and for an older guy, late thirties maybe, he's handsome. Not hot or cute, but definitely handsome in a chiseled jaw and scratchy face kind of way.

I can see why Elise is his lover.

"None of your business," I answer him after my pause.

His reaction is lost on me because I turn back to the window.

"Do you enjoy modeling?"

I shrug. "It's a job."

"Do you have a book?"

I have no idea what that means so I just say, "No."

This time his reaction is not lost on me because he bellows out a laugh. "No? If you're a model you have a book. Show it to me." He pulls out a card and offers it. "Here is my e-mail, send me your photos."

I take the card and meet his eyes this time. "I am not a model and I have no book, whatever that is. I just need a job. The invitation card said $100 an hour. I just need the money."

"Test shoots pay in pictures, child. You don't get paid for today, but I'll give you a CD with your images, just give me your address and I'll send it when it's ready."

I'm the one who bellows out a laugh this time. "Pictures? I don't need any fucking pictures! I need money!" I walk back over to the style station and Elise is watching me with a nervous expression. "Where's my bag? I'm leaving. What a waste of time. Pictures!"

My hoodie is still in the little changing area and I whip the tank top off and pull the thrift store bargain over my head. When I come out from behind the partition I thrust the shirt at Elise. "Here."

She accepts it and I grab my bag and walk out the door.

Pictures!

What a load of shit! I just wasted my whole day, I'm on the wrong side of town, I'll never get back to the shelter in time to get a bed, and I have no money to even take the bus because I needed a ten-dollar coffee from freaking Starbucks!

I descend the stairs as fast as I can and when I get to the bottom I just stand in front of the heavy oak door, unsure of what to do next.

I collapse on the bottom step and start to cry.

CHAPTER FIVE

Ronin

Her name is Rook. She's wrecked, those were Elise's words. She and Antoine are fighting over the TRAGIC campaign. Elise says no way, Antoine says she's the only one that can do it. With one look out his door, he picked her. He fell in photographer love with her.

I smile to myself thinking of his words, because I knew it.

We need her.

But Elise has power in this house. Elise, no matter what Antoine says, wears the pants in their relationship because if Elise is unhappy Antoine cannot live with himself. He falls to pieces when they fight.

So we work on her for almost half an hour inside the office. We wear her down, we make promises. We will watch Rook, we promise. We won't push her, we'll be careful. We promise all these things if Elise will let us keep this girl.

We want her that bad.

Of course, for very different reasons. Antoine wants to shoot her, I want to keep her. Antoine wants to take pictures of her gorgeous body and her fragile face, but I want to peel away her layers and see what's underneath. Antoine wants to make her famous and I want to hide her away in my room, under the covers of my bed, under me.

By the time we get Elise to agree to our plan, I'm half afraid the girl might've left, but as soon as we open the door she's there, next to the window where Elise left her. She's looking outside, so deep in thought she hears nothing. Not the dozens of workers who mill about in her immediate vicinity and certainly not us as we extract ourselves, full of longing (Antoine), pity (Elise) and desire (me).

We walk up behind her and still her gaze remains fixed on the people down below. You can just see she's not with us, that her thoughts are spinning and her life is chaos. It's written all over her face and Antoine sighs as he sees it too. I can read these girls almost as well as he can by now—that's my job. To get them worked up—to make these girls feel things—to bring those feelings out. Paint those feelings on their faces so when Antoine lifts his camera he's not capturing the body, but the mind.

That's why he's famous. It's not the body or face, it's the emotion. The emotion *I* make them feel.

I want to touch her right now but I hold back with Elise as Antoine starts shooting. The noise of the shutter snaps her out of her daze and I expect her to say something.

Anything—like *Am I doing it right? Is this what you want?*

But she says nothing. Antoine whispers to her, giving her small directions. She tilts her head when he asks, letting the light from the window fall across her face. It's late afternoon now, so the light is low and hazy. It bounces off her raven hair and her head turns in just the right way to catch some dying rays of sun, making her eyes sparkle. And that's how she's burned into my mind. The blackness of her hair, contrasting with the gray light behind her, and her bright blue eyes.

She catches me staring and I hold my breath. But neither of us turns away. We stare, unabashed, until Antoine's direction pulls her back into the shoot and she's lost again—guarded and unhappy, frowning and resigned. She's a blackbird sitting in a tree staring out at the world, daring the wind to come and knock her off the swaying bough.

She is wrecked, Elise is right. But she's not down yet. The look on her face is defiant.

When I look over at the clock it's well past five. Antoine has been shooting her for almost two hours. Elise left a while back but whether she's still here in the studio or up in her apartment, I have no idea. I lost track of her because my eyes are only on the girl.

Antoine does pretty well until the end. It's clear he's finished shooting and the girl is starting to look uncomfortable when he asks her what she was thinking about during the shoot.

I cringe. *No, you don't ask them! You make them want to tell you, you idiot!* I want to pull him aside and stop the crash and burn that's coming, but it's too late. She snaps at him and he pulls back when he realizes his mistake.

He turns the conversation to business and this is where it really gets interesting. She tells him she's not a model and has no portfolio. I'm just about to laugh when she starts yelling about pictures as payment.

I look back towards Elise's station and realize she forgot to explain the terms to her.

We are so off our game today. One tragic girl has disrupted all the carefully laid plans and protocols we've had in place for years.

The tragic girl storms off yelling. Antoine walks over to me and we wait together as she rants to Elise.

"You better fix this, Antoine," I say calmly, but inside I'm screaming too. "Pay the fucking girl, she needs the money."

He snorts like a fucking Frenchman. "I do not pay for test shoots."

"This," I say, turning to face him, "was no test shoot and you know it. You've got hundreds of shots in that camera. Pay her and make sure she comes back or I won't do the contract. I want her. I've put up with hundreds of stupid girls over the years for you and I've never asked you for a favor like this. I want this one, or I won't do it."

He fishes through his pocket and pulls out the cash that Clare never earned.

The studio door slams and we are all reminded that two models have walked out on us today.

"Elise!" Antoine calls, thrusting the bills out at her. "Catch her, pay her, and invite her back on Monday."

Elise grabs the money and flies out the door.

"We're in trouble, Ronin. She is trouble." He turns a little to look me in the eye, something he rarely does unless he's serious and wants me to consider his advice. "You should stay away from her, keep it professional. Or it might get messy."

I shrug. "I'll do what I want. And staying away from her isn't even in the top million things I want to do with that girl."

"Elise will hurt you if you ruin this one, Ronin. She won't tolerate another Mardee."

Fuck you, is what I think. But I don't say it, I just sigh and we wait in silence for Elise to come back.

CHAPTER SIX

Rook

My crying is not pretty, in fact, it borders on blubbering. It's a sobbing ugly cry, except I'm trying to be discreet so it comes out in weird half-silent gasps, in between hiccups and long draws of air.

When I hear footsteps I pull myself together, wipe the tears, and scoot over so whoever it is can get by. Instead they sit down next to me.

I look over at Elise and she holds out some money. "Here. He really doesn't pay for test shoots, Rook, but he likes your look and would like to extend another invitation." I take the bills and see that on top there is another little white card. I know I shouldn't, but I count the money as I sit there. Four hundred dollars in twenties. One hundred dollars for every hour I spent here today.

I look at her and start to cry again.

I know I should get up and just bolt out the door with my money, just make a quick getaway and leave this day behind, but Elise grabs my arm before I can stand up and I just don't have it in me to fight. I collapse back against the stairs and wipe my face frantically.

"Do you need help?" Elise asks after giving me a few moments to stop the tears.

I do. I mean, I really do. But I'm ashamed to have to ask for it. "No," comes out automatically.

She rubs my arm and lets out a small laugh. "OK. Well, would you believe that I am actually looking for someone to help *me* in the studio salon?"

I raise my tired and burning eyes up to her in surprise.

"Yes," she nods at me. "I am desperate, Rook. And I realize this is forward of me, but you did say you got fired today, so I was wondering if you'd like the job?"

"A job?"

"Shampoo girl. It's not much and it pays very little, but it does come with a small apartment out on the roof terrace."

"An apartment?"

"I know what you're thinking. Is the apartment nice? But I'm afraid, no, it's not. It's tiny really, and filled with old furniture. You'll probably hate it and I'm embarrassed to even offer it, but I figured you might take pity on me and accept the position and the apartment."

I just stare at her.

"What do you say?"

I cry.

She wraps her arm around me and laughs. "Just say yes, Rook. And we'll go back upstairs and you can go settle in that terribly ugly and small living space and try to forget this whole day." She stands and takes me with her and we begin to climb the stairs. "Except for the part where you got your hands on that invitation card and met us, of course. Because maybe tomorrow you'll see this was a stroke of luck for you."

She knew all along that wasn't my invitation, yet she pretended to remember me when I gave her my name. "Why are you doing this? I mean, I'm grateful and I want the job and the apartment, I really do. But you don't even know me."

"I've been you, Rook. I don't know the details, but we've all needed a twist of fate at one time or another and Antoine was mine. More than twelve years ago now. So today, I'll pay it back and be yours."

"Thank you."

"And one day, you'll be in my position and you'll stumble upon a lost girl, and you can help change her fate. And when you do, and she asks you why, you'll tell her about me."

We walk up the rest of the stairs in silence after that and when she takes me through the studio door we come face to face with Antoine and that Ronin guy again. Elise says something in French, and then they are all talking in French. But Elise does not wait for them, because she walks me around the other side of the salon wall and takes me through the massive glass doors that lead out onto the terrace.

It's one of the most beautiful places I've ever seen. Somehow, even though this is a rooftop terrace, there are two small groves of blooming cherry trees on either side. There's even grass on the ground under the trees. "How is there grass up here?" I ask as we walk past the trees and head towards a small brick building on the far side of the terrace.

"My Antoine is clever," she snickers. "It used to be a lap pool on one side," she points to the east where the sky is already getting dark, "and a family pool on the other." She points west now, towards the mountains and the setting sun. "Some developers bought this building from the city and made it into apartments back in the Seventies, but when we bought it more than a decade ago, the pools were a disaster, so instead of filling them in with concrete, we filled them in with dirt and planted those cherry trees and grass. We add something to the landscaping every year, usually another fruit tree."

It's like Mary Lennox's Secret Garden. Except it's on a rooftop in a trendy Denver neighborhood instead of the English countryside. I feel a little sad for a moment, because of all the people living in this city, only a handful of them will ever get a chance to walk through an orchard four stories up on the top of an old building.

Elise stops at the small apartment and punches in a number on the keypad. "All our doors have keyed locks. I'll bring you a code to use for the outside building after hours, but the garden studio apartment is all ones. Just five ones."

"OK." It sounds very fancy, but I can deal with five ones.

"And I might've lied a bit about the apartment."

"Oh," I say, the disappointment coming out.

"It's actually very cute. Not big, I didn't lie about that, but—" She opens the door and waves me inside.

It's the most darling place I've ever seen. The walls are painted a sunny yellow, the furniture is older, that wasn't a lie, but it's got a pretty flower pattern on it and it looks very comfortable. There's a couch, an overstuffed chair in the same pattern, a coffee table made out of oak, and two end tables. The kitchen is small, just one long counter against the far wall. There's a fridge and a small apartment-sized stove. When I look down the hallway I can see a bed dressed up in the same pattern as the living room furniture.

"It's not really a studio because it has a bedroom, but there's no door. So it's like a loft, I guess. The bathroom has a giant claw-foot tub."

I moan with happiness. "This cannot come with the shampoo girl's job."

Elise laughs. "No, I lied about that too. But if you play your cards right, Antoine and Ronin will choose you for the TRAGIC campaign and you'll be wanting to move out and get a penthouse apartment in New York like the last girl who lived here before you know it."

"The last girl?"

Elise nods. "She's the one who decorated the place, just secondhand stuff from consignment shops on the west side of town. But it's cute, right?"

It is, so I nod. There are many windows so even in the approaching darkness I can see how much light comes in.

"I don't even know what to say, Elise. I mean—" I'm truly at a loss for words. "I'm not sure how this happened. I didn't steal that invitation, I was just minding my own business over at Starbucks and these girls flipped the card away, and it hit me in the head, and—"

"It doesn't matter, Rook. That girl was never going to get asked back after her test shoot. She got an invitation as a favor to her agency. Antoine does not mess around with the models he uses. I told you he'd like your look and I was right. Now, my brother Ronin—"

Oh, I say to myself, blocking out her words but still smiling politely as she talks. Ronin is her *brother.* That's interesting.

"—so he's the one you'll want to worry about after Antoine makes his decision."

"Worry about?" I missed that. I hope she repeats it.

"Never mind him for now. Just stay out of his way, do what you're told, and don't act like the girl you watched storm out of here earlier."

"Clare?"

Elise rolls her eyes. "Yes, Clare. She's talented and has a long list of clients who want her for glamour and fashion contracts, but she's crossing lines with all of us, making Antoine very angry."

"And Ronin?"

"No, Ronin rarely gets angry with the girls. Now, I hate to do this to you, but Antoine and I are going up to the mountains for the weekend, so I have to rush out. But make yourself at home and I'll leave the building code with Ronin. I'm sure he'll be partying all weekend but Cookie's Diner down the street has a tab for our girls so you can go eat there. Just tell the hostess you belong to Ronin and it will be taken care of."

Oh, that makes my face blush! I wonder if I could even force those words to come out of my mouth? *I belong to Ronin.* It's sexy and sexist at the same time. Do I like that? I'm not sure. I'm definitely not Ronin's, that I know. I might like to look at his half-naked body, but I'm nowhere close to wanting him near me. He's one of those over-confident players, I can just tell.

And I'm not a player or even slightly confident, so I'd probably make my life a lot easier if I take Elise's advice and stay out of his way.

Before I can pull myself back to reality to keep the conversation going, Elise is making for the door and shouting out, "See you Monday."

And then I stand there. Alone.

Feeling very much like Cinder-freaking-ella.

CHAPTER SEVEN

Ronin

Elise is brimming with delight as she finds Antoine and I munching on apples in his office. "You want to explain what just happened?" I ask her.

She closes the door, still smiling. "I saved her, that's all."

"Saved her how, exactly?" Antoine questions.

"She's a mess, I think she's homeless or at the very least, not willing to go home. I gave her the garden apartment and a job washing hair in the salon."

"Washing hair!" Antoine and I bellow it together.

Elise puts her hands up like she's warding off our complaints. "She was too proud to admit she needed help, so I made it easier for her to accept it, that's all."

"So, she's not the new shampoo girl?"

"No, Ronin, she is. She has to be, or she might bolt and get a hotel room with her money or something."

"Elise, we want her for TRAGIC, she can't be shampooing hair. The other girls will swoop in like lions, she'll walk out!"

"Well, then I suggest you get those girls under control, Ronin. You let them get away with far too much. If they're mean to her and she walks out, that's your fault. Now." My tiny little sister rubs her hands together and seats herself in Antoine's lap and cups his face. "I'm ready for the mountains. Take me up there and rock my world."

"Oh, sick! You two!" Oh God, they're kissing now! "I'm leaving, does this girl need a babysitter, or what? I don't have to stick around, do I?"

I roll my eyes as Antoine and Elise finish their kiss.

"No, but she needs an exterior building code so she can come and go as she pleases," Elise says, breathless from her kiss. "Can you take her a code? I have to pack." And then she skips out of the office and heads for her and Antoine's apartment upstairs.

I look over at Antoine. His one brow is lifted all the way up to his forehead.

"What?"

"This girl, Ronin. You know what."

"Hey, you liked her too, it's not just me. She's perfect, right? She's the same type of girl you described to me last week, only that was your fantasy girl for TRAGIC. She's like a little modeling-god gift. Don't jinx it."

He's not convinced. "Elise wants to save her and you will ruin her. This will not turn out well."

"What do you mean? I have no intention of *ruining* her!"

"You know exactly what I mean. TRAGIC is named tragic for a reason. You're going to ruin this girl."

"You have no idea what you're talking about. I take care of *all* of these girls."

"You didn't take care of Mardee."

My mouth drops open, that's how stunned I am that he went there. "Antoine, dude, seriously, you're pissing me off now. What happened to her had nothing to do with me."

"No?" he asks evenly. "You brought her in here and she was swept up in the life. This Rook girl is Mardee all over again. I can see it. She's sweet and innocent now, but just wait until the money starts rolling in and the men start making offers. The agencies will be circling like vultures to get to her. It takes a strong person to navigate the maze of predators in this world, you know that."

"I told you, I'll manage her. Shit."

"You better, Ronin. Because Elise is invested in this one and that means I'm invested in her now, too. I won't stand by like last time."

"Get the hell out of here. You need a vacation. I take care of all these girls. Ask any one of them." He makes to protest and I add in, "Besides Clare! Clare doesn't count, so do not even start with me on her."

He gets up from his chair and points to his fruit basket. "Put that in the kitchen, will you? I don't want it to go to waste while we're out of town."

"Sure," I say, relieved that he's dropping the whole Mardee thing. I pick up the basket and head out, trying to shake off the feeling of shame that Mardee's name brings out in me.

She *was* out of control but I wasn't in charge of her personal life. Hell, I was only nineteen myself back then. I had just started managing the girls. It was hardly my fault that Mardee fell in with the neighborhood scum.

Besides, I've made a lot of changes since then.

I will not have a repeat of Mardee.

The kitchen is clean and quiet now that Friday afternoon has passed into Friday evening. I stick the basket of fruit in the fridge with the others so it will keep over the weekend. Antoine is a fanatic about his fruit baskets. My gaze wanders to the large window over the sink and I spy Rook's garden apartment. She has the curtains open wide and she's standing in front of it, looking out on the cherry trees.

I have to agree with Antoine. This girl is a Mardee waiting to happen and I should really make myself available tonight so she doesn't wander off and get in trouble in the rowdy neighborhood.

But why? She has no building code, so she can't leave. I smile as the idea comes to me. I'll just conveniently forget to take her the code and then I can enjoy my Friday night without having to wonder if her skinny ass needs saving. Yes, this might be easier than I thought.

I leave the kitchen, take the stairs three at time, and walk the hallway down to my apartment.

Rook can't get into trouble if she never gets the chance.

Sounds like a perfect plan to me.
What could go wrong?

CHAPTER EIGHT

Rook

Elise never appears with my building code and I'm starving. My stomach is churning with the emptiness, that's how hungry I am. The only thing I ate today was, well, a ten-dollar latte at Starbucks doesn't count as food, really. So I have not eaten anything today.

I peek out the window at the studio building. From the front room I can see the two-story windows on the fourth and fifth floors, and then on the sixth floor, there are smaller windows. There was a light on in one a few hours ago, but now everything is dark. I'm pretty sure there's a kitchen inside, but my code for the garden apartment won't open the doors that go into the studio.

So I'm like a prisoner out here in the secret garden.

I'm a secret prisoner.

It makes me uncomfortable. I mean, I really don't know these people at all. I met them today and the one I talked to has left for the weekend and the one who was supposed to take care of things is nowhere to be found. I wander the massive garden terrace. Pace, actually. I pace the terrace. And what's worse is that I can hear all sorts of people down below. This building is smack in the middle of a very active area of Denver filled with bars and all sorts of nightlife.

And I'm a secret prisoner in a secret garden.

I walk along the edge of the terrace and peer over to see what's happening down there. Lots of people. Lots of loud people which in my experience means lots of drunk people.

Down the street is a huge neon sign that flashes an image of a Fifties waitress and the letters, *Cookie's Diner!* If I get down I can go to Cookie's and tell them I belong to Ronin and get free food.

Screw that, I have money. I don't need to belong to Ronin to feed myself.

I huff out some air and start to get annoyed. My stomach hurts, dammit! I look up at the window where the lights were one more time and spy a fire escape. Am I that desperate that I'm thinking about using the fire escape?

My feet are already across the terrace and I'm hopping over the short iron railing that allows access to the stairs. I've never been on a fire escape. I grew up in foster homes and maybe Chicago isn't the best place to be a foster kid, but they always placed me in actual houses, I'll give them that.

But I've seen them on TV. You just hop over, climb down, and then hang onto that ladder thing at the bottom where it delivers you safely to the ground. Easy. My feet bang down the metal stairs and when I get to the last level there's a lever that looks like it wants to be pulled. I release it and the ladder drops down to the ground.

I am minutes away from food!

But voices down the alley stop me. There's a group of guys just turning the corner. If I hustle I can get down on the ground and be back out on the busy street before they get close. I climb down and they start calling out to me.

Shit, Rook! This is not a good situation to be in. I drop to the ground and make my way out to the street. The people are still loud and there's even more of them than there were before, but at least I'm not alone in a dark alley.

Cookie's is on the other side of the street, but that's the busy side where all the bars are, so I keep to my side and walk down the block, shoving my hand in my pocket to grab my money.

Shit again! I look back up at the Chaput Building wistfully. My money is still upstairs. I am so stupid. I turn around to go back up the fire escape to get my money and see the rowdy guys from the alley turn the corner.

I spin around and make my way to Cookie's. I guess for tonight I'll belong to Ronin. I weave my way through the crowds, looking back nervously as the guys follow me, and then cross the street when I get to the corner.

A hand grabs me from behind and I jerk away and turn. "Get your hands off me!"

The guy is tall and has a surprised look on his face. "Sorry, geez. We just wanted to see if you're OK. You look pretty shook up."

He's not one of the guys from the alley because they are still across the street. I turn away again, not caring if I was rude because I'm just totally out of my element right now and I just want to get something to eat. A crowd exits the diner and I let them jostle me away from the offended guy and push me inside. When the door closes behind me I let out a huge breath of relief.

Cookie's Diner right now is a haven for me. Some of the sound from outside is muffled and I give myself a moment to relax before the door opens and lets the noise back in.

"Can I help ya, honey?" the middle-aged waitress asks me as I stand there breathing hard.

"Um." Shit. I suck it up and force the words out. "I belong to Ronin and I just want some food to go, if that's OK."

The waitress smiles and winks at someone in the doorway behind me. "She belong to you, Ronin?"

I twirl around, my face hot with embarrassment. And yes, there he is, in all his top-model splendor, except with actual clothes on this time.

Ronin looks at me with a satisfied grin. "That's right, Angie. This one belongs to me all right. And we'll be eating here, so just send Cindy back when she's got time."

And then he hooks my arm around his and leads me towards the back of the diner. "Now, princess, do you mind telling me how you got yourself to Cookie's when I left you locked in your tower?"

"You left me up there on purpose?"

"How else could I keep an eye on you while I went out for drinks? You're not twenty-one, right? No bars for the baby. But I see you are resourceful. I might have to keep the reins a little tighter on you than the others."

I scoff at his boldness as he pushes me to sit in a booth at the back of the diner. Who the hell does this guy think he is? "Look, Ronin, I'm not sure how all the details of this deal will shake out, but I'm just going to go ahead and make one thing clear right now. I'm not in the market for a big brother, I can take care of myself, and if you try and lock me in the building again, I'm leaving for good. I don't take shit from any—"

"You all ready to order, Ronin?"

The waitress, Cindy I guess, is standing over us tapping her pen on her little order pad.

"Yeah," Ronin says, clearing his throat. "The usual for me, and bring one for her too, but make it well-done."

"Excuse me! I can order for myself. And I'd like—" I have no menu, so I make it up. "A grilled chicken salad."

The waitress eyes me, then bends down to write her ticket as she looks to Ronin for confirmation. What is up with that?

"She'll have my usual, well-done."

Cindy clicks her gum and walks off, ripping the order off the pad and clamping it up on one of those turn-style things for the cook in back.

"How dare you?"

"How dare I what?" He's grinning at me again and if he wasn't so damn irritating with his controlling bullshit, I might be tempted to gaze at him for a while. His eyes blaze with mischief, like I'm entertaining him or something, and then he leans back, kicks out his legs and pushes them against mine under the table. He drapes his arm over the back of the booth with a satisfied grin and my heart beats a little faster.

He's touching me.

I pull my leg back and he laughs. "Ah, yes, I forgot. Rook,

the only model in the history of Antoine Chaput studios who refuses to be touched. You're gonna have to get over that. Real fast."

"How dare you order for me?" I reply, ignoring his flirt, or threat, or whatever the hell that comment just was. "I have no idea what your *usual* is, and who are you to tell me to eat it well-done anyway? I just wanted a salad."

I get nothing from him beyond that confident smile. We stare at each other for a few moments and he looks me straight in the eyes. Like he can see through me or something. I try to keep his gaze, but I lose the contest and look away first as my heart does a weird dance inside my chest.

"Relax, Rook. This place is famous for their burgers so I ordered you a burger. Well-done, because that's how most people eat their burgers. I like mine medium-rare, but I don't like the idea of you eating undercooked hamburger, so I got it well-done, OK? Do you want me to change the order? I will if you prefer medium or rare or whatever."

I look away, embarrassed. Did I just overreact? Or did he just play me?

There's no time to answer because a girl dressed up like a biker straight out of Sturgis saunters up to Ronin and plants herself next to him in the booth. She ignores me completely.

"Ronin, my love. Does this outfit scream STURGIS, or what?"

It's like she read my mind. A laugh bursts out before I can stop it and the wannabe biker chick shoots me a dirty look.

"Sorry," I mumble.

"We're not casting for STURGIS until TRAGIC is over, Lisa. You'll have to come back in a few weeks."

"Well, I can do TRAGIC, too! I'm tragic, right?"

"Ah, you are, sweetie. But Rook here is our new TRAGIC girl, sorry. That job is taken."

My eyebrows shoot up. "I am?"

Lisa jumps on my indecision. "She's not signed yet?"

"It doesn't matter, Lisa, Antoine and I chose her this

afternoon during her test shoot. She's the girl we want." And then he looks over to me and smiles. But this time it's not cocky and bold. It's warm and seductive—a little crooked with a promise of something devious and a hint of dirty in it. Everything inside me goes warm in an instant. "So we'll do whatever it takes to keep her."

Lisa pouts and whines a little more but Ronin is looking straight at me the whole time. His gaze gets uncomfortable and I have to look away.

I take a deep breath and when I look up again, Lisa is gone and the food is here. Ronin helps Cindy with the plates and scoots my burger over towards me, says some flirty words to the waitress who looks exhausted and ready to go home, and then winks at me as he takes a bite of his food.

CHAPTER NINE

Ronin

This Rook is going to be a handful, I can tell. She's got a dark look to her, a look that says she's had some trouble recently. But she's not down, that's for sure. And her defenses are on high alert. Much too high for my comfort level. I'll have to work on that. If she doesn't trust me to order her food, then she's definitely not going to trust me to take care of her during a shoot.

And even though I told Lisa Rook is definitely the girl I want for TRAGIC, we won't get far if we can't touch her. *I* can't touch her, I correct myself. I'm the one who'll be touching her.

She has a good appetite once she settles in and starts eating, and that's a plus. I can only eat half of my burger, too many beers tonight, but Rook scarfs hers down and makes a decent dent in her French fries as well. I smile as she leans back in the booth. "Satisfied?" She blushes a bright pink and I have to stop myself from growling with desire. This girl does something to me and I'm not quite sure what to do about it.

"I was hungry," she explains. "I didn't eat all day."

"That's not good," I say, frowning at her. This might be an issue after all. "You want some pie? Cookie makes the best pies in town."

She laughs, as if this is absurd. "No, thanks. I've had enough."

I stand and hold out my hand to her. She looks at me funny but accepts it and I pull her to her feet and put my hand behind her back to direct her to the door.

"Don't we have to pay?"

"We have a tab, Rook. When you eat here you walk to the back booth, you order whatever you want and they bill us. No questions asked."

"Oh, then you take it out of our pay or something?"

I hold the door open for her and she murmurs a thank you as she passes through. I love her manners. She's a contradiction though, dark and defensive one minute, sweet and innocent the next. I'm not sure which side I prefer to be honest, I like them both at the moment. "No, this is just what we do for the models. We like you girls to look a certain way. Make sense?"

She looks over to me as we cross the street and make our way back to the studio. "I guess."

She has no idea what I'm talking about, and I'm really too tired to explain, so I just walk next to her in silence until we get to the door. "You can use my code for now, all right? It's 37351 I'll write it down for you when we get upstairs. It works for the terrace door too, so you're not a princess anymore."

She laughs at that and I have a sudden urge to put my hands all over her body, that's how much those little noises coming from her mouth turn me on. I can't even remember the last time a girl made me feel like that. Maybe never.

"Sorry for escaping, the hunger about drove me mad."

Oh shit. I feel bad. I'm such an asshole.

"But thanks for the burger. I really did like it."

We trudge up the four flights of stairs with just the noise of our footfalls to break the silence. Her little Converse sneakers are cute—bright red with little holes near the toes, like she's been wearing them since she was twelve and can't bear to give them up. I open the studio door and make sure it clicks closed behind us. "We've got the doors on a lock timer, so if you come in during business hours, it's always open, but after hours you need the code."

I open the terrace door for her and wait for her to walk

through, then follow her out onto the terrace.

"This place is so beautiful, even in the moonlight."

I look around at it. I'm so used to living here I don't even notice the cherry trees anymore. "Yeah, Antoine spends a small fortune on gardeners every month. We shoot a lot of stuff out here though, so it's worth it I guess."

She looks longingly at the grass and flowering fruit trees. "I spent most of my life in the city and there were some pretty places, I mean every city has pretty places, right? But they never quite made up for the ugliness."

Something tells me she's not talking about Denver.

"There's a swing over there near the first tree." I take her arm and pull her along with me over to the trees. "Get on. I'll push you."

I half expect a little fight out of her, but she's a lot calmer than she was when I found her in the diner. I watched her come out of the alley, get nervous about a group of guys following her, and then overreact when another guy asked her a question. She was wound up tight when I showed up.

But now—I listen to her stifle down a laugh as she settles down on the old wooden swing—she's calm and soft.

I think I prefer her like this. I can do without the dark Rook, but this girl, the one who says thank you when I open the door for her and who giggles when I push her in the cherry tree swing—this girl is sexy. Rook has Lisa and her Sturgis outfit beat by a mile and all she's wearing is some ripped-up low-cut jeans and an oversized sweatshirt that shows zero cleavage.

Her long dark hair floats out behind her as she swings forward, and then whips against her back as she returns to me. I catch a glimpse of her bare neck every once in a while and I get the urge to kiss her there. *Shit, Ronin, what's wrong with you?* Models are not girlfriend material, I remind myself. They are the farthest thing from girlfriend material there is. I try not to date the models, I try not to even look at them.

But Rook isn't a model. She might be one next week when

we start this campaign, but right now, she's just a girl.

And the only thing I know right now is that I want her.

"So Rook, tell me. Do you think you'll like modeling?"

"Yeah," she says, "I'll love it, as long as it pays me money. I just want a job, you know?"

She tilts her head back as she swings forward, making her whole body dip, and I imagine how she might look underneath me in bed—arching her back as I tickle her stomach with kisses. I snap out of the fantasy. "Do you have family here in Denver?"

"No."

That's all I get. *No.*

"Friends?"

"Nope."

Again, she offers nothing.

"So how did you get here?" I push.

"Fate." She laughs and jumps off the swing the next time it goes forward. She lands on her knees in the grass and then rolls down on her back. "That was fun, thank you." She gets to her feet and waits.

Despite her smile and her laugh, I recognize the move. She just ended the night.

"You're welcome. Want me to write the code down for you? So you can go get breakfast in the morning?"

"Yeah, sure," she says, already walking towards the garden studio. She punches in her code, which is all ones, so not a big deal, but she punches it in like she's lived here all year and not half a day. "Is there some paper and a pen in here? I haven't looked through everything yet."

"Yeah," I say. "In the top drawer next to the stove."

She shoots me a weird look, wondering how I know that probably, but I don't offer up an explanation and she simply hands the stuff over and I write down my code. "The doors are off hours all weekend, so you have to use the code at all times. OK?"

She nods. "Thanks."

Aaaaand… that's it. She's shut me down.

I take the hint and move towards the door. "OK, I guess I'll see you around tomorrow?"

She holds the door as I stand there waiting for an answer. "Sure."

I sigh and step out, feeling a little hurt as the door quickly closes behind me.

CHAPTER TEN

Rook

I lean my body back against the door after I force myself to close it on Ronin's face. It was so difficult to end this night but I'm not ready to get close to anyone, especially a guy like Ronin. He's dangerous, I can tell. He's some kind of supermodel, he runs the girls, whatever that means, and he's hot as fucking hell.

I giggle at my private swooning.

But it's true. My heart is still racing and it's not all because he scares me either. He does scare me though. I'm afraid of just about everything he represents. I mean let's be honest, all the best-looking guys cheat. That's a given. They know they look good, they probably spend all their time at the gym trying to maintain those bodies, and they only want one thing. But they want that one thing from as many girls as they can get, not just one thing from one girl. Because if I could find me a hot guy who only wanted that one thing from just me, I might think about it.

But seriously—Ronin is not that guy. He's practically got himself a harem of models that he claims like a caveman. Hell, even Elise told me to tell the diner I belonged to Ronin.

It's degrading.

And that whole ordering for me thing? I'm still confused about that. Because we both know it started out as a challenge, to see how far I'd let him walk all over me. But then he turned it on me with his logic and made me feel stupid for putting up a fight.

I huff out a breath and walk back to the bedroom and shuffle through my backpack to find my toothbrush. Everything I own is contained in this bag. And it's not much. Two pairs of jeans, besides the ones I'm wearing. And four more t-shirts. I don't even have underwear, because if you can believe this, someone at the shelter pilfered through my stuff and stole it all. They didn't just steal the underwear, that would be sick. They took all my clothes. So I had to get these all from the thrift store down the street from the shelter last week.

I grab what few toiletries I have and pull out a drawer to stash them away.

But the drawer is filled with stuff. Girl stuff. Make-up, lotion, nail polish. All sorts of things I'd love to buy on a regular basis but have had to go without for the past few months.

I sigh with satisfaction and then start to brush my teeth.

Rook, your luck has changed. This is a huge break. Last night I was holding a knife to my chest, ready to cut the pervert in the cot next to me if he tried to touch me again, and tonight I'm living—*living*—in a rooftop garden apartment on the trendy side of town. Is life weird or what?

It is weird, but I try not to think about it too much because if life can change for the better this fast, then it can change for the worse as well. I remember the money Elise gave me this afternoon and dash back to the bedroom to pull it out from under the mattress. I guess it's overkill to stash money in my own apartment that I live in by myself—this makes me privately squeal—but I can't help it.

Plus, I remind myself that I am making a list of why Ronin is not the guy for me, no matter how fast my heart thumps when he's near. That whole *I'll order for you* thing is cute the first time they do it, maybe. It's not for me, but if I was another girl, it might be cute. But in my mind, that shit is a red flag. Flying high out above his head. It says *I want to control you.*

And I'm not into that at all. Hell, I barely escaped the last boyfriend with my life, there's no way I'm getting involved with another guy who thinks he can tell me what to do.

And Ronin is flirting with the very edge of my boundary in that area.

I spit out the toothpaste and rinse out my mouth, then start the bath water and push the plug in the drain of the massive claw-foot tub. Maybe… yes! Bubbles under the vanity! I dump in a lot, far more than I need, but who cares. It's my tub and these are my bubbles! I can use as much as I want.

I worry about getting so excited about all this stuff, and getting used to it most of all. It sucks when you're used to something nice and then you lose it, but if you never have it in the first place, then you don't have to worry about losing it. Right?

That's how I think. And it works for me. Keeps my expectations low-key and my bullshit detector on high alert.

I peel off the clothes and slip into the hot water and enjoy how the bubbles feel as they float over my body.

I think I might be happy.

Maybe.

The last time I was happy I was fifteen.

And that is very sad. But tonight is not a night to be sad. Tonight is a night to have a private celebration that I made it. I'm OK. My eyes are not black and my body is not bruised. I'm OK. I'm safe.

And that asshole is one thousand miles away.

I smirk at this. *Asshole.*

I dunk my head under and shake my hair, then pop back up and relax.

Yeah, that Ronin. He's one cute guy and all. But he's not for me. Even if he is tall and has those amazing blue eyes. I bet if we had babies our kids would totally have the most cornflower blue eyes ever. And dark raven hair. Oh God, we'd make little model babies. They'd need agents at birth.

I am crazy!

Thinking about his little blue-eyed babies. It's fun, in a

sixth-grade fangirl kind of way. But I'd rather think about this TRAGIC contract to be honest. And the money that might come with it. I'm not sure how much it might pay or what it involves, but I'm definitely in. Antoine and Elise seem nice. At the very least, they seem on the up and up. So I think I will trust them. And anyway, Elise said I could shampoo hair for a job, so even if the TRAGIC contract doesn't pan out, I still have an apartment and a job.

For a little while anyway.

Ugh. The fear of losing good things creeps back in. I like this new life. I could get used to this very fast and I've never had anything that was even close to being this beautiful as far as apartments go. But Elise gave me the secret. She said keep your mouth shut and do what you're told. So, if that's all it takes to make Antoine happy with me, I can do that. I'll definitely do that.

I pull the plug with my toes and dip under one last time to wet my hair again. I'll wash when I wake up, but right now all I want to do is try out my new mattress. I giggle again as I get out of the tub, wrap a ridiculously extravagant towel around my body, and stumble over to the bed. I only mean to lie down for a second, but once my head hits the pillow, the thought of getting back up to change is just too much.

I slip into sleep already dreaming about Ronin pushing me on the cherry tree swing.

CHAPTER ELEVEN

Ronin

I spend the next hour on my own terrace that overlooks the large one down below, just watching the shadows move across her apartment. I can't see anything, so I don't think this is stalking or weird. I just want to see if she's OK. And to make sure she doesn't try to leave again.

Whatever. I want to catch a glimpse of her.

But I don't because the curtains, while sheer, are not really see-though. I see a shadow come and go, like she was in the bathroom for a while with the door open, because the light stays the same. And then no movement.

And the lights stay on.

I have an overwhelming need to find out why she has the lights on and I have to stop myself from going down there and asking her. Is she afraid of the dark? Did she slip and fall and knock herself out? Did she forget to turn them off and fell asleep?

I have to force myself to go back inside, undress, and lie down in the darkness.

But I cannot get her out of my mind.

She's got a past, that much is evident. And it's not a good one from the way she runs from it. But I want to know. If she signs the TRAGIC contract we'll get her social security information and maybe I'll run a background check.

That's devious. Maybe even stalkerish. But if she's an employee, it's my duty. I'd run a check on any new girl who came to us out of nowhere. Which has never happened before.

Antoine only takes referrals. Rook not only appeared out of nowhere, she has no agency, no book, and no interest in talking about her past. Bolt was the word Elise used. She might take her money and *bolt* if we don't tread carefully.

So if the shampoo job is a way to keep her, I'll make sure she's trained by Monday. That way we can keep her busy all day, do her second shoot after hours, and then explain the contract and get her to sign it that night.

At dinner maybe. Yeah, Elise and Antoine can make us dinner.

Us?

Shit, I really need to stop thinking of her like this.

This sounds like a plan and when I have a plan, I'm happy. My mind settles down from the day's activities, and I think about her huddled form in the hallway after watching Clare storm out. She was scared. I make a mental note not to scare her. Ever. And then fall asleep dreaming about pushing Rook in the cherry tree swing.

I wake up in the morning—well, after I reach over and check my phone, I realize it's late afternoon. And the second thing I do is pop up out of bed and start thinking about Rook. I wander out to the terrace to see if the lights are still on, but I can't tell. The whole building is awash with golden light from the afternoon sun.

I jump in the shower real fast, pull on some pants, and then head out the door barefoot and shirtless. I skip down the stairs and head straight to the garden apartment. When I get there I can plainly tell that the lights are still on. I cup my hands around my eyes and peek in through the front door window, but I can't see her on the bed, even though I have a straight line-of-sight from this door to that room.

I knock.

And wait.

And knock. And peer in again.

And then punch in the code to unlock the door.

"Rook?" Maybe she left? "Rook?" I walk back to the bedroom and stop short, my breath caught in my lungs.

She's sprawled out naked on her bed, the covers draped around her body, twined around her legs to cover her ass, and one breast is visible as she turns with a moan.

"Rook?"

She bolts upright and all her covers slip down her chest, baring herself to me. "What the hell?"

Her body is perfect. Flawless. Her skin glows in the light that flows into the western-facing window. She's still not fully awake yet and I take advantage of her indecisive moment to study her further. Her raven-dark hair is tousled around her face in waves and she rubs her eyes, breathing hard for a moment from the surprise.

There is no way in hell I'm leaving here without touching this girl. I tug her to her feet and smile as she realizes just how exposed she is and frantically makes a grab for the sheet. She looks up at me, or tries to, because her eyes get stuck on my own bare chest. I grin a little internally that I can shake her up like that. Eventually she pulls her eyes from my body and finds my eyes.

"What are you doing?"

Her voice is deep and throaty and I can't contain the chill she sends down my arms. I reach for her hair and she pulls away, gasping a little. "Shhhh. I won't hurt you, Rook." I have her full attention as my hand gathers the hair and pulls it down over her right breast, which is now hidden under the sheet. She relaxes under my touch and I get a wave of courage so I repeat the action, draping her long hair over her left breast.

And then I stop.

We stop.

The whole world stops.

And there is nothing but breathing, heavy with expectation.

"You're beautiful," I whisper as I take her hand and pull it down to her side. She whimpers a little and immediately grabs for the sheet with the other hand. "Trust me," I say. And then I tug on the sheet so that it slips down her stomach and falls to the floor. Her breasts are covered by her tresses, which tumble down her front like a waterfall. "Do you trust me?"

She shakes her head no and looks down.

I brush a finger down her front, lightly dragging it through the hair that covers her nipple, making her bite her lip and let out a whimper. Her eyes dart around the room, looking everywhere but at my face.

"Look at me, Rook," I command more harshly than I should.

I can tell she wants to put up a fight, but her will collapses under my pressure and she meets my gaze and then my smile allows her to relax.

"Why are you doing this?" she asks softly.

I gather some hair and drag it over her right shoulder so that it falls down her back and exposes her breast at the same time. Only the city lights streaming through the large window leave her bare. Just the one half of her body is illuminated, the rest is safe in the shadows.

I reach in my pocket and pull out my phone. "What do we do here, Rook? In this studio?"

Her eyes never leave mine. "Take pictures."

My phone makes a camera shutter sound.

"We're going to take a lot of pictures of you." I turn the phone around so she can see the picture. It's not the best, it's a phone camera after all, and the light is bad. But it tells her what she needs to know.

"It's pretty," she says, smiling at her first artistic portrait.

"Yes," I say, turning it back so I can look at it. It's fucking gorgeous. "And even though you're standing here in front of me with no clothes on, and even though everyone who sees this picture will instinctively know that you had no clothes on when I took it, they will only see what I allow them to see through the frame of this lens."

She bends down and pulls the sheet back up to cover

herself. "You broke into my apartment to teach me a lesson?"

I love her response, it tells me two things: She's not a pushover and she's game for this contract.

"No, I came to see if you were OK. No, that's not true either. I came because I haven't stopped—" My phone vibrates and I lose track of my words. I look down at it and read the text.

"Shit, I gotta go. I'll bring back dinner if you want." I look back at her as I leave the bedroom and catch her shrugging. "Just give me a couple hours," I call out behind me as I leave.

I grab a shirt and some shoes from my apartment and stare at the image of Rook on my phone all the way down to the parking garage. When I get to my truck I realize the real reason I went into her apartment. I don't want to ruin this girl but I'm not sure I can stop it now.

CHAPTER TWELVE

Rook

Holy shit!

Not only is this Ronin guy able to make all my girly bits shudder, he's got a flair for the dramatic as well. I can still feel his fingertips as they tracked down my breast. And I just stood there and let him do it!

What the fuck is wrong with me?

I laugh. This guy, that's what's wrong with me.

I need air, so I wrap the sheet around me and go out on the terrace. The spring breeze is nice and cool and my head begins to clear almost immediately. I peek over the wall and watch the people down below. It's not that crowded since it's still early evening. The sidewalks are mostly filled with families grabbing dinner. Something I very badly want to do as well.

A large black truck appears from under the building and I catch a bit of music leaking out from the cab. I bet that's Ronin's truck and I bet that text was from a girl. He'll be back with dinner my ass. I sigh and go back inside and start the shower. This tub is cool for baths, but as far as the shower goes, it sucks. There's like one of those kits they use to turn claw-foot tubs into showers, which means I have to stand there and use a hand-held sprayer every time I want to rinse.

"Oh, Rook," I say out loud as the bubbles stream down my body. "Last week you were showering in a homeless shelter twice a week if you were lucky. And now you're all high-and-mighty about using a hand-held sprayer?"

Yeah, getting used to things fast.

This is not good. I've been here two days and I'm being sucked up into this strange life of models and photographers and weird guys named after rogue Japanese killers who think they can order food for you and strip you naked after they break into your apartment.

I finish up in the shower and wrap the towel around me, anxious to get back to the bedroom. My hand slips under the mattress to the money Elise gave me yesterday. I haven't spent any of it and I won't, either. I'm saving this money, every bit they give me here, I'm saving it all up. Because if there's one thing in life I can count on, it's that eventually, no matter how freaking nice that rug is under your feet, someone always pulls it out from under you eventually.

I pull my jeans and t-shirt on and slip back out the front door to make my way into the studio kitchen. There's not much in there, just a fruit basket, some beer in the fridge, and a few frozen dinners in the freezer that have names on little sticky notes attached to them.

Apparently stealing someone's frozen skinny meal is verboten in this place.

I have no idea what goes on in a photography studio, or how models act, or what they eat, or how they stay so skinny or what happens if they get fat.

But I can take a good guess.

I'm thin because I was born this way. I'm tall because I was born this way. I'm not all that smart, I mean I'm of average intelligence I suppose, but I can't do much with math. And I don't pretend that I can understand politics or current events or scientific studies that tell me to stop blow-drying my hair or talking on a cell phone. Pretty much everything I know I learned from a movie. I'm crazy about movies and if I was pushed to describe my dream life, it wouldn't be modeling. My dream has always been to go to film school and make cool movies. Deep movies that have so many layers to them, people have to watch them a dozen times to get all the little inside jokes and nuances.

As a girl growing up in America you'd think I had it all. I mean, they fill you up with that we're-all-equal bullshit your whole life. *You can grow up to be anything*, my foster parents used to tell me. Right before they sent me back into the system, most of the time. But what they never mention is that dreams require money to fulfill.

They should just tell you this at the get-go if you ask me. Just state the facts and forget the equality crap. Because the facts are the facts. If someone had sat me down in the first grade and drilled it into my head that life is difficult, more difficult than I could ever imagine, and that success is neither guaranteed nor probable, and if they'd have followed that up with a step-by-step approach on how to get past all the pitfalls I might encounter along the way… well, I might not have tasted the poisoned honey my ex was selling when he found me, lost and desperate after running away from the tenth or twelfth foster home, and greedily accepted it as tasty.

Downright delicious, even.

They do us no favors, talking us up about women astronauts and lawyers and whatever. Because the cold hard reality is that none of those things apply to you when you're poor.

Unless you've got someone looking out for you—and most girls have this in their parents, but not everyone has parents and even fewer have good parents—you're screwed unless you figure it out yourself. And in my case, I did figure it out, but I took the long road to get here, that's for sure.

I have very few assets. But the ones I have I plan on using to my full advantage. I'm thin, I'm tall, I have long legs, blue eyes, and black hair. My tits are bigger than most models I've seen, but they're not porn-star material. I have straight teeth, a bright white smile and well-defined cheekbones.

I might not have much, but I have this. I have looks. I have The Look, if these people aren't blowing smoke up my ass. I have what they want. So I'm not interested in Ronin's games or Elise's attempts at big sisterhood, or the cushy life they're giving me here.

Beauty is fleeting. I know someone important said that, but I have no idea who it was. I just know it's true. So I'm gonna grab this second chance with everything I've got and I'm gonna ride this wave until it spits me back out on the beach of bullshit.

Because I know better now.

I've seen what being poor and stupid and scared does to you. I looked at it in the mirror and I'm never going back there. And maybe Ronin is a nice guy, maybe he's nothing like my ex, but I can't take the chance. I have my own dreams and Antoine Chaput's photography studio is just one more stop along the way to get to the place in life where *I* want to be.

I grab my phone and two twenties from under my mattress. I have no intention of spending them, but it's stupid to leave home without a phone and money, so I'm not about to do that. And I leave the safety and seclusion of the studio and go back out in to the real world to get my own dinner.

No boys bother me this time.

The words don't get stuck in my throat when I meet the hostess in Cookie's. I say "I belong to Ronin" because I have to. This is what I do to get by for now. I order a salad because while I might've been born thin, eating hamburgers every night is a guaranteed way to pack on the pounds and when your body is your money maker, you don't screw yourself over like that.

I eat and watch people and when the waitress comes by to check on me I order some scrambled eggs and bacon to take home and stick in the fridge for breakfast.

When the order's ready I take my free food and walk back to the studio and crawl in bed, thankful that I have somewhere to sleep, a bit of food to hold me over, and a general feeling of secure well-being, even if it is only temporary.

Ronin Flynn never shows up with dinner and instead of making me angry, this makes me happy.

Because I had him pegged right from the start. Ronin is a

player, a user, and a control freak. And I want absolutely nothing to do with him. I'm here to make money and that's all.

CHAPTER THIRTEEN

Rook

I wake slowly in the morning. I can hear the birds singing and recall leaving the door open to get some air flow through the screen door last night when I came home from the diner. It smells like spring. The air is cool and the gentle breeze travels all the way down the hallway to my bedroom and flutters the clean white sheets.

I think this is the best moment of my life.

Like ever.

I've never had my own apartment, I've never had my own bed, and I've never woken up in such a nice place two days in a row. I roll over and sigh, content. The sheets are wrapped around my body and it feels good. They are expensive sheets, I think. They are soft. Softer than anything I've ever slept on before.

My eyes open and I spy my pack on the floor. All my clothes are dirty and I really need to do laundry. This place even has a washer and dryer and I almost giggle aloud at this thought. No laundromats for me. For now anyway.

I push that moment of caution away because what's the point of having all this good stuff if I can't enjoy it while it lasts?

My legs swing out of the bed and I gather up all my clothes and stick them in the stackable washer in the closet just off the bedroom. The breeze caresses my naked limbs and gives me the chills, but I enjoy it. The goose bumps travel up my arms and spread out to my whole body. I shiver for a second and then head to the kitchen.

And stop dead in the living room.

Ronin fucking Flynn is sleeping on the couch.

What is he doing here? My eyes track to the front door and I suppose it's my fault, I left it open. There's nothing but a screen door between this apartment and the terrace. My gaze wanders back to the sleeping man. He's lying on his stomach, his one arm tucked underneath him, the other falling over the edge of the cushion, and he's shirtless.

And then I realize I'm naked.

"Shit!"

He stirs and I make a break for the bedroom. It's one thing to let him see me naked half hidden in darkness and quite another to be fully illuminated by the bright morning sunshine. I wrangle the sheet around my body and then head back to the living room, wistfully looking at the washer that contains every single article of clothing I own.

"Ronin!" I say loudly.

Nothing except a half-muffled snore from him. Lord, this man has the most perfectly chiseled and muscular back I've ever seen. Both hands pull up and go under his face, like he's blocking out the sunlight, and this gives me the perfect opportunity to study his flexing biceps. The muscles are thick and hard-looking near his shoulders. They curve down, dip into a little valley, and then climb once again.

I lean down and smell him.

"Why are you sniffing me?" he asks groggily.

"Uh—" *Because you smell delicious,* the inner Rook says. But luckily the outer Rook says, "I'm checking to see if you're drunk. Why are you sleeping on my couch?"

He peeks up, opening one eye in my direction, squints, and then croaks out some words. "I love your outfit." He grins, winks, and then drops his head back down into his arms.

"Are you leaving?" I ask, frustrated and confused at the same time. "I mean, why are you here?"

"I told you I'd come back with dinner. But when I got

here, the lights were on and you were in bed. I only sat down for a second to think up a rational excuse to wake you up, but I guess I fell asleep." He raises his head again, grins sheepishly, and then rolls over on his back, tucks his hands behind his neck, and flashes his perfect body at me as he closes his eyes, probably confident that I'll be checking him out.

I do check him out. It's quite hard not to notice that he's got the perfect six-pack abs and that absolutely adorable fuzzy happy trail you see on a shirtless designer jeans model. Hmmmm… maybe he *is* that model? "You have no shirt on."

Yes, after all that gawking, I finally manage the obvious.

He opens the one eye to look at me again. "Neither do you."

"I just put all my clothes in the washer. If I had known you were out here, I'd have saved an outfit to wear."

"Oh," he says, sitting up suddenly. "So you have to be naked until the clothes are finished?" He stands and we are only inches apart. He is so close I can feel the heat coming off his body. His hands find my hips under the bunched-up sheet and he sways me a little. "I'm still tired. Come with me." And then he takes my hand, leaving me scrambling to make up for the loss of one limb holding up my sheet, and tugs me back to the bedroom.

"Wait!" I say, resisting before we walk through the doorway. "What're you doing?"

"Going back to bed, Rook. It's early. Way too early to get up and worry about clothes." He tugs me to the bed and sits down. "Sleep next to me for a few more hours."

Holy crap. What do I say to that? "Uh," is all that comes out. He takes my indecision as a signal, which it is, if I'm being honest. Regardless of all those feminist she-nis thoughts I had last night lying here alone, this morning his self-serving idea sounds like a well-thought-out plan. So he pulls me the rest of the way down and I'm sitting next to his prone body.

"Lie down, come on. I won't bother you, I promise. Let's sleep for a little longer."

I give in. I'm weak, what can I say? He's hot, and not just in the looks department, he's got a heat radiating off his body that is calling me. It wants to wrap me up and it's been a while since I had that kind of affection, so I sink into the bed next to him and his arms open and then settle against my stomach.

I close my eyes. Because this feels good. This feels better than good actually, this feels perfect. He tucks his face down into my hair and takes a deep breath.

I smile because he just sniffed me.

"I'm just checking to see if you're drunk, ma'am."

I giggle a little.

"And if I wasn't so tired, I'd check you for drugs as well. Pat you down until I found your hidden stash."

"I'm naked, remember?"

"Awwww, come on, Rook! I'm trying not to think about that. Be good now, or I'll break my promise and bother you all up. Make you all bothered..." His voice trails off, already giving in to the call of sleep.

My entire body releases four years of tension and fear. And I snuggle against his chest.

And fall asleep thinking this is what people mean when they say they are content.

CHAPTER FOURTEEN

Rook

When I wake I'm alone, but I can hear the TV out in the living room blaring a baseball game, so I know I'm not really alone. I smile at this. He's still here, watching baseball in the living room. Like he belongs here.

Maybe he does belong here?

Rook, stop it. He's a player, he's a user, and he's probably got a million girls strung out all over this city. That's why he left last night and that's why he came back so late. And then you went and let him sleep in your bed and act like he's your boyfriend.

This has got to stop.

I roll off the bed, still clutching my sheet to my body, then pad over to the laundry closet in the hallway.

"I already took care of it." Ronin calls out.

"Took care of what?" I ask, peeking around the corner to see him. He's kicking back on the couch, feeding himself peanuts and drinking a beer. "Sheesh, comfortable much?"

"You know what the best part of living next to the baseball stadium is, Rook?" he asks, ignoring my snarky remark.

I shrug and simultaneously listen to the *Charge!* organ music on the TV and the fans outside in the stadium as they go wild.

He points to the bag of peanuts in his hand. "Baseball park peanuts at home." He grins a huge, wide-eyed, baseball-is-awesome-and-so-are-peanuts grin.

"You went over there to get peanuts?"

"No." He shakes his head. "I got a guy."

I laugh. "What? You have a peanut guy? Like a peanut dealer, who stands on the corner and sells peanuts from the curb as you drive by?"

"Nah, that's stupid. He delivers them to the freaking door. Anyway," he says, waving a hand at me. "I folded your laundry for you and do you know what I found out?"

"What?" I ask, shaking my head.

"That you do not own any panties."

My whole face goes hot. "*What?*"

"Panties, Rook," he says, pointing to the laundry closet with his bag of stadium peanuts. "I folded your seven articles of clothing over there so that when you woke up you'd have something to wear besides that sheet, and I found no undergarments."

I open the closet and there are my seven articles of clothing sitting on top of the stackable washer lid. Folded. "Uh…"

When I turn Ronin is standing next to me taking a swig of beer. He swallows and grins. "I can help you out with that, if you'd like."

"I'm lost. Are we talking about getting me panties, or taking them off me?"

He laughs. "Both, I think. Come on," he says, taking my hand and setting his beer down on the coffee table as we walk by. He pulls me outside and the only thing I smell is cherry blossoms. Every single cherry tree is filled with flowers, so many flowers every bough bends under the weight. It creates a heaviness that transfers across the terrace and pulls me into the scenery. Ronin catches my gaze and stops for a moment. "We're gonna take pictures of you out here tomorrow. It will be perfect, don't you think?"

I stare at the trees a few more moments and then mutter, "They're so beautiful I can barely stand to look at them."

"I know the feeling." His boyish charms are gone now as he looks down at me with a hunger I haven't seen on a man's face in a very long time. "And a picture of you surrounded by those blossoms will be enough to make a guy shed a tear over the perfection of it all."

I wait for the joke but it never comes. He just stares at me for a few more seconds and then squeezes my hand and pulls me into the studio.

"Where are we going? I have no clothes on!"

"Exactly," he comes back with. We enter a small hallway near the stairs and walk to the end of it and turn a corner to find a double door. It has a keypad and Ronin punches in his code, which I notice is the same one that opens the outside doors. The same one he gave me the first day I met him.

"That code of yours works a lot of stuff around here. You should maybe not hand it out to just anyone."

"I didn't." He grins and pushes against the frosted glass until the doors begin to open automatically. He waves me into the room and then flicks on the lights.

I gasp.

"Welcome to the Chaput Studios wardrobe and dressing room. You may choose anything you want from this side of the closet." He points to the largest area where racks are overflowing with clothes. There must be thousands of outfits here. "Those over there," his gaze goes to the smaller section, "are for the next week's shoot. And these right here," he says, pointing to a large chest of thin drawers, "are undergarments. These are all new, so take what you want."

"Am I allowed?" I ask, stunned.

"Allowed what?"

"To take this stuff."

"I just said you could."

"But won't Antoine or Elise get mad that I'm pilfering your stuff?"

"I run the girls, Rook. That means I run the closet too. This is like my little kingdom."

I laugh again. Shit, this guy has me laughing like an idiot this morning. "You're the King of the Closet?"

He bows. "The one and only."

"And you have spare panties for *me*?"

"Just shut up and pick some clothes, you goof."

"I don't know where to start, honestly. I've not had a lot of opportunities to shop."

He looks over at me as I take a seat on a long bench in the middle of the room. His expression is a little sad. "I'm not going to ask, because I know you've got things you're not about to reveal to me, not after three days anyway. But I'd just like you to know, that is not right. Whatever you've been through, whatever it was that made you so… sad. I'd just like to say you deserve better."

I swallow down some old hurt and mumble out a, "Thank you."

CHAPTER FIFTEEN

Ronin

"You're welcome, but you're definitely getting clothes today. This closet is bursting with shit so I'll tell you what, you look through the bras and panties and I'll bring you clothes. I have excellent taste anyway."

I go off to find her something comfortable. I pass by the sexy stuff, then grab a pretty nightie just in case, and continue on and find the casual wear.

Rook's clothes aren't that bad. I mean, she looks hot as hell to me. I don't look at that shit at all. Now her body, that's something else. I look at her body. But I work with girls every day. Beautiful girls. The most beautiful girls in the world, actually. And I know that when they wear pretty things, they feel pretty.

So I get Rook just about every pretty thing I can find, whether she needs it or not. I flip through the rack of jeans for some soft ones and grab several pairs. She must like jeans because that's the only thing I've seen her in, and besides, I like her in jeans and I'm the one choosing. If she doesn't like what I get, she can come shop for herself.

I grab some t-shirts like she's been wearing, but also some other stuff. Frilly things, tailored things, a few skirts, some shorts, tank tops, I grab all of it.

I catch myself grinning as I round the corner and come out of the circular closet behind her. "Here you go."

She spins around from the drawer of underwear, startled, like I scared the ever-loving shit out of her. And it hits me.

Something very bad happened to this girl, and it wasn't that long ago from the way she acts.

Slow down, Ronin.

"Here, try these on."

She takes the handful of clothes out of my arms and I back away. "I'll be out in the studio if you need anything, OK?"

To my surprise she comments to me on everything I brought, yelling out as she tries them on one at a time.

"How'd you know what size jeans I wear?"

We only have three sizes, and if she wasn't one of those sizes, she wouldn't have gotten past the door. She's not all bones like some girls, so the small size is out, and she's bigger up top than any of the models I've seen come through here, so I figure the larger of the three sizes is safe.

I say none of this out loud, I ignore that question altogether. That's a trap if ever there was one.

"Nice try with the nightie!"

Now this topic is safe. "I picked it because it's blue and I thought to myself, Ronin, that girl out there has the prettiest blue eyes, wouldn't she look spectacular in this little slip of see-through fabric that is a shade or two lighter."

She walks out of the dressing room as the last few words are coming out of my mouth.

Wearing the nightie.

I'm speechless and I'm pretty fucking sure my mouth is hanging open.

"I thought since you went to the trouble and put all that thought into it, you at least deserved to see it on."

"You are very bad, Rook. Very, very bad."

She laughs all the way up to her eyes and my heart is filled with… something. Something weird. Heat flushes through my body and I almost lose my train of thought when she begins to turn away.

"Hey!" I call. "Come back here a minute, you distracted me and I missed some parts."

To my surprise she turns back around and stands there,

her hip jutting out, one hand practically caressing the wall and an unreadable expression on her face.

She's not flaunting it, not modeling, or twirling around to hide her embarrassment. She just stands there and allows me to look at her. I almost feel guilty as my eyes travel down her body and then stop at the bottom and make their way up again. Half of her long black hair is flowing over one shoulder, but the rest of it peeks out from behind her back like a cape. "Miss Walsh," I whisper, "you've wiped my mind of everything right now."

I walk up to her and she averts her eyes but when I get closer she fights hard to meet my gaze. "I'm glad you're here," I tell her honestly. I want to take her face in my hands and kiss her so bad, but I make myself behave. "I hope you understand that. I'm a flirt and I joke a lot but—" I lose my train of thought as she starts breathing a little harder, making her chest rise and fall under the very sheer pale blue fabric that barely covers her breasts. "—but you *stun* me."

I finally find her face again and she's watching me closely, leaning in a little maybe—like she wants me to kiss her.

But then the moment passes and she turns away slowly. I watch her body move down the short hallway until she rounds the corner and starts talking again. "You're an excellent shopper, Ronin. I think I'll keep them all, but only if you take it out of my check." She comes back out a few minutes later dressed in a t-shirt and some jeans, holding the huge pile of clothes in her arms. On top is the sheer blue nightie.

"You're keeping the nightie?" is all I manage to say.

And then we both laugh because I am such a fucking pig.

"Yes, thank you for picking it out. I agree, it really makes my eyes look spectacular."

"Right," I breathe. "Your eyes."

"So you'll take this out of my check, right?"

"No."

"What do you mean, no?"

"No, I'm not taking the clothes out of your check. It's like the food, Rook. It comes with."

"Do you give all the girls free clothes?"

"No, but I would if they needed it."

"So I need it?"

"Don't you?" I see where this is going and a smarter guy would back off, but she's just being dumb.

"I don't really. I'm fine with the clothes I was wearing, it was you—"

"OK, whatever. I'll tell Elise to bill you for the clothes. Make you happy?"

She nods and I take the clothes from her arms and we walk across the terrace to her apartment. When we get inside I dump all her stuff on the bed and wait.

It's an awkward moment. Does she want me to leave? Stay? "Do you want to go get some lunch?"

"Um…"

"Before we train for tomorrow?" I stick that in to throw a wrench into her I'm-trying-to-get-rid-of-you plan, because I can see it coming.

"Train for tomorrow?"

"Yeah, I told Elise I'd train you at the shampoo station before she got back, you know, so she could relax on her romantic weekend getaway with Antoine. It's their anniversary. Well, sorta. They're not married, but they still call their first date their anniversary."

I'm fucking babbling.

"I need to train on the *shampoo station*?" is all she comes back with.

"Yeah, you know—the whole hot and cold water thing, shampoo versus conditioner. Detangler…"

I'm dying here.

"If you say so, Ronin. But I'm going to take a shower so why don't I meet you at the *shampoo station* in an hour and we'll talk about food afterward?"

CHAPTER SIXTEEN

Rook

Even though I should be thrilled at scoring a whole armful of designer clothes from the closet of Antoine Chaput's studio, I'm irritated as I wrestle with the stupid hand-held shower head thingy that won't let me relax and enjoy hot water at the same time. And Ronin. *Train on the shampoo station.* What kind of stupid way to spend a Sunday is that? I mean I get it, everything in my life is tentative right now, so I could do a lot worse than standing around listening to control-freak Ronin babble on about how to use the hot and cold water spigot.

I blow out a breath of air and rinse myself one last time and then give up on the shower being something fun. Next time I'll just take a bath, at least I can relax in a bath.

Who needs clean hair anyway?

Shampoo station training my ass.

I shake it off and go back into my room where all my new-to-me clothes are piled up on the bed. It is pretty cool that I got all this stuff though. I'll probably regret it when the bill comes, but that worry is for another day. Right now, I'm in underwear heaven. I fish out the prettiest panties I found and slip them on. They are black with little pink ribbons threaded through the butt and have tiny pink bows that accentuate each of my hipbones.

The jeans I wore out of the dressing room were perfect so I put those back on, and then wrangle my girls into the matching black and pink bra and add a black tank top to the ensemble. I look in the mirror. My hair is a bit of a mess and might even still have soap in it due to lack of proper rinsing, plus I have no make-up on to boot. But even so, this is the prettiest I've looked in years. Maybe ever.

I brush my teeth and then gloss up my lips with some brand new peach-tasting stuff I found in the make-up drawer. Imagine—three days of proper care and feeding can make up for four years of neglect and punishment.

It's amazing how little we humans really need to thrive and it blows my mind that a matching bra and panty set, coupled with the perfect pair of jeans, can lift my spirits up so high, it leaves me dizzy.

I sigh.

This is a lucky break. A total lucky break.

And even though I'm pretty sure I can handle the hot and cold water at the shampoo station, I'm going to be sweet and smile for Ronin as he explains these things to me like I'm an idiot. I can do that. And then I can ditch him and eat my leftover breakfast from Cookie's and spend a nice quiet evening watching TV alone.

Ahhhhhh… I let out a nice long breath and smile. I almost feel normal.

I slip my feet into my old Converse sneakers and head to the studio. Totally ready for shampoo station training. The weather outside is so perfect and the concrete is a bit damp, like it rained last night. I didn't hear any rain, but I was pretty dead to the world. The sweet scent of cherry blossoms wafts in the crosswind and even though there are all sorts of cars and people making noise and commotion down on the street, these trees cancel it all out. They make me feel like I'm walking across an orchard out in the country.

Inside the studio is bright and cheery and when I round the corner into the salon, Ronin's mood seems to match the atmosphere of the room. "Nice," he says.

I raise my eyebrows at him. Did he just use a player word on me? Ugh… how can such a good-looking guy be so irritating? "OK, I'm ready. Lay it on me, please explain all the technical details of how the hot and cold water handles work."

He grins. "You think it's easy, don't you? That shampooing doesn't require skill."

"Oh, I'm sure it does, but am I buying your whole I'm-an-expert-in-shampooing-stations act? No. But proceed. Teach me all I need to know about sinks."

"I think you've misunderstood, Rook. I'm not here to teach you how to use the sink. I'm going to teach you how to give a great shampoo."

I laugh. "OK, I'll ignore the fact that you specifically said hot and cold water and detangler earlier, but I've been shampooing my own rather lengthy, high-maintenance hair for a while now. I'm pretty sure I can handle it."

"But have you ever shampooed a man's hair? Huh? Because we have male models who need a shampoo here and Elise usually does her own shampoos. She's quite good at it, I hear, so they will be expecting the same treatment from you."

Is he for real? I look for the smirk that says he's joking but I can't find it. "O-kaaaaaay," I say, drawing out the last syllable.

"So I'm going to show you how to give a Chaput Studios-worthy shampoo and then I'll test you and see if you've got it down."

"Test me how?"

"You can do me after I do you."

Again I look for the grin that will let me know he's playing around, but there is no hint of innuendo there. He seems serious. I frown. "We're going to shampoo each other's hair? Like a Gidget sleepover from the Sixties?"

This cracks his facade for a moment and he squints his eyes at me. "A what?"

"*Please*," I beg in an exaggerated manner, "do not tell me you're ignorant of Gidget? I might have to walk out."

"Do you buy it in the App Store?" he asks innocently.

A laugh puffs out through my cheeks and I smile, because this is just too much. "No," I say, shaking my head. "And since you're clueless, you get to be Larue."

He shrugs like he could care less and points to the chair. "I do you first."

And there it is. Just as I'm turning away to sit down, I catch it. The smirk.

He is totally messing with me.

I sink into the soft leather chair and relax back against the sink. My eyes want to close immediately because this position is like a relaxation trigger. I never went to the salon much back in Chicago, but I went enough to know that Ronin is right—the shampoo comes with expectations. Elise certainly delivered the other day with me because I was willing to forget all my troubles for a few moments in her care.

Ronin gathers my hair and turns the water on. He messes around to get the correct temperature and stays silent, which makes this whole thing on the edge of awkward. "So," I begin. "Are you a certified shampooer?"

"I'm a total professional, Rook."

"Is that right?"

"Mmmm," he says as the warm water runs over the crown of my head and tickles me.

"Most professionals would put that little bib thing on their clients, though. Right?"

"Only the ones who plan on getting their clients wet."

"So… you don't plan on getting me wet?"

He chokes down a laugh. "Be good, Gidget, or I'll have to spank you." The water stops and I smell coconuts. He rubs his hands together and lifts my wet hair from the basin, massaging the sweet-smelling soap into the longest strands first.

"I used to be blonde, ya know. In my other life."

"Huh," he says.

"What?"

"I can't see you as blonde at all. What idiot made you do that?"

"Why would someone wanting me blonde make them an idiot?" And more importantly, I ask myself, why did he suspect I was forced so quickly?

"Because you're probably the most perfect natural beauty I've ever seen, so anyone who wanted you to have blonde hair was looking to ruin you."

"Yeah, you're probably right about that."

He stops the massage on the ends of my hair. "I'm probably right? Or I am right?"

I shrug as he takes his fingertips to my scalp. His touch has just the right amount of pressure and he rubs my skin in small circles, starting from my temples and moving back down my head, and then under my neck.

My whole body erupts in chills.

"Feel good?"

"So good," I murmur, enjoying it to the fullest.

"When you do me," he says as he takes his fingertips to the top of my head, producing another wave of chills, "I like it up here."

I laugh. "Is that right? That's your big shampoo training tip, Larue? Do me like this?"

He leans all the way down into my ear, so close that my eyes shoot open when his breath tickles the sensitive skin. "Do me just like that, Rook. Please."

Oh, fuck.

I swallow, trying to stall for a response, but I have nothing. I take a chance and glance up at him. He's laughing at me. "You're bad."

"You have no idea. Now, close your eyes so I can rinse. I might make you wet, so I apologize ahead of time for that."

Oh, he is so bad.

And I am in so much trouble because even though he's very careful with the water as he rinses my head, I am definitely wet.

"So, you're a model now. Or you most likely will be tomorrow. What's your big plan? Got one?"

"Yeah," I answer, thankful that we're done with the sexual banter for now. "I'm gonna ride it out while it lasts."

"So you think you'll like being a model?"

"Maybe, but it doesn't matter. If it pays decent money I'm gonna do it." He shuts the water off and I turn a little to look up at him. "It's a break I really need, Ronin. You have no idea. So maybe I'll like doing this stuff or maybe I won't. But I'm gonna get as much out of it as I can and then, when it's over, I'll go do something else."

"Like what?" The strong smell of citrus permeates the air as he starts working in the conditioner.

My hair is so long and thick, this usually takes a while even when I'm in a rush, but Ronin takes his time and I sink into the chair a little more, totally relaxed. "College, maybe. I never got good grades, and I took the GED when I was sixteen so I could quit going to school, but I know you can start out in community college and then transfer into a better place. That's my dream. It'll probably never happen, but you asked."

"What would you study?"

"I dunno," I lie. I could just tell him, but I don't feel like it. It's my dream and it's personal. It means a lot to me and I'm not gonna share that with some guy I just met.

"What if you didn't get this job? Or what if it doesn't last? Models are known for having a pretty sketchy schedule. Work one day, none the next. It's not real stable."

This question is even worse than the last one. "Yeah, well, I'm used to disappointment, so no big deal. If it doesn't work, I'll move on and do something else. I might be young, but I've learned a few good lessons in my day."

He goes still so I open my eyes and look up at him. He's frowning. "What lessons, Rook?"

"Don't rely on anyone to get what you want. You just gotta go get it yourself."

"That's kinda sad," he says as the water comes on again.

"Nah, just practical." I shiver as the water rushes over my head.

"So you're not the type who looks for a boyfriend to take care of her?"

I snort. "Fuck. No. The last thing I want right now is a guy who wants to take care of me."

"Huh. Well, what do you tell them then?"

"Tell who?" I ask, looking up at him again.

"The guys you date? Do you tell them you're just interested in casual stuff, or what? I don't get it."

I'm tired of this conversation so I shut it down. "I tell them nothing, Ronin, because I don't let anyone get that close."

"Because someone hurt you?" he asks, trying to sound nonchalant.

"Is this a psych couch or a shampoo station?"

He smiles down at me and shuts the water off, then wrings out my hair and drapes a towel over my head. "Sit up." He fluffs my hair with the towel for a few minutes, then tosses it into a basket across the room and hands me a comb. "So, was it everything you thought it would be?"

The innuendo is back and I smile as I drag the comb through my hair and stand up next to him. He's tricky, this one. Knows just when to light me up and dim me back down. "It was so much more," I gush, "I have no words to describe it."

"Try," he says, suddenly serious.

His hands begin to wander around my waist, tugging on my belt loops, a safe way to make contact but not put his whole hand on my hip.

I'm holding my breath and it comes out in a soft rush. "It was gentle."

He smiles.

"And it made me tingle."

"Tingle?" he asks. "Really? That good?"

I nod as I watch his lips. His mouth opens a little and I draw in a deep breath.

"Well, I'm not sure you're ready to step into my shampoo shoes, but give it a go, OK? And if you get nervous, just take a deep breath and I'll hold your hand the whole way through. From working the faucet to rinsing the conditioner, I have your back, Rook."

Never once does he crack a smile.

I nod and become very serious. "I really appreciate your confidence in me, Larue. Now, please, lie back in my chair and I'll do you just the way you like it."

CHAPTER SEVENTEEN

Ronin

Rook's hands on me almost drive me over the edge. I take a deep breath as she sprays the water down my head, then leans down to talk in my ear, just the way I did with her. She's totally on to me and this makes me smile.

"What's funny, Larue?" she quips.

"You, Gidget. You think I don't know who Gidget is? *Please*." I say it the way she did earlier, with mock exasperation. "I fangirled on Gidget *before* she was on RetroTube every night."

"You do not watch RetroTube!"

I cross my heart with my fingertips. "I swear, Gidge was my girl back when I was a boy. She's hot."

"It's the pigtails, isn't it?"

"Mmmmm, and she did this thing with her tongue…" Rook covers her mouth with her hand to hide her laugh. God, she's beautiful when she's laughing. "… and her feet. When she talked on her little pink phone her feet had this whole other conversation going on."

"Oh my God, you *are* a Gidget fan! Who would know that?"

I open my eyes and enjoy her delight. "We have a contract coming up soon. The one you're doing is called TRAGIC, right? We have the STURGIS one and then the GIDGET one. I've been researching that little teen-flake for months now."

"So which one, Sandra Dee or Sally Field?"

"Definitely Sandy but Sally has way more episodes, so…"

"Yeah, I agree. When I was a kid I wanted to be Gidget so bad. Who's got the contract for that job?"

I look at her and it sinks in.

"Let me guess, you can't be both TRAGIC and GIDGET."

"Two totally different worlds, Rook."

She just shrugs and goes back to my hair. "How am I doing so far?"

"Magic, your fingers are magic." I close my eyes and relax again, content with how this afternoon is playing out. She's fun and easy-going. She's not offended when I flirt and she flirts back.

Water rushes down my neck and I jump out of the chair and turn back to look at her. "You got me wet!"

"Sorry, Larue. But I'm just a trainee, you can't expect me to be a professional like you on the first try."

I whip my shirt off and wipe the water off my neck. "Are you done with me?"

"I'm not sure," she replies, tilting her head coyly. "Did I do you right?"

I walk towards her and she holds her hands up and shrinks back into the corner. She's laughing so I know it's all in fun, but the defensive positioning bothers me for some reason. Like she's used to being stalked. Like she's used to guys coming at her with fists.

She starts to shift, uncomfortable with my silence and staring.

"Would you like to come upstairs with me?"

"What's upstairs?" she asks, trying to play innocent.

"My apartment. I could make you lunch." I look at the clock on the wall and it's almost dinner time, then nod towards it. "Or dunch, since it's late now."

"Dunch?"

"Yeah, you know, lunch and dinner. It's like brunch, but it's dunch."

"You cook?"

"No," I laugh. "Not really. But I can buy food and bring it back and put it on a plate and pretend I made you dunch." I walk a few paces towards her and she takes a deep breath but holds her ground. Yes, someone definitely hurt this girl in the past and that makes me angry. She catches my change in mood and I smile to ease her back down. She's perceptive.

"What else would we do?" she asks as I take her hand and pull her out of the corner.

"Watch a movie?" I offer. This piques her interest and she brightens as I bring her towards me and push her wet hair off her shoulders. It leaves drops of water behind on her bare skin.

"Which movie?" she breathes as I pull her into my chest. I can feel her heart hammering against my body and I take her face in my hands.

"Any movie you want. We have a database of pretty much everything." I lean down and caress her lips with mine and then groan when a tiny moan escapes her mouth.

She pulls back, her hand firmly against my chest to keep me at bay. "Why are you kissing me?"

"Because I can't stop myself. And because I'm the only one who knows you, and you're just Rook, the girl who appeared out of nowhere. But tomorrow, you'll be Rook, the face of TRAGIC. And I don't think you're tragic at all, Rook. I think you're Gidget. But what I think doesn't matter, because things will move forward once you sign that contract and we'll just have to wait and see where it all ends up."

"You don't want me to sign the contract?" She scowls at me, like I'm trying to steal her future away or something.

"No, that's not it. I want you to have your chance at that dream you have, but there's a reason this campaign is called TRAGIC and not GIDGET and I'm guessing you already know that, because you look like a smart girl to me. So, just for tonight, I'd like to treat you like Gidget and have you over for dinner and a movie."

She swallows down a sad look and then paints on a smile. "OK, dinner and movie. I'd like that."

I lean down again and brush against her ear with my lips as I whisper, "But no matter what happens—you will never shrink back into a corner from me again. Because I will never hurt you."

She stiffens a little as I hold her close, but I wait for her to relax before I let her go. And then I take her hand and lead her towards the stairs.

CHAPTER EIGHTEEN

Rook

Oh shit. I'm not sure what I'm doing here. Ronin is all over the place with me this weekend. Last night he had me standing in front of him naked so he could take a picture and hint that he'll take care of me. He leaves to go take care of someone else apparently, then lets himself back into my apartment and sleeps on my couch. He gives me a boat-load of free designer clothes, tests the waters with some not-so-veiled flirting, and then kisses me and invites me up to his apartment.

And I'm going!

Even though my head is screaming *stop*, my feet keep going. My hand is grasping his just as hard as he is clutching mine. My heart is pounding and if he wanted to take me to bed right now, I'd probably let him.

And on top of all that, he's got some well-formed opinions on what might have happened in my other life.

He stops at the top of the stairs and I try to rein in my wild emotions.

"Everything OK?"

I swallow and nod and this makes him frown. "What?"

"You look scared out of your freaking mind, Rook. You don't have to come up here, you know. We can go eat at Cookie's if you want."

I take a deep breath. "No, no, I want to watch a movie with you." That's not a lie either, the thought of picking a movie to watch with him actually sounds fun. "But I'm not interested in anything else." I look away, embarrassed.

"I don't want anything else, Rook. Just dinner and a movie."

I nod and snap back to reality, noting the hallway we've ended up in at the top of the stairs. Ronin notices my new interest in the place and points to the massive wooden double doors down off to the right. "That's Elise and Antoine's apartment. I'm this way." He redirects my attention to the left, where the hallway goes on for several yards and ends at an equally massive single door.

He keys in his security code and the door beeps and then clicks when the mechanism unlocks. Ronin opens the door and waves me in. I take a tentative step forward and then move out of the way so he can get past me. "Come on, I'll show you the movies."

He lets go of my hand and I scramble to take it back. He smiles over his shoulder and tugs me farther into the room. "Here's the remote," he says, motioning at me to sit on the couch. "Push that turquoise button to get to the movie database."

I push it and a search screen comes up along with a menu for different genres. "What kind of movies do you like?" I ask.

"Your pick tonight, I'll get dinner, and," he stresses, "I get to pick your food. And you can pick the movie."

"What's with you and the choosing food thing? I don't get that. Wouldn't you rather I get something I like?"

"Did you hate the burger I got you?"

"No, but—"

"But nothing. Give me a chance. I promise, I'm good at this."

"Yeah, but it's weird."

"What's weird about ordering you food?"

"It's not the ordering, it's the control."

"Oh, I get it. You're one of those."

"Those what?"

"Control freaks. You have to be in control all the time,

right?"

"What? That's so far from the truth it's bizarre."

"What else could it be then? I mean, if I pick what you like, then why do you care if I order you food?"

And I'm trapped. I can only shrug because to tell him the truth will spill all my secrets and to deny it will just keep the conversation going. Luckily he's one of those graceful winners and shoots me a wink.

"I'll be back in like twenty, OK?"

I nod and relax back into the overstuffed couch as Ronin walks down the hallway and comes back with a clean shirt, then heads out. My gaze wanders around the room and I take it all in. It's definitely a guy's apartment because the color scheme is nothing but shades of brown with some black thrown in for variety. He has the biggest TV screen I've ever seen hanging on the wall and I get a little chill of delight as I think about watching movies on that thing. He's got surround sound speakers placed strategically around the room and through the sheer curtains I can see the city lights across what seems to be a pretty significant terrace.

Man, these people definitely have money.

I take my attention back to the database and enter the movie I want to watch. I've been thinking about this movie since I met him actually, because of his name. It's a movie both of us can enjoy—a touching love story with beautiful scenery—cherry blossoms even. And it's a war movie with lots of blood and gore.

I think he'll love it. This makes me warm because if I'm honest, I want him to love it. Because I love it.

I really don't have a lot of experience with men but I can say with absolute certainty that no man has ever looked at me the way Ronin Flynn did when I came out of that closet wearing the blue nightie. His eyes swept down my body in hungry desire and then they climbed back up so slowly my heart started pounding with the anticipation of what his expression would say when he finally found my face.

If I spoke the language of his eyes I'd know for certain, but I'm at a loss with this guy. I'm fumbling around in the dark trying not to look or act like a complete child and I hope I'm not wrong about my guess, but those eyes looked like they wanted to touch every part of my body.

In the few seconds we twined our gaze together I heard myself ask him to kiss me a million ways in my thoughts, and if I spoke the language of my own desire then I'd know for certain that I almost begged him to do it with the look on my face.

Touch me, I should've whispered. *Kiss me*. Because my whole body is humming with the realization that this is how a man makes you feel when you actually like him. This is what girls mean when they claim a man makes them feel weak. They don't picture fists hovering over them as they cower in the corner, hoping and praying that those hands never connect with their cheekbone.

I press play on the screen and then pause the movie and go over to the terrace to wait for Ronin. It's not warm out, but it's tolerable for a spring evening so I slip out and leave the door open behind me. It's a pretty large square terrace filled with patio furniture and a grill off to the side.

I walk over to the railing, bend down a little, and rest my chin on my hands. The view of downtown Denver is stunning—the tall buildings are lit up and everything seems to twinkle. I have no idea what any of the buildings are, but I don't care either. They're pretty. It's amazing, when I think about it, how fast things can change. Three months ago I was an abused girlfriend, beaten to within an inch of her life. Three days ago I was a scared girl with very little money in a strange city and living in a homeless shelter.

And tonight, even though I'm still scared and I still have very little money, it's all flipped around. I'm in a fantastic apartment with a beautiful man. I'm wearing some pretty nice clothes that I'll probably regret asking for when I see how much they cost. And I might even have a job as a model for a photographer who is important enough to own an entire building and pay girls a hundred dollars an hour to sit for him.

I hear the soft footsteps but I don't turn.

"Find a movie you like?" he asks as he comes up behind me. He puts his hands on either side of the railing, my body between them, and then takes a chance and leans in to close the distance between us.

"Yes," I reply as his mouth dips down to my neck, sending a tingle all the way up my body.

"What're you thinking about, if you don't mind me asking?"

I sigh. "Just how funny life can be. How things can change in a moment and how you never know when that moment will come. It's occurred to me over the past few days that I'm not really in control of very much. I mean, I can make a decision to get on a bus and move to a new city completely alone. And I can make the decision to walk out of a job where I was being falsely accused of stealing. And I can make the decision to spend my last ten dollars on a coffee where a bunch of models fling a little white card at my face and I end up with an invitation to sit in front of Antoine Chaput."

I turn my body so I'm facing him. I wonder what he thinks of that little revelation? That I wasn't invited, but stole an opportunity to test for Antoine from another girl. He eases up to let me turn, but as soon as I'm settled he presses against me again, only this time his chest is touching my breasts instead of my back, and his hands slip under my hair and begin to caress my neck. If he has an opinion on the invitation, he holds it back.

"But everything after that was luck," I continue. "I can't control other people. I couldn't make Elise take me into the studio, or Antoine like the way I look, or get offered a fake job shampooing hair just so I'd stick around."

He grins at that last remark.

"And I have no control over how you feel about me or why you want to let me stay here." I stare into his eyes and shrug. "I'm totally at the mercy of the universe for these parts. And it's a little bit scary not to be in control, don't you think?"

He pulls my face closer to his and my heart pounds with the thought of another kiss. But he doesn't kiss me, at least not where I expect him to. He brings his lips to my forehead and crushes himself to me, breathing in deeply. And his hands play with my hair, still stringy and damp from my shampoo.

"It's very scary," he whispers as his mouth travels down to my ear. "And I don't know the whole story with you but if you really did all that then I'm in awe of your courage, Rook."

"I think you overestimate me, Ronin. It wasn't courage, it was desperation and fear."

He pulls me all the way into him then, pressing me up against his chest, his hands wrapped tightly around my head and neck in a protective embrace. "Even so. You came up with a plan, and that is courage. Because if this guy you're running from did the things I think he did, then I know first-hand how scary that is."

I push back and stare up at him. "How?" I ask.

He smiles but it's sad. "Because my father used to beat the shit out of my mom back when Elise and I were kids. And one day he hit her with a baseball bat and she never got back up. Elise was eighteen and I was ten when they took my dad to prison. He's still there, I think. I have no idea really. When Antoine showed up and wanted to date Elise and take me in, we stopped being those tragic kids and just went back to being us again. It was scary as fuck those first few years, having to trust that Antoine was good and that he'd stick around. He and Elise never married and this bothered me for a very long time. I always felt that my new life was a rug that was about to be pulled out from under me at any moment. But then, slowly, things started to change. Antoine is a good guy, he loves Elise, and yeah, I'd like him to marry her and give her more security—but if what they have is good enough for Elise, then I just have to accept it."

It's my turn to wrap my hands around his neck and pull

him close. I can't reach his forehead so I kiss his chin instead and he laughs. "Sorry," I say with a smile. "I can't reach your forehead but I wanted to kiss you."

He leans down and takes my lips this time, a soft, slow kiss that makes my toes feel warm. The heat climbs up my body as his mouth opens a little and I'm throbbing between my legs in seconds.

I pull back.

"Ronin Flynn, you might undo me."

"I'm already undone, Gidge. I'm just hoping you'll stick around long enough to put me back together."

CHAPTER NINETEEN

We go back inside and get our food. I got her another burger. Since I flapped my mouth about picking something she likes, and I know she likes burgers and salads with chicken on them, I got the burger again. She laughs and calls me a cheat, but eats every bite and this makes me so happy I can't stand it.

Even though my general rule is no models in the bedroom, I've dated them before and I know each and every one of them has an eating disorder. Maybe it never gets serious, maybe it only manifests as small, barely noticeable rationing, but we all know that if the girls get too big, they can't wear the clothes. And if they can't wear the clothes, they're out of a job.

Rook doesn't know this yet, but it won't take her long to figure it out. And I like her the way she is—her body is fucking hot. And I think it might break my heart if she traded those curves in for bones.

"So what movie are we watching?" I ask.

"*The Last Samurai*," she says with a coy grin.

"You think you're clever, don't you, Gidget? Got it all figured out?" She plops down on the couch and I sit just far enough away to make her wonder what my intentions are. I have no intentions. Well, maybe I do, but they are fairly innocent right now.

"I have no idea what you're talking about. This movie has Tom I-have-no-shirt-on-and-I-kill-people-with-swords Cruise in it."

She's got me here. "So you have no idea what my name

means?"

"Hmmm," she says. "Larue, that's French, right?"

I laugh. "Really? You have no idea?"

She smiles and leans back into the couch, her cute little bare feet doing a dance as they rest on the coffee table. "Everything I do is done with purpose, Ronin. The waitress wrote your name on the ticket that first night I ate at Cookie's, so I knew right then it wasn't Irish, even though your last name is Flynn and that *is* Irish. But I didn't choose this movie to impress you with my knowledge of your name."

I laugh again. Like hell she didn't.

"I chose it because it's got cherry trees, is deeply philosophical, and is cinematically beautiful."

I just stare at her.

"And because Tom Cruise gets to kick ass with a stick."

"Bokken," I correct her as I smile with satisfaction. I kick my feet up on the coffee table next to hers and click play on the remote. Every time she opens her mouth she surprises me. "So tomorrow, you have any questions about tomorrow?"

"Just wash the heads, right? And do them like I did you?"

My grin is so big now I have to hide it with my hand as I look over at her. "You're bad."

"No," she says as she lies down and rests her head on my thigh. "I'm good, I swear. I'm Gidget, remember? Not tragic."

I play with her hair and watch the movie and before I know it, we're curled up together on the couch, her back pressing against my chest and my arm tucked around her middle, breathing deeply and falling asleep.

CHAPTER TWENTY

Rook

I've always been a deep sleeper but how Ronin got his hand under my shirt and cupping my breast is a little beyond the scope of any past sleeping experiences I've ever had with an almost complete stranger. I'm not sure what to do. Besides his hold on one of my girls, he's got his other hand very low down on my belly. Pretty much slipped inside the waistband of my jeans, it's dangerously close to descending past a point of no return.

And I'm basically lying here with a racing heart from these simple touches. I cannot even imagine how turned on I'd be if his fingers slid between my legs.

I'd be undone for sure.

He's also pressing himself up against my ass, making it hard to ignore a feature of men in the morning the world over. The wood.

I giggle a little at my thoughts and he stirs awake.

Oh, shit! Now he's gonna wonder why I didn't move his hands!

I'm saved by a loud knock on the door.

"Shit," Ronin says, obviously awake because that was not a husky I-just-woke-up voice. He disentangles himself from me and makes his way to the door.

It's Elise. I can sorta hear them, but not really because they talk low. I do catch something about me being here and then it sounds like Elise is asking a bunch of questions. I sit up on the couch and straighten out my shirt, feeling a little bit like an intruder as I wait for the conversation to be over.

The door closes with a quiet little click and then Ronin comes around the corner and smiles. "Sorry, didn't mean to wake you."

"What time is it? I can't believe I slept here on your couch."

"It's five thirty, and I enjoyed you sleeping here. I hope you'll do it again tonight, actually."

"Oh," is all I can say to that.

He shoots me a grin. "But right now I'm gonna walk you back to the garden apartment so you can sleep in. Mondays are crazy busy and Elise just excused you from shampoo duty. She says for you to come by the salon around two o'clock. That sound cool?"

I make a face. "So I have to spend the whole day in my apartment?"

He shrugs. "You can spend it here if you want, but it's gonna get noisy."

"No, I didn't mean that, I just meant…" What the hell did I mean? "Never mind, yeah, it's better to go back to my apartment. I need to hang up all those clothes anyway. What should I wear when I show up for Elise?"

"Jeans, whatever. She'll tell you what she wants you to wear."

"Oh," I say again. "I thought you ran the clothes?"

"I do, but I have to take care of something today. That's what Elise came to tell me. So I'll miss your big debut and we'll do those cherry tree pics tomorrow."

I shrug on the outside, but inside I'm wondering just what this is all about. He's got to leave for an entire day? I slip my Converse on and he opens the front door for me. I feel a little cheap as I make my way down the stairs and then when he says goodbye at the terrace door, holding it open for me so I can pass through alone, I almost feel dirty.

I'm not even sure where this feeling is coming from, I mean I didn't sleep with him or anything. I just feel like he's trying to get rid of me before anyone figures out I spent the night at his house.

I turn to say goodbye, but the door is already swinging closed. So I pad over to my own place, let myself in, and flop down on the couch, trying very hard not to feel used.

But Rook, the internal monologue starts, *you know he's a player. He's a male model for Pete's sake. His job is 'running the girls' at a major photography studio.*

Maybe I should take the money I make today and leave?

I can get on the bus and go to Vegas like I planned. Denver was never my original stop anyway. I was on the bus to Vegas but—well, it's a long story but I never intended to stay here in Denver. I mean who lives in Denver anyway? Not that it will be any better in Vegas, but I feel like my life is out of control right now. Like I'm not in charge of myself. And the last time I felt this way it was because my ex was the one controlling me.

I don't want to be controlled so if I made the decision to leave, then I could take that control back. If I stay here, then Ronin and Antoine and Elise have control over me, no matter how subtle.

Ughhh. Why can't life be simple?

I start picking through my new clothes, hanging up the ones that need hanging and folding the ones that need to get put away in drawers. It occurs to me pretty quickly that I have one pair of shoes and that's it. My Converse will not cut it if I want to go somewhere in a skirt.

After I hang stuff I tackle the dresser drawers. I open up the top drawer to put the underwear away and get a surprise.

This drawer is full.

Of underwear.

What the fuck?

I mean, I realize Elise said another girl used to live here, but she left her underwear? And that explains the make-up in the bathroom. And all the shampoo and soaps and stuff. Yeah, another girl lived here, but she left so fast she didn't even bother to take her very expensive-looking undergarments?

Wait a minute. These underwear are all brand new, they have tags on them.

I sit down on the bed and shake my head. What the hell can that mean? They stock this place with new underwear and makeup for… what? What reason could they have?

Maybe they have so many girls come through here I'm just another temporary occupant?

I am so confused. I mean, when Ronin is around everything feels right about this place. I feel comfortable around him, he makes me laugh, I make him laugh. We have what appears to be an easy friendship.

But every time I get away from him, all these things that might seem cozy and comfortable start to make me claustrophobic and paranoid. And I'm not really in a good place right now to be able to distinguish between the two. I can't really trust myself to see the difference between what is normal and what isn't because I've lived with abnormal for too long.

The only thing I really do know is that I need this job. No matter what's going on here, I need this job. And then once I get some money I'll bail and head west like I planned and forget all about Ronin the rogue samurai and the whole Antoine Chaput debacle. Maybe I'll go to LA, that's where people who want to go to film school live, right? I'll find a cheap apartment, get a roommate, live there for the required year to get in-state tuition, and then get my ass into some community college and finally get my life on track.

Ronin Flynn might be hot, he might have manners, and he might have a soft side—but he's definitely not settle-down material and he certainly seems to have a problem with letting a woman make her own decisions. And I'm not ready to hand that back over again.

I'd rather spend the rest of my life alone and lonely than give up my freedom again. I need to keep my eye on the prize. And that means no more flirting with Ronin, no matter what.

CHAPTER TWENTY-ONE

Rook

I lie in my new comfortable bed for a while and then let myself doze for a few hours before I have to go meet Elise. When I get up I take a bath but don't wash my hair because I figure I'll get the whole hair treatment in the salon. Plus, the same claw-foot tub that looked vintage and charming when I first saw it now looks old and dingy.

It's not charming, it's a major pain in the ass.

When I'm clean and dressed I head out to the terrace and steady myself for the day.

It's only one, so I have an hour before Elise needs me, but I figure I can get acclimated to whatever it is that's going on in the studio. I pull the doors open and I'm immediately assaulted with the bustle of people. There is laughing, talking, cameras going crazy, lights being moved, a few squeals from the girls, frantic rushing into and out of the dressing room and pretty much every degree of chaos you can think of crammed into this one room.

There are several photographers and that surprises me. I expected that Antoine was the only one who worked here because of how quiet it was last week. But today there are no fewer than four people taking pictures as I stand there.

There are also girls, in various stages of dress, everywhere. Two are naked. Granted, the naked ones are all in the middle of a session with their respective photographers, but still.

Naked.

I am not doing *anything* naked.

A few of the girls look over at me and point, then whisper to each other. I look around, then down. Not sure what to do.

"Rook!" Elise's voice bellows out of the cacophony of noise. "I'm ready, sweetie, come in here!" She disappears behind the salon wall and I follow her.

"Did you sleep well?" Elise asks as she takes me by the arm and leads me over to the shampoo station, then pushes me into the chair.

That question sounds loaded, but I choose to ignore that and answer honestly. "Yes, great, thanks."

If she's interested in that answer she doesn't show it because the water is streaming down my head and she's busy doing her job. It's not relaxing like it was last time, it's tense. My whole neck is tense, even as she does a little scalp massage.

"Ronin won't be back until tonight. He asked me to tell you."

"OK, thanks," I manage to say as she rinses and then applies some conditioner to my long tresses.

"I'm going to have Josie trim your hair. You need it badly."

"OK." I agree because what am I gonna say? I figure that was not really a question, just a statement of facts. *Rook, I control you now, so I'm going to have someone cut your hair.*

"Then you'll sit for Roger. Antoine has to do some retakes, so he can't shoot you today. Roger is good, though. That's one thing you can count on here—everyone does their job well or they are asked to leave."

This sounds like a warning, but maybe I should be thankful? It gives me some control back. If I do my job well I can stay. If I don't, then I can go. It's up to me really. I'm not exactly sure what's all entailed in doing a good job at modeling, but I imagine it has a lot to do with following directions.

And that rubs me wrong too. Because that takes away the control I'm trying to talk myself into thinking I have.

Who am I kidding? I'm not in control at all.

Elise is done with my hair so she pushes on me to sit up. The water drips all over my t-shirt and she rubs the towel over my head, but my hair is so long it spills out and drags the water along with it.

"I like your shirt. I have one like that too, we did a shoot for them a few months ago."

I look up at her to see if she's joking, but she's not paying attention to me, she's calling for Josie to come do my trim. "It came from your closet, Ronin said I could have it," I confess.

She looks back at me and smiles. "Oh good. We have hundreds of them left. I like it but shit, ya know? A hundred of them is too many. All the girls took what they wanted, you take as many as you like."

She introduces Josie and I don't even bother contradicting the fact that Elise just told her to remove four freaking inches off the length of my hair. I just sit still and let them control me because all I can think about is how Ronin picked this shirt for me, so maybe he knew they had so many no one would care? I thought it was nice until I learned it was unwanted.

I snort out a laugh at the absurdity of my reasoning.

"You OK, sweetie?"

What's with the sweetie stuff around here? Is this how grown women talk to each other? "Yeah," I mumble. "Just thinking of something." I sit quietly after that and just let Josie do her thing. When she's done cutting she starts blow-drying, Elise is busy with another girl on the other side of the salon, but when she's done she comes back and begins to wrap my hair in hot rollers. "Roger wants big bouncy curls, he said. So, that's what you get today."

"OK." That's pretty much the extent of my vocabulary right now. *Just agree, Rook. Just agree and take your money and then you'll have more choices, but right now, you just have to do what you're told.*

When she's done Elise ushers me over to another part of the salon and someone applies makeup while another girl does my nails. "You need toes today, honey?"

I shrug. That's not a question I can answer with OK. The would-be pedicurist leaves to ask Elise, and I can hear Elise become frustrated and tell her to get busy on my feet.

I've never had a pedicure, and maybe if I was paying for it and I was somewhere I could relax, I might enjoy it. But right now the last thing I want is this woman touching my toes. I balk a little when she starts rubbing cream on them, but she mistakes that for being ticklish. "Don't worry, hun. I'm not a tickler. You'll be fine."

I suck in a deep breath and let them do their thing.

When I'm done my hair is filled with loose bouncy curls, my nails and toes are both cherry red, and my make-up has me looking like I should be walking Colfax with the whores.

Elise comes back as I sit there, feeling stupid and fake. The other girls are on a break and the place has quieted down considerably since my arrival. For some reason I imagined models and artsy photographers as being afternoon people, but what do I know?

"OK, Rook. You're up." She thrusts a garment bag at me. "Since you've met the dressing room, go on and get dressed—only put on what's in the bag. When you're done, go find Roger, he's the blond one."

I don't even get to say OK this time. She walks off, calling for someone else.

CHAPTER TWENTY-TWO

Rook

The dressing room has a few girls in it, but they ignore me and concentrate on themselves.

I take the hint and do the same.

Or I try to, because they are all naked and I'm just not ready to get naked in the middle of the room with these girls.

A tiny girl, someone who looks like the opposite of the image you have in your head when you say the word model, stops in front of me and smiles. "First day?"

I try not to notice she's got no shirt on, but I think I fail. "Yeah."

She nods her head towards the other side of the room. "There's privacy stalls over there if you need one." And then she saunters off, her long blonde hair bouncing along her butt.

Modest these girls are not. I look down at myself and get a sick feeling. I'm not sure I can get naked in front of them so I opt for the private dressing rooms.

The outfit was not what I was expecting. In fact, I almost laugh when I take it out of the garment bag. It's a pair of well-worn jeans and a dark red t-shirt. Both of which look like they came from the men's department so they are monumentally too big for me, but I do what I was told, pull on the jeans, and slip the shirt over my head. There's no bra or panties in the bag, so I'm commando on both ends.

When I study myself in the mirror I can only sigh. Why did Elise get me all made up just to wear some old, half-ripped jeans and a cruddy t-shirt?

I walk out barefoot, because there were no shoes in the bag either.

At first I figured finding Roger could not be that hard, but there are no blond guys with cameras, so I just stand there until one of the girls comes out of the dressing room and I grab her attention real quick. "Roger?" I ask, as if that explains everything. She points to a guy who is sitting on a table on the far side of the studio. I turn to say thank you, but the girl is gone.

I take a deep breath and walk over towards Roger. He spies me coming from a distance and walks to meet me.

Well, that was nice.

"Ruth?"

"Ah, no. I'm Rook."

"Rook, right. That's what I meant. OK, Antoine just wants the standard portrait shots and then if we have time, I'll take some artistic ones of you and Billy since he has the other half of this outfit on."

He points to a shaggy-haired guy across the room who is also wearing an old pair of weathered jeans and a red t-shirt. Only his are much smaller than mine. "Maybe they got the clothes mixed up?" I say out loud before I can stop myself.

Roger laughs. "Why do you say that?"

"Well, his clothes look awfully tight and mine are awfully loose. It makes no sense."

He eyes me cautiously. "You're really new, aren't you?"

"First day," I reply as the nervousness appears in my stomach as a billion butterflies. "Why? Is there some secret about the clothing sizes that I should know about?"

He shrugs. "Ready then? Go stand over there and then we'll adjust the lights." I do as I'm told and stand on a little x taped to the floor. He's got four helpers just for us and they bustle around with lighting things and the background image, which is just black.

And that's pretty much where my thoughts stop. The rest is just turning and looking, and changing position, and closing my eyes, then opening them. I do a whole lot of things—standing, sitting, kneeling.

But the one thing I never get asked to do is smile.

Again.

This is weird to the point of almost being creepy because the last time I was here Antoine never asked me to smile either.

"OK, Rook, go grab Billy over there and we'll set up for the artistic shots."

I nod out a yes, but this makes me jitter with nervousness. I walk slowly over towards the Billy guy. His shoot is over and he's just hanging out with a girl.

A girl who looks pretty pissed off that I just walked up to them and interrupted.

"Uh, sorry. Excuse me, Billy? Roger asked me to come get you."

The girl sneers at me then kisses Billy, drags her fingernail down his chest, and whispers, "Call me later," as she saunters off. I watch her for several seconds before turning back.

Billy is watching me.

I smile.

He sighs and walks over towards Roger.

Shit, these people are not as friendly as I'd hoped. Even Elise was kinda short and testy with me today. I look up at a giant clock on the wall and wonder when the day will end. It's already almost six o'clock and I'm very hungry. I munched on my take-home breakfast from Cookie's the other day, but that was right after I came home from Ronin's and I didn't have any lunch. Maybe this is why models are so skinny—there's no food around!

I reach Roger a few seconds after Billy and they are already positioning him on a bed that has somehow materialized. My heart beats a little faster and my eyes dart around to try and figure out what we're doing.

"Relax, Rook. There's a reason for the loose clothing, it's so that when Billy here gropes you the clothes show some skin. So go ahead and sit down next to him and we'll get this started."

Gropes me? I'm thinking I'm saying that out loud, but I'm not. So no one explains, but Billy does get up and takes my hand and leads me over to the bed.

"First time?" he asks casually as we stand there.

"What?"

"For an artistic shoot? I haven't seen you around before and you look pretty nervous."

"I am," I confess. "I've never done this before."

He slips his hand up my shirt and all I hear is the rapid clicking of a camera shutter. I look around and the shoot has started.

"Don't worry, it'll be quick." He tugs on my shirt, exposing my belly, then pulls it up and leans in to kiss me. I don't know what I'm thinking but I let him. This is work, right? This is what they do? Kiss each other?

I have no idea, but his hands are all over me, his mouth is traveling down my neck fast, and I'm starting to shake.

"Easy," he whispers. "He won't shoot long. Just listen to me, OK?"

I nod.

"Just let me do my thing, pretend you're in love with me and my hands are a gift from God, and he'll get his shots and we can go eat or something."

Is he asking me out? I am so confused but I do what I'm told. It's not that hard, Billy is doing all the work, really. His hands do the groping, pulling the red shirt this way and that, exposing my skin, my belly here, parts of my breast there. It's OK. This is work.

"OK, Rook," Roger says, interrupting my thoughts. "Take his shirt off, *slowly*."

Oh, shit.

"Any day now, Rook."

I nod. OK. I lift up the bottom of his shirt—

"Slower, Rook."

Right. Slowly.

"Now look at him while you do it."

This gets very personal, very fast. Because Billy here has a hard-on, I can feel it as he presses his leg against my hip, and his eyes look like he's about to throw me down on the bed and make me scream his name right here in front of the whole studio filled with people.

"Keep working, Rook."

I tug the shirt up again and Billy lets out a moan. "Shit, Rook," he says. "You're sexy. I don't even have to try."

I do try… and ignore him, that is. But it's pretty hard when Roger is constantly telling me to look Billy in the eyes. Finally, *finally* I get the shirt over his head and then he starts on mine.

"Am I supposed to take my shirt off?"

"Just go with it, Rook, or we'll be here all fucking night."

Billy leans in to kiss me and the shutter goes wild again.

"Slower this time, Billy. I need lips for stock art."

Billy slows down and takes his time coming at me.

"Rook, either respond or we'll have to do it again."

I do my best, but I'm not that great of a kisser and Billy here is doing enough for both of us. His hands slip around my waist, pulling me close. "Touch me, Rook, let the man get his photos."

I allow my hands to travel up his torso and feel a shiver burst from his skin. My body responds the same way as his hand slips under my shirt and then he spins me around, lifting the loose fabric up as his hand explores my breast. He's kissing my neck and tugging on the jeans. They are so loose, they almost fall down my hips. This makes Roger call out a "Nice, Billy! Do that some more," to which Billy responds by slipping his hand right between my legs.

I let out a giant gasp and Billy is about to swipe my shirt clean off when Ronin is up in his face screaming. "What the fuck are you doing?"

I'm discarded by Billy, instantly forgotten as the two of them push each other.

Roger is trying to run interference and then Ronin pushes Billy so hard he comes hurtling towards me, knocking against my shoulder, and sends me crashing to the ground.

Everything stops.

Everyone looks.

And then Elise is pulling me up and shoving me towards the stairs as Antoine and several other people pull Billy and Ronin apart.

"I fucking told you portraits, Antoine! What the fuck is going on here?"

"Go upstairs and wait for Ronin, Rook," Elise says sternly, like this is somehow my fault.

I start walking, watching them fight.

What just happened?

I get to Ronin's apartment but the door is locked, so I go back and sit on the top step because I can't even remember my birthday right now, let alone his security code. I just sit there and listen to them all argue inside Antoine's office. The door is closed, I can tell by the muffled voices, but it's not sound-proof.

The yelling gets louder and then the door opens because the voices are like right there, echoing off the massive walls of the studio. Almost everyone has cleared out now, and then I watch Ronin as he takes the stairs three at a time. When he gets to me he stops.

Just stops. There are no hurried words or fast actions. He is just still.

"I'm sorry, I told Antoine what I wanted, but he forgot to tell Roger. It was a mistake. I'm sorry."

"What was a mistake?"

"That shoot with fucking Billy!"

He says it like he can't believe I had to ask, so I just nod. "Right, OK."

He takes my hand and leads me towards his apartment, then he must spy my bare feet. "Where're your shoes?"

"The dressing room, with my clothes."

"OK," he says, pushing me through the apartment door, "I'll get them, you stay here."

I stand in the middle of the room, watching the empty space where he just was.

This whole thing is getting weird. I might need to go back to the shelter. This thought makes me swallow down a giant lump in my throat because I really do not want to go back there.

Ronin takes forever, so I just take a seat on the couch and wait. Still, he does not come back. I lie down and close my eyes. I have to admit, even after all I've been through in the past few months, this has been one of the longest and most confusing days of my entire life.

CHAPTER TWENTY-THREE

Rook

I wake abruptly as Ronin adjusts my body so my head is resting in his lap. "What?"

"Sorry," he says. "You fell asleep and I just wanted to sit with you. Rook, I am so sorry about earlier. Antoine said he was going to do the shoot himself, I asked him to keep an eye on you. It shouldn't have happened."

I sit up, the make-up from earlier making my face feel caked with filth, and I'm almost positive that it's totally streaked all over my face. I have like a ton of goop in my eyes and it's taking every ounce of self-control not to rub them red. "What *was* supposed to happen?"

"Just some portrait pics, that's all. I told him."

"Well, that Roger guy did take a bunch of those. I know that for sure. Then he said I was dressed for an artistic shoot with Billy and—"

"Yeah, fucking Roger knows better. We don't stick new girls with Billy."

I take a deep breath and turn to look at him. "Ronin, why don't you tell me exactly what you guys do here? Is it porn, or what?"

"No," he says quickly. "It's not porn, it's… erotic art."

"Uh-huh. Erotic art. So what exactly do you guys want me for? Just so we're clear."

"Pictures."

"Of me naked?"

"No… I mean… well, somewhat naked, yes. We're not

doing cock shots or shit like that, Rook. It's tasteful nudes and stuff."

I laugh as I stand up. "OK, I'm probably gonna have to leave. I mean, I'm not against doing some pictures, even some racy ones, but I need to think about it and see how much money it pays and I'm not comfortable doing that here. So I'm gonna go back to the shelter for a while and you guys call me if—"

"Absolutely not, Rook! You're not going to a fucking homeless shelter. We're having dinner with Antoine and Elise in an hour to sort it all out, you can't leave before you at least get all the details."

I hesitate because I don't want to go back to the shelter, I mean, I would almost rather sleep anywhere else but there, so I hesitate.

"Just go take a shower, put on your own clothes, and let's have dinner, OK?"

I am seriously starving and my rumbling stomach wins the night. I can at least hear them out. "OK." He sighs with relief. "I would like to take a shower, actually."

His eyes light up. "That's the best news I've heard all day. Follow me, I'll introduce you to the beast."

I follow him into the bathroom off the hallway and he's not kidding. The shower is a beast. It's a massive work of tiled art with more knobs and shower heads than I can even imagine are necessary.

He sees me eyeing them suspiciously. "Don't even ask, Rook. I have no idea what they all do. But if you press this button here"—he points to something that looks like a security system control panel—"then they all come on at once and I'll just warn you now, that shit is better than sex."

"Oh," I moan, "that's too bad. I totally thought the only way I'd feel better tonight was if I could just get me some sex, but now that I have this here shower, I guess I'm good."

"You're OK, then?" He takes my joking as a good sign, but honestly, it's my default setting. When I get nervous and

I'm not in danger of getting my face punched in, I tend to turn into a smart-ass.

"I'm really not, but I'm trying real hard, Ronin."

He walks over to me, doesn't touch me, but gets close enough so that we don't need to touch to understand what's going on. I can feel his presence, like his body has an electric field around it and I've suddenly found myself inside. I have to look up at him because now that we're standing right up next to each other I realize how tall he is. At least five inches taller than me and I'm five nine.

"Just give us a chance, OK? If you don't want the job I'll understand. But this day should not have happened this way."

He watches me intently but I'm not capable of talking about this right now. I need some space. "Can you go get me some clothes from the apartment? I'll even let you pick them."

"Yeah, sure. I'll just turn on the shower for you." He messes with the control panel and water starts spraying out in all directions. I smile a thank you and he leaves, closing the door behind him.

When I look in the bathroom mirror I was right about the make-up—it is totally smeared under my eyes. The beastly shower feels better than ever right now. My body is tired and not eating right is not helping. I hope they are having something good for dinner because if it's some French shit, I might scream and throw a fit until they feed me a burger or take me to the baseball stadium for a hot dog.

When I'm done I wrap the towel around me and open the door cautiously, I can hear Ronin talking on the phone. I listen for a few seconds, but it's all in French and I only catch the name Clare. There's a small pile of clothes on the floor in front of the bathroom and I grab them and disappear back inside. He picked me out a very sweet white bra and panty set, some pink capris, a pink tank top, and a white cotton button-up sweater. I slip on my beat-up old Converse because they're all I have. When I look in the mirror my long black hair contrasts with the cute outfit and I suddenly feel like biker Gidget.

He was so right last night—I'm no Gidget. I'm definitely a tragic if ever there was one.

Ronin is sitting on his couch watching sports when I come back out.

"Feel better?"

I nod. "Yeah, I do."

He gets up, takes my hand, and then we walk down the hallway towards the stairs. It's so quiet compared to earlier I almost don't recognize the studio as we walk past and continue down the hall. Ronin punches in a code, opens the door and waves me in first.

Antoine and Elise are nowhere to be found, so I take a moment to study the apartment. It's like stepping back into the Roaring Twenties. The whole inside looks like something off *The Great Gatsby* movie set, it's all curves and contrasts—art deco from top to bottom. The furniture is ultra-modern but old and stylish at the same time. The chairs and couches have high curved backs, and the black piping on the cushions perfectly sets off the white fabric.

The far side of the room is one giant circular window that has pocket glass doors to allow access to the terrace. This is where the voices are coming from and Ronin leads me through the portal-like door. Exiting onto the terrace is like stepping into another world. There are twinkling white lights strung everywhere and the terrace itself is massive. Like bigger than the first floor of the house I lived in back in Chicago. It's furnished like the inside, except with weatherproof fabrics.

Ronin calls out a, "Hey." And both Antoine and Elise pull apart from an embrace like two school kids caught necking in the hallways.

Did I just use the word necking?

The Gidget outfit is getting to me, I think.

"I hope you like kebabs," Ronin says. "Antoine makes some of the best kebabs ever."

"If it's meat, I'll eat it," I reply, my stomach growling like mad with the smell that wafts off the grill and teases my senses.

"You wanna beer?"

"Sure." This is already turning out to be way better than I imagined, so why not relax a little. In my head dinner with the Chaputs involved a white tablecloth, crystal glassware, and eating snails drowning in butter with tiny little forks.

Ronin grabs a Corona from a box filled with ice and twists off the cap, then hands it to me and takes one for himself. He grabs two lime wedges from a little silver bucket in the ice, and shoves them down the neck of each beer. I enjoy the smell of a fizzy lime-infused beer and then take a long gulp.

Elise walks over to us. "How old are you, Rook?"

"Twenty-one."

"Really?"

"Shut up, Elise, like you waited until you were twenty-one to drink. Leave her alone, she's here to relax."

Elise narrows her eyes at Ronin and then looks over to me. "I wasn't asking because of the beer, I just need to know for our contracts. Are you really twenty-one?"

"No, I'm nineteen," I say, a little ashamed as I try and hand the beer back to Ronin. He shakes his head at me and I keep the beer.

"I'm not interested in policing your alcohol habits, Rook. This is a working dinner, sweetie, and it involves contracts so I just want to make sure you are legal to sign them. We need to get some things straight and we need to know what you will and won't be doing for us while you're working here."

I swallow. Boy, she really gets to the point.

"Because while we feel what we do here is art, not everyone agrees and you need to know what it means for you to agree to model for us. OK?"

I nod.

"So Ronin, why don't you go keep Antoine company while Rook and I go over the particulars."

"You OK with this, Rook?" he asks.

"Yeah, sure. It's business."

He smiles and walks over to Antoine, who has switched the conversation to French. I can hear Ronin say, "English, you ape," as he approaches.

"Have a seat, Rook." I look back to Elise, who is all business right now. Gone is that little fairy woman who took pity on me as I cried on the stairs and I'm sorta sorry she got to see me in such a weak position, it puts me behind right now. Like she knows I'm not strong so she automatically gets the upper hand.

I sit like I'm told and wait for it.

"OK, I'm not going to sugarcoat it because I'm hungry and I try and treat everyone the same, and I don't sugarcoat it for any of the other models, so you are no different just because Ronin wants to keep you."

"What?"

"He likes you, Rook, I think we can both agree that is true. So what I want you to know up front is that we are an erotic photography studio, we supply photos, *tasteful photos*," she enunciates, "to companies like publishers, producers, large marketing firms and the like. They typically come in an order that asks for something specific, but if we have images we can't use, leftovers and such, we sell them to stock art companies. Do you know what that is, Rook? Stock art?"

I shake my head.

"It's a database of photos on a large website that allows anyone to buy the images for a fee and use them as they see fit for projects, with certain restrictions regarding print production. So this means, should you sign our model release form, your body could end up pretty much anywhere. On the cover of a book, in an advertisement, a CD cover, things like that. Do you understand this?"

"Yes, I understand."

"Good. So here's the deal. You don't have to do nudes. We have some work for you that is straight portrait and fashion, a bit of glamour stuff every now and then like Clare does. You'll make twenty dollars an hour and that's it. You work by the hour and the work for these types of shots is not steady, but since Ronin seems compelled to take care of you, you hardly need the money."

I'm not sure why, but I take offense to this statement.

"Ronin would prefer this option, but you should know that if you get a private contract—for instance, if you agree to do the TRAGIC campaign we are setting up—you will make thousands of dollars. Many thousands of dollars. This contract has a budget of two hundred and fifty thousand dollars and a portion of that is for the models. If you're chosen and you agree, you'll make a lot of money. This is what we do here. We make a lot of money, but there is a price to pay. Your images will be all over."

"OK."

"OK? That's it?"

"What do you want me to say?"

She takes a deep breath. "Let me give you some advice, Rook. Because if you like Ronin, and I know this from my own experience with Antoine, he will not want you to take those contracts. So if you do, you might pay that price too."

I take a swig of my beer and look away for a moment, over at Ronin and Antoine as they fool with the grill and the food. I'm not sure why, but this whole thing with Ronin is bugging me. "Elise, I like your brother. He's one sexy man, pardon me for saying that as you're his sister. And he's a model, and he's got a lot of money, but I've known the guy for four days. I'm not ready to base a life-changing decision off a potential relationship with him. So if you have a contract I'd like to read it and then I'd like to think about it."

Elise smiles, maybe for the first time since I got here. "Good girl. I was hoping you'd react like that. Ronin is my brother, but he's a twenty-two-year-old guy, you know? They are what they are, and something tells me you need stability right now, am I right?"

I nod. "Yes, I'd very much like to be stable."

"Well, twenty-two-year-old guys aren't known for their

stability, if you get my meaning. Antoine was a lot older than me when we met and even then, it took me almost a year to trust him, so I get it." She lets out a deep breath and closes her eyes for an extended period of time. "It was very hard to trust that he would take care of me and to be perfectly honest, I still have panic attacks over it because we never married. So, think about it all very carefully." She pauses. "And if I could make one suggestion?"

"Yeah, sure."

"Be careful how much time you spend in Ronin's apartment. You have a place, I gave you that place, so use it. Please."

I think about this for a moment and it's like she's reading my mind.

"Yeah, OK."

Her face lights up. "Yeah?"

"I can see the wisdom in that. I crave some private space so bad, I can't even explain it."

She leans over and hugs me and then Ronin is up next to me. "What's going on? Girl hugs are a bad sign."

CHAPTER TWENTY-FOUR

Ronin

Leave it to my sister to fuck everything up. Dammit. Rook is so skittish, she really is like a bird in that respect. Ready to take flight at the slightest hint that something is up. And I can't blame her? If I had her past I'd be skittish too. Hell, I damn near did have her past and I am just barely recovered from it. It took Elise and me years to get over that shit.

But I do not want her down in the studio apartment.

We walk across the large lower terrace and I shake my head.

"What?" she asks.

"I just don't like the idea of you being down here alone. It's too far away, it's dark, it's creepy, it's—"

"It's four stories up and there's a keypad on the studio door."

I smile as I take her hand. She's brave. "I know, but it's far."

"Far from where?"

"Far from me, you little shit." She squeezes my hand and I feel a little better because she's still sending some token I-like-you signals.

I open the door and find the light switch on the side of the wall, not ready to leave her yet.

"So what should I expect tomorrow?"

"Well," I say, trying my best not to ravish her mouth as I watch her chew on her lip. "If you sign the contract then we'll do a practice shoot, in private, well, semi-private. All the technicians will be there and probably two or three photographers."

"Why so many?"

"Antoine likes to get a bunch of angles, and he can only work one camera at a time, so he makes the other guys come in sometimes. Since we're planning on using you for TRAGIC, he'll want as many views as he can get."

"Will you be there with me? Or will I be alone?"

"I'll definitely be there, Gidget. We're submitting the two of us together for the contract."

"So I'll be naked with you?"

I tread carefully. "That's not quite how it works. It's all about the mood of the models."

She walks back to the bedroom and starts fixing the covers on the bed.

"Does that bother you?" I ask. "If I see your body?"

"I'm nervous," she confesses. "I've never done anything like this before, I'm not sure what to expect."

"Well, after tomorrow you'll know exactly what to expect. I won't let anything happen to you, OK?"

"OK," she says. "Thanks for walking me home and—" She stops abruptly. "Well, thanks for everything really."

I back away before I tackle her and rip that adorable little Gidget outfit right off her body. She catches me staring and smiles. "I'm on to you, Larue."

"Yeah," I say, closing the distance between us despite my inner warnings. I wrap both hands around her hips and pull her a little closer. "I don't see how you're on to me when I'm innocent, I have nothing to hide."

"Well, I appreciate the Gidget outfit anyway. It's very cute. And I really expected you to come back with the blue nightie, so it was a huge step up in my mind."

I grin like an idiot picturing me dressing her up in that nightie and then taking her to dinner.

"Ah, I see your mind spinning with that thought. So, I

appreciate your self-control in that area."

I back away again, because I see the stop sign she's getting ready to put up. "Tomorrow we'll do the cherry tree shoot. It will be completely different than what you experienced today, OK?"

"Well, that's if I sign the contract, right? I have to sign that first."

My eyes dart to the papers she set down in the nightstand and I have a moment of hope that she'll wake up in the morning and say screw this contract. But that will never happen, so I just exhale a long breath and force myself to smile. "Yeah, but I think you'll sign it, don't you?"

She studies me for a moment and her brows crease a little in thought. "I need the money," she says almost apologetically.

"Yeah, I get it."

"Well—"

"OK, goodnight, Rook." I turn and walk out of the garden apartment and make my way back upstairs. Maybe she *will* walk away from that contract tomorrow, who knows? I wish she would, because the minute she signs it I have to treat her like all the other models and I have a feeling she's not going to like that one bit.

CHAPTER TWENTY-FIVE

Rook

After Ronin leaves I change into a pair of shorts and a t-shirt and slip into a long peaceful sleep. In fact, when I wake up in the morning I feel rested and at peace with my situation for the first time in like… forever. Even going all the way back to my childhood, before my mom overdosed and I went into foster care. She was a mess. Your typical teen mom. Broke, craving attention, no clue how to take care of a kid.

And my life was never peaceful. It was nothing but chaos. In fact, now that I think about it, my life has been one long chaotic episode after another.

When I first decided to put some thought into getting the hell away from my ex, Jon, I would go to the library and use their computer so I didn't have to worry about my browsing history being detected. I could never trust that anything I looked at on our home computer wasn't being traced because that was Jon's job. Computer forensics. He wasn't a cop but he worked with them all the time.

Scary shit if you're his ex-girlfriend trying to make a clean getaway.

Anyway, the library had all kinds of material on domestic abuse. It took me several visits to finally accept that was the situation I was in. Domestic abuse just sounded so clinical. I just knew he hit me, mostly for no reason, but sometimes I defied him on purpose just to make him do it and get it over with.

It turns out that men who abuse their partners go through

a cycle—it starts out fine, then the tension builds and builds, he snaps and gets violent, and then the make-up stage is the only time he's reasonable.

So even though I didn't really understand this before reading that pamphlet, I could feel these phase changes. I could feel the anger and the tension building to a peak. And it drove me insane, how I had to just wait for him to release it. On me, of course. So sometimes I'd do something on purpose just to get to the make-up stage where I could relax for a few weeks.

Except there's just one problem with that rationale. After a period of time the abuse gets worse and worse and the make-up stage gets shorter and shorter until it fades away entirely. Then there's only tension and violence.

That's the stage Jon and I were in.

Twenty-four-hour tension and violence. If he wasn't hitting me he was yelling at me or calling me names. He especially liked 'whore,' even though he knew damn well he was the only man I'd ever been with. And the last time was the end of the line for me.

After that I knew he was going to kill me next time. Of course I could've called the police and stayed in Chicago, letting the system work it out. But the statistics were not in my favor. Most women went back and even if they did get a restraining order, the guys almost never respected it. There was even a pamphlet on the different methods the men would use to get the women back after incarceration or legal action.

I might still be pretty weak right now, but I am a hundred times stronger than I was back then. I know for sure—I'd have been one of those dumb girls who went back. I would've. So the only way out for me was escape to somewhere else.

I sigh and let all this bad stuff out with the air.

It's over now, so I can let it go. It's been months, he gave up, he's moved on and found someone else to beat, or maybe he got himself thrown in jail for hitting the wrong person. Whatever happened after I left, it didn't happen to me.

I smile at this even though I sorta feel guilty that I didn't put him away so he couldn't hurt anyone else. I am only one girl. And even now I'm not strong—just strong*er*—back then it was incomprehensible that I could do anything to stop him. Maybe someday I'll have it in me to fight back like that if it ever happens again, but right now I'm fragile.

But I'll take fragile. It's a hell of a lot better than broken.

And that's what I was back in Chicago. A mess of shattered emotions and irrational feelings that had no hope of understanding that what he did to me was not love.

That's the one thing I accepted pretty quick when I started to realize what was happening to me internally—the way I justified his acts and allowed him to keep me there in the house after his abuse. I was just as sick as him, but in a different way. I had a psychological disorder that grew over the years until I was incapable of understanding what a healthy relationship was.

I was sick. The abuse had conditioned me into some strange state of acceptance and I can remember every detail of the day it all became clear. I was sitting at a computer in the library and I suddenly looked around.

And asked myself an honest question.

Is this all there is for me?

I mean, I was a kid once. I had dreams. I had plans. But there I was. In a public library looking up facts about domestic violence when I had a state-of-the-art computer at home in my living room that I was afraid to use.

I was broken, beaten, and scared of pretty much everything.

And it hit me.

If I wanted to change my life then I'd have to do it myself. Because no one was coming to protect me, or save me, or heal me.

There was just me.

There is no such thing as heroes, no such thing as being rescued, and if I had a domestic violence problem, then I better be able to figure it out myself because if I didn't, I was going to end up dead.

And while Ronin seems like a good guy, he has triggered a lot of red flags that keep me guessing. And guessing about my safety isn't something I can afford to do right now. Because in the end there is still only me.

I need to keep this in mind as I make choices about what I will and won't do while I'm here living in Antoine Chaput's erotic photography studio.

Because if I'm not careful, the tide of abuse will wash over me again, and this time I might sink instead of swim.

CHAPTER TWENTY-SIX

Rook

Elise's knock disrupts my reality check and I smile at her face peeking in through the window next to the door. I trot over and let her in.

"OK, big day today, Rook. I've got a lot to tell you, so let's get started."

Elise is all business and I kind of like that because she seems like a straight shooter, she just lays it all out and steps back to let me react.

"I'm ready."

And I am. I listen to every word, she points out every single stipulation in the contract. Nowhere does it say I will take off my clothes, and nowhere does it say I can't refuse to do certain shots. I like this part. What it does say is that if I don't cooperate and allow the photographer to produce what he's asked to fulfill for the contract, I will not be paid. And if I don't follow the rules of conduct for the models, I will be fired and asked to leave.

It's my choice.

I initial each stipulation without blinking. I can do this, I've decided. I will be cautious and think clearly and make decisions based on facts and not emotions. And the fact is that right now, I want that money. If I can get a few thousand dollars together, I can really make a go at starting again.

I'm not stupid—I know modeling is a short-term thing. This is not a career, just a stepping stone.

So I initial every stipulation and sign the contract.

Because I've thought about my second chance a lot over the past several months. I've dreamed it. I want it very badly. And for whatever reason the Chaput people have decided they want to help me get it. So I'm taking this chance and running with it until I'm out of breath. And when I've gotten all there is to get from it, I'm out and onto my own dreams.

Elise hugs me after my hand swishes the final letter of my name on the contract. "OK, Rook, let's go make some big money, shall we?"

"We shall," I say, laughing.

Elise and I walk into the studio together and I'm surprised at how calm things are compared to yesterday. She reads my expression. "Mondays are crazy," she explains. "We have to get all the contracts for the week settled and everyone is tense until the schedule is cemented. Most days are not like Monday, but they can be if we get something in that's on a short deadline."

She directs me to the salon chair and today we are the only ones, like it was last week when I first showed up. Has it only been five days since I met these people? Since I was homeless? Since I spent my last ten dollars on a coffee and had that little white card flipped at me in the coffee shop?

It can hardly be possible, but it is.

I have only really known Ronin for three days and change. The first day doesn't count because we never got a chance to talk until the day was over. He only said that one phrase about not making it here if they couldn't touch me when I first showed up.

Oh. God.

What am I doing?

Elise, the ever-perceptive older sister, picks up on my

apprehension. "Take a deep breath. I'll be watching the whole thing, Rook. No one will take advantage of you here. I see everything."

I believe her and my heart rate calms.

"Besides," she says as she sprays water down the side of my face. "Ronin is your partner today, and I might be his sister, but it's hard not to notice. All the girls like him—"

I open my eyes and let some water splash in just so I can pay better attention to what she's saying.

"—*because*," she emphasizes, "he is very patient and gentle when the situation calls for it. He will take care of you while you're here modeling for us, trust me."

I relax and decide to go with it. I signed the contract, the money has been promised, the shoot is set up, I'm getting my hair done, and Ronin's hands are the ones that will be on me, not some stranger's.

That sends shivers all the way up my body.

Elise adjusts the water temperature, thinking I'm cold, and I decide that she really does see everything.

When Elise is done I change into a thin wraparound robe that ties in the front. She styles my hair straight, then braids it loosely so that it falls down the front of me. She paints on some make-up while another girl removes the cherry-red polish on my nails that was just applied yesterday and exchanges it for a pale pink.

When they turn my chair around so I can see myself in the mirror I'm a little taken back. "I thought the theme was tragic? I look… sweet."

Not at all how I imagined.

"Well, this is pretty much how tragedy takes hold, right, Rook? You start out all sweet and innocent and then bam, your world is ripped apart. So for this shoot you are happy and yes, sweet. I have your clothes set out in the dressing room, you won't have to worry about your hair, it's a zip-up."

And that's my cue to get up and get ready. My stomach is a ball of knots as I make my way into the dressing room. There's only one garment bag on the rack and it's got a slip of paper on it that says, ROOK—TRAGIC.

"Ready?" Ronin's husky voice whispers down into my neck as his hands brush against my shoulders for a moment, then take hold and turn me around.

"Yeah, I think so."

"OK, first things first. I need you to step on the scale." He points to a large stand-up scale in the corner. It looks like it belongs in a doctor's office.

"Why?"

He raises his eyebrow at me.

"I mean, why do you need to weigh me?"

He pushes on the small of my back and guides me over to the scale. "Because, Rook, this is my job here. I run the girls, I run the closet, and I take it very seriously. So now that the contract is signed, I have to keep track of you. Please, step on the scale."

I think I feel sick. He gets to weigh me? "What if I don't?"

"Why do you care if I weigh you?" he asks with an annoyed look on his face.

"It's degrading. You're reducing me to a number."

"It's not just a number, it's an indicator."

I turn as my whole body goes hot with anger. "Indicator of *what*?"

"Of whether or not you are following the rules we have in place for keeping the models looking a certain way."

He waits as I process what he just said and then reads my silence as acceptance and pushes me until I step on the scale. He steps around to the other side and writes the number down in a tablet. I can't see the number because it's hidden from this side.

"Well?"

"Well, what?" he asks, pushing me to move off the scale and shaking the garment bag at me.

"How much do I weigh?"

"It's just a number, Rook. I never tell the girls how much they weigh."

"Why not? It seems pretty stupid to weigh people and then keep it a secret if you ask me."

"Because I'm not interested in what you weigh, only in whether or not you change from the weight you are now."

I snatch the bag from him and walk away. I am so fucking glad I did not decide to rely on Ronin Flynn, because he's an asshole. I choose the same dressing room as I did yesterday and unzip the bag to look at the clothes.

It's a pink knee-length dress and it's straight out of Gidget. I stand on my tip toes and peek over the door.

Ronin smiles and waves his finger at me from down the hall.

There's no underwear or bra again.

I slip out of my clothes and pull the dress on. It's got a squared-off neckline that plunges right down to my girls and a wire underneath so they are pushed up high on my chest.

So I guess I'm skanky Gidget today.

"There's no shoes," I call out.

"Just go barefoot," Ronin says, peeking over the door at me.

"Do you mind?"

He responds by opening the door and stepping into the dressing room with me. "Turn around," he says, twirling his finger at me. "I'll zip you up."

Oh. I turn and he zips. "I thought you were shooting with me?"

"I am."

"Then how come you're not dressed?"

"I am."

"You're wearing jeans and a t-shirt, like you always do."

"Rook, no one gives a shit what I wear. They want me

naked and if I'm not naked, then I'm just there to make you look good until we do get naked."

My face has got to be scarlet red. "Oh."

"Ready then?"

"Ready as I'll ever be, I guess." Ronin takes my hand and leads me out to the terrace and when I step over that threshold I feel it in my bones. Nothing about my life will ever be the same after this. I'm just not sure if that's a good or bad thing just yet.

CHAPTER TWENTY-SEVEN

Rook

I am lost in my own thoughts as Ronin leads me across the terrace to the cherry trees. Antoine and Elise are sitting at one of the picnic tables, chatting and smiling. There is no one else around, not even a light person. This makes me let out a long exhale and Ronin squeezes my hand. "You OK?" he asks, stopping for a moment to get my response.

"Yeah, I'm just glad there's not a lot of people around."

"I set it up that way, Rook. Just let me take care of things now, OK?"

I nod so he'll drop it, but this control stuff with him is really setting me back. He acts like I'm not allowed to question him.

We've reached Antoine and Elise now and they are talking, both to me and to Ronin, but I just nod my head and agree because I have no idea what they're talking about. Technical stuff. Natural light, Antoine says. I look around and yes, sure enough, the sun is shining right into the middle of the cherry trees on the east side of the terrace.

I study the 'set' and notice that the swing I was sitting in the other night is not even attached to the tree branches, it's attached to a long green pole that spans the entire grove. There's a picnic set up on the grass, complete with wine glasses, cheese, and a bowl of cherries. The blanket isn't checkered though, it's a crisp white with cotton lace on the edges, and there are cherry blossom petals all over the place. I'm not sure if that was planned or not, because each time the wind blows, those boughs, heavy with the sweet-smelling flowers, release dozens of them at a time.

Everything about these trees says climax. The flowers are mature, falling off and getting ready for the tree to bear fruit over the summer. It's a single moment in time that will be captured on digital film for eternity.

And I'm part of that.

I get the chills and Ronin, still talking to Antoine and Elise, absently pulls me closer to him, like he senses my needs and wants to keep me warm.

It's all very confusing. I like that he notices when I'm having a problem and need something, but I don't like relying on him for stuff and I hate the fact that he's allowed to make decisions for me. It's too personal.

But that's what this contract is all about though, isn't it? I've basically given them my body in exchange for money. And I just have to trust that they will not take advantage of me.

They are finished with their conversation and Ronin leads me over to the cherry tree and leans up against the smooth bark of the trunk and then puts his hands on my hips. We are not that close, there's a good eight inches between us, but I can feel his heat and his hands instantly warm the skin under my dress.

"You OK?" he asks.

"Yeah, I'm good. So what's the plan?" I nod my head over at the blanket. "Besides the picnic?"

"We're gonna get some straight couples shots right here against the tree. We gotta be quick to catch the light just right though, because Antoine likes natural light." He stops to nod at Antoine and the camera shutter begins to click as Ronin continues to talk. "And then we'll just have a little romantic picnic. Sound good?"

"OK, but what do I do? I don't get it."

"Just what you're doing right now, Gidget." He smiles at my new nickname and I blush a little. "See, that right there is what Antoine is looking for. An honest reaction to the situation. So I'll flirt with you and you react. That's pretty much it."

"I think I can handle that."

"Good," he says as his grip on my hips tightens and he pulls me into him. His hands sneak around behind me, not quite on my ass, but not quite *not* on my ass either. They are hovering just on the edge of inappropriate behavior.

Of course, I signed up for this so he's already got permission. I swallow and pull my upper body back as he continues to bring us closer.

"Relax, Gidge. I've got you."

I do, I relax and he pushes my pelvis against his groin. I look up quickly and he's almost laughing at me. The shutter is still clicking away as Antoine moves around us. He speaks to Ronin, but it's all in French, so I have no idea what he's saying and Ronin doesn't reply or translate for me. His attention is one hundred percent on my face, watching everything I do, searching my eyes for questions, his hands still hovering just at the edge of sexy as they caress my hips, then move down a few inches and return.

It's not so bad really.

Shit, who the hell am I kidding? Ronin Flynn's hands on my ass feel spectacular. I grin up at him and he smiles.

"Good, now let's move on to the next shot, OK?"

"What's—"

I stop mid-sentence because his mouth is nuzzling into my neck, his breath hot as it sweeps up into my ear, making me shudder and let out a little moan. "You OK?"

"Mmmmhmmmm," is all I can manage, because a chill rockets down my spine and my head involuntarily tips back and gives him permission to suck on my neck.

Holy shit.

He pulls back for a moment, just long enough to say, "Touch me, Rook," and then his mouth is back on my neck. He takes my left hand, which has a firm grasp on one of his belt loops, a safe move if ever there was one, and flattens my palm against his waist. I move the other hand in a feeble attempt to be an active participant instead of a dead fish who only reacts.

"More of that and we can put this scene to rest."

I take a deep breath and slip my hand under his t-shirt and then we both let a little gasp together as the chills travel up his body now. Antoine is talking in French again and Ronin leans down and takes my mouth.

It's a soft kiss at first, but as soon as I open up for his tongue his hands go behind my neck and it turns into something way beyond soft. He crushes my mouth with his, drawing in a breath that says he's absolutely turned on. This excites me and I kiss him back with just as much force, our tongues probing and twisting, our breath coming in gasps and long draws, like there is not enough air in the world to fuel this kiss. His hands are all over my body now, one still grasping the back of my neck to keep me close to him, the other, the one not on the side where Antoine is clicking away at the camera, slips under my skirt and travels up my thigh.

I moan and then catch Elise moving in out of the corner of my eye and Ronin withdraws his secret hand, bringing it out in full view once again.

"Take my shirt off." It's not a sweet request, it's a command. For like a fraction of a millisecond I wonder if he's allowed to command me, but I slap that cautious Rook away and do what I'm told.

"Slow?" I ask him.

"As long as you drag your fingers up my body as you do it, slow is just fine with me."

Oh fuck!

I take the thin fabric between my fingertips and slide my palms against his body as I lift and then roll it up, inch by inch. I'm driving him crazy, I can tell, mostly because he's practically biting my ear and whispering, "You're driving me fucking crazy, Gidget." I only make it up to his chest before he releases his hold on my neck and whips the shirt over his head in one sweeping motion, then bunches it up in front of him and throws it over at Elise who is still standing guard off to the side where the offending hand was wandering a few minutes ago.

Antoine barks in French again and then Ronin pulls back and leads me over to the blanket.

"Lie down," he says in that throaty command he gave earlier.

I'll debate whether or not I should be putting up with that later, but right now, I'm all in. I kneel down, smooth my dress out a little and then lie back on the cool cotton blanket. My skin is so hot and feverish from the kisses and touching that the blanket soothes me. Everything around me smells like cherry blossoms, and when I turn my head I realize that they are all over the blanket now because Elise swoops in to adjust my hair and place the flowers in strategic locations. Ronin is messing with the food and pouring the wine into glasses.

And before I know what's happening he's lying down next to me, leaning down and pressing himself over my stomach. I sigh at the dress, because it's the only thing separating my bare skin from his. "Just a few shots like this, Rook, then we'll sit up and have some fun." He's got a devilish grin as the words come out.

"Finally," I say with mock exasperation. "I'm starting to get bored."

He growls down at me and then goes back to kissing my neck so he can whisper in my ear, "I'd have you naked by now if Elise wasn't here."

"Ohhh, you're being bad," I whisper back, being equally discreet. "I bet she grounds you if I tell her what you just said."

We stare at each other for a few seconds, his eyes searching me for a moment. "Date me, Rook."

"What?"

"Let me take you out."

I look over at Elise who is distracted by an assistant who has joined us. "Are we allowed?"

"Pffft." He rolls off me and sits up, then pulls me up and sets me on his lap. I'm breathless with the quick change of position and almost gasp when he leans in to whisper in my ear again. "Pay close attention, Gidget." And then Antoine is giving orders and Ronin is fixing my dress so that it flares out around his legs.

It occurs to me then… I have no fucking underwear on.

And the reason it occurs to me is because his excitement is right underneath my completely bare girly parts.

Antoine is on Ronin's left, so Ronin's left hand begins to caress my foot with small circles, a touch so light it actually makes me squirm because my feet are totally ticklish. He takes the hint and slowly sweeps up my calf, which is just about the most sensual feeling I've ever experienced. I moan out a little and his bruising kisses are back, crushing against my mouth.

Just as Antoine takes his attention to our lips Ronin's right hand also begins at my foot, swirling his fingertips around the soft pad of my arch. I laugh into his mouth and he pulls me close, my hair hiding our faces for a moment, and says, "Shhhh, now. Be good, Gidge." And then his right hand sweeps up my leg and under my dress, caressing the same small circles along my inner thigh.

"Oh, shit," I whimper as I bury myself in his neck. Just a few more inches and I'm going to come undone. My neck tilts back as the sensations all crash together and he takes his kisses to my plunging neckline, his left hand, the one still out in the open, slips up to my breast just as the hidden hand drops down a little farther, just a flutter of a touch against my crease.

He reaches over, not with the hidden hand, and picks up a glass of wine and hands it to me.

My fingertips barely understand what to do with the glass because the only thing on my mind is where his other hand is. We each take a sip and then he bites into a cherry, taking half of it in his mouth, and spits out the pit.

Antoine barks something harsh in French and Ronin laughs. "It's a fucking pit, Antoine, it's not *litter*." He rolls his eyes at me. "Sit still now, Rook, and keep your mouth closed for a moment."

My mind is still on his fingers as they caress my inner thigh, but I do my best not to squirm.

He brings the cherry to my lips and I keep my mouth closed. This makes him smile and then he traces my lips, dripping juice as he paints them. I'm just about to let my tongue dart out and get the juice when Ronin's mouth reaches up and licks it off, stopping to suck on my bottom lip, and then gives it a little nibble that makes me cry out.

He bites into another cherry and again, to Antoine's disgust, woofs out the pit into the grass. Spitting is a skill only boys really acquire. They are so good at it. It might gross out Antoine, but not me. I think just about everything Ronin is doing with his mouth is astonishing right now. The secret hand under my dress appears again. He lifts my left hand and paints each fingertip pad with cherry juice, then sucks it off, nibbling them one by one, just like he did my lips.

I just stare at him and his eyes never leave mine. "What?" he finally asks.

"You—" I say.

He raises his eyebrows.

"—are bad."

He laughs. "If you were naked right now I'd drip this juice all down your belly and let my tongue—"

"OK, that's enough," Antoine says. "Excellent job, Rook."

Fucking Antoine.

I bite my lip as Ronin licks my fingertips one more time and then grins up at me like an idiot. "Want to come over and watch a movie, Gidget?"

I nod enthusiastically as Elise helps me up, and then Ronin bounces to his feet and puts his arm around me protectively. "You fell asleep pretty quick last time, are you sure you're up for a movie?"

I'm not sure if a movie is the code word for sex or not right now, but either way, I'm definitely up for it.

CHAPTER TWENTY-EIGHT

Ronin

"Hold on, stud!" Elise calls out before I can swoop Rook back inside and up to my apartment.

"Go change and I'll meet you outside the dressing room, OK?"

Rook nods and walks off and I watch her until the glass doors close behind her and she turns the corner. I turn back to my meddling sister who is already shaking her head at me. "What? That was some shoot, eh? Don't you think? She's perfect. I can't wait till tomorrow." I laugh a little because while I really am excited for tomorrow, I know mentioning it like this is pissing Elise off.

Bad.

"You are not dating that girl, Ronin. I mean it. She belongs to the studio for now—when this contract is up, you two can talk about having babies and all that shit. But for now, you stay out of her pants, do you hear me?"

"I'm offended, Elise. Really. I'm a professional."

She eyes me cautiously for several long seconds. "If you do, I'll know. And I will be pissed, do you understand?"

"It's a movie, Elise. I'm gonna feed her some more fruit and get her a little drunk, what could possibly go wrong?"

"I'm not kidding. I saw your little stealth hand move, by the way. Next time I'll pull the plug, but Antoine is exhausted tonight so I ignored it." She stops to glare at me. "I won't ignore it again. And she's not even legal, Ronin. You will *not* get her drunk."

"Would you relax, Ellie! It was a joke, since when do I get minors drunk? Fuck, I don't know why you're going all batshit about this. I'm gonna take care of her just like I take care of all the rest, except I'm gonna enjoy our photoshoots just a little bit more than usual." I grin, thinking that remark is fantastically fun in my mind, but Elise is not amused.

"That's what I'm concerned with, Ronin. We don't need another Mardee on our hands."

Oh... buuuuuurn. What a bitch. "You know what? Fuck you, Elise. I was nineteen fucking years old when she came through here. I had no idea what she was doing."

"And that's my point, dumbass. This girl is nineteen too, she's had some kind of very recent upheaval in her life, and you're fucking with her head right now. Stay out of her pants, do you understand? Or I will pull you from this project so fast your dick will spin."

"Whatever." I wave her off and go back inside. I am not responsible for Mardee, that's one thing I've come to terms with since all that shit went down. I could no more have stopped her than anyone else. And Elise insinuating that I dropped the ball when she was modeling for us just pisses me off.

Rook is already dressed when I get back inside. She's waiting by the door, biting her lip.

"What?" I ask, a little impatiently as I direct her up the stairs.

"What was that about?"

"Nothing, don't worry about it."

"I put the dress back in the bag and hung it up on the rack."

I shake Elise's words off and take my attention back to Gidget as we round the corner and head to my apartment door. "Perfect, I'll take care of it in the morning. Are you still up for a movie?"

She nods. "Yeah, sure."

Rook is not Mardee, in fact, Rook is the anti-Mardee.

There is not one thing I can think of that might link the two. They don't look alike, they certainly don't act alike, and I never thought of Mardee as anything more than a fun interlude between girlfriends.

And she thought the same of me. We were mutually apathetic towards each other.

"But Elise didn't look too happy."

I push Rook inside the apartment and close the door, then take her face in my hands. "Who cares?" I kiss her again but she's not as interested as she was down on the terrace. "She's just overprotective, that's all. She worries about the girls, especially the ones I date." I stop here to make a point. "But I'd just like you to know, I don't bring them home, Rook. Ever."

She shoots me an incredulous look.

"I swear, I'm not saying I'm celibate or anything, but I don't bring them here to this apartment."

"So where do you take them?"

"It's a four-story building and we're the only people who live here. There are lots of places downstairs."

"Oh," is all she says to that and I take a deep breath, feeling stupid for admitting that I fuck girls in random rooms in our building.

"You have to be hungry, are you?" I ask, trying to change the subject.

She pushes me away from her, then ducks under my arm, walks into the living room and takes a seat on the couch. "I am. What do you have?"

Yeah, that moment during the photoshoot is pretty much gone. I go into the kitchen and open the fridge. "Fruit," I call. "Apples, Cuties, grapes, and pomegranate seeds."

"That's quite a selection," she says from behind me.

I spin around, surprised. "I love fruit. I blame it on Antoine. He gets fruit baskets delivered every week. I'm not even sure where they come from, like maybe he's got a subscription to one of those Fruit of the Week Clubs or something? I'm not sure. But for the last dozen years or so I've been eating fresh fruit out of a basket that sits on Antoine's desk in his office."

She's smiling again and my heart lifts. Maybe I didn't fuck it up?

"You've never asked where they come from?"

"Nope."

"Why? If you've always wondered."

"Because it's gonna be something stupid like Mamie Chaput or the fucking Fruit of the Week Club. And I'd rather imagine something more exotic, like maybe it comes from some long lost love who lives in Fiji—and she misses Antoine so much, she sends him fruit every week to remind him of what they might've had?"

"You have a Mamie Chaput?"

I laugh. "Yeah, well, Antoine is French, in case you haven't noticed. I kinda got sucked into the family by extension."

"Wouldn't that be weird for Elise if there *was* some woman sending Antoine fruit baskets every week?"

"Yeah, probably. But I like picturing this girl in a string bikini, lying in the sun on a tropical island, pining over the one that got away. I never said it was practical, just exotic."

I hand her a Cutie and take out a container of pom seeds for me.

"So all you eat at home is fruit?" she asks, looking at my fridge.

"Nah, I eat everything, but I never go grocery shopping, so I just steal fruit from the baskets downstairs."

"But you have beer?" she adds, looking at the many different Colorado microbrews I have stashed in the fridge.

I grin at her. "OK, enough of your questions. Go eat your orange."

"So you make it to the liquor store and the fruit basket, but that's it? And you don't bring girls up here, but you do take them to some hidden harem room downstairs?"

I'm not sure if she's joking at this point.

"That's some picture you've painted in my head, Ronin."

I take her orange back and start peeling. The sooner she can eat it, the sooner she stops psychoanalyzing me. "That's not the picture I want you to have at all, Rook. I'm just your typical twenty-two-year-old guy."

"OK," she says, taking the orange back half-peeled. "I get it."

"Get what?" Somehow this whole day has turned against me and I'm not quite sure where it all went wrong. "I wasn't sending any messages, so I'm not sure what you get."

She hands the orange back and walks away.

"What?"

I let out a deep breath as the front door closes.

And I sit on the couch, absently flipping through channels, wondering how the fuck I just blew this whole day with a conversation about fruit baskets.

CHAPTER TWENTY-NINE

Rook

OK.

I'm certifiably stupid for just walking out over a fruit basket, but it's not about the fruit. It's about Elise's warnings. Both the one she gave me last night and the one she just gave Ronin downstairs. I only caught part of it, and maybe I don't know who Mardee is, but whatever happened to her, Elise thinks Ronin was the cause and Ronin was immediately defensive.

I'm no shrink, but I'm guessing that defensiveness comes up when you're playing defense. Which means he had something to do with the bad thing that happened to this Mardee girl, regardless of what he says.

I head straight for the door and skip down the stairs to get my own food from Cookie's. There's no baseball game today and lunch is technically over, so the streets are fairly quiet. I walk the block over to the diner in thought, then tell the hostess inside that "I belong to Ronin" and head back to the table. It's empty so I sink into the booth and grab a menu sitting behind the salt and pepper shakers.

Elise also said I needed stability and maybe Ronin doesn't fit that criteria. I think that bothers me a little more after he got all personal in the photoshoot than it did before. Before the shoot we were just flirting, but his hand went beyond flirting today. And then there was the little remark about Elise being protective of the girls he dates.

Why?

I mean, I don't consider us dating, but beyond that—why does Elise need to feel protective towards the girls he dates?

I order a salad and watch people as I wait. This place is still pretty busy for being almost three o'clock. A guy comes in who catches my eye. Not because he's hot, even though he is hot, but because from the minute he comes through the door he's watching me. I look behind me just to make sure, but there are no people dining behind me. He takes his attention to the hostess. He's got short messy hair, not quite blond, but not really brown either, and a little bit of facial hair. Enough to make him look rough, but not unkempt. The waitress points back to me and I watch the hot guy smile.

What the hell?

He starts walking towards me and once the counter is out of the way, it's hard to miss the fact that he's a biker. He's got the tell-tale biker boots on and they sound off a manly thud on the polished concrete floors as he approaches my booth. When he pushes up the sleeves on his white thermal I see what else he's got. Tattoos all over. Like everywhere.

He stops right in front of the booth and smiles down at me.

"Let me guess," I say sarcastically, "you belong to Ronin?"

He slides into the booth across from me and laughs. "Hey, if it gets me a seat here with you, I'll belong to that dickhead for an hour." He offers his hand. "Spence."

"Rook," I offer back as I shake his hand.

"Yeah, I figured. Antoine described you on the phone, but shit, he really played you down. You're perfect."

I twist my eyebrows at him. "Perfect for—?" and that's when Ronin walks into the diner. The hostess points back to us, but he doesn't need an invitation, he's already halfway down the aisle. I watch him very carefully, but whatever his deal is, it's got nothing to do with me because his eyes are blazing at my new dining companion.

"Spencer Shrike, what the fuck are you doing sitting in my booth talking to one of my girls?"

Oh, really! If these asshole men weren't about to throw in the diner I would be so offended at that comment!

Spencer Shrike gets to his feet and claps Ronin on the back. "Good to see you too, asshole. Now sit the fuck down. You know too fucking well I'm here on business. And now that I've met Rook, I'm more convinced than ever you guys deserve the STURGIS contract."

Ronin motions for me to move over and pushes on my upper arm a little to make me hurry. I shoot him a dirty look as I scoot, but he ignores me. "Rook has a job, sorry. I've already set up Bonnie and Val for you to try out tomorrow."

Spencer takes his attention to me as my salad arrives. We all sit back and shut up until the waitress leaves, but then Spence picks it up right where it left off. "Is that so, Rook? You're booked up through August?"

"August? I have no idea," I admit. "When does this job end, Ronin?"

Ronin growls and it takes all my self-control not to spit out a crouton as I laugh. Oh, shit. He might start pissing on me soon.

I shake my head. "I highly doubt I'll be busy until August. Is this another modeling job?" I take another bite of salad and chew methodically as I watch the silent bro-down going on at the table.

"She's busy," Ronin says through clenched teeth.

"I'm not busy, Ronin. Let the man speak."

Spencer smiles and then scoots down his booth bench so he's across from me again. "It's a complicated deal, Rook, but I'd love for you to attend the meeting I have with Antoine in about," he checks his phone, "thirty minutes. You in?"

"How much does it pay?"

"Not set in stone, so don't worry about that. We've got studio money behind us for this job," now he's talking to Ronin, "so think about that before you turn into a Neanderthal, Flynn. Can I expect to see you in the meeting?"

His blue eyes track back to me and I shrug. "Sure, what do

I have to lose?"

Spencer Shrike slips on some very dark sunglasses and shoots me with his finger. "See you then, Blackbird."

I smile at the nickname. A rook is a blackbird over in Europe. Not many people know that. Most of them think I'm named after a chess piece.

Ronin catches my pleasure and even though every defense mechanism left over from my previous life tells me to hide that smile to avoid a confrontation, I don't. I flash it even bigger, daring Ronin to make a big deal about getting my pants charmed off by a biker.

I take another bite of my salad and then Ronin gets up and follows Spencer out the door, leaving me alone.

I show up fifteen minutes late for the meeting. On purpose. I figure they're all in there acting like dicks and that's not something I need to be a part of. Chaput Studios might own me for the TRAGIC contract, but I highly doubt this thing lasts for three months, so there's no way they can stop me from doing this STURGIS job if I really want to. It's best to just let the men-folk fight that out in private, come back to reality when they figure out none of them are in control, I am, and then settle back down in the world I live in.

The one where I call my own shots.

I knock softly and Ronin opens the door.

There are like ten people in the room, some suits, some bikers, and of course, Ronin, Antoine, and Elise. It doesn't take a genius to understand the STURGIS contract is about bikes. Obviously the only thing associated with Sturgis is bikers. So this should be interesting. I'm game, that's for sure.

Everyone goes silent as I enter, then Antoine takes over.

"Sit, Rook. Spence invited you, so you're welcome to listen in, but there will be no model negotiations for this meeting."

I almost do shut up and sit down, because that's basically

what Antoine just told me to do. But that's dumb. "Well, I'm not about to sit in on a tense meeting when it has nothing to do with me, so if I'm not going to be provided with any useful information, I'll just take off."

They all stare at me.

Spencer stands and takes control. "Rook, we're going to offer you the contract. I've been told that TRAGIC wraps up next week…"

Next week? That was quick. I figured this job would last a little longer than that. Ronin was not kidding about modeling being erratic. I think I might actually *need* this job.

"… so we'll talk more then."

Wait—what did I just miss? Everyone is looking at me, waiting for an answer, and I break into a sweat. "OK, yeah, sure. I'll leave you guys to it then." I pull the door closed behind me and go back to my apartment, still thinking about how quick I could be homeless again. I mean, this is their place, I'm no one, just another model among hundreds who have probably come through here, and they are letting me stay here because I have a contract with them.

Which will run out next freaking week!

I plop down on my couch and watch TV for a while, my gaze absently wandering to the front window, waiting to see if Ronin will come by for a visit tonight.

But he doesn't.

And I don't blame him.

Because I was a total bitch today.

I bite my lip and watch RetroTube until Gidget comes on. And that just makes everything worse, because even though I've been trying to talk myself out of it for the past week, I think I might actually like Ronin Flynn.

CHAPTER THIRTY

Rook

I wake early the next morning. Elise came by late last night and told me to be downstairs at seven AM, so I make my way into the studio ten minutes early to find everyone is already working. It still amazes me the early schedule these people keep. The dressing room is buzzing with girls. And every single one of them is naked.

I'm not talking topless, I'm talking *naked.*

They are chatting and laughing and generally acting like being nude is just another day on the job. And I guess it is when you work here.

I stand there a little lost when I hear Ronin's call.

"Over here, Gidget. Get on the scale and then Elise wants you in the salon for hair and make-up."

I forgot about the fucking scale.

Ronin doesn't smile at me, in fact, he barely notices me as I walk over to him. I step on the scale and I'm about to say something to break our awkward silence when a girl storms in, fully clothed and looking like she never went home from a party the night before, screaming at Ronin in French.

Ronin walks away and takes the girl by the arm, trying to shove her out of the dressing room. It's only then that I recognize her. The screamer from the day I came for my test shoot.

Clare.

Ronin's voice rises with hers and they stand toe to toe, yelling right up in each other's face. She pushes Ronin and he spins her around and drags her out into the studio, where her French threats echo off the tall ceilings.

"Fucking Clare," a naked blonde girl huffs out next to me.

"I know," another naked girl, this time a redhead, says with disgust. "I don't care who that bitch is, I'm glad Ronin canned her ass. She thinks she can break the rules, do whatever she wants, and still have a job?" The blonde girl snorts at this. "No," Red answers herself emphatically. "She's under his thumb just like we are. Right, Rook?" She smiles over at me.

"Whose thumb?"

"Ronin's, of course. Unless, you two have some deal going." She narrows her eyes at me.

"What deal?"

"Well, I find it interesting that you got the garden apartment and don't have to be at work on time. Why is that? Ronin keeping you or something?"

"What does that even mean?"

They laugh and go back to their clothes and it's only then that I notice every girl in the dressing room is staring at me. "What?" I ask them.

They turn back to their business but I'm left there feeling stupid so I just turn on my heel and go find Elise in the salon.

Thankfully things in the salon seem a little more amicable. I don't generally care if the girls I work around are friends with me or not—typically when I have a job I'm there to work, not socialize. But that blonde girl asked if Ronin was *keeping me.* And Elise said something very similar the other night when we had dinner with her and Antoine. She said, *You're not any different from the other models, just because Ronin wants to keep you.*

What the fuck does that mean?

I'm not sure but the alarms are going off in my head again. I could let it slip by as a cute way to say he likes me, but now this girl said it too. Not to mention the whole *I belong to Ronin* thing they have going on down at the diner.

"Over here, Rook." Elise points to the shampoo chair and I ease back, ready to relax for a moment, even if it is in a shampoo chair and I just woke up an hour and a half ago.

It takes several hours for them to make me up, not so much because what they're doing to me is complicated, but because there are so many girls here today they have to keep trading us off like an assembly line. One does toes, one does hands, one does hair, one does make-up.

It's total insanity.

But I kinda like it. Everything goes fast, people are talking fast, walking fast, the girls come and then they go. The photographers are busy calling out directions, the camera shutters are clicking wildly.

It's all very exciting.

Everything I imagined a big important photography studio would be. Before I came here and found out it wasn't, of course. But today it's all business. After Ronin gets rid of that Clare chick, no one has time to think about anything but doing their job. Finally, when it's well past lunch, Elise pronounces me ready and ushers me off to the dressing room to get dressed, then tells me to meet them all out on the terrace.

I head into the dressing room, which is eerily quiet compared to the chaos I just came from, and find my clothes on the rack. Ronin is nowhere to be found and for a minute I miss him being there for me. He's not been around all day. The girls gossiped about him all morning though, talking about Clare.

I'm getting the impression she was an ex-girlfriend.

It bugs me that I feel jealous over that, but I really haven't had time to think about it much.

I lift the bag of clothes off the rack, expecting it to weigh—something—but it's like air. Like that bag contains almost nothing. I walk over to the armless couches that span the middle of the room and open it up.

It's a men's dress shirt. White.

And a pair of little boxer shorts that were definitely not made for a man.

It takes me two seconds to put the new clothes on. I

button the shirt all the way up, then feel a little stupid and unbutton three of them.

Even though the shirt drops down to my mid-thigh, is long-sleeved, and goes up to my neck—I feel exposed. I exhale a long breath and force myself to walk out into the studio. Ronin is the first face I see because he's standing in the doorway as I turn the corner that hides the dressing room from onlookers.

He smiles and all the tension just evaporates.

"You're so fucking sexy."

I actually blush at that.

He takes my hand and leads me over to the terrace, then opens the door and waves me through like a gentleman.

There are about a dozen people outside and the afternoon sun is shining down on the terrace. It's shedding a lovely pink light and I can only assume that Antoine is in love with how it drapes over everything, washing out the drab harshness of the city and making it all soft.

Once I'm noticed everyone snaps to attention and then lights are on and those black umbrella things they use for diffusing it come out, and people are all busy. Ronin leads me over to a nook in the side of the building. There's a flowering cherry tree in a massive pot in the middle of the nook and the branches reach out and soft pink petals brush my cheek as I follow him under the canopy. "This is where we're shooting today, OK?"

All the camera shutters start clicking and I look over at the photographers.

Ronin directs my gaze back to him with a light touch on my chin. "I'm right here, Gidge. Forget about them, understand? You're not posing for them, you are reacting to me today. OK?"

I nod.

"They will not interfere unless it's time to stop. Otherwise you will only look at me or where I tell you to look. Ignore them completely. They do not exist."

"OK," I say, gulping down some air. That makes all the cameras start clicking again and it takes all my self-control not to look over at them.

"Good girl," Ronin says smiling. "Now, let me explain the rules. We both have power here. I have power to tell you what to do, to make you react, and to get the shots we need. Does that makes sense?"

"Yes, you're here to help me give them what they want."

"Yes, that's a good way to put it. I take care of you in the shoot, Rook, but my hands will be all over your body. Are you going to be OK with that?" I nod. "Words, please," he prods.

"Yes, I'm OK with that."

"And if the situation calls for it, meaning if we're getting the reactions we need, if everything is working, I might undress you."

"Might?"

"We make art here, Rook. We want the models to exhibit feelings that can be felt immediately when people see the pictures—we are not making porn."

"OK." More clicking shutters almost make me look but instead I find Ronin's eyes and ask him instead. "Why are they shooting already?"

"Because today is the first time you've ever done this and right now you're looking very sweet and innocent." He grins and wraps one hand around my waist, pulling me into him. The cameras go wild again. "Your reaction right now, as we do this for the first time, is priceless."

I blush and try hard to tuck the smile away, but I fail and try and forget about the cameras. They're doing their job, Ronin is doing his job, and I need to do mine.

Which is, as far as I can tell from yesterday's fully clothed version of a shoot, letting Ronin make me feel good.

"OK, now on to your power. You can give me direction in how quickly I proceed. Fast is not generally something we want. We want to make it all slow so the photographers can get their shots. But sometimes we get going and things move too fast, or maybe you're feeling uncomfortable. When that happens you can tell me one of two things. If you say the word *slow*, I'll change direction until you're comfortable again."

"OK, slow. Got it. What's the other one?"

"You can tell me to *stop*. And then the shoot ends and we all go home. Understand that, when you say stop, the shoot ends. So use it when you want things to be over. Not because you want things to change direction. Use slow for that, OK?"

He slips his hands under my shirt and caresses the skin just above the waistband of my shorts and while I know the cameras are clicking, suddenly I stop hearing them. My focus is one hundred percent on Ronin. His touch sends shivers up my entire body and my nipples perk to attention.

He smiles, like he knows, but he can't possibly know. The shirt is big and there's no way to see them.

Still he grins like he knows.

"Now, there's one more thing you can tell me." His hands retreat and start undoing the lower buttons of the shirt. He stops at the button just below my breasts and then returns his hands to my waist, but this time he pulls the shirt back, exposing my belly in the process. He looks down at my little boxer shorts.

"I love those," he whispers before looking back up at my face. He licks his lower lip. My tongue darts out and mimics him before I can stop it.

"What's the other thing I can tell you?"

He leans down to my neck and kisses me softly. I know the cameras are going crazy, but all I hear is his breath in my ear. Heat fills my lower body and I have to inhale deeply, making my whole chest rise and then fall with my exhale.

"The other thing you can tell me is *go*, Gidget." His hand wraps around my neck and massages my jaw line with his thumb while his words tickle all the way into my ear canal. I swallow down the desire that's building in me. "When you're done with slow, you tell me to go."

His mouth pulls away from my neck and finds my face.

He's so close our lips almost touch, my mouth opens a little in anticipation and his hand glides up my torso and tenderly grabs my breast.

And then his mouth is on mine, his tongue flicking in, his mouth closing, then another flick. I close my eyes and my head drifts back a little as I respond. He's pinching my nipples now, ever so slightly, just enough to know his fingers are on me, are in control of me.

He teases me with his kiss over and over. I let him at first, I let him control me with his movements, his hands still drifting up and over my breasts, a little more forcefully now.

But then the desire inside me takes over and I reach up and wrap my hands around his neck, I pull him to me, I let my fingertips glide down his chest. He's bare on top and is wearing jeans on the bottom. Just a pair of old and faded jeans, but he is so fucking hot I can barely contain myself.

He laughs a little and I pull away, my hands still touching him, still caressing him. I slip a finger inside his waistband and he actually gasps.

"Do you like that?" I ask.

"You're trouble, Rook." He smiles and takes my hand and pushes it down farther and I feel the little hairs that run the length of his belly. I pull on one and he takes my mouth again. His hands are on my ass now, slipping inside the little boxer shorts and squeezing my cheeks.

A moan actually escapes my lips and the camera shutters are so loud I almost have to look at them.

I'd forgotten they were there to be honest.

Ronin won't tolerate the distraction, his hand dips between my cheeks and his finger tickles me between my legs.

My head drops back as I gasp and then he's holding my face again, his mouth taking me completely. I begin to rake my fingers through his hair when he abruptly spins me around so I'm facing forward, straight at the cameras.

"Do not look at them, Rook. Forget about them, OK?"

The throb between my legs is making it very hard to even

open my eyes at this point, so I have no intention of looking at anyone, let alone the photographers. Ronin's fingers resume their undoing of the shirt buttons and I know this is the scary moment. Up until now it's just been a public makeout session. A heady one, for sure. But nothing obscene.

"Tell me what to do, Rook. You're in charge."

I don't even have to think about it. I turn my head up to him and he leans down in response, tilting his ear towards me. I breathe out, and I feel him shudder as it tickles him like he just tickled me, then whisper, as softly as I possibly can, "*Go*."

"I'm going to bare you to them, are you sure?"

"Go," I repeat.

I expect him to rip the clothing off me in a rush, but he doesn't. Two fingers grasp the collar of the shirt and tug it slowly, fractionally, down one shoulder. He leans down and nibbles my neck and I almost lose it right there. My clit is throbbing, pulsating to the beat of my racing heart.

I reach my arms up and back so I'm grasping the back of his head. This must be magic for the photographers because they go wild at this move. I tip my head back so far, I'm almost looking at Ronin upside down. He claims my mouth and pulls one arm down and slips that half of the shirt off. I pull my arm out, exposing my breast. His fingers are instantly there, flicking my nipple and then pinching it, making me whimper.

I bite his lip in response and he growls, forcing my other arm down.

The shirt slips all the way off and drifts to the floor.

He claims my wrists and brings them back over his head and I respond by pushing my ass into him. He is so hard.

I wiggle against it and then one hand is caressing my breast while the other travels down my belly, slips inside my boy shorts and goes right between my legs where the throbbing is so profound I think he might actually be able to feel the pulsations against his wet fingertip.

He flicks my clit and pushes his finger inside me and a feeling I have never felt before begins to build in me.

The moan escapes my mouth and it is *loud*, but all I can think about is Ronin's fingers as they play with me and then that feeling is there, like a wave getting ready to break on the beach, rushing forward, building and building, just beginning to crest and—

"Stop!"

What?

Who the fuck said stop?

"Ronin, what the hell are you doing? Rook, this is over now." Elise drapes a white robe over my shoulders and escorts me away from the crowd of people. Everyone stares at me, their eyes wide and their mouths gaping open as I pass.

"What? What happened? I don't understand!"

"He's got you way too worked up, Rook, this is not how we typically operate."

"I don't get it, isn't that his job? To work me up so you guys get good pictures?"

She opens my studio apartment door and pushes me inside but doesn't follow.

"He's supposed to make it feel real, not bring you to orgasm in front of a dozen people!"

And then she slams my door and leaves.

And I'm standing mostly naked in my new apartment, very pissed off that my clit is still throbbing like crazy and Ronin's magic fingers are outside and he is at this very moment—I know because I'm peeking out the front window—being bitched out by his sister.

CHAPTER THIRTY-ONE

Ronin

"What the fuck, Ronin?"

Elise is so angry she's stabbing me in the chest with little staccato pokes of her finger. Her nails are long and pointy, so this does not feel pleasant. I glance over at Rook's window and find her face and grin.

"Ronin, stop smiling at her! I assured her this wouldn't happen and you made me a liar."

"She told me to go, Elise. Why would I stop? She was enjoying herself."

She pulls me along until we are back inside the studio. I'm assuming so Rook cannot see us.

"Ronin, this girl is fragile, do you understand? Much too fragile to make a rational decision about what is and is not appropriate on her first serious modeling job. You are the professional here and you know better!"

"Yeah, but this one's kinda like my girlfriend."

"All the more reason to protect her from this, you stupid piece of shit! Why do you think Antoine has me doing make-up and hair?"

I sigh and scrub my hands across my face. She's right. What the hell was I thinking? "OK, I get it. It's just that she drives me crazy and she said *go*, so..." I have no excuse. "Sorry, I lost control." I look down at Elise and nod. "I won't let it happen again, OK? I promise."

Elise and I both stop talking as the photographers come back inside. Roger laughs as he passes. "Way to go, Flynn.

That was quite a show. This campaign is in the bag."

When I look back to Elise she's shaking her head. "You better make this right, Ronin. She's all worked up with the passion right now, but once she realizes these pictures are going out to clients, she's gonna be pissed."

I walk over to the terrace window and peek through at her window. Her face is gone now and I wonder what she's thinking. "Will you go talk to her?"

"No way. That's your job. You did this, now you fix it."

She looks at me for several seconds, her head tilting. I know this look, it says she's got an idea. "What?"

"Antoine and I have tickets for a fundraiser at the zoo, but he's meeting with Spence and the STURGIS team tonight."

"Oh, that sucks. Sorry, sis."

"Take Rook instead."

I shoot her a dirty look. "Now you want me to take her out, but yesterday you were threatening my manhood if I got anywhere near her? What's the deal?"

"Spencer is here and he's got that look, Ronin. Don't let him swoop in because you know he'll try. Let her choose a dress from the closet and take her to the fundraiser. I have a feeling she'll enjoy herself. Oh, and write a check on your way out. A big one."

And then she pats my cheek a few times and walks off.

A night at the zoo. For a fundraiser. I'm not sure about this. It sounds like I have to wear a tux. I think about this for a second, then wander into the closet. It also means I could pick Rook out a nice sexy dress. I make my way over to the evening gowns and start looking for something red, long in length, and plunging at the neckline. I grab the dress and some shoes that look like her size, and then put it in a garment bag and hang it on the rack with Rook's name tag.

I hope she likes it.

Next on the list is the girly stuff, so I head over to the salon and talk Josie into making Rook up for the occasion. She agrees if I tip her generously, which I do because I figure if

Rook has to worry about hair and make-up she'll probably say no.

Walking across the terrace makes me nervous for some reason. This girl who has not even been in my life for one week completely dominates all my thoughts. I mean, she's on my mind every second of the day. Even when Clare and I were fighting this morning, the only thing on my mind was how Rook was going to perceive that manic display of insanity from Clare.

I told Antoine I'm done with that girl. If Clare wants to jump off the ledge, fuck—there's nothing more I can do. I cut her loose and that's the end of it. Antoine was not happy, but whatever. He's never been able to control Clare and I've only ever had a tenuous hold on her at best. But all of that has left the building these days.

I can only hope that Rook doesn't read too much into it.

I stand at her door and knock, again feeling just a little bit off balance from all the recent changes. Rook answers in a pair of shorts and a halter top. My eyes take her in, from her perky nipples standing at attention, to her long legs, to her bare feet.

Which have painted pink toenails and are fidgeting around like she's Gidget talking on the phone or something.

I take a deep breath.

"Hey," she says, seductively leaning against the door jamb, jutting her hip off to the side and twirling her long raven-black hair around a finger. All she needs is some gum and she'd be the Gidget of my dreams.

"Hey," I say back, like an idiot. "Uh, I was wondering if you'd like to go to the zoo with me tonight?"

That sounded lame.

She coughs down a laugh. "The zoo?"

"Yeah, it's a fundraiser. Antoine and Elise were gonna go, but they have to work tonight. So she gave me their tickets."

"What are we raising funds for?"

"I have no idea." *Fuck, all I want to do is take you upstairs and throw you on my bed and hold you down while I make you scream my name*. I hope to fucking God I did not just say that out loud.

She doesn't laugh or squirm, so I guess I'm safe. "Is it fancy?"

"Yes, very. But I have a dress for you and Josie said she'll do your hair and make-up. What do you say?"

"You picked my dress?"

Oh, shit. I probably fucked up with that move. "Uh, well, you can pick something else if you want, but it's sexy as hell." I waggle my eyebrows at her and grin like an idiot, hoping to defuse that blunder.

"Does it make me look like Gidget?"

"No," I say too quickly. "Not at all."

"Well, in that case, I'll go. What do I have to do?"

I take her hand and tug her out the door. "I'll take care of everything, just relax and I'll meet you outside the dressing room at seven."

I drop her off with Josie and get the hell out of there before she can change her mind or ask me anything else about fruit baskets and vacant bedrooms on the lower floors of the building, then take the stairs up to my apartment three at time and go searching for my tux.

CHAPTER THIRTY-TWO

Rook

Josie does my hair in an up-do. It doesn't take long, all she has to do is brush it out and pin it up, swooping it over to one side, while the top and back are sufficiently poofed up to give it some height. When she shows me in the mirror I let out a small gasp. Even without the make-up and dress, I already look better than ever before. The hair is sleek, not messy and half falling out like most up-dos end up, but shiny and pulled tight.

Josie smiles when I look over at her. "That's how fashion models do the up-do, Rook. Don't ever let them give you those wispy tendrils again!"

As if I ever had wispy tendrils to bag on. "Thank you, it's perfect."

"Now, for make-up, you don't need much. Some foundation and bronzer, then red lips. Ronin said the dress was red, so you must have lips to match. I'll put a sealer coat over it, so it will last."

She does it just like she said and then sets me off to find my clothes in the dressing room. It's past six now, so the whole place is quiet. I find my bag and take it over to the upholstered benches in the middle of the outer dressing area where all the naked girls were earlier. This time I get shoes, and I'm relieved because my ripped-up Converse would never do for the absolutely stunning red creation I pull out of the bag.

Maybe Ronin is a control freak, but he has good taste in

dresses. I hold it up to my body and it falls to the floor like it was made specifically for me. I guess it was, really, since I'm a standard model size and all these clothes are made for people who have a shape and height like mine.

It's strapless and has two slits that go all the way up to my mid-thigh on each side. The neckline is not low enough so my girls are hanging out if I move and the fabric is incredibly soft. I have no clue what it's made of, but it's soft. The bodice is trimmed in a few clear sparkles, just enough to make it twinkle in the lights, but not enough to make me look like a disco ball. After helping myself to some new panties from the underwear drawer, I wiggle into it and reach around to draw up the zipper. I only make it halfway, but I'm sure Ronin won't mind finishing that off for me.

I chuckle when I think about him. Gah, this man! I'm not sure what to do with him. He made me feel incredible today. Seriously, I've never had an orgasm. Sex was not something I enjoyed in the past, but after experiencing what he can do to me, I'm hoping that is about to change.

When I slip my feet in the shoes and realize they are not only my size, but comfortable to boot, I almost give in to his controlling ways. He really does know what he's doing. Is it so bad to trust someone to take care of you?

"Rook?"

"Come in," I yell back.

He walks in and I about have a heart attack. He's wearing a tux. "Oh, my," we say at the same time. And then we both burst out laughing.

"I feel like a grown-up," he says, looking down at himself.

"Mr. Flynn, you definitely look like a grown up." His tux is the kind that rock stars wear to those award ceremonies—black on black with slim-fit trousers. He walks straight over to me without hesitation and wraps his hands around my hips. His touch releases a fire that travels all through my body.

"Do you need a hand with the zipper, Gidge?" he asks, leaning down into my ear.

I want to say *yeah, but not the way you think*. I want him unzipping me right now. I want him to lift me up, slam me against the dressing room wall, and take me right here. Fuck this dress, this fundraiser, and everything else!

"Yes, please," is what really comes out.

Darn stupid inhibitions.

He turns me around, his hands trailing around my waist, and then his fingertips dance along my bare back for a moment before he gently lifts the zipper. I twist a bit at his touch and let out a gasp when he leans in to kiss the back of my neck.

"Did I tickle you?" he asks, leaning in closer as I turn back to face him. His breath teases my throat and then his lips travel up and flutter against the soft skin under my ear.

"No, you excite me, Larue. You make all my Gidget parts tingle." I giggle as his tongue continues to tease my throat and then I have to shake my whole head to dampen down the shudder of pleasure that runs through my body.

"You're gonna make me want to forget all about this night out if you're not careful. And then I'll have Elise mad at me for wasting the tickets and Josie mad at me for wasting the beautiful job she did on your hair and makeup. Now, hold still."

Something cold slides against my chest and Ronin's hands clasp together a piece of jewelry around my neck. I look down and bite my lip at the gemstones as they sparkle in the overhead lights of the dressing room.

He turns me around and steps back, hands never leaving my body. "I have no words for you, Rook Walsh."

"Try," I whisper back as I stare hungrily into his eyes.

He brings his palms to my face and tilts my chin. "I could describe what you look like, but that's not what I see. You are so much more than a body inside a dress, Rook. You fit me. When I saw you crouching in that stairwell last week I felt like I knew you. You stopped me dead in my tracks, you wiped my mind. And I reached out to touch you that day because I couldn't resist. I needed to do it and I plan on touching you all night, on the way there in the car, through dinner, as we walk around the zoo and do whatever the hell it is they do at a nighttime fundraiser, and all the way home."

"And then?" I prod.

He lets out a soft laugh. "Oh, Miss Walsh, I plan on doing many more things to you tonight, but most of all, when I finally get you back to my apartment and into my bed, I plan on making you whimper into my neck, begging me to make you come."

Whoa! I think I need a new pair of panties. I breathe in deeply and wait for him to laugh or do something to break the mood.

But he doesn't.

He stares at me and then dips down to my neck again to whisper in my ear. "I'd crush your mouth with kisses right now if I thought I could get away with smearing your lipstick."

And then we do laugh. I take another deep breath and he offers me his arm. I grab hold of that arm like I never want to let go. We take the elevator down instead of the stairs and when we exit the garage, there's a town-car waiting to take us to the zoo.

A long breath escapes as the driver holds the door open for us. I get in and scoot across the butter-soft leather seat, then Ronin joins me and the door closes with a soft whoosh.

"What?" he asks.

"Just wow." I look over at him and laugh a little. "I mean, I've never…" The sentence just drops off because I seriously have no words for how I feel right now. "I've never been on a date like this." I look over at him and he's got a crooked grin on his face.

"Then you're long overdue, Gidget."

The car pulls out of the parking garage and I watch the street outside as Ronin puts his arm around my shoulders and pulls me a little closer to him. "How far away is the zoo?"

"Not far, just over in City Park."

"So have you lived here in Denver your whole life?"

"Yeah, Five Points, born and bred." He shrugs, like he's apologizing.

"Is that a good thing? Or not? You seem to be leaving something unsaid."

"It's not Park Hill, let's just leave it at that. Elise and I grew up in a house just down the street from our building. It was a total shit hole."

"Oh. Does it bother you to be in the same neighborhood?"

"No. I can't explain it, but even though there's a lot of nasty shit that happens on our side of town, it's home for me. And where we are, things are more quiet than in some places. I can see the draw of moving over to Cherry Creek or Park Hill or Highland's Ranch, but I'm not ashamed of where I started. You can't choose your parents." He shrugs.

I internalize this for a few moments. "You could be talking about me."

His eyes come back to me and he waits a few seconds before speaking. "I wasn't though. I have no idea how you grew up."

I swallow down the bad memories. "Pretty much the same as you, except for the French knight in shining armor thing. I never got one of those."

"*Vous avez tort, mon amour. Je suis juste ici.*"

"What's that mean?"

He leans in and nuzzles my ear. "It means the bad stuff is over now, Gidget, and the good is just about to start." My whole body flushes and he laughs in my neck as the car stops. "We're here. When's the last time you were at a zoo?"

"Never," I admit.

He pulls back as the driver gets out to open our door. "That's criminal! How can a child grow up in America and never go to the zoo?"

I shrug. "My childhood was a long string of foster homes and crack houses." I watch his eyes as the door opens from the outside. "Sometimes," I continue, "I had both at the same time. The Chicago foster care system is not ideal."

He's crushed as the words sink in. His hand reaches over and grabs mine off my lap and he shakes his head. "I had no idea, Rook. Maybe we shouldn't go in?"

"Why?" I ask, startled, my heart racing in my chest.

"Because this fundraiser is for foster care kids. I didn't know, I swear. If it's not something you want to think about I'll take you somewhere else. Anywhere you want."

He raises his hand to brush against my cheek and for a moment I lose control. A little wave of hurt and sadness sweeps over me and I feel the pool of tears that threaten my perfect night. But I swallow it down. "No," I say, shaking my head. "No way. I'm not responsible for where I came from. I didn't choose that life, I chose this one. This night isn't about me, it's about them," I say, pointing to the zoo entrance. "I want to go in." He hesitates, but I nod and say it again. "I swear, I want to go in. Come on, let's go."

We get out of the car and walk towards the entrance where Ronin hands our tickets to the ushers. They point us down a pathway that veers off to the right and then hand us a program.

"Want to walk around a little?" Ronin asks. "We have about twenty minutes."

"Yes, please. What's close by?"

Ronin studies the map on the back of the program and leads us past the event center. "Elephants!" he says with a laugh. "Once, Antoine took Elise and me to India for some big fashion thing. We'd just met the guy, we'd known him for like three months I guess. And he sprang this trip on us and even though I thought Antoine was a total dick because he refused to speak English to me, that trip to India was awesome because I got to ride an elephant. Of course," he says, looking sideways at me, "I tried to pretend I was unimpressed with the whole thing. Kids, right? They never appreciate anything."

"Wow. India. I can't even imagine how cool that would

be."

"Well, you know, they've got their problems, the shit's the same the world over. Some places are nicer than others. But Antoine was photographing some important people so we got special treatment. It was cool."

We stop in front of the elephant enclosure and stare at nothing. There are no elephants in sight. "Oh, look, you have to go inside," he says.

I'm not sure I want to go in the pachyderm house in this dress, but Ronin pulls me so I'm forced to follow. Inside there is a table set up and two zoo workers are chatting with the event visitors about sponsoring an elephant. The elephants just munch on hay and give us all dirty looks.

Ronin grabs some literature as we shuffle though with the other guests, then find ourselves outside where the hint of rain becomes a light drizzle. We get caught up in the wave that brings us back to the event center, get escorted to our table, and take our seats as the presentations start.

I've never been to a charity anything, let alone some big production put on to squeeze money out of the pockets of Denver's rich and famous. There are quite a few presenters and Ronin actually knows a few people who appear on stage.

Which is weird. Because I just don't see him as the rich and snooty type, but I guess Chaput Studios is a major player in this town. There are a few kids who give their touching stories and a few older kids, the same age as me probably, who talk about the great families they had in foster care.

After the presentations and plea for money, dinner is served. Ronin chats easily with the other couples at our table between bites of prime rib. They are all friends of Elise and Antoine's and they don't seem at all disappointed that Ronin and I had to step in and take their place for the evening. They ask us a ton of questions about pretty much everything. It's funny how once you get older, questions that normally seem rude become standard. Like, *So when's the wedding?*

I almost snort some ice out of my nose at this one.

Ronin doesn't even flinch, he just promises to send the couple an invitation once we nail it down.

I smile into my water glass at that.

The night just flies by and before I know it Ronin is writing a check and then we're huddling underneath a large black umbrella as we make our way back to the parking lot in the pouring rain.

We both scoot into the back into the car and breathe a sigh of relief.

"Was it fun, Gidge?" Ronin asks me as he brings my legs up over his lap, then slips my shoes off my aching feet and starts to rub them.

"Yes, it was fun… oh, God, that feels good!"

"I told you I was gonna touch you all the way home."

And all during the night, which he did. I can barely recall a second when his hand was not on me in some way. If it wasn't draped over the back of my chair, gently teasing the back of my neck, it was on my knee, squeezing lightly as the other couples did their best to embarrass us with questions about babies.

But the really interesting thing about all this touching is how I feel about it. A few days ago I might have seen it as possessive, but tonight it felt like affection. Maybe that means I'm getting over some of the bad things that happened to me in Chicago?

I hope so. Because I like Ronin Flynn for sure now.

"What're you thinking about?" Ronin asks me as the town car makes its way through the traffic in the parking lot.

"Just kinda reevaluating my thoughts on certain things." I shoot him a sideways glance. "About you mostly."

"Yeah? Is that good or bad?'

"Good, I think. I mean, I'm still a bit of a mess personally. But maybe I was wrong about you? Maybe you are a good guy?"

"Did you really think I was a bad guy?" he says, his brow in a furrow.

"No. Yes. Well," I sigh. "I'm probably not the best judge right now, Ronin. I'm tainted by past experiences, so I'm not sure I can tell the difference anymore."

"Well, let me ask you this, have I ever hurt you?"

"No."

"Did the last guy hurt you?"

I look away and let the question hang there as I take a deep breath. "Very badly," I finally manage.

"So now you doubt your decisions? About choosing the right guy to date?"

"Sorta."

He waits because we both know that's not an answer.

"I just never want to get in that situation again. I never want to be controlled like that. What I do want," I say, looking him in the eye now, "is to be myself and not get mowed down by a boyfriend's personality, or dreams, or needs. I want to make my own money so I never have to depend on a guy again. Does that make any sense?" He nods, slowly. His hands are still massaging my feet and I lean my head sideways on the back of the seat and try to relax as I listen to the rain pound the roof of the car.

"I get it, Rook. I have the same problem, except in reverse."

I open my eyes and look at him. "What do you mean?"

"Well, I have this rule that I won't date a model, right? I mean, I break it all the time," he laughs a little, "obviously. But the part I won't break is where these encounters will end up. I want a normal life with a normal family. I don't want to bring kids up in Antoine's studio. I don't want my wife taking her clothes off so I can touch her in front of the camera. I want *boring*. I want kids in Catholic school and a minivan filled with car seats. And I have no idea how long this thing with Antoine's studio will last, but I'm pretty sure that I'd rather die than be the father of a teenage girl who runs the models at an erotic art photography studio."

I smile a little at that thought. He's right. That's a disaster waiting to happen.

The car pulls into the studio parking garage and Ronin slips my shoes back on. We wait for the driver in silence, then make our way to the elevator and head on upstairs.

"So where's that leave us?" Ronin asks.

I shrug. "I dunno," I say honestly. I have never fantasized about getting married and having children, not even as a child, because I have no good memories of that kind of life. But this seems to be a big deal to Ronin and I don't want to ruin our perfect night, so I follow up my shrug with something evasive. "I guess we'll just have to wait and see what happens."

CHAPTER THIRTY-THREE

Ronin

When the elevator doors open Rook and I are bombarded with studio lights and general chaos. Elise is barking orders at technicians and Antoine spies us from across the room and is already yelling out in French as he crosses the distance.

"What's going on?" Rook asks me.

"Rain shoot," I say, picking up every third word coming out of Antoine's mouth due to the scraping of a ladder across the floor. I feel Rook tense at the screeching noise. "We have to get a shot in the rain for TRAGIC." I should've anticipated this, really. But I stopped thinking about work hours ago.

I put my hand up as Antoine approaches, but I know it's useless. There's no getting out of it, we have to shoot tonight. Now. "Go with Elise, she'll get you ready."

"Wait." She grabs a hold of my arm. "We have to work *right now*?"

"Yeah, sounds like fun, huh?"

She rolls her eyes at me.

"Rook, nine times out of ten, being a model sucks. Better get used to it if this is the life you want." I push her towards Elise and sigh. I know it's a dig at her declaration of independence, but I can't help it. The last thing I want is this girl half naked in the cold rain at night. But it's in the contract that we get a rain shot, so it must be done.

Elise whisks Rook off to the salon to wash her makeup off and take her hair down. I take the stairs to my apartment three at a time and head straight for my closet.

I hang up the tux and try not to let the disappointment wash over me as I trade my expensive clothes for an old pair of jeans and a white t-shirt. Rook will be wearing the exact same thing, except she'll have a nice black bra on so that when she's soaking wet it will show through the fabric for everyone to see.

And that just pisses me off. Elise was right, I should be protecting her from this life, not encouraging her to give Antoine what he wants.

I take a few deep breaths to dampen down the anger and then pull on a pair of boots and head back downstairs. Antoine is waiting for me, still barking orders, but clearly waiting for me because he's blocking the stairs. He sends the technician off and turns as I try to push past him.

"Ronin, wait."

I shake my head. "Tonight, Antoine?"

"It might not rain again."

"It's called a fucking shower. We could just do it inside, in the warm fucking shower room."

"I want city lights," he says, like this explains everything.

"So fucking what?"

"Her contract is with me and I decide what we shoot. If you're too attached to her, then I can get someone else to finish the job."

"You're funny tonight, ya know that?"

"The quicker we get started, the quicker we can be done. Go."

He pushes me and I pull back out of his reach just as Rook comes out of the dressing room. Just as I predicted, white t-shirt, faded jeans, and a nice black bra that everyone can see. I smile at her because she looks worried.

"Hey," I say, accepting an umbrella from one of the techs standing by the terrace door. I open it and we walk outside together. The rain is pelting down with such force against the umbrella I have a hard time hearing what she's saying.

"What?"

"This sucks," she screams in my ear.

"Yeah," I agree, squeezing her arm a little.

"And I'm freezing!"

"It just gets worse, Gidget. So better to just put on the game-face and push on, because the sooner fuckwad Antoine gets his piece-of-shit pictures, the sooner we can go to bed."

She looks up at me. "We?"

I smile and let the anger wash off me, but I let that question hang there. It's hard to predict how this will turn out. Maybe good, maybe not.

We have a special platform that we do the city light shots on. It's raised up about six feet off the terrace floor and basically it's just a slab of concrete that has a railing, so it looks like you're on a terrace, but it gives Antoine lots of different ways to approach the photo. Tonight we have a tarp set up to protect everyone except Rook and me from the rain, and all the exterior lights are on. We have a mock street lamp and spotlights that are mounted on the ground. We slip under the tarp and I hand the umbrella off to someone who looks like he's about to pass out from fatigue. It's after two in the morning, so I can't blame him, I feel the same way.

"OK, Rook, let's just get this done as quick as possible. We go out in the rain, they adjust the lights, we make out, wiggle around a little, start undressing each other, I get you down to the bra and panties, end of shoot. Got it?" She starts shivering the minute I say the word undressing, and by the time I'm done talking her teeth are chattering.

"I'm f-f-fre-eeeezing," she repeats, her arms all drawn up against her body.

I hug her close and she melts into my chest. "I know. As soon as we're done I'll warm you back up, OK?"

She nods, but the chattering continues.

"OK, let's go." I pull her out into the rain with me and the shit is coming down so hard it actually stings my skin. I look over at Rook as I get into position and she's frantically trying to straighten out her wet hair. Elise appears in a rain slicker and begins adjusting her hair, leaning in to tell her encouraging things as she does it.

When Elise leaves I lean against the fake light pole and pull Rook into me again. She's very willing and this makes me smile. "Put your arms around me, Gidge. You'll get warmer, and besides, mauling my body is part of the job assignment tonight. This job has awesome benefits, doesn't it?"

She laughs and wraps her arms around my waist. Antoine is already shooting, so I slip my hands inside the edge of her t-shirt. It's plastered against her body already, we are fully soaked.

Antoine barks orders at the techs to adjust the lighting, but I tune them all out and concentrate on Rook. I lean down into her ear as her body trembles with cold against me. "Forget them. Forget the rain. Forget the job. Look at me."

She looks up.

"It's just us. Pretend we're in the warm car, all dressed, and we can't wait to get home so we can rip each other's clothes off."

"You have mind-reading powers, don't you?"

"What?" I laugh.

She winks at me. "You were reading my mind back there in the car, weren't you?"

I lean down and kiss her, just a soft flutter kiss to let her know I'm interested in playing. "You're on to me, huh?"

"I am," she coos back. "But do you know what I was thinking *after* I fantasized about ripping off your clothes?"

I nod.

"Tell me."

"You were thinking that maybe I'd take my hands and slip them inside your shirt, like this." My fingers travel up her ribcage, a light drag that makes her gasp and hold in a giggle, and then I push against her breast. "And I was thinking about how I wasn't allowed to kiss you all night because of your lipstick. But now, it's all gone."

"Mmmmhhhmmm," she moans as I take my kisses to her neck.

"So now, I can ravish your mouth properly." I withdraw my hand from under her shirt and I absently log Antoine complaining that he wants me to take the damn shirt off, not lose focus, but I grasp Rook's face with both hands, lift her up to me, so all her attention is on my face and nothing else. And then I crush her lips with my kiss. The heat of her mouth and the twirl of her tongue against mine makes me hard in an instant. I grind against her a little and she moans back at me, that little thrum of her voice against my palm driving me crazy.

I rip my own shirt off in one fluid motion. Antoine goes crazy with this move, and not in a good way—he likes the girls to play with that a little, but fuck him. Rook's hands start in on my chest, tracing a stream of water that is racing down my body. Her fingertip starts at my shoulder and then falls down, the water bouncing off it, splattering a little, as she traces over my muscle, then continues as the tiny river is lost in the waistband of my pants.

Her finger slips in, just a tiny fraction, just enough to drive me up a fucking wall with desire. I feel her laugh a little and I pull back.

"You think you're in control here, Gidge?"

She nods, blushing.

I begin lifting her shirt away from her body, it's so wet now, it's plastered to her skin. I rub it against her belly as I lift and she moans, making me rush a little, showing her bra. It's a demi, so it dips very low, almost exposing her nipples. The shirt comes off a few seconds later and I can hear Antoine telling me what to do, but I dismiss him.

I know exactly what I'm doing. I take her whole breast in my hand and squeeze until she whimpers, then drop my mouth to her nipple and drag the fabric down with my teeth. She fists my hair and I lift her up until her legs wrap around my waist. I turn and push her against the light pole, and she is panting into my ear as I suck.

"Pants! Ronin! We're all cold here!" Antoine barks.

I shift Rook until I have her weight distributed against my hip, just the one hand holding her up, then lift my other hand towards Antoine.

And flip him off.

And then I gather Rook against me, pushing the heat between her legs into my thick hardness, walk off the set, down the stairs, and over to her apartment. I crash her against the outside wall as I punch in the codes and whisk her inside. My foot comes out and kicks the door closed, and then I carry her down the short hallway and throw her down on the bed.

"If you want me to stop, please," I beg, "say it now."

She licks her lips as I stare down her with hungry eyes, and then whispers, "I don't want you to stop, Ronin. I don't want to take it slow or change direction. I just want you to go. *Please*, I'm fucking dying here, just go!"

CHAPTER THIRTY-FOUR

Rook

He laughs at my plea, but shit! I've never had an orgasm and right now I'm on the edge. It's like I can feel that fucker ready to explode, I need the teeniest bit of pressure in just the right spot and I will gush all over him.

All the caveman shit from outside is gone now and he watches my face as he works on the front clasp of my bra. My breasts fall out as he unfastens it, and then I sit up and wiggle my arms out and he tosses it across the room.

"Lie down," he commands.

I do.

His hands go to my jeans and after some unbuttoning, he grabs them by the waist and pulls them down so fast they end up inside out because they are wet and plastered to my legs. His fingers go to my panties and he tugs a little until I lift my hips. He slides them down my legs and drops them to the floor.

I lie still, completely naked, as his eyes take me in. "Your turn," I say in a throaty whisper.

His fingers unbutton his jeans and unzip the fly and then he steps out of them and his boxers in one movement. He's well-built and I try not to stare, but I don't entirely succeed. When I look up at his face, he's smiling.

"What?"

"You, Gidget. You're blushing."

"I'm not very experienced," I admit. "I'm not a virgin, but it was all pretty boring and I've never—"

He waits a few seconds and then prods me on as he lies down next to me. "You've never what?"

His hands caress my stomach and I relax against the pillows. My wet clothes have made everything damp on the bed, but I do not care. "I've never had an orgasm."

I expect him to laugh or make a joke, but he doesn't. He just leans over my body, pressing himself up to me, his erection grinding against my hip. I am desperate to get him inside me, but he's slow now. "I might not be able to make many guarantees in this world, Rook," he says as his hand travels down and traces the crease between my legs. "But I will say with one hundred percent certainty that you will come tonight."

He leans down to my face as his fingers probe into my entrance and teases my lips with a nibble as he pushes one finger inside me, and then uses his thumb to gently caress my clit. I squirm as his kiss becomes bruising, my whole body on fire with the desire I have.

"Oh, God, Ronin. Please, I am so close." My hands reach down and grab his shaft, pumping him, making him breathe heavy and moan out my name. That talented finger of his flicks against me in just the right way and the agonizing throb that has been building for the last week suddenly explodes. I shove my face into his neck and bite his ear, which only makes him work my clit harder and send a wave of wetness between my legs.

He lets me pant there in the crook of his neck as the tiny flutter waves flow through me for a few more minutes, and then he lies back and pulls me on top of him, his erection peeking out from between my legs. "You can be on top, Gidget. Do you like it on top?"

"I have no idea," I admit again.

"I think you will. Lift up for a second."

I lift my hips and he slides his cock back and forth across my slit, murmuring approval as he enjoys the wetness he created with his fingers. And then I feel the pressure. His hands have a hold of my hips now and he urges me to push down on him and I feel him stretch me as he pushes up.

"Fuck, Rook, I can't believe how good you feel." Ronin stares up at me, his eyes barely open as I lift up and then push down one more time. I shift a little as I come down, my clit rubbing up against the base of his shaft, and holy fucking shit, that feels good. I do it again and this time I exert a little more force as I come down, making Ronin growl out a few unintelligible words.

His hands thrust me up and then slam me down, and everything I just experienced is magnified, I can feel the pressure building inside me again. I lift up, getting into his faster rhythm, and we slam together harder and harder with each movement and just when I think I'm going to come again, he slows it down, and instead of the thrusting, he draws me down onto his chest and grabs my ass with both hands, sliding me, sliding my clit, back and forth across his body. We come together this time, a collective of pleasure and panting, as his mouth crashes against mine once more, our tongues still desperate for each other.

When the shock waves subside I burrow my head into his neck again, then collapse against his chest. He turns me over so I'm on my side and then slips his arm under me, pulling my ass up against his stomach. "It was better than the fantasy, Rook. I'd just like you to know that."

I lie there for a few seconds, so happy I can hardly stand it. So satisfied with his body pressed up against me, his breath lingering on my neck as he relaxes. And I fall asleep with a man I might love for real, for the first time ever.

CHAPTER THIRTY-FIVE

Rook

A loud knock jolts me out of my sleep and I turn so fast, I fall out of bed.

I'm naked.

And when I look around in a half-asleep daze, I also realize I'm alone. I'm pretty sure Ronin was here when I fell asleep.

The knocking comes again and I wrap the sheet around me and hustle my ass down the hallway to the door. I can see Elise's face peeking through the window so I relax a little.

"Jesus," she says. "Heavy sleeper or what?" Her hands are clasping a clipboard piled with papers.

I can barely see her though the gunk in my eyes, so I don't answer, but that should be her second clue that yes, indeed, I am a heavy sleeper.

"Why are you here?" I manage to croak out.

"Time to work."

"What time is it?" I ask, confused. I look around, still trying to put things together.

"Seven-thirty."

"What the hell? I just went to bed a few hours ago, Elise! You guys had me out in the freaking rain in the middle of the night!"

"Yeah, well, today we need to make you look like shit for this shoot, so what better way to look like shit than to feel like shit? Besides, Ronin is gone for the day and Antoine wants to shoot you with Billy for this."

"Billy! But—"

"Hey, don't push it right now, Rook, you guys pissed him off last night pretty bad. He needs some slutty shots and he wants someone to take care of you in the shoot, so that's Billy for today."

"Yeah, because that went so well last time," I mutter.

"That was a misunderstanding, Billy is just fine. He's worked for us for almost two years so relax. Don't shower, just put some clothes on and come right to make-up."

She turns on her heel and some of her papers flutter off the clipboard and float down at my feet. I reach down, still slightly dazed from sleep, and go to hand them back to her when I realize what I'm holding.

It's a contact sheet filled with pictures. Pictures of Ronin and me from yesterday.

The view in each one is from below, like whoever took this shot was on the ground looking up at us. Front and center is Ronin's hand inside my boxer shorts and there is no way to miss the fact that his fingers are definitely between my legs. The other hand gropes my breast with a force that appears to be bruising. My head is tilted back, my mouth open in what I can only imagine was a groan of pleasure, but it's Ronin's face that stops me cold.

He's looking straight at the camera. His electric blue eyes blazing like a predator, his brows furrowed together, and his lips in a snarl. He looks like an animal ready to take down a kill. And I get it, it's theatrics for the sake of art. Or whatever. But he made such a big deal about not looking at the camera, and here he is, staring directly into it?

It feels like a betrayal.

"What the fuck is this?" I ask Elise.

She draws in a deep breath and takes the photo back. "That is the winning image, Rook. They loved it. Congratulations, you're about to be famous."

And then she turns around and walks off, leaving me standing in the doorway.

Is this what I signed up for? Of all the images they got of

us yesterday, that was the one they have to use? Where the hell did Ronin go? That's really not cool. And slutty shots? I don't even want to know what that means.

"Hurry up!" Elise calls out as I stand there thinking.

I slam the door and go put on some clothes, brush my teeth real fast, slip on my ratty old Converse, and head over to make-up.

Why I am sent there I have no idea because when Josie turns me around to look at myself, I look like shit. Just like Elise wanted. I have raccoon eyes from the smeared eye shadow, my lipstick is splotchy, and she has applied some kind of make-up in just the right way to make my face look hollowed out.

I am a crack whore.

I am my mother.

In that instant I see her. The same eyes, the same raven-black hair, the same look of impending death.

I look over at Elise, who is impatient to get me in the dressing room, and shake my head.

"Yes, we need this shoot and we need to get it done quick."

"Why? Why is it such a rush?"

She ignores me as we walk quickly into the dressing room. Everything about this day is wrong.

My clothes aren't in a bag, they are splayed out on one of the benches in the middle of the dressing room. It's only then that I realize there are no other girls around. "Elise, what's going on? Where is everyone?"

"We have meetings with the STURGIS people, the suits are here again, they're nailing down the specifics of the contract and Antoine is not happy, so please, just do what you're told and you'll be done fast and you can have the rest of the day off. Now put those clothes on and meet us down on the third floor."

Again, she walks out.

I look over the clothes and almost laugh. The shirt is dirty and torn, the jeans are the same, and the underwear—yes, I actually have underwear this time—is black. It comes with a demi bra, like the one I had on last night, and some boy shorts. I put the underwear on and then the clothes. The rip on the shirt goes right between my tits so the black bra is visible.

When I turn to look at myself in the mirror, I am a homeless crack whore.

I swallow down the bad feeling I'm getting about this day, slip my feet back into my sneakers, and walk down the stairs to the third floor.

Billy is waiting for me, checking his phone for a text or something. He looks up after his fingers finish their swiping, and smiles. "You look great!"

I'm not sure if he means I look great for this part I'm playing today or if that was a total joke, so I just say nothing.

"Oh, calm down, Rook. It's a simple shoot, no nudity or nothing, Antoine said. Although I'm disappointed at that, to be honest. You are very hot. So I'm just supposed to tell you what to do. Antoine thinks it's weird if he tells you himself, so I'm playing moderator today, I guess. To keep Ronin at bay once he finds out we did this while he was busy with Clare."

"With Clare?" I ask, my heart beating fast.

"Yeah, he's down in the first floor apartment with her, sleeping it off or whatever."

Sleeping it off? What the fuck does that mean? "What first floor apartment?"

Billy opens a door and ushers me in with a wave of his hand. "One of the extra ones Ronin uses for his girls."

Holy shit. I feel like a total idiot.

"Rook!" Antoine barks. "Over here." He points to a makeshift bedroom and I do as I'm told because all I want right now is to finish this shoot and get the hell out of this place. He talks to Billy in some amalgam of French and English and then Billy is telling me what to do. He touches me, has his hands all over me, kisses me a few times even, but nothing about this shoot is anything like the ones I did with

Ronin. Billy is all business, and I suppose that's good. I mean, if a strange guy is getting paid to maul you, I guess you'd want to keep it professional. But nothing can stop the horror of him stripping my clothes off, fondling my breasts, and then sitting me down in his lap, only in the underwear now, and placing my own hand between my legs as Antoine's camera clicks away.

And then it's over and I'm putting my clothes back on.

I have no idea what just happened, but I have never felt so fucking dirty in all my life.

Thankfully Billy takes my arm, chatting away pleasantly like this is just another day, and walks me out to the hallway. I stop at the stairs and come to my senses.

"I'll see you later, huh?"

He just continues to climb the stairs and calls out, "Sure thing!"

I walk down the stairs slowly, talking myself into believing this is just a big misunderstanding. Ronin is not sleeping it off with Clare. He was with me last night. We didn't go to bed until three in the morning, at least. I woke up at seven thirty. When did he find the time to sleep with another girl?

I've never explored the other floors before but Ronin freely admitted to taking his fuck buddies into these rooms. When I get to the first floor I walk down the hallway and try every door. They are all open, they are all shabby, and they are all empty. When I get to the last door, the one near the back of the building right next to the fire exit, I see a keypad.

I punch in Ronin's code and the door clicks as it unlocks. I twist the handle and push it open quietly, listening for sounds of people. Nothing. I open it more and step inside, leaving the door open behind me.

And I hear a faint moan.

I force myself to walk into the living room. It's pretty clear someone is living here because this place is furnished, maybe not nicely, but adequately. And there are old food containers that have the Cookie's Diner logo on them.

And there are clothes strewn about the floor. Underwear.

I walk farther in, towards the sound that has since ceased, and stop at a bedroom door that is slightly ajar. I can see in and I can see a bed.

And on that bed is Clare and Ronin.

Sleeping it off.

My heart beats wildly as I back out of the apartment, quietly close the door behind me, and push open the emergency exit door to get away as fast as I can. I push through a second door and then I'm in the parking lot out back near the freight elevators.

There are a whole bunch of people loading motorcycles and I weave my way through them, bumping into people, almost knocking down a bike, just doing anything I can to get away from this place. I push past a big guy and he grabs me by the arm as I flee. I turn to fight him off when I realize it's Spencer.

"You OK, Rook?"

I just stare up into his blue eyes and shake my head. "No, I don't think I am." I look back at the building and shake my head again. "I'm not OK. I need to get out of here. I need to go." I pull away from his grip and start running down the alley but he catches me and pulls me back, almost yanking me back, until I slam into his chest.

"Hold on, what's going on? Did someone hurt you? Why are your clothes all ripped?"

I look down at my outfit and laugh. "Oh, fuck." He lets go of my arm and waits as I take a deep breath. "Sorry, no, no one hurt me. This was from the photoshoot, that's all, but I can't stay here right now. I just need to go someplace, anyplace. I just need to go."

He takes my arm again and guides me over to a big red Ford F-250 with the logo of his bike shop on it. "Here, take a seat, we'll go get some lunch. I wanted to talk to you about the contract anyway, before Antoine and Ronin exaggerate it all out of proportion. I want you to make up your own mind about whether or not it's a good fit, because frankly, I'm tired of hearing them tell me you're not interested when I think you might be. So sit tight, sister." He waits for me to settle in the passenger seat and then closes the door and heads over to his buddies who are unloading bikes from the back of a semi.

I watch the back door nervously, afraid I'm going to get caught. Where is this feeling coming from? I didn't do anything wrong!

But that's never stopped you from getting punished before, Rook.

I shake my head. Ronin is not Jon. Antoine is not Jon.

But they might not be the people I thought they were either.

Spencer comes back a few minutes later, climbs in, and turns to me. "Where should we go?"

"I don't care, I have no idea, just get me out of here. And not Cookie's, OK?"

He laughs. "I'd never take you to Cookie's, Blackbird. I'll take you to my favorite restaurant, how's that?"

I nod and chew on my nail as we drive away, my whole world spinning once again.

CHAPTER THIRTY-SIX

Rook

Spencer and I end up at a biker bar that is nowhere near Denver. And really, I asked for this, right? *Get me out of here* is code for *get me the fuck out of here.* I laugh at this as I eat my burger.

"What's funny?" Spence asks.

"Nothing, it's just… where the hell are we?"

He leans back in the booth and stretches his arms out to either side, obviously proud of himself. "My bar." He grins like an idiot now.

"This is your bar? Shit, dude, you're like loaded or what? You can't be any older than Ronin and you have all those bikes, some TV show people paying for a major deal with Antoine, and you own a bar?"

"You forgot Shrike Bikes showroom next door. Which is really where I want to take you so I can show you what this contract is all about."

"Why not just tell me? I mean, why's it such a secret?"

"Well, it sounds bad on paper."

I eye him suspiciously.

"But it's not, Rook. I swear, just let me show you because if Ronin and Antoine get to you first they'll blow it all up and make it sound dirty." He stops to lean forward and raise his eyebrows at me, but not in a joking way, he's almost pleading for me to understand. "It's not dirty. It's art. And it's a hell of a lot less exploitative than what you're doing for TRAGIC, I'll tell you that right now."

I pout at this, because today was just wrong. I had to wash my face in the bathroom when I got here and change into a spare biker shirt Spencer had in his truck because the whole crack-whore thing was not working for me. If this is what modeling for Antoine will be like most of the time, I'm not interested. "I'll keep an open mind, how's that?"

"Perfect, that's all I ask."

After we eat we walk over to his shop. It rained a little while we were inside, so water sloshes inside my worn-out Converse as we splash through some puddles. There are no sidewalks around here, just dirt. Spencer opens the door to the showroom for me and I'm a little taken aback by the beauty of it all. "Wow, you have some nice bikes, Spence. I had no idea."

"You're into the bike scene, Rook?" he asks, a bit surprised by my genuine interest.

I shrug and sigh at the same time because I was into the bike scene once, if only because of the person who got me interested in the first place.

"Which one do you like the best?" he asks me as I walk between the aisles of bikes lined up, headlight to headlight, facing each other. There must be like thirty or forty bikes in here.

"I like the retro ones, like this one right here," I say, tapping the glossy gas tank. "It looks like an old Triumph."

"Ah, you are a biker chick!"

The smile creeps out with the memories this time, I can't help it. "I had a boy once. He liked bikes."

"Yeah? Where's he now?"

I shrug and swing my leg over and cop a seat on the pretty turquoise one I was eyeballing.

"Do you ride?"

"Dirt bikes," I say under my breath.

"This boy teach you that?"

I look up at him and change the subject. "So spill the details on the contract, Spence. I'm dying to know if this will work for me or not."

"OK," he says, taking a deep breath. "Come with me." I get up off the bike and follow him towards the back. There are a few lingering customers and one cashier helping people out, but the shop seems to be winding down for the day. He opens the door to an office that has his name on it. It says, *Spencer Shrike, President.* Which totally trips me out.

I walk in and Spence directs me to take a seat at a round table surrounded by cheap vinyl chairs that look like they belong in a VFW and not the Shrike Bikes president's office. I do, and then wait patiently as he gathers up some binders on the filing cabinet behind his desk. I look around the office as I wait. It's a typical biker office. Eagles and American flags, and of course, black velvet girls with tits hanging out, adorn the walls. I have to chuckle behind my fist because seriously…

I take my attention away from the artwork and study the furniture. The desk is a monstrosity of dark wood, mostly scratched and filled with paperwork. His office chair says a lot about him as well. It's leather, but not pretentious, and it looks well-worn, not new.

Spencer is a clash of contradictions. But this is a good thing. It says he's a down-to-Earth guy, not some asshole who gets off having the word *president* stenciled on his door.

He brings the binders over to the table and then takes a seat and looks over at me with a grin.

"What? You look nervous," I say.

He opens the book and there's an eight-by-ten glossy photograph of a naked girl. Except it's very hard to tell that she's naked on first glance because her entire body has been painted to look like she's wearing the sexy female version of an Elvis jumpsuit, complete with rhinestones and a nice sparkly belt.

I grin. "What's this?"

He turns the page and it's the same girl, only now she's wearing a roller derby outfit. He flips the page again and she's a cowgirl, complete with Wrangler jeans—it's an ass-shot—

and a red checkered shirt.

The next page makes me gasp. Because it's a picture of Spencer, painting the girl.

"You!" I say, jumping up and grabbing the book from him.

"Me," he says proudly. "I paint on girls." We both laugh at that, hysterically almost. "I paint on girls," he says again. "And I want to paint a girl to match the custom bike I'm making for the Sturgis Rally this summer."

"Wow, you have blown me away, Spencer. Holy shit! Never in a million years did I think this was your secret. You're an artist!"

"Yeah, and I want to paint you, Rook. For the contract. I want to paint you to match all my bikes for the portfolio and advertising, but mostly, I want to paint you to match the custom bike I'm making special for Sturgis, because it's called the Shrike Raven. When I heard your name was Rook, well, that was it, girl. I just need it to be you."

"Wow," I say again. I nod at him. "I think I'm in, Spencer Shrike. This looks like the most fun I might ever have in my life."

"You'll be completely naked, Rook, just so you understand. When we do public performances, your nipples will be covered with those pasties, and you'll wear a thong, but that's only for the public appearances. In the photoshoots and in the private show at Sturgis, you'll be painted everywhere. And even with the pasties and thong, you have to be painted up nude, first. So it matches up perfect."

I flip through more pictures. Each one is perfection. You cannot tell these girls are naked. Not one bit. "I'm OK with that, Spencer. I'm in."

"Ronin is not going to approve."

"Who cares?" I reply, still flipping through the book.

"Well, I got the impression he liked you yesterday, so I figured you liked him too."

I can't hold it in anymore so I spill it. "I think he's seeing that Clare girl, Spencer. I saw them together today, in a bed.

And we slept together last night. I thought we were, I don't know, together or something? But he obviously doesn't see it the same way. Maybe he *will* hate it, but I can't be bothered with that right now. I have to make my own decisions."

"Fair enough. I'm not gonna stop you, so you wanna see the bike you'll be painted up to match?"

"Yeah!"

We go back out to the showroom and it's empty now. He takes me to a book on the front desk and opens it. "This here is the showroom, but I build the bikes in a shop just north of Fort Collins, about a half hour from here. I'm almost finished with it, so we'll shoot you on the other bikes first, all painted up to match each one, and then we'll take the new bike to Sturgis and do a presentation to kick off the Biker Channel show we're gonna film for next year's spring TV season."

"Wow. I realize I've said that like three times already, but Spencer, you're amazing. This bike is the shit." Most of it is still in pieces, but the rendering is beautiful. It's got curves, and chrome, and the gas tank has been molded and painted to look like a raven's head.

"Which bike out here, Rook? Which is your favorite? You can pick one to be in the show too, then keep it for yourself."

I turn around and check them out carefully. "Are you serious?" I look at him, astonished.

"It's no big deal, these are showroom bikes, not special customs like the Raven. But I'll have it customized a little and we'll take it to Sturgis for you."

I walk between the aisles, my fingertips lovingly touching the tanks of several very nice specimens. But if I get to keep it, I should be practical so I can actually ride it. I don't want a chopper, that's for sure, they look difficult. I go back over to the turquoise one I was sitting on earlier and try it out again. "This one," I say, looking up at Spence's beaming smile. "I like this one."

"Can you really ride?" he asks as I lean forward on the tank and rest my cheek against the cool metal. I let my arms drop and a long sigh comes out.

"Yeah, I had a boy. He was wild about bikes."

"Hold on, be right back."

He leaves and comes back a few minutes later, pushing a cart filled with art supplies down the aisle. "Stay just like that, but lift your shirt up a little."

"What?" I laugh.

"I'll paint your back, just to make sure you know what you're in for. Just something simple."

I have to admit, this is exciting. "OK." I lift the back of my shirt up a little and lean back down on the tank. He sits behind me on the bike and grabs his supplies. First he washes my back with a wet cloth and then he dries it with a soft one.

"Now," he says, "tell me about this boy with the bike."

And I do. He paints while I talk. "Wade was his name. I was fifteen when I went to live with him. I was in foster care after my mom died, and this was literally like the tenth foster home I'd been in. I wasn't even a troublemaker or anything, it's just... I don't know, no one wanted me. Wade was two years older than me and he was a motocross racer. He taught me to ride a dirt bike and then he got a motorcycle when he turned eighteen and it was such a big deal. We had started messing around a little by then, and well, his mom figured I was bad news, a baby-maker waiting to happen maybe. She sent me away. But even though we never did anything beyond second base, he was my first love."

I wiggle a little at the soft touch of his brush on my back and he growls out a "Stay still, Blackbird," at me.

"And after that, Spencer, nothing in my life was ever good again until I found Antoine, Ronin and Elise last week." I stop for a moment to consider things, and then continue. "You too, I think. I mean I realize I barely know you, but shit, Spencer, you made my life today. Seriously, this whole offer is like a dream. And I've been pretty short on dreams these days, so it's a big deal to me."

He swishes his brush in a can of water and turns on a fan

to air dry the paint on my back.

"Yeah, well," he says as he gets up and takes a seat on the bike next to me. I turn my head so I can see his face as we talk. "I have to admit, at first I just wanted to piss Ronin off and get you to agree, not that I didn't immediately think you were perfect, because Antoine described you over the phone. But Ronin and I used to be close and we're not anymore. So I was just being childish."

"So how do you two know each other?"

"We went to Catholic school together."

I almost choke on my own spit. "Oh shit, Ronin mentioned Catholic school last night, but I figured it was, I dunno, a weird suburban fantasy. How the hell did the two of you end up in Catholic school?"

"I always went to Saint Margaret's, since fucking pre-school. But Ronin showed up in eighth grade, just before we were about to graduate over to the Catholic high school. I lived in Park Hill and he lived over in the studio with Antoine. Ronin was a trip, ya know? He showed up out of nowhere speaking French like he grew up in Paris instead of Five Points, leaving school every few months to go travel the world for photoshoots. It was a strange life for a kid, but Ronin was never a kid. I found out about his parents a few years later when someone dug up the police report and plastered it all over school."

"Oh, that sucks. He told me about his father."

"Yeah, you'd think that would really piss a guy off, but not Ronin. He never even blinked. He said something in French, which roughly translated to *I am not my father's son*, and went about his business. That was tenth grade. We spent the next three years inseparable."

"What happened?"

"Ahhh," he says, getting up off the bike, "it's a long story. I better get you back before he goes apeshit. I have no idea what you saw today, but Ronin's not a cheater, Rook. He's just not. He's dated a lot of girls, I know that for sure, but he's never dated them at the same time. That's not him, so maybe let him explain."

He checks my back and pulls my shirt down after determining the paint is dry. I get up, feeling a lot better than when I left the studio, and I realize something.

I'm ready to go home.

CHAPTER THIRTY-SEVEN

Rook

The studio is still bustling with activity when we arrive. It's hard to believe that it takes so long to unload bikes and roll them into the elevator and park them upstairs, but it must, because there are still two bikes in the truck.

We take the stairs and I'm exhausted because this day has been long and teetering on the edge of unpleasant since it started. If Spencer hadn't made this STURGIS offer, I'd probably be very depressed right now. We reach the fourth floor and the door is open, I can hear Antoine yelling in French about something. I'm really glad that guy prefers to get pissed in a foreign language, because it saves the rest of us from listening to his big-ass mouth.

"Rook! Where the fuck have you been?" Ronin yells, storming over to us.

"Spencer and I—"

Ronin pushes Spencer in the chest, sending him backwards, and then before I even understand what's happening they are throwing punches. "Wait!" I yell, grabbing at Ronin's arm. "What's the—"

Ronin reacts to my grab and pushes me away. I go flying backward and end up on my ass.

Again! That fucker!

Antoine pulls me up and asks me politely if I'm OK, and two of the technicians break up the fight.

"Where the fuck were you?" Ronin demands.

I ignore his question and turn to Antoine. "Spencer said

he wants to offer me the STURGIS contract, so I'd like to sign that *right now.*"

I look over at Spencer, hoping I'm not overstepping my boundaries, and he smiles at me, still breathing heavy from the fight.

Antoine doesn't move, Ronin just stares at me, and Elise is the only one with enough sense to speak. "I'll get the papers."

"Rook, I think you need to wait on that, we can talk about this tomorrow."

"No, Ronin. I don't need to discuss anything with you. I got all the details from Spencer and I'm signing that contract tonight." *Because*, I don't add, *I'll be damned if I'm gonna get stuck here with an asshole who has pushed me down to the ground twice in the past fucking week while he was angry at another guy.*

Elise calls me into the office while the guys just stand around staring at me like idiots, so I walk off, then close the door behind me once I get inside.

"Sit," Elise says.

I do.

"Now, what happened? Last night you and Ronin were practically screwing each other in the rain, and today you disappear with Spencer and come back pissed off. What's going on?"

"It's got nothing to do with Spencer, if that's what you're after. I'm just not sure I need a guy in my life, and to be honest, Elise, you're the one who warned me to stay away from Ronin. So I should be asking you the same question." I snatch the papers out of her hand, grab a pen off the desk and start skimming the stipulations. The contract looks like the last one so I assume it's standard and initial and sign in all the designated places.

I throw it down on the desk and take a deep breath and say in my most polite voice, "I'll move out as soon as I get paid for the TRAGIC contract. Can you give me an approximate time frame for that?"

She just sits on the corner of the desk frowning at me for a few seconds. "We have three more shoots to do, you can do them all tomorrow and we'll give you half. Then the other half once the final contract is delivered. But it will be a long day of non-stop work, Rook, and it's not the sweet kind either."

"I'll be fine. What time should I report?"

"Six AM."

I don't even nod this time, I'm just ready to be alone. So I spin on my heel and leave, walk past the men who stop arguing mid-sentence as soon as I emerge from the office, and head straight to my apartment. I set my phone to five AM so I can wash the crack whore off me before Elise and Josie can turn around and make me up as a meth fiend.

I'd forgotten all about the paint job Spencer did on my back yesterday, and I can't quite reach it to scrub it off in the tub. It doesn't help that I have to hold that damn shower head the whole time either, so I just leave it alone. I sigh, because I'm pretty sure this will piss everyone off if this is a naked day. I try to look at it in the mirror, and I can see that it's a dark bird that might be a rook or a raven, but it also has lettering down at the bottom, near the small of my back, and that is way too little to read backwards.

Well, what can I do?

Nothing, that's what.

When I walk out on the terrace it's still slightly dark, but all the lights inside the studio are on. I go inside and Elise, already busy with that tiny blonde girl, points to the dressing room and says, "See Ronin first."

Wonderful, he's the last person I want to see.

I walk into the dressing room and it's busy and filled with girls. All half-naked, all lining up at Dr. Ronin's scale to be weighed.

The bile comes up in my throat, that's how sick it makes me to think about this weighing-in stuff. And it's not because I'm worried about gaining weight. I might gain some, I might lose some, but I have a natural size to me and this is it. I'm not a fluctuator. It makes me sick because I can't stand the fact that he gets to invade me like this. It feels so…

"Get in line, Rook," Ronin says as I begin to wander off toward a bench that is not yet claimed.

I do what I'm told. I'm weak. There are only two girls ahead of me so it goes fast. I step on the scale without looking at Ronin.

He lets out a small laugh.

"What?" I ask.

"You gained two pounds." He laughs again.

"And you find that funny?" I ask, the irritation with him building.

"No, not funny. Just satisfying."

"Ugh! Where are my clothes?"

He points to a bag hanging from the rack with my name on it and then whispers, "Don't get too comfortable in the clothes, though—it's TRAGIC, remember? Most of this day will be spent wearing nothing. And you better get used to it, *Blackbird*, because the entire STURGIS contract is nothing but full-body nudes."

I admit, this does make me uncomfortable, but then I remember the beautiful paint on all those nude girls in Spencer's book and relax a little about my decision. Besides, it's done. I signed the contract, it can't be undone without a huge production. And that's not something I'm interested in making.

I step off the scale and look around, not sure what to do next.

"Why are you doing this, Rook?"

"Doing what?" I ask, not looking at him.

"Taking another contract. It's clear that the shoot

yesterday set you off, so why do more when you don't have to?"

I turn and meet his questioning gaze. "I do have to. I already told you, Ronin, I want to be independent and take care of myself. This," I say, waving my hand at the naked girls in the dressing room, "is a job that pays me money. And nothing more."

"So why disappear yesterday?"

"I did not disappear, I was with Spencer the entire time. Now, if you could just tell me what to do so I can finish this job and get the hell out of the garden apartment, I'd really appreciate it."

He watches me for a few more moments, then throws up his hands. "Go see Elise for make-up, then come back here and get changed."

Elise is shaking a thin white robe at me as I enter the salon, I grab it, go behind the partitioned wall to change, and come out wrapped up and ready.

"Shampoo," Elise says, pointing to the chair. I lie back and she turns the water on and begins, talking as she goes through the motions. "So, Spencer is nice, huh?"

I sigh. "I'm not interested in Spencer, Elise. Just his contract."

"Then tell me what happened. Ronin likes you, two days ago you liked him… how did you get to this place right now? It makes no sense."

She turns the water off and begins the shampoo. This time she is gentle, like the first time I showed up here. That was a week ago. One week, and this is what happens to my life. "I just don't think Ronin is the guy for me, that's all. I don't really feel like discussing it."

"And?" she prods, her fingers massaging the back of my head. "You have trust issues, right?"

I snort. "Elise, don't pretend you know me, because you don't."

"Well, I know Ronin found you huddled in the hallway

like Clare was gonna kill you or something—" I bristle at the name and Elise senses this and stops talking for a second, then resumes her psychoanalysis. "And Ronin did manage to land you on your ass twice now out of jealousy, so I can see why you'd be pissed at him about that. And I know you were homeless when you ended up here, you admitted that to Ronin. And I know you've been hurt. So actually, Rook, while I might not know all the details, I think I know you better than you think." The water comes on again, saving me from responding, and I lie still as she rinses my hair. When she's done she squeezes the excess water out and applies the conditioner. "Today will not be pleasant, so just be prepared. I know you were unhappy yesterday with Billy, so at least it will be Ronin today, but it's going to be hard for you."

"Well, I'll get over it, Elise. Don't worry, I always do. By the time I have my life back on track and your door is hitting me in the ass, I'm sure exposing myself to cameras will seem second nature."

"But it doesn't have to be, Rook. That's what I'm saying. Ronin likes you a lot, just go with it. Why do that STURGIS contract? I can get you out of it, Spencer will be mad, but he won't make you—"

"Don't you *dare* try and talk him out of it! I will be so pissed!" Jesus! These people have some nerve! "I want that job, dammit! How many ways do I have to say it?"

She sighs heavily and rinses my hair out for the final time, plops a towel on it and sits me up. I get up and take a seat in her stylist chair so she can blow my hair out.

It's a long morning that bounces between uncomfortable silences and short curt responses and by the time Elise is finished with me, my musing about being made into a meth fiend is not far off when I look at myself in the mirror.

And that mirror is speaking to me.

It says, *Rook Walsh, you really* are *TRAGIC.*

Tragically stupid for agreeing to all of this stuff in the first place.

CHAPTER THIRTY-EIGHT

Rook

Back in the dressing room I realize today's fun has only just begun. Ronin is nowhere to be seen, so I grab my bag and head over to the privacy stalls. Most of the girls are out in the studio by now, but I'm not interested in seeing anyone so the privacy stall it is. Inside the bag is the pink dress I wore for the very first shoot with Ronin. Well, maybe not the exact same dress, but at the very least, it started out looking just like it.

It's just that it looks nothing like that dress now.

Because the previously knee-length hem now falls just below my crotch and has a torn jagged edge. To my utmost delight the entire bust has also been modified, if you can call it that, because it's been cut out and replaced with black lace. Mix that all together with my tweaker make-up, some knee-high white stockings and black Mary Janes, and you've got Skanky Gidget Goes to Porn School.

My thong underwear barely qualifies as a postage stamp and since the bra is non-existent, it's just my nipples peeking through that, *cough*, amazing black lace.

Gross.

I turn around to look at my ass in the mirror, tug on the dress a little, and realize hoping for coverage is a lost cause.

"Well"—I spin around and find Ronin looking over the stall door—"I have to say, Gidge, I've seen you look better."

He opens the stall door for me and I scoot out and walk down the hall to the dressing room, then turn and give him a look-over. He's got different clothes on this time too—a pair of faded jeans, a white t-shirt, and black biker jacket. So he just gets to look like a hot greaser right out of *The Outsiders.* He's Matt Dillon as Dally and I'm still Skanky Gidget Goes to Porn School.

When I meet his gaze the sad expression on his face makes me feel shame.

But I'm a trooper, so I rally and paint on a smile. "Just tell me what to do so this day can be over and I can get paid."

"So that's all this is to you, a paycheck? That's all I was to you the other night? A paycheck?"

"I'm not talking about this, Ronin." I push past him and walk back out to the studio. Antoine, Elise, and a bunch of technicians are all waiting around for me. I catch Elise wince as she takes in my new look, but I ignore her and tip up my chin.

Ronin and Antoine are talking in French, not quite arguing, but not being amicable either.

Elise comes and takes me by the elbow, leading me over to the terrace. "Back under the cherry tree for you," she says as we walk outside. There are a lot fewer flowers on the branches now, most of the blossoms are on the ground, withered and wet from the recent rain. Elise lets go of me when we get to the swing and motions for me to take a seat. The technicians are already messing with the lights and those umbrella things, and then Ronin, Antoine, and the other photographers come out. I guess we wouldn't want to miss a single angle of my ass-crack, so yeah, why not get every single photographer we can, right?

Ugh. I want to die right now, and I'm not even naked yet.

Antoine doesn't speak a lick of English as we get ready, he talks only to Ronin and Ronin repeats everything he says in English for the rest of us. They start shooting right away and Ronin stays out of the picture for most of these. Then he stands behind me, tells me to move this way or that, and then kneels down in front of the swing, parts my thighs and lays his head along my leg. He's got a perfect view of all my goods and I just want to die all over again.

His hands reach under my ass and he turns his head up. "Look at me, Gidge. Antoine wants you to look at me."

I do as I'm told and I have to admit, it was a lot easier to do this when we were flirting with the possibility of a relationship.

"He wants you to be angry with me, but you already are, so I guess that's not a problem, is it?"

I just stare down at Ronin, my mind going a mile a minute.

"You mind telling me what I did?"

"I saw you," I say, as the cameras keep clicking.

"Saw me do what?"

"I saw you downstairs, in that apartment with Clare."

"Oh, fuck."

"Yeah, oh, fuck."

Antoine barks out an order to Ronin. "Get up," Ronin repeats after Antoine.

I do, and his hands are immediately around me, tugging me towards the tree. He leans back and pulls me into his chest. The cameras are clicking and Antoine continues to talk as Ronin's hands wrap around my ass and start to cup my breast. "It's not what you think, Rook," he whispers into my neck as his lips begin to kiss me.

I move away from his kiss and Antoine growls out something unfriendly.

"I have to, Rook, it's part of the shot. So just try and forget about all that stuff for now."

I keep my mouth shut and try to act like this is OK, but then he's unzipping my dress and pretty soon he's got one of my arms out, exposing my breast.

"You can say stop, you know," he reminds me.

"I know," I whisper. "But it's got to get done, right? So just go, just get it over with."

He continues with the other arm, slowly dragging the dress down until it falls to the ground and the tears are starting to build from the humiliation I feel.

"What the hell is on your back?"

Ronin's sharp words bring me back from the edge and I cover myself with my arms and turn away from Antoine. "The painting Spencer did yesterday."

Now Antoine is up next to me as Ronin spins me around so they can take a good long look at my body art. They both talk like I'm not there. And it's not even in French this time.

"Ah, fuck, Ronin! What the fuck is this?" Antoine growls.

"I didn't see it, she had clothes on at the scale!" Ronin retorts.

"Well, how the fuck are we going to shoot her with this paint all over her back? Huh?"

"We'll just have to wash it off."

"It will make her skin red!"

"You guys do realize you're speaking English, right?" I ask. "I mean, I'm right fucking here!"

They switch to French and Elise brings me a robe so I don't have to stand there naked. "Come on, Rook, this shoot is over. We'll do it another day."

"But—"

"I'll still pay you half today, you can leave if you want, but we need to wash that paint off and this shoot is a disaster, so I'm calling *stop*."

That one word is all it takes. The crew begins packing up immediately, Antoine stops yelling, and Ronin grabs my hand and leads me back into the studio. He bypasses the dressing room and tugs me up the stairs, and before I can even string together a valid argument on why I should not be going into his apartment with him, I'm already there, sitting on the couch almost in tears.

CHAPTER THIRTY-NINE

Ronin

I sit down on the chair opposite Rook in the living room and let out a long sigh as I drop my head into my hands, scrub my face and then look back up. "Tell me something," I ask, trying not to look at her in that make-up, "why do you think I weigh the girls? I mean, you've hinted that I'm some sort of control freak, so is this why you think I do it? So I can control you?"

Rook wraps her arms around herself. She's still naked under the robe and I take a minute to go get her a blanket from the hall closet. I offer it to her and she squeaks out a barely audible "Thank you," then pulls it up to her neck.

"You think I'm—what? Looking for girls who gain weight so I can fire them?"

"Aren't you?" she asks.

I laugh and shake my head. "Holy shit! No! I'm not looking to fire anyone for gaining weight, Rook. I told you, I don't care how much you weigh, I only care if you *lose* weight."

"You never said that, you said you were looking for a weight *change*."

"Right, not weight *gain*." I stop again and lean back in the chair so I can look up at the ceiling as the guilt comes back. The guilt always comes back, and it always comes back to the same girl.

"There was a model who came through here a few years back. Mardee." I look over to see what Rook thinks about this, but she has her knees drawn up to her chest and her face is hidden in the blanket. "Mardee and I dated, I was only nineteen and she was just barely eighteen. Too young, really, like you, to be taking her clothes off for Antoine's camera. But like you, she did it anyway. And she was good at it.

"She got a lot of offers and pretty soon there were agencies and clients calling, she dumped me and started dating older guys, she got herself mixed up in a lot of bad shit and the worst of it was the drugs. In case you haven't noticed, this neighborhood is not the best. Sure, it's family friendly during the day and when there's a game in the stadium, but the reality of these streets is just half a block away. So she met some of the locals, all people I've known since elementary school, so you know, I was at the very least hesitant to tell her they were all a bunch of losers."

"What happened to her?" I have Rook's attention now and her eyes watch me carefully even as she tries to continue hiding her face in the blanket.

"She did a lot of heroin, that's what happened to her. She wasted away to nothing just as she started to make all her dreams come true. She ruined her life, she gave it all away for drugs. She'd show up here high as fuck and I pretended not to notice because I was in denial, or too busy to see how bad it was getting, or maybe, if I'm being honest here, I just didn't give a fuck about the girl beyond sleeping with her in one of the old rooms downstairs. And three months shy of her nineteenth birthday, she was dead."

"Oh, I'm sorry, Ronin."

"She died in one of our artistic rooms on the third floor. I fired her but I felt sorry for her after and let her stay in a room we rarely used. I found her down there, a tie-off still strangling her arm, the needle still sticking out of her vein."

I take a deep breath and then let it out and take responsibility for what I did. Maybe for the first time ever, I admit that this girl is gone because of me. "And not only did I know she was using, but I saw all the signs that she was *losing*. And the weight loss was the first clue. The weight loss, Rook, is the first clue in this business that something is wrong. And not just with drugs, either. With depression, and eating disorders, and all kinds of nasty things that plague people who rely on how they look to make their living.

"So that's why I check the girls every day. I'm looking to make sure that if they lose a pound or two, they gain it back pretty quick. Otherwise I start paying more attention to their habits and if I find out they're using, I fire them. That's the deal you signed on both of those contracts. I keep an eye on you for your own damn good."

I see her eyes flash, ready with the retort, but I'm way ahead of her.

"And if you think you can navigate this business alone, you're already dead, Rook. Because you *can't*. This business will use you up and throw you out like trash."

"So you think I'm stupid for signing Spencer's contract?"

"No, I get it. I really do. You got caught up in something bad and now you think money will save you from it ever happening again. And maybe it will, but money, from the way I see it, is the fucking cause of all the bullshit that happened to Mardee. If she had no money, she wouldn't have been able to buy drugs, or accept dates with rich losers, or sign contracts to do porn and whatever else she was doing at the end. Money won't save you, Gidge. Money is a tool and nothing else."

"Maybe," she admits. "But it's better to have bad options than no options. And people won't save you either, ya know."

I shake my head and let out a long breath. "God, that is the saddest shit I've ever heard."

She looks away now, her eyes glassy with the threat of tears. "No one came to save me. No one gave a fucking shit about me and the only reason I'm still alive right now is because I got myself out. I saved me, Ronin. Me."

I get up and join her on the couch. She turns her back to me so I push the blanket away and pull the robe down to look at the painting on her back. "Did Spence tell you what he wrote?"

She shakes her head and looks over her shoulder at me. "What'd he write?"

"He wrote, *I belong to Ronin and Spencer Shrike knows this.*"

"Oh, God!"

"It was meant for me, not you, Rook," I say, tracing the outline of the bird on her back. "He was sending me a message. We fought over Mardee. Spencer and I were best friends in high school and halfway through college, but I found out he was the one who introduced Mardee to the local scum dealers. Even though he grew up in Park Hill, he spent enough time down here with me to get to know them all. I pretty much poured all my guilt into hating him"—I stop to look Rook in the eyes—"so I could forget that it was really me who killed her. With my indifference."

She drops her head and sniffs.

"And I'd do anything to prevent that from becoming your future. But I can't stop you and honestly, I'm just a big fucking hypocrite because this is how I've made all my money too. This is how I bought into the partnership Elise and I have with Antoine. How I paid for this apartment, the cars, the truck, the bikes, the trips. I enjoy a lot of nice things in life because girls like you take off your clothes for guys like Antoine and me. So I've got no room to judge."

She sniffs again and the last thing I want is for her to feel defeated so I give her what she needs to hear right now. "But if you're going to take another contract, this body painting one with Spence is probably the best-case scenario because I know for a fact that Spencer Shrike is a good guy."

She looks over her shoulder, confused. "So you're not mad about that?"

"Fuck yes, I'm mad! But the truth is, Rook, you *don't* belong to me. You're free to do whatever you want. I can't stop you. I can give you my honest opinion, I can warn you when I see the dangers—but I can't make you do anything.

"And Rook, just so you know, I'm not looking for a girl to corner, or control, or use up and throw away. I've had that, I can get that anywhere. What I can't get anywhere is a partner who trusts me and loves me. So if you think I'm trying to trap you, you're wrong. I'm not interested in a girl who wants to get as far away from me as she possibly can."

She sits in our silence for whole minutes before turning her body so she can look me in the face. "I might like to belong to you, Ronin," she whispers. "Someday. But right now, I'm still running scared. A few months ago I looked at myself in the mirror and I had no idea who that girl was."

CHAPTER FORTY

Rook

"You wanna hear a tragic story?" I ask Ronin, feeling ready to talk about it. "Because I really do have one."

He leans forward and kisses me on the top of my head, and then pulls me back into his chest. "Tell me, Rook."

"Well, one thing before I tell you, I just want you to know that I'm OK now." I wait to see if he has anything to add but I can tell he's just going to let me talk it out. "It's over, I'm gone, and I'm never going back. So, I'm not looking for anyone to go back and get him for me, or take pity on me, or any of that. But if I act a little distant or I make decisions that maybe don't fit with how you think, well, just know that I have my reasons. OK?"

He nods beneath me and I take a deep breath.

"Last year I was pregnant but I had a miscarriage. My ex caused it actually, and as terrible as this sounds, it was a blessing because not only did it prevent an innocent child from being born into a family of abuse, but I also got one of those implant birth control things while I was in the hospital." I pull the blanket away and rub my finger along my fleshy upper arm. "I knew what a baby with Jon meant and it wasn't an extension of our love or a chance to create something beautiful." I look up at Ronin. "It meant eternal captivity. He kept me locked in a prison—not the kind with bars and locks, but the kind that takes over your mind and holds you hostage. So I got the secret birth control implant because that was his plan. Get me pregnant and then use that baby against me for the rest of my life and hold me like a prisoner."

"Rook, I'm so sorry." He pushes some hair out of my eyes and kisses my head again.

I take a deep breath and continue. "I kept it secret for a while but one night while we were having sex, his hand was gripping my upper arm and he felt the little matchstick-sized implant. And he beat the living shit out of me. Pulled me up off the bed by my hair, slammed me down onto the ground, kicked me in the back so hard I thought I was paralyzed. Except I could feel the pain radiating up and down my spine, so I knew I wasn't paralyzed. I don't even know how many times he punched me in the face, I only know that both of my eyes were swollen shut long before he was done.

"When I didn't get up, he carried me to the shower, dropped me in the tub and turned the cold water on to wash away the blood. I could only lie there, motionless, or at least trying not to move because of the shooting pain going up my back. The water turned a dirty red color from all the blood spilling out of my nose.

"Usually, I never looked at myself afterward, but the next day I made myself. My face was unrecognizable—just swollen and—well, not me. And that's when I knew. If I stayed here with this man, he'd kill me. I'd be giving up my life if I stayed."

Ronin hugs me tighter and whispers into my neck, "And you left on a bus, all alone."

I nod. "After I was healed I left on a bus and ended up in Denver. It took exactly thirty-one days for my face to go back to the way it was. I wasn't working at that point, he made me quit my job long before then. So no one even knew. I had no family, I had no friends, I couldn't even ask a neighbor for help because we lived out on some land his family had. There was just this dumpy house in the middle of nowhere.

"But he gave me money every week so I could go shopping, before that beating anyway. And for three years I'd been planning for the day I'd have to leave because even though before that last incident I was too scared to really do anything about it, I knew that one day I'd have no choice. I knew that eventually he'd kill me. So I saved a few dollars from that allowance money he gave me when I could get away with it. Sometimes he checked my receipts and he kept a running inventory of all the food in the house, so it was very difficult to get enough to even buy that bus ticket, let alone a bit of money to get me through once I got away. He checked the mileage to make sure I never went anywhere in the car and he logged keystrokes on the computer to make sure I wasn't using it while he was gone. So I couldn't talk to guys or some stupid shit like that."

"He controlled everything."

"Yeah," I say. "He *owned* me." I turn around now so I can see Ronin as I talk. "And that's why I need this, Ronin. I need this, or I swear I wouldn't do it. You have to believe me. I don't want to do drugs, or stop eating, or make modeling my career. I have my own dreams and I'm not ready to give up on them yet. I just want the money so I can make my own decisions. And maybe this contract with Spencer is a mistake. Maybe I'll regret it, but I don't think so, because Spencer Shrike was gentle and he makes *art* on nude bodies. It didn't feel... dirty."

"Like TRAGIC."

"Yeah, this contract is definitely dirty. I mean of course I'll finish what I need to do to get paid, but I'm not interested in this modeling stuff, Ronin, I'm not interested in the clothes, or the attention, or anything like that. I just want the money so I can move on."

Ronin lies back on the couch and pulls me down with him so that my cheek rests on his chest. I'm still naked under the robe, but I don't care. He feels good.

"So you don't trust anyone."

"Right," I breathe. "I mean, I'm pretty well-adjusted I think. When I was at the shelter I talked to some counselors. It was very difficult at first, but every day away from him I healed a little more. And I know I have issues and maybe I'm making all the wrong decisions right now. That's possible, I get it. But even if what I'm doing is all wrong, I still need to do it. I need to be in control, I need to have these choices and I need to make my own mistakes. It's the only way to really make things right with me."

"But Gidge, you have to let people help you. You can't live in a vacuum."

"I know, I get that too. And maybe one day I'll trust someone else and let them take care of me again, but not today." I turn and look up at him. "That day is not today. I need a little independence, Ronin. I need to be able to think for myself. And honestly, I was about to give in to you after our date at the zoo and the night we spent together afterward. But then I saw you with that other girl and I realized that I'm just not ready yet. I'm way too vulnerable right now. I need a little more time, I need a little more control."

I relax back into his chest and we think things through in the silence.

"Well," he says a little while later, squeezing me a little tighter. "I'm sorry you had to see Clare and me like that, but I'm not dating her, Rook. I've never dated Clare. She's Antoine's niece and she's a mess. She came home high yesterday morning, that's her apartment, by the way. She lives here in the building. Antoine called me yesterday morning and I should've just told you what was up before I left you in bed, but I didn't. I'm sorry. Everything that happened yesterday was my fault."

He pulls back so he can see my face and I give him a little smile.

"Anyway, Clare has got a lot of problems and we were very close to getting her to check herself into rehab, so I stayed with her to make sure she didn't leave before the people came to pick her up. She's up in the mountains right now, hopefully she'll stay there and complete the program, but to be honest, she's been there before and nothing's helped."

He shrugs underneath me.

"She stresses us all out, you know? It's like, on the one hand we just want her to go away and kill herself somewhere else so we don't have to watch. But we can't let go. We let her come back, we take care of her, but it's not working. I don't think she's gonna make it, Rook, she's not strong like you. That day you showed up for your test shoot was the first time we let her model in months. And even though Antoine never lets her do anything but fashion and glamour shoots, we set her up for that sexy artistic shoot for one reason only. So I could check her body for indicators. And if I found anything that even hinted she was still using, we were gonna fire her for good.

"You take away the job, you take away the money, you take away the drugs. That's how it's supposed to work, right? How it should've worked with Mardee, too. The tough love routine. And maybe Clare just goes and finds her drugs somewhere else, but at least we're not contributing to it." He stops to exhale a long breath of air.

"But that day you showed up here I checked her over in the dressing room and she had fucking track marks between her toes."

Ronin just shakes his head and pauses for a few seconds. "That's a pretty bad sign. And we have no delusions, but Antoine figures we can't give up. So, I'm sorry she was the reason you were angry. If ever there was a girl who was tragic, it's Clare Chaput, not Rook Walsh." Ronin sits up and takes my face in his hands. "You're not tragic, Gidget. You're the sweetest thing I've ever seen. And I never want to see you in that ugly-ass TRAGIC costume again, but if you need this, and if you want to do the Shrike Bikes body art bullshit so you can stash a shitload of money away in some secret bank account and get some control over your life again, then just do me one favor."

"What?" I ask.

"Let me help you. Because I can make sure you get through to the other side intact."

I smile and whisper, "Thank you."

"But make me one promise, OK?"

"Now what, Larue?"

"That you'll listen and take my advice when I offer it. Because I can't help someone who doesn't want to be helped. I know better than most that it just doesn't work."

Even though I'm trying to joke, his face stays dead serious. I swallow down my shame and give him what he needs. What we both need. "I promise, Ronin. I will listen and make good decisions based on your advice. Just don't give up on me yet because I really like you."

He pushes me off him and gets up, peels the blanket off of me and reaches down to slip off my clunky Mary Jane shoes. His hands glide up my calves and then tug down the white schoolgirl stockings. It takes all my willpower not to squeal at that, because it tickles so bad.

When he's done he takes my hand and pulls me to my feet, then leads me down the hallway. "Where are we going?"

"To wash the TRAGIC off you, Gidget. I can't stand to look at it for one more second."

He leads me into the bathroom and turns to the mission control panel that powers on all the shower heads. They don't all come on at once this time, but a fine mist shoots out from the ceiling along with a puff of steam. He slides the robe down my shoulders and it drops to the floor in a soft whoosh and then undresses himself as I watch.

When we're both naked he opens the shower door and enter the mist of steamy water. He sits on the tiled bench against the wall and holds his hand out to me. I take it and climb into his lap as his hands dip down to cup my ass.

"I think you might've told a lie, Larue," I say playfully as I look down on him.

"Yeah? What'd I lie about, Gidge?" he asks innocently as he nuzzles my neck.

"This shower."

He tilts his head back and I smile.

"There is no way this shower is better than sex."

His laugh fills me up and suddenly I'm totally in the moment. I tip my forehead down to his and squeeze my eyes shut to stop the happy tears.

The contracts can wait, Elise and Antoine can wait, life can wait. Because right now there is nothing else—there is no one else—in this world except us.

Rook and Ronin.

I'm not sure what's going to happen. Maybe we make it, maybe we don't, but if there's one thing I've learned, it's to appreciate the good when it happens. And having this man accept and want me the way I am right now is a good thing, and it's happening right this second.

So I'm gonna enjoy it.

Manic

Rook & Ronin Book Two

JA HUSS

Edited by RJ Locksley
Cover Design by JA Huss

Dedication

For those crazy Bombshell friends who show up at just the right moment.

Thank fuck.
For you.

CHAPTER ONE

Rook

There's a cool breeze swimming up my bare legs and Ronin's feather-light touch just compounds the tickle. I try my best not to squirm, but I don't entirely succeed. I stuff my face into the pillow and stifle a giggle and I hear him sigh behind me.

"See?"

"See what?" I ask, half turning. "You're doing it that way on purpose. If that was Spencer, he wouldn't be *trying* to turn me on."

He squints down at me. I rest my gaze briefly on his eyes, those electric blue eyes. They are amazing. Actually, all of Ronin is amazing. His chest is… perfect. He's got very little hair on it and that's something I quite like. What I like even more is the little trail that trickles down the middle of his abdomen and disappears down his boxer shorts.

I realize my fingers just walked their way down to the waistband of his shorts right along with my eyes and when I look up at him he's grinning.

"That's a naughty look on your face, Gidge."

I snicker and sit up. I'm wearing the blue nightie he gave me from the studio closet when I first came here. "You do that to me sometimes."

"Only sometimes?" He tackles me and rolls me over until I'm on top of him.

I know it's just your basic flirt, but actually, Ronin does it to me at all times. I have to take a deep breath to quiet my heart rate a little because everything about him sets me off. "Kiss me."

He does. He kisses me like he hasn't seen me in weeks. Months. Like he didn't just make love to me an hour ago. I embrace that kiss and drag my fingertips down his back. He takes the paintbrush in his hand and sweeps it slowly down my chest, making me buckle back.

He pulls me forward. "Oh, I like that," he moans in my ear. "But I don't like to think about Spencer having that effect on you at all."

"Ugh. You ruined it! I was just about ready to give in and you ruin it!"

He rolls us over again and places himself on top, in control. He holds me down by the wrists and then leans down and kisses my neck with little fluttery breaths that carry up into my ear and make me squirm. "I give! I give!"

He kisses my lips once, just a quick one, then rolls off me. "You're so ticklish, he's gonna be tickling you all up, Rook. I hate it."

I know he hates it and he's been so perfect pretending that he doesn't. He's been supportive and understanding about the whole mess. We finished the TRAGIC contract about a couple weeks ago, which was its own little nightmare with all the nude crack-whore pictures those people wanted, then went on a little mountain vacation up to Granby Lake for a week to try and forget the whole experience. I wonder if all contracts require a vacation to put it behind you?

I really hope not. Although I don't see myself taking another contract. I think I've had my fill.

I thought this whole body art stuff with Spence would be OK, but it is what it is. Sure, I'll look like I have clothes on when he's finished doing his thing, but the reality is—I won't have clothes on. I'll be completely, one hundred percent nude.

"Ticklish isn't the same thing as turned on, you know." I smile to try and make him feel better, but honestly, he has every right to be jealous and worried. Not because I'm going to do anything with Spencer. I'm not interested in Spencer at all. But the guy will have his paintbrush all over me.

Like *all* over me.

And if some girl was painting my boyfriend all up for the sake of making a walking billboard, yeah, I'd be pissed.

"Just because I wiggle a bit doesn't mean I want to have sex with him, Ronin." I say it gently because I'm so in the wrong in this one. I have nothing. I take my hands to his face and rub the stubble on his cheeks softly. "I know it bugs you, and I'm pretty sure I already regret signing this contract, but it's done. They've got it all set up, it's three months, then I'm out and we can make real plans. I'll go back to school and we'll make real plans." I kiss him and he responds with a half-hearted nibble on my lower lip.

Everything he said to me that day we finally opened up to each other is turning out to be true, and I figured he was right at the time anyway, I knew that. But I never expected to regret things so quickly. Right now I have more than fifty thousand dollars in my bank account. Accounts, actually, because Antoine took me to his accountant and they explained all sorts of money shit to me that made no sense, and then they told me to put my money here and there, and I signed the papers and then we went to a bank with some other money and I got a little plastic card with my name on it.

I've never had one before because Jon, my psycho ex, always kept the money in his name. So even though I have receipts in a folder that say I have accounts with many thousands of dollars in them, that card carries more meaning.

Ronin was right. I don't need the money. But I had no idea that TRAGIC contract was paying so much. I really thought five grand was pushing it, but the total was actually fifty-seven thousand and it blew my fucking mind when I heard that number. Ronin got a bunch too, even Billy got some because he did that one shoot with me.

Maybe I'm not rich long-term, but I'm looking pretty good right now as far as money goes.

I laugh a little and Ronin makes a face. "What?"

"I have more money than I need, I think."

"Yeah," he sighs. "You just sock that shit away and don't touch it. Save it."

He's said this before and what he's really saying is that he's paying for everything and my money is no good here. Maybe that would've bugged me a few weeks ago, it might've felt like he was trying to control me, but Ronin's not like that. He's just trying to take care of me, and even though that was a huge red flag because of Jon's controlling ways, I think I'm coming around to it because he took care of everything during our lake trip, which was so much fun. We had this little cabin that we shared with Antoine and Elise in the forest and we rented a boat for a few days and went fishing. Which was really just everyone drinking beer and pretending we gave a shit about fishing.

Then we went to this little bar in the mountains that was famous for hosting big-name bands even though it was in the middle of nowhere. It overlooked the Poudre River though, and was a fantastic place. A local band played that night, but still, they were good and the shows were all ages, so it didn't matter that I wasn't twenty-one. There were two universities not very far away, so there were lots of college kids, and lots of underage kids like me. I watched them and wondered if I'd ever get my chance at school or if that would just remain a dream.

"For school," Ronin continues, like he's reading my mind. "UCLA is pretty expensive, but I think you'll have more than enough when this contract is up."

I'm not one hundred percent sure what this contract will pay, it depends on a few factors like total production costs. But if I got paid fifty grand for that stupid TRAGIC stuff which was less than two weeks' worth of work, then this should be a lot more. It's thirty painting outfits with thirty different bikes, plus the trip to Sturgis and the show up at some big campground venue.

"I don't have to go to UCLA, you know. It makes no difference to me where I go to film school. I mean, didn't those *South Park* guys go to Boulder? That's not far, right?"

"No, it's not too far to commute. I finished my degree up there after quitting DU to get away from Spencer. He transferred to Fort Collins to get away from me and I guess that's why he keeps his workshop up there. But you said UCLA, and if that's where you want to go, you should go. Don't let me stop you."

It hurts a little the way he says that. Like we're not quite in this together. Like it's just me going to LA. "Well, I have no chance of getting into any of those schools unless I put in at least two years of community college, so I guess that's a conversation for another day."

He pulls me close and kisses me on the cheek. "That's the best thing I've heard all morning. Two whole years of you in school, forced to stick around and fall in love with me."

I am so totally in love with Ronin Flynn right now, it's scary. He doesn't say the L word and neither do I, but I have never felt this way about a guy. Not even my first love, Wade.

I turn and rest my head on his chest. "This is a really good moment."

"Yeah," he breathes. "Let's go back to sleep and make it last a little longer."

My eyes close and we breathe in and out together like we're a team.

And the last thought I have as I drift off. I want us to be a team. We're not just a couple, we're a team.

CHAPTER TWO

Rook

Pounding on the door wakes me just as Ronin slips out of bed and rushes down the hallway to take care of things. I ignore him and the pounding. Whatever's happening, it most likely doesn't involve me. I know we have a meeting with the STURGIS people today, but it's not until four and—I pause my internal monologue to look at the clock on Ronin's nightstand— it's only five-thirty.

I laugh.

Oh, well. So what? Don't stars get to be bitches and come in late and generally act like assholes towards all the little people who—

"Get your ass up, Rook! You're late!"

Guess not.

He rips the sheet off me and I shield my eyes from the blazing-ass sun that pours into the bedroom as he lifts the blinds. "Shit, Ronin. Give me a second."

He sighs. "The producer is pissed off and honestly, I'm not in the mood to fight your battles for tardiness. You signed, now you're in. So get up and get to work. They wanted permission to install the cameras in your apartment, they've been waiting down on the terrace for almost two hours, banging on the door. Finally Elise and Antoine got back from visiting Clare and came up here looking for us."

"Well, no one told them to show up early, and—hey, wait a minute. What cameras?"

He sneers down at me as he shakes his head. "How could

you not know this?"

"What cameras?" I repeat slowly.

"The reality show, Rook, it was in the contract you signed. They get to follow you around for three months."

I sit up and shake my head. "No, Spencer said the show was about the STURGIS Rally, I'm sure of it. He said they were filming the rally for the kick-off, so why do they need cameras on me now?"

"Because, Gidge, it's a two-hour pilot that follows the whole process of Spencer painting the girl, that's *you*, and making the bike to match her."

"Oh."

"Get up and get dressed." He throws me some jeans and a t-shirt from his closet. "Hurry, this guy's a dick and he can dock your pay if you screw around."

"Well, fuck. The only reason I'm doing this is for the money."

"Right, so fall in line and do what you're told." And then he disappears in his closet and gets dressed.

"Fall in line," I mutter as I watch him. "I don't like that."

"No?" Ronin asks, coming out of the closet pulling on some boots. "Well, you're in the wrong business, Gidget. Because doing what you're told is pretty much the only way to succeed as a model." He pulls me up out of bed and smacks me on the ass. "Chop, chop, my little money-maker."

"You're funny today, Larue. I will definitely punish you for that crack later."

He leans in and kisses me on the neck as his hands cover my hips and sway me back and forth a little. "I can't wait. Now hurry, if we get this meeting over quick we can go grab dinner somewhere nice. I'll meet you down in Antoine's office."

And then he's gone in a rush. Say what you will about Ronin—I mean, he's a male model, he's somewhat bossy and controlling, and he's got some very Sixties opinions on what he's looking for in a wife—but he is not lazy. The man works his ass off around here. I guess I didn't notice it much during most of TRAGIC because I was too busy being confused and defiant, but he starts his day very early.

Ungodly early.

In fact, this whole studio is filled with those driven A-type workaholic personality people who live for their jobs. Granted, most of them go home, but Elise, Antoine, Ronin, and now me, we stay here twenty-four seven.

I'm not even remotely interested in investing so much of myself and my life in this stuff. Now, maybe if my job was film school or making movies, I might feel the same way.

That brings my attention back to the whole reality show thing. I did not read that contract, I skimmed it in a fit of rage after Ronin started a fight with Spencer and then I got knocked down to the ground by accident. I wonder if the cameras have to be in my bedroom?

That makes me want to throw up.

But I totally asked for this. This was my big declaration of independence. It was a temper tantrum of Rook pointing to herself and screaming, *Look at me, look at me! I'm in control now!*

What a dumbass I am. Seriously, what was I thinking? Taking all my clothes off for three months of nude body painting. I must've been on some serious instability emotions that night. I sigh as I pull on the clothes Ronin left. Everything is huge, but I've made a big deal about not moving my stuff up here to his apartment so I can retain my freedom. So it's either wear the dirty clothes from yesterday, or his stuff.

I choose his stuff because it smells like him and his smell is delicious. I snicker at this as I brush my teeth and hair, then slip on my old Converse sneakers and head downstairs. The studio is empty today because they've scaled down the regular shoots for the summer. They still have a few jobs going, but no other contracts like STURGIS. They want me to have privacy so it's not weird, but that's pretty stupid since the cameras are gonna be there. My naked body will be on the Biker Channel next year.

I shudder at that.

Bikers staring. DVR-ing me.

Yuck.

I take the stairs down to Antoine's office slowly, listening to the conversation that leaks out. They're not saying anything important from what I can tell, but one guy who has a snooty clip to his speech sounds a little put out about me not being on time. I picture him in my head as my sneakers creep down the concrete steps. He sounds like he's wearing a suit.

When he comes into view as I turn the corner to head back to the office, I put the visual together with the voice.

Yup. He's a suit.

He watches me as I walk towards them, then Ronin, who has his back to me, turns and smiles. "There you are. See, told you, Ford, she's here, she's ready."

Ford—what a stupid name first of all—looks at me dubiously as I approach Ronin, who is now my manager. We decided this on vacation out at the lake. Elise said I had to have someone and I could either go get an agency to represent me, or hire my own manager. I hired Ronin. Of course, he's not taking money from me, but he's in charge of everything, which, yeah, sounds like I sorta just gave in and let him take control, but it's different. It's only for business.

Since Ronin feels the need to kiss ass with this Ford guy, I stretch out my hand and say, "Nice to meet you."

He glares at me from light brown eyes under his furrowed brows. He does eventually reach out and shake my hand, but it takes a few seconds for him to decide to do this. I look over at Ronin as we shake and he smiles. His smile says, *Be nice.*

"It's a pleasure to meet you, Rook," Ford says unconvincingly. "We were given permission to install the cameras in your apartment, so the crew is in the process of doing that now."

"Where's Spencer?" I ask after looking around. "And everyone else?" It's just me, Ronin, and this asshole named after a truck.

Ford checks his watch. "Well, Ms. Walsh, you're quite late, I made special reservations at an exclusive restaurant downtown to celebrate our partnership, so they all went ahead." Then he disdainfully looks down at my clothes and winces. "You'll need to dress."

My face heats up with embarrassment at how this man is treating me. "Who the hell—"

"She's got an outfit, don't worry," Ronin says, pulling me towards the dressing room. "We'll meet you there."

"What the hell was that?" I ask once we're safely on the other side of the dressing room doors.

"That was called a pissed-off client, Rook, and typically when people are paying you a lot of fucking money to do a job, you try to avoid the pissed-off client. He was never on board with you in the first place, said you were too young, but Spencer insisted and he had a clause in his contract that he was in charge of picking the canvas."

"The canvas." *Wow.*

"Come on, now, put on the game face. You're in the contract, but this guy is just looking for a way to make you screw up and have to pay him a bunch of money, so if you want to keep the cash you just made for TRAGIC, you'll have to be on your best behavior. Got it?"

"Got it," I say as he hands me a pencil skirt, a crisp long-sleeved white shirt, and some low black heels. "This is what I'm wearing?" I'm a librarian. "Can I safely assume the accessories will include glasses on a chain and my hair in a bun? Should I shush people tonight?"

These people have no middle. It's either sweet or trashy.

"Just put it on, OK? We don't have time. Just trust me for once, will ya? I've been dressing models for five years, I know what I'm doing."

I grumble, but after I put the outfit on and Ronin hands me a brush and a clip to keep my hair neat, I decide some librarians can be sexy and I'm definitely one of them. When I turn from the mirror he's exiting from the men's side of the closet buttoning up his shirt cuffs.

We smile at each other.

"I can't wait to get you in bed again," he growls.

"Why wait?"

He smacks my ass and pushes me out of the dressing room. "Be good tonight, it's important."

I smile at that as we hop down the four flights of stairs that lead to the parking garage and then get in his truck. I take a deep breath as we exit onto the busy street outside our building and say a little prayer that this contract was a good choice.

CHAPTER THREE

Rook

The restaurant is at the top of a very tall building in downtown Denver. I have no idea what this building is called or anything else about it, but I don't dwell on it because as soon as we give the valet guy the truck, Ronin is practically dragging me to the elevator.

"Shit, Ronin. Calm down, will you? You're making me nervous."

"Sorry," he says, squeezing my hand. "Ford is pissed and that means Antoine is pissed, and not to sound like a jerk, but Antoine is pretty serious about the business side of the studio, it's got his name on it after all, so we try to keep clients happy and this is a huge contract, Rook. Huge. So play it cool, be nice, and smile sweetly. *Please*," he adds at the last second.

I've never seen Ronin so... *on*. I'm thinking about how I really don't know him that well when the elevator doors open and he places a calming hand against the small of my back and gently guides me forward. He talks to the maître d' in French and they laugh like they're old friends, and then we're led past all the other diners and into a private area. Spencer's boisterous laugh fills the room as we enter as all heads turn to us. Antoine stands and walks over and takes my arm to place me in a seat next to him. Ronin shakes hands with all the suits and Spencer as he walks around the table to find his chair across from me.

I look to my left and there's that Ford guy. I smile sweetly like I was told, then look past Antoine to Elise. She's prettied up in a dark red dress that looks like someone made it specifically for her tiny little frame. Her short blonde crop is gelled up to make little wisps of hair curve against her cheeks and forehead. She smiles at me and raises a glass, her champagne and dimples both sparkling at the same time.

She's adorable.

I pick up my champagne glass and raise it back, then take a sip and realize it's water.

Ford leans into me a little, making me pull back. "You're underage, right?"

I catch Ronin's glare across the table and put on the game face and talk in my sweetest voice. "So, tell me, Ford—is that a family name? Or did your parents just like trucks?"

Spencer spits out his beer all over another suit guy and barks out a laugh. "Oh, Rook, I think the next three months with you will be the best of my life."

I look over at Ronin and he's not happy. I look over at Elise and her dimples are gone. I try not to look at Antoine, and it's not that hard because he's directly to my right so all I have to do is look straight, but I don't need to see him because he leans down and whispers in my ear, "Behave, Rook."

I turn to Ford. "No, seriously, it has to be short for something, right?" I bat my eyelashes at him and the rest of the table settles down and starts talking again. "Tell me, I'm interested. I have an unusual name myself."

He smiles but it's so fake I want to tell him he needs to practice that shit in the mirror before he unleashes it on the world. "It's short for Rutherford. A family name, as you said."

"Nice," I say. "I'm named after a chess piece myself, the rook. You know what the rook does, Ford?"

He laughs a little. "Yes, Rook, I know. But Spencer told us you're named after a bird. Which was why he fell in love with you and insisted that you be the nude body he gets to paint up this summer."

He says the last bit as he looks at Ronin, and this makes my heart beat a little faster. What's going on here? "Well, that too," I say, watching Ronin stare at Ford. "Uh, do you guys know each other?"

"Oh, yeah," Spencer says from down the table. "Ford, Ronin, and I go way back. High school."

"Oh, Catholic high school, right?"

"That's right," Ronin says. "Ford was two years ahead of us."

"Uh-huh." I wait for Ronin to continue but he drops it and starts talking to the suit guy next to him.

I look up at Ford and he's smiling. But it's not a good smile and I feel a little protective of Ronin. It doesn't take a mind reader to get the fact that Ronin and Ford are not friendly.

There's like a team of waiters just for us and they appear and talk to each of us personally about what we want. They don't have hamburgers or grilled chicken salads here because this place has nothing but French food.

It's like my worst dining nightmare come true.

Ford gets something I can't even pronounce and Antoine chats in French with the staff and then chooses a whole bunch of shit I can't pronounce. Finally I look across the table at Ronin and he's smiling.

"Would you like me to order for you?"

"Please choose the hamburger," I say, grinning.

I'm pretty sure I'd understand hamburger in French, so I'm also pretty sure that's not what he gets me.

After the food is ordered Elise announces she needs to go to the restroom and then walks up next to my chair and waits. "Oh, you want me to go with? OK." I get up and know she's gonna chew my ass out in there. Ronin lifts up his glass and gives me a cheers as I look at him for help.

I suppose this is what I get for being mouthy.

She whooshes the ladies' room door open and right there in front of that towel person who stands around waiting for tips, she lays into me. "Do you have any idea what this contract is worth, Rook?"

I shake my head.

"Two point five million dollars."

I almost choke. "Elise, I'm sorry. But he's kind of a jerk. He's baiting me."

"He's baiting you," she says between clenched teeth, "because he wants you to screw up and forfeit the money. We got the contract, so as long as we fulfill it we get paid. But do you understand that he can dock us for things like being late?"

I shake my head.

"I'm only going to say this once. You work for us, you have a contract. You will be polite when you speak to him, he's your producer now. You will also be considerate of his time. Do you understand me?"

I nod like a kid and Elise hands the towel person a twenty-dollar bill and walks out.

I stare at the door as it whooshes closed and then look over to the attendant. She's a middle-aged woman in a tight uniform. "First time with the big shots?" she offers helpfully.

"Yeah."

"Yeah," she repeats as she pockets her tip in a crisp white apron. "Hope it's worth it."

I follow Elise out and find her taking deep breaths just outside the door. "OK, I get it. I'll shut up and do what I'm told."

She smiles. "Perfect. Now, please, use your talents for good, Rook. You're likable, he'll like you, just be nice. It's Ronin he hates, they've never been friendly, just tolerant." And before I can ask her about that she hooks her arm in mine and we walk back to the table like old friends.

Dinner is a boring nightmare from my perspective, but from Ronin, Antoine, and Elise's perspective, it goes swimmingly. Ronin gets me some kind of meat—duck, I think. He's too busy chatting with the suits to pay much attention to me. Duck is not really my thing, so I skip most of the main course and concentrate on being polite to Ford. Everyone leaves happy, my transgressions are forgiven, and it's not until Ronin gets into his side of the truck that I let out a deep breath. "That was no fun at all."

He gives me a long look, then puts the truck in gear and pulls out of the valet area. "I think you're going to be sorry for taking this contract, Rook, but there's nothing you can do right now. Even if you wanted out, they'd probably fine you."

"Fine me for what?"

"Breach, of course. You're stuck and just so you know, while we were all at dinner, those cameras went into your apartment. You're stuck for three months."

"Can't I just stay with you?"

"You don't get it, do you? You signed a contract, Rook. You agreed to be in the show and be the body painting model for Spencer. You also agreed to walk down the main drag at Sturgis with nothing on but a very small thong and what amounts to two band aids over your nipples. In addition, you will appear on stage naked in front of five thousand drunk bikers for the final show. So whether you like it or not, whether you want to do it or not—you're stuck. You signed up for this and they're gonna hold you to it."

I turn away and look out the window as we stop at the light in front of the baseball stadium. "I should've listened to you, right? That's what this is about. I should've taken your advice, let you make decisions for me."

He drives forward at the green light and then eases us into the parking garage under the studio. He pulls into his spot and turns the truck off and we sit in silence. "Well, yeah. I would've told you to do something else. Less money, but less exposure, too. But," he says, taking my hand, "I have more bad news. I have to drive up to Steamboat tomorrow to see Clare. She's causing a whole bunch of trouble apparently and she needs some support. She's got a couple months left in treatment and if she leaves now, she'll just go back to it and we might never get another chance to save her again."

"How long will you be gone?" My heart suddenly feels heavy. "I don't want you to go."

He gets out of the truck and comes over to my side and opens the door. "You'll be OK, Antoine will take care of you. Elise is coming with me, but Antoine has to stay, of course."

We walk slowly to the elevator. "OK," I say. Because it's not like I have a choice in this. He's leaving to help Clare and I'm stuck here working on a job I probably never needed and very much do not want to do. "Can't I stay with you one more night?"

I expect him to agree. I mean, how could he deny me that?

"No, Rook. You have to stay in your apartment, babe. You have to or they'll fine you for that too. And look, I know it's hard, but it's temporary. Once this is over you won't take another contract without a lawyer, OK?"

"Yeah," I say as the elevator doors open and drop us off on the fourth floor. He walks me out on the terrace and over to my garden apartment door and we stop. "I'm done signing contracts."

"Good, Gidge. Because even though you hate it, I really do know what's best for you right now." He leans down and kisses me, his hands lingering for just a moment on my hips, then pulls back. "I have to go pack, but I'll come by in the morning and say goodbye before I leave, OK?"

"OK."

"The cameras are in every room except the bathroom, but there's one outside the door—they wanted to be able to see you getting ready, I guess."

"Lovely."

"Just keep the door closed and you'll have privacy."

Great, so the only place in my tiny apartment where I can be alone is in my bathroom with that godawful claw-foot tub that I hate.

"You're gonna be OK?"

I sigh. "I'm sure I will, I mean, I'm not happy, but I'm gonna live, right?"

"No more contracts," he whispers as he kisses me again. "No more." I nod in agreement as he tears himself away and opens my door. "See ya in the morning, Gidge."

I give him a smile for being so helpful and concerned. "Later, Larue."

He laughs and walks back to the studio.

I go inside and find each and every camera. They are little mirrored dome things. I walk up to each one—three in the living room, one in the hallway outside the bathroom, and one just outside of the bedroom, pointing at my bed. I stick my tongue out at each one, then rearrange my bedroom furniture so that camera that thought it was gonna watch me sleep has a very limited view.

It might not give me total privacy, but at least that eyeball isn't beaming directly down on me anymore.

I change in the bathroom, then turn out the lights and lie in bed, totally creeped out.

CHAPTER FOUR

Ford is waiting near the studio windows when I walk in, his back to me, his stick-up-his-ass posture as erect as ever. It's been years and still the sight of him makes me want to punch his face in.

"Where'd you find her?" he asks without turning around.

"She found me."

"What's wrong with her?"

"She's a nice girl, Ford. So stay back. She'll do her job, don't worry."

"I'm not worried. So, where are you off to?"

"Clare. She's in rehab up in Steamboat—"

"Again?"

"Shit, Ford. Way to be an asshole. Have a little sympathy."

"She's been broken for how long now, Ronin? Three years? More? Hell, maybe she was never right, did that ever occur to you?"

"This time's different. She just needs some support."

"Like all the other times?"

"OK, I'm done here. You hate her, she hates you—shit, I hate you. I'll see you when I get back. And don't bother Rook, she's not handling things well right now." I don't wait for an answer, I just walk over to the stairs and head to my apartment.

"Feels like old times, don't you think?" Ford calls out after me.

"No, Ford. It doesn't." *Asshole.*

When I get to the top of the stairs I can hear Elise and Antoine arguing in French. I head over and punch the code on the door. They hear the beeping and immediately stop the argument. When I walk in Elise is so angry her face is bright red.

"God, what? Seriously, Elise? Stop it!"

"What's going on, Ronin? If this is part of one of your jobs, leave us out of it!"

"It's not! Antoine, tell her. This whole project is legit! I had nothing to do with it. Do you really think I want to work with Ford and Spencer? Shit, you guys are the ones who wanted the fucking contract! I'm the one who said no! Now my fucking girlfriend's stuck in the middle, she's got no idea what I used to do, and the whole fucking thing is about to blow up in my face! There's a lot of shit that really *is* happening, Elise, so I do not need you accusing me of shit that's not!"

She pours herself a shot from the bar and downs it, slamming the glass on the polished wood for emphasis. "If I find out the three of you are working again, I will turn you in. Do you understand? I will not risk everything we've built here for these stupid schemes you guys cook up!"

I take a deep breath because Elise is trippin' right now. She's got every right to be wary, pissed off, even. So I just try and remain calm so she'll get over it sooner. It's no use arguing with her, because she's right.

"And I'm not about to hang out here and watch," she says, looking at me. "I'm going up to Steamboat, so you assholes stay here and do your jobs." She looks over to Antoine. "I'll go save your niece."

She storms off and leaves us alone. Antoine wipes his face with his hands. "She's angry," he says in English. "She was not expecting Ford to be part of this deal."

"No, Antoine, she's pissed. I had no idea Ford was in on this shit either, Spencer never told me dick and he told Rook even less. And look, I love Clare just as much as you guys do, but I'm obligated to help Rook for this contract. I have to be here for her."

"Ronin, please. You're the only one Clare listens to. Give it a few days, that's all. Just a few days of your time to see that she's getting the care she needs and she's on her way back to us."

I sigh. How the hell can I say no to that? I mean, this guy—he picked Elise and me up after our lives fell apart. He's been there for me since I was ten years old. And even though I've never thought of him as a father, or even a brother for that matter, he's the closest thing I have to family aside from Elise.

"And keep an eye on Ellie for me. She's got her opinion on this job and she's not letting it go."

"Why, though? I mean, where'd she even get the idea?"

He sneers at me. "Please, Ronin. The last time the three of you were together I bailed you out of jail."

"Hey." I throw up my hands in an innocent gesture. "Those charges never stuck." And before I can stop it, before I can hold it together to prove that I'm not that guy anymore and Elise has nothing to worry about, I grin.

No.

I chuckle.

Antoine sneers again. "You better stop that right now, Ronin."

I grin wider. "You have to admit, it was perfect, wasn't it?"

And even though Elise would verbally castrate him if she was here and saw it, Antoine grins widely as well.

Because Spencer, Ford, and I got away with a whole load of shit back in college.

And if we wanted to, we could do it again.

CHAPTER FIVE

Rook

I wake up to Ronin's kiss.

"You came," I croak out in a sleepy voice.

"You doubted me? Rook, please. You should know me better by now. I'm reliable."

I open one eye and snort. "Maybe with most things, but not when it comes to Clare. Every time you ditch me it's for her."

"Not true. I never ditched you, I just have to take care of things. Antoine's been good to me, Clare is his niece, and all that aside, I like her. When she's not high and freaking out like a psycho, I like her. She's nice and she's funny. You'll like her too, Rook. Once she gets well again, I mean."

"Maybe," I say, but that declaration doesn't make me feel any better. In fact it makes me feel worse.

"Love what you've done with the place, by the way."

I open my eyes and remember the cameras. "Yeah, well, I'm good at getting by, right? I'm sure they can still see me over here in the corner, but at least it's not in full-on spy mode anymore." He kisses me again and then gets up. "You're leaving already?"

"Gotta go, sorry. Elise is already down in the garage waiting for me. I'll call you when we get there. Keep your phone on you, OK?"

I nod and then he's gone.

And I'm pretty sad about that. Even though I've been telling myself for months now that I'm number one, I don't need anyone, and settling back down is the worst possible option for me, I'm starting to have doubts.

Ronin is nice. He's more than nice, he's good. Not everyone is good, but these people are. I can feel it. Sure, Antoine is a jerk sometimes, and it pisses me off that he mostly speaks French and makes Ronin translate, but he's still been pretty cool. I should probably make an effort to learn some French, that way he could talk to me like he does Billy in a mixture of both languages, because it's obvious he only speaks English when he has to.

And even though Elise is a real hardass, she's nice too. She's firm when she has to be and gentle when she thinks I need it. I could do a lot worse in the world than these people, even if they make their money off erotic modeling. I'm one of them now anyway, right? I'm an erotic model. I haven't looked online, but Ronin did and he said those TRAGIC photos hit Japan a few days ago. That's where those TRAGIC people were from. The photos were for serial book covers and the first one with the cherry tree shoot is already for sale. There's ten in all and they are releasing the story in parts. Each week a few chapters go out with a picture of me on the cover. From Sweet to Tragic, that's the theme.

Hopefully the books flop and no one reads them and sees me on the covers, but with my luck I'm sure this author is the Japanese version of EL James. At least they are confined to Asia right now. Ronin said they have no immediate plans to distribute the books in the US, so, phew. Dodged a bullet there.

I laugh at this because it's ridiculous to be worried about my body on the cover of erotic romances in Asia making their way over here when I'm about to be photographed naked with thirty bikes. This will probably turn into full-page ads in major motorcycle magazines, maybe billboards around freaking Denver for Spencer's shop, not to mention the nude walk of shame down the Sturgis strip and the private performance to end the rally in August. And then I get the pleasure of reliving every moment in hi-def on the Biker Channel next spring.

I decide to let all this shit go. What can I do? The contract is signed, the painting starts tomorrow, this is my last day off for three months. I should go back to sleep and enjoy it.

I take my own advice and pull the covers back over my head.

No one pounds on my door today. No one calls on my new iPhone I bought with all my new money either. But it's only four PM, maybe Steamboat is a long drive? I grab my phone and bring up the Internet, then type in 'drive time from Denver to Steamboat'.

It says about four hours. He should've been there by lunch.

I drag myself up, then barely catch myself before undressing in front of the camera. I sneer up at my spies and grab some clothes and go in the bathroom to clean up and dress.

The studio is busy but not bustling too bad for a Monday. Usually it's crazy busy, but this STURGIS contract is taking up the whole summer, so I guess Antoine had to cut back on other stuff. I do catch a glimpse of Billy and he waves from across the room. I wave back. He's not as bad as I thought. Ronin and I went out with him and his on-again off-again girlfriend a few times. If you picture what kind of life a male model lives, Billy fits that stereotype perfectly.

Ronin is the complete opposite. He's not a big drinker, he doesn't do any drugs at all, but he does gamble a little at a place in the mountains called Black Hawk. That place is not far—I know because I've gone with him once. I'm not twenty-one, so pretty much all the fun stuff up there is off limits to me.

It sucks being underage when all your friends aren't.

Antoine and Spencer are chatting next to a bike on the far side of the studio and when Antoine sees me, he waves a hand, gesturing me to come over.

"Hey, Rook," Spencer says as I approach.

"Hey, what's up with you guys today?"

"This is our first bike, Rook," Antoine says. He points to the Shrike bike. It's not anything extraordinary, so I'm not sure what I'm supposed to do with that information.

"Cool," is about all I can manage.

"We'll photograph this bike tomorrow, just the one," Spencer says. "So you and I can get used to each other. It'll probably take me most of the day to get the artwork right, then Antoine will want to fuck with the photo gear, so just one bike tomorrow. But we're hoping we can do more than one for each session after that."

"Oh? Sounds like a lot of hours."

"It will be," Antoine says. "Long days, but Spencer's decided he can be more efficient with his projects, use the base paint and only change the colors on some, to get the catalog shots over with quickly."

"Yeah," Spence chimes in, "I need to get the fuck back to Fort Collins and work on the Raven on the weekends, so the sooner we can get these catalog shots done, the better it'll be. I have a lot of work to do still. Plus, I need to spend some time on the final design for your body. After painting you up for the catalog shots I'll be pretty familiar with it, so I can plan better."

"Uh-huh, sure. Sounds like a plan to me."

"So what we were thinking, Rook"—Antoine picks it up again—"is that we'll shoot for a week getting as many bikes down as we can, then take the weekends off while Spencer works up at his shop."

I shrug. "OK." I mean, really, like I have a choice? I'm

the hired help. I'm a walking billboard sign.

I leave them there talking about bikes and stuff and hop down the stairs to get some food from Cookie's. I don't know why I continue to go over there, I have a ton of money and I could eat anywhere I want, but I like that place. And it reminds me of Ronin. I miss him already. I sigh as I press the button at the crosswalk that leads to the diner, then wait for the light to change before making my way across the street.

I enter the diner and the hostess is Cindy. She recognizes me and nods, so I take that as I'm a regular now and I can seat myself at the back booth that is reserved for Ronin's girls. God, how that bugged me when I first met him. Having to come in here and declare that I belonged to Ronin was humiliating, especially since all that stuff with Jon was so fresh.

I feel better about it now, plus I don't say that anymore. I don't have to. They know I belong to Ronin.

I grin at that as I take my seat, then grab a menu and start looking it over for something different. A shadow appears at my booth and I'm just about to tell the waitress I'd like the turkey club on a Kaiser roll when I realize it's Ford.

"Can I help you?" I ask rudely, then check myself and smile.

He smirks back and takes a seat across from me. "Rook, I had no idea you enjoyed diner food."

He's dressed in a suit, just like he was last night, and his day wear looks just as expensive as his evening shit. "Ditto, Ford. You look like a French restaurant kinda guy to me."

Cindy does appear then and I order the club while Ford asks for a coffee.

"What do you want?" I ask.

He tsks his tongue. "Why are you so combative with me?"

If this asshole thinks he's gonna win this little game of wits with me, he's mistaken. I might not be college-educated and produce reality shows—*yet,* I secretly say in my head—but I'm not a fool either. "Look, Ford, I already know you never wanted me on the show, so save it. I know you don't like me."

I pretend to people-watch and ignore him as Cindy brings him a coffee.

"Well, that's not what's going on here, Rook," Ford says after Cindy leaves. "I do like you. You're pretty to look at, that's for sure. And I know that Ronin and Spencer both like you, so why would I not like you?"

"Then why are you being a jerk to me?"

"When was I a jerk?"

"*Oh, Rook,*" I say in a fake voice, "*You're underage, right? So sad, you have to drink water at dinner.* Save it, OK," I say, returning to my normal voice. "Because I already know you don't want me on the project. You think I'm too young."

He smiles and it disarms me for a second. He's got nice teeth. *Teeth, Rook?* I shake my head a little as he starts talking again. "You *are* too young. If I were Ronin I'd forbid you from doing this contract."

"Forbid me? Pfft. Ronin is not in any position to forbid me from doing anything."

"No? I thought the two of you were together."

"If you mean are we dating, then yes. But he's not my keeper, Ford. I make my own decisions, thank you."

We sit in silence for a while. He looks around, interested in anyone but me, so I take out my phone and check for missed texts and voicemail. It's pointless, I have the ringer on and it never went off, but I check anyway to pretend like I have something else to do besides talk to Ford. I'm the modern-day version of the girl sitting by the phone. I snort a little at that, because pining women have come a long way if you think about it. We can go out and have fun and impatiently wait for our boyfriends to call all at the same time.

Cindy appears again and slides my plate over to me. Ford is still nursing his coffee and covers the top of it with his hand to keep her from filling it back up. I thank Cindy and then start eating. I feel like a starving lumberjack. I barely ate any of that French shit last night at dinner and then I forgot to eat when I got home. Add in my missed breakfast and I have to stop and thank my lucky stars Ronin didn't want to weigh me this morning. I probably lost a few pounds. He's a total freak about the models losing weight and if it's me losing I can only imagine the freakout would triple.

"So let me get this straight." Ford continues the conversation from ten minutes ago, like he's been pondering my answer the whole time. "Ronin is your boyfriend but he's not allowed to tell you not to do harmful things?"

I shrug. "Yeah, I guess. We're dating but he's not my father, Ford. I think I can identify harmful things just as well as he can." This is a total lie. I was stuck in an abusive relationship for three years and the guy almost killed me before I finally figured out I needed to leave. But I don't want Ford to know any of that, so I play it cool and just take a bite of my sandwich.

"Hmmm..."

"Hmmm, what?" I say with my mouth full. Maybe I can gross him out and make him leave me alone.

"You're close to his type, but not quite."

What's this guy's deal? "OK," I say, still chewing. "I'll play. What's his type, Ford? If I'm not it, then what's he usually go for?"

"Clare. She's his type, Rook."

"Oh, well"—I swallow—"something tells me the whole junkie thing's not working for him these days."

"No doubt. But she wasn't always a junkie. She went to school with us for a while my senior year. Her mom died and her father wanted her to go to school in the US, so Antoine let her come for a summer and then decided to keep her here. She and Ronin have been tight for a long time now. He crushed on her hard for a while back in school. Then Mardee came along. He wanted her more, I suppose, so Clare was forgotten. But they're all forgotten eventually, so Mardee became just another junkie. He likes the lost ones, Rook. He likes to swoop in and save them. Or think he's saving them, because let's face it, his track record is pretty bleak. But you have a little more sense to you, and I always thought Ronin liked the dumb ones, you know? The ones who don't know any better. Or the young ones."

I just stare at him with my mouth open.

"You come off as pretty smart, plus you don't seem to have any life issues that he can fix, so I just can't picture the two of you together. The only thing that interests him is your age from what I can see. Unless you have some secret fucked-up life I don't know about."

"Wow, Ford, you're a total asshole, aren't you?"

"If you say so," he says, continuing on like my opinion of him hardly matters. "I guess it shouldn't surprise me that he's allowing you to do these nude modeling contracts because that makes you need him. He's your manager, right?"

"You know he is," I sneer.

"Well, if you were dating me," he says standing up and reaching for his wallet. "I'd forbid it. It wouldn't even be up for discussion. And if you did go and sign a contract without counsel, one that required you to pose nude several dozen times, I'd have ripped Spencer a new asshole if he didn't talk you out of it." He throws a twenty down on the table as he waits for my reaction.

"Food's free here," is all I have to say.

"Nothing's free, Rook."

And then he walks out.

CHAPTER SIX

Rook

Ford's words sting. Like bad.

Because not only am I young, too young to do anything fun with everyone else Ronin hangs out with, I'm also pretty fucked up in the life department. I mean, that was my whole deal, right? I was tragic. So tragic they had a campaign with my name on it. So fucking tragic I was living in a homeless shelter when I turned up here.

My appetite is gone after four bites of my sandwich and my stomach roils with the thought of eating anything else right now. I grab my phone off the table and leave the diner, walking slowly back to the studio. The doors are locked since it's after hours so I key in my code and then start to walk up the stairs, but change my mind and take a seat on the bottom step. I can hear a whole bunch of shit going on up there—lots of people here still. But I feel pretty alone.

I basically have no friends.

I have Ronin, but he's a boyfriend, so I'm not sure if that counts. Plus he's far away.

I have Elise, but she's more like a boss than anything else. Plus she's far away too.

I have Antoine, but he's... I don't even have another relationship to compare Antoine to. I can't even imagine in my wildest dreams of approaching Antoine and asking him if he wants to catch a movie or something.

None of the other models talk to me. Val, that tiny blonde girl who walks around naked every chance she gets, is sorta nice. But she's never asked me if I wanted to do anything after work. Plus, she's on vacation with almost everyone else while we do this STURGIS contract.

Billy is OK, but I'm too young to participate in his brand of fun.

Spencer is really cool actually, but he's running like four companies. He's got a bar, the Shrike Bikes, the TV show, and the painting. He's got no time to be my friend.

And that's pretty much it as far as my social circle goes. It's pathetic. And even though Chicago holds the worst memories of my entire life, I suddenly wish I was there so I could at least attempt to look up an old friend. Maybe Stacy Juniper who was my foster sister for almost a year at one house. Or even some of my old foster parents. They didn't all hate me, some of them just had bad luck, not enough time or money to keep other people's kids. Stuff like that.

It's dangerous to have only one friend, who in this case for me is Ronin. Dangerous because you start to depend on them too much.

"Rook! There you are," Antoine calls from above. "Come up to the third floor, we have to go over the show details."

"Yeah, OK." I drag my ass upstairs and when I get to the third floor it's just Ford, Spencer, Antoine, and me.

"Are we ready, then?" Ford asks me.

"Sure," I reply, even though I have no idea what we should be ready for.

"OK, command central for the show is down here." He waves his hand and we all walk forward, then Antoine opens the door and waits until we all enter before pulling it closed behind him.

It's a huge room, not as big as the studio upstairs, and the ceilings are only ten feet tall instead of two stories, but it's still pretty big. There's nice light coming through the windows even though it's starting to get dark outside, and there's a table and a shit-load of art supplies packed onto one of those red tool boxes professional mechanics have.

"This is where I'll do all the painting, Rook," Spencer says. "So you can have some privacy, then when I'm happy with the art, we'll go upstairs to shoot."

I nod out an OK.

"Over here, Rook"—Ford takes over—"is the production center for the show. All painting sessions will be recorded."

For the first time I notice there's a whole team of people over on the other side of the room. There's also a massive bank of monitors, wires going everywhere, camera equipment, and microphones. I look back to the guys and Ford continues.

"Each of you will have a team assigned. Antoine gets team one, Spencer gets team two, and Rook gets team three. I won't even tell you their names, they don't exist. If you need anything, you ask me. That guy over there sitting at the console"—I look and a big guy wearing a black Metallica T-shirt waves to us—"is our director, Larry. Larry runs pretty much everything but you three. You shouldn't ever need to talk to him, but he'll be talking to me to make sure we're making something people will want to watch when we're done."

I stop listening after that. I just smile and nod. *Uh, huh*, I tell them. *Sure, yes, I totally have it. No problemo. I'm in. Yes, sounds about right.* I give Ford every meaningless affirmation I can think of because I do not give one stupid shit about this show.

Basically what he said was, I have three dumbasses who get to follow me everywhere. Two cameramen and a sound guy. Plus Ford, because what kind of fun would this be if Ford wasn't tagging around all day long? Of course, Ford assures me he won't be around all the time—sometimes Antoine will need him or Spencer might have a question, but I'm probably the one who will need his guidance the most, you know, because of how young I am.

He is such a dick.

The only bright spot of this whole meeting is the revelation that my crew is not allowed in my apartment, but that's only because they have it all wired up anyway, so there's no point in cramming us all in that small space.

When I'm all out of nods and Ford is finally tired of hearing himself talk, I am excused.

By this time it's nine o'clock and Ronin never called me. And since Ford was so thoughtful this afternoon when he informed me I'm not Ronin's type, Clare is, I think the worst. I end the day sitting all by myself on my bed, literally huddled in the corner as I try to stay out of the camera. *Tomorrow,* I tell myself, *tomorrow will be so much better than today.*

Today is just a day that had a lot of new stuff in it, a day filled with confusing things, so it felt weird and scary.

But tomorrow those things will be less new, so I'll be less confused and it will be so much better than today.

At least I tell myself that.

But it's a lie and even my damaged psyche understands this, because tomorrow I will be naked in front of all of them and I'm sure, even compared to the whole groping experience I had with Billy that first time I did anything here at Antoine Chaput's erotic art photography studio, this will be scary as hell.

Because this time I know exactly what's happening.

And I signed on for every single second of it.

CHAPTER SEVEN

Ronin

"***She didn't respond*** to the buprenorphine treatment."

That's it. That's all this asshole doctor says. Like I know what the fuck this drug is and what it means that Clare's not responding to it. I want to punch his fucking face in.

I take a deep breath instead. "Can you explain that to me? I'm not quite sure what it means."

"Oh," he says with a smile. "Sorry, I just figured you'd be familiar with treatment. Sorry."

I stop listening for a second because I'm pretty sure this fuckwad just insulted me. Just assumed because of who I am, I'd be a drug addict, too. Elise grabs my arm and shakes me.

"... but she's a heavy user, so we think a long-term methadone taper would work better."

"Right. So what's the problem? Put her on it."

"She's refusing. She might need to leave. She's playing with us, Mr. Flynn. She thinks she can force us to give her euphoric levels of opiates to relieve her withdrawal symptoms, so she's refusing everything. She's thrown herself into rapid detox four times in the last two weeks, then accepts the methadone to come out of it, and it starts all over again. This is not what we do here. In fact, her manipulation is unacceptable."

I rub my face with my hands. Now I just want to strangle Clare. "Where is she?"

He points down the hallway. "Room 23."

"Wait here, Elise." I disentangle Elise's clutching hand

from my arm and head down the hallway. I knock once, then walk in.

The TV is blaring People's Court and Clare is slumped over in bed, obviously high off her ass from a large dose of opiates. "Well," I say in a soft whisper. "It's gonna be pretty hard to have a conversation with you if you're constantly fucked up."

Her head slowly tilts in my direction. "Help me, Ronin."

I sit down on the bed and push her hair away from her hollowed and black-ringed eyes and my heart hurts for her. This is so difficult, I hate seeing her this way. She looks nothing like the girl who came to live with us in tenth grade. All I see is Mardee, the day before she overdosed. Clare tugs on my heart in so many ways. It kills me to see her like this, but it's a pain that I'm ready to let go. I can't take it anymore. "I'm trying, sweetie. I'm trying. But you're being bad. They might kick you out and seriously, Clare. You can't come home if they kick you out."

Her head rolls to the side and the tears spill out. "It hurts."

I've never taken drugs. Like ever. I'm probably the only fucking person alive who's never smoked a joint. Hell, even Antoine and Elise toke up every now and then. But I've never had the desire. I don't understand this not wanting to get better. I'm clueless. I've read the pamphlets that tell me this is out of her control. Her body chemistry has been changed by the drug and she can't fight it. It's too powerful.

But I still don't get it.

"Clare, they're gonna put you on a new treatment and you will agree to it, do you understand me? I can't fucking take this anymore. Why do you *want* to be sick?"

"It hurts!"

"Yeah, that fucking sucks. But you know what? Who gives a shit? It's either take the hurt or die. Do you understand that? You either take it or *die*."

"I'd rather die." And then she turns away and mumbles it

again. "I'd rather die."

She calls my bluff. Because I can't let her end this way. I can't.

I get up and walk out, heading back towards Elise and Dr. Assface, and come in at the middle of a conversation about getting Clare to sign new consent forms. "Mr. Flynn, I was just explaining to your sister that if she had family members here to make sure she signed all the consent forms and followed the program, we'd consider letting her stay."

Elise looks at me, her eyes pleading. "Please, Ronin. I've had enough. I can't watch another girl die from this shit. I can't do it." Assface walks off mumbling something about privacy and I run my hands through my hair as Elise continues. "I've seen too many girls go down this path, I've had it, Ronin. We need to *make* her get help. If we stay, she'll listen. We can drag her though this program, she'll get better."

"And then what, Elise? When she gets back to Denver and she's got all her fucking friends taunting her with drugs? It'll start all over again."

"Just let Antoine and me handle that part, OK? But I need you to stay here, Ronin. She's always listened to you."

"Rook is just starting her contract, Elise. I can't stay up here in the Buttfuck Mountains. I need to get back, she's got a shoot tomorrow and I'm her manager."

"Rook is not dying, Ronin. Rook is getting her picture taken. She signed that contract, you told her not to. So if she's big enough to make that decision, she's big enough to deal with the repercussions. Teach her a lesson about signing shit just to spite you."

And Elise is right, of course. Rook asked for this, she wanted to do it. She made a big deal about it. It was her decision. "But she never really understood the deal, Elise."

"Yeah, like I said. Repercussions for being stupid. Clare made stupid decisions too, and if Rook was in dire need, I'd say fine. Put her first. But Clare is family and she is *dying*, Ronin. If you walk away from her I'll never forgive you."

And there it is. The ultimatum. Rook or Elise.

And as much as I hate to do it, I choose Elise. Because what choice do I have? What choice do I have? This tiny woman is my only true blood family left.

CHAPTER EIGHT

Rook

Even though I woke up several times during the night remembering to squish myself up against the wall to avoid the camera in my bedroom, I'm ultimately sprawled out, ass cheek fully exposed from my crooked shorts in the morning.

Note to self: Wear pants to bed from now on.

I'm annoyed, tired, and in no mood to fight the pathetic excuse for a shower that is my claw-foot tub sprayer system, so I grab some clothes and head over to Ronin's apartment to take a shower in the Beast. It's early, barely five AM, but Chaput Studios will wake soon because these people are morning freaks. How in the world can Spencer be a morning person? I mean, I can see Ford getting up at the butt-crack of dawn, he's got one of those sketchy A-type personalities, I bet. But Spencer?

Nonetheless, there are a bunch of people already in the studio when I enter and make a mad dash for the stairs that lead up to the apartments. I spy the camera crews and several of the guys—Team Rook, from the panicked look on their faces—scramble together their equipment.

I run down the hall, press in Ronin's door code, and rush inside before they can catch me. It's stupid, I know, they'll get enough footage of me this summer to embarrass my non-living relatives from the grave, but I can at the very least have an hour of personal time with Ronin's better-than-sex shower.

The control panel running the multitude of shower heads might as well be in French, that's how much sense it makes to me, but I push several buttons and enough jets come to life to manage a few minutes of relaxing hot water.

I'm showered and dressed far too quickly, but the clock says it's been almost forty-five minutes, so I make my way down to the studio where everyone is standing around looking at me when I appear. They have a buffet table with food on it and just about everyone has a plate filled with fruit and pastries.

Spence walks up to me and I try out a forced smile, so, so nervous about what's about to happen. "Hungry, Rook? Grab some chow and we'll get started in about twenty minutes. I've already eaten, so I'll meet you down in the art room, OK?"

And then the only friendly face leaves me there, his camera team scurrying to keep up with him. Now I'm alone with Ford and my "crew."

Ford smiles.

I go grab a plate and pile on some grapes, because the pastries are apple and I hate apple pastries. I think they expect me to go chat with them, but I take my stuff outside instead. The air is still very cool and that is definitely something I enjoy about Colorado. The summer nights are almost never hot. I cop a seat at one of the picnic tables and don't look over my shoulder when the doors open and my team appears. They stand around me, one guy holding a long stick with a microphone on it, the other two filming.

They don't say hi, and I guess that's normal, we're not supposed to interact with the crews. So I just ignore them and try to eat my grapes. The door opens again and I look back, hoping it's Antoine, but it's not. It's Ford.

He bellows out, "Good morning, Rook! Ready for today? I can't wait to get started!"

I bet he can't. I mean, he gets to gawk at my naked body all day, what's not to like?

"Oh, and by the way, no sneaking off to Ronin's apartment. That's a breach of contract. If we had cameras in there, then you could go about your business, but Ronin refused." He gives me a shrug that says, sorry, out of my control.

I ignore him.

"Oh, come on. You have to talk, that's in the contract too. You agreed to interact."

I get up, dump my plate into the trashcan near the door, then go back inside and make my way downstairs. The crew scurries along after me, but when I look back as I make it to the third floor, Ford is gone. I smile a real smile for the first time since Ronin left.

Spencer is whistling as he sets out all his art supplies and he's got his own camera crew, so now we're eight people in this place. Spence catches me sighing and squeezes my shoulder. "Want some tunes, Rook? I like to listen to music when I paint."

"Sure, put on whatever you normally listen to."

"Comin' up." He plugs his iPod into a speaker tower and messes with it for a few seconds. "This is what I call my *Gettin' Ready for Sturgis* playlist."

"Yeah? Who's on it?"

"Oh, everyone good, man. Deep Purple, some Zeppelin, some Priest, Sabbath, Seger, Skynyrd… you name it, I've got it."

I laugh. "I'm not really up on all the cool kids' music these days, but I know an old fart playlist when I hear it." His jubilant mood degrades into something somber, maybe even hurt—so I backpedal. "Uh, well, I like Freebird."

He shoots me with his finger. "There you go, Blackbird. Freebird suits you. I'll put the whole *Pronounced…* album on."

"Well, shit, that's like a whole day's worth of music right there."

He laughs. "You're a lot smarter than you let on, Rook. Ford over there better be careful with his baiting."

It takes all my self-control to ignore that creeper Ford. He deserves my undying indifference. "So Spence, how is it you're twenty-two and you still call it an album?"

Lynyrd Skynyrd blares through the tower and Spence turns it down to a conversational level. "Twenty-three, but I got a vinyl collection that would make your grandfather cry, Rook."

I sigh again. Thank God for Spencer. He's a good guy, he's easy-going, and he's happy. All three very good qualities when he's gonna have his paintbrush all over my body in like twenty minutes.

"OK, you ready then?"

I'm not really, but that's not the answer they're looking for. I try for words, I really do, but all I can manage is a gulp and a nod.

"Here," Spencer says, holding out a short white robe for me. "Just go get undressed and put this on, and twist your hair up or something, keep it out of the way."

I grab the robe and follow his pointing finger to a partition that has concept drawings tacked to it and is doing double duty as a makeshift dressing room for me. When I go behind it, I can still see everyone, and they can still see me, because this thing only goes up to my neck.

"Well, that's not quite privacy, is it?" I say to no one in particular. Which is good, but no one in particular is paying any attention to me, except for my camera crew who seem to think they get to follow me in here. I smack the microphone away. "Get the hell out. You'll see my goods soon enough, you assholes."

They back off, still filming, microphone hovering above.

"Rook," Ford starts in, "I won't tolerate things like that. So please, just be amicable."

Amicable, my ass. But he's right, it's not their fault I made a bad decision. "Sorry," I say as I strip out of my shorts and tank, tie the robe around me, then twist up my hair in a makeshift bun. I have sixteen eyeballs waiting anxiously for me, so I put on a brave face and step out from behind my partition.

Spencer comes over and takes my hand. "OK, it's gonna be weird, I get it. But Rook, I swear, this is just a job for me. OK?"

I nod.

"Besides, today is the catsuit, so what I'm gonna do is spray you up in black, so even though you'll be naked, you won't *feel* naked. Once the paint goes on, Rook, it feels different. Trust me, OK?"

"I do, Spencer. I trust you."

He smiles. "Good." And then he turns and walks over to Ford and they whisper to each other for a few seconds. Ford looks past Spencer's head and eyes me suspiciously, then nods an agreement.

"OK, both crews, let's take five. Rook," Ford says as he eyeballs me, "this is the only time we'll do this. Understand? The whole point of the show is to watch the girl get painted up naked."

I say nothing because I'm not sure what he agreed to, and even if it's what I think it is, I don't want to let him know I appreciate that, because he's a jerk.

When the room is cleared, Spencer motions me over to stand on top of a white canvas drop cloth and then turns to grab his airbrush. "OK, disrobe, girl. I'm ready. He's not gonna ask to come back in, right? He's just gonna have them sneak in. So how about you face the back of the room and I'll keep an eye on the door? That way, if they do their job right, you won't even notice when they come back in. Deal?"

"Deal." I let the robe drop. I'm not as scared as I was a few weeks ago of getting naked—those last few TRAGIC shoots cured me of that—it's just I hate the thought of men leering at me in person. And I don't even have Elise here today to keep an eye on me. She was a big comfort through all the other shoots. And when she wasn't there, Ronin was. Now they're both gone.

Spencer doesn't do anything stupid like whistle or even stare, he just primes his airbrush on a piece of cardboard, then begins spraying my body. I watch, fascinated at how my skin soaks up the paint. The mixture of color and air makes a cool breeze across my skin and I shiver, which is sorta unfortunate since I'm naked, but what can you do.

I catch Spencer smiling as he takes note of my new perkiness.

"So you *are* a man," I say with a grin.

He looks up at me with a wink, but true to his declaration of professionalism, keeps his mind on his work. He asks me to lift my arms, and I do, but besides that he is silent. I stay still and he makes his way around me. Spraying up and down my legs, a few long swipes of air across my nether regions, which are smooth because Elise made me get a thorough waxing a few days ago. She even waxed up my arms. I'm hairless everywhere except my head.

And then Spencer starts on my backside.

It's not that hard really, and Spence was totally right. Now that my body is covered in black paint I don't feel so exposed. He kneels down and asks me to spread my legs a little, then his paint goes up and down my inner thighs.

It's sorta erotic.

In fact I have to bite my lip at this one and I am so glad I'm facing the wall, because Ford and the crews came back in a while ago. That's all I need—Ronin watching TV next spring and figuring out this was almost a turn-on. It's not really my fault, having my body all squirted up with paint is a new sensation, and it's getting done in front of a whole crowd of people to boot. Not that I'm an exhibitionist or anything, but let's be real.

"OK, daydreamer. You can put your arms down and relax for a few minutes. I gotta mix up some colors and then we'll get started on the zippers and make the whole thing slutty as hell."

I surprise him with a laugh. "Gee, Spence, I can't wait." When I turn around the first thing I see is Ford. He's sitting in a chair not five feet from me. It's a bit of a shock, but the nosy camera guys take my mind off Ford. They are zooming in on my tits. I roll my eyes. "You boys are so predictable." The camera pans up to my face and I decide to tell the audience a thing or two. "I mean, am I right, girls? All these assholes think about are tits."

I chance a glance at Ford and he shoots me a thumbs-up. I get a little tingle of satisfaction from that to be honest. I guess talking shit to the audience isn't out of bounds. Which is sorta cool. That means as long as I'm not being a bitch to Ford or the crew, I can take all my frustration and fear out on the viewers.

Spencer comes back after a few more minutes and begins to paint a zipper on my new outfit. His paintbrush is minuscule, like that thing has two hairs attached to it, that's how thin it is. And Spencer knows just what to do with it. I watch as he loads it up with a silver paint, then he strokes it back and forth between my breasts.

He stops and dabs on more paint every now and then, but he's pretty efficient because that silver line down my front is looking like a zipper in about thirty minutes. He cleans the brush and adds some more color to his palette, then mixes it in with the silver, making a darker gray.

He dabs this color on, little pinpricks of dark in between the silver, and I'm so fascinated with his technique, watching him create a lifelike zipper from color, that I jump a little when Ford speaks next to me. "Wow, Spencer, I've seen the pictures, but I had no idea." Spencer is glaring at him because my little jump made him screw up. "Sorry," Ford says, looking at me apologetically.

Everyone is entranced by Spencer's skill and we all just stand there watching him paint for hours. After he finishes up the main zipper he paints on some zippered pockets. One on each breast, one on each hip, and then some zippers running down the side of my legs, from knee to ankle. He even adds glare to certain strategic places with a bright white color, making the entire outfit look like shiny latex instead of flat paint. When I look in the mirror I realize he's added a sharp collar around my neck, and he used solvent to remove some paint and make the outfit more revealing around my breasts. There are even realistic wrinkles in the zipper as it goes down my front.

The next time I look up at the clock it's after two and not only am I hungry and exhausted, but I have to pee as well. It took us almost eight hours to do this 'outfit'. I cannot imagine doing more than one in a day.

"OK," Spence says, swishing his brush in the paint cleaner. "We're ready for makeup. You need a restroom break, Rook?"

"Yes," I say emphatically.

"OK, no sitting down, squatting only and aim accurately. It won't come off easily, but be careful just the same, got it?"

I blush, but nod out a yes.

"Use the restrooms upstairs, then meet Josie in makeup."

"OK," I say, making my escape. I'm amazed at how not naked I feel. Team Rook follows me as I walk past all the crews and Ford like it's nothing. Then I bounce upstairs and fail to get even a second glance from anyone who happens to be working, not even Billy. He looks at me, lifts his head in a greeting and gives me a little wave.

He has no idea I'm naked.

I secretly grin as I make my way into the dressing room and find the bathrooms. Squatting isn't the easiest thing to do, especially when I'm all anxious about messing up Spencer's art, but it all works out. I almost forget and try to pull up my panties, then have to laugh at that.

Even *I* forgot I was naked.

I meet Josie in makeup and she oohs and ahhs at me so much everyone comes over to take a look. This time the fact that I'm naked is not lost on Billy and he grins. "Finally, I get to see Rook naked!"

"Shut up, Billy. Besides, if you remember, you groped my goods that first shoot we did."

"Oh yeah," he says thoughtfully. "Forgot about that. Sorry. I really didn't know you were that new, Rook, or I would've never been so aggressive."

Every girl in the makeup cubby groans and rolls her eyes, but I think it's cute that he apologized.

Hair and makeup is quick because I have Josie all to myself. She's now my personal makeup artist, no one else is allowed to use her until this contract is over. That means no leaving me sitting in the chair while she goes to attend to something else.

She pulls my hair back so tight I almost look bald when she's done. She leaves the ends in a long ponytail and then goes to work on my face. Mostly it's just your basic toner stuff and some bitchin' long eyelashes. I can barely see past them, they're so long.

She tops me off with a dark plum lipstick then adds some shine to it.

And I'm ready for Antoine. When Josie spins me around he's standing just outside Elise's salon, smiling. "You look beautiful, Rook, should we send Ronin a picture?"

I nod, embarrassed at his compliment. He's never said anything about how I look before, which sounds funny since that's pretty much the only thing he's concerned about around here—how we all look through the lens of his camera. It's almost like he's got a sort of professional detachment from us girls.

I like it.

But I also like his compliment, because he'd never say that to me unless it was true.

He takes my hand when I approach and leads me over to the bike under the afternoon light shining through the massive two-story windows. There's a bunch of studio lights as well, and about ten people to help him get what he needs. But I ignore all that. He lets go of my hand when we reach the bike and then asks me softly in a mixture of French and English that I only half understand to do things.

And the shoot begins.

CHAPTER NINE

Rook

At first it's just Antoine telling me what to do, but everyone else is there as well. Since Spencer plays many roles in this contract, he's not only the artist, but the director of the catalog photo shoots, and it doesn't take long to figure out he and Antoine have very different visions about what these shots should look like.

Antoine is not happy about this and I can see his point. People usually hire him for his artistic interpretation. But Spencer is an artist too, so there's a whole lot of polite disagreement going on.

"Hey," I interrupt Spencer telling Antoine how he wants my body to hug the line of the seat and the tank. "Spencer, I think you should take five. Let Antoine do his job. Because I'm really tired here, and you guys just wasted like forty-five minutes with this bullshit vision stuff."

Ford snuffs out a laugh in the corner.

I might have stepped over the line. "I mean," I say, walking up to Spencer and putting on a pouty face, "he's famous, Spencer. His talent is the whole reason you guys chose Chaput Studios, right?"

Spencer shrugs.

"Just let him do it his way today, it's just one bike. We've got plenty more for you guys to make adjustments."

"Yeah, OK, but make sure you get the details of her body, Antoine, don't hide the sexy parts, man. We want guys zooming in on her, ya know? We want them to zoom in for tits and see the details on the gas tank, or the chrome on the tailpipe when they look at her legs."

Antoine responds angrily in French but Billy is the only one who appears to understand what he's saying, and he throws his hands up and says, "Leave me out of it."

But whatever Antoine said, Spencer walks out and Antoine refuses to speak English after that. He uses Billy and this time Billy does get involved, because even I know the French word for dollars.

"OK, Rook," Billy says after Antoine whispers something and then starts messing with his camera crap. "Sit on the seat backwards, then lie back on the tank." I do what he says and this makes my back arch and my tits stick way up. "Now turn your upper body slightly, so we get the"—Antoine says something here—"tank shot."

Right, I sneer to myself. *The tank shot.* It's got nothing to do with my nipples.

I just stop thinking and do what I'm told—that *is* the secret to being a good model. Billy moves me around like a mannequin, Antoine stays in French, and Spencer never comes back. Team Rook keeps far back from Antoine, maybe guessing he's about to morph into super-asshole at any moment over this shoot, and Ford, to his credit, says absolutely nothing. He just sits in a director's chair far off to the side, almost in another set, in fact.

Antoine finishes up pretty quick and I'm not sure if that's a good thing or a bad thing, but either way, Spencer returns, like he was standing outside the studio door just waiting for it to be over, and walks up to me. "Come with me, Rook, I'll wash the paint off you and then we're all going out to dinner."

I do not want to go out to dinner, but I'm too tired to argue at the moment. He puts his hand on the small of my back and leads me back down to the third floor, but this time we don't go back to the art room, we go through a set of double doors at the end of the hallway.

It's a shower room and there's already a bucket and a large

sponge waiting next to one of the shower stations.

He turns the water on and waves over to the stream coming down from the shower head. "Rinse off and then I'll scrub you down with this paint remover. Sorry it's so personal, but it was either me or Billy and Antoine said me. So..."

He looks guilty.

"Doesn't anyone ever ask me about these things? I mean, maybe I can, you know, shower all by myself?"

He sighs. "You can't reach the back, Rook." He points to the bucket. "That's the paint thinner we use for this special body paint. It needs to be scrubbed."

I go stand under the shower and wet myself down and Spencer enters the room with me, staying out of the water blast as best as he can, and begins to scrub the paint off. It runs down my body in long ribbons of inky black streams.

"All that work, gone. It's sorta sad, huh, Spence?" I look over my shoulder at him and he's smiling.

"Yeah, this part sucks, but that's why we have Antoine. You were right earlier, I should butt out. I know this is hard work for you, believe me, I understand how hard models actually work. So I'm grateful you were so patient today and you did real well, for it being your first time."

"It wasn't bad. I think the outfit helped, you were right, I never felt naked." But now that the paint is being stripped away and there's no black buffer between Spencer's wandering eyes and my body, it does make me squirm a bit.

"And just so you know," Spencer says, interrupting my thoughts, "I'm not taking advantage of you, OK? It's just that we get one chance to capture this artwork, ya know?"

"Yeah, I know. Wait, who said you were taking advantage of me?"

"Antoine, that's what he said when he was speaking French back there because I want all your sexy parts in the photos and he was going out of his way to cover those bits up. It's just, I get it, he's making *art*. But I'm selling bikes to horny guys, so I need those shots, Rook. I'm not trying to take advantage."

Now that my back has been scrubbed clean, he bends down to scrub my butt and the back of my legs. I turn around and look at him because, yeah, that's a bit personal.

Spencer ignores me, either he doesn't care that it's personal, or he's trying to pretend it's not. The sponge is rubbing all over my ass when it dips between my legs a little making me gasp.

Spencer stands up. "OK, you can do the rest." He plops the sponge down in the bucket and walks out of the shower room, leaving me there to manage on my own.

These people get more and more confusing with every job. How am I supposed to process this? Spencer gets to paint me up then wash me down. All of me, my entire body. He gets to touch my ass and put his brush between my breasts. And Billy gets to manipulate my body into weird contortions so my nipples are standing at attention in every shot, even for the fucking fender—that was some feat, but that Billy is resourceful—and Antoine gets to take pictures of all this, while Ford and the crew stand around and record every facial expression on each of us as we do these things and try to remain professional.

I'm pretty sure my relationship with Ronin is over. Because no man, I don't care what kind of Catholic saint he is, would ever put up with this arrangement. Elise was right, I'm paying the price for this STURGIS contract, and I'm paying up front, because this is day fucking one and I have to do this shit all summer long.

I pick up the sponge, soak it with the remover solution, and scrub as fast as I can. All I want is to go back up to Ronin's apartment and take a real shower, but I can't do that until the paint's all gone. And Ford can go fuck himself, because I need that shower. It's not a luxury or a way to hide, my shower just isn't adequate enough to deal with the amount of cleaning my body will require at the end of these shoots.

Luckily Spencer left me a nice soft towel, so I wrap myself

up in that and head back to the studio to make a break for the Beast. No one is around when I slip in, so I tiptoe as best as I can with my wet feet, and head upstairs. As soon as I turn the corner towards Ronin's apartment, I see Ford.

He wags his finger at me and smiles. "I knew already, Rook. Nice try, but the crew is waiting on the terrace, go shower in your own place."

I punch in Ronin's code as I ignore him.

"You can do this, I can't stop you, but I *will* fine you, Rook. The deal is that you live at your apartment, not here."

I sigh and run through my options. Ford is a control guy, even if I was wrong about Ronin, I know for a fact I'm not wrong about Ford. He thinks he's Mister Dominant. I turn around and smile at him. "Ford, I swear, I'll shower in my own place on days that have no body paint, OK? It's just my shower isn't really a shower, it's a claw-foot tub with this pathetic sprayer system and I can't..." I stop to pout and open my eyes a little wider as I stare up at his face. "I just can't relax in that thing. And now that I have all this crap on my body, I can't even get clean in it!"

I'm not sure what I expected, I don't know him that well, but "Nice try, sweet cheeks," definitely wasn't it.

"Fine, I'll pay you to use the shower, bill me for it."

"People watch reality shows because they think they'll get to see something personal, the whole shower setup is part of that. It's a big part of that, in fact."

"How much?"

"How much what?"

"How much do you want to let me take showers at Ronin's place? Just give me a number."

Ford actually covers his mouth with his hand to hide his smile. "You're trying to pay me off?"

"Just tell me how much the fine is, asshole. This job will probably ruin my life, so I'll be damned if I'm gonna spend one more second worrying about getting a decent fucking shower."

"OK, would you like to make a deal, Rook? How about you go to breakfast with me tomorrow morning. Five AM. If you do that, I'll look past the shower this time. But only this time."

"Breakfast? You want to buy me breakfast?"

He shrugs like he's playing innocent, but he's got a devious gleam in his eye.

"Whatever." I push the door open and then quickly close it behind me.

I wash off the paint thinner in the Beast, and I tell you what, I'd have breakfast, lunch, and dinner with Ford to keep using this thing. I figured out how to make the steam come out from the ceiling and it makes the whole experience feel like a tropical island. It's only after I'm all done that I realize I have no clothes.

I don't keep clothes at Ronin's place because that would imply that our relationship was more than just dating, and now I regret that. I search through his closet—which is spectacular—and find a pair of old jeans and a dark green t-shirt. The pants are way too loose, but there's plenty of belts, so I grab one of those too. I have no bra, but I can change just as soon as I get back to my place.

Dinner is not something I'm really up for but they are all waiting for me down in front of Antoine's office. I try to sneak by, but Team Rook is waiting just off to the side of the stairs, like they were trying to ambush me. I hustle out to the terrace, they follow, but I smile in satisfaction when I go inside my apartment and they have to wait outside. I grab some clothes and then pull on some shorts and a tank top and complete my outfit with my old Converse sneakers. I don't care how many pairs of expensive shoes I get, nothing beats a well-worn pair of Converse.

When I go back out the crew follows me again. I huff out an annoyed breath, but they ignore me like a good crew.

"Rook!" Antoine barks as I enter the studio again. "Good, we're starving. I sent Ronin a picture, he said he's tried calling you, but you never pick up."

"Oh, duh. I don't have my phone on me. I'm not used to carrying it around in here."

"You can call later."

"How's everything, did he say?"

Antoine gets a worried look on his face as Ford and Spencer join us and we walk down the stairs. "Clare is OK, Ronin is the only one she's ever listened to, she's always been difficult. I'm just glad he's there."

"Yeah, I'm glad too," I say, but I catch Ford's smug look out of the corner of my eye.

We walk over to Cookie's then take our booth in back like normal. Antoine scoots in and then Spencer takes the seat next to him, so I'm stuck near the window with Ford on the other side of me. The waitress, not one that I recognize, brings us drinks and I order the Big Breakfast Special instead of dinner. Antoine and Spencer get the diner version of steaks, and Ford orders an egg-white omelet.

I sigh as we sit. I'm tired of these guys already and it's the first day, but I do notice one thing. "Hey, where's our camera crews?"

Ford points up to the ceiling. "We paid Cookie's to let us tap into their security cameras and we have a microphone hidden nearby. So as long as you come in here, no crew will follow."

"Good to know," I say dryly. "Anywhere without a camera crew is good."

"OK, I'm just going to go ahead and ask, Rook. Because I don't understand. Why the hell did you take this contract if you didn't want to be on camera?"

I look over at Spencer and he's wincing, but Antoine's the

one who answers. "Spencer left that part out when he explained the terms to her. She didn't know, Ford."

"Hey, I never thought she'd take the contract that night. Rook, tell them, you were a little impulsive, remember?"

"I was," I admit. "It's not Spencer's fault. Ronin and I were fighting and I overreacted and signed the contract without talking it over first."

Ford just looks at me but says nothing. The three of them talk about bikes and photo shoots, and even old times, since Antoine has known both Ford and Spencer since they were in high school. I don't participate much and I'm just too tired to think about making meaningless conversation.

After we eat Antoine and Spencer head over to a sports bar to watch the Rockies play the Padres in San Diego and Ford and I walk back to the studio in silence. I punch in my code when we get to the doors and then stop and turn to him when he tries to follow me in. "Aren't you going home?"

"I need to check on Larry's crew before the day's over." He holds the door open wider and beckons me to enter. We walk up the stairs in silence again, then he heads off at the third floor, waving a gesture back at me which might pass as a goodbye.

I continue up to the fourth floor and then make my way out onto the terrace. It's a beautiful night and since it's Monday, it's also quiet. I go inside my garden apartment and grab my cell phone. Sure enough, there are seven missed calls from Ronin. I press redial and walk back outside to sit on the grass under the cherry trees.

He never picks up, of course. He's probably mad at me for forgetting my phone, or maybe he took one look at that photo Antoine sent him of me in the painted-up latex suit and decided Clare the junkie was a much better fit for him.

Being jealous sucks. I hate it. I hate the feeling you get when all you want is to hear your boyfriend's voice on the other end of a phone. It's a horrible feeling and I don't even understand how something as little as getting someone's voicemail can ruin a perfectly fine day. And this day wasn't so bad, really. I mean, it was better than the first day I was groped by Billy. That was a weird day. I lie back on the grass and look up at the canopy of leaves on the cherry trees and then close my eyes for a second.

"Rook?"

"Huh?" I sit up, confused. "What?"

Ford is kneeling down next to me. "Why are you sleeping outside?"

"I just dozed off, Ford. Shit, cut me a break, will ya?

"Are you sure that's all it was?"

"What else would it be?"

"Not wanting to sleep inside under the cameras."

I laugh and sigh at the same time. "Yeah, forgot about them, thanks for reminding me though. I appreciate that."

"Well, if you prefer to sleep under the cherry trees let me know, I'll put some cameras up there too."

I glare at him. "You probably would, too." I get up and brush off my shorts. "Well, I'm heading in."

"We're still on for breakfast tomorrow?"

I snort out a laugh this time. "Yeah, we're on."

"Wear something comfortable," he calls out as I walk away. I leave him there and make my way inside, not even bothering to turn the lights on. I just sleepwalk back to my bed and crash, not even remembering to squish myself into the corner or wear pants to bed so the audience can't get a good look at my ass in the morning.

CHAPTER TEN

Why, God? Just why? Why do people insist on pounding on my door at the most ungodly hours? "I'm coming!" I scream. The pounding stops and I reach for my phone. It's five after five in the morning.

What the fuck?

I roll out of bed and stumble down the hall, then throw the door open and shield my eyes from the morning sun.

"You're not ready." Ford frowns down at me.

I look down at my shorts, then up at him, and shoot him my own frown. "Give me a second." I leave the door open and shuffle back to the bedroom, grab a clean pair of shorts and a tank top—

"I said comfortable and loose, but you'll need a good bra."

"What?" I shake my head at Ford, who is peeking his head around the corner of my closet.

I look down at his clothes and recognize the garb of trendy exercisers the world over. His outfit looks like he pulled it off the rack at Sports Authority this morning. "Ford, you said breakfast. I do not work out."

"It is breakfast, you'll see. Unless you want to take showers in that claw-foot monstrosity down the hall?"

"All right, get out. I'll meet you outside."

He backs off and I grab some sporty stuff that Ronin gave me from the Chaput closet when I first got here. The tank top has a built-in bra and it's a pretty coral color. The sport shorts are black with a matching coral racing stripe going up the sides of my thighs. I look the part until I put on my shoes, and that makes me laugh because all I have for my feet in the way of sneakers are my Converse.

I brush my teeth and pull my hair back in a ponytail, then head outside. Ford is talking with Team Rook over by the picnic tables. I guess that means we're not going to Cookie's, since the crew isn't necessary for that eatery.

"Ready?" Ford asks as I approach. "Nice shoes," he says, shaking his head.

"What are we doing?"

"You'll see, just follow."

I do what I'm told—I'm used to that anyway—and we walk down the stairs and go outside using the back door that leads out into the parking lot, then cross Blake Street and we're at Coors Field, the baseball stadium where the Rockies play. Ronin loves baseball and we've gone to two games together already. "We're eating breakfast at the stadium?"

"Yes, afterward, anyway."

"After what?"

He never answers, just walks us around the side and stops at a plain gray metal door that has no windows at all. He knocks and it opens immediately. The Mexican guy on the other side greets Ford in Spanish and they act like old friends, laughing and joking and shaking hands. He finally turns to us. "Rook, this is Jose, he's the head guy back here. I've known him since I was a kid. I used to come to the stadium every morning until I graduated from college a few years ago." Then he looks over at Team Rook and says, "Sorry, guys, only one guest allowed."

I smile at that and follow Ford into the dark hallway. So whatever we're doing here, we're doing it in private. I'll take any privacy I can get at this point. I follow him through the convoluted hallways until he pushes through a door and we come out on a stairwell. "Which way, Rook? Up or down?"

"What are you up to?"

"Just pick, up or down."

"Down," I say, "because climbing stairs is not my idea of fun right now."

He stifles a chuckle and leads the way down the stairs, then we get to another landing and he pushes through a set of double doors and we're in the stands, about midway up.

"Cool," I say, still not sure what the hell is going on. He walks over to the railing and looks out. I follow of course. There are a few other people here, all running up and down the stairs spread out across the seats across from us. "I sincerely hope"—I stop to snort here—"that you do not expect me to *run*, Ford. Especially up and down stairs. Because I'm not a runner. I'm a slow walker at best, possibly a shuffler, or an aimless wanderer, but never a runner."

He's just smiling.

"I'm serious."

"I can tell, but so am I. So I'll make you a deal, OK? You run stadiums with me every morning and I'll let you shower at Ronin's any time you want. As long"—he stops to give me a stern look—"as you don't take advantage and start spending all your free time in the shower."

"Why?"

"Why what?"

"Why do you want me to run these steps with you? There's a reason, you're just not telling me, so maybe I'll agree, but I wanna know the real reason you want me to do this with you. Are you coming on to me? Trying to piss off Ronin? What?"

His smile falters for half a moment, then it's back, brighter than ever. "Are you sure you want the real reason? Because most people prefer white lies to truth."

I roll my eyes. "Just tell me. There's no need for drama, Ford."

"Fine." He shrugs. "I want you to run with me in the morning because you're too young to take this job and maybe I don't know your whole story, but I'm perceptive enough to see that there's something *wrong* with you. I'm not sure what it is, I don't even want to know what it is, but this job will change your life. So instead of letting you dwell on how much it sucks and how big a mistake you really made when you took this contract, or beating the shit out of Spencer for letting you, or belittling Ronin for not being able to control you better—I'm just gonna take it upon myself to save you." He stops to pan his arms wide at the empty stadium. "With exercise. Because it will help, take my word on that."

"That is the dumbest shit I've ever heard."

He busts out a laugh. "You're a fighter, that's for sure. And I'm not gonna ask, Rook, so don't wait for that moment. I do not care why you come off as broken, I really don't. I'm just not gonna be the guy responsible for making it worse."

"Well, I'm not gonna exert myself, Ford. I'll *walk* up the stairs."

He turns his back and starts running up the steps. "Fine with me, just don't stop climbing until I do. That's the deal."

I huff out some air and drag my feet up the steps. When I look up to see where he is, he's already finished this set and is running down the middle landing to the next set. He descends those stairs with just as much enthusiasm. I trudge my way up to the landing, then find him again. That asshole is like four sets of stairs away from me now.

It's like reverse psychology or something, right? He thinks he can shame me into putting in more effort, but he's wrong. I'm naturally lazy when it comes to athletic pursuits. I like sitting in the stands at the baseball game, not playing. Or running stadiums, for God's sake. I reach the bottom of my second set and then walk over to the next one. When I look up to find Ford, he's like a million miles away now.

We do this for a good while before I notice him starting to make his way back towards me. My legs are a little sore, but I do exactly what I said I would. I practically mope up these steps. I only cover a few aisles, that's how much I mope, but Ford, he does almost half the stadium, *at a fucking run*, before he turns back towards me.

I wait for him on the landing as he bursts up the last set of stairs and then stops to breathe hard, bending over a little in the process.

Damn, the guy really made an effort, he's dripping sweat, and I'm still fresh as can be. Not even thirsty. "I thought you said we were gonna eat, Ford?" He laughs, but he's still very much out of breath. "Shit, dude, you really take this stuff seriously, don't you?"

"Feels good, Rook. It feels good to run it off every morning."

"No," I say, shaking my head. "Mornings are for sleeping in and eating breakfast. Speaking of which, I'm starving, where's my food?"

He waves a hand at me to enter the stadium doors, not the way we came, but the way you go to get snacks during a game. We both go inside and Ford whips his shirt off and starts dabbing it across his wet body.

I steal a look. I'm a girl, I can't help it, he's not bad-looking. His hair is lighter than Ronin's, but not blondish like Spencer's. He's got a bit of scruff on his chin left over from yesterday. But I bet he shaves it when he gets home because he's more of a clean-cut kinda guy. The complete opposite of Spencer, who is one hundred percent biker, and Ronin, who comes off as hip and edgy.

Ford's look says *goal-oriented* or *I come from a long line of bankers*. I tuck down a laugh at those thoughts and sneak a look at his body. It's very nice. Maybe not Top Model Ronin nice, but still nice. He obviously takes very good care of himself.

He catches me looking and smiles as I turn away quickly.

We walk along the interior corridor for a while and the smell of breakfast food wafts into my nose. "Food!"

"They keep a stand open for us in the morning. Breakfast burritos."

"So, let me get this straight, you bust your ass to burn calories, then come eat breakfast burritos? That makes no sense."

"We're not here to lose weight, Rook. People who have access to the stadium are training, which means we eat a lot of food when we're done."

"What are you training for?" I can't help myself, he's made me curious with his secret endorphin-rush addiction.

"Life, just like you," is all he says before we come to the counter and he's ordering us food and orange juice. He pays, then we walk back outside and find seats in the empty stands.

The burrito is good and even though I didn't expend much energy, I do feel awake and have more pep than I usually do in the morning. I better be careful or that reverse psychology shit will start working on me and before you know it, I might turn into one of those annoying freaks who thinks all manner of physical activity is *fun.*

We don't say much after that. Just eat. Then he takes my trash and throws it away and we walk back over to the studio building and part ways. He goes to his car and I walk upstairs, grab some clothes to stash at Ronin's, then head up to his place and enjoy my totally legal kick-ass shower.

Smiling.

CHAPTER ELEVEN

Rook

Team Rook was nowhere to be found when I made my way to Ronin's apartment door, but when I emerge freshly showered, they are waiting outside in the hallway. We all act like I'm the only person there and all I hear is the scuffle of their shoes as they follow me downstairs to the third floor art room.

Spencer is already rocking out to that Bad to the Bone song, singing along quite loud for a guy, and messing around with some paints and brushes. "Yo, Rookie! I'm glad you came back for day two. Sometimes the girls skip out after the first session, but I guess I played it cool, because here you are!"

"I signed a contract, Spencer. I can't skip out. And please, do not ever call me Rookie again. I will go apeshit on you."

"Noted. But I played it cool, right? That's the real reason you came back, right?"

"Right," I say, smiling. It's hard not to enjoy being around Spencer. He's a clown, and a hot one at that. He's got on his usual garb today, a Shrike Bikes t-shirt, old faded Levis, and biker boots. Even though I've seen him like a bazillion times, I've never seen him wear the same t-shirt twice. And they are cool designs, not your typical black and orange Harley eagles or big-titted girls with American flag bandannas wrapped around their heads screen-printed on those cheap-ass black polyester shirts.

The designs on Spencer's shirts look like someone drew them with a charcoal pencil. This one is a light gray and has a blackbird on it, beak open like it's cawing, bending down with wings half open, like it's about to take flight. It says *Shrike Raven* in big bold letters on top, and at the bottom it has the new Shrike motto, *Not Your Daddy's Ride.*

I know that's a dig at Spencer's father because Ronin told me. He retired a few years back and left the business to Spencer, and Spencer, wanting to make his own name, came up with that tag line to let everyone know this was his game now.

And he's done pretty well. The guy's not even twenty-five and he's taken the company from small pop-and-son to mega-commercial in like two years.

Spence notices my gaze and points down to the raven on his chest. "This is one of the designs we're gonna use to promote the bike, but I'm gonna make one of you too."

"You're part of the merchandising package, Rook." For the first time I notice Ford sitting in the corner in that director's chair. "I just thought I'd let you know that, in case Spencer conveniently forgot to mention your face will be made into dolls and put on clothing." He says it in an irritated voice and then Spencer flips him off and turns away, busying himself with his art supplies again.

"Wonderful," I say to no one in particular. "How lucky am I? Don't all girls want to be turned into Barbie?"

"Yeah," Ford says, again with the irritation, "but I'm pretty sure Biker Barbie was never part of your girlhood fantasy, was it?"

I scowl at him. "What's your deal, Ford? I'm a big girl, OK? I'm fine with the doll shit. It's a fucking doll. Who cares, they'll probably make like five hundred of them, people will buy them, break them, lose them, destroy them—whatever—and it will be over. It's not like someone's naming a fucking battleship after me."

Ford says nothing, just keeps his bad mood to himself over in the corner.

"OK, well, what's the plan today, Spence?"

"Bikinis, four of them."

I shake my head trying to imagine four paintings and photo shoots. 'That sounds like a long day."

"Well"—Ford is back in action again—"it's not really, Rook. Because the term bikini is used loosely here." I mouth the words *shut up* at him, but he looks right at me and continues talking. "Because those little postage stamps Spencer is going to paint over your nipples barely count as clothing, or paint for that matter."

Spencer turns around, his eyes blazing, his whole demeanor screaming *fuck you.* "That's it, Ford, I warned you. Out. I'm not putting up with your bullshit."

For a second I figure this is some theatrics for the sake of the cameras, but when I look over at Team Spencer, they start to get uncomfortable. Team Rook steps back, like these two are about to throw. "OK, what's going on? Are you guys fighting? I mean, I just saw you an hour ago, Ford. What's the problem?"

"The problem is what Spencer plans to do with you today, even though Antoine told him there's no one to help you between shoots, that's the problem."

"Spencer?" I ask, totally lost.

Ford continues, not even giving Spencer a chance to talk. "Well, let's walk through this, Rook. Spencer's gonna paint you up in a bikini, but he wants to do four shoots today, so that means that paint will have to be washed off four times." He stops to stare at me. "I think you can put two and two together from there."

"So Spencer will have to wash me off? Is this the problem?"

I look over at Spencer and he shrugs. "Rook, I gotta get through this catalog and get back up to Fort Collins by Friday, so we have to get as many shoots as we can. The bikinis are popular, easy, and quick."

"Hey, I could care less, Spencer. I'm not sure what Ford's problem is, but I'm pretty sure you're not painting on bikinis to feel me up." I roll my eyes. "Let's just do this."

Ford actually gets up and walks out.

I look back over at Spencer and he throws up his hands and turns back to his supplies. "Just get naked, OK? Twist up your hair and we'll get started."

I take a deep breath and look over at the camera people, then say an internal *fuck it* and whip my shirt off right there. What's the point? They're gonna see me naked whether I strip in that pathetic excuse of a dressing room or right here in front of them. I watch them as I do it too, daring them to even snicker. My look keeps them professional and when I glance back at Spencer he's laughing at me.

"You are something else, I swear. OK, first up is the *white bikini*." He says this last part loud, like he wants Ford, who is all the way across the room talking to Director Larry, to hear him. "White, so we can *paint over it*," he yells. "And not have to *wash it off*."

Spencer and I do a collective eye roll and try not to laugh.

"OK, Rook, just come stand here in the middle of the sheet." Spencer checks for Ford and drops his voice to a whisper and winks at me. "It might get a bit personal, but just know, I'm a licensed professional, Rook."

"Where have I heard that before? Oh, yeah, Ronin, when he was teaching me to shampoo his hair."

Spencer gives me a stupid look and I shrug. "Never mind."

Spencer's got his paints and brushes all laid out on a rolling cart this time. He catches me eyeing them and explains. "No airbrush today, right? It's all detail. So it goes a little slower at first, but the bikinis are so small, it won't be bad this time."

"This time?"

"Yeah, well," he says, kneeling down in front of me. "The other outfits aren't so easy. I've got something spectacular planned for Sturgis, that job will take all day, in fact we'll probably have to get up in the middle of the night in order to have it ready for the public presentation, which is later in the afternoon."

I think about this for a minute, trying to picture what that last shoot will be like, but even though I've seen all sorts of pictures of Sturgis, I've never been there before. And even though yesterday was pretty long, I can't imagine what it might take for Spencer to actually paint me all night long and into the morning.

His paintbrush on my lower stomach snaps me out of my daydreaming and I gasp as he drags it across my skin. His face is like right *there*. He's practically breathing on my sensitive little button!

"Sorry," he says, looking up at me. "There's just no good place to start this project. It's here, your ass, or your tits. Might as well get the hard part out of the way, right?"

I say nothing. Because honestly, I really didn't think this through.

I twist my head a little and find Antoine off to the side, his hand over his mouth trying to hide a frown. "Hey, Antoine. What's up?"

He stays right where he is, which is really too far away to have a normal conversation. "Ronin called. He can't reach you, he said. He wants you to call him right away."

I look down at Spencer but he's practically got his head buried in my girly parts, and if he cares that Ronin wants me to call him, he doesn't show it. I shrug a little, which makes Spencer grunt at me to stand still. "Can you dial the phone and hand it to me?" I'm secretly dying to talk to Ronin, it's been days and even though I was the one who said things should stay casual, I miss him. Like bad.

Antoine shakes his head. "No, not now. After we finish the first shoot, I'll call him back and tell him." And then Antoine walks out.

"Well," Ford says, from behind me. "Here we go."

"What's that mean?"

"Ignore that dickhead," Spence says, clearly irritated.

"He's just jealous."

"Rook," Ford says, grabbing a chair and positioning himself off to the side, just out of my peripheral vision. "You do realize as soon as Ronin sees what's going on here, he's gonna be pissed? You do realize this, right?"

"Are you trying to make me feel bad on purpose?"

"Ford," Spencer growls, "I fucking told you to get the fuck out of here. No more talking to Rook, follow your own goddamn rules for once, will ya? She's just doing her job and if Ronin has a problem with it, he can take it up with me."

"Why would Ronin have a problem with it? It's not a secret." I don't get this weirdness going on with Ford and Spencer. "He's OK with the job, Ford, we talked about it."

"Did you talk about having Spencer between your legs drawing bikini bottoms?"

Spencer rushes Ford and they both crash through the flimsy partition pretending to be a dressing room. Spencer throws a punch that lands squarely on Ford's jaw, and a split second later Ford is back up on his feet and he pounces on Spencer. They grapple on the floor, landing punches and doing weird shit with their legs, trying to get the upper hand. All the crew on the other side of the room and Team Spencer start pulling them apart. Team Rook keeps filming.

They both stand there, breathing heavy, red-faced and lips bleeding. "Out!" Spencer growls. I've never pictured Spencer mad before, but right now he's scaring the shit out of me. He looks like he might kill Ford.

When I look over to Ford, he's the complete opposite, his tie is a little crooked, but generally, he looks calm. Spencer's anger barely touches him.

I think I have a new respect for Ford.

Antoine and his team enter just then and he is roaring, not really in French or English, but a strange mixture of both. He's talking to Spencer and the only word I really catch is *stop*.

I look over to my team and they look just as scared as I feel.

This studio has one rule. Just one. And that rule involves the word stop.

"Are we done for today?" I ask Antoine.

"Yes. Put your clothes on, go home, and call Ronin. *Now*."

I do as I'm told. Fuck these guys. I don't know why every single fucking time the men around here get in a fight everyone always acts like it's my fucking fault. I stomp away like a baby, my team doggedly following, then leave them all outside when I go back inside my apartment. My phone is still on the night table next to my bed, and when I wake it up I have seventeen missed calls.

No voicemails.

I press redial for Ronin's phone and he answers on the first ring.

"Shit, Gidget, it's about time!"

"Sorry, I keep forgetting to keep it on me. You're never gonna believe what just happened!"

"Let me guess, Ford and Spencer?"

"Yeah, how'd you know?"

"We have history, that's all. I don't even know why Spencer took this gig, he knows Ford will just piss him off."

"Antoine called stop, so I guess we're done for today."

"Well," he laughs. "That's a first. What'd they do? Get in a brawl?"

"Yes, Spencer charged him like he was Juggernaut. He kinda scared me, Ronin."

Ronin breathes out slowly on the other end and I can't really tell if he's frustrated with me, or just trying to remain calm. "He'd never hurt you, Rook, OK? He never would."

"Well, I just want this contract to be over. Can't you call Antoine and tell him to let Spencer finish these outfits today?"

I can hear Elise talking in the background, then a muffled noise, like Ronin's covering up the phone. "Yeah, OK. I'll have Elise call him. We won't be home until Sunday, Gidge, so just hang tight, OK? Clare's not doing well, she needs us right now. She really needs Antoine, to be honest, but he's got the contract. It's just really fucked up."

Sunday? I privately pout, then immediately feel guilty because Clare is physically sick trying to get over her addiction and I'm just caught up in my own stupid decisions. "Don't worry about me, OK? She's way more important than this job."

There's a loud knock on the door and I peek down the hallways to see who's there. "Ford's at my door, I guess I better go."

"All right, Rook, call me before you go to bed, OK? Antoine said he's taking you to dinner tonight, so don't let Ford or Spencer talk you into anything."

"OK."

"I miss you real bad, ya know that, right?"

I smile into the phone as Ford's knocking becomes pounding. "I miss you a lot, too. I really do."

"See ya Sunday. Love you."

I sit there, my mouth hanging open, wondering if I'm supposed to say it back. But before I can decide, I hear the line click off. He didn't wait to find out.

I let out a long breath.

Then smile.

I'll be ready next time.

CHAPTER TWELVE

Rook

"What can I do for you, Ford?"

He runs his hand through his hair and grimaces. "I'd just like to apologize, I was out of line. I'll keep my mouth shut from now on. Antoine has revoked the stop order. We can proceed."

Well, that's not what I was expecting, but nonetheless, just looking at him is pissing me off. "You know what, Ford? I don't really care why all you guys hate each other, I really don't. But I'm just trying to make a living. This is a job, Ford. A job I actually need, or else I wouldn't be doing it. So if you assholes can't control yourself, just don't hang around, OK? Because the next time you guys fight in front of me, I'm calling a lawyer to see how difficult I can make your life, you got it? Maybe it's too late to quit, but I promise you, I'll make you regret you ever met me if you try this shit again. I'm not interested in your big-brother routine, I have a boyfriend, I'm not looking for your brand of friendship, so butt the fuck out!"

He just nods as I walk past and hurry across the terrace, trying not to smile at Team Rook as they hide their chuckles, and then hoof it back down to the art room.

Ford does not follow.

Antoine is still half-yelling at Spencer, in French, so apparently he understands him, and Spencer's expression is a cross between irritated, angry, and embarrassed.

I clear my throat when I reach them and Antoine turns around.

"Spencer, I'm gonna tell you the same thing I told Ford. If you pull this shit in front of me again, I'll make you sorry. I'll hire lawyers, I'll ruin this show, I'll be the worst model you can imagine." I drop the robe and stand there as Antoine turns away and walks out. "Now, paint the fucking bikinis. Do not breathe on any sensitive areas. Do not even talk to me right now because I'm pissed. We just wasted a whole bunch of time, and I'm ready to get the fuck back to work."

He shrinks back a little as my words get sharper, but then nods and goes over to his supplies and starts getting it together again. I look back at my team and wink and then catch Producer Larry and his people on the other side of the room snickering.

A few minutes later Spencer is back kneeling on the floor in front of me, painting furiously fast, not being all that careful if you ask me, and not saying one word.

And that's OK with me.

I stand still, I turn, I kneel, I even lie down and spread my fucking legs at one point, but I could care less.

This outfit is boring compared to the last one, but Ford was right about one thing, there's not a lot of paint involved.

Today when I go back upstairs for the first photo shoot I absolutely feel naked. My nipples are white stars that have bikini strings attached to them. It looks real enough, Spencer did his magic and painted wrinkles in the fabric and shaded it just right so it tricks you into believing the illusion, but I don't feel dressed and I don't feel sexy.

Josie bundles up my hair in something that looks like an old-ass bathing cap and then slaps on a blonde wig cut into a flirty bob with straight bangs. She brushes my cheeks with bronzer and a little bit of pink to give the illusion of a slight sunburn after a day in the sun, then drags some mascara through my lashes. It's all very natural, except for the wig.

Billy has materialized from somewhere and to be honest, I'm happy about that. Billy and I got off on the wrong foot, but he's very professional and after spending time with Ford and Spencer, I can appreciate the tight ship that Antoine normally runs here. I miss Elise's watchful eyes and Ronin's calming gestures. These guys would've never pulled this shit if Ronin and Elise were here.

Billy doesn't make one crack about me being naked this time and I'm not sure if Antoine warned him to keep his mouth shut or if he's just smart enough to figure that out himself, but either way, he makes me feel better. "Ready, Rook?" he asks in a low voice.

"Yeah, I'm good." I go over to the bike we're shooting today. It's an old-school soft-tail that sorta reminds me of those classic Fifties cars, with the white walled tires and the off-white colored frame. The gas tank really sets it off because it's fat and has a pretty powder-blue Shrike logo on it, which is never the same thing twice. Each custom bike gets its own custom logo to match. This one is a spiked skull and crossbones, but painted up with fancy lines and swirls. It's kinda girly.

I almost wish I had chosen this bike as my ride, since Spencer promised to customize a bike for me from his showroom.

This bike only has one seat and it sits low. Billy tells me to cross my legs, then put them up on the handlebars. I sit sideways, then lean over and flash my ass, then back around to push out my tits. Even though Antoine's pictures will show a lot more skin in this shoot than they did yesterday, in my opinion it's not nearly as sexy as that catsuit.

"OK, Rook, that's enough." Antoine stops talking and looks behind him at Spencer. "She needs to wash this paint off?"

Spencer looks uncomfortable. "No, I can paint over this one. Next time, though, yeah."

"Billy will take care of Rook in the shower until Ronin returns."

I smile all the way back down to the art room because these asshole men have been put in their place and Antoine must have really been pissed to tame Spencer like that. Ford never even came back up to the studio.

This next painting goes very quick because Spencer just adds to it, turning the stars into flowers and making the bottoms yellow and white stripes. I'm back up in the studio in less than an hour.

Josie just does touch-ups on my makeup and since I never took the wig off, the hair only needs a quick comb.

This time the bike is a sunny orange and it has a sandy floor and a beach backdrop behind it. Antoine has props for me now too, a wide-brimmed hat and a pair of orange sunglasses. Spencer appears after changing into some board shorts. He's got no shirt on and all his tattoos are now in plain sight. I guess I never paid much attention before, but all of Spencer's tattoos are red and black. I've never seen anything like it. It's clear that Spence plans his body art just as meticulously as he does his body painting.

Most of his tats are skulls and birds. And I guess this makes sense, a shrike is a little bird infamous for impaling insects on thorns. I looked his name up because it was so unusual. The birds on his arms and chest are not all shrikes, because those are little robin-sized birds. So despite their cool name and impressive impaling capabilities, they are not really suitable as the starring avian in Spencer's artwork.

No, most of his birds are large. I can see an eagle, an ibis, and lots and lots of ravens.

Or maybe they are rooks?

His front piece is the most beautiful blackbird tattoo I've ever seen and there are ribbons of red and smoky gray weaving around it, camouflaging skulls in the swirls. "Who does your art, Spence? It's incredible."

He snorts out a laugh but doesn't answer, just takes my hand and leads me over to the bike.

"Oh, are you in this shot with me?" I ask, trying to sound nonchalant. I'm a little surprised because no one ever mentioned that Spencer and I would model together.

"Yeah, I'm the owner, right?'"

I squint at him. "Did you just pull rank on me?"

"Spencer," Antoine warns.

Spencer throws up his hands. "She asked me a question. Fuck! What am I supposed to do? Ignore her?" He takes a seat on the bike and then pats his lap. "Sit down here, Rook."

I hesitantly sit on his leg and he grunts. "Now look, Antoine, I'm paying for this fucking shoot, I need her to be natural, you've got her all wound up. Rook"—his attention goes back to me—"just pretend like you do in your other jobs. I'm your boyfriend, we're sitting on the bike at the beach, and you *like* me."

I wrap my arms around his neck and scoot back on his lap a little more, which makes him suck in his breath—and makes me snicker a little if I'm honest—and then lean into his neck and whisper, "I do like you Spencer. But you scared me. I don't like that fighting stuff."

"I'm sorry," he says. "But I'm not taking advantage of you and I'm sick of everyone thinking I am."

Antoine is busy shooting as we talk and then he's barking out orders in French, which Spencer seems to understand.

"Do you speak French, too?"

"It's hard to know Antoine without learning French, he hates to speak English. And I took it in school so Ronin couldn't talk shit about me behind my back." He grins a devious smile down at me. "I know enough and Antoine says if I want good pictures I gotta get you to act like you're having a good time in my lap."

"Spencer!" Antoine barks.

Spence winks at me as he wraps me up in his arms. "I made that last part up, but it's true. Just give me some good pics, Rook. I saw the ones you did with Ronin and those were fucking hot."

I bite my lip a little. They are paying me a butt-load of money, a lot more than the TRAGIC contract was worth, so fuck it. If I'm gonna do this job, I might as well do it right. I lean in and kiss Spencer and Antoine's camera clicks like crazy. Spencer rubs my back a little and then he wraps his hands around my neck and pulls until we bump foreheads, our lips very close but not touching. I look down at him and smile.

"Thank you," he whispers.

"It's my job, right?"

"Right." He leans in and kisses me again. It feels… weird to do this and not have it be cheating. Is it cheating? I pull back and then Antoine tells me to stand on the other side of the bike and lean down on Spence's shoulders, draping my arms around his body.

The plus side to this pose is that it's not an ass-shot. But my tits are practically dangling right in front of Spencer's face. I try to pretend it's just a job, but the truth is, Spencer is excited, and while I am flattered to have that effect on him, I'm also kinda worried, because I'm a little turned on too.

Antoine asks for a few more poses, all of which compound the energy between us right now.

I do not like him that way, I tell myself emphatically.

That's not a lie either. I want Ronin.

But there is a purely physical part of me that can't help but respond.

When Antoine finally gets what he needs I get up quickly and trot downstairs to wash this paint off. Billy dutifully follows me.

"So," he says, grinning, as I turn on the water and grab the sponge that is already in the bucket of paint cleaner on the floor of the shower room. "It's not as easy as it looks, is it?"

"What's not?"

"Keeping it professional."

"Did it show?"

He laughs. "Uh, yeah, Rook. We're not blind."

"Ronin's gonna be so mad."

"Hey, look at it this way, Rook. Ronin's been doing this for years now, longer than me, that's for sure. And if he tells you he's not turned on in those shoots, probably every single one of them, he's a liar. It's natural, it's sexy as hell, Rook. It's the whole purpose of erotic photography, right? If we're not turned on, we don't give Antoine what he's looking for. So as bad as Antoine feels about needing Spencer to make you feel that way, that's his job. To give you a partner who turns you on so he can get his photos."

I think about this for a few minutes as I scrub. Billy stands off to the side, not facing me so I have an illusion of privacy. "Do you sleep with them, Billy? After you're done? I mean, what's it mean afterward?"

He shrugs. "I sleep with some of them, sure. But sometimes it's just a thing, ya know? Just a physical reaction, and nothing more."

I finish up with the shower and Billy hands me a towel and walks me upstairs to the studio.

Just a job, Rook. It's just a job.

CHAPTER THIRTEEN

Rook

Ford is back when I enter the studio, but he's on the other side of the room, sitting in a chair next to Director Larry looking at the wall of screens. I ignore him and walk over to Spencer. His shirt is back, but he's still got the board shorts on. "Are we modeling together for all the shoots, Spencer?"

He doesn't turn, just keeps messing with his brushes and paint. "Does it bother you?"

"Um." Does it? "No, it doesn't bother me, that's not the right word." My camera team zooms in on me. I guess this is what Larry is looking for, because I can hear a tinny voice coming out of the earpiece of my main camera guy. "I'm just worried about what Ronin will think."

Spence turns now. "Ronin will just have to learn to deal, Rook. I picked you because you're beautiful, you're the girl I want to represent my bikes. And if that makes Ronin uncomfortable, too bad. I won't be in all the shots, but we have to get a few, at least. I mean, that's just reality, Rook."

"I know," I say, sighing. "I should just forget about Ronin, huh?"

Spencer laughs. "Why? Why would you say that?" He points me over to the sheet and grabs his stuff, then starts painting my breast. "You like him, he likes you. What's the fucking problem?"

"If our roles were switched and Ronin was the model being painted up by a sexy artist, I'd be mad. I'd never put up with it, to be honest."

"So, you think I'm sexy, eh?"

I laugh. "You know what I mean."

"Well, you can't change that, Rook. You're the model, I'm the artist, he's the boyfriend. He can deal or not. But I'm still the artist and you're still the model. And if he's smart he'll just shut the fuck up about it, stay out of the way until the contract is over, and then forget it ever happened."

"Do you have a girlfriend?"

He winces.

"What?"

"She broke up with me."

"How come?" I suck in a small breath as he paints a string along my upper ribcage and around my back.

He ignores my question for so long I'm ready to ask it again when he finally looks up, smiling.

"What?"

"She broke up with over this contract. She was jealous."

I can't help but laugh with him. "Well, I guess she didn't mean much, huh? You don't look broken up about it."

"Well, I do miss her hands because she's the one responsible for my body art. But I'm not a relationship kinda guy, Rook. I like to play the field. So if she wants to be a bitch about it, get jealous over you and me spending so much naked time together, then she can take the fuck off."

"Have you known her long?"

"Yeah, she's the model in all the other pictures too."

"Holy crap! That's just rude, Spencer!"

He doesn't even look up from painting my nipple. "What's rude?"

"She's your model and you chose me!"

He shrugs. "Your name's Rook and in case you haven't noticed, I've got quite a thing for blackbirds going on. Besides, this was a business decision. She wanted the contract money, that's all. She allowed me to paint her so she could make money. I let her be my canvas because she was willing. She used me, I used her, and to tell you the truth"—he does look up now—"I'm pretty fucking pissed off that she turned it all personal. I never promised her this contract and as you now know, this is way beyond a modeling job, right? It's a TV show, it's a marketing campaign, it's my entire fucking business. And if everything goes well, you'll be part of this franchise for a long time. I have long-term plans, Rook. And she was never part of them."

"But I am?"

"That's right," he says in a soft whisper. "You're definitely part of them."

Both our sound guys move the mics closer to us and I can only hope they missed that last part. Because I think Spencer Shrike just made some kind of declaration to me and I'm having hard time thinking it was professional because now his paintbrush is practically caressing me between my legs. He uses broad strokes, so it's not like he's trying to excite me on purpose, but he's a man, kneeling down in front of me, staring at my most private body parts.

I inhale, close my eyes, and think about how I'd feel if I walked in on Ronin doing this to some girl. Or even worse, Ronin getting his manly parts painted up by some hottie chick.

I snicker internally, proud of myself. That image was all it took.

"OK, on the floor with you, Blackbird."

I cringe. I was mad the last time he painted up my girly parts, but now I'm confused. And worried about Ronin and my physical reaction to Spencer.

"Problem, Rook?"

"No," I say as I kneel down, then lie back and fold my hands over my stomach. The camera crew backs off for this and it makes me wonder if Ford told them to do that. The first bikini was just white, so Spencer didn't spend a lot of time down here. It was quick and easy. The second one only required that he paint the stripes on.

But this time I'm bare again and Spencer wants to paint the suit up to look iridescent, so he spends more time than he did the last two times put together.

"Hurry up, Spencer, this is weird. If Ronin was here, he'd be having a fit, you staring right up into my—"

"Hey now! I'm painting, Rook!"

I snort. "Whatever, I'm standing up in ten seconds. I'm not spreading my legs for your motorcycle ad, so you don't need to get carried away with the details down there."

When my private count gets to ten, I push his head back and stand up. "I wasn't kidding."

He ignores me and continues painting a shadow under the string that wraps around my hip to the little piece of fabric on my ass.

"I don't like doing more than one outfit in a day. This sucks. I'm ready to be done—"

"We still have one more, Rook. Better settle down, sister."

My irritation comes out as a growl. "Well, I don't like it. I'm hungry, I want to pee, I'd like to take a nap, or read a fucking book, or—"

"Here, Rook."

Ford is standing a little behind me thrusting a tablet in my direction. I take it automatically. "What's this?"

"Books. I like thrillers and classics, so maybe not your thing, but you can shop the store and find something you like."

"Oh." I take a moment to calm down from my rant and then smile. "Thanks, Ford. I definitely need to get one of these. In fact, I need to go shopping, maybe I need a car? When will Elise be back? I'm tired of hanging out with men, why can't this show have more girls on it? And what's up with having no girls on the production team too? Not one girl can run a microphone or camera?"

I get silence. Straight-up crickets.

"Hello? Are you guys listening to me?"

"No!" they all say at once. Even Director Larry's team on the other side of the room yells it out.

"Well, shit. I guess I better find me a book then." I open

the leather flap that covers the device and it comes to life. I swipe my fingers to unlock it, then browse the little carousel that holds all Ford's books.

Talk about eye-opening. "Ford's reading *Gatsby, Deeply Odd,* and *Making Babies for the Billionaire.*" I get snorts from everyone, even my team.

"Funny, Rook," Ford says dryly from across the room.

"You know what's funnier? The fact that all you dumbasses got the joke. I know what you're reading at night."

"Someone please, turn on the fucking tunes."

"Spencer, that was not nice. How about I read from the billionaire book? You guys should like that."

Spencer stops painting and looks up at me. "Does he really have that on there?"

We all bust out laughing. "Oh, Spencer."

"All right, I'm done. Let's get this over with, give you something else to bitch about for a while."

I race out and head straight to the bathroom, then make my way upstairs, totally oblivious to the fact that I'm one hundred percent naked. It was less than a month ago that I stood in the Chaput dressing room wondering how all the girls could just walk around naked, but here I am, traipsing around the entire building like that.

My team is waiting for me upstairs and Spencer is shirtless again, but he's changed into some faded jeans with holes and grease all over them, like he's been working in a garage all day. He's sitting casually on the new bike, messing with the grips as he chats to Billy. This bike is like psychedelic. It's got swirls of light blue and purple on the frame and the tank. The Shrike logo is a thick bold black outline, the total opposite of the girly one from the last shoot. The set is still beachy, but the backdrop spills over onto the floor and it makes it look like we're on the side of a road. When I sit down for Josie, she takes off my blonde wig and exchanges it for a black one. The cut is shorter now, the bangs severe, and it frames my face. She removes the old makeup and paints on new. This time I get the glossy treatment. Red lips, dark eyes, and plum blush.

I also get some spiky pumps that probably require a personal injury insurance policy to walk in, and after about thirty minutes I'm stumbling my way over to the guys.

Antoine is in his office, and when I'm ready Billy goes to get him.

"What's all this?" I fan my arms out to the set, curious as to what message we're sending.

"You're a hitchhiker, I'm your knight in shining armor."

"I'm hitchhiking in a bikini and fuck-me pumps?"

"Biker fantasy, Rook. Trust me."

"O-kaaaay."

Antoine and Billy appear, and as usual, Billy does all the talking. I wonder how I'm going to fill in a whole evening of conversation when Antoine and I go to dinner. I wonder if he'll take me to Cookie's. I'm so fucking hungry.

"You're thumbing, Rook, step behind the bike and act the part."

I do as I'm told, then pretend to have a conversation with Spencer as he ogles my tits. I'm not sure if that's pretend or not, but it makes me frown and Antoine barks out something harsh and Billy tells me to look happy. I do, then climb in front of Spencer, facing him, and wince as I realize I'm in yet another position that will have Ronin breaking up with me as soon as he gets back. Spencer sneaks a peek down.

"Really, Spence? I mean, you've been looking at my goods all day, you haven't seen enough?"

"That's totally different, I'm not supposed to get turned on when I'm painting, but this is different."

"*Spencer.*"

Spencer glares at Antoine this time. "Look, she asked me a question, *again*. So why does she get to talk to me, but I'm not allowed to talk to her?"

"Who said you're not allowed to talk to me?"

"Antoine. I'm supposed to keep it professional, but that's a fucking first. The whole reason we hired you, Antoine, was because you're famous for getting the girls to be as unprofessional as possible."

"OK, let's just move on. What should I do? You're the one in charge, Spencer. I need direction here because I'm not all that good at this shit."

Spencer shoots Antoine a look. "See, she wants me to tell her what to do." He looks at me, his hands wrap around my middle, then slip down to the top of my ass. "Take the pictures, Antoine," Spencer growls.

I hold down a laugh because these babies have no idea what to do with me right now.

Antoine starts shooting and Spencer's one hand stays down, while the other one slides up, picks up my arm and drapes it over his shoulder, then cups my breast. "Kiss me again, Rook."

I look at him, the shock plastered across my face, I'm sure. I swallow, not sure what to do with myself right now, either.

"Rook," Spencer repeats, a little harsher now. "I want kissing, I want mad fucking passionate kissing. The kind of kissing I've seen in all those other photos of you, the kissing that is so filled with emotion and longing and lust, I'm instantly hard. Kiss me like that, Blackbird."

I gulp some air and stare at him, right into his eyes. We hold that moment as Billy translates encouraging things from Antoine. I lean in a little, slowly, never breaking eye contact, then touch his lips with a soft kiss, and pull back.

He smiles.

I do it again and this time he's ready, his hand leaves my breast and wraps around my head, pulling me towards him. His mouth opens and I respond by doing the same. Our tongues flick against each other, then I pull back as his grip releases, trying to catch my breath.

"That's more like it," he whispers. "Now turn around, Rook."

I stand up and turn around, my ass against his thighs.

He's very excited.

His hands go to my shoulders, then his fingertips drag down my arms. One hand grabs my breast, while the other slides across my stomach, then drops very low.

"Arch your back and tip your head, Rook."

I do, and his hand drops even lower with the change in my body position. I have to admit, for being a bike designer, he's pretty good at this sexy modeling stuff. His mouth is suddenly heavy against my neck, his breath slow, but louder than before.

I moan.

Oops.

He laughs behind me and I relax a little.

We're still acting, I tell myself.

CHAPTER FOURTEEN

Rook

Billy follows me downstairs to the shower room again and this makes me wonder. "What's the deal with this whole bodyguard thing, Billy? How come you have to follow me around?"

"Rook, this building is unlocked during business hours, you do realize that, right?"

"Um…"

"I wasn't gonna say anything because you've got enough going on here today, but Antoine was pissed that you didn't wait for me to walk you to the bathroom. You can't just traipse around naked outside the studio. At the very least, have your camera crew around. You need to wait for someone to go with you, even if it's just walking upstairs."

"Oh, well, yeah, that makes sense." I can't argue with that. It was a little weird walking around naked all alone, anyway. "Thanks, Billy. I'm really glad you're here. It makes a difference."

He smiles and turns around. "Hurry up, I'm starving and we can't eat until we're done. Hopefully the next painting will go fast."

"Oh," I say, squeezing out the sponge and rubbing down my chest. "Are you coming with us to dinner? Ronin just said I was eating with Antoine tonight."

Billy laughs. "Antoine doesn't go anywhere with the models alone. Ever. Not even you, Rook. He keeps a healthy distance from all of them, that's why he's got Ronin. To run interference."

"Makes sense, I guess." I scrub the bikini bottoms off my front and then get as much of my ass as I can before holding the sponge out to Billy. "Get the rest of it, hurry."

He does as I ask and I just have to privately shake my head at what my life has become. It's weird. All these guys looking at me naked. Getting my picture taken. Being a sort of girlfriend to Ronin, yet my job is allowing his former best friend to touch and kiss me. And Billy here, washing paint off my backside.

"OK," he says, turning me around so the water washes off the soap. "You're good. Let's go." He hands me my towel, I wrap myself up again, and we go back to the art room.

Ford is back in his director's chair in the corner of Spencer's space, Spencer is messing with the music, and Team Rook is looking tired and bored. I'd hate to be the camera person for a reality show. It's like you do nothing but hang out until something exciting happens. Even Ford looks bored out of his mind. He's holding the tablet in his lap, reading.

I walk over to him. "*Gatsby, Odd,* or *Billionaire?*"

He grins and I notice that there's a dimple in his chin when the smile reaches his eyes. "Guess."

"*Gatsby,*" I say.

"Correct."

I shrug, "It was the first one on the carousel."

"Do you like *Gatsby,* Rook?"

"Never read it. I pretty much dropped out of school at sixteen, so I never got past *Lord of the Flies.*" He's scowling at me. "What?"

"You didn't finish high school?"

"I took the GED. Why? Is there an educational requirement to pose naked with bikes?"

"It surprises me, that's all. You come off as smart, like I said earlier."

Yeah, Ronin likes the dumb ones. I shake my head at him. "You know, Ford, every time I start to like you, you act like a pretentious asshole."

He points his finger at me. "See, that right there is what trips me up. Most drop-outs don't use the word pretentious."

"Never mind him, Blackbird, disrobe, let's go. This is a one-piece, let's get a move on."

Ford huffs out a laugh under his breath.

"What?" I ask, looking back at him again.

"You'll see," is all he says.

Ford chats with me as Spencer paints, calling out book titles to see if I'd like to read them. He starts with classics, none of which appeal to me. He turns his nose up at every rejection, like he's taking it personally. Which I can totally see. He looks like a classics lover.

"Just skip to the romance, Ford. Why torture yourself?"

"Billionaires?"

I laugh at that, along with Spencer's new fascination with my armpits. He's painting bikini strings in very interesting places. "No, I'm not into fantasy billionaires. I've got Ronin, remember?"

My team chuckles at this dig. I think I like my team, they seem to be on my side.

"Right, yes, I do recall that."

"Just try the regular romances, or the ones they write for kids my age."

He cringes at the word kid, but fuck it. Why pretend? I'm still a kid. I like being a kid, I missed a lot of kid time in my earlier life, and I'm in no hurry to grow up now, even if I am standing here naked in front of a whole room full of men.

Ford's brow twists a little as he searches. "Coming-of-age or college life?"

"Um, the last one I guess. Just read the description for the number one book, let's start there."

"*Ashley, the only virgin in her freshman dorm…*" He stops and looks up at me. "Seriously?"

"Keep going, it sounds good." My team is having a hard time hiding their amusement now.

"... *is desperate to be deflowered by long-time crush, Eaton Fuller.* Eaton? What kind of name is that?"

"Says the guy named Ford."

"*But that's before hot and dangerous Rowdy Breaker saves her from a spelunking adventure gone wrong.* This is stupid. Spelunking gone wrong? It's so cliché."

"One-click that sucker, Ford. Any guy called Rowdy has gotta be hot. You don't get to be number one for no reason. I'll read about Rowdy and his cave-dwelling tendencies. Hand it over."

"We're done here, no time for books, Rook."

"Done? You just started!"

Ford laughs.

I look down and if this suit was real, it'd be nothing but a bunch of rope winding around my body in strategic places. None of which happens to cross my private parts. "This isn't a bathing suit, it's rope. I look like I'm being tied up for... Oh."

They are all laughing at me now.

"Come on," Spencer says. "I'll walk you up."

"Are you modeling with me this time, too?"

Snickers from Team Everybody.

"What?"

"Nope, not me this time, Rook. Billy's got this privilege."

Billy is the sexiest cowboy I've ever seen. I've never pretended the guy wasn't gorgeous to look at, because he is very easy on the eyes. But sporting all that western gear, the tight jeans, the hat, the chaps, and the boots, in combination with a new rough expression I've never seen him wear before, plus his bare chest, makes him look like he's about to bind my wrists and take me from behind.

Whew. I have to stop and take a breath after that thought.

This bike is a work of art. It's got a custom seat shaped like a western saddle and an entire scene depicting a bad-boy cowboy meets helpless half-naked female airbrushed on the top of the fat tank. The whole frame is a smoky black with barbed-wire running down the fenders like racing stripes.

"Wow."

"I love this bike, Rook," Spencer says as he stands next to me. "I've been waiting to get decent images of this one and put it online. It's not a showroom model, but a one-of-a-kind custom. I'll be sorry to sell it actually." He laughs a little under his breath. "Until I get the check, that is. Because this one's a sweet ninety-five grand."

Holy shit.

"Over here, Rook," Josie calls.

I walk over to the salon and she removes the makeup from the last shoot and reapplies. I get another wig, only this time it's Farrah Fawcett à la Charlie's Angels hair, all frosted blonde highlights in big bouncy curls that fall halfway down my back. I get the natural look as far as makeup goes, and then I slip my feet into the cowgirl boots and plop the hat on my head.

When I walk back over to the guys Spencer buckles a gun holster around my waist and then slides two revolvers inside.

So I'm wearing boots, guns, and a hat. And my body has been painted to look like I've been tied up.

When I look up to see what's next, every mouth is hanging open.

Except Antoine's, because he's just coming out of his office, trying to pretend I'm fully clothed.

"What're you assholes looking at? I've been walking around here naked all day, quit it!"

They mumble out some incomprehensible words as I walk over to Billy.

He's smiling. "That is fucking hot for some reason. I'm not sure why, it just is, Rook."

I shrug. "You're pretty hot too, Billy. Maybe it's the hats?"

He chuckles. "Yeah, the hats. OK, for this one you're my bitch. So bend the fuck over the seat, ass to the camera, and let me whack you a few good ones so your cheeks turn pink."

"*What*?"

"I'm kidding, Rook." He sits down on the western saddle seat and pulls me toward him. "Just sit in my lap to start, wrists together, because if you do that, you'll see it looks like I've bound you up."

I put my wrists together, then Billy reaches down and adjusts them. He puts his arm around me as Antoine starts the shoot. Billy is not Spencer, he knows exactly what to do and when to do it, so I relax and just do as I'm told. I lean against him as his hands rub the side of my body in long strokes. He leans down and begins nibbling on my neck and then whispers in my ear. "Antoine liked that moaning you did last time, but he's not gonna ask for it, Rook. So give the man his photos and you'll be done sooner. That's the secret to this job. Give him what he wants and right now he wants you to look the same way with me as you do with Ronin."

"Can I move my hands? Or do I have to pretend to be tied up?"

"Do you want to move them?"

"Yes."

He repositions my body so I'm straddling the tank, leaning back on his chest like I was with Spencer. Billy has either had a lot of bike sex before, or he's got a very creative on-the-fly imagination because I'm pretty hot and bothered in a matter of seconds. He opens my legs right up, places one on the handlebars, and then reaches around to cup my breast. "Touch me, Rook."

I reach back and grab his head, thrusting my upper body up and out. Billy's right hand caresses the leg propped up on the handlebar, then slides down and slips right up under my ass. His other hand is squeezing my breast until I squirm from the pressure. "Turn towards me, Rook." His voice is a low rumble.

I turn and his mouth is right there, his kisses are just as passionate as any Ronin gave me, and his hands just as daring. His fingers are between my legs, not past any point of no return, but hovering right there, right on the edge. He rubs my lower abdomen a little, slips down, then brings his fingertips back up just when I think he's gonna slip them in farther.

It's driving me fucking crazy. I am so horny right now it's not even funny.

I lose track of time, of the camera, of everyone in the room. I feel his kisses, I kiss him back, but I'm not even inside my body right now, that's how worked up he has me. I'm not sure what it means, but none of this can be good for a brand-new relationship with a man who is not the one fondling me right now.

"OK, great shots, Billy and Rook. We're done for today."

And that's it. Antoine takes his camera and walks away.

"You OK, Rook?" Billy asks, his voice totally normal, like he always is after a shoot.

"Um..." *Wow.*

He lifts me up off him and sets me on the ground. "Come on," he says, taking my hand as he gets off the bike. "I'll walk you to the showers."

I have no words as we go back downstairs. Like none.

We go in and he starts the shower for me. "You wanna talk about it?"

I blow some air out of my cheeks. "I don't think I can do this, Billy."

"What are ya talking about? You did great."

"I mean, I don't think I can keep all these feelings separate."

He laughs. "Oh, you're hot for me now?"

"No, it's just, that felt so..."

He grins as my words trail off. "It's OK to admit it, Rook."

"Good, it felt good."

"It's supposed to feel good. That's what people want to see in the pictures."

"So you don't want to really jump my bones?"

"Well, fuck yeah I do, but you're seeing Ronin, right? So you're off limits. I'm not an asshole, I'd never do that."

I've got nothing for that response. I'm not sure if it helps or makes things worse.

"Rook, when I'm working, you're just a naked body, OK? And I guarantee you, Spencer is the same way. He's got a naked girl in his lap and he'd like to finish her off and get himself some too. That's just how it is. But when the shoot stops, you're Rook again. And that's not the same thing as a naked body in our laps. It's work, Rook. Not love."

He takes the sponge from me and starts washing my back and I just stand there and let him. When he's done he thrusts it at me until I take it from him. "You can finish now, right? I'll be in the hallway."

He walks out and leaves me standing there. I snap back to my senses and wash the rest of the paint off, then wrap myself up in a towel and go out to meet him. We walk upstairs together and then he drops me off in front of Ronin's door.

"Be ready in an hour, we're having dinner, remember?"

Right, dinner. I nod and go inside, ready to be alone so I can begin to process this day.

CHAPTER FIFTEEN

Rook

Dinner with Billy and Antoine wasn't terrible, but I spent most of the time just listening to them talk about sports. It was pretty boring. And now that I'm back home in my apartment, I'm simply exhausted. I can't imagine working like this every day. My phone buzzes and I smile at Ronin's face on my screen.

"Geez," I say after answering, "I figured you forgot about me."

"Nah, I knew you were eating with Antoine, remember? How'd it go today?"

I hesitate. "Well, it was… weird, confusing, exciting, long, demanding, and… weird."

"Why weird twice?"

I thought about this conversation all through dinner. I need to get this out in the open, because if Ronin is gonna break it off with me over this contract, I might as well understand that now. "When you model with other girls, does it…"

"Does it what?"

"Feel good?"

He lets out a small laugh but I'm not convinced that it's a happy one. "Did it feel good today with Billy and Spencer?"

"You knew I was modeling with them?"

"Rook, I'm your manager. I know what every painting looks like, we're not making this shit up as we go. This has all been planned. So yes, I know what you did today. And my question is, did it feel good?"

I swallow. "It did. I can't help it, when they're asking me to kiss them for the photo shoot it got personal. I felt turned on."

He says nothing for several long seconds.

"Do you get turned on when you're with other girls?"

"Yeah, I do."

"So, what I'm feeling is… normal?"

"It is."

"So you're OK with it?"

"Would you be OK with it? If it was me doing a contract like this?"

Oh God. He's totally breaking up with me.

"Rook? Would you?"

What do I say? *No, I'd break up with you.* Or, *Yes, I would, so you should be OK with this too.*

"Rook, it's not a hard question."

I take a deep breath and then let it out. "No, I wouldn't be OK with it."

"I'm not either, but it's too late for that. You signed, I decided to stand by you and wait it out, and this is what that looks like."

"Are you mad at me?"

"Yeah. I am, I'm not gonna lie, Rook. It pisses me off and it's even worse knowing I'm not there. Antoine isn't paying attention during the artwork, is he?"

"No, he's upstairs the whole time."

"So who's in there? Ford?"

"Yes."

"Spencer, obviously. Camera crews?"

"Yes, and the director people."

"Billy?"

"No, but he walks me to and from the studio and he's in charge of helping me wash the paint off." He grunts at this. "That was Antoine's call, Ronin. Not me. It was him or Spencer, and Antoine said Billy. And if it makes you feel any better, I'd prefer Billy because Billy knows exactly what he's doing and he keeps it professional."

"So Spencer tried something with you?"

"No! That's not what I said. It's just Billy understands this is pretend."

He lets out a long controlled breath but stays silent for a while. I have nothing to add, so I just let him think it through. "Well, I told you, Rook. I warned you and now it's all playing out exactly as I feared."

"What's that mean? I'm not interested in Spencer, Ronin. And I don't know what his deal is, but he's been one hundred percent professional with me during the painting. It's really only the photo shoots that bother me, because he wants me to kiss him and stuff."

Silence.

"Did you hear me?"

More silence.

"So we're fighting? That's what's happening?"

"What do you want me to say, Rook? It bothers me, but I'll get over it? Is that what you want to hear?"

"Well, yeah. That's perfect actually. But I know you're messing with me, so it's also pretty fucked up."

Silence again.

"So I'll see you Sunday, then?"

"Sunday, yeah. We'll be home late afternoon probably."

"I miss you. And you didn't even give me a chance to say anything when you said you loved me earlier."

"It just slipped out. Sorry."

Long, dreadful, agonizing silence.

Now what the hell am I supposed to do with that? "I'm tired, exhausted really, and Ford will be here at five to make me run stadiums with him, so I—"

"What?"

"Ford. I made a deal with him so I can use your apartment to shower and get some privacy. I hope that's OK."

"Which part," he growls, "the fact that you're running

with Ford in the morning or using my apartment while I'm gone?"

"OK, I'm hanging up now." I press end on my phone and lie back on my bed. He's got every right to be mad but I don't have to listen to that shit.

My phone buzzes.

"What?"

"I'm sorry."

"Look, Ronin, let's just break up then, OK? Because as you pointed out to me the other night, I'm stuck. This job needs to get done. I'm committed to it, and there's nothing I can do. So let's just call it off and maybe we can try again later or maybe we just say fuck it. You can take care of Clare for the rest of your life and I can move on and go to school."

"Is that what you want?"

"Yes. Because I spent the whole fucking day worried about *you*, Ronin. I worried about every single thing I did, and even though Spencer told me I was being ridiculous and Billy assured me you would understand, I couldn't stop thinking about how mad you were gonna be. And I can't live like that. So, I won't use your apartment, OK? And you just take your time coming home. Bye."

I end the call and then look up and realize every single bit of this was just caught on camera. I stow my tears away until I make it outside and then I go sit under the cherry trees and cry.

It's one of those poor-me, silent and tearful, pity cries. And it gives me a headache. But this day has been too much for me all of a sudden and I can't hold it in. And the last thing I want is for Director Larry and his people to watch me fall apart after that stupid conversation.

I'm not sure how long I've been lying out here when the studio door opens. I listen to the click of expensive shoes across the concrete. "What now?" I say, annoyed.

Ford stops and looks down on me. "What are you doing?"

"Crying. What does it look like I'm doing? And I'm sure you guys got all that on camera, so don't waste my time with your feigned innocence, Ford. I'm not in the mood."

He smiles and sits down on a nearby picnic table. "See, feigned, that's another one. Most drop-outs don't use feigned, either."

"Go away."

"We were listening to the conversation, Rook."

I turn away from him and close my tired eyes. "Go away."

"Your phone's been buzzing since you hung up on him, so why not just go answer it?"

"I'm not running with you tomorrow, I don't need to take a shower up there anymore."

"You're just being bratty, Rook, he's jealous, that's all. Go inside or I'll have a technician come down and hang a camera." He gets up and walks away. "I'm dead serious about that, you have five minutes."

I wait until he goes back inside, then I count to sixty and get up to go back to my apartment. My phone has seven missed calls and no voicemail messages. I figure that means he's not interested in a call back, so I just turn the ringer off and slip into bed, fully clothed.

CHAPTER SIXTEEN

Rook

Someone is rocking me back and forth. "Whaaaaaat?"

"It's almost five, Rook."

"Grrrr... Ford, I told you I'm not running with you because I'm not going to be using Ronin's shower."

"Right, but I have another offer you might be interested in."

I pull the covers over my head.

"I'll take the camera out of your bedroom."

I slide the cover back down. "Why? Why do you want me to run with you? It's weird. I know this is some sordid plot to make Ronin jealous and hate me even more. Go away."

He laughs. "Sordid, that's three. Where did you get that one?"

I open my eyes and stare up at him. Ford is a strange guy, but I have a good answer for him, so I say it. "*Sordid Lives*. Ever seen it? That movie is hi-*lar*-ious. I didn't actually know what sordid meant before that movie, but I looked it up."

"*Sordid Lives?*" he says with a little question mark at the end. "Unusual choice of movie for a girl your age."

He sits down at the end of my bed and waits to see if I'll tell him anything else. I wasn't planning on it, but then I remember what his job actually is. He's a producer, he's into this stuff, he might, in fact, understand why I'm a movie freak. "I like comedies. They... always made me feel better." And this one is about white trash, and that's me in a nutshell. But I leave that part out.

His mouth makes an O, like that explains everything. "Come running, Rook. It's good for you."

"I'd rather pout."

He smiles and a chin dimple appears. "Yes, that's always fun for children, but you're a grownup, Rook. So get up and come running with me."

"That won't work, you know."

"What won't work?"

"That reverse psychology bullshit you're trying to pull on me. Call me a child, tell me I'm childish so I'll do what you ask. Run your ass off up and down those stairs to make me feel lazy so I'll put in more effort. It won't work, I'm not stupid."

"Well, I'll tell you what. Get up and mope along with me and tomorrow I'll show up with all kinds of statistics that will convince you this is good for you."

I pull the covers back over my head. "I'm too tired today. Yesterday was hard and long. I want to go back to sleep."

"Today will be quick, Rook. Antoine told Spencer just one outfit today, he's going up to see Clare and won't be back until Sunday. So you can take a nap after work."

"What? He's going up there and didn't even invite *me?"* That last word barely makes it out of my mouth before I'm crying. "Ronin never even said anything about Antoine going up today!"

"Rook, it's not a vacation, his niece is addicted to heroin, she's not doing well, he's sick with worry. It's got nothing to do with you."

I try to stop my crying because it's so embarrassing, but once I start holding it in I make weird noises. Ford drags the covers off me. "What the hell are you wearing?"

"Clothes."

"To bed?" He asks this with a weird cock-eyed look on this face.

I point up at the camera.

"OK." He pulls me by the feet and drags me until I fall

off the bed. "Run with me every day and I'll take out all your apartment cameras."

"You will?"

"Yes," he says nodding. "You're not adjusting very well, Rook. Go change, I'll be outside."

He walks out and leaves me there on the floor. *Not adjusting well, my ass. I'm the queen of adjusting.*

I get up, find another sporty outfit, tug it on, then step outside and walk over to Ford. He's sitting at the picnic table over by the cherry trees, holding out a box to me as I approach.

"What's that?"

"Running shoes. You can't wear those things, Rook. They're unacceptable."

I look down at my Converse. Then peek in the box. And change shoes. Might as well look the complete part. We walk over to the stadium, minus the camera crew. I guess they figure they'll sleep in if they can't follow us inside. We start at the same place we did yesterday, Ford trucking up and down those stairs like a pro, me dragging my feet up while expending as little effort as possible.

I watch him to take my mind off Ronin. He runs hard, like he's really racing someone, or like he's running for his life. I make it almost nine rows before he stops, checks his watch, and then turns and heads back my way at the same break-neck pace. When he's only one row away I stop and wait.

He's breathing hard again, sweat dripping off his body. He takes off his shirt and starts wiping himself off.

"You need a towel, Ford."

He smiles. "Hungry?"

I shrug. "Not so much this morning."

"Well, you might change your mind once you smell the food."

I follow him inside and this is a repeat from yesterday as well. Two breakfast burritos, two OJ's. We eat in complete silence and he doesn't make any move to start a conversation with me or even look uncomfortable because we're so quiet.

I think this is more of his reverse psychology, so I forbid my mouth from saying anything. He's not gonna win this, he won't. When I'm done with my burrito, which did hit the spot even though I didn't think I was hungry, he simply picks up my trash, throws it away, then waits for me to get up and join him by the trashcan.

We walk back to the studio in silence and then he gives me a half-hearted goodbye at his car.

I go inside and go straight to Ronin's apartment to take a shower. I'm feeling like a creeper because I'm really not supposed to be in here today, but that's not enough to stop me from starting the water and taking off my clothes. I look at myself in the mirror and wonder if this mistake will ruin my life.

I press a bunch of random buttons on the shower control panel and wait to see if any good jets will come on. I don't like the rain shower, but I'm not really sure which button works that one, so sometimes it comes on and I have to press more random buttons until it stops. But this morning I get the steamy mist and two hard streams that come out of the corners and meet together to make one blaring jet of water. I stand underneath it and let it pound against my neck and upper back.

It feels good so I close my eyes.

A hand touches my shoulder and I whirl around. "AHHHHH!"

"Rook! It's me!" Ronin grabs me and pulls me towards him.

"You scared me!" The sudden rush of adrenaline has my heart pounding like a jackhammer and I really have to try hard not to cry. I put my hand over my face and take a few deep breaths.

"I'm sorry." He wraps his arms around me and holds me against his chest. "I'm sorry, I didn't mean to scare you."

"What're you doing here?"

"It's my house, silly."

I pull away and enjoy his naked body for a second. God, Ronin has a terrific body. "But you never said you were coming home."

"I left in the middle of the night. I shouldn't have been an ass on the phone. Antoine is leaving this afternoon to see Clare, then coming home with Elise on Sunday. I told them I had to come home because I'm not at all interested in breaking up with you over this contract. I'm not happy about it, I'm not happy about Ford, or Spencer, or Billy or any of it, actually. But I'm not ready to say goodbye over something so *temporary*."

I hug him. "I'm so glad you're here. I don't want to break up with you, either. I just feel so guilty for what I have to do in those shoots."

"We'll get through it, OK?"

I nod into his chest.

He pries me from his body and grabs the soap. "We gotta get an early start, it's the sexy Elvis painting today. I'm gonna take over from here, if that's OK."

"Take over how?" I say as he lathers my arm with the soap.

"In the shoots. I called Spencer and told him I'd model with you, no pay."

"What—" His soapy hands move to my breasts and I lose track of my words.

"I don't need the money, believe me. It's not a big deal to work for free and I have to be around all day with you anyway, to keep an eye out. Besides," he says, rubbing my other breast now. "I'm not sure any man would call what I'm doing a job."

I look up at him and he leans down and kisses me gently. He drops the soap and pulls me right up against his full erection, still gently caressing my lips. My hands slip around his waist and then up his muscular back. I drag them back down his arms and then up his chest. He pulls me with him as he steps back a few paces, then sits down on the tiled bench on the far side of the shower, away from the punishing jets and right into the thick mist of steam coming from the ceiling.

He leans back against the wall and I climb into his lap, positioning my hips over his thickness, then easing down until he fills me up. We stay still like that for a few seconds, me leaning against him, my head on his shoulder, him dragging his hand down my wet hair, and then we start rocking. Just a little at first.

I close my eyes and tug on his hair a little, making him groan. He reaches up and fondles my breast, gently rolling my nipple between his fingertips. I pull my head back and look down, deep into his eyes. "Do you love me?"

He smiles. "I do."

"I wanted to tell you back, but you hung up."

"You scare me, Rook."

"Why?" I ask, puzzled.

"Because your future is making itself right now, this very moment. And you have no idea it's happening. I want you so completely it hurts. But you and I are in two totally different places."

My whole body shivers with a chill as I absorb his words. I swallow. "That sounds like the beginning of a break-up speech. Are you breaking up with me?"

He scoots my bottom closer, thrusting himself inside me a little more. "I love you, Rook. I'm not breaking up with you. But it's all bad timing, you know?"

I shake my head. "No, not really."

"My career started when I was seventeen. I've done everything you're just getting a taste of now. I've traveled all over the world, I've made a shitload of money, I have pretty much everything I want."

"But—"

"Except the only thing I really want."

I wait for it, but he lets out a long sigh and holds it in. "Is it a secret?"

He lets out a soft laugh and rocks himself into me again.

"No, it's not. I already told you that night we went to the zoo."

"A family," I say, a little breathless now because what he's doing, this serious conversation combined with the sensual lovemaking, is making my heart pound.

"Yes. I'm done, Rook. I can live off the money I've made for decades. I'm ready to do something else. Start something new."

"Well, how is that a problem for us?" I ask, lifting up and slipping down on him. It's his turn to become breathless. "I'm not against the idea, you know."

He smiles as his hand reaches up to cup my breast.

I shiver again, but this time it's a good one.

"Not against the idea is not the same as on board." His fingers stop and his hands wrap around my waist as he slides me back and forth across his lap. My whole body flushes with heat and I tip my head back and close my eyes.

"I'm looking for a partner."

I swallow. "I'd like to be that partner, but—"

He waits.

I open my eyes. He's watching me very closely, his hands still gliding over my body, slowly—so, so slowly. My clit throbs against his friction.

He waits.

"I'm scared too, Ronin. But of very different things."

He wraps his arms around me completely and buries his face in my neck, tasting the water on my skin left over from the misting shower spray. "I'll take care of you, Rook."

I take a deep breath and let it out. "I want you to take care of me, Ronin."

His palms slide up underneath my wet hair and then he fists it, just a little, like a claim. It makes me hesitate, but then he pulls me forward until my cheek touches his. "Then let me, just let me put it all together for us. I can make you happy."

Our rocking becomes thrusting, just small movements at first, and then more forceful. I lift up and then ease down on him, making him growl a little. I smile at that, do it again, then again. His left hand fists my hair just as the other slips down to my neck, not a squeeze, but a gentle full palming against my throat, soft and light.

I don't panic at this move. He's done it before and it's always this gentle.

I know him now.

His hand continues down to my breast where he squeezes my nipple until I turn into his mouth and his tongue flicks against mine. My whole body is aching with these small touches. My hips continue their movement, but now I lean forward and then pull back, resting my forearms on his muscular shoulders as I rub myself against him.

He knows me now, too. He knows what I want, what I like. His fingers leave my breast and trace down my stomach, stopping at my crease. He slides his thumb back and forth against that tender spot and I bite my lip as the pleasure rockets up my body.

His other hand drags down my back and slips under my ass, urging me to lift up higher and rock down with even more force.

I let him guide me because even though I'm on top, he's in control.

He's always in control.

He pushes his thumb against my clit, hard, then soft again, repeating the pattern, knowing it drives me wild. I can feel the wave building in me and he does too, so he pulls back and makes me whimper.

"No, Ronin. Stay where you are."

He laughs softly into my ear, his breath hot. My whole back arches, opening myself up to him and then his thumb is back, pushing and making the little nub pulsate against him. He leans down as my arching back thrusts my breasts up to him, and he responds to the invitation by sucking on a nipple.

I lose it. The pulsations turn into short bursts, then explosions. He rocks me up and down harder, more forcefully, then growls against my neck, biting me just hard enough to make me squeal when he releases into me.

We stay still for a second, breathing hard, our hearts hammering against each other.

"Mmmmm," I say.

"Mmm-hmmm," he responds. "I'll make you a deal, Gidget."

I push my face into his neck, my tongue playing with his earlobe. "What deal?" I say, my blow of breath just enough gets a tiny shiver out of him.

"You don't pose with anyone else but me and I won't pose with anyone else but you."

"Oh, I like that deal. That deal sounds like a deal."

"And after this contract, we walk away from modeling."

I sit up straight and look down at him. "Serious? But what about Antoine? Your job here?"

"I actually do have a degree, Rook. I didn't go to college to be King of the Closet, it was just too good of an opportunity to pass up. But we can talk about it after this contract is over, OK? Forget about everything and let me handle it. Can you do that?"

I let out a huge sigh of relief. After yesterday I'm not sure being in control of everything is the way to go. Sure, I still like making my own decisions, but I'm an amateur in this business. Everyone seems to be in on the joke besides me. It would be so much better to let Ronin deal with things.

"I can do that."

He kisses me on the nose and slaps my ass, the smack echoing off the shower walls. That probably shouldn't make me giggle, but it does.

He grins at me with a knowing smile. "All right then, let's go get this job over with, then we can do this again when I wash all that paint off you."

CHAPTER SEVENTEEN

Rook

Everything about this day is different. The mere presence of Ronin changes attitudes and actions. Ford never appears in the art studio and the camera and sound guys are never even supposed to get within ten feet of me. "They have zoom lenses for a reason, Rook," is what Ronin says. Plus, and this really makes me feel stupid, they're not even allowed to shoot me full frontal during painting, only when I'm on exhibition.

That phrase sucks, by the way.

Ronin knows all this stuff and I don't. Of course, I should probably be mad he didn't warn me, he *is* my manager. But whatever. It was my fault for not reading the contract properly. Pretty much everything about this contract is my fault for that reason alone.

Ronin sits off to the side as Spencer paints me up. Spencer is the same, he was never out of bounds during painting. And this outfit is quite interesting.

"Have you done this one before, Spence? You're quick this time."

He looks up from painting the sparkly sequins on the bodice and winks. "I painted Veronica up like slutty Elvis about a dozen times."

"Veronica, that's the girlfriend who didn't get the job?"

"Yeah, we did the Elvis Fest in Vegas last year. She won a pretty big costume contest, even though she's a girl and she wasn't even wearing a costume. That was hysterical, people were pissed. But hey, you can't deny the talent of these fingers."

I look over at Ronin and he's smiling and shaking his head.

"Do you miss her?"

He stops painting. "Little bit. But not enough to give her a job as the Shrike Girl just because she's my girlfriend. And it pissed me off that she wanted that contract so bad she'd fight with me over it. I liked her for her, she liked me for Shrike Bikes."

I have nothing to say to that. I doubt it's true because Spencer is very good-looking and he seems like a funny and easy-going guy, but what do I know? Maybe she's a total gold-digger and he's right?

"Anyway," Spencer continues, "I've painted this outfit more than any of the others. And the bike that goes with it is pretty fucking cool as well."

"Does the bike have a cape?"

He laughs. "No."

"Do I get a cape?"

"Yes."

"Oh, I like that. I'm like a super-sexy naked Elvis girl."

"Yeah, and thanks to your temper tantrum last night, I get Ronin the supermodel as your Elvis counterpart for free." Spencer looks over at Ronin, clicks his tongue, and shoots him with his finger.

"Right," Ronin replies. "But from now on the only lap super-sexy naked Rook will be sitting in is mine." He shoots Spencer back. "So I win."

Spencer mumbles under his breath.

"Are you guys friends again?"

Mumbles from both of them.

"OK, let's change the subject. Let's talk about Ford. Why don't Ronin and Ford get along?" I hear people muttering behind me, back where Director Larry is with Ford. "What'd Ford do?"

No one wants to tackle that one because all I get is silence.

"OK, moving away from things that require you men to talk about your feelings. How'd you get started doing this painting stuff, Spence?"

"Took art since I was a kid. But you know how you were born looking like a model?"

"Yeah." That's true too. I didn't do anything to look this way. It's just how it is.

"Well, I was born to paint up naked girls. That's the only explanation I have for it. I know how to do it, I know how to mix up colors, and I see perspective. I've taken lots of classes and even did a fancy summer apprenticeship with a big-name *trompe l'oeil* body paint artist. She was pretty cool and she never took students, but my dad paid her well, and I wasn't too stupid—her words, not mine. Plus, she was French, and I already spoke French by that time, thanks to Ronin. But, mostly, I just always knew how to do this shit, Rook. Everyone has one God-given gift and painting naked girls is mine. Maybe I'm not curing cancer, but whatever. This is what I got, so I just needed someone to point me in the right direction and show me how to use the gift."

"So you majored in art at school?"

He almost snorts. "*No*, are you kidding? My old man is a filthy rich bastard, but private university prices for finger-painting was beyond even his wasteful tendencies."

"So what'd you major in?"

He looks up at me. "Business, what else? You can't run a business without knowing what the fuck you should do with it."

"Well, you're pretty good at this business stuff, Spence. You have a lot going on professionally. What'd you major in, Ronin?"

Ronin just smiles, like he's keeping a secret.

"What was it, Spencer? Accounting, right?" I look over at Ronin and wink. "Spencer the Businessman Biker and Top

Model Ronin the Accountant. Seems about right."

"Marketing," Ronin says. "I majored in marketing. And that's what I'm gonna do when we quit after this contract."

"Quit?" Spencer is appalled. "You're not quitting, are you, Rook?"

"Afraid so. We're done. Gonna buy a minivan and get desk jobs."

Spencer looks over to Ronin. "Did you do this on purpose?"

"Do what?" I ask.

Spencer stands up and puts a hand towards my face. "Hold on, Rook." He walks over to Ronin. "Did you talk her out of the next deal I was gonna offer? That was confidential."

"I didn't talk her out of anything, Spencer. And as far as I know, she has no idea what the next deal is."

"What deal?"

Spencer ignores me. "I told you, motherfucker. I wanted her for *all* the deals."

Oh shit, what just happened?

"And I told you, she's my fucking girlfriend. She's not a goddamn toy to parade around your shop for the next few years."

"Wait, what?"

Spencer takes a deep breath and then comes back to me. "OK, Rook, since Asshole over there pretty much ruined the surprise, I might as well tell you. If they like how things go in Sturgis and we give them a compelling reason to believe this show will fly, they're gonna offer us a twelve-episode season contract and we'll start filming in September. What we're doing right now is the two-hour pilot. It's a test, really. So if we got that deal, I was gonna ask you to come work for me up in the shop."

"Doing what? Sitting in the showroom naked?"

"Not the showroom, the *shop*. Where I build the bikes."

"But I don't build bikes, Spencer, so what would my job be?"

"Parts girl. You're like a pick-up girl, drive around and get us stuff, drop frames and tanks off at the painters, answer the phone and talk to clients."

"Hmmm." I think about it. I picture myself doing all that normal boring stuff, then look over at Ronin. "It's not modeling. Are you against this?"

I can tell by the look on his face he is, but he's in professional mode right now. "We'll talk about it in private, Rook."

Spencer growls at that answer but just goes back to work on the belt. The rest of the session is very quiet and very tense, but he was almost done anyway, so we're ready for Antoine before it gets old.

This time Ronin is the one who walks me upstairs.

If Elvis was a bike, he'd be this bike. It's even got lights on it—all sorts of gold and white and blue lights, and of course it's painted white, just like the outfit I'm wearing. I catch a glimpse of myself in a mirror and I look so much better than I did yesterday in those bikinis. This outfit is like Elvis if he were a girl and he had on a sexy one-piece bathing suit covered in gems instead of a bell-bottomed jumpsuit. I have the huge sparkly belt, the long pointed collar wrapping around my neck, and just as I'm starting to wonder where the cape is, Ronin appears and shakes it at me.

"Sexy, huh?"

I nod. It really is.

"OK, Rook. Sit for Josie and I'll go change and get ready."

Oh, my heart flutters at that. Ronin in a costume. Josie is watching me as I approach and take my seat in her chair.

"Yeah," she says. "No offense, I'm not sure if you're the jealous type, but seeing Ronin dressed up for his jobs is like the best perk this place has."

I laugh. "Well, I probably should be jealous, but I'm too busy picturing him all up as Elvis!"

We giggle at that and suddenly I wonder if Josie and I could be friends. She starts brushing my hair and I decide to fill in the silence.

"Are you married, Josie?"

"Thirteen years now," she says brightly. "So when you finally meet my husband, hush on the fawning over Ronin stuff. All the boyfriends and husbands around here think us girls are secretly in love with Ronin." She winks. "But it's no secret, Rook. We are!"

I laugh at that too. I can see why. Ronin is a total catch. "Do you have kids, Josie?"

"Four."

"Really? But you look so young and I'd never be able to tell, you're so tiny and cute."

"You have the model genes and I have the baby-making genes." She shrugs. "I like it, so I'm not bitter about starting out as a teen mom. My husband was my high-school sweetheart. We weren't all that bright and well, let's just say I wasn't partying on my graduation night, I was seven months pregnant.

"We got married, and you'd think we were doomed, but it all worked out. I went to beauty school and landed a job here with Antoine and Elise almost right away. And we own a tow-truck business. That's how I met Elise, actually. She was the night dispatcher for us around the same time she was trying to decide if Antoine was the right guy for her. She said she'd give him a chance if he gave me a chance. I was just getting ready to graduate beauty school, no experience or references. And, well, the rest is history."

She's standing in front of me doing makeup and I can just tell she's thinking about her life. All the years that she's spent here in this studio. How Elise changed her luck, maybe.

"Elise is a good person, isn't she?"

Josie smiles. "She's the best, Rook. The absolute best."

I knew this the day I met her. Before she offered me the fake shampoo girl job and saved me from homelessness. I knew Elise was nice by the way she talked to me when she took me into her salon and washed my hair.

But it would've been so great to get a second opinion from someone I trusted. It would've been nice to go grab coffee with a best friend or a mom so I could run everything by them first.

Since I don't have a mom—and even if she was still alive she'd be the last person to ask for advice—and since I have no friends to double check my decisions with either, I decide to trust Josie's opinions instead. Almost everyone who works for Antoine and Elise has worked here for a significant amount of time. I think that counts as a reference.

CHAPTER EIGHTEEN

Rook

Ronin is hot.

Ronin is so fucking hot dressed up as Elvis, I can't keep my hands off him as we sit here on the amazing Shrike Elvis bike. The lights are blinking, Antoine's camera is going crazy, the shutter snapping like wild as he captures this mood we're in, and I'm about to abso-fucking-lutely lose control.

My fingertips trace down Ronin's chest, then begin unbuttoning his shirt.

"I never knew you had a thing for Elvis, Gidge," Ronin says playfully.

I lick my lips as his hands slip inside my cape and grab my ass. I have no idea what we're supposed to be doing on this bike, but no one seems to care that we're just sitting here flirting. The camera keeps clicking and the one time I managed to pry my eyes away from Ronin I-am-sexier-than-Kurt-fucking-Russell-in-*3000-Miles-to-Graceland* and glance at Spencer, his teeth are practically glinting in the sunshine, that's how big his smile is.

He catches my gaze. "Now this, Rook, is what I'm talking about. I'm gonna sell a shitload of bikes with this shoot!"

I continue my task of undressing Ronin, ignoring Ronin's question about Elvis and Spencer's remark about sex selling bikes, but Ronin's still talking. "I mean, shit, Gidge, I might have to wear a costume everyday if this is what it does to you."

I laugh a little, but nothing will deter me from getting him out of this shirt right now. The last button comes undone and

I slip the shirt down his shoulders a little. I suddenly notice Antoine's positive remarks. Of course, I don't understand them, but his tone is pretty clear. He's happy with my performance today as well.

I go for that big belt next, unclasping it and letting it drop to the floor with a thud, then drag the shirt down his arm, the pads of my fingertips caressing his biceps as they fall with the shirt sleeve.

He withdraws his arm and then I repeat this move on the other side, so the shirt drops to the floor next to the belt.

Now we're both naked on top, but being dressed up in paint makes it hard for me to consider myself nude. I *feel* dressed.

Overdressed, in fact.

As is Ronin.

When I look up Ronin's eyebrows are lifted up to his forehead. "What?"

He stretches out, easing himself down on the back fender, blue and yellow light flickering against his face. "Go for it, Gidge."

I lean down on his chest, moving forward just a little, just enough to tease myself, then sit back up, the palms of my hands dragging along his chest, across his abdomen, and then to the snap on his Elvis pants.

It clicks as I undo it.

Ronin draws in a breath.

I unzip his fly.

He lets out a moan.

I bite my lip, thinking about my next move just as Antoine barks out, "OK, we're good."

It's like he does it on purpose.

Ronin sits up, grabs me under the ass, then lifts me up as he stands. He carries me up the stairs to his apartment and sets me down outside the door so he can punch in his key code, then whisks off my cape and tosses it to the floor and leads me down to the shower.

"I'm having déjà vu. How about you?"

He winks back at me. "Give it a minute. This will be nothing like this morning."

And it's not.

Ronin finishes what I started downstairs, his pants dropping to the tiled floor. He pushes some buttons on the shower control panel on the wall and brings up his favorite setting. Steam and drizzle.

When we shower together, it's like being on a tropical island.

The bucket and sponge are waiting, ready for Ronin to wash me off. He swishes the sponge in the bucket and then takes my left arm and drags the sponge down in one long swipe. My head tips back as I open my mouth to suck in a breath. Holy shit, this is just my arm!

He does the other arm, then bends down to caress my legs. "Open them a little, Gidge."

I am immediately wet right where he wants me to open up. But I do as I'm told.

He slides the sponge along the inside of my thigh, then up against my slit, parting it slightly, just enough to make me gasp. When I look down, he's smiling up.

He repeats this motion several times and each time I am so close, but just as I'm about to let it go, he pulls back, relieving the pressure. He doesn't let me come, but instead finishes my legs and moves on to my back. The sponge slides down the middle of my spine, then across my ass, and right between my legs. My clit practically has its own heartbeat right now.

When my back is clean to his satisfaction he turns me around and starts with my stomach, massaging little circles around my belly button, then sweeping down between my legs, just enough to remind me that I'm ready.

He drops the sponge in the bucket, swishes his hand around a little in the solution, then removes the paint from my breasts with his fingertips.

When all the paint has been cleaned, he repeats every single motion with the soap and by the time he's rinsing me with the detachable shower head, I'm about to explode all over him.

It's only then, when the paint is all gone and my body is soft and sweet-smelling, that he presses himself up against me. He's been hard the entire time but when he grinds against my hips, his hands on my ass to guide me along with his motions, he is more than hard. He is solid and thick.

"I love you."

My eyes search his as I take this all in. "I'm not sure what I feel, Ronin, but I really want to say that back to you."

He slides his hand behind my neck and laces his fingers into my wet hair. "So say it."

"I love you, too."

His kiss is immediate, almost before I'm finished uttering the words he was looking for. His mouth opens and I flick my tongue against his. He devours my mouth and for a few minutes we are breathless, moaning, and grasping for one another's most sensual parts. Then he draws back and leads me out of the shower, punching buttons on the control panel to turn it off as we walk by.

I'm still dripping wet when Ronin sweeps me off my feet and sets me down on the bed. He gently lifts my legs up and pushes my thighs apart, then delves down and devours me again.

I'm writhing in seconds, my back arching, my hands fisting the sheets. He pushes my thighs higher, exposing me further, and then sucks gently.

My moans are louder now and I squirm as the feeling becomes too intense.

He slips a finger inside me, sliding back and forth gently at first, then pumping harder as his thumb and tongue swirl against my nub.

I lose it.

I come hard against his mouth, my hands fisting his hair.

He waits, his tongue dipping down as I continue to pulsate from the explosion of sensations. When I'm done he scoots up towards me, his thick erection in his hand, ready to enter.

But I push him back. "Not this time, Larue. My turn. Lie back."

He laughs. "It's not a *quid pro quo*, Gidget."

"I know." I've resisted giving him oral, I have bad memories of it from my ex. But I push that thought away and concentrate on the beautiful, caring man in front of me. He is a gentle lover. So, so gentle. "I want to, Ronin."

CHAPTER NINETEEN

Ronin

I didn't think it was possible to be any more turned on right now, but I am. Her words have turned me up a thousand decibels.

Rook watches me. "I want to, Ronin."

Her eyes are still half-mast from coming hard, her taste still on my tongue. I swallow because this girl—this girl makes me feel more than good. It's like every touch, every look, every sound that comes from her mouth is something sensual and perfect.

"Lie back," she says again.

My crooked grin makes her smile as I lie down next to her. She twists her body, pressing her breasts against my chest, then stretches up and kisses me, just little kisses at first, as if she's deciding if she likes the taste of herself. Then she straddles me and opens her mouth, her tongue done probing, ready for more.

Just as fast, she stops, her body sliding down, her chin rubbing against my stomach muscles as she descends. She plays with my hard-on for a second, then her tongue slides along the slit in my head and dips in for a taste.

Before I can even process how fucking good that feels, her mouth is desperate to wrap me up. She pumps again and again, sucking slightly, tonguing me as she pulls back, then massaging me with her lips as she descends down my shaft.

I give up.

The breath comes out of me in a soft rush as I relax back into the pillows and enjoy her. Fully enjoy her and everything she's doing right now. My whole body is on fire for this girl, my arms ache to flip her over and take her from behind, make her scream my name over and over again.

But I calm myself and suck in a breath between my teeth as I try to maintain control. I moan as the hot air of her laugh tickles the tip of my cock.

"Gidge," I say in a throaty whisper. My hands go to her head, pushing her slightly, compounding her rhythm as she evokes so much more in me than just a desire to come.

"Gidge," I repeat. "Climb on, baby."

She continues with her pumping and sucking but I'm not about to come this way. I sit up and toss her over on the bed next to me, then crawl up between her legs.

She's laughing at me.

"What's funny, Gidget?"

"You love me."

I laugh back. "I do, and I'm going to show you just how much every chance I get." I push her thighs open wider and flick my cock against her swollen clit a few times, back and forth, making her moan. She likes that.

I slide inside when she's in mid-gasp. She's so wet, so ready for me again. I ease in and out, slowly, then harder. Slow pumps become short thrusts, and then deep, penetrating, plunging assaults. Her back arches and her fingernails dig into my shoulders.

This is her signal. Her signal that she's gonna come and there's no way to avoid it.

At least that's what I think it says to her. But to me it says, *Do something spectacular right fucking now, Ronin, and I will make the most amazing noises for you.*

I reach down and play with her, slip between her folds and then sweep up to her clit and twirl my thumb, pushing it around gently in little circles.

She screams this time.

And I can't help it, this girl just does it for me. I lean down and growl into her neck as I come with her.

We fall asleep like this, me clutching her around the waist, her legs twined around mine in a way that makes me feel both wanted and whole. I wake once when she gets up to use the bathroom. But as soon as she returns to my bed I tug her ass up against me and fondle her breasts until we drift off again.

When we wake it's late afternoon. "Hey," I say, squeezing her breast a little. "Wake up, let's not waste the day."

She moans and turns away and I just have to smile. I've never met a girl who sleeps so soundly. She's not a naturally early riser and she's not easy to wake. Ever.

"Rook." I try again. This time I breathe into her ear and her shoulder draws up against my face.

She growls at me.

"Come on, I have plans for us."

"What plans?" she moans.

"Bike ride to the mountains."

"I don't wanna go to Black Hawk, I can't even gamble or drink. It's boring."

"Not gambling, Rook. A ride up to Lookout Mountain. Come on, it's romantic. Besides, it's good practice for the road trip to Sturgis."

She turns. "I thought we were taking an RV up there?"

"We are, but you can't ride into Sturgis in an RV, Gidge." I laugh as I picture Spence RV'ing into Sturgis. "Spencer would be laughed out of town. He said he's working on your bike too, says it's real nice."

"When you'd talk about that? He never said anything to me."

I shrug. "I talked to him last night after you hung up on me."

She reaches out and pokes me in the arm with her fingernail. "You were checking up on me."

"Of course I was. That's my job."

She tilts her head and gives me a dirty look.

"It's not weird, Rook. It's normal. That's what boyfriends do for their girlfriends. This fear you have is unreasonable, ya know."

"I know," she pouts. "But I can't help it. When you say stuff like that it scares me. It feels invasive."

I lie back down and pull her close. The bike ride can wait. "It's not, though. It's normal."

"I don't like people talking about me, it bugs me." She stops and turns her head to look me in the eye. "It really bugs me."

"Well, you're not gonna be able to avoid it, Rook. Your face and body will be all over the world soon. You're in a reality show, you're on book covers in Japan, and a half a million people are gonna be talking all about you at the rally."

She wrinkles her nose at this.

"So I think it's OK if I ask Spencer what's going on. I'm still not sure what to think about what you said last night, about being turned on. I mean, I get it. I've been there. I get turned on too. But I've never had to talk about it with a girlfriend because the only other model I dated who was working with us at the time was Mardee. And I already told you, I was not all that nice to her. I never got jealous over her jobs."

Rook leans over and kisses me softly on the lips. "Sorry," she whispers into my mouth. "I just wanted to be honest. I just wanted you to tell me what it means. I want *you*, Ronin. Not Spencer. Not Billy. You."

"Yeah, well, I hate to disappoint you, but I'm not sure

what it means."

"See, that's why Billy was so helpful. He told me it means nothing." She throws her hands out a little to illustrate her point. "He said he's always turned on, that's what Antoine wants and expects. But that it's meaningless. Even when he sleeps with the girl after, he says. It's meaningless."

"Huh." Billy's a fucking whore. The absolute last guy I want giving my girlfriend advice on what is and isn't normal in an erotic photo shoot. "You wanna do the bike ride?"

"Yeah, it sounds fun. Besides, I think I need to get out of this place for a while. I never go anywhere. I might need to buy a car."

"Why?"

She shoots me a dirty look.

"No, I mean, why *buy* one? I have two cars I never use. Just take one when you need it." Her silence tells me she's got a problem with this. "Rook, I swear, if you say something stupid like *I need my own car so you can't control me,* I'll handcuff you to the bed and show you what domination really looks like."

Her whole face screws up in disgust. "Don't joke. You know that's never gonna happen, right?"

"Yeah, I figured. But that doesn't mean I can't picture you like that. Your bottom bright pink from being spanked." She blushes and I am immediately hard. "Sounds fun, doesn't it?"

She doesn't answer that either way.

Progress.

CHAPTER TWENTY

Rook

The evening with Ronin passes much too quickly. And he was right, as usual. Lookout Mountain has an amazing view of Denver. It's not even that far away, it barely took us thirty minutes to get to the freeway exit, but the winding road that climbs up the side of the mountain—foothill, Ronin corrects me, he scoffs at me when I call these rolling hills mountains—takes a whole lot longer. But I don't mind. I enjoy the vibrations of the bike beneath me. I press my cheek up against Ronin's leather jacket and gaze out at my new hometown as dusk takes over.

By the time we get to a little pull-out along the road, it's almost dark and the city lights down below are twinkling.

Ronin and I both look the part tonight. Matching leather jackets, courtesy of the Chaput closet, faded jeans, and black biker boots. My hair is in braids to keep it under control, and Ronin has one of those WWII helmet knock-offs for protection, but I'm wearing a proper one with the full face guard.

When I'm no longer pressed hard against Ronin's heat, I notice the chill. It's almost always pleasant down in Denver at night, but we're a couple thousand feet higher now, so the temperature dips as soon as the sun disappears over the peaks.

We don't stay long. I know enough about bikes to understand what a ride is and what it isn't. It's not a way to get somewhere, it's about enjoying the journey.

It's fitting for me, really. The journey is the only thing that counts because once you reach your destination, there's always somewhere else to go. Another journey to take.

Life is like that too.

I took a journey when I left Chicago. I struggled with homelessness and hunger. I feared for my safety and eventually, that journey ended with Antoine, Elise, and Ronin.

And now I'm on a new journey. I'm not sure where I'm going just yet. Maybe college. Maybe somewhere else.

Maybe marriage—eventually.

I know that's what Ronin wants, he's not kept it a secret about how much he wants a family. And I'm starting to think about what that means for me. I'm not on board yet, so I don't ponder it too seriously. But I watched Antoine and Elise when we were up at Granby Lake and it's nice what they have. They know each other so well and they're still very much in love.

I'd like that, too.

Someday.

But I'm only nineteen. It's just way too soon to think about forever. I like Ronin. Might even love him. I think he might be the one for me. But my life just started. I just got here. I'm not ready for the things he wants. Maybe I'll never be ready for kids. I'm not even sure about that.

I sigh into Ronin's back as he turns into the parking garage below the studio. We stopped at an Italian place in Golden to eat, and my day is finally catching up with me because I'm dead-ass tired.

I hand my helmet to Ronin and he locks everything up in the garage lockers, and then we take the elevator up instead of the stairs.

He knows I'm tired.

I like this about him. He made an effort to understand me after I told him what happened in Chicago. He pays very close attention to me. And I like that.

Most of the time, anyway. Tonight is one of those times.

When we get to the studio I try to walk up the stairs to his place, but he tugs my hand over to the terrace.

"Awww," I moan.

"Sorry, Gidge," he whispers into my ear as he opens the door. "But we have time for a swing, if you want."

"I do." God, can he be any more perfect? We walk over to the cherry trees and I plop down on the swing as he takes his position behind. He pushes me and my whole experience here at Chaput Studios comes rushing back with the wind as it whips my hair around.

"So, opinions on Ford. You guys getting along better yet?"

"I guess. He's OK."

"How about Spencer?"

I twist around as the swing goes back so I can catch a glimpse of Ronin behind me. "He's funny."

Ronin laughs. "Yeah, he is. He's not a bad guy."

"Is Ford?"

"I hate Ford. Really, seriously, hate his fucking guts."

I'm not surprised. But I am surprised he told me that. Ronin is a professional and the relationship we have with Ford right now is business. Which means what he said was unprofessional. "Wanna tell me about it?"

"Nah, he's not worth it." Ronin stops the swing and takes my hand so we can walk back to my apartment. "Ford said they want you up on Fort Collins this weekend to film you hanging out with Spencer."

"Oh, that sucks. I figured I'd have the weekend off."

"Yeah, me too. But Ford—never mind."

He stops. Maybe because we're at my door or maybe because he realizes he's not supposed to talk shit about a client.

Either way, I don't push it. "Are you coming up there with me?"

He cups my face in his hands and kisses me tenderly on the lips. Just a small, slow kiss with no tongue. "I wouldn't miss it, Gidget. We'll ride up in the truck after breakfast."

I kiss him back a little more forcefully.

He laughs and pulls back. "I'd love to take you in there

right now and make love to you, Rook. But I have some work to do and want to call and check on Clare before bed. So I'll come by in the morning, OK?"

"OK," I say, nodding.

He leans in and kisses me softly again. All the urgency of our earlier tryst is gone and now it's just easy and long. I kiss him back and then lean my head on his shoulder. "I love you," I whisper.

His fingers thread through my hair and he kisses me again, only this time it's on the top of my head. A protective, emotional kiss. "I'm so in love with you, Rook. So fucking in love with you, it scares me."

"But it's a good scary, right?"

He chuckles. "Yes, definitely a good scary." He turns, holding my hand until the last possible second, our fingers not quite willing to let go, and then he slips away and goes back to the studio.

I go inside and plop down on my couch and flip on the TV and channel-surf for a while. It's been a long day, but a good one. It's still pretty confusing. I'm not sure what to make of my job. I'm not sure if getting painted up naked and kissing other guys as part of work is cheating or not. If I was on Ronin's end of things I'd certainly be jealous. And I'm sure he is, but he's got a lot of self-control.

He deserves lots and lots of points for that.

And I'm pretty sure he's pissed off about Ford and Spencer making me go up to the bike shop this weekend, but he handled that well, too. We haven't had time to talk about the next job Spencer wants to offer me, but I'm open to considering it. It's not modeling, and that's good. I don't want to model any more. I've had enough. This contract will pay me a lot of money and I bet if we really do get a whole season of shows on the Biker Channel that will pay pretty well too. Granted, the show is about Spencer and his bikes and body painting, but if I wasn't an important part of that I wouldn't be Spencer's first choice. Plus, by the time that contract comes up I'll sorta be famous all on my own. They'll have to offer me something nice, or else why would I take the job?

They don't know how much I hate this naked stuff. In fact, I should stop whining about it so they think I *want* to take another job, that way I'll have a better chance at negotiating more money if I do get the contract. I could just tell them how much other offers would pay and make them match it.

I smile at this and then turn the TV off, change into some shorts and a t-shirt, and slide into bed.

Exhausted, but not scared.

CHAPTER TWENTY-ONE

Rook

I'm ready right at five this morning but Ford never comes to my door. I can see him out on the terrace, sitting backwards at one of the stone picnic tables on the side of the building, not facing me. He's just kickin' it, like he's got all the time in the world. I watch him for a couple minutes to see what he does if I don't come out. He never checks his watch or even hints that he's waiting for me. Just sits, his arms resting comfortably on the table, his legs stretched out in front of him.

I open my door and he looks over at me and then gets to his feet. "I was beginning to wonder."

"Wonder what?" I ask as I walk over to him.

"If you would show up or blow me off because you have Ronin to run interference now."

"Hey, a deal's a deal, right? And besides, I was watching you for like five minutes and you never once looked like you cared if I came or not."

"I'm not forcing you to come."

"Well, technically, Ford, you are. You asked for this deal and I agreed."

"Yes, but do you really think I'd put the cameras back in if you refused to run with me?"

"Yeah."

He looks over at me with a crooked grin on his face. "I wouldn't, Rook. So if you'd like to skip out, feel free."

I say nothing, just follow him over to the studio door. He holds it open for me, and we walk down the stairs and cross the street. We go to the upper level seats this time and Ford doesn't say a word. Just sets his watch, to time himself I guess, and takes off running up the stairs.

For some reason starting at the bottom and going up seems harder to me. When we run the lower stairs we start at the top and it feels different going down. I trudge up, walk over to the next set, then stomp back down. I'm not as winded as I was the first day, so by the time Ford stops to check his time and head back towards me, I've covered a significant number of rows. I watch Ford's expression as he runs towards me. It's flat. Well, no, not really flat. It's more like a grimace. Like he's determined or something.

When he gets near he stops to catch his breath, leaning over like he always does, like he's about to heave. "Why do you run like that, Ford?"

"Like what?" he asks, uprighting himself briefly, then bending over again. He's so sweaty it drips off his face and plops to the ground.

Surprisingly, this does not gross me out. "Like you're trying to catch someone."

He doesn't look up this time. "Maybe I'm running away from something?"

I shake my head at him. "No, I don't think so. You're not someone who runs away."

He smiles and straightens up, his breath back to normal now. Which means this guy is in awesome shape. Because if that was me, I'd be on the ground gasping like a fish on the beach for like an hour. "You're right. I'm not running away. I never look back, I only move forward."

"Interesting," I say before I even realize the words are coming out.

"What's interesting about it?" He moves forward towards me, his eyes locked on mine. When I back up I find the wall behind me. I press against it as Ford takes a few more steps towards me. "Are you a runner, Rook? Or a chaser?"

I swallow because he's very close now, only a few inches.

He's as tall as Ronin, easy. So I have to turn my head up a little to match his gaze. "A runner," I whisper.

He places his palms against the wall on either side of my body, but he keeps those few inches between us. "Do you look back?"

I shake my head, still transfixed by his stare. "No," I say, gulping a little bit of air. "Or, at least I try not to."

He removes his hands and waves me towards the door that will lead inside to the breakfast burritos. "And how successful are you at moving forward right now?" he asks as we pass through the door and walk down the lobby hallway that curves around the stadium, following the smell of food.

"Well…" I let out a deep sigh. "I'd say average. I'm not dwelling, but I'm not over it yet, not completely, anyway."

He stops walking and grabs my hand. "Over what yet?"

I laugh it off a little and shake my hand free. "I've had a rough life, Ford. I'm new money."

"Ah," he says, like I just gave away a piece of vital information. "So that's why Ronin likes you so much. You *are* damaged."

"Hey, that's fucking rude. I'm not damaged. I had a problem, I took care of it, and now I *am* moving forward."

"Then you're a chaser, Rook. Own it, if that's what you are."

"I'm neither, Ford. Or, maybe I'm both at the moment. I'm not ashamed that I ran. It was the best decision I ever made."

"How did you get here?"

"Where?"

"This moment in time. How did you end up *here*, inside Coors Field, running with me? Where did you grow up?"

It takes me back a minute because I'm so used to Ronin avoiding my past. I watch Ford's eyes as I consider if I'll answer him and he waits me out. Not making a move, not making a sound. Just calm. He exudes patience.

"Chicago," I finally say.

"OK, now tell me how you got *here*."

"I walked across the street with you."

He chuckles a little under his breath. "Did you fly? Drive?"

"Bus."

"Ahhh. That makes sense. So why Denver? What made you want to come to Denver of all places?"

"Well…" I go over to a table near the windows and Ford follows me. We sit across from each other, him facing the sun, and me with my back to it. "I was actually on my way to Vegas but I was sitting across the aisle from these boys going to Denver. And they were watching *South Park* on their tablet the entire ride." I stop to laugh because I love *South Park*. "And that stupid Cartman, he gets me very time, so I was eavesdropping, trying to listen for him to say one of his funny lines."

Ford's serious expression falters and he smiles with me.

"Anyway, they were talking about how those guys who made *South Park* went to the university in Boulder and since my dream has always been to go to film school, I figured it was a sign and maybe Denver was where I was supposed to end up, so I took a chance on fate and just… stepped off the bus."

I wait for Ford to say something but he just shakes his head and smiles.

"What?"

"I went to Boulder and majored in film."

"Hmmm. That's sorta weird."

He stares at me, his eyes bright as his mind takes this in. "Fate, you say?"

"Well, weird, at the very least."

"So you were compelled to get off a bus in Denver because of *South Park* and the CU Boulder film department?"

"Yeah, that's how it happened. I had nothing to lose, ya know? So why not? Why not take a chance here?" I shrug. "It seems to be working out OK."

Ford stands and I stand with him. "Thank you for telling me that, Rook. It's a great story."

"No problem. I'm hungry now, can we eat?"

He smiles and we start walking down the corridor towards the smell of food and when we get close to it Ford guides me over to a table with his hand on my back. I take a seat but he stays standing. "I'll get your food. Stay here."

I sigh. Ronin would probably not like me talking to Ford about personal things, but Ford said Ronin likes damaged girls. No, correction—*young*, damaged girls. And that's me for sure. And I can't help myself, I feel the need to know more about this. If I'm just another project to Ronin, I'd like to figure that out sooner rather than later. I like him a whole lot and I don't want to get hurt.

Ford comes back and hands me my burrito and OJ, then takes a seat across from me and begins to chow down. I do the same and we are too busy chewing to talk for a while. He finishes before me, because he's a guy and every guy I've ever met has been a scarfer when it comes to food. He balls up the foil burrito wrapper and finishes off his juice and then starts with the questions.

"How long has it been?" he asks. "Since you ran?"

I think back and count the weeks. "About three months," I finally say with my mouth full.

"How long have you known Ronin?"

"About a month." I stay quiet, waiting for his next question, but he looks away, like he's thinking about my answer. "Why?" I finally ask.

"I'm just trying to figure out what it means that he claimed you."

That word almost makes me choke. "He didn't *claim* me, Ford. We're dating. That's it."

"Huh." He looks over at me now. "How many men, Rook? Not to get personal, but I'm just curious. How many men have you been with?"

"What's that got to do with anything?"

"Because you come off as very, *very* inexperienced. That's why. It makes you seem far younger than you really are."

I snort. "OK, I guess you're the expert in sexual experience, then?" I just shake my head at him. I'm not answering that question. It sorta pisses me off, in fact. I wrap my burrito back up in the foil and get up and walk away.

He catches up with me as I'm going down the stairs.

"Too personal?"

"Yeah, Ford. I'm sorry I told you that story now. You're gonna do something dirty with it, I can tell." I stop and look at him. My face feels so hot I wonder if I'll start crying. "Just leave me alone." I start to walk off but he grabs my arm firmly and doesn't let go, even when I try to jerk away.

"Wait. I'm not trying to upset you, Rook."

I whirl around. "Like hell you're not! And you're doing a good job of it too, because I like Ronin, OK? I like him and you've told me twice now that I'm nothing to him aside from some sort of project. That he's only interested in me because he has a sick hero complex. And it makes me feel…"

Jesus Christ, Rook. Why are you telling this guy about your feelings? Get a grip.

I yank my arm away and continue down the stairs.

Ford follows me but stays a few steps behind, then catches up and holds the door when I throw it open and go out to the parking lot.

"Makes you feel what, Rook? Used?"

I stop again. "Yeah, OK? You make me feel like he's using me. And he's not, you are! You're using me to mess things up between us and…"

"And what?"

I hold that in and keep walking.

"And keep you for myself? Is that what you think, Rook?"

"No, Ford. That's not what I think."

"Then your instincts are off, because that's exactly what I'm doing."

I stop again. "Holy shit! You are such an asshole!"

And then he smiles. And it's not a smile I've ever seen on him before. It's like all his other smiles were fake and I'm just now seeing real happiness on his face for the first time.

It disarms me. Completely. And he knows it because he moves closer to me, not touching me, but very close. It makes me uncomfortable and I look around, feeling guilty. There's no one else in the parking lot. There are a lot of cars on the street, but we're still a good hundred yards from the street.

"I won't touch you, Rook, don't worry," he whispers. "I'm not a runner and I'm not a cheater, either. Life is long, you are young, and I'm very, *very* patient."

My expression hardens, all traces of insecurities disappear in an instant and I look him in the eyes. "I'm not worried, Ford. Because if you touch me, I'll knee you in the balls so hard it'll be weeks before you can run stadiums again."

CHAPTER TWENTY-TWO

Ronin is waiting for me in the garden apartment when I get back. He's kicking back on the couch watching some news channel. "Hey," I say as I walk through the door.

He throws his hands wide. "Where the hell did you go?"

"I run stadiums with Ford in the mornings now, remember? It's a deal we made to get the cameras out of my bedroom."

"Stadiums." He thinks about this for a second. "Why?"

I huff out a breath. "I just told you to keep—"

"No, why *running*?"

"Well, *I* don't run," I snort. "I mope, shuffle practically. But Ford runs like a maniac. Like he's chasing—" I stop. Because Ronin has a weird look on his face. "Um, I'm not sure what's going on with you guys, you and Spencer and Ford, but you all could use a lesson in poker faces. That's all I'm saying. Because obviously there is something you three are not telling me and it's getting weird."

He turns away from me, hiding.

"Ronin," I say, sitting down next to him. "What's the deal? Is something wrong?"

He looks back to me and sighs. "No, nothing's wrong. It's just we have a very complicated history and—"

I wait a few seconds, but he turns away again, like he needs a moment to think of what to say. "And what?" I prod.

"This whole project is a bad idea. I don't know what Spencer was thinking."

"Because you and Ford don't get along?"

For a second I think he's about to tell me something really important. Like he's got words just aching to get out. But then his expression hardens. "What do you and Ford talk about? When you run together?"

Oh shit! Is he psychic or something? I suddenly feel guilty, even though I did nothing wrong. I'm not responsible for Ford's words. I walked away, threatened him even. "Nothing, really. He just said that I was too young to do this contract, it's probably a very big mistake, and he's not gonna be the one responsible if things turn out bad."

Ronin just stares at me.

"He says there's something wrong with me"—I leave out the part where he said Ronin only likes broken girls that he can try to save—"and exercise will help me cope or some shit like that."

Ronin is absolutely still and quiet, but I only have to watch his eyes to see that his mind is going crazy on the inside.

"Ronin?"

He lets out a long breath. "Stay away from him, Rook. No more running."

"Why?"

"Does it matter why?" He gives me a sideways glance. "If I tell you to stay away from him, isn't that good enough?"

I laugh. "No, it's not. I'm not your pet, Ronin. Maybe I'll run with him tomorrow and maybe I won't but either way, I won't be making that decision based on your orders."

"Since when is asking my girlfriend not to spend time with a guy I don't trust out of bounds?"

He's right, of course. Ford just made a move on me. Maybe not in a normal way, but that was definitely a move. "Ronin, I'm not a piece of property, OK? If you've got information about him that I should know, or you think he' s gonna hurt me—"

"Don't be dramatic, Rook. He's not going to *hurt* you."

"Oh! Me? I'm not the drama queen here, Ronin. That's

you and Ford." I get up and walk outside, not really sure where I'm going, but fuck him. I knew it. I knew as soon as I let him have some control he'd start this caveman shit with me. And I've been there. I see the signs very clearly and right now they're flashing bright red just so I can't miss them. I walk over to the cherry tree swing and then the screen door slaps closed behind me and Ronin follows me over.

I settle in the seat and he's already apologizing as he walks.

"I'm sorry, Rook. OK? I don't mean to set you off like that—"

"Set me off like what? I walked out the door calmly, I'd hardly call that *setting me off.*"

He stops in front of me and my feet scuff against the grass as I wait for him to answer. "You're a runner, Rook. You learned that if you've got problems you can make them go away by walking out. Or getting on a bus and just disappearing. So you walking out of our conversation *was* the perfect example of you being set off."

I laugh. "Sorry, my mistake. I didn't realize marketing degrees required psychology classes as well."

He walks over to me and takes my hand. "OK, just answer me one question then. What part of me asking you to stay away from Ford bothers you? Why do you care?"

"You didn't give me a good reason. If you want me to ignore him then tell me why."

"I—" His phone buzzes and he reaches into his pocket to check the text, saying nothing for several seconds. Then he texts back and turns to me. "Fuck. I have to go back up to Steamboat."

"What? Why?"

"Clare escaped."

Fucking Clare. It's like she's doing this shit on purpose.

"They found her in the nearby woods, so she's OK. But Elise says she's asking for me and the doctors are so pissed off right now, they might kick her out. I'll just stay one night, I'll be back tomorrow, OK?"

"Just like that? Clare's in trouble so you drop everything, drop *me*, to go save *her?"*

He steps forward, takes my hand, and pulls me up off the swing. "Rook, if you were the one who needed help I'd drop everything for you, too."

"But I'm good now, right? I don't need help. Now Clare needs you."

He shrugs. "That sounds like a loaded question, but I'm not sure what you're getting at, so yeah. That's about it. You know where the cars keys are, Gidge. Help yourself to the cars, or whatever else you need, OK?" He drops my hand and turns to leave.

"Wait! Why can't I come with you?"

He turns and gives me a weird look. "It's not a vacation. She's addicted to heroin. She doesn't even know you. She's sick and she doesn't want to see anyone but us. "

"You, you mean, right? Because Antoine and Elise are already there. So she just wants to see *you*."

He leans down and kisses me on the cheek. The fucking *cheek*. "I'll be back tomorrow morning and we'll drive up to Fort Collins together, OK?"

And he turns and walks away.

I swear, I'm so stunned I can't even move. I don't even know how long I sit there out on the swing before I go lie down under the tree. And after that, I have no idea how long I lie there alone, staring up into the canopy of leaves and branches, before Ford is suddenly standing next to me.

"What?" I ask.

"There's a camera in the trees."

"So you heard all that."

"Just agree with him, Rook. I don't care if you ignore me. Don't fight over something so stupid."

I sit up and shield my eyes from the sun so I can see his face. "He thinks you're some creeper, Ford. And you're OK with that assumption?"

He shrugs. "Yes."

And then he turns and walks off. His steps even and emotionless as he crosses the terrace and makes his way inside.

I laugh a little under my breath. This contract was a mistake, but fuck it. I'm making bank right now. When this is over I'll have enough to go to California if I want. Just move to LA and fight for my dream. Because in the last twenty-four hours I've thought about breaking up with Ronin twice and that's not a good sign as far as potential long-term relationships go.

CHAPTER TWENTY-THREE

Rook

Ford is sitting outside promptly at five minutes to five the next morning.

For half a second I consider not going. But I'm already dressed in the stupid athletic shorts and tight-ass top. As soon as I go out he stands and walks to the studio door and holds it open for me. "You surprise me, Rook," he says matter-of-factly as I walk through, mumbling out a *thank you.*

"Why? Because I keep my promises?"

"No, because even though you're smart and capable of a whole lot more than posing naked and accepting your fate as Ronin's project, you choose this life and let people walk all over you."

I snort but I do not even dignify that with a response. Fuck him. He says nothing else the entire walk over and when we get inside he waits for me to choose top or bottom stairs.

I head through the door that leads to the bottom seats because I prefer to start at the top and go down. As soon as we get inside the stadium he takes off and leaves me there. I watch him as I shuffle down my section of stairs. He starts off at a faster pace than usual, like he's turning it up a notch. I shake myself out of this fog Ford has draped over me and concentrate on my own workout. It's not as difficult as it was the first day and when I get to the bottom and start to climb the next section I make a little bit of an effort.

Just a little.

I decide to see how fast I can go and for how long, so I

take off booking it up the stairs. At first it feels good to exert myself like this because I've been angry since yesterday morning and I need to burn it off. I run hard all the way up to the top, then dash down the aisle to the next set of stairs and go down as fast as I can and repeat the mad dash over to the next set. I climb again, fully exerting myself, but soon my thighs are burning and about three-quarters of the way up I have to slow down because they are on fire. I stop and look behind me and let off a little smile. Maybe I'm a total stadium-running loser compared to Ford, but this is a challenging exercise and I didn't do too bad.

I look over to find Ford and to my surprise he's not running. He's watching me. I walk up the remaining steps and he starts heading my direction.

My stomach flips a little at this change-up in our routine.

"What are you doing?" I ask when he gets close enough so I don't have to yell.

"You're ready now?"

"Ready for what?"

"To work."

I'm tired of his cryptic messages. "Whatever, Ford. I just wanted to see how fast I could go for how long. Don't get excited, I'm not about to morph into some health nut. I come here because we made a deal. If you want the deal to be over, stop fucking showing up outside my apartment at five AM. It's real simple. If you're not there, I don't go." He smiles that hidden smile again, and it confuses me for a second. Why is he smiling now? "Are we done for today or what?"

"Do you want to be done?"

"It's up to you, Ford."

"No, Rook, it's up to you. I'm not done, but you're free to go if you wish."

More psychology bullshit from him. "Why are you so weird? What kind of game are you playing with me?"

"Just run the stadiums, Rook. Is that what you want me to tell you? Give you orders? Are you waiting for orders?"

Am I?

I turn and walk away.

Because I might be. I might actually be waiting for him to tell me what to do. It makes me sick when I think about it.

A hand grasps my upper arm and I whirl around.

"OK, wait," Ford says as he looks down at me. "Just answer this, Rook. Do you want to come here with me in the mornings?"

Silence from me.

"Well? It's either yes or no."

I laugh at that. Because it's not that easy. If I say yes and mean it, then I'd have to start asking myself a whole bunch of other questions. If I say no, well, that's just a lie. Because the fact is, I do want to come here with him. I sorta like it. I like the fact that he's outside every morning. He's weirdly reliable. And strangely persistent. "Yes."

He smiles that smile again and my whole stomach flutters. "OK, so get busy then. If you're going to spend time here, don't waste it. Make it count."

And then he turns around and starts running again.

I turn as well and start down my set of stairs at a faster clip. Going down isn't easy at a run because the steps are not even, it's like you have to take two steps forward and then step down. It's an odd rhythm. My legs hurt when I get to the bottom, but not in the same way as when I go back up. I'm slower this time, my muscles more strained, but I have to admit, when I get to the top I feel pretty exhilarated. I continue this way, and with each set I get slower and slower. By the time Ford turns to head back my way I'm sitting down leaning up against the cinder-block wall.

He leans over and lets the sweat drip as he catches his breath.

"So you gonna tell me who you're chasing? Or are you the only one who gets to ask questions?" Two can play this game.

He straightens, just like he did yesterday, but instead of

turning away he slides down the wall and sits next to me. "You have no idea who Ronin is, Rook."

Everything inside me does a little flip. "What?"

"It's not a disparaging remark. Just a fact."

"But you do? That's what you're saying?"

"I do," he says matter-of-factly. "I've watched him in some very stressful situations, and he's seen me under the same circumstances. We know each other well."

"So when he tells me you're fucked in the head, then that's just as true as you telling me he's only using me to play out his hero fantasy."

That smile again. I have to look away and wait for his answer.

"My father was a famous psychiatrist. I was a weird kid, I liked reading and computers and I wanted to be like my dad, so I read all his books on human behavior and psychology and I used to freak people out in school by diagnosing them with clinical disorders and fucking with their school records online."

He laughs and when I look over at him I can't help myself, I smile at his huge grin.

It's the first personal thing he's ever told me. "Are you using that psych bullshit on me right now? By confiding in me with this sincere admission of childhood nerdiness?"

He grins again and this time his smile lights up his brown eyes. "You know, you're very smart. You don't belong here. And I might've come across a little strange back in school, so I can't blame Ronin for his opinion, plus I pulled a fucked-up prank on him once. It was stupid and childish, and not something he'd forget easily. But I'm not trying to make your life difficult, Rook. I'm just trying to make you stronger."

"So I won't need Ronin."

He turns to look at me and now the smile is gone. My stomach knots up as I meet his gaze. "Yes. That's why. I have a disadvantage here because I don't want people to need me like Ronin does. I don't want to slow down for someone,

Rook. I want someone to keep up with me."

"But that's selfish."

"Why?"

"Because if you like someone you should want to help them."

"I am helping you."

I roll my eyes at him. "Not me, specifically. I just think that if you like someone you'd be willing to give up a little piece of yourself to keep them. If you really liked someone, you'd be OK with slowing down."

"All right, then why did you insist on taking this contract when Ronin was against it? Why not give up that choice to please Ronin?"

"Because I like making my own choices, Ford. So if I want to model nude for a butt-load of money, so what? I'm allowed to do that and it's no one's business but mine. "

"Just because you *can* make that choice doesn't mean you *should*. There's a big difference between being in control of your future and making bad decisions."

I shrug. "So?" But I laugh a little because I sound like a two-year-old.

"OK," he sighs. "Would you like my childhood psycho-babble interpretation of what you're doing right now?"

I swallow. Do I? Not really, but this conversation with Ford is oddly compelling. "Go for it."

"You resist Ronin's advice because you're not ready for it yet. But at the same time you need someone slow and controlling very badly right now. Just like I need someone free and fast. Whatever it was that happened to you, you're looking for someone to make it better, but for some reason you're having a hard time admitting that to yourself. So you're in this weird in-between stage that justifies mistakes in the name of freedom. And whatever it is you're trying to fix, I'd just like to say Ronin's not the answer. Because there's only one person who can fix that mistake you made, Rook."

"Me?" I ask in a whisper as I watch his eyes.

"You," he answers softly. "I'm not trying to fix you, I'm just trying to give you the tools to fix yourself."

"I actually already knew all that stuff, Ford. And besides, I've already saved myself."

He chuckles under his breath. "Not quite, Rook. You're like Clare right now. In treatment but resisting. It's a long road to recovery."

He gets up and offers me his hand. I accept it and he pulls me to my feet. We skip breakfast and walk back across the street and despite the very personal nature of our conversation today, we part ways in silence when he gets to his car.

Ford is one weird guy.

I go home and climb back into bed, tired and relaxed from the morning exercise.

CHAPTER TWENTY-FOUR

"Hey," Ronin whispers in my ear as he settles against my body later. "You awake?"

I roll over and look at him. "Yeah, how's Clare?"

He sucks in a long breath. "She's iffy."

"She can't kick the heroin? Or what? I don't understand what's going on."

"It's not an easy habit to kick, Gidge. It's got something to do with brain chemistry, she thinks she's dying but it's the withdrawal symptoms. We're just trying to get her over the worst of it." He pulls me into his chest. "What'd you do while I was gone?"

"Ran with Ford, slept, moped." I look up at him and smile. "Waited for you to come back."

"How is Ford?"

"He's weird, Ronin. He's a weird guy."

His whole body stiffens underneath me for a second, then relaxes. "What'd he say?" He sounds worried.

I sit up and look down at him. "He said I like being told what to do."

This makes Ronin pull away. "What?"

"Yeah, some crap about waiting for orders."

"That guy is unbelievable."

"Why?"

"Never mind, Gidge. But if you're interested in taking orders, then take mine. Stay away from him. He's not a nice guy."

I say nothing.

"Let me guess, he said the same thing about me?"

"Yeah, sorta. He said you like broken girls so you can fix them. Do you think I'm broken?"

He nuzzles into my neck. "You're so strong, Rook. You're the farthest thing from broken I've ever seen. Please stop running with him. He's a mind-fuck. He does it on purpose. His father was some big-shot psychiatrist, just as nasty as Ford before he died. Ford is one fucked-up dude. And you wanna know why I hate his fucking guts? Because when I was in the tenth grade and he was a senior, he looked up the police report about my father, made copies of it, and then plastered it all over school. Antoine went ballistic, but Ford's father donated a bunch of money to the school and nothing ever happened to him. He's a total asshole."

But this revelation has lost its shock value because Ford preemptively confessed all this. "Then why do this project, Ronin?"

"Antoine and Elise wanted the contract and I'm only one-third partner. They're socking money away like crazy for something they're not sharing with me. So there was nothing I could do. It's not Ford's money, anyway, it's the Biker Channel people. But enough about Ford. I missed you and I'm sorry I just walked off like that. Antoine's desperate to make things right with Clare. This is our last chance, you know? She's just a total mess."

I snuggle into him. I really want to love Ronin and I'm not sure Ford knows what he's talking about. He hasn't seen Ronin in a long time. So even if Ronin used to be looking for a girl to save, that doesn't mean he's still like that now.

His hands slide up my t-shirt and I gasp as he pokes my ribs. "What," he asks innocently, "is the problem, ma'am?"

I twist and squirm as he continues to poke me, giggling as I try and get away from his tickling touch.

"Ma'am, are you resisting arrest?" He leans down to sniff me. "Have you been drinking? I might have to taste you to find out." He kisses me, just a little tease to see if I'm interested. My mouth opens and our tongues tangle and tumble together.

Oh, I am so interested.

He nuzzles into my neck, then bites my earlobe gently and kisses his way down my throat, cups one breast while he sucks gently on the other.

"Wait! I have to confess something."

"Ma'am, I'm gonna have to ask you to remain silent." He tips his head up as he slides down the bed then positions himself between my legs.

"But I have a confession."

He looks up at me and grins. "I'll use it against you, ya know."

"I understand."

"OK, confess."

"I'm hiding drugs," I say with a stupid grin.

"Really?" His eyebrows waggle at me.

I bust out a laugh and nod. "Yes."

His hands go for my shorts. "I'm gonna have to strip-search you then. Sorry, ma'am. Just following procedures." He pulls down my shorts, taking my panties at the same time. "Take off your shirt, Rook." He breaks character and it comes out as a command.

But it's pretty hot the way he says it so I sit up and pull my t-shirt over my head. His gaze falls to my breasts and then he leans forward and sucks on my nipple again, using his fingertips and tongue at the same time to make it bunch up and get hard.

"I love that," he says as he drags himself back down my body, sitting up slightly to grab my legs under the knees and push them forward. His tongue teases little circles around my nub and then dips inside me, twisting and tasting. His hands slide up my ribcage and he palms both breasts, hard, then softly. My hands go to his hair and I fist it and push his mouth into me. His hot breath on my most tender parts is about to push me over the edge.

He pulls back just as the intensity starts to build and I moan. He slides back up and kisses my mouth. I draw my legs up and grind against his erection through his boxer briefs.

"Take those off," I say. If he can command, then so can I.

He grins and laces his fingers through my left hand. I'm just about to think that's totally sweet when he lifts it slowly over my head, gently lets go and wraps my palm around the wrought iron bars of the headboard. He repeats this exact same move with my other hand until both are above my head grasping hold of the bars.

"Stay still, Rook."

I know what he's doing and even though it sorta ticks me off that he's pulling this dominant shit with me, it also sorta turns me on. So I do stay still. I watch him as he gets up and rummages through my drawers until he comes up with a silk scarf.

"Ronin—"

"Shhh. Just quiet now," he says as he comes back over to the bed. "You're not being restrained, Rook. You wanna take it off, just take it off." He waits to see what I'll say. "OK?"

He's waiting for me to give him permission. I've modeled with him enough to know if he asks me a sexual question like that he wants an answer. "OK."

His grin is immediate. "Lift your head up a little." I do and he ties the scarf around my eyes. The scarf is yellow, so it's not dark. I think he did this on purpose because I know for a fact there are black scarves in that drawer. He picked a yellow one so while my sight will be restricted, it won't be dark.

When he joins me in bed he's missing his boxer briefs. He slides between my legs and I feel his firm erection against my thigh. My heart rate kicks up a few notches as the excitement begins to build.

I'm definitely turned on and that surprises me because I just handed him control. I suck in a sharp breath between my teeth as he starts with kisses. This time they are hard and desperate. My breathing gets all ragged and I push myself against him, rubbing a little. He enters me and we find our rhythm. There is nothing scary about this at all.

"Rook," he whispers into my neck. "I want you in my bed every night." He thrusts into me and I gasp and buckle my back, holding onto the iron bars so tight it almost hurts. He repeats that move over and over—our bodies hard and fast one moment, then still, or slow the next. He pulls out, almost completely out, then slides back inside me. And again, he varies the rhythm so just as I'm getting used to his motion, it changes and the new sensations demand my attention.

He leans down into my neck and lets out a steamy breath of desire. "It feels good to give in, doesn't it?"

"This feels good." I can feel his smile against my skin and I smile too. "But maybe next time I can blindfold you?"

"You wanna be on top, Gidge?"

He likes me on top and I like it too. "Yes, please."

He growls against my neck again. "You have nice manners, Miss Walsh. Now let go of the headboard." I do and before I know what's happening he flips us over and I'm straddling his waist. My hand goes up to the blindfold. "No," he says, stopping me with a firm grasp. "Leave it."

I obey, then lift up and wrap my palm around his thickness. We are both very ready. I guide him inside me and then let myself dip down. His hands are on my hips, encouraging me to move back and forth instead of up and down. This drives me crazy and he knows it.

"Come here, Gidge." He gently grabs my shoulders and pulls my upper body down on top of his muscular chest. "Stay right here." And then he takes over, alternating between thrusting and sliding me against him in just the right way so that my clit is throbbing with the friction. I draw my knees up a little so I can push myself against him.

"God, you feel so good, Rook." His hands are on my ass now, squeezing, and then he lifts up and gives me a small smack. Not enough to hurt but definitely enough to make me want more. The next time he does it I moan and increase my movement, lifting up and then slamming down on him. "Yeah, that's nice," he says and when the hand smacks down for the third time I explode.

I come so hard I can't stop the scream.

CHAPTER TWENTY-FIVE

Rook

Fort Collins, or FoCo as Ronin likes to call it, is a about an hour's drive north of Denver. Spencer's shop is just northwest of the city outside a tiny town called Bellvue. It sits on a large piece of land that bucks up against the Cache La Pouder River and the shop is really a large barn behind a massive white farmhouse.

This place is totally cute.

Ford, being the asshole that he is, put a car cam in Ronin's truck for the ride up so we dutifully said next to nothing the entire time just to piss Ford off. Now that the crew is back I'm less enthusiastic about being chatty, so I let Ronin do all the talking. He's discussing things with Spencer and Team Rook is messing with the microphone when Ford walks over to me.

I do my best to ignore him, but it's not easy because he just stands there and waits out my silence.

"What?" I finally ask as I turn to look up at him.

He shakes his head at me. "Don't let him talk for you, Rook. Stop moping about the cameras and make decisions. This is your life they're discussing." And then he walks off.

He's right, I have to admit that. I should be over there talking about this. I walk over to Ronin and Spence and Ronin puts his arm around my waist and pulls me close as he continues talking. "Two places," Ronin says to Spencer. "That's it."

"Two places, what?" I ask.

"Four, Ronin. I need her to meet everyone on this trip so

we get a good rapport going with the locals. I get that you don't want her doing the whole season, but she already signed a contract for the pilot, and the purpose of the pilot is to generate good footage so we get the whole season."

"What places?" I ask again.

"Spencer, she was contracted to do modeling, not be your errand girl. She's a *model*, not your bitch."

"What's going on?"

"Yeah, but the modeling included the reality show, so technically she is my bitch."

"Spencer—"

"Rook," Ronin says, a little exasperated. "Please, just let me manage the contractual stuff, OK?" He kisses me on the head and points over to the far end of the shop. "There's your bike, go check it out."

Hmph. I walk off. Should I be mad at that exchange? He's my manager, he's just doing his job. I look back for Team Rook to see if they've sorted the microphone yet, but they are still busy setting things up. I stop and check out the bike I chose last month when I was at Spencer's showroom and he painted my back up. It was just a plain bike back then, reminiscent of a classic Triumph with a flashy turquoise tank. Now it's all turquoise. The frame, the fenders, and even the long classic leather seat.

But the thing that really makes this bike stand out now is the logo. Every bike gets its own logo and my bike is called the Shrike Rook. It's so perfect I can hardly contain my glee! It's got a cool swirly feathered blackbird in the middle of a blood red circle and the letters are in a font most heavy metal bands could appreciate. The girly feathers repeat on the fenders and are embroidered on the seat.

"It's nice, huh?" Ford asks.

"God, yes! He said he'd customize it a bit, but I never imagined he'd go to all this trouble. It's… *stunning*." I laugh a little and look over at him.

He's not even smiling.

"What?"

"That was underwhelming, Rook. You didn't even get them to look at you."

I let out a long breath. "Ford, he's my manager, that's his job. Now leave me alone."

"Rook!" Ronin barks at me from across the room. I can see Ford give me a look out of the corner of my eye but I ignore him.

"Yeah," I reply, turning to walk back over to Ronin.

He meets me halfway, throwing a pissed-off look at Ford who is still back by the bike. "OK, we've agreed to three stops at the different vendors. They're putting the cameras in the truck right now. You drive to three places around town. The painter, the chrome guy, and the upholsterer. Just drop off some bullshit parts, it's all fake, so don't worry about that. Chat the people up, flirt a little maybe, then come back. Ford and your crew will follow in the van. When you get to the shops, let the crew do everything first so they can get shots of you pulling in the parking lot, entering the building. Got it?"

"Yeah, sure. Are you coming with me?"

"Ah…" He hesitates. "No, Elise called, they need me up in Steamboat again, so I'm just gonna drive up there real fast and I'll be back soon. Tonight, probably, tomorrow at the latest."

"What? But it's far, right? You'll never be back that fast!"

"It's only three hours from here, Gidge. I swear, this is the last time, OK? She's just being a freak. I'll be right back. You'll be working anyway, you'll never miss me." And then he does it again. He leans down, kisses me on the cheek and walks off, calling out some last-minute bullshit to Spencer as he goes.

I look back at Ford and he's frowning. He walks over to me. "I'll ride with you, Rook."

"No," I say. "I can drive myself, thanks."

The parts truck is a big-ass mother, red, with a huge ol'

Shrike Bikes logo on it. It's like a twin to the one Spencer drives. It's even got flashy chrome exhaust pipes and rims. When I get in, I feel powerful.

I laugh. I have a thingy in my ear so I can hear Ford and a necklace with a microphone on it. They're worried about me getting lost even though they've punched all the addresses into the GPS, so he's talking in my ear as I get situated.

"What so funny?" he asks.

"I love this truck. I might have to buy me one. Ask Spencer if I can have it."

Ford repeats what I said and I can tell he's laughing. I barely make out Spencer's retort, but Ford repeats it for me. "He said if you help him get the full season, this will be one of the many signing bonuses he offers up for the contract."

I buckle myself in, then turn the ignition. The beast rumbles to life and I let out a little squeal. "OK, I'll do my best, Spence." Thankfully this thing is an automatic, so I put it in gear and gun it out of the parking lot, Ford and Spencer following along in the van with the crew, yelling in my ear to slow down.

But my foot has other ideas. I haven't driven in a while and I've never driven a truck. My lead foot is getting even heavier now, so the beast lurches forward with power. I roll my window down and pump my fist back at them as I whoop it up.

And promptly get flashing red and blue lights for my trouble.

"Oh, shit! The po-nine's here!"

"Rook," Ford says very seriously in my earpiece, "do you have a license?"

I pull off to the side of the totally abandoned road. How the hell did the cops even see me out here? We're like ten miles out of town. "Yes, but it's still Illinois."

The cop pulls in behind me and then the van pulls in behind the cop. Spencer jumps out and tries to run interference. He shakes hands with the cop and they walk up to my window together.

"Ma'am—" I'm suddenly having flashbacks of Ronin checking me for drugs and a laugh bursts out.

Spencer and the cop look at me funny.

"I'm not drinking, I swear."

"What?" the cop asks.

"I'm just saying, I'm not drunk or anything, officer. It's just I've never driven a truck like this before and it was so much fun, I got a little carried away." I stop to bat my eyelashes at him. "I'm sorry, I'll tone it down, OK?"

"License and registration."

Fucktard. I reach into my pocket and pull out my license and hand it over. Spencer's already on the other side of the truck fishing through the glove box for the insurance card and registration. When he finds them he hands the papers to me and I pass them along.

The cop takes them, eyeballing Spencer as he shuffles through the glove box, trying to hide a gun under some Dairy Queen napkins. "Please tell me that's not what I think it is."

"It's permitted, Scott. You wanna see my concealed carry card?"

"Only if it has *her* name on it, Spencer. She's the one driving the truck."

I glance over at Spencer and raise my eyebrows. He just shakes his head until the cop walks back to his car and gets inside.

"Goddamn it, Rook! You're on the road thirty seconds and you get pulled over!"

"Am I gonna get busted for that gun in the glove box?"

"I'm not sure. He could be a dick about that, but it's not technically illegal—we could fight it. I forgot it was in here to be honest, I have guns stashed everywhere. And you driving like Danica Patrick isn't fucking helping the situation. This might be the Wild West, but you can't piss off the locals like that, Rook!"

"That's not fair, Spencer! It's the middle of nowhere!" I

look around trying to figure out where the cop came from but all I see is a little dirt road that leads up a hill and some cows munching on grass across the way.

"Well, if you'd listened to me when you were busy gunnin' it, I would've told you that a cop lives right up that road and that's where he eats his lunch every day."

"Oh."

Ford walks up and leans in my window. "This is good TV, Rook. Nice going."

"It wasn't a plan, you dickbitch," Spencer growls at him. "This guy hates my guts and he just saw my fucking piece in the glove box, so let's not piss him off, OK?"

We wait there in silence for what seems like eternity and then the cop finally comes back, writing something down on a pad of paper.

"Scott," Spencer says, trying to begin the negotiations that are surely coming. "Don't be an asshole. You know my trucks are legal, you know that gun is mine. She's new, she was having a little fun, she's—"

"She's got a missing person's report out on her in Illinois. Some guy who says he's her husband, Jon Walsh."

I lean out the window and puke right on Ford's shoes.

CHAPTER TWENTY-SIX

Rook

"Rook?" Spencer and Ford are saying my name together but all I can do is try to remember how to breathe. "Rook? Stop, Rook. Look at me!"

"Get her out of the truck. Take her out!" The cop is pushing Ford to get out of the way and trying to open the door but I'm grasping onto the window and pulling in the opposite direction because I feel like I'm dying.

I'm dying.

He's found me.

I grab at Ford's shirt, pulling him towards me as I gasp for breath. "Help me! I can't—"

"She's just hyperventilating. Rook, look at me." I look up at the cop and he's pointing to his eyes. "Look at me, OK? Can you look at me?"

I nod, my breathing becoming harder and harder.

"Do you have any breathing conditions? Do I need to call an ambulance?"

I shake my head as I continue to sob and gasp for air.

"OK. Listen, I'm not going to hurt you, I'm just going to put my hand over your mouth and pinch one nostril closed. Then you can only breathe through one side of your nose. This will help you calm down, OK?"

I nod and he does what he described. I struggle at first because it reminds me of being suffocated by Jon, but he keeps a firm hold over my mouth and talks to me in soft, soothing words. "Slow down, OK?" He looks me in the eyes.

"Slow."

I try, but it's very hard to stop the chain reaction inside my body. I shake all over as I try my hardest to get my breathing under control. And then slowly, after many minutes, he removes his hand and I am not gasping.

And then I just cry. "He's gonna find me!"

I just cry.

"Rook," the cop says. "Don't cry, OK? No one's gonna find you. You're OK. If you start crying, you'll have another attack. Just calm down."

I stop the sobbing but the tears still come. They pour out in rivers and roll down my cheeks. "He's gonna find me. He's gonna know where I am!"

"Who, Rook?" Ford pushes the cop out of the way and puts his hand on my shoulder. "Who's gonna find you?"

"My ex, Jon. He's gonna know." I look over at the cop. "You ran my name and it triggered the report, right?"

"Yeah, but he won't have access to that, you don't—"

"He's a computer forensics specialist for the Chicago PD!"

The cop is stunned silent because I'm sure he's seen this scene play out a hundred times. There's only one reason for a girl to act this way about a man from her past.

"Scott, can we just take her home?" Spencer asks from the passenger seat. "If you're gonna write a ticket, do it fast, OK?"

"No, you're good." He looks past me, over to Spencer. "Sorry, dude. I had no idea. It was just a stupid traffic stop."

"Get in, Rook," Ford says, taking my arm. He opens the door to the back cab and pushes me in, then follows me. "Drive, Spencer."

Spencer climbs over the console and plops down in the driver's seat and starts up the truck. He turns around and takes us back to the shop. When we get there, Ford talks into his little microphone and tells the crew to turn off the cameras. Then he and Spencer take me into the house and sit me down on the couch.

"OK, I'm not gonna fight with you about this, Rook," Ford says with a hard edge to his voice. "I'm only gonna ask you once. Is this man dangerous?"

I nod and the tears start again.

"How dangerous? Does he fight men? Or just women?"

"Just women, I think."

Both Ford and Spencer exchange a sort of conspiratorial look.

"Is he really your husband?"

I cry harder as I look up at Ford and nod. "He is. He made me!"

"OK, that's enough, Ford. She's had enough now. I'm calling Ronin. He's probably not even halfway yet." Spencer pulls out his phone and messes with the screen. We listen together as it dials Ronin on speaker.

It goes straight to voicemail.

"Shit, no service in the mountains. I'm not leaving this kind of message on voicemail, Rook. So we'll just have to wait until he gets back in range near Steamboat and I'll try again later."

I am suddenly exhausted and I just nod and lie down on the couch, my face buried in the pillow.

Ford sits down on the coffee table as Spencer goes outside to run interference with the camera crew coming up the front steps. "You're safe here, you know that right? You're totally safe here."

"I don't feel safe, Ford. I feel the opposite of safe."

"This is your damage, isn't it? You ran from *him*, didn't you?"

I nod my head into the pillow.

"And somehow you found Ronin, and he figured it out. Because I know you didn't tell him. You're not a teller, are you, Rook? You keep secrets, don't you?"

"Just stop, Ford. I'm not in the mood."

He hesitates for a second, then takes a deep breath. "I

have to confess, I've never seen someone have a panic attack like that. I thought you were dying."

I turn over a little so I can look up at his face. I'm not sure what I expect, but it isn't sympathy like I get. "I felt like I was dying, too. I thought you were a mental psychosis prodigy, Ford? How could you never've seen a panic attack?"

He laughs out a little bit of air. "I'm an armchair therapist—"

I watch him struggle for words for a few seconds and his eyes dart back and forth as he looks me in one eye, then the other. His expression becomes very serious. "What?" I ask.

"You really scared me."

"Sorry."

"You need to get a divorce."

"I can't see him again, Ford. I can't. I'm not just not capable of handling that. I'm not."

He looks away and looks off into the distance. "Just leave it to us, Rook. We'll handle it."

"What's that mean?"

Ford shrugs, like this is nothing. "I'm sure Ronin's going to ask for favors when he gets back."

"I don't understand."

"Just relax, OK? He won't hurt you again. You should just stop worrying about that right now."

"The hurt's inside, Ford. He doesn't need to be here to hurt me." I watch his expression carefully as he absorbs my words. This uncharacteristic version of Ford. The one who says he's scared and who talks soft and reassures me. I'm not sure who this guy is and it's making me nervous.

"Do you want me to leave you alone?"

I nod yes because my chest hurts with each hiccup of air left over from crying and hyperventilating and my eyes are burning so bad I can't keep them open anymore. "I just want to close my eyes, OK? Just for a minute."

"We'll be right outside if you need anything."

I turn away and face the back of the couch, running

through all the bad days of my previous life. The psychological torture Jon put me through, the verbal lashings, the physical punishment. My head is throbbing so bad I almost want to throw up again.

But I think of Ronin instead. Of all the ways he's treated me nice since I met him. Even Ford, who is still a very weird guy who probably has some not-so-innocent intentions with me. But he's nice too, and he seems to care.

And Spencer, and Antoine, and Elise. Even Billy and Josie.

I have a whole new life filled with people who are nice. People who don't think it's OK to hurt me.

But what if Jon decides he needs to hurt them too?

I start crying again, because I can handle him hurting me, but I would never be able to live with myself if he hurt one of my new friends.

CHAPTER TWENTY-SEVEN

Ronin

Clare's sleeping when I finally make it to the treatment center just past two. Antoine and Elise are already back at their little apartment and I'm not even gonna bother stopping in there, I just want to make sure Clare knows I'm still around. I sit down next her and smile when she begins to wake up. She's so much better than she was last week. Not out of the woods yet, but definitely better.

"You're back," she mumbles, still very drowsy from the methadone treatment.

"I said I would be. You didn't need to panic, you're gonna give Elise a heart attack, making her call me and threatening to stop treatment if I don't come."

"I was afraid you'd ditch me for that girl."

"Well, I wouldn't ditch you. It's not an either-or choice, Clare. You'll like her, you'll see."

"Are you staying?" She's having a hard time keeping her eyes open now, it's only a matter of time before she dozes off again.

"No, sorry. I have to get back. But I'm rooting for you, you know that right?"

She's out. And it's a good thing, too. Because if she was at the tail end of her dose instead of at the onset, she'd be a lot harder to deal with. It sucks to say it, because it's all kinds of wrong, but she's so much nicer when she's sedated.

I go back out and tell the reception girl I'm leaving, then get back in my truck and start the three-hour drive all over again.

I've been trying not to think about Spencer's phone call, but it's hard not to, now that I'm heading back and there's nothing else to occupy my time. This makes the drive back to the Shrike Shop agonizing because all of the calm that came from seeing Clare asleep and getting better has been wiped away by Spencer's words. They just repeat over and over in my head. Panic attack. Missing person's report. Married.

That fucker *married* her.

The rage inside me as I picture her being legally tied to that violence is almost too much and by the time I pull the truck into the driveway, I'm ready to kick someone's ass.

Ford and Spence break from the crowd of crew members out near the shop and start walking towards me. I just stand still, trying to calm myself. Spencer recognizes the look on my face and jerks his head out towards the woods.

It's like *deja vu* as the three of us veer off the driveway and head north towards the little bend in the river. Even when we meet up, we say nothing, just continue walking until we are under the cover of the trees. Once there we follow the little footpath down to the river bank— the sound of rushing water just loud enough to layer over our words and make them unintelligible should anyone be listening.

Old habits.

I look at Ford, then Spence, and state matter-of-factly in a low voice, "This dude's gettin' wiped. Let's vote."

"I'm in," Spence says.

"I'm in," Ford says.

"I'll wait and talk to her, of course, but I don't see a way around it. It's done."

We walk back out, part ways in the middle of the yard, and I head to the house and they veer off back to the party.

I stand outside for a minute to calm myself, then reach down and pick a pink daisy from the front garden. It's just a weedy little thing, half wilted from the afternoon sun, but I want to brighten up her day and this is all I have.

I open the door quietly. Spence said she was asleep on the couch the last time I talked to him on the phone, so I make my way over to the living room and ease myself down in the large leather chair across the room.

When she told me what happened to her back in Chicago I processed it, then tucked it away. I've met lots of asshole guys who hit girls. I've met lots of girls who get hit. But I've only ever dated one besides Rook.

That's how I caught on to her erratic behavior so fast when she showed up. I knew the first moment I saw her crouching down in that stairwell outside the studio door that someone had mistreated her. But I had no idea how sick that fucker really was until she told me about the beating that finally convinced her to leave.

She made it clear that she wasn't interested in getting the guy back or putting him away. And I don't blame her one bit. But I should never have agreed to her request. And I have no excuse. Spencer was right there. Ford was on his way. It was almost too perfect.

But maybe a blessing in disguise. We know what we're up against now. Computer forensics specialist with the Chicago PD is nothing to dismiss and had we not known that little detail before making plans, we'd almost certainly be fucked.

But we are far from fucked now.

Rook inhales quickly several times, proof of her earlier panic attack betraying her resting body.

I'm shaking, that's how pissed off I am. I want to kill someone.

I rub my hands across my face and take out my phone to text the accountant. I instruct him to move all her money to her bank account, put it all in plain sight—to hell with the penalties, just move that shit now. I'll pay her back.

The secret to the perfect job is to keep it easy. Very predictable.

I've thought about this job all the way down the mountain. And I might not know him all that well, but if he's a hacker he's into two things. The thrill of penetrating security firewalls and money.

Rook's got a nice little stash of money right now. Only fifty grand or so, but still. If you could steal fifty grand in an afternoon and be guaranteed to get away with it, you would.

And he will.

Men who hit women are also easy to read, I know this from the very first job Spence, Ford and I pulled just before Mardee died. Those assholes think their women are property. This Jon guy sees Rook as something he owns.

In my opinion this is the perfect combination. Half money-lusting hacker, half misogynist woman-beater.

Because that makes him vulnerable to money and sex.

Two things I can most definitely dangle in front of him, then twist it around so bad, he'll never know what hit him.

This is what we used to do.

Your first impression of Spencer should be dumb. There's just no way around that, in high school he always looked the part of the big dumb jock. And now that he's all tatted up, he's just switched over to being the big dumb biker.

Your first impression of Ford should be well-dressed asshole, but maybe a little on the weak side. Not buff like Spence, but lean and fast. He plays that part well. Snooty, rich, privileged, soft hands, soft words, living off his name and his family's wealth.

Your first impression of me should be honest, trustworthy guy. Good-looking, charming, happy, and eager to help and please. A rule-follower who wants to forget where he came from.

Your first impressions would be dead-ass wrong in all three cases.

Because Spencer is a certifiable genius, Ford is as ruthless as they come, and I'm an accomplished liar.

Together we pulled off a series of con jobs in college that netted us tens of millions of dollars—in secret, untraceable bank accounts, of course.

And I have a plan for this Jon guy.

Oh, yes, I think to myself as I twirl the pink daisy by its stem between my fingers.

I most certainly do have a motherfucking plan for this guy.

CHAPTER TWENTY-EIGHT

Rook

I wake suddenly, the rush of my earlier panic attack making me sit straight up before I realize where I am. The dying sunlight from outside filters through the sheer curtains but it's dusky inside as well. Ronin is sitting across the living room from me. I smile at him, trying my hardest not to cry as the words come out. "You came."

He gets up and walks over to the couch, then sits down and sets my head in his lap. "Of course I came, Gidget. I'm so sorry I wasn't there for you." He drags a piece of hair off my forehead and then tucks it behind my ear with a little pink daisy.

My hand goes to the flower and I am overwhelmed with how much he means to me. "I'm sorry," I choke out between half-hidden sobs.

He lets out a soft chuckle and leans down to kiss my forehead. "What in the world do you have to be sorry for?"

"For not telling you I was legally married."

He sighs. "I won't pretend, it hurt a little to find that out from Spencer over the phone, but Rook, we barely know each other. It's not like you lied, it just never came up."

"So you're not mad at me?"

"No, Gidge. I'm not mad. We can talk about that stuff later. How are you feeling?"

I swallow down all my feelings and paint on a happy face. "I'm OK." He's staring down at me with a scowl. "What?"

"You don't look OK, Rook. Tell me the truth now."

The tears build up again and my whole face scrunches up as I try to stop them. "I'm scared, Ronin." He strokes my hair and waits for me to continue, so I take a deep breath. "Why can't he just go away? Why? How arrogant can he be? To put out a missing person's report on me after what he did? It's like he's still claiming me, you know?"

"He's not getting you. Ever. He's never coming near you again, Rook, so just put that thought out of your mind, OK?"

"But now he knows I'm here. There's a missing person's report, what does that mean? Will I have to go back?"

"No, Rook. The report has been cleared now, he knows it was cleared here in Larimer County, and that's it. Spencer and Ford already talked to the deputy who pulled you over and he said they have to file a report because they cleared the missing persons out of the database, but that's all they're required to do. They won't mention Spencer or the shop or anything."

I breathe out a little sigh of relief, but Ronin's not done talking yet. "But the problem is, you told everyone he's a computer forensics specialist?"

I nod up at him as my stomach roils with this 'but'.

"He *has* to know where you are. There's no way he doesn't know where you are. You've done nothing to hide yourself, your social's on record as working for us, you have a bank account…"

My whole face crumples under this news. "Oh, God."

"But look at it this way, Rook. He hasn't bothered you so he's probably given up."

I snort through my sobs. "He didn't give up. You don't understand. He threatened me! He tried to—"

I stop, because even though this is Ronin and I know he's one hundred percent on my side, admitting that I allowed this monster to do these things to me is so hard. It makes me feel so weak and stupid.

Ronin strokes my cheek. "He tried to what?" he asks softly. "Just tell me, Rook. I'm not gonna judge you and I know it must be hard to talk about, but we need to know what we're up against."

"I didn't want to marry him." I look up at Ronin, pleading with him to believe me. "I didn't. But he took me up to this island in the lake near Michigan, some stupid island where they have no cars. And he told me it was for my birthday, when I turned eighteen. Before that we sorta had to hide because he was already twenty-one when we started dating." I stop and meet Ronin's worried eyes. "I was only sixteen. But I was in a bad foster home and I ran away. I'm not even sure how it happened, but the next minute I was on the streets homeless, just wandering around. And I begged enough money to go inside this diner and get some food, and he was sitting next to me at the counter. I knew it was stupid then, but I was desperate. So I let him take me home.

"It was OK for a while. I turned seventeen a few months later, and he moved us to that dumpy house his uncle left him when he died. And then all the violence and weird shit started. He was always talking about marriage and at first I said no, I'm too young. But after a while that got me a smack and a long lecture about how I belonged to him. So I just agreed. Then he booked this trip to that island for my eighteenth birthday and when we got there we were staying in the honeymoon cabin at this crappy campground on the lake. And—"

I shake my head as I remember it.

"Tell me, Rook."

I look up at Ronin and just blurt it out. "He tried to drown me. He held me under the water that night, he choked me. I thought I was gonna die, Ronin. I swear. He said he'd kill me if I didn't agree to marry him and if I ever tried to leave him, he'd torture me. And I believed him because he had already done so many terrible, *terrible* things to my body by that time, drowning and torture were just the next logical steps."

Ronin brings his hands up and scrubs them across his face a few times but he says nothing.

"Please, Ronin, tell me what you're thinking right now.

Do you hate me?"

He leans down and kisses my forehead one more time. "No, Rook. Hating you is the last thing I'm thinking about. I'm thinking about how easy it would be for us to kill that motherfucker."

"Us? As in me and you?"

He's got a far-off gaze now, just staring out into space. "No, Gidge. Us, as in Spencer, Ford, and me." He looks down and his eyes are blazing with anger. "It would be so easy, you have no idea."

I think back to what Ford said earlier. *I'm sure Ronin's going to ask for favors when he comes back*. "What do you mean by that, Ronin?"

He sighs and ignores my question. "You wanna stay here tonight? Or you wanna go home? It's only an hour and a half drive home. Wanna go home?"

"What about the footage we need for the show?"

"Fuck the show. We can do that another day."

"But we have to do it though, right? So let's just stay here and do that tomorrow and then it can be over with."

He gets up and takes my hand, pulling me up with him. "Come on, then. Let's wash your face and get something to eat. You hungry?"

I nod and let him take care of everything. There's nothing about this night I want to be responsible for, I just want him to do all of it.

After I splash some cold water on my face and wash off the dirt and tears, Ronin leads me out to the fire pit near the shop where the crews have a big BBQ going. Everyone is standing around joking and drinking. Even Spencer and Ford have eased in with the crowd. No one seems to know that I had a major meltdown or that my ex is a piece of shit woman-beater and is looking for me so he can come back and finish the job. So I just pack all that bad stuff away and quietly stick to Ronin's side.

It feels normal.

Ronin does this.
Ronin makes me feel normal.

CHAPTER TWENTY-NINE

Ronin

We finish filming late the next day and then we all pile into our vehicles and go back home. Spencer stays one more night since the frame came in from painting and he wanted to start the assembly, but he's back on duty with us bright and early this morning.

Ford has given in to Rook completely. She gets to stay with me. No cameras in the apartment.

Ford is weirdly affected by all this Rook stuff. It hits us all pretty close to home, watching her fall to pieces. It brings back a lot of very bad memories of Mardee and how all that shit went down in the end.

How Ford lost and I won.

But really, no one won. We all lost.

I got Mardee, I took her from Ford, and I lost her anyway.

Rook was wrong the other day when she asked what Ford did to start our fight. It wasn't Ford who did anything. It was me. I'm the one who took Mardee from him, brought her into the studio, then let her get caught up in the life, the money, the drugs, and the sex—only to discard her and leave her to find her own way back from all the scumbags that hover around the periphery of the modeling and entertainment worlds.

He never forgave me, and up until right now—maybe even right this second as I run all this through my head again—I never gave a fuck. I could always take or leave Ford, he was barely an acquaintance and never a friend.

But despite that he was a partner in the business the three of us ran during college.

That was just before Mardee died. Just the one job, we said, just the one guy, the dealer who turned Mardee on to the heroin. We were all feeling guilty. Spence for bringing her around the guys in this neighborhood, Ford for letting me take her away, and me for not caring enough about her to stop what was happening right in front of my face.

But we were all a little lost after Mardee died, and that job was too easy, because regardless of what Spencer looks like on the outside, the fact is, he's a fucking certifiable genius on the inside.

Ford might just be a well-dressed asshole to most people, but if you saw the guy's psychological profile, you'd shit your pants. I've seen it—that's how I know he's one fucked-up individual. He showed it to me, walked me right into his old man's office, hacked into his computer, and let me read what his own father wrote about him.

Incapable of emotion—high-functioning Asperger's Syndrome with areas of prodigious savant skills.

Like Spencer, Ford is a genius, but unlike Spencer, Ford's brand of intelligence is scary high. Off-the-charts evil-genius kinda shit. The kind of intelligence that comes about once every few hundred years.

But even though Ford has some emotional limitations, he's perceptive to fitting in. He started failing his intelligence tests long before I ever met him. In fact, that file in his father's computer was created when he was only seven years old. Ford never passed another test after that. He hides both his limitations and abilities well.

Showing me that personal file was his way of making things right for that fucked-up prank he pulled on me in high school. But we can all thank his solitary childhood computer geek stage for the special skills he brings to the table now.

Me? I'm not a genius, I'm not a hacker, I'm just the face. But every operation needs a front man, right?

And this Jon Walsh asshole is a worthy opponent. It might even be fun.

I watch Rook and Ford cross the street and then part ways at Ford's little sports car. Rook looks up, sees me watching, then drops her head. I'm not jealous of Ford. If she wants to work out with him, that's her deal. I won't interfere. But that doesn't mean I won't keep my eye on her as she does it.

I stay on the terrace until I hear the door in the apartment beep, then go inside and meet her in the shower.

"Have a nice run?"

"Yes," she says as she takes her clothes off and then gets in. It's just a regular single stream of water, so I take it she doesn't want company and go get dressed. Today is the cyborg bike shoot. It's an amazing custom chopper that's been in the inventory the longest since it was Spencer's first custom bike, and I know he's really counting on this photo to sell the thing soon. So Rook and I will have to be on today.

Trouble is, she's not on at all. She's so off, it's getting dark in there quick. She said almost nothing on the way home yesterday, and it wasn't because of the cameras, because Ford took them out of the truck before we left.

When we went to bed last night I wasn't expecting sex, not after her fucked-up weekend. But I wasn't expecting the cold shoulder either. I had to tug her up next to me. She settled after that, but up until last night, I've never had to encourage it. I don't even want to think about what that might mean.

I wait patiently in the living room as she exits the shower and dresses in some shorts and a tank top. She doesn't even bother with shoes, just grabs my hand when she gets to the door and we walk downstairs together. "You OK?" I ask as we cross the empty studio.

"Yeah, I think so."

I squeeze her hand. "It's a long day. You're a cyborg today."

She smiles but says nothing.

Spencer is messing with the tunes when we walk in and all the crews are busy checking sound and lighting and all that other bullshit they do for the TV show filming. I take a seat on the couch I had a crew member move in over the weekend. I figured if Ford and I had to sit around and watch, we might as well be comfortable. He's not around when we come in, probably still down the street at his corporate apartment.

"What do ya want to listen to today, Rook?" Spencer calls out to her as she goes into the half-hearted attempt at a dressing room and changes into the little robe.

"I don't care. Whatever you want, Spence."

Spencer looks at me after she turns away from him. I shrug.

"Well, that's not an answer, Blackbird. I need an answer. Choose a band."

She turns back, clearly confused at his insistence. "Um." She stops to think. "Lady Gaga?"

I hold down a snort.

"What?" she asks me, annoyed. "I like her."

I throw up my hands in an *I surrender* gesture, then kick my feet up on the coffee table as Ford walks in.

"Did you just say Lady Gaga, Rook? I love her."

I turn and sneer at him. What a dick.

"But I have a better idea."

"What?" Rook asks, a little defeated by my reaction to her choice in music. I'm the dick and now I feel like shit.

"I'll read to you."

Rook immediately smiles and I'm like, *What the fuck? Read to her gets a smile, but me wanting to take a shower gets a big fat nothing?*

"It's a joke, Ronin. Relax," Spence says. "Rook was making fun of his reading list last week."

"Yeah," she says. "You were gone that day. With Clare."

Ouch.

She takes her attention back to Ford. "Is it a billionaire book?" She smirks at him.

Smirks.

And everyone laughs but me. Not in on the joke again.

"No," Ford says through his smile. "It's *Gatsby*. You interested? You never read it, you said."

She sighs and shrugs. "I'd rather you read that one about Rowdy the hot spelunker, but whatever."

Ford is either an evil genius for reminding Rook that I left her last week, or a clueless dumb fuck.

I think we've already established which of those he is.

"OK," he says, taking a seat next to me. "Oh." He looks over my way this time. "I've catered lunch. Rook looks thin, she's not eating enough."

I look over at Spencer and he's shaking his head at me. "Don't do it, Ronin. He's baiting you."

I look over at Rook and she's waiting to see how I'll handle this little remark. What can I say? "Awesome, looking forward to Ford footing the bill for lunch."

Maybe I should go running with them in the morning, because clearly they had quite the conversation while I was back at the studio. And yeah, he's right. She looks a little thinner, but he's implying I'm not keeping track of her. He's implying I'm too busy with Clare to notice.

And he'd be right. Because I haven't weighed her in weeks.

Ford starts reading, Spencer grabs his paints and brushes, and Rook disrobes.

Our day begins.

Ford is adept at narrating books. He really missed his calling in voiceovers. He brings the book to life as Rook listens, cocking her head at all the right moments, internally questioning all the carefully planned foreshadowing, and even stopping him on two occasions to ask a question.

Fucking Ford.

He finishes the book long before Spencer is done painting up Rook's cyborg body and this is the perfect time for everyone to take a break. Spencer offers to walk Rook over to the bathrooms down the hall so I take my attention to Ford as he messes with that stupid e-reader.

"What?" he asks, without looking up at me.

"What are you doing, Ford? You trying to steal her right out from under me, or what? I mean, come on—Mardee was a long time ago…"

He looks up at her name. "Don't," he says, shaking his head. "Don't you fucking dare accuse me of that shit. I'm worried about Rook—"

"You're forgetting something, Ford. You're incapable of being worried about anyone, so save your bullshit for the person who doesn't understand you're an emotionless freak."

"I've invested a lot of time and money, not to mention my reputation with this show, in *her*. Maybe you don't care about this project, but Spencer and I do. So I'm not going stand by and watch her fall apart because you were too busy with that pathetic drug-addicted princess of yours to give a fuck."

I stand up and Ford follows.

"You want to fight, Ronin?" He stares me in the face. "I'm the guy you *need*, remember? I'm the only guy who matters in all this. So sit your ass down and shut the fuck up."

My head is throbbing, that's how pissed off I am. The blood is rushing to my head and I feel like I'm gonna explode if I don't just put my fist through his teeth. I poke him in the chest, a provocation, but Ford has a lot more self-discipline than I ever did. He can't be baited. "You better make it happen then, because I'll tell you what, if I have to put up with you pulling this stealthy girlfriend-stealing bullshit all summer, then you better come through."

He smiles. "If she *can* be stolen, then she was never yours to begin with. And do not insult my skills or question my ability to *come through*. I always come through."

Rook and Spencer come back in, chatting about the bike. I guess they went upstairs to see it real fast. Or maybe Spencer knew Ford and I were gonna get into it and he took her far enough away so she didn't have to see it.

"What now, Rook?" Spence asks. "Story or music?"

"What else you have on that thing, Ford?" She wanders over and sits down next to me. I put my hand on her shoulder and rub her back a little. She shudders and then leans into my chest.

"Watch the paint, Rook!" Spencer calls.

She sits up and looks back at me apologetically. "You're bored, huh?"

"Not at all, Gidget. Not at all." I smile at her. She's totally naked, but she's covered in so much paint right now, it's easy to forget. "Pick—story or music."

"Story," she says, glancing back at Ford. "Rowdy the Spelunker and that virgin chick."

"Ashley," Ford chimes in.

Rook laughs. "You've been reading it!"

He shakes his head and she giggles at him. Giggles.

"How about *The Secret Garden?"* he asks in a low voice.

Now she loses it, her laugh is so big even I have to smile. I look over at Ford and he knows he just won. He knows it.

"You'll read *The Secret Garden* to me?" She squints her eyes at him in disbelief.

"Yes, go, let Spencer finish so we can be done."

And Ford does read that stupid girly childhood book to her. Every motherfucking flowery word of it. And this time Rook's face is more than interested and questioning.

She's enchanted.

CHAPTER THIRTY

Rook

Spencer has painted me up as a cyborg.

It's one hundred percent awesome. As in, I might die from feeling so cool right now. He's such a master with that paintbrush, he knows just where to put the colors to make his art look 3D. He paints tubes and stuff all down my midsection, then fills in behind that with shades of black and blue, so it looks like I'm hollow. Like my midsection is nothing but these tubes and wires. He does the same thing to my arms, making them look like pistons and mechanical parts in some place, devoid of skin. Then purely human in others.

When he takes me up to see the bike after our bathroom break it's a cyborg too, only the opposite of me. I'm mostly girl with machine parts, but the bike is mostly bike with girl parts. In fact, this bike is a girl. Well, a girl of the cyborg persuasion. She's bent over at the hips and her arms reach down, acting as the front fork that holds the tire. Her head acts as the headlight, and her back is the tank, but it looks a lot like my stomach at the moment. Parts of it are painted in just the right way to make it look like it's got a huge hole in it, with tubes and pistons visible.

I actually clap at this one and make a remark to Spencer that it's very *Terminator 2*.

He loves that and has to stifle a proud grin with his fist.

Today I'm really happy to be a part of this project. Spencer is amazing. The Shrike bikes are stunning. And his artwork is incredible. I hope Antoine gives me some of these photos, because this is something I'd like to remember forever.

Maybe the bikinis were pretty boring and exploitative, but this is definitely more like movie FX.

And then there's Ford.

This morning at the stadium we talked a lot. Much more than usual. Not about me, not at all. But about him. I asked him about his schooling and he told me all about CU Boulder and their film department. He even went so far as to say he could get me in to talk to someone.

He even hinted at an internship next summer.

How incredible would that be?

I jerk back to reality as Spencer asks me to tilt my head up so he can paint my face. Ford is still reading.

And I tell you what, this whole *let me read to you* thing is just about the most tender expression I've ever experienced with a man. I'm not sure why, maybe because of the book. It's such a sweet book, so opposite of Ford in every way, that the fact that he's willing to read those words out loud, just to make me happy, well—it does something to me.

It doesn't want to make me jump his bones, but it does add to the ever-growing, and ever-changing, view I have of Ford.

Ronin is not happy. But I don't care. I don't want Ford. I'm not in love with him, I'm not even fantasizing about kissing him or touching him or anything like that. I'm just not interested in him that way. I'm interested in Ronin that way. So I don't feel bad about these new feelings for Ford. Ronin will have to get over it because Ford and I might become friends.

"OK, Blackbird. You're ready for your close-up."

I smile at the movie reference. I look over at Ronin and he's asleep.

"Should we let him get his beauty rest?" Ford asks. "I can walk you upstairs and fill in for Ronin in the shoot. You haven't posed with me yet."

"Um, that's a big negative, Ford. Ronin?" I shake him a little.

"I'm awake!" he says, sitting up.

"Right," I laugh. "We're ready to go upstairs." Ford heads out ahead of us and Ronin gets up and takes my hand, still not fully awake. "You're tired from all that driving, huh?"

He smiles. "It's catching up with me. But we're in the home stretch now, Gidge. We'll crash soon."

"I'm pretty tired too, that was the longest painting session yet. Do you have to get ready?"

"Just your basic futuristic road warrior shit, nothing like you, my cyborg sex kitten."

"I love this one. I feel like…"

"A cyborg sex kitten?"

"Yeah," I say, snickering. I really am a cyborg sex kitten because my girls are painted up with huge blue nipples and the clothing Spencer painted on is more like small strips of metallic blue fabric that criss-cross my body in all the wrong places. Which means, to the men, all the right places. None of the fun bits are covered by the fake fabric in the least. My legs are painted up to look like I'm wearing ripped blue leggings, and I have painted boots that come up just past my ankle. "I don't really *look* like her, but I *feel* like a cyborg Tank Girl."

"Mmmm, I crushed on her pretty hard back in the day. She's hot."

We part ways in the studio, I go to Josie for hair—no makeup because Spencer painted my face this time—and Ronin goes to the dressing room to change. We meet in front of the bike about thirty minutes later and Ronin is absolutely the sexiest Terminator that ever existed. "I need your clothes, your boots, and your motorcycle," I quote from the movie, snickering under my breath.

"What'd you say, Gidget?"

"Oh." I blush. "Did I say that out loud?"

He grins down at me and takes my hand. "Let's make this fun, wanna make it fun?"

"I could use some fun, actually."

He leans into me and begins to kiss my neck, his hands lightly exploring my body, just barely skimming my skin so he doesn't disturb the paint. I arch my back and tip my head and his hand slides up and caresses my throat.

"Sorry," he says as he moves his hand away.

I'm just about to ask what he meant by that when Antoine starts giving us directions in French and there's no time, because I lose track of everything but Ronin's words. They are soft and slow, not anything like our last shoot when it was his hands that got me excited. He's tender with cyborg sex-kitten Rook. I slide against him and he strokes my cheek with the side of his index finger and then he leans in and kisses me.

It's not bruising or deep, but just a flicker, his tongue darting forward just enough to tease me, twisting against my lips, then pulling back so I'm left wanting more. He strokes my hair as he watches me with a question in his eyes.

"What's wrong?" I ask.

He shakes his head and scoots my whole body forward so my pelvis is pressing right up against him. But it's what I don't feel that surprises me. He's not excited. "What's wrong, Ronin?"

"Nothing's wrong." He takes his nibbles down my neck and then over to my ear, breathing a soft breath against the tender skin, and sends a chill through my whole body. His hands circle my waist and then he whispers, "Lean back, Gidge."

I do as he asks. His strong hands keep my lower body firm against his groin while my upper body lowers down onto the tank. I'm an arch, the blue nipples pointing straight up. Then Ronin's mouth is all over my stomach, licking and nipping the skin on my belly, teasing me and sending little chilly flutters shooting up my arms.

One hand moves away from my waist and he slides one finger up my ribcage, tracing the bones one at a time in such a way that I actually squirm away and giggle at the tickle. The other hand moves away from my waist now too, only this one slides up my stomach and grabs my breast just as the weight of his body lowers down on me.

Every time we shoot these erotic scenes together he surprises me because it's never, ever the same scenario twice.

And while the heady, lustful passionate shoots are fun and say *I want to jump your bones right now*, this one is soft and sexy in a very tender way that says *I want you to be part of my life forever.*

CHAPTER THIRTY-ONE

Ronin

I'm not sure what possesses me to palm her throat like that in the shoot, but as soon as I do it, I'm ashamed. And then the last time we made love hits me hard. When I blindfolded her and wanted to assert more control.

She tried to tell me she wasn't into that crap but I pushed.

And now I'm so fucking ashamed.

I've been thinking about her relationship with that Jon fucker since she told me he tried to drown her and it's taken a lot of self-control to keep it tucked away. As soon as Antoine dismisses us I take her hand and lead her upstairs to my apartment and walk her over to the shower.

"God, it's such a shame to wash this all off right now, don't you think, Ronin?"

She's worried about Spencer's artwork. It kills me how this girl forces herself to cope. "Yeah, but that's why we take the pictures. Spencer will always have the pictures."

She looks at me funny. "What's the matter with you?"

"Nothing, why?"

"You're being weird."

I turn on the shower and start stripping. "What makes you say that?"

She looks down as I take off my pants. "Well, you're not excited to see me." She laughs a little at this. "And nothing we were doing out there was turning you on. Are you mad at me?"

I kick off my boxers and lean down to kiss her. "Absolutely not, I'm not mad. I'm just sorry about that choke move out there. And the whole blindfold and spanking thing we did last time. I'm not sure why you put up with me."

"Wait, what'd I miss? What choke move? And I sorta liked that spanking stuff."

I guide her into the shower and start washing off her paint. It's thick this time, her whole body is covered. I start with her back. "I'm just not comfortable with it, Gidge. Not after what he did to you for all those years."

"What're you talking about?"

"The rape. I'm surprised you can even tolerate me kissing you, let alone that dominant bullshit I tried to pull."

"Ronin, he didn't really rape me."

"No? So you gave him permission to have sex with you after all that violence?"

"Well, no, but I was his wife. And before that, I never told him no."

"Because you wanted to have sex with him?"

"No! Of course not. Even before he got violent I never wanted to sleep with him. I was a virgin."

I turn away to hide my anger but the words still come out. "He took your virginity by rape?"

"He didn't rape me, Ronin. I never told him no."

"Did you tell him yes?"

"Well no, but—"

"Rook, he *raped* you. Repeatedly, for several years. You're just so used to being mistreated you can't even comprehend what happened."

She stares at me, the water running down her face, streaking it with black and blue paint that slides down her body and swirls together in an inky pool of color at her feet.

"He raped you."

She shakes her head. "No."

I reach out and pull her close, hug her tightly. "Yes. That's what happened, Rook. And while I'm very proud of you for how well you've been dealing with the past, you need to know, in case it ever happens again, that if a man intimidates you into sex, that. Is. Rape."

She pulls back, squinting her eyes up at me as she tries to process my words. "I don't think I can talk about this."

I nod and pick up the sponge, then swipe it down her arm. She stands still as I wash her. Just thinking about what I said.

We meet Spencer and Ford for dinner, and even though they both keep up their ends of the conversation with some crude *South Park* talk, Rook is unable to hide her reaction to the facts that are suddenly becoming clear.

The doctors say the brain finds way to cope with stress and one of those ways, a very popular way actually, is denial.

This girl has been in denial for so long, she can barely process the truth.

When we go to bed that night she's quiet and clingy. I like her clingy because that just means I get to touch her more. But she's not snuggling, she's desperately holding on to me. She sighs against my chest and I sigh with her.

It hurts me—physically hurts me—to think of what she went through as a teenager.

She was a child when that monster found her, desperate and needy. Homeless and hungry, alone on the streets.

And that pathetic excuse of a human is nothing more than a pedophile rapist.

It takes hours for Rook to slide into her normal deep sleep, but I wait patiently until her breathing evens out, her clenched fist releases my shirt, and she turns a little to sink into the pillow. I slip out of bed, grab my phone and text Ford.

He's standing down in the studio near the far windows, like he never went home. He knows better than to speak about work unless the conditions are right, so he walks to the center of the room and flips on one of the fans we use for windy shoots.

"What'd ya got?" I ask, my voice barely audible over the vibrating hum.

"A nibble. Small withdrawal."

"He's testing?"

"Yes, that's my guess."

"So did you make a grab?"

He sneers at me. "If we just established he's testing, why the fuck would I grab him now?"

"I'm just asking, Ford."

"Be patient. It's a waiting game. He knows where she is now, the ball's in our court. I'll put the website up this week and set up the accounts. See if we can't tempt him to move fast."

"Do you think he will?'

Ford looks out the window as he thinks. "No, I think he's gonna wait. I think he's one paranoid motherfucker, but stratospherically ballsy at the same time."

"Why?"

"Because his first transaction was ninety-nine cents. He went inside and paid for a cup of coffee at Cookie's with a card from Rook's account with his name on it. I found it on the security footage we have access to for the show. I don't want to risk invading Rook's account because I'll muddy the tracks, so I can't be sure of how he got it without asking Rook to check things, but there's only one reason for him to be that ballsy. And that's because he ordered that extra card right from her online banking account. He's definitely had access to that for a while now."

"What a dumbass."

"Yeah, that's what *we* think because we know the food's free at Cookie's, so she'd never pay for a cup of coffee. It was a dead giveaway, we couldn't have asked for a better tip-off. But in his mind, that's about the safest transaction there is. A cup of coffee at her local haunt. If she did pay for food there, she'd never suspect it."

"How long do you think? Before he moves on her?"

"Hard to tell." Ford shrugs. "But he's quite good, it takes some skill to deal directly with banks."

"What about the other stuff?"

Ford smiles his nasty evil genius smile and nods his head. "Setting it up. He'll regret ever stepping into my little sphere of vengeance."

I get the shivers as the words come out because Ford is diabolical when it comes to these jobs. "What do you want me to do?"

"This is a non-personal con, Ronin. You're not really necessary until the very end. Just keep your eyes open, I don't trust this man. He's devious. And we all need to be carrying from now on. He was issued a concealed carry weapons permit out of the JeffCo Sheriff last week."

"Fuck. That means he's been here for a while."

"Probably as long as Rook has. That's the only way he could get that permit so quickly, and even then, he probably had someone pull strings."

I just nod, hoping we're not putting her in more danger as this plays out.

Ford turns and walks off and I flick the fan off and take the stairs three at a time back up to my apartment.

Rook is still sleeping peacefully, unaware of the deal Ford, Spence, and I are making. Unaware of who I really am, what I used to do, and what I'm capable of.

Unaware of what I'm gonna do for her now.

CHAPTER THIRTY-TWO

Ronin

And that's pretty much how our summer passes. We put the entire studio on lockdown, no public hours at all anymore, entrance by appointment only. Spence, Ford and I hold secret meetings under cover of bubbling rivers or oscillating fans. Rook is painted up to match the bike of the day and then photographed alone or sitting in my lap. We spend our weekends up at the Shrike Shop, filming fake deliveries and goofing off for the cameras. I visit Clare up in Steamboat a few times as a reward for good behavior. She finally begins to make progress towards a real recovery.

And we wait it out.

We wait for that sick fuck to make his move.

But he is so very, very patient.

And it's making me very nervous, because there's no way around it. Somehow, some way, this asshole knows we're setting him up. Ford was supposed to move on to part two of the con more than a month ago, but Jon Walsh disappeared and we had to hold back, then start all over again when he finally resurfaced.

Ford says it's normal for a guy with his credentials to be wary, but I'm not buying it. There's no way this is normal.

So I worry, and pace, and most nights I sit up in bed, watching Rook sleep, my Ruger in hand. Like I am right fucking now. Maybe this started out with him paranoid, but I have a bad feeling that he's turned the tables on us, like somehow he knows. He knows who we are and what we do and he's taunting us.

And our road trip to Sturgis starts today, so that means we're gonna be out of state, on the highway, in a campground with five thousand other strangers—all badass, all mean as fuck, all drunk and horny—and this is not going to end well. I can feel it.

I drag my hand across my forehead to wipe the sweat and Rook breathes a little heavier than normal, like she's dreaming. She's a perceptive girl, that's one thing I noticed about her immediately. She reads body language like a librarian reads books. She's on to us.

But anytime she asks, we shut her down. And something tells me she's OK with that. She's at the very end of her coping capabilities, she wants us to handle it for her.

She still runs with Ford in the mornings, but now Spencer and I hang out over there too, just in case. The AM training program at Coors Field is not something most people know about. It's private, reserved for big shots in the know. But this Jon guy seems to be in the know more often than not.

The waiting is killing me.

My phone buzzes with a text and my heart jumps at the noise.

Fucking Ford. I read the text and it simply says: *Nibble, nibble.*

He's such a child. I text back: *Don't fuck it up this time.*

I didn't fuck it up last time, asshole. Part two, commencing now. Website accessed.

I click the link Ford sends and almost get physically ill when I see Rook's picture advertising a live sex cam. I grimace and look over at her again. If she knew, she'd probably hate me. I close the web browser down and sneak out of bed. Light is already filtering through the windows and since we're leaving for Sturgis later this morning, I might as well just get up and go find Ford and talk this shit out with him in person.

"Rook," I whisper down in her ear. "Wake up, Gidge."

"Hmmm."

"I'm going down to the studio for a second, but the alarm is still set, so if I'm not back, don't ignore it. We gotta get ready to go in about an hour. OK?"

Nothing but snores.

"Rook!"

"Mmm-hmmm. Heard you."

"And do not ignore me if I text."

More snores.

"Fuck it, I'll be right back, OK?"

She's out.

I slip some jeans on and walk out to the hallway and make my way down to the garden terrace, texting Ford as I go. When I get outside he's over on the far side, craning his neck to see something down the street. The edginess is back and my heart beats a little faster. "What's up?" I ask softly as I near him.

"Saw someone. Maybe him, actually." He takes his attention to a ping on his tablet, scans the message, then turns back to the street below.

My heart rate jacks up as I process his words. "You're fucking kidding me? Now?"

"I said *I think*, Ronin."

"Where's Spence?"

"I sent him down the street, that's who I was watching."

"Did Walsh make a purchase?"

"Not yet, but I've had seventeen nibbles on it in the past several hours."

"Define nibble, Ford. What's that even mean?"

Ford stops his intense concentration on the street and turns to me. "He's tried to hack it repeatedly over night. But my friend is mistaken if he thinks he can crack past my firewall machine before I'm ready to let him in."

"So he wants cam access but doesn't want to pay and leave a record."

"Pretty much," Ford says, turning back to the street. Spencer is in plain sight now, walking back towards us.

"Well, that pretty much defeats the whole fucking

purpose of having that site in the first place, doesn't it? If he gets access, we're fucked."

"Relax, Ronin. Let me handle it. It's my ass that will burn if he does that, not yours. You do your job and that's it."

Spencer enters the building downstairs and we go inside and wait for him in the studio, turning on the fans to keep the conversation muddied. Just in case. We are paranoid fuckers and that's why we're not in jail. The keypad on the door beeps out his code and then Spence enters, a little out of breath from running up four flights of stairs.

"Nothing," he says to Ford. "There's a few vagrants down there, that's all."

"I'm not buying it," Ford says. "He's down there, he's just hiding. It's definitely today. He's watching us, waiting for us to fuck up."

"Should we cancel the trip?" I ask Ford.

"Fuck that, we're not canceling the trip," Spencer retorts in a huff. "The sooner we get on the road the better. Keep her confined in the RV. That's better than hanging out here in this huge-ass building. Besides, everyone's ready. The crew are all packed and they'll be here in a few hours."

"Maybe," I say, but internally I'm thinking about all the ways we're sitting ducks inside that RV on that long, almost empty highway leading up to Sturgis. All the way through Wyoming. It's not good.

"You got anything else, Ford?"

"No, it's dead now. Nothing. I got seven proxies to query, though, so I'm gonna go back to Rook's apartment and work on that. Let's just move on like there's nothing out of the ordinary. Pack up the RV, pack up the trucks, when the crew gets here, just keep them busy. We'll decide what to do next on the road."

He walks off towards Rook's apartment and Spencer heads for the door. "I'll be down in the art room packing up the last of my supplies."

I'm like a deer in front of a Mack truck at night. Not sure

what to do, paralyzed by the possibilities that are barreling down upon me.

CHAPTER THIRTY-THREE

Rook

Ronin is a manic mess this morning and I'm standing here in the middle of his apartment, trying for the life of me to figure out why. We're packed, we're on time. The RV is gassed up. The crews aren't here yet, but they're not due for another half hour or so. We ate breakfast. The bike is on the truck. Spence is downstairs getting his supplies together and shutting down the art and production studio.

We're ready. And I'm not even nervous—in fact, I'm looking forward to this trip. I'm gonna get blind-ass drunk up there in Sturgis, I do not even care that I'm underage. I figure if I'm old enough to parade my goods in front of half a million people, a few shots of tequila and some fizzy Coronas aren't gonna make a bit of fucking difference. If I have to sit in the RV and get drunk alone, I will.

The rally officially starts tomorrow, but we're not scheduled for the downtown walk of shame and Shrike Raven unveiling until the day after. It's a long day, one that I'm very anxious to be over. But being naked barely bothers me anymore, I'm so used to wearing nothing that when I do put clothes on for dinner every night, it almost feels weird. I might become a nudist.

I laugh. Right out loud.

Fuck that, I can't wait for winter so I can put on layers of clothes.

"Hey?" I call out to Ronin. He's out on the terrace talking fast and low to Ford, I think. Ford has been texting and calling him all morning. It's starting to drive me crazy because each time Ronin gets more and more wound up. Ronin puts one finger up towards me, then turns and continues his conversation.

Whatever. He's not gonna ruin my trip. I've been stuck in this place all summer, thinking about Jon and all the what-ifs. But he never showed. I figure I'm safe. Ronin was right—he probably did find me, saw I was already involved with someone else, I'd started over and all that, and then he left.

And Ford has been working on the divorce stuff slowly. He tells me a little bit about how we might take care of this every now and then, but he says we should wait until things calm down and then we'll talk about the plan. Annulment, he hints. Sounds good to me. I still run with him every day, it's actually one of the few things in my life that is stress-free and predictable. It allows me to think about nothing for thirty minutes every morning, clear my head. Ford was totally right about exercise. It's good for me.

I can't keep up with him when we run, but he slows down for me a little bit before taking off and going ahead on his own now. He's been talking a lot about the Biker Channel season going through with Spencer, so I've been mulling that over. It sounds a lot better than anything I've ever done, so—

"Rook!"

Ronin comes busting in from the terrace and interrupts my thoughts. "I've gotta go downstairs for a second. Stay here, I'll be right back." He leans down and kisses me on the cheek, then rushes out the door.

"OK," I say to no one, since I'm alone now. I go to the fridge and grab some blackberries from the fruit basket I took from Antoine's office yesterday. I can take or leave his apples and pears, but berries… that's another story.

The doorbell rings and I almost pee my pants, it scares me so bad. I didn't even know we had a doorbell, and for that matter, who the fuck would ring it?

I walk slowly around the corner of the kitchen and then

just stare at the door.

Who would ring the doorbell?

I swallow hard as my heart rate picks up.

Who would ring the doorbell?

We're on lockdown, have been for months. No one in or out without a code. Everyone's code was changed when we came back from FoCo after the missing person's report was cleared. And no one who's allowed to be in this building needs to ring the doorbell, because everyone has access to Ronin's apartment via a second code, just in case Jon did come back and somehow make his way inside.

My heart thumps so hard with this thought my hand goes up to my chest. I feel like I have to hold it inside or it will burst through.

It's Jon.

Oh, God. I rush over to my cell phone and push the preset for Ronin. The little icon at the top of the phone says no service.

Oh, fuck.

He's messed up our service.

He's inside the building.

Where can I go?

He must not have the code for Ronin's apartment, either that or he's fucking with me, trying to draw me outside. I tiptoe over to the door and peek through the little peep hole.

There's a sign taped to the wall across from the door.

It says, *Where's Ronin?*

My arms reach out for the wall before I faint. *Do not faint, Rook. Do not faint*, I tell myself over and over.

He wants me to go outside. It's a trick. I know this, I know it's a trick. I lived with this man for three years, this is how he plays his game. And now that I think about it, that's what that phone call was with Ronin, something to do with Jon.

I stand up and catch my breath. Still, if that freak thinks he's gonna hurt Ronin… I take another deep breath and push my ear to the door. Nothing.

I tiptoe back to the kitchen and grab the biggest knife we have, then walk calmly back to the door.

I twist the handle on the door and cringe as the locking mechanism automatically releases. I wait for the door to burst open, I'm prepared for him to come at me from the hallway.

But nothing happens.

I open the door a crack and wait. Again, nothing.

I throw it all the way open and rush forward into the hallway.

Silence and emptiness.

Where the hell is everyone? We're leaving in like half an hour, where's Elise and Antoine?

Oh, God, please, please, I beg. Please do not let them be hurt or worse, dead, by this monster's hand.

I have to stifle down a cry before I remember that my own life is in danger if he catches me. I walk down the hallway, and for once, my old Converse sneakers are the perfect footwear for the job. I stop just before I get to the stairs and push myself up against the wall the way you see people do in the movies, just before they flash their eyeballs around a corner where Charlie's waiting to pump their guts full of lead.

I peek around the corner.

There's a girl down there smoking a cigarette.

"Hey!" I call. "Who the fuck are you?"

She slides her shades down her nose and blows out a ring of smoke. "None of your fucking business. Where's Spencer?"

And then it hits me, this is the other model Spencer used. His ex-girlfriend. "Veronica?"

"Who's askin'?"

I run down the stairs and she spots the knife and starts backing up. "Hey, look—"

"Shhhh," I say. "How the hell did you get in here?"

"Door was open."

"No, the door was *not* open, we're on lockdown."

"It was open," she snorts at me. "And if you try anything

with that knife, I've got a gun in my purse and my shooting instructor says I'm the best natural shot he's ever seen."

"You do! Oh, thank God. Get it out, Please. There's a crazy guy in the building, Veronica. He's gonna kill me, please get out your gun!"

"What's going on—"

"Rookie!"

I spin around, the bile in my stomach already exiting my mouth. Green shit splashes across the floor and I cough, my whole body shaking just from the sound of his voice.

"I've been looking for you, baby."

Veronica's backing away from my vomit, screaming obscenities at me.

"Run!" I scream back. And then, because she's got a gun and I don't, I grab her hand and head for the door. She resists for a moment but my panic is contagious. I throw the door open praying that someone, anyone, one of those fucking camera stalkers that have been around all damn summer, is within hearing distance. I scream, "Help!"

I'm still tugging her behind me, but her shock is wearing off as I get to the first landing between the fourth and third floors and she plants he feet firmly on the floor. And I just know, if I save this girl, I'll die. So I yank at her purse as Jon comes into view above us. She resists. "Let go of my purse!" she screams at me. So I let go and run down the stairs, then dash into the art studio. I figure that's where Spencer is, packing up his shit, but when I get in there it's pitch black.

And now I'm trapped.

I stumble across the floor, tripping over some light cords, fall on my face, scramble to my feet, and fall again, then settle for crawling towards the back of Spencer's space.

I scramble around the partition that served as my changing room all summer, then lean back against the back wall, desperately trying to silence my gasping breaths. I can hear Veronica and Jon fighting out in the hallway, she's bitching him out, and then a gun goes off and I have to cup my own hand around my mouth to shut myself up.

CHAPTER THIRTY-FOUR

Rook

The gunshot is still echoing through my ears and the smell of powder invading my nose when I catch the creak of the door opening. I almost shit myself this time. I clamp my mouth shut and pinch one side of my nose together just like that cop did when I had my panic attack.

If I panic now, I die.

I die.

I close my eyes and concentrate on my breathing, listening for footsteps at the same time. I can hear them, but they are not coming towards me, they are walking over towards Director Larry's station.

The lights come on and laughter is blaring through the speakers on the other side of the room.

"Funny, Rook," Ford's voice says.

"You know what's funnier?" my voice says. *"The fact that all you dumbasses got the joke. I know what you're reading at night."*

He's been watching me since I started this job. He's been here since the very beginning. He probably tapped into the camera system. He saw everything, he saw me standing naked in this room, five days a week for the last three months.

A slow clap sounds off from the crew station. "Very nice, Rookie. You look very nice in that bikini. Oh, no wait. That's not clothing, that's *paint.* You're posing nude for these sick freaks. I always knew you were a whore."

The vomit wants to come up again, but I swallow hard and keep very, very still—and I'd like to say quiet as well. But my breathing betrays me. In my own head my breath sounds like a raging tornado. The talking covers up most of it, but it also covers up Jon's footsteps.

I have no idea where he is.

Please, Ronin. Please, please—find me!

"I know you're still in here, Rookie. I'm going to take you home now. We can work this out. Of course, there's a price to pay. And you know, I'm always sorry about that, but you're mine. And you make me do those things. Those terrible, terrible things."

He is closer now. I can't hear his steps, but his voice is near. By the couch Ronin and Ford sit on when I'm being painted. I sit up on my haunches, ready to spring up if he finds me, fisting the knife handle.

Something goes crashing across the room, Spencer's artist lights smashing to the ground, shattering, more things go flying and something hits the partition in front of me.

It shakes.

And he laughs.

"Clever little Rookie. You always tried to hide, but you were never very good at it, were you."

I whimper.

"That's right, love. I've caught you. But I'll make you a deal. You come out and say you're sorry, and I'll wait until we get home to teach you a lesson."

I'm nodding. *What the hell is wrong with me?* I'm nodding! I shake my head and grip the knife harder. Then I stand up.

I can see him over the partition.

He's smiling.

I swallow. "I'm sorry."

"Oh," he laughs. "I'm *sure* you are, Mrs. Walsh. I'm *sure* you are."

He waits to see if I'll say anything else, but I just stand quietly, trying to stay as still as possible.

"Is that it? That's the extent of your apology?" He unzips his pants and points to his crotch.

I swallow hard again and force my feet to move, just far enough to get to the edge of the partition wall. Then I stop and wait.

"All the way over here, *right now*!" He growls out the last two words between clenched teeth.

But I don't move. I know what's gonna happen if I go over there and it won't be anything as simple as a blow job apology.

"Now!" he bellows.

I jump a little in fright, but I stay right where I am and shake my head at him. "No, you're going to hurt me," I say in a shaky voice.

"I came all this way to find you, why would I hurt you, Rookie? I'm not gonna hurt you. Not as long as you apologize correctly."

I take a deep breath and repeat Ford's words in my head. No one can fix this mistake for me, I need to fix it myself. Jon has no right to be here, let alone make demands of me. No right. He's lucky I let him go, not the other way around. He's the dick who abused me, not the other way around. I'm the one with the power of righteousness on my side, not him.

So I count to three, stand up a little straighter, and smile at him.

He smiles back. "That's more like it."

"That's more like it?" I ask. "That's more like it? Look, Jon," I say in my most brave voice as I think up a kick-ass way to really piss him off. I can't take this tension. I can't, I'd rather get it over with. If this is my end, I'd rather just go out fighting like a ballsy street bitch and not whimper and fade away like some pathetic loser. So I force his hand and dig around in my brain for one of my God-given gifts. "I'm real sorry you came all this way to get me, but… even if I were blind, desperate, starved, and begging for it on a desert island, you'd be the last thing I'd *ever* fuck."

His face betrays him. He doesn't know what to do with that remark and I almost laugh. I stole that line from *Scarface* and his dumbass woman-beater brain is struck stupid by it. And then it occurs to me, I've got a million of these movie insults in my head. How many times did I imagine telling this prick off? "And I'll tell you something else, *Jon*, the day I need a friend like you, I'll just have myself a little squat and shit one out." Thank you very much, Frank Darabont and *The Mist*.

And now I do laugh, because that was damn funny.

He charges me, I raise the knife just a second too soon and he sees it, knocks me in the head and sends me flying against Spencer's art supplies. I crash into an art cart, lose hold of the knife, and go sliding across the floor. He picks me up by the hair and starts pulling me towards the exit.

"We're leaving now, Rookie, and you won't be back. So take a good look around and—"

"Just who the fuck do you think you are, you crazy ass-faced bastard?"

Veronica is standing in her ripped-up fishnet stockings, her lipstick smeared, her cigarette dangling out of her mouth, and a bloody gash crossing her billowing white blouse at the waist, like a bullet just missed some very vital organs a few minutes ago.

I laugh again. "Ha! Shoot his ass, Veronica! Shoot him!"

And then shit happens so fast I can't process it. Veronica nods and I can seriously see her finger getting ready to squeeze that trigger when Jon pushes me to the floor and charges her. He hits her dead in the chest, knocking the wind out of her and kicking her ass at the same time, and the gun goes off.

Veronica screams.

My feet know what to do and even though I'm ashamed to leave Veronica there, I scoot around Jon before he can get back on his feet, dash through the door and book it down the stairs.

"Help!" I yell, but this fucking place is totally empty.

Jon is right behind me, only a few steps off actually, and I jump down an entire flight of stairs to the next landing, my exercise with Ford finally paying off, and I gain a few seconds on him. When I get to the first floor I head to the back where the crew should be packing the RV and the vans for our trip. I burst through the first security door and I'm pushing on the long silver bar that will open the second door and take me outside when Jon grabs my shirt and we both go down.

I don't even think, I elbow him in the nose, wince at the sound of cracking cartilage, and I'm back on my feet, stumbling out into the parking lot.

No one. There's no one. I stand there, stupid for a second, then focus on Spencer's truck.

I scramble over to the driver's side door, pull it open and launch myself inside. Jon's got me by the ankles, pulling me back out. And I know, if he gets me out of this truck, I'm dead. I kick out hard and crack him in the mouth with my sneakers.

I reach over and open the glove box, praying that there's a gun in here. I pull out a map and some bullshit papers, my palm searching. I feel the cold hard metal of the weapon, slide my hand around the grip, cock that bitch-ass safety back, then point it right at his face.

"I will blow your motherfucking head off, I swear."

He hesitates and I open the passenger side door, jump down and run back to the building. I'm keying in my code before he comes to his senses and realizes I didn't shoot him. I swing the door open again, running all balls out now, and then smack right into Ronin.

I mow him over and we go down together. Jon catches up, but now he's not worried about me, he's focused on Ronin.

And there's no fucking way this batshit-crazy woman-beater is gonna hurt my new friends.

So I shoot that fucker.

And the gunshot is so loud, it rings in my ears long after Jon falls to the floor, screaming.

CHAPTER THIRTY-FIVE

Ronin

The smoke is still spilling out of the barrel of the revolver in Rook's hand and that psycho rapist is writhing on the floor, his knee blown out and blood pooling under his body. Rook and I are all tangled up and she's shaking uncontrollably as I try to move her aside and figure out what the fuck is going on.

Spencer comes barreling in from the back door, while Ford enters from the front.

"Yes," Ford says into his phone. "I need an ambulance, there's been a shooting at Chaput Studios… "

Rook gasps and looks back at me. I put a hand on her shoulder. "Keep calm, Gidge. I'm not fucking around right now, let me handle this." I hold out my hand. "Give me the gun."

She looks down at the gun, then over to her ex. He's moaning on the ground, blood is still spilling out at an alarming rate.

My little Gidget might've hit an artery.

I smile at that, then turn back to her. "Rook, look at me. We've got about three minutes before the cops get here."

She nods her head and hands the gun over.

"You are in shock, OK? Do not say anything. You are in shock. Do you understand me?"

She nods again.

"The whole building is wired, we've got it all on tape. But you are in shock, you will not make a statement until the shock wears off."

I get up and then pull her up along with me.

"Is he gonna die, Ronin?" Her voice is very small and shaky as the reality of what just happened sinks in.

"No, Gidge, we're not gonna let him die. Death is too good for that prick." I take her hand and walk her out the back door. There's people everywhere now. Elise and Antoine are talking to the crew, just getting back from breakfast. Elise is bordering on hysterical, while Antoine catches my gaze and rushes over babbling frantically in French.

"She's OK, she's fine. Let us handle this, Antoine. You two were at breakfast across town, you never saw anything, so step the fuck back and just say *I have no idea* over and over until they get sick of asking you questions."

I open Spencer's truck door and sit Rook down on the passenger side. "Pay close attention, Gidget." She's scared out of her mind right now, so I lean in and kiss her on the head just as half a dozen Denver police pull in the back alley. "You're in shock, remember? Just stay quiet until I'm done talking."

I'm not the genius who perfected this plan.

That's Spencer.

I'm not the hacker who executed this plan.

That's Ford.

I'm the liar who cleans up the mess.

And my job starts now.

"Threatening text messages," I tell the cops. Because that's innocent, really. Easy. And you always want the job to be easy. "If you check his phone, you'll see he sent her text messages this morning, threatening to kill her, me, all of us."

The law about searching cell phones is iffy at best, so we needed a fool-proof way to make sure his phone would be checked on scene—no room for mistakes, no way to hide what he's got on there.

Jon is too smart to send threats by text. But Ford took care of that because sending threats, followed by his genius plan of breaking and entering and attempted murder, means no search warrant is required to access the phone and look for that evidence.

And guess what pops up on the home screen of our friend Jon as soon as the cop swipes his chubby fingers to wake it up?

No really, just guess.

It's almost a giveaway, the Feds use this one all the time. Our version is a new take on the long con bait-and-switch, because we're super-awesome lying, hacking geniuses like that.

Possession of kiddie porn in this day and age is the equivalent of tax evasion last century. That's how they always got the bad guys back then, all those mobsters. Something stupid simple like claiming too many dinners on your taxes.

And let's face it, our boy Jon is one hundred percent guilty of pedophilia, right?

Sure, we set up the photos the cops are confiscating from his phone right now.

But this fuck deserved it.

And believe me, they'll find a whole shitload more at his apartment down the street. Not to mention a transaction, executed less than an hour ago, where he tried to buy more illegal porn, thinking he was purchasing a live cam peek at Rook.

I might love Ford right now.

Rook listens carefully as I talk, I can tell. But she keeps her head down and her mouth shut.

"Shock," I say again. "She needs a doctor. Maybe a psychiatrist. He damaged her for years—violent, horrific beatings. Torture. She's not capable of talking right now. We've got a team of lawyers here to make sure she's competent to give a statement."

That shuts down the questioning, because she's not in any trouble here, not at all. All they want is a way to dot the i's and cross the t's so everyone can get the hell out of this parking lot and go grab some lunch.

If you're stupid enough to break into someone's home and attack the occupants in Colorado—and Chaput Studios is most certainly Rook's home at the moment—you're gonna get your ass shot and the person who shot you will never be charged.

Make My Day, it's called.

Make My Motherfucking Day Law. That's what we do with losers like Jon in Colorado when they try to attack us in our homes.

We shoot them. Most of the time we kill them, but Jon deserves his day in court and a very long prison sentence.

He so, *so* deserves that.

And Rook was definitely fearing for her life when she pulled that trigger. She was on the ground, he was coming at her, she was in her home, he broke in.

This is a clear-cut case. It's a textbook case, actually. The cops have no chance of charging her with anything, because we got every second of it on camera.

Of course no one was supposed to get shot. We could've killed him, but that would be way too easy. And not even close to the kind of punishment he deserves. We did underestimate that sick fuck a little because he baited us, got us out of the building chasing after a fake transaction down at Cookie's so he could make his move.

But I think Rook will be OK in the end. She didn't kill him either, she's not a killer, she's far too sweet for that. She only did what she had to do to protect herself. She should have zero guilt going forward.

The paramedics find Veronica swearing and enraged upstairs and she comes out of the building with her arms around two men as they help her hobble across the parking lot to an ambulance. Her fishnets are a bit ragged from her struggle, she's missing a stiletto, and she's got a trickle of blood running down her side. But her hair's still in place and her cigarette's still hanging out of her mouth. Jon's strapped to a stretcher, ready to be loaded into the ambulance when Veronica passes by. Her fist darts out and she whacks him in the nose. "Bastard," she spits.

You have to love Veronica. You have to. She's like a live-action cartoon character. She's the real-life Jessica Rabbit.

Spencer is a bit shaken that Veronica ended up being involved and he hovers over her as the medics check the flesh wound just above her waist. He's got a weird strained look on his face.

Personally, I think those two are made for each other, but Spencer's not a relationship kinda guy, so Veronica's sorta out of luck.

We could not have planned this part better if we tried because Veronica sucks up attention like it's a precious commodity. She's got the entire parking lot filled with medics and cops twisted around her little finger as she moans about her injury. They all take turns lifting up her shirt to check her flesh wound—scrape really. That bullet scraped her as it flashed past her waist.

Spence catches me watching and smiles at me from across the parking lot, then shoots me with his finger. "We're still road trippin'? Rook? Ronin?"

I look over at Ford. He's busy with the lawyers now, explaining with his hands, smiling, and even laughing a little. The way he always does when things are nearing the end and he knows we just pulled off the perfect job. We're gonna get away with it. Again.

"You wanna stay home, Rook? I think even Ford will understand if you flake on this deal."

She finally lifts her head and looks me in the eye. "You set all this up?"

I nod. "Well, I came up with the general idea, Spence made it real, and Ford hacked the shit out of that loser all summer trying to get him to take the bait. Of course, I didn't know he had access to the building or I'd never've left you upstairs. I'm so sorry it ended wrong, it was only supposed to be a virtual crime."

She gets a little misty-eyed and I hug her close. "It's over now, OK? It's all over. He's going away, he'll never walk right again, and he's gonna spend a very long time being some thug's prison bitch."

"Thank you," she says in her most serious and sincere voice. "Thank you."

"Any time, Gidge. Any time. Oh, I almost forgot. You might be exactly four hundred and fifteen thousand dollars richer." I laugh as the number rolls off my tongue. "And it might be sitting in non-traceable off-shore bank accounts. Because we might've stolen all his money while we were at it. Serves him right since the only reason he got caught is because he tried to steal yours. Paybacks are always a bitch."

CHAPTER THIRTY-SIX

Rook

Elise, of all people, is driving the RV up to Sturgis. It's only a six-hour drive, so not a very big deal. But just seeing her tiny hands clutching that huge-ass steering wheel makes me laugh.

"What's funny?" she asks me as she blows past a slow car on the highway. There's hardly anyone on this road. Not many people live up this way. Not many would want to.

"You," I say. "You constantly surprise me. Elise."

A loud roar from the back signals a winner of the current hand of poker. It's just us in this RV—no camera crews allowed. Ford's orders. It's just me, Elise, Spencer, Ronin, Antoine, and Ford. Just us.

My new family.

I cannot even explain how great it feels to think of them this way.

Elise winks at me and then eases the massive vehicle back into the right lane and slows down a little. "I keep everyone on their toes, Rook. If I wasn't here, the whole place would fall down."

I believe that, too.

I chat with her like this for the entire drive, occasionally spotting some wildlife I never even knew existed in the US. Like antelope. Who knew? The cops kept us occupied most of the day yesterday, so we just decided to head out early this morning instead. We still have time to settle in before our show tomorrow. Spencer said he changed his mind about the final painting, he didn't even show Ronin.

I never knew what the original one looked like, so I could care less. This summer I've been sexy Elvis, a cyborg, a slutty hitchhiker, a slutty beach girl, a slutty Catwoman-ish thing… well, just insert slutty in front of all the rest… Fifties waitress, roller derby girl, motocross rider, the tattooed woman—that was cool because Spencer painted me up to match him—rodeo queen, tied-up BDSM rope girl, superhero, go-go dancer, policewoman, mermaid, snow leopard, soccer player and a whole week of slutty lingerie models.

Let me tell you, painting fishnet stockings—the worst. It took the entire day.

But even though I'm still real nervous about the final painting and the show tomorrow night—this has been the best summer of my life. No matter what happens to me, no matter how things go after this is over—whether Ronin and I make it or not—no one will ever be able to take what we created together this summer.

It's very special.

I start to get excited as we get closer because there's lots of other RV's on the road now, plus all the bikers. They come out of nowhere, all of a sudden. One minute we're on this desolate highway in Wyoming, and then, bikers everywhere. All of us heading to the same place. I notice a few motocross racing team transport trucks. "Is there a motocross race here this week?" I ask Elise.

"Yeah," Spencer answers from the seat behind me.

I look back at him.

He winks because he must remember that I told him my first boyfriend was a motocross racer back in Chicago.

I shake my head. "Just asking, Spencer. I was pretty big into it when I was a kid."

"Yeah, good thing, too. Otherwise I'd be teaching you how to ride that beautiful Shrike Rook bike tonight."

I smile and secretly kiss him in my mind for not telling on me in front of Elise.

We ease into the campgrounds about an hour later. It's all pretty primitive, but since we're headlining a show, and Spencer needs a private place with access to water in order to paint me, we get to stay in the executive cabins. The big luxury is that it comes with a bathroom.

How lucky are we!

The whole day just flies by with all the settling in. The campground is a madhouse and we're still a few miles outside Sturgis. Ronin and I turn in because I have to get up at three in the morning so Spencer can start painting.

Ronin pulls me up to him in the bed, wrapping his arms around me and kissing my neck. "How you doing, Gidget?"

I turn so I can see his face. "You know, not anything like I should be. I don't understand how I could've shot someone yesterday and today, I'm just camping up in Sturgis like it never happened. And the weirdest thing, Ronin? I could care less. What's that mean?"

He tucks a wayward strand of hair behind my ear. "It means you're gonna be just fine, Rook. You owe that guy nothing. Not one second of remorse or sympathy."

"Yeah," I sigh. "That's what I figure too. I'm just gonna forget about it, Ronin. I'm just gonna let the past go, move forward with you."

He squeezes me. "You make my heart happy right now, Rook. So totally and completely happy."

We cling to each other, but not in a desperate way. We cling to each other and fall asleep in a way that makes us feel complete.

And when stupid Ford comes pounding on our cabin door at 3AM, I wake up feeling complete as well.

"OK, Rook, last painting."

Ronin and Ford went to the campground general store to get coffee for everyone, so right now it's just Spencer and I in his cabin. He's moved the beds out of the way to give us room, and he's got the music going. I'm pretty sure no one in this campground but Ronin and I bothered to go to sleep, because the party is still raging outside. It's loud as fuck and if I wasn't such a heavy sleeper, that might've prevented me from getting some shut-eye. But as it happens, I can sleep through the Sturgis rally no problem.

"Are you gonna tell me what it is?"

"Nope!" he says, grinning like a teenager. "You'll just have to discover it as I go."

He gets his airbrush out and a smoky gray color goes on first. I watch patiently as he winds the paint around my body in ribbons. He switches to another airbrush so he doesn't have to keep cleaning it between colors and sprays on some black, blending it together. After that there's more gray, some shades lighter, some shades darker, and white to bring it all together. Even though he's only done background colors, it already looks amazing.

Ronin and Ford come back with the coffee and take a seat on the couch to watch, but even with the caffeine and the roaring sounds of motorcycles outside, not to mention Spencer's airbrush, neither of them last long because Spencer is building the scene in a really cryptic way to keep us all guessing.

It becomes too boring for the tired babies and they are out.

It's late morning before I figure it out, that's how well-honed Spencer's craft is. He's applying the red, the only other color besides the shades of black, gray and white, when it all starts to click.

"It's us."

Spence shoots me with his finger, just like he did when he sat across from me in Cookie's and offered me this job all those months ago. "It's you two. It was a helluva summer, huh, Rook?"

"Yeah, it really was. But you know what, Spencer? I'm so glad I did this with you. My whole life has changed and you're a big part of it."

"Same here, Blackbird. Same here. We got the contract for the first season of Shrike Bikes. It's your job, but I'll live if you say no."

"I'll talk to Ronin and see."

When Ronin and Ford wake up they are stunned silent by the artwork on my body. It's all in shades of black and red, just like Spencer's tattoos, and the front piece is a beautiful composition depicting a Samurai warrior and a blackbird sitting in a cherry tree. For the first time, in all the paintings Spencer Shrike has completed on my naked body, my girly parts are not emphasized. The painting flows flawlessly over my curves, hiding every inch of skin underneath. The blossoms take me back to the first day I arrived at Chaput Studios, broken, scared, and barely holding myself together.

And a gentle man named after a masterless warrior pushed me in a swing and started the healing.

But that moment in time was fleeting, just like those flowers.

That girl blew away in the wind and this girl took her place.

If I thought the catsuit made me feel beautiful and fully dressed, this is a hundred times that.

I feel like a goddess.

And when I get to town, I walk down that Sturgis strip

with my head up, feeling loved and pretty.

And no one whistles or talks to me rudely. They say hello, they compliment Spencer's talent, they take pictures with me, and they treat me like a piece of art.

I see him in the crowd. Watching me, following our progress down the street, but from the opposite side. Trying to be stealthy, I guess. And a small part of me wonders if he's the real reason I took this job so quickly. I knew as soon as I saw the motocross transport trucks on the highway he'd be here. So did Spencer.

He comes to the show that night too. Stands right in front. Here the crowd is more rowdy, they are all drunk after all, but Wade stands still, his eyes never moving from me while I'm on stage.

He was my first love. I thought he was the one. I cried over losing him for years after his mom sent me away.

But when he finally lifts his hand to wave I don't wave back.

Because I'm not a runner anymore.

I'm a chaser.

Panic

Rook & Ronin Book Three

HJ USS

Edited by RJ Locksley
Cover Design by JA Huss

PROLOGUE

Rook

Day 1,110 in Captivity
Six Months Ago
Wayne, Illinois

Thirty-one days.

That's how long it takes my face to heal.

I watch the girl in the mirror, looking for marks. She tilts her head this way and that, lifts her chin, stretches her neck for any sign of fingertip-shaped bruises, and then she sighs.

They are all gone. I can see a tiny scar on the edge of my lower lip, but it's not as bad as it could've been if Jon hadn't rigged up a rudimentary butterfly bandage so he didn't have to take me to the hospital. It should've been stitched, but it wasn't.

My pack is waiting on the floor of the bathroom. I wasn't sure if today would be the day. I tried last week but there were still a few purple splotches on the skin under my eye and the lip was scabbed.

It's been torture waiting to heal. And I kept thinking—what if he does it again? Before I heal? Then I'll be stuck here even longer.

But enough of that. It's healed now and I have an appointment. I take one more look in the mirror and give myself a little pep talk. "You're going to live, Rook. You're going to *live*. You might not have the best life, but it will be better than this one. No matter how bad it is at first. Things will get better."

I really believe it too. Before all this mess with Jon—that's what he calls it, the mess—I was what some people might call an optimist. A half-full kind of girl.

I think I can be that girl again.

I think I can.

My suitcase contains all my worldly possessions. It's not much really, just some clothes and trinkets. A few softcover books I never finished, and some crap that meant something to me at one time or another, but no longer matters.

I just want to leave it all behind. Every bit of it. But I don't want Jon to have anything of me. I want to leave this house and leave no trace of myself.

It's impossible, I'm not delusional. I'm all over this place. I picked out the dishtowel hanging on the stove. I found the dishes at an antique store not far from here. I'm the only person to ever have used the oven. And I'm leaving behind an entire room of things I can't bear to look at.

But I can't change any of that. I can't erase the imprint I'm leaving here.

All I can do is remove the few very personal items I have and stuff them in this suitcase.

Jon left the car keys today. And a list of errands he wanted me to do. Go to the store, buy his favorite foods, pick up a package at the post office—he was pissed about that, that it had to be picked up instead of delivered. But it was his fault. I couldn't exactly open the door with my face all purple.

I take one more look down the hallway to the last door on the left. It's closed. It's always closed.

I hope it stays closed forever because I'm so tired of thinking about it.

The suitcase is very heavy since it contains all the things I'd rather throw away than leave with Jon, but I manage to get it in the backseat of the Toyota, then plop myself down in the driver's seat and put my pack on the passenger side.

I'm remarkably calm for a girl who is about to run away. I expected my heart to beat wildly, like the last time I tried to leave.

I didn't make it that time. But that was two years ago now. He's made a mess of me so many times since then and I never tried to run away again, so I guess he figures I'm beat. He's won.

The car protests with backfires and clouds of smoke when I turn the key. I just press the gas until it gets over it. It will work today, I know it will. I'm not worried about the car breaking down at all, and typically I worry about that even if I'm just going to the supermarket in town.

Today it doesn't matter.

I pull out of the driveway and never look back.

The first thing on my checklist is to ditch the suitcase. I have no use for all that crap in my life anymore. My pack contains two extra day outfits, seven pairs of underwear, one pair of pajamas and some personal hygiene items.

I pull up to a dumpster just inside the Chicago city limits, then lug the suitcase out of the backseat and throw it down on the ground. There's a few homeless people sleeping nearby so I call out in a friendly voice, "Free stuff in this suitcase. Take whatever you want."

Most of them just stare at me looking pretty miserable. But a few get up and mumble out a 'thank you.'

I shrug and get back in the car and weave down a number of streets filled with cars and people walking. Going places and generally being busy on this Monday morning.

Monday is the perfect day because Jon can't work from home on Mondays. He has to go into the office downtown and work on the servers and stuff at the police station. So even though I won't answer his calls all day, he won't be able to figure out what's wrong until he gets home tonight. By then I'll be long gone and he won't be able to find me easily. His thing is computer forensics, so he's like a god in the virtual world. But I don't do anything virtual these days, so that's a total dead end for him. I have cash in my pocket that I've been stashing away, little by little, down in the basement for years.

And my bus ticket isn't even purchased yet, so he can't

track me that way.

I park the car in a trendy neighborhood far away from the bus station and check the mirror one more time.

I smile. My lips pull back from my cheeks and I look like a skeleton. I've lost a lot of weight, probably fifteen pounds, and skinny is in my nature, so right now I could probably stand to gain at least twenty to fill out my frame. I smile again and try not to see my life in my eyes.

This time I look almost OK. When you ignore the fact that my soul is crushed and my eyes really are a mirror inside. I don't look so bad.

But like the car, it doesn't matter today. I'm not worried about how people see me. If they see my fading bruises, or my cut lip, or the lost, tragic look in my eyes—I do not care. I exist alone in this world as of today.

There is just me.

The smile stays on my face as I enter the beauty salon.

And when I come out two hours later, I'm someone else. There's no sign of the limp blonde hair I've been dyeing since Jon took over my life. The tragic eyes are only half full of sadness and despair, the other half is hope. My hair is as close to its natural brown-black as you can get and not look fake and I changed into my other outfit before I left. All the ladies in the salon made a big deal out of me because I told them I had a special first date tonight and they chuckled and smiled and congratulated me and told me to 'go get him.'

What I left out was that my first date was with myself.

I end day one thousand one hundred and ten sitting on a Greyhound bus heading to Las Vegas. It's a two-day trip and I've been sitting in this seat for less than half of that and my back already aches and my legs are going numb.

But I don't care.

It's nice to meet me again and I can't wait to get to know me better.

CHAPTER ONE

Rook

Six Months Later
Denver, CO

The music pounds in my ear as I force myself up one more aisle of steps at Coors Field. This song always gets me trying a little harder. I hop the long step, then take a stride and pump my legs to go up two steps at once. I can't do this very long, I'm still no Ford when it comes to running stadiums, but I almost make it to the top before I have to slow down and then finally stop.

I look for Ford, but he's doing the lower sections today. Just a blur of a black shirt running much harder than me up his current set of steps. I jog in place until the song winds down and realize I've used up all my energy. So I stop and enjoy the view. This is why I come to the upper section these days.

The view. These mountains are gorgeous and I never get tired of looking at them. I'm off to the far right of first base. I'm not a baseball person, so I have no idea what that area on the field is called. Right field? I dunno. I'm not on the field anyway, I'm up in the stands, so it hardly matters.

The only thing that matters is that I can see the mountains and the way the reflected sunrise from the east lights them up all pink. Sometimes when Ronin and I are up there for the weekend or just for a ride, I have to pinch myself, that's how pretty it is.

Colorado changes once September arrives. One minute you're grilling outside and the nights are pleasant, the next it's freezing-ass cold. Well, fifties and sometimes forties, anyway. Too cold to hang out at night in shorts anymore.

But the new crisp air feels spectacular on my sweaty skin right now. In fact, I get a little chill because I'm starting to cool down. I enjoy the relative quiet for a few minutes. The traffic down below is pretty loud, but it's tempered by the ever-constant wind whistling across my ears. Colorado should be nicknamed the Wind State because it's a regular thing.

Life is so weird. I still can't get over how much things have changed for me since I stepped off that bus six months ago. I have a lot of money. Well, maybe not a lot compared to Ronin, but to me, a million dollars is too much to even comprehend. STURGIS will pay out at just under six hundred and fifty thousand dollars, plus the fifty grand I had from TRAGIC, plus the money the guys took from Jon when they set him up. I've got over a million, actually.

And I've bought nothing since before the STURGIS contract started besides food and gas and stuff like that. Not one thing. Not one article of clothing—I have way more clothes than I need. Not a stick of furniture—Ronin purchased all my furniture. Not even a car. Although this is gonna change very soon. I'm just too content to think about spending right now. I've never been a shopper and money has not changed that in me.

"Why did you stop?" Ford has made his way across the stadium and into the upper level while I was daydreaming. He's even carrying burritos and drinks.

"I'm done. Besides, I wanted to enjoy the view. It's our last time here, Ford."

He smiles. He does that a lot these days. And not just at me. I'm not one hundred percent sure if this is normal, but I'm guessing not. September has rolled in and everyone in my new little family is suddenly a lot happier.

Elise is pregnant, so she's one of those glowing moms-to-be. She's tiny everywhere but her stomach where she's just getting her fourth-month baby bump. No wonder she was so crazy all summer worrying about Clare. She was just as surprised as the rest of us when she did the pregnancy test the day we came back from Sturgis. Good thing Elise is not a partier or she'd probably be insane with worry because her mothering instinct is already kicking in. Antoine is beside himself with pride. He even asked her to marry him but she said, and I quote, "After twelve years I refuse to accept your proposal knocked-the-fuck-up."

He's still working on her, but she hasn't taken his ring.

Ronin is happy too. He's in charge of the GIDGET contract, which is not erotic modeling. Well, not really. It's a retro pin-up catalog shoot for a new lingerie company. They aren't really new, they're some subsidiary of another huge lingerie company, hence the cash flow for this kick-off.

Spencer is back up in Fort Collins doing his thing. But I'll see him tomorrow when Ronin moves me up to the shop for filming of the first season of Shrike Bikes for the Biker Channel.

Ronin and I talked about this decision *ad nauseam* after Sturgis. I won't go into the boring details, but he was managing the GIDGET contract so it was only fair that I got to do the show with Spencer because they start at the same time. It's perfect really. Our last flirt with this crazy world of modeling, then on to vague new things.

We haven't gotten that far yet, so I'm not sure what that means other than not what we're doing now.

"Here," Ford says, handing me a water and my partially unwrapped burrito. I take it and dig in. "We'll find something to take its place when we get up north. Don't worry."

"Hmm," I say with my mouth full. "I don't see what, Ford. That place is in the middle of nowhere. And winter is coming."

He smiles at the film reference. "Snowshoeing. Cross-country skiing. Extreme croquet."

I spit out some eggs as I laugh. "What. The. Fuck. Is. That?"

"It's croquet, but not." He sighs. "It's all relative, I guess."

"Sounds like my kind of game, actually. It's for stoners, isn't it? Like Frisbee?"

Ford laughs. "Maybe. We can skip the extreme croquet then. I'll figure something out. How's school coming?"

School. I'm in school. Sometimes I have to pinch myself, that's how excited this makes me. Ford, ever the stealthy hacker genius that he is, rigged my mandatory placement test for the community college up in FoCo and got me registered for fall semester. It's all online, so it's not really life-changing like if I was living on campus at Colorado State, which is the big FoCo university, but I'm stoked. I'm taking basic shit. English composition, History of Western Civ, biology, and pre-algebra.

Yes, I'm a total math loser, but what can you do? One baby step at a time.

"How's math, in particular?" Ford asks, like he's reading my mind. "I know you hated that I put you in a non-credit class, but it was the right decision, wasn't it?"

"Yes," I reluctantly admit. "I'm barely keeping up to be honest. It's confusing for me. I'm not a math girl."

"Well, luckily you need very little of it for film school, so don't dwell. Just do your best."

Ford is very supportive of my academic pursuits. *Very* supportive. It makes me wonder sometimes. It's not like Ronin isn't supportive, he is. He wants me to follow my dream. But Ford is supportive in a different way. Like he's invested in it or something. Like his success is dependent on mine. And that gets me thinking back to what he said a few months ago. About how patient he is. About him giving me the tools I need to fix my life, so I'll stop looking for Ronin to do that for me. He wants me to be strong all on my own. Not need anyone.

I like that about Ford. It's like he trusts me. Like he's got faith in me.

It makes me have faith in myself.

"How come you don't have a girlfriend, Ford?"

"What makes you think I don't?"

"Oh," I reply, embarrassed. "Do you?"

He looks away. "I have... women." He looks back, smiling. "But they're not girlfriends."

I'm not even sure what to say to that, so of course I choose something totally inappropriate. "Are they... whores?"

He laughs. "No comment." And then he takes a big bite of his burrito and shuts that conversation down.

"Clare's coming home tomorrow." I'm not sure why I fill in the silence with that tidbit of information—

"You're nervous about meeting her."

—but apparently Ford has a pretty good handle on my psyche these days. "Yeah. I still think about what you said, you know."

He shrugs. "I'm not going to say any more about it. Ronin's your boyfriend, you like each other. That's all that matters."

I stare at him for a few more seconds and let this sink in. "Good, that means you've lost interest in me and all that shit you said last summer about wanting me to leave Ronin is over."

He laughs. "We're friends, right? I'm happy with how things are going between us. It's perfect actually."

Hmmm. That's weird. In fact, I'm weird right now. I shouldn't be asking him this stuff but I can't help myself. "Because you're... what? Emotionally incapable of intimate relationships? This friendship is as far as you go? There's nothing after this but the physical act of sex?"

"Yes, yes, and yes. You missed your calling. You should've been a psych major."

"I cheat. Ronin told me about... well, he told me why he was so insistent on me not talking to you."

"And do you agree with my diagnosis?"

"Not really," I say, shaking my head. "You're a bit on the

strange side—"

He laughs again, his eyes darting around the stadium, like he's thinking about this.

"—and I'm guessing you really are some scary smart genius. I totally see that. But you've done a lot of very nice things for me, Ford. And I never asked for it. I'm not always nice back to you, but I hope you know I really, really appreciate it."

He drops the smile now and stares hard just past my head, like he's thinking. I hold my breath as I wait for him to say something and when he finally begins to talk, it's soft and low. "We fucked Mardee up pretty good. We were all tight—Mardee, Ronin, Spencer, and me. A sort of unit. Even though Ronin and I never got along well, it was different when the four of us were together. It was… just different. And you stunned me last summer when you asked me that question, Rook. I didn't know what to say."

"What question?"

"Who was I chasing." He lets out a long breath. "Her. I'm chasing her. I'm trying to catch up with all the mistakes we made. It's funny how you take people for granted." He looks me in the eye for this part. "We took her for granted. We used her, we…"

I wait him out, patient, like he is with me.

He takes a drink and swallows hard before continuing. "Ronin blames himself for not paying attention to her, and Spencer blames himself for bringing her around the drugs, but we all played a part. You two really have nothing in common, but every time I look at you, I see her. And it just…" He stops to shake his head. "I just want you to succeed so badly. It feels good to watch you grow stronger."

I'm not sure what to say. I knew this Mardee girl weighed on Ronin's conscience, but it seems to go much deeper than that. There's a lot more to this story than they've told me, but Ford was right about something else he told me last summer. I'm a keeper. A secret-keeper, just like they are. And I'm not sure I want to keep their secrets as well as mine. I'm not sure I can handle that right now.

So if these guys do have more secrets, they can keep them. I'm totally OK with that and I take my chance to change the subject before I learn something I might not want to know. "I am getting better, though. And you're helping me. All three of you are helping me, actually. You with the running and school, Ronin with trust and relationships, and Spencer with the jobs. I'm so lucky to have you guys."

"I'm enjoying you too, Rook. You've taught me a few things as well."

I choke down a snort. "Like what?"

He begins to talk, but stops the words at the last second. His gaze sweeps across the baseball field below, then rests back on me. "Emotions have been… very difficult for me. It's true what Ronin said. I wouldn't say I have none, or that I'm incapable like my father thought. It's not that I *don't* or *can't* feel things like that. It's that I don't want to. I just don't care about people." He throws up his hands. "That's my dirtiest secret and now you have it. I just don't give a fuck about people, I really don't."

I can't help myself because these personal conversations with Ford are not common, so I ask. "Did you care about Mardee?"

"I did," he says with a sigh.

"And she preferred Ronin?"

He's the one who almost snorts this time. "Don't they all?" He looks over at me. "Don't you all prefer Ronin?"

I rest my elbows back on the concrete step behind me and then stretch my legs out. "You're a nice-looking guy, Ford. So is Spencer. I'm not sure one could actually choose between the three of you. You're all good catches. Equally desirable in different ways."

He screws up his face. "How is *Spencer* desirable? I have never understood what girls see in him."

I laugh. "Well, he's like a big fun-loving goof-ball, but

powerful and dangerous at the same time. He's the bad boy girls fall in lust with and don't mind taking orders from."

"And Ronin?"

"Ronin's just hot." I grin over at him. "He's the player all the girls want to settle down with. But he's nice too. If Spence is the bad boy, then Ronin is the good guy. The knight in shining armor, like you said."

"And me?"

I don't look at him this time, but I can feel his stare like it's heat. Waiting. "You're… predictable."

He belts out a laugh. "Well, I appreciate the ego stroke, Rook. Thank you." He gets up and starts to walk down the stairs.

"I wasn't finished."

He stops but keeps his back to me.

"Not predictable as in boring or repetitive, but predictable as in safe. Even though I'm always adjusting when I'm with you, reevaluating things about myself and… you. You're like an open book, Ford. What you see is what you get. So I'm not sure why your father thought that about you, I'm not really qualified to think too hard about it and make a better observation. But I'll just say this. The reason I like you is because you're honest. I know what I'm getting with you even though you keep me guessing. Because I always know that when you give me something, it will be good and you're only thinking of what's best for me. Ronin and Spencer are not better-looking than you, that's for sure. You guys are just desirable in different ways."

He turns around and smiles. "Good to know. Ready?"

I shrug because I can see through his act now—he avoids talking about himself in personal ways most of the time. He'll tell me all about his college days, his jobs, professional things like that. But he hides from the emotional stuff, the things that cause him to feel too much. Not everything, mind you—he opens up every once in a while—but that open book has closed for today and I know this is his signal that talking is over.

I'm OK with that because I, too, am patient.

CHAPTER TWO

Rook

There are a ton of girls milling around the building because Ronin is having an open casting call for the GIDGET models. I'm actually relieved I'm not GIDGET. Not that there's just one, he needs like a dozen of them, I think. But I'm so over modeling, it's not even funny. I can think of hundreds of jobs I'd rather do right off the top of my head. Like rodeo clown. I'd rather be a target for a raging bull than be a model.

The girls are here early to line up and they wind around the corner and spill over into the back lot. They are all dressed up, full make-up, heels, and they look cold. I'm still warm from my morning exercise, but I can feel the chill in the air. And just looking at their shoes makes my toes sad. I'm so glad I'm the new parts girl for Shrike Bikes. I get to wear jeans, and hoodies, and sneakers.

I totally got the better end of the deal.

Ford and I walk towards the parking lot as per usual and he gets annoyed at a girl who is standing too close to his vehicle. He always parks in the same spot in the back of the lot, just off to the left of the back door. He just got a new car—well, I'd never really call it new, but last week was the first time I've seen it. He used to drive a sporty little black Beamer but then he showed up with this… thing. "I liked the old car, Ford."

He's just about to open the door when this comes out and he stops to look back at me. "Really? Why?"

I crack a smile and so does he. "It suits you. This circa 1986 Bronco is just all kinds of wrong."

"I needed a truck for winter. I still have the BMW, I just parked it in my mom's garage."

"You have a mom?" I laugh as the words come out.

"You thought I was a demon spawned from hell?"

I nod and laugh again. "I might buy a car. I'm gonna get something totally inappropriate for winter. Like a VW bus."

"Or a convertible. I could totally see you in a Roadster."

We both stop for a second. I'm sure the irony isn't lost to the armchair psychologist in him. I just compared myself to a beaten-up old has-been and he compared me to a classic beauty. I smile. "Yeah, I love those. But I'll probably end up with a truck too. It seems that's the vehicle of choice around here."

Ford nods in agreement. "What time are you and Ronin driving up tomorrow?"

"Well, I think Clare is supposed to get here tomorrow around noon, so we should make FoCo early evening, maybe? I'm not sure."

"OK, see you then." He turns back to his hideous truck and I notice that there are a lot of girls in the back parking lot now. They're all staring at Ford and me. I make my escape to the back door, punch in my code, and then take the stairs up to the fourth floor.

There's lots of people here today even though it's a Friday. Typically Fridays are dead, but it's open casting. Ronin already hired two models who have worked for Antoine before. And Billy is the only male model. But since they're doing a catalog shoot with hundreds of clothing articles, they need a lot of girls. Plus, once the shoot is over they're having a special fashion show in LA for the kickoff just before Christmas. It's kind of a big deal for the models. A career-making kinda job.

I wave to Ronin across the studio, but don't stop and chat. He's busy talking to Roger, who is the main photographer for this contract. Antoine is officially on hiatus so he and Elise can keep an eye on Clare when she gets home from the clinic.

She was up there at that treatment center for four months and she's barely out of the woods. My mom was a crack addict, she never did heroin that I knew of, so I'm not all that up on the consequences of that particular drug. But after hearing about Clare's struggle this summer, I just can't understand why anyone would even try that shit once. She had a terrible time. It made her slightly insane for a while. And she was in a lot of pain, I know that for sure because Ronin left some literature out in the living room once and I read it. The withdrawal from heroin is so bad, so painful, that most people just can't do it.

Clare is lucky. She has Antoine, and Elise, and Ronin. And they're all very rich. She got the best treatment money could buy. She was sequestered up in the mountains, away from all negative influences, and she was dragged through the program by people who love her until she could manage the commitment herself. It's a miracle she got this far and we had a very serious conference call with the treatment facility yesterday about what she needs to do going forward. They've finally weaned her off the methadone, which is a long-acting opiate that alleviates the pain of withdrawal without getting her high.

Her last dose was two weeks ago and the doctor insists she's done very well, but it only takes one slip-up. Just one and all that hard work will be for nothing. She'll always be addicted to opiates, she can never take them without risking the possibility of withdrawal pain. "She will never," he stressed, "be normal again." The drug has changed her forever. She will always be tempted to take it, remembering the euphoria of the high and not the pain that comes after.

It scares the shit out of me just thinking about it.

I punch in Ronin's apartment code and head to the shower and then peel off my clothes and start the jets.

Clare's lifelong addiction issue scares me for two reasons. One, of course, is that it will be so difficult for her to stay clean. I feel sorry for her and I really do want her to succeed. But even more than that, it scares me because it practically guarantees Ronin a girl who will need him forever. And even though Ford won't bring it up again, I'll always be wondering if I'm just a project for Ronin. If I'm just a broken girl who needs a knight to save her.

I'm not broken. In fact, I've never felt so together in my entire life. I have everything going for me. I've got money, a cool job, friends, a place to live… I have it all. And I'm pretty sure my damsel-in-distress moments are over.

So if that was the reason he liked me, I'm gonna figure this out pretty fast.

I'm not convinced that Ford's characterization of Ronin is correct. I mean, Ronin has said over and over that he thinks I'm strong and brave and I'm not getting the liar vibe off him. Not at all.

But still.

I'd rather know sooner than later if this is the case. I don't want to ignore the warning signals that things are going off track and then wake up three years later and realize I wasted my time—it's over.

I check the clock and realize I have to get downstairs to help out with the casting, so I pull on some jeans, a t-shirt, and a little zippered hoodie just in case I get cold. I slip out into the hallway and see Antoine and Elise standing down at the end of the hall in front of their apartment.

"Rook!" Antoine calls. "Ellie is going back to bed. Can you check the girls in today?"

I walk over to them and look down at Elise. "What's wrong?" So far she's had a pretty easy pregnancy, but she's practically green this morning.

"Just queasy, that's all. I need to go back to bed for a little bit, I'll come help later."

I take her hand and pat it gently. "I can do it, Elise. Just go rest." I turn to Antoine. "Ronin and I can handle it, Antoine."

"Are you sure?" he asks doubtfully. "There are hundreds of girls already lined up."

I shrug. "Well, it's a casting call, not anything life-threatening. We'll manage. Just go relax, you guys."

I don't have to say it again—they are outta there. I smile as I go downstairs. The front door is still closed but everyone is already busy. Ronin and Roger are chatting over some notes when I walk up to them.

"Antoine said I can check the girls in since Elise isn't feeling well."

Ronin turns to me quickly. "What's wrong with her?"

I take his hand. "She's fine, just morning sickness." I smile up at his worried face. I think it's cute he worries over Elise so much. He's really gonna be a fantastic uncle. When Elise told us after we came back from Sturgis Ronin was so happy he could hardly contain his excitement.

"You sure? I'm new at this baby stuff, I worry about her."

"Antoine's with her. If she needs help he'll come tell us."

He thinks about this for a few seconds and then puts his arm around me in a casual embrace. "OK. Billy!" he yells. "Show Rook how to check in girls up here and you can do first cut downstairs."

Billy nods and I kiss Ronin real quick and head over. Billy is fussing with a laptop that is set up near the door. He points to it. "OK, Rook, it's pretty simple. When they come up you check them in in groups of five. We put out an international casting call, so we will have hundreds of girls outside today. I'll choose which ones can come up for a group interview and give them a number bracelet." He points to the computer. "Then you fill in the form with their names and stuff, then hit enter. Ronin and Roger will get it over at the set"—he points to the large black partition segregating us from the interview section of the studio—"and they'll send you a message when they want you to send them over. Then it's just lather, rinse, repeat. Got it?"

"No problemo," I answer back.

"OK," Billy says, checking his phone. "It's five minutes to nine now, so I'll go start choosing and then send them up one at a time. Check them in as they come because pretty soon there will be a lot of girls lining up on the stairs."

I salute and he heads down to the street level. The computer is set up on a tall cafe table and there's a stool for me to sit on. But I take advantage of the silence and wander into the kitchen and grab a cup of coffee from the massive automatic machine, then make my way over to the computer table and wait for the first girl to arrive.

It takes five more minutes before the main door whooshes downstairs and the first girl's heels click up the stairs. I bet she is a nervous wreck. I know I would be. I picture myself as I made my first trip up these stairs and I barely recognize that girl in my memory. I'm lost in my own recollection of weakness and fright when the girl comes into view.

I'm not sure what I expected, but this was not it. The girl is a few inches taller than me, which is saying something because I'm five foot nine, and her hair is long and naturally blonde. It's got streaks of brown in it, like people pay salons hundreds of dollars to replicate, and her eyes are a striking blue-green. Blue-green. Who has blue-green eyes? She is so beautiful I'm almost speechless. I swallow. "Hi, I'm Rook and I'm gonna check you in."

"I'm Océane," she says. Her accent is French. I have to turn away to stop the sneer. What did I expect? Antoine has beautiful girls walking around here every day. I'm one of them, actually. But even though Billy said they put out an international casting call, I guess I just expected Denver girls to show up. I take a deep breath and start checking her in, trying my best not to worry about Ronin being around all these beautiful women for the next few months while I'm up in the middle of fucking nowhere prancing around in my t-shirts and jeans, picking up parts for Spencer's bike shop and playing extreme croquet in the snow with Ford.

It only goes downhill from there. One extraordinarily beautiful girl after another walks up those stairs. Billy knows what he's doing sorting the wheat from the chaff, because they are all stunning with a capital S. I'm still mulling this over, half-heartedly checking in girls as they come up the stairs and sending them into the studio in groups of five, when the freight elevator dings.

We hardly ever use the freight elevator. Most of the time everyone just takes the stairs because the elevator is slow and clunky. So this ding actually makes me stop what I'm doing and turn around just in time to see a thin blonde girl exit with a man in a suit. It takes me a minute to recognize her because of the cute outfit and lack of make-up. She's wearing pink sweatpants, a white tank top, and a cropped pink zippered jacket to match her pants. Her fresh face is glowing, her eyes are bright, and she is the picture of health. Her long hair is tied back in a ponytail and she looks like she's about to model for Victoria's Secret *Pink* line. She walks past me, never even looking in my direction, and the white letters splash across her ass. Yup. *Pink* all right.

"Who's that?" someone asks from behind me.

She disappears behind the tall black partition wall put in place for the interviews and I can hear Ronin's roar of delight.

"Clare Chaput," I reply absently in a whisper. "That's Clare Chaput."

CHAPTER THREE

Ronin

GIDGET is the first project that Roger and I are working on exclusively. The first project where Antoine is not involved at all. So everything is just slightly more important than normal. At least for me—I'm a perfectionist ninety percent of the time and I've been obsessing over this contract since I won it a few months back. If I play my cards right I might be able to make a go of fashion marketing. Not that Rook and I need the money. Work stopped being about money a while back. I've lived in money for a dozen years now and at least half of those years I was earning a significant amount on my own just from modeling. The con jobs don't even factor into my bank account bottom line because it sorta creeps me out.

Stolen money. We stole all that money. Ford, Spence and I ruined more than one family over it and I do feel a little bit guilty about that. People's children should not have to suffer for the misdeeds of their parents, but we had our reasons.

I don't touch that money. It's in so many different trusts and offshore accounts I might not even know how to find it all again, should I ever want to.

I laugh at that internally as I pretend to listen to the group of girls in front of me. Ford would know how to find it. We might hate each other most of the time, but he's got his skills, and manipulating money and keeping track of bank accounts is one of them. The three of us made a pact after that last job. No spending any of our new money until we all had careers that would justify the lifestyle change and avoid any scrutiny, because I'll be honest here, we barely got away with one a few years back. It was a technicality really. Rules of evidence worked in our favor.

There was no paper trail because we were strictly virtual criminals, but one detective got nosey with a computer that was not part of the crime scene and he found a teeny-tiny nugget of info which led to something Ford had taken great care to hide. But because the detective had no warrant, meaning he'd accessed that computer illegally, nothing he got from it was admissible as evidence when the grand jury was asked to indict us.

We walked away free and clear and that little bit of info was sealed and not given out to the media, but the cops know what we did.

And they are patient. They watch everything, I'm sure.

Which is why we're working our asses off. We're patient too, and besides, all our cons, and that one in particular, were for revenge, not paying bills or vacations.

Ford, Spencer, and I all have the same work ethic and that's one of the things that bind us so tightly. Each of us has been given opportunities through luck or paternity, and we never took them for granted. We're professionally successful because we work hard, not because we steal. I don't need to work, I have a shitload of honest money saved up, but I will be working once Rook and I leave this life behind because sitting on my ass is not an option.

I scroll down the laptop screen as the next group of girls walks in. So far there are maybe one or two who might fit with what we're looking for. Tall and thin are a given, but beyond that I'm looking for fresh. Exciting. Clean-cut. And wholesome—it's a retro pin-up type shoot, after all. We like to use pouty and depressed girls for the dark erotic shoots because they sell better, but this is a catalog shoot. Lots of bright artificial lighting is a must so the girls typically at the top of my model list are not really suitable.

I look over this group, absently smile at them as Roger does the interview, then we dismiss them and I choose no one. "Did you like any?" I ask Roger.

"Nah. Next."

I'm just about to message Rook so she can send the next group when another girl walks into our makeshift room. It takes me a moment to recognize her because I haven't seen her in over a month, but once I do my happiness is immediate.

"Clare!" I get up and scoop her up in a big hug. "We're supposed to pick you up tomorrow!" She squeezes me tight as I lift her and everything just melts away. I put her down and hold her out at arm's length so I can look her over. "You look so good, sweetie!"

She sighs and then flashes me an embarrassed smile as she blushes. "Thanks. Hey, Roger, long time, eh?"

"Yeah," he says, standing up and coming over to her. He plants a kiss on her cheek and pulls her into a hug. "You really look great, Clare. Really great."

"Do Antoine and Elise know you're here?"

"No, I wanted to surprise you guys, I wanted to—"

I grab her hand and pull her towards the stairs. "Oh, you're gonna make them so happy, Clare, come on!" I drag her upstairs, totally ignoring the guy she came in with, punch in the code and rush her into the apartment. Elise is lying on the couch with her feet in Antoine's lap. It takes them a moment to recognize Clare too, but both sets of eyes go wide when it kicks in and Elise jumps up faster than she should for someone with morning sickness. She flings her little arms around Clare and hugs her tight.

"You sneak! We were gonna pick you up tomorrow!"

Clare starts crying as Antoine joins the group hug and then pulls her into his arms and buries his face in her hair. "I'm so glad you're home. So glad you're home."

Clare is like a new person. I just stand there and shake my head. I can't remember her ever looking this good. Ever. She's put on at least ten pounds, her hair is sleek and her blue eyes are bright and alert.

How long has it been since I saw her clean?

Years. It's been years since this girl looked healthy.

I just smile at them as they chat and Elise and Clare wipe away tears. "Oh, Rook! You have to meet Rook, Clare." I jog through the door and stand at the top of the stairs. "Everyone—take thirty, please. Clare's home!" I hear a smattering of claps from the regular staff and take a deep breath and let the happiness wash over me. *It worked,* I think to myself. *We fixed her. She looks better than ever. It worked!*

"Rook!" I call down. "Come up here, Gidge! You have to meet Clare!"

Rook smiles and sets down her clipboard, then pushes the girls outside the door and closes it before walking slowly over to the stairs. I take her hand once she reaches me and let out a long sigh. "Did you see her come in? Doesn't she look great?" I don't wait for an answer, just tug her into Antoine's apartment with me and spread my arms wide. "Rook, this is Clare. The *real* Clare," I add. "Not that psycho bitch you saw in the dressing room that day last spring."

Clare swats me on the arm. "I deserve that, but I'd rather not be reminded."

I pull her into another hug before she greets Rook, then lean down and kiss her head. "I am so happy, you have no idea!"

She swats me again and pulls back as she offers her hand to Rook. "I've heard a lot about you, Gidget." Clare winks at her and when I look over at Rook she's blushing.

Rook extends her hand out and shakes it. "It's so great to meet you, Clare," Rook says. It comes out polite and sweet, like all her words. But I detect something underneath. She can't be jealous of *Clare*. Can she?

Clare turns back to Elise and Antoine and they talk excitedly in French. When I look back to Rook she's frowning. "Hey, English only when Rook's here, guys. She can't understand and it's rude."

"That's OK, Ronin. I don't mind."

This is a lie, but I'm not about to push it here. I pull her close and then lean down to kiss her. "Let's get back to work." I look over to Antoine and nod. "We're still on for tonight?" He nods back and I smile down at Rook again. She's uncomfortable with Clare, I can tell. Maybe jealous, maybe even intimidated.

"What's tonight?" she asks.

"Oh, just dinner at your favorite French restaurant."

She moans and follows me out the door. I stop at the top of the stairs. "You don't want to go fancy with me tonight? I'll pick you out a sexy dress from the closet." I waggle my eyebrows at her to try and play innocent, but she's irritated on two fronts now. My choice in restaurants and insinuating I get to choose her clothes.

It takes all my self-control not to laugh at her, but I manage because she's right where I want her. So I say nothing, just drag her back downstairs and drop her off at the front door and then take my place back on the other side of the room with Roger.

Yup. I've got her right where I want her.

CHAPTER FOUR

Rook

The rest of my day goes like shit. I check in hundreds of girls. Hundreds of beautiful girls who make me look like some homeless person living out of a garbage can in my zippered hoodie and my last year's jeans.

I'm not kidding either. I know I'm not ugly. Hell, I'm pretty enough to get two major modeling contracts, so that's not what this is about. It's not about me, or my degree of pretty. These girls are drop-dead, can't-take-your-eyes-off-them, stunningly beautiful—gorgeous.

They have perfect skin, toned bodies, designer clothes, professionally applied make-up, and exotic accents. Almost all of them have some sort of accent, even if it's just Southern Belle Sweet or Valley Girl Annoying. None of them sound the same.

And then, of course, there's the really exotic girls. The ones from Asia and Australia and Europe.

I wonder if my barely-there Chicago accent qualifies as exotic?

I snort quietly to myself. I'm pretty sure that's a big fucking no.

And if all this wasn't enough to make me feel super insecure and plain, Clare is here.

Clare. The first beautiful person I encountered the day Luck changed my life. The one girl who commands Ronin's attention like no other. Not even me. Sure, he shows up and saves me when I need it, but if Clare and I had an emergency at the same moment, I'm just not sure he'd pick me every time.

I sigh and send the last group of girls over to Ronin and Roger.

These girls look tired and worn down. It's past six now and they've been standing around for the better part of twelve hours. They must really be in denial because there's no way Ronin and Roger, exhausted and sick of looking at girls and reading resumes, are even remotely interested in these last five girls. But maybe they like the girls enough to keep their names on file for something in the future. I guess if you're desperate to be discovered as a model, this is one way to do it.

Less than five minutes later Ronin comes out from behind the walled-off partition stretching his arms as I let the sad group of girls out and then make sure the door clicks to indicate it's locked. A knock scares the shit out of me and I open the door again.

"Delivery for Chaput?" the man with a clipboard says.

"Um…"

"That's us," Ronin says. He signs the paperwork and points over to the kitchen or maybe the terrace. "Over there is fine, thanks." And then the freight elevator dings and Ronin has me by the arm and he's leading me upstairs.

"What about my dress?" I ask as we flash past the dressing room.

"I told you, I got you covered."

I scowl at him. "I seriously thought you were kidding. You're not kidding?"

"Trust me, Rook." But I'm not sure I should, because his face does not look trustworthy, it looks… *devious.* If my silence bothers him, he doesn't show it, just pulls me down the hallway to our apartment, unlocks the door, and whisks me inside.

"What's going on?"

"Wanna have living room sex or kitchen sex?"

He winks at me and I let out a long breath and laugh. "What?"

His hands slide around my hips, dipping down to caress my ass a little through my tight jeans, then slip under my shirt. "Or patio sex?"

"What's wrong with shower sex?" I ask, smiling. *What's gotten into him*?

"We have shower sex every day, let's spice things up."

I blush a little because it has gotten a little predictable lately. Ronin has been cautious with our sex life all summer over all that Jon stuff, but I'll be honest and admit that I prefer the sexually adventurous Ronin over the sexually cautious one any day. "Well…" I say, dragging out the word. "What do you have in mind? And how long do we have before we have to meet everyone for dinner?"

He leans in and kisses me, sliding my zippered hoodie down my arms and letting it drop to the floor. I never know what I'm in for when he gets in the mood. Sometimes he acts like he's starving for my lips, desperate and wanting and rough.

Tonight it's like he's afraid of breaking them, that's how soft and tender he is.

I like it and I kiss him back just as tenderly, our tongues twisting together as he lifts up my shirt. He pulls back for a moment to slip it over my head and then resumes the kiss as the shirt is discarded. One hand cups my breast and then reaches behind to get rid of my bra while the other one unbuttons my jeans. "Kitchen or living room?" he breathes into my mouth.

"Right here," I reply as I lift his t-shirt up—dragging my palms against his muscular back—clear his head and drop it in the pile of clothes at our feet. He pushes me a little until I take a step back. The back of my knees bump up against the leather couch and I am forced to sit down, coming eye to eye with his hard thickness through his jeans.

I smile up at him.

He smirks down at me.

I go for the button on his jeans but he gently takes my hands and pushes them away. "No, Gidget. Not tonight." He pushes me back on the couch, unzips my pants, grabs them by the belt loops, and pulls them down, taking my panties with him.

He looks down on my naked body with hunger. Like he's never seen it before. He licks his lips and kneels down.

"What are you up to?"

"It's present time," is all he says as his head dips between my legs. He lifts one leg up and pushes it towards my shoulder and his lips find the dent behind my knee.

I laugh when he sucks and nips the tender skin there, and then arch my back because holy fucking shit, I had no idea that spot was so, so, so… erotically sensitive.

I close my eyes and moan as he nips just a little bit harder, making me immediately wet.

And then his fingers are inside me. Fucking Ronin always did have magic fingers. What he does with those fingers, oh, God. I could write books. I try my best to calm down, but it's very, very difficult to ignore the way he makes me feel. Just as I'm about to get it back under control his tongue joins the party and I can't help it, the orgasm explodes against my will.

When I open my eyes and look down at him he's grinning so big I have to laugh. "What?"

"You," he whispers and lets out a sigh. "You are the hottest fucking woman I've ever laid eyes on. I saw hundreds of girls today, each one prettier than the last. But I compared each and every one of them to you, Rook. And not one—" He stops to look me in the eye as he stands up and takes off his pants and boxers, then pulls me to my feet, sits down where I just was, and places me in his lap. I drape my arms over his shoulders. "Not one of them even came close to measuring up to you, Gidge."

I blush as all my insecurities melt away.

Like instantly.

I lean down and kiss him, another tender one. He responds in the same manner, not hurried or desperate, but slow, and patient, and soft. "I am so in love with you, Ronin

Flynn. So very, very much in love with you."

"OK, wait," he says with more urgency that is necessary. I have a little panic attack thinking he's gonna say he's not in love with me anymore, but that melts away when he cups my face and looks me in the eyes. "I can't call you Rook Walsh anymore."

I laugh. "What?"

"I can't say it without feeling sick. So what's your last name?"

"Corvus," I say in a whisper. "My name is Rook Corvus."

He smiles, like he's in on the joke, but he keeps it to himself if he is. "Miss Corvus, I am so far beyond in love with you, I can barely function. I want to marry you. Like yesterday. But I know that's not gonna happen just yet, so I just want you to know, I can wait." He studies my face as I take all this in. "I will wait."

CHAPTER FIVE

Ronin

Even though Rook and I have had quite a bit of downtime over the past few months, it's not enough. I wish for endless days of doing nothing but making love, feeding her fruit, and sleeping with my arms wrapped around her.

Right now we're both spent from the mind-blowing sex. Her cheek rests on my shoulder as I lean my head back on the couch. "I could fall asleep right now."

"Let's stay home," she mumbles into my neck. "I'm too tired to get dressed up and go to dinner."

"We can't skip this one, Gidge. It's our last dinner until next weekend."

She moans but doesn't lift her head. "I'm gonna buy a car and commute to Fort Collins. It's not even that far."

"I'm one hundred percent on board with that." And then I smack her ass cheek playfully and make her squeal. "Come on, let's take a shower real fast. It'll wake you up so you can enjoy the evening."

I stand up, still cupping her close to me, and she reluctantly untangles herself and kisses me on the neck. "Don't get me the duck this time, OK? Maybe pasta."

I laugh. Poor Rook. "Don't worry, I promise, you'll enjoy dinner."

She livens up in the shower when I wash her, but it's hard for her to get excited when she thinks she's being forced to wear a dress she'll probably hate and eat food she knows for sure will make her hurl.

I almost feel bad. But not quite.

She's sitting on the bed wrapped up in a white towel, just moping, as I pull on my tux trousers. "The dress is in your closet, Gidget. And it doesn't have legs, so it won't come to you."

She makes a face at me and then hoists herself up and walks into the closet. I slip my crisp white shirt on and wait for it.

Silence.

Little itty-bitty tip-toe footsteps behind me.

My grin is huge as she drapes her arms over my shoulders and breathes her words heavily into my ear. "What is that absolutely gorgeous gown doing in my closet, Larue? That's not something you wear to dinner, no matter what kind of food they serve."

I turn around and look down at her. "No? Well, you must be the expert, so tell me… what kind of event warrants a gown like that?"

"A Cinderella ball," she coos in my ear.

"Oh, fuck, Rook. Do that again and I'll never let you out of the apartment tonight."

"Fat chance of that now! I'm wearing that damn dress. I'm not sure what you've got planned, but whatever it is, I'm going."

She skips away making happy squeals and calling out guesses about where we're going. "A fundraiser?"

"Nope," I say as I button up my shirt.

"A private jet to… well, shit, there's no classy cities close to Denver, so… Albuquerque?"

I laugh. "Only Bugs Bunny goes to Albuquerque."

She snorts for real at that remark. "That's funny." I tuck my shirt in and go for the bow tie. "Somewhere in the mountains?"

"Try again."

I grab my suit coat and slide it on, then check myself in the full-length mirror. There's no way I'll be able to live up to how beautiful Rook will be tonight, but it will have to do.

"Zip me," she says quietly from behind.

I turn and take her in. I didn't pick this dress, Elise did. In fact, Rook has no idea, but it was made especially for her by a fashion friend of Antoine's. We've been planning this night for more than a month. It's a floor-length strapless white gown with the slightest mermaid shape to it. Not enough to make her look ridiculous, just enough so that the smooth fabric hugs every curve on her body and flares out near her feet. And Rook has all the right curves in all the right places. She's nothing like the skinny models who came through here today and I love everything about her shape. The tail drags just enough to make her look like she's floating when she walks, but not enough so that it will cause problems in a crowd.

"What's the occasion, then?" she asks coyly. Clearly she knows what the occasion is, but she's fishing to see if *I* know.

"The occasion? I don't need a special occasion to take you to the ball."

"So it is a big event?"

"Yes," I say as I turn her around and slide that zipper up her back. I lean in and nibble behind her neck. "Leave your hair down tonight, OK?"

"Yes, sir," she says with a wink as she pulls back.

But she's not getting away that easy. "You can't *yes, sir* me and then expect to walk away without a reminder of what's to come later." My hand reaches behind her neck and I press her whole body into mine, then kiss her, raking my fingers up into her long dark hair and fisting it a little as she moans and throws her head back. I know she likes some of the dominant stuff we do in the bedroom, but I don't try it often. It took me all fucking summer to get over what her ex did to her as a teenager. But that awkward feeling is beginning to fade. And I'm not sure it was ever a real problem with her, so maybe tonight she'd like to do something fun.

"I hope that's a promise, Mr. Flynn."

When she says my name like that it takes my breath away.

I want her to be my Mrs. Flynn so bad it makes my heart ache, but I refuse to pressure her. I want her to come to me when she's ready. "Miss Corvus, don't ever doubt me." Her blue eyes sparkle when she looks up to me and for a moment I can actually picture our beautiful family. A whole gang of little blue-eyed cherubs running around.

It makes me sigh.

"What are you thinking about in there, Ronin? I see the wheels turning."

I slip my arm around her waist and dip her backwards, making her squeal. "You, that's all." I lift her back up and smack her butt to end the flirting and get us back on track, because we are already fashionably late and people are probably tired of waiting.

She goes into the bathroom and chats to me non-stop about the dress and her make-up, which she applies as she talks. My phone buzzes and I check it, then text Antoine back and let him know we're coming in five minutes.

When she's done with her make-up she fluffs up her damp hair with the blow dryer, making it cascade down her back in loose raven curls, and then pulls a brush through it. Her feet slip into the white satin shoes and she looks over to me and smiles. Rook hates heels and if she had her way I'm sure she'd be wearing those old-ass red Converse with the holes in the toes. So I made sure her shoes for tonight are comfortable ballet flats. She turns her back to me so I can clasp a necklace around her neck. The only time Rook wears jewelry of any kind is when I put it on her. Otherwise she won't bother. I hand her some earrings to match the necklace and she puts them on and turns to the mirror.

"Wow. I look great."

I laugh. "Yeah, you really do, Gidget. You clean up nice."

"I almost feel like a bride, wearing this white dress."

"Don't taunt me with that image, please." I take her hand and lead her out of the apartment. "But I'd be more than happy to pretend this is our wedding reception if you like."

"OK, spill it. Where are we going?" We walk down the hallway towards the stairs. "Why's it so dark in here?"

"I dunno, but you better hold my hand a little tighter so you don't fall down the stairs."

We get to the bottom without killing ourselves and we're just walking past the terrace when I notice the light out in Rook's old apartment. "Who's in your place?" I ask.

"What?" she asks, craning her neck to see outside. "Huh. I have no idea. Maybe Ford's in there doing something?"

"Let's check it out." I urge her to follow me over to the terrace doors and punch in my code to open the door. "After you," I say, waving her forward.

"It's dark—" The words are just leaving her mouth when the whole place lights up. Every cherry tree is sparkling with white lights.

"Surprise!"

I laugh when she jumps back at the shouts. And then everyone appears from the various alcoves and nooks. Rook's hand goes up to her mouth. "What's this?"

I pull her close as she takes in the scene. Everyone we know is here. Spencer and Veronica, Clare, Ford and his… *woman.* Antoine and Elise, all the camera and sound crews from the Shrike Show, Director Larry, Billy and his girlfriend, Roger and his wife and a few of the other photographers, the Chaput models, and all the salon girls and their husbands.

Every man is wearing a black tux and every woman is wearing a white dress.

"A black-and-white affair for my Gidget. Because Rook, you are one batshit insane chick if you think you can have a birthday around here and not be embarrassed with a huge over-the-top production!"

She cries.

And I hug her close as everyone comes over, smiling and laughing at putting one over on her and making her tear up with happiness.

She turns and hugs me hard, then dips her mouth to my

ear. "Ronin Flynn, you are my forever guy. I'd just like to say that right now. You are my forever guy."

"I fully plan on holding you to it, Gidget. One hundred percent. Now let's have some fucking fun with our family and friends."

CHAPTER SIX

Rook

I'm living in a fairy tale.

Seriously.

The entire terrace is something magical. The cherry trees are awash with soft white lights, the late September air is crisp but not cold, and for once, there is not even a hint of wind. I just look around and take it all in as the musicians play a soft string piece. I burn the sight, the sound, and the smell into my memory for safekeeping. Because one day, when life is hard, or ugly, or depressing, I'll be able to think back on this night. Even if I never have another moment as special as this for as long as I live, I will be OK because I will always have this memory.

Ronin's arm tightens around my waist and then he pulls me in close, turning my body so I'm pressed against his chest. He takes my hand in his and we dance.

I don't even know how to dance like this, but it doesn't matter. I just drop my head on his shoulder and let him lead, my feet making small steps as he whispers in my ear. "Do you like it?"

I don't even look up because I can't bear to lift my head from the place on his shoulder where it fits perfectly. "I love it, Larue."

His chest rises a little with his chuckle. "I have a gift for you too."

"Isn't this party the gift?"

He kisses me on the head and pulls me in so close, we are

like one person. "Hardly, Gidget. A party isn't a gift, it's a celebration. Mine is with all the others."

I do look up now. "What others?"

He points over to a table near the door and sure enough, there's a pile of pretty presents. "Oh, wow. Why did you make them bring presents?" I complain on the outside, but inside I'm clapping like an idiot and screaming *presents, presents, presents!*

"I didn't make them, Rook. They just wanted to."

I'm so happy I could cry, but I don't want Ronin to get the wrong idea, so I squeal instead. "Let's open them now!"

He laughs. God, I love when he laughs. Those blue fucking eyes sparkle and his whole face beams. How did such an amazing man fall for me? I don't get it. "Not now, Gidge, I'm trying to monopolize your time and keep that creep Ford from cutting in."

"May I cut in?" I laugh as Ford's voice comes from behind me. "I promise to give her back."

Ronin smiles down at me. "I dunno, Ford. She's looking pretty content right now."

I peek back at Ford and smile. "Oh, absolutely, Ford. Because I want to know all about that date you brought. Like every single detail."

We all look over at her at the same time. She's… older. Mid-thirties, older.

I turn to Ronin. "I need that story. Come save me from His Weirdness in five minutes."

He hands me off and Ford slides in next to me without even breaking the little shuffling dance Ronin and I were doing. "Is she the… *girlfriend*?"

A smirk from Ford. "I told you, I'd never call them girlfriends."

I look at her again as Ford turns us on the patio. She's tall, blonde, thin, and wearing an elegant white dress that goes just past her knees but hugs all her curves. Her hair is piled into a sophisticated up-do that even Josie would envy. "What's her name?"

"She has no name."

I laugh. "*Ford.*"

"I'm serious. I never get their names."

"Is she a call-girl?"

He scowls. "No, I don't pay for sex, Rook."

"Hmmmm. I'm not sure what to think."

"I told you, I do not give a fuck about people. I wasn't kidding. I use them, they use me. Everyone is happy."

"But you're not using me."

"Of course I am. You're filling the friend role for now."

I look up at him and he winks.

"I'm not sure if you're serious."

"I am serious."

My thoughts are racing as we continue to spin slowly.

"But just so we're clear, I do like you and I'm oddly drawn to what you do with your life. I'm not sure why, but I feel like I need to participate in it. So, I'm sorry, but you're stuck with me."

I shake my head as Ronin comes back. "OK, I can see him morphing into psycho Ford in real time, so that's enough."

Ford drops my hand and backs off. "I have a present for you tonight, Rook. But I have another one for you as well. I'll give it to you tomorrow at Spencer's place."

And then he just walks away.

I look over at Ronin and he just sighs. "I give up. I can't predict him, I can't control him, and I can't compete with him. He's *your* weirdo friend now, Rook. I wash my hands."

I lean up and kiss Ronin's soft lips. He responds with his twisty tongue and I melt a little. He does this to me every time. "Ford *is* weird. He says he doesn't even know that woman's name."

"Well, that I believe. I'm not sure how he even gets them to participate in his—" Ronin stops before he completes the sentence. "Never mind, I'm not sure I want to go there." And then he literally shakes his head and grabs me by the waist and pulls me close again. "I had the caterers prepare the perfect dinner for us tonight. Guess what it is?"

"Snails and goose liver?"

He laughs. "You peeked!"

I lean up and kiss him one more time because his lips are like the siren's song, they call to me, they blind me to everything around me. "I don't care what you ordered me tonight, I'll eat it because you want me to have it."

"Ah, that's a good little Gidget." And then I squeal as he spanks my ass, drawing the attention of all the partygoers.

My cheeks go hot and I turn back to Ronin. "I will have to punish you for that later, Larue."

"Promises, promises."

The terrace is sprinkled with round tables and real white linen tablecloths set with so many utensils I get a little overwhelmed. But Ronin leans in to my ear as he slides my chair in and whispers, "You can slurp your soup with the butter knife if you want, Rook. No one gives a shit, so stop thinking about it."

Veronica is two chairs down on my left and her boisterous laugh fills the night air. "Too true, Ronin. No one here gives a fuck what fork you use, Rook!" She leans past Spencer who is next to me, picks up my champagne glass, clinks it with her own, and then thrusts it towards me so I'm compelled to take it. "Cheers, sweetie. Since you're not trying to steal Spencer from me, and I *did* take a bullet for you a few weeks ago"—everyone groans at her over-exaggeration—"I think we'll be friends."

And even though Veronica scares me a little with her perpetual smoking—which isn't even real, she only smokes ecigs—and her over-the-top self-confidence, I feel warm inside. I like Elise and Josie, but they have been besties for a long time so there's not much room for a new girl who's a lot younger than them. I'd like to have my own package deal, so maybe Veronica and I can be like that. We're closer in age, she's twenty-two and I'm twenty now. Plus, she lives up in FoCo, and I'll be close by at Spencer's place. I'm sure she'll be around a lot, so making her my new BFF is probably a smart idea.

Our table has Ronin and me, Veronica and Spencer, and Ford and no-name. We're going boy-girl tonight, so I'm in between Spencer and Ronin. Ford's woman is on Ronin's right, so that puts Ford across from me with Veronica on his right. Everyone seems to be ignoring Ford's date and I sorta feel bad. "So," I say, loud enough to draw her attention. "I didn't get your name earlier."

Her eyes sweep past me, over Spencer and Veronica, and then rest on Ford.

Ronin leans in. "She's not allowed to talk, Gidge."

And this is when I notice the thin diamond choker around her neck. At first glance it looks like a piece of jewelry with a little charm on it. But… it's not.

It's… a collar.

"Hmmm. Well, that's interesting." I look over at Ford and he looks pretty proud of himself. "Should I drop it?"

All the guys chuckle as Ford nods, then Veronica takes over. "She's a pet, Rook. If you make her break the rules Ford will have her bark for us, and as fun as that sounds, I'm really not up for it tonight. So just pretend she's not there."

"Okaaaaay. I'm ready for dinner."

The waiters arrive and begin placing silver domed plates in front of us. Ronin stands just as they finish and taps his glass with a spoon. "A toast for Rook." He pulls me to my feet and when I look around I get a little embarrassed with all the attention. Every face has turned to me. "Rook." Ronin brings my attention back to him. "Four months ago you literally appeared on my doorstep. And the minute I saw you, I knew—" My heart flutters for a second and I have to take a deep breath because I'm not sure what he's gonna say. "I knew"—his voice softens as he looks me in the eyes—"that you were something special."

The whole terrace erupts into a collective, "Awwwww."

"And this party is just a way for all of us"—his arms spread out towards all the tables—"to show you how much we care." And then he leans down and kisses me, whispering "I love you," as he pulls back. "Cheers!"

Everyone cheers as Ronin and I take our seats and then Spencer cries out, "Let's eat!"

I lift the silver dome off my plate and bust out laughing. "Ronin Flynn, you are a sneak."

But he's *my* sneak, and I love him for it. Because on my plate is the most delicious-looking cheeseburger I've ever seen, nestled on top of a giant mound of French fries.

CHAPTER SEVEN

Rook

"What are you laughing about?" Ronin asks later as his hands slip around my waist and slide down to rub my stomach.

I'm standing over by my old garden apartment looking down at the people on the street. It's Friday night, so it's really busy. I turn to face him and casually drape my arms over his shoulders. "You know me pretty well, Larue. I thought for sure dinner would be something funky and French."

He chuckles. "It was either salads with chicken on them or hamburgers. And guess who made the final decision?"

"Um, the pregnant lady over there stuffing her face with strawberry shortcake?"

"That'd be the one."

We both watch Elise chew and chat with Josie at the same time. Antoine is also watching her from across the terrace and you can just tell he's dying to say something to her about talking with her mouth full. He hates that. But his hand scrubs his scratchy chin for a moment and he thinks better of it. Wise man.

"I'm falling hard for you, Rook. I hope you know that."

I look up at this incredible man and I have no words for what I feel. I'm not falling for Ronin, I'm laid out flat on my face. He is the perfect man. He's put up with so much from me. He's stood by me when I insisted on making mistakes, and planned an entire con job so that Jon would get his karmic payback. He deserves so much more than the indecision and distance I've given him over the past few months.

"I told you a while back that I'd like to belong to you, Ronin. *Someday.*"

His hand cups my face and his thumb traces the curve of my chin.

"I think someday has come and gone because I think I've always belonged to you. From the very first moment we met in the stairwell, I wanted you. And even though it took me a while to understand my feelings, I guess I'm better late than never."

He laughs and pulls me into a hug. "I'll take late, Gidget. I'll take late."

Clare and Ford walk past us and then enter the garden apartment. It just occurs to me that the lights have been on inside there the entire night. "What's with those two?" I ask Ronin.

"Exit interviews for the pilot. Ford figured he'd have all of us together tonight, so why not do interviews. Two birds kinda thing."

"Oh." No one told me about any exit interview, but shit. No one tells me anything unless I ask. Maybe I should start asking? "But why Clare, then? She wasn't in the show."

"Well, technically she was. Since you were the female star and I'm your boyfriend. And I kept leaving you to go see her."

"Wait, so all that's gonna be in the show?" Oh, fuck. That sucks. I guess I shouldn't be surprised. Most of my angst came from jealousy of Clare. I just didn't think she'd be quizzed on it at the end. "Did you get interviewed yet?"

"Ford said I'm last. He needs your reactions first or some shit like that."

"He's setting us up. We should refuse to do them, Ronin. I'm not gonna do it. My contract is over, isn't it?"

He squeezes me tight. "Did you get paid yet?"

"You know I didn't."

"Then it's not over, Gidge. Ford likes you, he won't set you up. Just answer his questions. Lie if you want. No one cares. It's a stupid reality show."

But that's not true. Ford *would* set me up. Ronin never knew the extent of our conversations while he was busy with Clare last summer. Ford never came out and said he wanted to date me, but he did hint around to wanting *something* from me. I'm not really sure what, especially after this morning's conversation about his girlfriends. Not to mention the collared pet he brought with him to my party.

Ronin and I wander back into the crowd and chat casually with people, me leaning into his chest and his arms wrapped around me. He talks with Spencer and Veronica and I nod my head pretending to pay attention, but I'm focused on the garden apartment. The curtains are sheer, but I can't see any movement in there. He must be interviewing her in the other room.

Clare comes out and Ford calls for Spencer. Veronica claps for this and then looks over in my direction after Spencer walks off. "I get to be interviewed too, Rook! Because I saved your life and took a bullet for you!"

"Cool!" I say, but I'm still thinking about my private conversations with Ford. What if he brings them up on camera? What will I say? I didn't do anything wrong, I never cheated or anything. But Ronin might see my omission of facts as lying. We circulate around the terrace, talking to different people. I watch Veronica go in after Spencer. Then Antoine, then Elise. Ronin still seems so unconcerned, but by the time Ford dismisses Elise and looks over in my direction, my nerves are shot.

I look up at Ronin but both he and Spencer are laughing hysterically about something. I look back at Ford.

He beckons me with a finger.

Fuck.

I break away from Ronin and he pats my ass and says, "Have fun, Gidge."

CHAPTER EIGHT

Rook

I walk slowly over towards my old apartment and give myself a little pep talk. *He's not gonna trap you, Rook. He's not interested like that, he said so this morning. He sees us as friends only.*

"Ready?" Ford asks as I approach.

"How come you didn't tell me about the interview this morning?"

He waves me inside and then closes the door behind us. "Yes, I should've said, 'I'll see you tonight at your surprise party where I will conduct your exit interview.' Besides, my payoff in this friendship is getting to watch you react to me honestly."

I don't even know what that means, but it sounds very personal. Almost sexual. I look back at him for a moment and catch him smiling as I enter the bedroom. He's got two plush red chairs set up across from each other and two tripods with cameras. One facing each chair.

"Are you on camera, too?"

"For this interview I am."

My heart pounds in my chest. "Why?"

"Sit, Rook, and relax."

I take a seat and he follows, leaning forward in his chair as I lean back. He rests his elbows on his knees and steeples his fingers under his chin.

And waits.

"What?" I ask. "What are you doing, Ford? Don't get weird with me, please." I look nervously up at the camera.

"It's not on yet, Rook."

"Well, turn it on and let's go."

"I'm making you nervous?"

"You know you are. Why didn't you tell me about this? What are you gonna tell Ronin? I thought we were friends."

"There's nothing to tell Ronin. What could I possibly tell him that he doesn't already know?"

"Know? He knows you told me you were trying to make me not need him? So you could, I dunno, swoop in and claim me as your pet, like that woman out there with the collar? Did you tell him *that*?"

"Do you want to be my pet?" he asks seriously.

"No!" I scoff. "No! I'm not in the least bit interested in becoming your fucking sex slave!"

He goes silent again, watching me as the grin creeps up his face.

I shudder. "I'm counting to five and then I'm leaving. One—"

He stands and moves toward me, his leg brushing against my dress as he reaches behind me to flip the camera on. The heat of his touch makes me dizzy for a moment. He steps back and then turns on the camera behind him before taking his seat. "Did you enjoy being Spencer's canvas, Rook?"

"Yes," I say truthfully.

Ford leans back and retrieves a clipboard on the small table next to him. "What did you enjoy about it? Oh, and talk in complete sentences, so the audience understands the question without having to hear me ask it."

"Well, I had a good time working with Spencer. It was a little weird at first because I had to model with him, and that was… confusing because I was just starting to date Ronin. But once that part was over and Ronin was my partner, everything went real well."

"Why did Ronin make it better?"

I squint my eyes at him but hold my tongue. I refuse to let him bait me on camera. I refuse to allow him to get ratings because I'm uncomfortable. In fact, I think it's my turn to make him uncomfortable. "Everything was better with Ronin because he knows my body. He's got a very personal relationship with it. So having him touch me and position me and kiss me for the photo shoots was easy. It felt good and I didn't have to worry about making him jealous."

"Did the shoots with Billy and Spencer feel good?"

I walked right into that, didn't I? "The photo shoots with Billy and Spencer were erotic, that's for sure, but not like they are with Ronin."

"And what did you think of our running routine?"

"I loved it, to be honest." Ford smiles and my heart rate increases when I realize Ronin will see that smile on TV next spring. "Running with you every morning was—well, I wouldn't call it fun, but I would call it helpful. I liked getting up early, and believe me, that was a huge change for me. But I like the feel of dawn. When things are just getting ready to stir and life is still on pause from the night before."

Ford stares at me for a second, a look of contemplation on his face. "That's a very poetic way to put it." Then he chuckles and moves on. "Tell me more about the shoots and the painting, Rook. And then you can be finished with the camera work. Just say whatever you want, I'll have it edited down."

"OK." I swallow, a little relieved at that. "Well, Spencer is incredible. His talent is beyond words. My favorite painting was the tattoo woman because he painted all his tattoos on me just like they were on him. And his own body art is exceptional. I've never seen tattoos planned out like that, it's not just a front piece or a sleeve, it's a whole upper-body piece. The birds—oh my God, even if my name wasn't Rook, I would fall in love with them. And the final painting at Sturgis was like the greatest gift I could ever ask for. I told him that this was the best summer of my life, and I wasn't kidding. I learned a lot about myself this summer." I stop and smile because he's smiling now.

"What else made you happy, Rook?"

"Modeling with Ronin in costume," I say, blushing. "He was that sexy Elvis and wow. And actually, Billy was a pretty hot cowboy, too." I shrug. "I loved it. I probably shouldn't have loved it, I should probably be embarrassed about what I did for money, about having Spencer paint up my body like that, not to mention the photographs and the rally show. But I'm not embarrassed about it. I'll never forget this summer. I'll never regret being Spencer's canvas, and I'll never regret becoming a model for Antoine Chaput."

Ford stands up and turns the cameras off again and then sits back down.

"That's it?"

"That's it for the questions I want on film. But I have a few more for you, Rook."

I gulp some air. "Ford, let's not, OK? Let's just leave it here."

"No," he says firmly. "I have a few questions for you and since the Biker Channel wants me to have two roles in the full season I want to get this out in the open."

"What two roles?"

"Well, I'm still producer, but they want me interacting with you guys like I did in the pilot. So I'm a character now as well."

"Oh." I'm pretty sure this is bad for me. And I'm also pretty sure Ronin does not know this yet.

"So my first question is, why did you run with me all summer? Was it because you loved the exercise or because you did it with me? And no lies, Rook, I'm not interested in lies."

"Ford, please. *Please* don't ruin this for me. I love Ronin, I like you too, and I'm not sure what those feelings are, but I love Ronin. Don't mess it up."

"Why would I go out of my way to make you happy only to do something later to cause you pain?"

I shake my head. "I don't know. You're playing with me, you're messing with my head, you're—"

"I'm not, Rook. I'm not playing with you at all. Every intention is sincere, I promise."

"But I'm seeing Ronin, I can't—"

"I can't either. Do you know why I brought that woman here tonight?"

I swear my heart stops for a moment. "Why?"

"Because I wanted you to see me and maybe accept me for who I really am. I'm not a good guy, Rook. I'm not even close to a good guy. I want you to succeed, I want you to be happy, and that happiness will never come from me. I just want you to know that what I am doing, these little things—like reading to you, the exercise, bringing you breakfast, talking—it's the only way I know how to care."

A lump starts forming in my throat, my face goes hot, and I can feel tears. Actual tears starting to form. I have to breathe deeply for several seconds to shut down my body's visceral reaction to his words.

"And," he continues, "I want you to know that I care about *you*. I care enough about you to leave this conversation here in this apartment when you walk out that door and go back to Ronin. I want you to make your dreams come true and I'll do whatever it takes to help you. That is the only way I know to express… love. But I will never kiss you."

I look up and meet his gaze.

"I will never do anything physical to ruin what you have with Ronin. I would just like you to *talk* to me. Be honest when I ask for it, trust me, and be my friend. Is that too much?"

A little laugh comes out at Ford's question. "Of course not. I'd love to be your friend, Ford."

He pulls his hands back and smiles. "Good. Then we're done here. Just send Ronin in, I won't keep him long."

"I thought you wanted me to talk about Clare?"

"Why would I make you do that?" He grins and that chin dimple appears. "Why would I make you talk about her? On this night, of all nights? I only want you to be happy, Rook. If

I had information you needed to know about *anything*, especially about Ronin being a lying, cheating piece of shit, believe me, I'd just tell you straight up. He's not, by the way. Ronin is a pretty straight shooter despite being the most convincing liar I've ever come across. I am not playing games with your feelings, I'm not trying to trap you and force you to interact with me or fuck up your relationship. I want you to *want* to be my friend. I want you to *want* to trust me, and come to me for help. I have no desire to corner you into doing anything. I just want to be the safe guy, like you said this morning. The person who will point you in the right direction and you can feel comfortable taking my advice."

"A friend."

"Yes. A friend."

I let out a deep breath. I can actually picture myself doing all those things with Ford. I like Ford. And if I don't have to worry about him making a move on me, I like him even more. "Thanks, Ford. I'm not sure why you're so interested in helping me, but… I'm glad you are."

"So we're straight with this now? No more weirdness?"

I nod. "OK, yeah. We're good."

"Great. Happy birthday, Rook. Next year we'll finally get to take you out in public and celebrate like grownups."

"Asshole."

But I laugh on my way out.

Yup, Ford is one weird dude. I'm just glad he's on my side.

CHAPTER NINE

Ronin

I close the door behind me as Ford pulls the blackout curtains across the front window of Rook's old garden apartment. "We're gonna throw in here, or what?"

Ford glares at me under his slanted brows. "I'd win that fight."

"*Riiiight.* Rook came out happy, what'd you say to her?"

He takes a seat on the couch and beckons me to the chair across the coffee table. I follow suit and ease down into the overstuffed chair.

"I told her I consider her a friend and if she needs anything, she's welcome to come to me for assistance."

"Uh-huh. That's all?"

"You don't trust her?"

"I don't trust you, Ford. I see the flashes of insanity inside your brain that pass as ideas and I'm worried that you've decided to make Rook your next victim."

He folds his hands in his lap and leans back a little more, giving off an air of being totally comfortable in this setting. "I'll be truthful, Ronin. I like her. A lot. Maybe more than any person ever. I'm not sure why, maybe because she's unavailable, maybe because she refuses to put up with my shit, maybe because she listens to me when I give her advice. I'm not sure, but it hardly matters why. The fact is, I like her and she likes me."

I start to say something but he puts a hand up to stop my words.

"I think we both know what that sick fuck was doing with her. And if you're still delusional I'll spell it out for you. I recognize her behavior. She hides it pretty well, but she's quite easy to control once you know her triggers. I manipulated her all summer when we went running. They were all unconscious reactions, of course, and if I pointed it out to her, she backtracked and did everything in her power to prove she wasn't under my control. She was something to Jon, but a girlfriend wasn't one of them. Not from his point of view, anyway. What really happened?" He lets out a long sigh. "Well, we won't know that until she's ready to tell us. And that might be never, that might be tomorrow. We just can't know."

I have to swallow to keep my dinner from coming back up. I guessed this too, but Ford is seriously involved in that shit, I'm not. BDSM is just a game to me, it's something I play at. To Ford, it's a lifestyle. And if he says Rook displays all the characteristics, then I'm gonna have to defer to his expertise. I feel it to be true anyway.

"She will never admit this to you because she has yet to admit it to herself."

I lean back in the chair and rub my temple a bit. My head fucking hurts.

"She needs serious help. She needs a lot of time. And she needs a lot of freedom. I know she likes you, maybe even loves you, but if you keep her too close she'll fall back into the same patterns. And do you really want to get her by default?"

I pinch the bridge of my nose, trying to make the shooting pain go away.

"She's running blind right now. She wants to do something, anything to erase what she was. So to prove to herself that she's not the same girl who put up with that life for three years, she's ready to jump on just about every opportunity that comes her way."

"I'm not breaking up with her."

Silence.

I lift my head and look over at Ford. "I'm not gonna do

that. I'll back off, I'll give her space, I'll support her decisions, but I'm not breaking up with her."

Ford shrugs. "I'm not asking you to. She'll check out soon, though, Ronin. Write this down. She's not ready for you. She's not ready for anyone right now. What she needs is to start over. She needs to figure out who she was before Jon came along if she's to have any hope of figuring out who she is now."

"Is that your professional opinion, then? We done here?"

"Not quite. That ex-boyfriend is in town."

"Who?"

"Wade Minix, a boy from her childhood. Spencer said she lived with him as a teen in a foster family. This guy was her first boyfriend, or love, or something. His mother got worried when the relationship started getting serious and sent her back into the system. After that her status as ward of the State of Illinois goes cold. I figure Jon picked her up soon after. Before the Minix family she was in twelve other foster families."

"Yeah, she told me this part. Not good ones, either."

"Not good is an understatement. Almost of all them have been stripped of fostering privileges." Ford gets up and grabs a folder off the kitchen counter, then takes his seat and opens it up. "Rook Camille Corvus entered the foster care system at age five when she was found wandering the streets of Chicago barefoot in the middle of January. She didn't speak to anyone for months and when she finally gave up enough information to determine who her mother was, it was too late. The woman had OD'd and was already a cremated body in an unmarked grave. I could go on, but if you use your imagination, I'm sure you can fill it all in. She never got involved in drugs, prostitution, had any illegitimate babies, or did porn." He stops to laugh. "Until you guys, that is."

"Fuck. You."

Ford smiles one of his evil grins. "Sorry, I couldn't resist. But as I was saying, Wade Minix is in town. He hasn't contacted her from what I can tell. I saw him wave at her at the show up in Sturgis. He followed her all over the strip the day of the show. Then ended up standing in the front row that—"

"What? How come you didn't tell me this?"

"Because Rook never responded to his wave and never made any move to reach out to him. She ignored him. But I'm telling you now because he's back. And I think she should reconnect with Wade."

"Yeah, I'm sure you do."

"Well, Ronin, he's gonna get his chance to speak to her no matter what you do. Face that fact. He's here, he's here to see her, and he's not leaving until he does. So you might as well just embrace it. Because you can't stop it, that's for sure. And if you make a big deal about it, she'll just do it anyway. And she'll break up with you because you forced her to make a choice."

I hate it when Ford's right. "So I'm just supposed to sit down and shut up? That's what you're saying?"

"Yes. This is not about you, it has nothing to do with you, in fact. She likes you, that's for sure. Otherwise she'd take that money, buy herself a car, and be on the road to anywhere but here. Because that's just how she works. I call her type the Leaver."

Ford and his fucking labels. "Yeah, I think you're right about that. She's got no fear of the road. I could tell that immediately. What kind of teenager gets on a bus alone knowing she'll be homeless when she steps off? She's not afraid to chuck it all and start again."

"Exactly. And I'll go one further. She told me she had no intention of getting off the bus in Denver. She was on her way to Vegas but she thought fate was sending her a message via *South Park* and got off on a whim. No plans, no home, no money, no friends, and no prospects. She stepped into the unknown because of a fucking cartoon. Now she has all of those empowering things and more, how hard would it be for her to just leave now? If you pressure her, she's gone."

I hold my head in my hands, trying to stave off the headache with a last-ditch brow pinch.

"Just give her some freedom, Ronin. I'll keep an eye on her up at Spencer's place."

I get up and walk to the door, then stop. I don't turn and say it to his face, but I say it just the same. "Thanks, Ford. And dude, just so you know, I'm sorry. About… Mardee." I don't wait for an acknowledgment, I just plaster a smile on my face and walk through back into Rook's birthday party.

CHAPTER TEN

Rook

"Did you have a nice birthday, Rook?" Ronin unzips my dress and I wriggle out of it, just an itty-bitty bit drunk. He laughs as I wobble. "I'll take that as a yes."

Once the dress is gone all I have on are my panties. I watch helplessly as Ronin hangs the gown up. "This was the best birthday of my life. And thank you so much for the camera. You did not have to do that for me. But I love it. I'm gonna start filming tomorrow and I'll never stop. Ever."

That camera is like something else. It looks like a mini-version of the cameras the film crew use for the show. I have no idea how to use it but how lucky am I? I have a film team at my disposal to teach me. I smile at this as Ronin guides me over to the bed and pushes me until I sit down. Once I get some momentum going it's hard to stop and I end up lying all the way back.

"I'm drunk," I say, laughing.

The lights go out and then Ronin's bare skin slips up next to my own. "I know. It's a good thing we had mind-blowing sex before the party." He nuzzles into my neck and pulls me close to him, just like he does every night. "I love you, Rook. I hope you know that."

I sigh into his perfect muscular chest and then trace my fingertips down the length of his stomach. "I know that."

And that's it for Rook. My night is over.

I wake early, dying of thirst. I swallow down my cotton mouth and disentangle myself from Ronin.

"Where're you going, Gidget?" he asks groggily.

"Water," I croak.

I get up, slip on a dirty t-shirt draped over a chair near the window, and pad out to the kitchen and grab a bottled water. I gulp it all down and then fill it back up with the tap water and do it again. My gaze wanders over to the dining room table and I spy my presents. I have no memory of carrying them upstairs, but here they are.

I got a bunch of stuff. Some clothes, girly hair accessories, and some sapphire earrings from Elise and Antoine. A journal and two tickets to the opera from Ford and his pet. Spencer gave me a custom-painted black leather biker jacket with zippers. It has Gidget painted down one arm and Blackbird down the other. Like each of these men have made a claim on me. The back of the jacket is a giant blackbird logo with the words *Shrike Fucking Bikes* painted inside a red circle that surrounds the bird.

Even Veronica got me a gift. A gift certificate for a free tattoo at her shop up in Fort Collins.

But it was Ronin's gift that touched my heart.

The camera. A camera I can make movies with. I open up the box and start unpacking. It's got interchangeable lenses. I don't know a whole lot about camcorders, but I do know that it's not normal to be able to change lenses on them. Which means this camera is a BFD. When I check the clock it's only five fifteen AM. I do a search for my phone and find it on the little table over my the front door, and then call Ford.

"Miss Corvus, we do not have a date this morning."

I laugh. "I know, Ford. But I'm looking at my camera that Ronin got me and I want to start filming now. I have things to capture before I leave this place. Can you come help me set it up?"

"Did you charge the battery last night?" he asks with doubt.

"Um, no," I say, disappointed.

"OK, well, I'll grab a camera and bring it to you. How's that?"

Happiness overtakes the disappointment. I guess he's serious about this friend stuff. "Thank you."

"Meet me on the terrace in fifteen minutes."

I wash up, change into some jeans and one of the Shrike Rook shirts Spencer made for me, and then pull on my red Converse shoes. I keep waiting for these things to fall apart, but they never do. They have holes in the top near the toe and there's even a little hole in the bottom of the left one. So my feet totally get wet in the rain. But I don't care. Besides the backpack I left my last foster home with, these ratty shoes are the last thing I own from my life before Jon. I take it as a sign that the old me is still around. Somewhere.

By the time I get to the terrace Ford is ready. He's got a camera like mine upstairs and he's pointing it at me as I walk towards him.

"You're up, Rook. I'm your cameraman. Say what's on your mind."

"Oh, now I'm nervous." I giggle. "OK, well, I just want to show…" I stop and take a deep breath and start again. "I just want to capture what's happened to me. What this place did for me and how it all started."

"All what started, Rook?" Ford asks from behind the camera.

"The journey back." He says nothing to this, just waits for me. "The journey back to myself." And then I point to the swing. "And it all started right there." I walk over to the swing and take a seat. "It started under these trees last spring. When they were filled with flowers and they smelled so incredible, the scent was almost overwhelming. And the very first night I spent here at Chaput Studios Ronin pushed me in this swing." I look up at Ford and he's smiling. I lean back and kick my feet out in front of me, pumping my legs to gain some momentum to push myself in the swing.

"And then he started asking me personal questions and I jumped off." I jump and land on my feet this time. "That was my very first night in the garden apartment. That's how my new life started." I take Ford over there and we go inside and I sit in each room and tell the camera some memory about it. Afterward we go back out on the terrace and he shoots me standing with a view of Coors Field behind me and I talk about our running.

We go through the whole studio. We hit the two-story-tall windows where I had my test shoot with Antoine, the dressing room where Ronin gave me all those clothes, and the salon where Elise washed my hair. Then make our way upstairs where a sleeping Ronin jumps up in surprise when we enter the bedroom.

"What's going on, Gidge?" he asks, still groggy.

"I'm recording my life here with you for posterity, that's what." I jump into bed with him and Ford sets the camera down on a chair and walks away.

"I'll see you two this afternoon. That camera is still on, Rook."

Ronin tackles me and rolls me over on my back. "You're trying to make a sex tape with me?"

I laugh. "No! I just want a little film of us in private. That's all."

"Mmmm," he growls. "But in private we do lots of naughty things, so that means right now we have to be sweet."

"I like sweet."

"Me too," he says, nipping my earlobe until I squeal. "I'm gonna miss you real bad, Gidget. I'm gonna go crazy down here thinking about you up there with Spencer and Ford."

"And I'm gonna go crazy up there thinking about you down here with Clare and the GIDGET models."

"There's only one Gidget for me and that's you."

"And I belong to you, Ronin Flynn."

He flops back and pulls me onto his chest. "God, I want to hear you say that again."

"I belong to Ronin."

His lips find mine, kissing me softly, his hand slipping inside my t-shirt to tickle my stomach. "And I belong to Rook."

CHAPTER ELEVEN

Ronin

"How?" Rook asks me with a totally sincere expression on her face. "How will I ever survive until Friday afternoon without you?" Her fingers dance along the arm of the new couch I bought her, along with all the other furniture in her little basement apartment. "I'm gonna be bored to death."

"You won't be. Spencer and the guys will keep you busy. Besides, I bet Veronica will be here all the time."

"Unless Spencer gets sick of her because he's got commitment issues," she sneers.

I finish up with the surround sound set-up and then grab the remote to check it out. The TV comes on and I flip through the guide until I see a movie she might like. *"Yippee-ki-yay, motherfucker!"* blares from eleven strategically placed speakers in her large basement apartment in Spencer's farmhouse.

Rook turns quickly. "Bruce! Oh, I love Bruce. And this *Die Hard* is the best!"

It's the second one and I agree. "See, you forgot about me already."

She saunters up to me and wiggles against my leg, making me laugh. "You're the one who hooked up the movies. All I need is a popcorn machine and I'm set."

"I'll put it on the list, ma'am."

"You can't call me ma'am and not jump my bones, Mr. cute-total-stranger-cable-guy-who-just-showed-up-to-hook-up-my-surround-sound."

"I jumped your bones twice today already. But if you need it again I'm happy to oblige." I wink at her. "Ma'am."

"Will you miss me?" she asks, suddenly insecure.

"More than you'll miss me, that's for sure. You have Ford and Spencer, they're already friends, so it's not like you'll be alone. I have no one."

She snorts. "That's not true. You have *Clare*."

"I can't hang out with Clare. What do we have in common? Nothing."

"You're her boss now, right? She's the main Gidget model?"

"Yeah, but she needs that job, Rook. She needs to stay busy until she's confident that she won't slip back into her old habits. If you're jealous, you should save yourself the angst because I'm not interested in Clare. At all. She's like a fucking sister to me now."

Rook wraps her arms around me and whispers, "Thank you. I just needed to hear it one more time."

I kiss her sweetly. "You're welcome. Now walk me up, because I have to get back to Denver and you need to settle in. I guess there's a big party planned for tomorrow with all the Shrike cast members, so that will be fun, right?"

"Yeah, I guess."

We walk up stairs and meet the guys in the living room.

"Hey, you leaving already, Ronin?" Spencer asks from the kitchen. "Not gonna stay for the Let's-Embarrass-Rook welcome dinner?"

"Ha, ha, Spencer," Rook says as we walk past.

"No, I gotta get back. Roger and I have casting bullshit tomorrow. We need to sort through the audition pics and figure out if we can fill up all the spots for GIDGET."

"Don't strain yourself, Ronin," Ford says dryly from the dining room where he's messing around with a tablet. "And don't worry about Rook, I'll take care of her while she's here."

"Ford—"

"Relax, Larue," Rook interjects as she rubs my arm. "He's

messing with you. Come on, let's go outside, I have a gift for you."

She tugs on my hand and when I look at the expression on her face I know she's up to something, so I follow. "What's that look for? You're being sneaky?"

We pass by her Shrike Rook bike as we walk to the truck and I catch her eyeing it with longing. "You gonna ride that thing, you think?"

"Absolutely. I can't wait."

"Hmmm, I'm not sure about that, Rook. It makes me nervous. Don't ride it alone, OK? Make sure you've got Spence or one of the shop guys with you."

I lean back against the truck as she pushes herself into me and purrs in my ear, "You worry too much, Larue. I'm a big girl. I'm only gonna ride it for a few weeks before it starts snowing. Besides, I have the Shrike truck to hold me over until I figure out what kind of car I want."

"And that's another thing—"

"Don't start with me! I'm buying my own car, I already told you that."

I lean down and kiss her gently. "What were you gonna give me, Gidget?" Her hands slip under my t-shirt and chills ride up my body. "Fuck, I'm gonna miss you."

"Well," she coos in my ear. "I'm gonna miss you too. But the gift I'm giving you before you leave is my heart."

And then she turns her bright blue eyes up at me and I feel it.

I'm not a romantic, I'm really not. I believe in love and all that shit, and I like to make girls happy with presents and careful attention as far as sex goes. But this is something else entirely. She makes my heart ache. Literally. My chest feels like it's gonna be ripped apart from the longing, that's how much I love this girl. "I'm totally taking that gift, Rook. And I'm never giving it back, so please don't ask for it."

"I'm not sure where we're headed, Ronin. I have to be honest about that. I know you're ready to settle down, but I'm not there yet. So I hope you're patient with me. I just started school and parts of it aren't fun, so maybe I don't have what it takes to get a college degree. But I need to figure that out. I might need to go and do all that stuff before I'm ready to settle. Will you be OK with that?"

"Gidget, I'm ready to stand back or step in. You just tell me which one you need and I'm there."

"Just love me, because I love you. I really do. And tonight, when the reality of today sets in and I have to crawl into that cold bed alone, I'm gonna cry my eyes out."

Awwww. I lean down and feather little kisses across her lips. "You better call me if you do. In fact, you can call me any time you want and I'll be there, OK? You need me to drive up, just say so. You need to come down for a day, just show up. I don't care what time it is, what day it is, or what else I'm doing. You're my life, Rook. You're my future, but I'm not in a rush, babe. I'm not. I can wait, so just do your thing, OK?"

She kisses me and the whole world disappears. Just blips out of existence for me. When she kisses me there is nothing but her tender lips and my pounding heart. There is nothing but the buzzing of her essence coursing in my blood and penetrating my soul. There is nothing but us.

"We're an us," I say impulsively and she giggles into my mouth.

"We're definitely an us."

I gather her face gently into my cupped hands and tip her head up. "If you need me, Rook. I'm here, OK, babe? I'm here. You can come to me with anything."

We hug one last time and then I reluctantly get into the truck and drive away, my eyes flickering between the road in front of me and the beautiful girl waving goodbye in Spencer Shrike's driveway.

I hope Ford is wrong, I swear. Because I might die, that's how bad this makes my heart ache. I might die if she checks out on me and walks away.

CHAPTER TWELVE

Rook

I watch Ronin drive off and suddenly my stomach is twisting into billions of knots. This is probably a mistake. I have so little confidence in what I'm doing with my life, and now that he's gone and I'm here all alone, every decision feels like the wrong one.

"You coming inside? Or you just gonna stand outside and cry?"

Ford is over by my bike. He's wearing jeans and a Shrike Rook t-shirt, which I'm hoping Ronin didn't notice because that's weird. "Why are you wearing that shirt? To piss Ronin off?"

He looks down at his shirt, pretending to be surprised. "It's a blackbird, Rook. It barely looks like you at all."

And then he flashes me that chin dimple and I laugh. "Save it, you're a horrible actor. Besides, the blackbird has blue eyes and the fucking shirt says Rook right across the top."

"Yes, but that's the name of the bike. This one in fact." He smiles smugly as he points to my bike.

"Whatever."

"I have a present for you, come inside."

Ford doesn't wait for me to agree or watch to see if I follow, he simply turns and walks off. And even though I know what that means, I follow anyway. It's not like I really have a choice. I have to go back inside at some point. Might as well do it his way and get a gift out of it. I end up in the great room that connects to the kitchen. Spencer has been cooking all freaking afternoon and it smells awesome. Ford is back at the table flipping through a stack of papers.

"Hmmm," I mumble as Spencer hands me plates and silverware.

"Hmmm, what?" Ford asks, not bothering to look up at me.

"I live with two guys. I never really thought of it that way, but it's pretty clear now."

"We promise not to walk around naked too much, Blackbird."

"Or bring stray pets home." Ford smirks, still concentrating on his work.

"Set the table, Rook, and get the drinks. I won't card you because it's your first night, but just remember I'm doing you a favor and you owe me."

I shake my head and pass out the plates and silverware and then get us three beers. Spence only has one kind and it's from the microbrewery in FoCo, which is kinda cool. "I might regret staying here with you guys. Ford, get your shit off the table, we're eating now."

"See, Ford. Told you, she's already bossin'."

Ford stacks up his stuff and puts everything but one large yellow envelope over on the living room coffee table. "What's this one?" I ask, pointing to the thick package.

"Your gift. But let's eat first."

I look over to Spencer as he sets the basket of bread on the table and then goes back to get the spaghetti. "Don't get excited, Rook. It's not something cool like a motorcycle. I mean, he gave you opera tickets last night for fuck's sake." Spencer practically snorts. "His gifts are as lame as his personality. No wonder he has slaves instead of girlfriends."

And then Ford glares at Spencer so hard I wonder if it might come with a growl.

"Sorry," Spencer says quickly, looking over at me. "Sorry, that came out wrong."

I swallow and try to ignore the awkward moment by grabbing some bread as Spencer dishes out pasta on my plate.

"Well—here we are," I mumble into the silence.

"Yeah, well, let's toast. Rook, I knew you were my blackbird when I first laid eyes on you"—I blush a little. I didn't expect something personal—"and I was right. You were the perfect model for my paintings and you're gonna be the perfect addition to my new show. I'm so glad you talked that caveman boyfriend of yours into letting you come join me here. I'd kiss ya, but something tells me you liked it a little too much when we did that last summer, so I'll spare you the embarrassment of fawning all over me and keep it professional." He winks and I laugh.

"I still don't see it," Ford mumbles. "How? How is that desirable, Rook? If I were toasting I'd say—" He clears his throat. "To Rook, the girl who got back up. The girl who never looks back. I hope you find your dream and it's everything you ever wanted."

"Awwww, Ford."

"And to the end of her first failed fucking marriage because it's official! May you never have another!" We all shout "Cheers!" together and clink bottles. I knew Ford was working on it, but he never said anything about it happening so soon. "Annulment, Rook. Like it never happened. You are hereby legally a marriage virgin."

"Thanks so much, Ford. Is that what's in the envelope?"

"No, that shit's over there in the living room. This," he says, holding up the envelope, "is your future."

I hold my breath for a moment and then let it out. "What's in it?"

"Everything you'll need to apply to CU Boulder and an interview with the film department head."

"What?" I'm stunned. "How? And why? I'll never get in so soon, Ford. I'm not even done with one semester. And I might suck at this college stuff, I'm not doing well in math, so maybe—"

"Stop," Ford says in a serious voice. "You'll be fine. I've already chatted with the higher-ups and they're giving you life credit for the reality show work. That's enough to declare film your major. You *will* have to actually get in. But really, Rook, if I did all this, do you think I'd leave you hanging?"

I shake my head. He never would, I know this to be true.

"I've got a lot more in this envelope but we'll do that later this week."

"Good," Spencer says through a mouthful of spaghetti. "Because this school shit is boring the fuck out me. Let's talk about bikes. Or tits."

"How did I get here? We're *Three's Company*. Spencer is airhead Chrissy, Ford is intellectual Janet, and I'm pretending to be gay so I don't notice that you two are roommate eye-candy."

Spencer looks over to Ford. "What the hell did that have to do with tits?"

Ford just shakes his head and laughs.

God, I love these guys.

CHAPTER THIRTEEN

Rook

After dinner Spencer goes out to the shop to work on his bikes and Ford kicks back on the couch, setting up my camera, as I do dishes. Every other word out of his mouth is 'fuck'.

"How's it going in there?"

"Fuck."

"You don't have to do that, you know. I can ask one of the camera guys tomorrow."

He grunts in response.

"You know, I think that white thing on the floor by your foot is actually the manual."

He looks up at me slowly and screws up his face, then goes back to pretending to not need said three-hundred-page book on the floor.

Typical man.

"Tell me what this school stuff is about, Ford. I'm starting to freak out a little. I'm not ready for that. I'm barely making it in math and—"

"I hired you a tutor, stop worrying," he says as he messes with a camera lens.

"What tutor?"

"At the community college. Mondays, Wednesdays, and Thursdays at seven PM. Just show up, I already set it up and he'll show you exactly what to do so you pass the tests."

I'm staring at him over the bar that separates the kitchen from the living room. "Him who?"

"Um—" Ford gets up and grabs the envelope and shuffles though the paperwork. "Gage something. He's a senior in engineering. Sounds like a real nerd, which means he's perfect." Ford goes back to the camera gear and snaps in the battery. "There, I think it's ready now. But *you* will need to read the manual, otherwise you might as well be using your iPhone to make movies."

I start the dishwasher and go plop down on the couch next to Ford. "Thank you. I'm so excited about this. I'm gonna start making movies like now."

He puts his arm around me and gives me a squeeze. "You're gonna be good at this, I can tell. You wanna go shoot Spencer in compromising positions and then edit the shit out of it to make him look stupid?"

I lean over and kiss Ford on the cheek. It's impulsive and he almost has a small freakout before he shuts it off. "Sorry, didn't mean to make you uncomfortable, but you're awesome."

He disentangles himself from me and gets up, pulling me up with him. "I enjoy it, Rook. Being with you feels normal. I should be thanking you."

We grab all the gear and spend the rest of the evening fucking around with Spencer in the shop. We even get him to lip-sync that *Bad to the Bone* song into a socket wrench. And by the time I get back to my basement apartment I'm feeling a lot better about my decision to come up here and live with Spence to do this show. My phone beeps an incoming text just as I settle back on my couch and turn on the TV.

My heart flutters a little as I read the text.

Dear Rook (AKA Gidget),

I've never had the urge to write a love letter but I'm lying in bed, looking over at your side, wondering if I can somehow change your mind about this whole deal and talk you into coming the fuck home. (I'm a selfish asshole, I know.) But I get that you need this so I'll just say this instead: I felt like I was leaving a piece of my soul behind the moment I left. And every second that passes, I miss you like that, times a million.

Love,
Ronin (AKA Larue)

I press call under his name and he picks up on the first ring. "Ronin Flynn, you are like a door."

He laughs. "It was that touching, huh?"

"Not a window where you can see through to the other side and be sure of what's coming. But a door, still closed and leading to every opportunity imaginable and requiring a leap of faith that the risk is worth it. You are my doorway to endless possibilities and I'm ready to take that risk."

I can hear him swallow on the other end and when he's done his words rumble out in his deep, sexy voice. "Rook, I'm not a risk, I'm a sure thing. You're the only girl I want to build a future with. Ever. You're the one, Rook. The love that only comes around once in a lifetime and I refuse to settle for anything else."

He's perfect. Simply perfect. "I love your love letter, Larue. It made me sigh like a schoolgirl."

"Well, you *are* a schoolgirl, right? I think I'm gonna have to go looking for a little tartan skirt and some knee socks. Dress you all up in a sexy outfit this weekend."

"If you do that, I might have to be bad on purpose, Mr. Flynn."

"Don't tease, Gidget, or I'll spank you."

"You promise that so much and never come through. I hardly get excited about it anymore."

He guffaws this time and I can practically picture his gorgeous smile lighting up his electric blue eyes. "I can't fucking wait until Friday."

I giggle a little as I picture our Friday. "I might just ditch class early, Mr. Flynn."

"And that will earn you two spankings, Miss Corvus."

"Promises, promises."

After Ronin and I hang up I read the text over and over again. A letter. It's sorta old-fashioned and sweet. I look over at the camera and the idea that started this morning with saying goodbye to my latest journey through life with a wrap-up of Chaput Studios gives me another one. I set up the camera on the small kitchen table, sit down in front of it, and turn it on. I take a deep breath and begin to talk.

"Dear Rook at age fifteen. Your life is not over. Wade Minix was not your one. I wish you'd stop crying and being depressed and just make yourself get over it, because I'm Rook at age twenty and I know better. I know that your one is waiting for you five years in the future and his name is not Wade. I wish I could warn you to stay far, far away from that diner where you meet Jon. I wish I could warn you that moving out to that house with him in the country will be the biggest mistake of your life."

I take a deep breath and then continue.

"I wish I could tell you what to watch out for, when to say no, when to walk out, and when to never look back. But I can't. Because you need to do all those things without my help. You need to learn all those lessons. You need to experience all that fear and pain and desperation. You need to see all that stuff. Because at the end of all those bad things, there is a sweet and gentle man named Ronin Flynn."

The tears start to flow down my face as I allow myself to feel a small fraction of the emotions I've bottled up in the name of survival since I left Chicago.

I get up and turn the camera off and take another deep breath.

I'm ready.

I'm ready to accept what happened and let it go. I'm not quite sure how I'm gonna do that and I'm not quite sure what will happen when I confront the past and take a good hard look at all those memories. I just know that I'm tired of pretending that girl is not me. Ronin deserves a girl who is whole. He's done so much for me that I owe him this. I owe him a whole girl who can accept his protection and love without constantly being afraid she'll make the same mistake twice.

CHAPTER FOURTEEN

Ronin

After Rook and I hang up I lie on the couch and halfheartedly watch *The Last Samurai* as I think about making love to her this morning. She's definitely getting more adventurous, but I still feel the need to be careful with her.

A knock brings me out of the daydream and I jump up and jog over to the door. It can only be one of three people. Clare, Elise, or Antoine. That's one thing about living in a secure building. No unexpected visitors.

The door lock clicks as I open it and Clare is smiling at me from the other side of the threshold. "Hey, what's up, little chick?" She's wearing some pink shorts and a white tank top, looking totally cute.

"Can I come in?"

I throw the door open wide. "*Mi casa* and all that shit, right?"

She laughs. "Right." She eyes my outfit now. I'm only wearing a pair of baggy black sweatpants cut off mid-thigh and her gaze lingers on my bare chest a little too long. I clear my throat and wave her over to the couch. She takes a seat in the middle so I plop down next to her and put my arm around her shoulders. "You came to hang out and watch movies? Or you have something on your mind?"

She looks up at me with those blue eyes of hers and I can't help but smile. "I just needed to say it in person, that's all. When I'm not high, or crying, or a total mess in all the other ways in which I'm normally a total fucking mess."

I squeeze her a little. "Say what?"

"Thank you. I really mean it, Ronin. I know you put up with a lot from me last summer. I was a total pain in your ass and I probably made your life more difficult than it needed to be. So I'm sorry for that."

"Hey," I say, taking her chin and lifting it up so she has to look at me. "You're family, right? I love you. You're part of me now and I'm not gonna let you give up. I never understood what that drug was to people, but I know now. After watching you struggle and go through all that pain, I know. But you're a fighter, Clare. And I have an idea about what you're feeling, so just put those doubts out of your head. You're gonna make it. You're over the worst and now it's just maintaining, right?"

She swallows hard and leans back against my chest. I automatically sit back into the couch cushions and pull her in next to me.

"You're a good guy, Ronin. I totally messed up when I blew it with you back in high school."

"Yeah, well. Bygones, OK? Don't dwell on my silly high-school crush. I'm happy with how things shook out. You'll find the right guy, Clare. You're fucking beautiful, and smart, and French."

She laughs and then turns her head up to look at me. "But—maybe, if things don't work out with you and Rook, you might give me another chance?"

I laugh a little. "Well, I hate to disappoint you because I'm gonna marry Rook. But I promise, if things go bad, I'll call you first, OK?"

Her fingertip traces along my lower arm and sends a chill through my whole body. "I miss you."

I push her off and get up because this is not gonna happen. "I'm tired, OK? I gotta get some sleep so Roger and I can get everything ready for the test shoots on Monday. Maybe you can help us choose the girls, eh? You have a good eye for that, right?"

Clare drags herself up from the couch and walks off

slowly, not turning back until the front door is open and she's about to walk through. "Everyone can see she's a mess, Ronin. She's not gonna stick around."

Clare pulls the door closed behind her before I can object so I just stand there, holding my breath as I internalize those words. Ford pretty much said the same thing. *She's checking out, Ronin.* That's what he said. And even though Clare knows nothing about Rook, she's right. Rook *is* a mess. She's looking pretty good on the outside, but the stuff she's covering up on the inside is another matter. I grab my phone off the coffee table and press Spencer.

"Yeeeello."

"Yello? Dude, you sound like a fucking eighty-year-old grandpa."

"And your point is? Grandpas are cool, everyone loves a grandpa."

"Pfft, obviously you've never been to the Chaput family compound in France."

"I hear that papi of yours is a real killer."

"Yeah, like literally. He ran over the baker last month with his fucking bicycle. There were baguettes everywhere, made the guy sprain his ankle. He's lucky he's not in jail."

Spencer laughs. "OK, well, what the fuck do you want? I got nothing to tell you, really, Rook seems fine. We had dinner, she did the dishes because I cooked and you know Ford, he's not about to lower himself to do domestic work. Then they came out to the shop and filmed me with her new camera, trying to bait me into saying something stupid so they could edit it down and embarrass me. She's OK."

I let out a long breath. "I dunno, Ford said—"

"Why the fuck, Ronin—after all these years, after all the bullshit between the two of you—why the hell are you even wasting one fucking second on what that asshole has to say about *your* fucking girlfriend? I mean seriously."

"Because he's been noticing some really fucked-up signs, Spencer. Stuff that only he would see, stuff that makes me sick to even think about."

"Oh."

Silence.

"Yeah, *oh*. And I have to say, now that he's put it out there, I can sorta see it too. I think she needs real help, Spence. She pretends like none of those years with Jon Walsh ever happened. Or actually, maybe she's not pretending. Maybe she's legitimately blocked it out and she can't remember? And Ford said she's gonna leave. He doesn't think she'll stick around."

More silence.

"Spence?"

"Yeah, I'm here. Just thinking is all. God, I fucking hope he's wrong. Do you think he's wrong? It was just your run-of-the-mill abusive relationship, right? I can't even think about that other shit."

"I want to believe he's wrong too, I really do. But I don't think he is. I mean, Ford knows. And they are very close right now. He spends a lot of time with her. She trusts him. They might, in fact, be BFFs or something."

It's Spencer's turn to let out a long breath. "Well, maybe she needs a new best friend? I'll call Veronica and see if she'll invite Rook to hang out. Plus, she's got that coupon for a free—"

"Spencer, do not tat up my girl, OK? I like her the way she is."

"Yeah, well, I'll call up Ronnie and see if she'll take her shopping or something. Rook needs girlfriends anyway. It's not good for her to hang out with so many guys."

"Yeah, tell me about it."

"I'll keep my eye on her. I think Ford's gonna—oh, hold on, here he is—"

There's some shuffling sounds as the phone is passed to Ford, then some muffled talking.

"How can I help you, Ronin?"

"I'm not sure. I'm just worried about her."

"She seems fine for now. She was in a good mood tonight. She's in bed. I'll wake her up early to run stadiums in town, and she's got the party tomorrow night, and schoolwork. Her days will be full. She might just settle down and be fine."

"Or she might not."

"Right, well, we'll have to wait and see. I'll do my best to see if I can persuade her to seek help, but it's touchy. She won't put up with a lot of pushing from me. She walks away angry."

"She walks away from everyone. Including me. I can't push her either."

"So why are you?"

"What choice do I have? Just let her hold it all in until it explodes?"

"I told you about Wade. I think she should talk to him. Maybe that will spur her in one direction or another?"

Silence from me now.

"If she chooses him, then there's nothing you can do, Ronin."

More silence from me.

"She won't choose him, though. I've spied on him, sifted through all his online records. He's not her type anymore." He waits a few seconds to see if I'll respond, but I don't. "Well, it's been fun. Here's Spencer."

"Yeeeello."

I laugh a little. "You're a dumbass."

"Hey, if it'll make you feel any better, I'll go kiss her goodnight for you."

"Asshole. OK, I'll check in tomorrow."

"Later, Larue."

The line goes silent before I can respond to Spencer's dig.

Nothing I can do. Ford is right, this is all about her and there's just nothing I can do.

CHAPTER FIFTEEN

Rook

I'm up with time to spare the next day. I throw on some black yoga pants, a black running tank, a Shrike Bikes zippered hoodie, and my running shoes. Ford lives above the shop, so I grab my camera and head down the driveway to see if he's awake and ready.

Spencer has all his doors coded like Chaput Studios so the crew and other employees can get access when they need to, so I punch in my code and walk through the shop reception area. This is where I'll be working. Answering phones, making appointments for clients to Skype in with Spencer and place a custom order, driving around town picking up and dropping shit off.

Your basic receptionist-slash-delivery driver position.

Right now the shop has eight bikes in progress. Spencer and another guy named Ryan build the custom bikes, while Fletch and Griff make the showroom bikes. Customers are allowed to ask for modifications, so they do a little custom shit too. What Ford will be doing here is beyond me. As far as I know, he doesn't build bikes. But he's been known to surprise me before. He lives upstairs above the shop in another apartment. I walk to the far end of the work area, picking my way between half-built bikes and tool chests, then climb the steep steps.

I knock.

I hear a faint, "Come in," from behind the door.

"Ford?" I call back as I open the door.

"You're early," he says through a mouthful of toothbrush. He's wearing a pair of old jeans that hang low on his hips, exposing his happy trail because he has no shirt on.

Hmmm. Ford is not a bad-looking guy. He's all muscle, but not the same way that Spencer is. Spencer is bulky and buff. Ford is lean and taut.

Taut. What a great word. I laugh internally at that, then realize I laughed externally as well.

"Stop staring at me. I never stared at you when you were prancing around naked all summer."

"I didn't prance! And I'm not staring," I reply, blushing. "I was comparing your body to Spencer's."

He walks back into the bathroom to spit and rinse. "How do I stack up?" he asks, walking across the hallway to his bedroom to change.

"Umm—" I shouldn't even go there.

He peeks his head around the corner and tugs a black shirt on. "Well? You can be honest because let's face it, I'm much better built than Spencer." He ducks back into his room and I laugh.

"Well, you're certainly more full of yourself."

"Right. That's a good one. I'm humble compared to Spencer." He comes back out into the little living room with his shoes and sits down on the couch. His jeans are gone now, and replacing them are his usual black running pants. "Why do you have that camera? Is this gonna be your thing? You're one of those film students who records every moment of their life?"

I shrug. "Maybe. What's it to you? I'm eager, that's all."

He looks up from lacing a shoe and smiles. "Yes, I can tell."

I'm not sure if that was innuendo or not, so I change the subject. "Where are we going, anyway?"

"CSU Football stadium. It's southwest of FoCo, but there's a back road we can take from Bellvue, so it shouldn't take too long to get there. It's a scenic drive, that's for sure.

So you can film that if you want something nice for B-roll."

"I love it when you talk film to me, Ford."

He smirks up at me as he finishes up his shoes. "You're not allowed to be this happy at five in the morning. I will train that smug smile right off your face in about twenty minutes, you wait."

He grabs his keys and one of those trendy running jackets and we hop down the stairs and walk outside to his Bronco. I get my camera ready just in case there is something pretty to shoot for B-roll. You never know when you'll need a shot of Colorado back country.

We drive in silence—well, that's relative because this hunk of junk is not exactly quiet. But neither of us mind letting the rumble of the engine fill the silence. I just watch out my window, filming the scenery. We go right through Bellvue and come out on an empty road south of town. It takes us past a lake on one side and a bunch of university buildings on the other. "Research stations," Ford says, pointing to the buildings. "Horsetooth Reservoir," he says, pointing to the lake.

A few miles later the stadium comes into view. We have to go past it and double back on another road to get there, but it really didn't take that long. "Wow, there's a lot of cars here. They must have quite the AM training program."

"Homecoming weekend stuff," he explains. "But we've got permission as long as we're out by eight."

"How do you get permission for all this, Ford?"

"Money," he deadpans. Then he looks over at me and laughs. "How else?"

"You have to pay for us to run? Did you have to pay for me at Coors Field?"

He ignores me and pulls the Bronco up to a security guard at the parking lot entrance, then reaches into his jacket pocket and flashes two ID's. The guard waves us through. "Money," he says again, looking over at me this time. "And hacking skills."

I'm not sure if he's serious, so I leave it. Because I'm not interested in his hacking activities or anything else Ford does with Spencer and Ronin as part of their 'business'.

I hide my camera under an old jacket that Ford hands me from the backseat and then we head over to the stadium entrance. We pass several more security checks. Each time Ford flashes those badges and each time we are waved forward. Ford seems to know where he's going so I just follow. We come out in the stands, about halfway up, like we used to at Coors Field.

"OK," Ford says once we get inside and choose a spot that's not being used by other runners. "I will slow down for you. From now on, we run together. But I won't slow all the way down, you need to meet me halfway. So you have to actually push yourself. No more slacking off."

"Well, that's no fun. I'm a moper, remember? I come to shuffle."

"Your shuffling days are over, Rook. And I'm sick of your moping. From now on, you're training with me. So keep up or I'll find ways to make your life uncomfortable."

"Ha! Like how?" I cross my arms in front of my chest in defiance and before I can even process what he's doing, he leans forward into my personal space and slips his hand under my hair behind my neck, drawing me close to him. His touch affects me immediately and I flush with heat. I can probably count on two hands the number of times Ford has actually *touched* me, and most of them have happened in the past few days. His mouth dips down to my ear, his breath hot against my skin, and for a second I think my heart will actually stop from the shock of it all.

I swallow.

"Like this, Rook." Ford's soft words vibrate into me. "I like you. I'd like to show you how much, actually. I'm being a gentleman to make life easier for you, but believe me, it's not really in my nature to be so accommodating. I typically just take what I want."

A shudder erupts as his fingertips drag lightly across the back of my neck. He pulls away smiling. "So keep the fuck up or I'll make things very confusing."

And then he turns and takes off running up the stairs.

What the hell just happened?

But I don't have time to think because he's already halfway up this aisle. I follow, running hard for a second to try and catch up, but once I match him he slows a little so that I don't have to exert myself too much. He continues to adjust our pace like this, running harder for ten or twenty seconds, then slowing down for a minute or more.

And I realize something.

Ford knows me. He knows exactly what I'm capable of at my current fitness level. He recognizes the sound of my breathing when I'm getting winded, as well as the sound of it when I'm too comfortable.

He pushes me to do better and try harder in just the right way.

Not too fast, not too slow.

But just right.

We run this way for almost an hour. Much longer than we normally did at Coors Field. That was always thirty minutes or so. I'm starting to lag behind severely, and no amount of threatening me with uncomfortable sexual touching will make me keep up, so he slows to a walk. "We'll do two sets like this, then we can be done."

I wait for my hard breathing to slow and my heart rate to come back to normal and then I figure I *have* to say something. Because the entire run, all I thought about was how his hand felt on the back of my neck. "Are we playing again, Ford?"

"Playing what?"

"Are you gonna try and make a move on me? I thought we were friends?"

"I thought you said you trusted me to do what's right for you?"

"Yeah, as a friend, I do! But that was before—" I'm not sure what the hell that was back there so I don't even have a word ready to describe it. Ford doesn't offer any help, in fact I can sorta see him smirking out of the corner of my eye. "I think you just came on to me."

He laughs, then stops and stands in front of me, forcing me to look at him. "Believe me, Rook," he says with a serious expression. "If I was coming on to you, you'd have no trouble recognizing it." He turns and continues walking.

"So I should just—what? Ignore that exchange back there?"

"Just keep up in training, Rook. And you'll have nothing to worry about."

I stop and throw up my hands. "OK, I'm done then. I'm out." I turn around and start walking down the stairs.

He follows and when he gets alongside me he jumps down several steps and cuts me off. He starts walking back up, which makes *me* almost fall, but he grabs my arm and then lets go when I'm steady again. "So that's it?"

"What's it?" I ask, annoyed.

"That's your boundary? I can push you to run past your current endurance level just fine. You adjust and work harder without one complaint even though I doubled our running time and had you gasping for breath on four occasions. But when I push emotionally, you shut down and run away immediately. You know, I'm the guy who supposedly has no emotions, I'm the one who's supposed to be incapable of feeling. I'm the one who doesn't give a fuck about people. But you, Miss Corvus, are really giving me a run for my money. You want to play as long as you're in control, right? You stare at my chest then freely admit you're checking me out to compare to Spencer. So I might ask you the same question.

What are you doing with *me*?"

"You said we were friends. I was joking about Spencer."

"You spend time with me why, Rook? Because I'm your friend? Or because you like this game we're playing? You say you love Ronin but you argue and rebel against all his good advice, yet you do almost everything I ask whenever I dangle the smallest carrot in front of your face. Why?"

"I just want you to be my friend."

"That's not an answer to my question. Answer the question."

I get flustered for a second and don't have anything to say. "Why do I like you? Is this what you're asking? You need me to stroke your ego a bit, Ford?"

He laughs. "Hardly, Rook. I just want the truth from you."

"I just need a friend. I want you to be my friend."

"I am your friend."

"But that back there was not what friends do, Ford. It *did* confuse me. I already have a boyfriend. We're in love."

"Yeah, a boyfriend who's desperate for me to figure out what the fuck is going on inside that messed-up head of yours because he's terrified you'll walk out on him if he asks you himself."

"What? You assholes are talking about me? He's asking you for advice and you make a move on me?" I shake my head and start walking off again, but this time Ford grabs my wrist.

"Stop!" he commands.

I stop.

And then I realize what he just did and attempt to yank myself free. But each time I struggle he pulls me closer until I'm pressed against his chest, fighting off tears. He leans down again and whispers in my ear. "I was wrong about you, Rook."

I swallow and look up at him, meeting his gaze.

"You're not inexperienced, are you?"

My heart is ready to jack itself right out of my chest and I try my hardest to break free, but he holds me tight and close.

"You're not inexperienced, you're submissive. You just spent the last few years unconditionally following orders, didn't you?"

"You have no idea—"

He grips my wrist hard enough to cut off my words and make me cry out. "I'm the guy who brought a *pet* to your birthday party, Rook. Don't fucking tell me I have no idea."

I turn off. That's all I have left, I just turn off. I stop struggling as my eyes glaze over. I concentrate on a point out on the sidelines where a cheerleader is doing tumbling moves. A few of her friends join her and—

"Look at me."

"Fuck you."

He lets go of my wrist and I lower my head and count the seconds to see what he's up to. When I get to ten and he has nothing to say, I jump down the stairs and head for the parking lot.

CHAPTER SIXTEEN

Rook

My face is hot and it takes all my willpower to prevent the tears from coming out with the anger and frustration. Ford is weird. I need to stop this. Ronin was right, he's got emotional issues. Or lack of emotion issues, I'm not quite sure. Either way, I think I'm done with Ford. I reach the Bronco and yank on the door handle to get in and realize it's locked.

Of course it's locked, you idiot. Your eight-thousand-dollar camera is in there.

I lean against the door and watch Ford walk towards me across the parking lot. When he reaches me he says nothing, just pushes his key into the lock and then opens the door.

I climb in as he goes around to his side and does the same.

He sinks back into his seat and I turn my head and watch the various groups of people bustling around the stadium.

"You ran."

I shake my head. "I'm done here and I'd like for you to start the fucking truck and drop me off at Spencer's."

He lets out a sigh. "Too far, then?"

I look over at him now. His face is expressionless, just passive, like this isn't some monumentally fucked-up moment in time for me. "So you're fucking with me? Is that it, Ford? Your job here is to rip apart my brain and do what? Use me up and spit me out like the rest of your pets? Am I a pet to you? Your project? You know what's fucking funny? You say Ronin's the one with the hero complex, but from what I can tell, that's you, Ford. Ronin doesn't fuck with me like this, he just accepts me for what I am."

He laughs. "Is that right? Do you have any idea what Ronin *does* in our little partnership?"

"I do not give one fancy fuck about Ronin's part in what you guys do together."

Ford looks away and sighs. "I'm sorry, then, OK?" He looks back over at me and waits a few seconds to see if I'll respond. But I keep silent. "I didn't realize it would affect you like that, OK? I'm sorry."

I continue to stare out the window. "Whatever. You know exactly what you were doing, so save it. Just take me home."

"Rook, I swear, it was a little harmless flirt, that's all. I didn't realize you'd get all…" He stops. "Well, I don't really understand what happened, actually. Do you *like* me? Like that?"

Oh, my God. I am so completely fucking humiliated. "Just take me home."

I catch him scrubbing his hand down his face from the corner of my eye, like I'm frustrating him. "OK, I'll start then. How's that? Because I really didn't mean to have this conversation with you, like ever. But since I've unleashed it—maybe unconsciously, maybe not—I'll just say it."

Holy fucking shit, he's gonna go there.

"I want you. I have it pretty bad, in fact. I knew the fucking moment I saw you come into Antoine's office that day we went out to dinner. I went out of my way to make sure you were sitting next to me. And you, you… you just… there was just something about you that drew me in. I had no idea what it was. At least back then." He stops and swallows and then looks over at me and stares hard, straight in my eyes. "But I do now. I know what it is that draws us together and I think you do too."

"I'm not talking about this."

He ignores me and continues. "I'd never make you cheat on Ronin, Rook. I'm not like that at all."

"Take me home."

"But you'd make my year if you admitted to me that you feel this too."

"Oh. My. God! Shut the fuck up and take me home!" I shout it and I expect some reaction to this lapse in emotional control, but a laugh isn't quite it. "Why are you laughing?"

"You do like me, don't you? Enough to leave Ronin? Not that I'm asking," he adds hurriedly. "I'm not asking you to do that, OK. I'm just—"

"You're just playing with me, right? You think you've guessed something about my past and that gives you the right to mess with me? Play concerned friend, take me running and then flirt and make me uncomfortable. Get me to spill my guts and then stomp all over my feelings and rub it all in. That's what you're doing, right?"

"Rub all what in, Rook?" he asks, confused.

"The fact that you could dangle that teeny-tiny carrot in front of me and I'd jump."

"Do you like me?"

"Of course I like you. Why else would I spend so much fucking time with you?"

"Do you *want* me?"

I take a second to think this through because this question is much harder to answer.

"Do you, Rook?"

"No, Ford. I don't." I look over at him and let my defenses drop a little. "You have this power over me, you make that rotten carrot look like spun sugar. And I've been there already. I know it's an illusion. I'm not looking for that kind of relationship again, OK? But..." I'm not sure I want to say the, rest, so I stop and chew on my nail as I watch the people in the parking lot.

Ford stays silent for a while, but there's no way I'm getting out of this now, so when he pushes I'm not surprised. "But what? Just tell me, Rook. If you want me to keep it from Ronin, I will. I won't tell him any of this."

I continue my silence, my mind racing with what Ford is asking me to admit. I'm not sure I'm ready to do that, in fact, I might never be ready to do that. But I need to tell him something. I swallow down my fear and turn to look at him. "If you were to ask me to leave with you. To just walk away from all of it. The show, Ronin, school… all of it."

He raises his eyebrows in surprise.

"I'd go. Because you're right, there's a part of me that finds that dominance shit attractive and you control everything. Every encounter we have, you are always in charge. So that draws me in, and I'd go if you asked because you… you know how to make me *want* to do what you ask. And giving in to what I was is so much easier than taking control and becoming something else."

Ford huffs out a laugh and turns in his seat to stare out the front window.

"But if I actually did that, you would ruin my life."

He looks back, any pleasure he got from my revelation instantly gone.

"You'd ruin my life because there's a huge difference between you and Ronin, and regardless of whatever insecurities you have about your looks, that's not what's different, Ford. You're plenty good-looking. You practically sweat sex, and there is something very frightening, yet compelling about you that makes me want to… to give in to you—to *submit*." I throw up my hands. "There, was that what you were waiting for? That word? Fine, you can have it, consider it a gift. It changes nothing for me, because the difference between you and Ronin is that you're looking for the girl I was and he's looking for the girl I want to be."

I wait for him to respond but he's the one who looks away now.

"Yes, you have it in you to compel me to do a lot of things, Ford, simply because you know the right way to ask for it, you know how to manipulate my emotions because of the way I was tr… tr…" I search for another word because that one just won't come out of my mouth. "You know how to manipulate me because of how I was *treated* in the past. But if you did decide you wanted me, you'd get that other Rook and you'd be stuck with her forever, because regardless of what you think, I *did* save myself back in Chicago. I did it once, but I'm not sure I could do it again. And I'm not saying you're anything like Jon. Maybe you treat that pet of yours nicely. Maybe she even loves you and maybe I would too, but I'd never have it in me to walk out again. Being with you would be a total surrender for me. You would *ruin* me."

He thinks about my words for several seconds and then looks over to me. "I'm so sorry."

"For what?"

"For what I said and did earlier. I was just having some fun with you back there. It really was just a flirt. I never expected it to make you feel like this. I do like you and if you wanted to be with me, I'd be in for that. I would. But I don't want that other Rook." He stops to sigh and look out the window for a few seconds before continuing. "I want nothing to do with that Rook and I'd never be able to live with myself if I dragged you backwards and made you surrender. I'm into your potential, I love your strength, and I'm in awe of your struggle to overcome these things in your past and be a new person."

"I'd rather die than go back to being that other girl, Ford. I'd rather die. I need Ronin's gentle hand and I need to make these mistakes because I had all my choices taken away from me back in Illinois. I had no free will at all. So to answer your question about why I refuse to accept Ronin's good advice, it's because he gives me the *choice* to refuse. He lets me be me. And he stands by me, even if he's unhappy with what I'm doing. I need that so *badly* right now. I need all this freedom but I also need to know someone will set me straight when I stumble. And that someone is Ronin."

We sit in the silence for a while, his eyes darting back and forth as he takes his turn watching people in the parking lot.

And then he abruptly shoves the key into the ignition and starts the engine. "Would you like to go see the math building at your little college so you know where to meet your tutor tomorrow night?"

I huff out a breath. "Yeah, sure."

"And then we can take a drive down to Boulder and look at the university, it's not that far. I'll show you the new building they have for film studies. It's a great facility."

Fucking Ford. "Sounds like a plan, let's go."

"Well, first we have to get breakfast bagels." I release the built-up tension as a laugh and look over at him. He's smiling at me. "Because this stupid fucking CSU stadium has no open concession stands for its early-morning trainees." He pulls the Bronco out of the parking lot and looks over at me. "We miss Coors Field already, don't we?"

"Yeah, we do." I pick my camera up from the floor and turn it on, recording some B-roll of the drive as Ford talks about application deadlines for CU Boulder and summer internships.

Ford and I have a lot in common and one of those things is denial.

We do denial well.

In fact, we're exceptionally good at denial when we do it together.

I like that about Ford and I have a feeling he likes that about me too.

CHAPTER SEVENTEEN

Ronin

"I think these girls will be a good fit."

Clare leans down over my shoulder, her hair brushing past my cheek as she touches my arm with one hand and rests the file folder gently on the desk in front of me. I look up at her and she smiles. It's not seductive, and believe me, I know that look well. She's never done sexy shoots like the other models, but you don't need to be naked to have bedroom eyes. This is not her being seductive. And even though she said straight up the other night that she was still very much interested in having a relationship with me, the typical game-playing I could expect from the old Clare is missing.

"Thanks," I tell her with a genuine smile. I flip through the folder and look at each girl.

"I chose seventeen, do you want me to set them up for test shoots this week?"

I shuffle through the resumes. All these girls are beautiful and they are all experienced. "Yeah, we'll probably keep at least twelve, just in case someone doesn't work out. Nice to have back-ups. And make sure they understand the contract before the test shoot, OK? I don't want any surprises. Find out if they have any… issues." I try to be gentle, but she knows what I'm saying. If they're on drugs, I'm not interested. "And make sure to tell them about the scale. Billy's in charge of the closet and the girls for this shoot."

"Got it," she says, then dips down and pecks me on the cheek real fast and skips out of the room.

Watching her makes me happy these days. She is so pretty. Her blonde hair is long and lush, her eyes are blue and bright, her body is curvy instead of rail thin, and her skin is glowing. She's not the girl I knew back in high school, not at all. She's better. "Hey, Clare?" I call out before she gets too far away from the office door.

"Yeah?" she asks, turning around.

"I'm glad you're home."

She beams at me and lets out a long sigh. "Me, too."

I kick my feet up on Antoine's desk and think about Rook. I know she's running with Ford—this is a habit I've come to accept, even if I don't like it. She likes him, it's clear. But how far that affection stretches, I'm not sure just yet. Her attitude towards me hasn't wavered. She's always interested, she's always happy to see me, and her playfulness has only increased since the whole Jon thing before Sturgis.

But I'm desperate for more from her. I'm desperate for something more permanent. And I do understand that it's totally selfish of me to expect her to give up her dream to make me happy, so that's something I'd never ask her to do. But it eats away at me. Her lack of permanence. It's like she's fleeting, like she's a moment. Something that comes and goes. I want marriage, I want kids, I want everything I never had as a child, and I want it desperately.

But I want her more.

I will wait, that was not a lie. I'll wait forever if I have to.

"Elise is back!" Clare yells from the studio.

I jump up from the desk, rush out to the studio and wait in front of the elevator with Clare. It dings pathetically just before the doors open and Elise and Antoine appear.

"Well?" Clare exclaims.

"I told you, they won't know for another month. This ultrasound was just to check on things."

"Oh, please! I happen to know for a fact that they can tell at seventeen weeks. My roommate Jamie from rehab was pregnant, so I heard all the scary details of bun-baking while I was up there."

Elise smiles coyly. "Well, the tech did give us a hint."

"What is it?" Oh fuck, I'm so excited I can barely stand it.

Elise defers to Antoine who lets out the biggest fucking smile I've ever seen on that asshole's face. "Boy," he laughs. "It's a boy!"

"Ahhh! That's great!" We high-five and then clap each other on the back, then look down at Elise, who is frowning. "A girl would be good too! But it's a boy, so hey, what can you do?"

"I'm just happy it's OK. I'm so stressed out. I'm tired, my feet hurt, my back aches, and I'm not even five months yet. I don't think I'm a very good mother."

I look up at Antoine to see what this is about but he's got a strange look on his face. "Oh, come on, Elise. It's normal to be all those things when you're pregnant, right, Clare?"

Clare's about to shrug it off, but she catches my look. "Oh, yeah, Ellie, mothering is natural, right? You'll be a natural."

But I can see Elise's mind whirling as these words sink in. Our mom was not a natural. She was pretty terrible at it, actually. And she picked a bad dude to have babies with, hence the whole beaten to death and prison sentence outcome. I take Elise's hand and tug her towards the stairs. "Come on, I'll watch girly TV with you if you want." She smiles at me and lets me lead her away. I steal a look back at Antoine as we walk up the stairs and he mouths 'thank you' at me.

"Let's watch at my place, sis. I have a better TV and besides, you never visit me at home anymore."

"I'm sorry, Ronin, I'm a bad sister too."

"*Please.* This is definitely hormones talking." I punch in my code and unlock the door, then wave her into the living room but she heads straight to the bathroom. I plop on the couch and kick my feet up on the table, then flip through the DVR and find some Ellie shows. She likes all the typical shit that I'd normally never be caught dead watching, but this is how I spent my childhood. Sticking to Elise's side like glue as we navigated our way through a very fucked-up home life. She had a little TV in her room and six nights out of seven I was in there sleeping with her instead of my own bed. We'd watch Jenny McCarthy and *Jackass*, then the Top Model show later, after Antoine took us in. It was kind of a joke, right? Since we lived with Antoine and half the time I had famous models taking me on tours around foreign cities and Elise was in a position to make and break careers with a whisper in Antoine's ear.

She had wanted to be a model, even though she's so small. She knew the high fashion stuff was a no-go, but the erotic stuff didn't have those kind of requirements. And that's how she ended up here. Well, Antoine had a much smaller studio over in North Denver, so that's where Elise dragged me that afternoon, about six months after our family disintegrated. She was so nervous and I was only ten years old, too young to understand what she was about to do for money. So I was just scared. And when Antoine came to get her from the front room Elise started to tremble and I just flipped out and refused to let her go with him. I tried to fight him, in fact.

I can laugh now, but I was so fucking afraid for her. I thought for sure this guy was gonna do something horrible, why else would she be so scared? And then I'd be alone, totally alone.

But Antoine let me come back into the studio and he took so many pictures of her that day—fully clothed—that I fell asleep on the floor. The next thing I knew, I was being homeschooled in India while he photographed important people and used Elise as his make-up artist.

It was surreal how Antoine changed our lives.

When we came back from India he bought this building. We lived in a high-rise apartment during the renovations and I had private tutors because every few months we'd pack up and go somewhere else. I've been to more countries than I can count. And we always did fun tourist stuff when we were there, even though I could tell Antoine hated all that shit. He took us anyway.

I tell myself he's not like a father to me, or a brother. And that's true. Because there isn't a word to describe how much Antoine means to me. Father just doesn't cut it because my father was such a bastard, I'd never saddle that moniker on the guy who literally saved me and my sister. Antoine is like… like a best friend more than anything else.

When the building renovations were finally over three years later, Elise and I grew accustomed to this life and forgot all about the violence and fear we left behind. That's when Antoine enrolled me in Saint Margaret's for the end of eighth grade and I met Spencer. Ford was already in high school, so I didn't meet him until the next year when Spence and I started ninth grade. Antoine, Ellie, and I still traveled, but not as much. Things settled down little by little, and pretty soon Antoine was just… sorta famous. I'm not even sure how it happened. He was well-known in certain circles before this transition, but at some point he became someone you had to book a year in advance to get your fucking picture taken. That's when all this contract shit started. And that's when I started modeling seriously myself.

I'd been discovered way back in India. Everywhere we went someone wanted a picture with me in it because, well, I was a handsome fucking devil, what can I say? But when I was almost seventeen I was approached by big-name designers. Jeans at first, then underwear, then sportswear, and once I turned eighteen, some of the more tame erotic shit. Then the woman who was running the closet got pregnant and quit. So I was in. After that the FIRE contract came up and they wanted Clare and me to model together, but Clare opted for fashion and glamour contracts and signed with an agency that took her all over the world for the next two years. And she came back an anorexic addict. So the girl I ended up doing that FIRE contract with was Mardee.

Mardee.

You know when you see a group of guys and they have the token girl? The tomboy who they never see as a girl, so she gets a pass into their inner circle? Well, that was Mardee. The little sister in our con circle. Spence, Ford, and I were only doing stupid pranks back then, not the major hacking we did later. And we used Mardee for a shitload of small-time money-grabs. I liked her, sure. But Ford *really* liked her, and Mardee and I were a little bit drunk one night… so. Yeah. We did the drunk fuck and were too young to understand we were supposed to back away gracefully the next day. She wanted to give modeling a try and Antoine actually thought she was perfect so… the rest is history.

I've spent the last few years trying to understand all the mistakes I made that year, but even after all my recent hardcore introspection, I'm still not sure I could have changed things. I could've let Ford have her, but I'm not convinced she would've listened to him if he told her no modeling because the girl could only be described as a whirlwind. She blew into our little group and twisted us all up, then left all the damage in her wake.

And all four of us participated in it. It wasn't just her, it wasn't just me, or Spencer, or Ford. It was all of us. We got caught up in the shit and the shit kicked our asses.

Us guys share that regret and I suppose that's what keeps us so connected. Her death mixed with the knowledge of how much power we have as a team. How much damage we're actually capable of. Because after Mardee died, we wielded that power to the extreme for the better part of a year.

Until we conned the wrong guy.

The bathroom door opens and I drag myself out of the past. Elise comes back with red eyes and a sniffly nose. "What's wrong, Ellie?" I asks her softly. She drops down next to me and I wrap her up in my arms and pull her close. "You're just emotional because of the pregnancy. Don't cry."

She cries harder.

I should know better. When you tell a girl not to cry, they really think you're telling them to go for it.

"Tell me," I say in French, because French is the language of Antoine and our charmed life with him. It's a reminder that we are good, and happy, and normal. "You can tell me, Elise. I'm a good listener."

"I'm gonna screw up this kid, Ronin," she replies in English. "I have no idea how to be a good mother."

"Oh, come on." I tsk my tongue at her. "You're just being silly now. And you know what?"

She looks up at me with her red and watery eyes. "What?"

"You did a pretty good job with me. You raised me since I was a baby. You changed my diapers and fed me and made sure I took baths and brushed my teeth. When people used to ask who my mother was when I was a kid, I'd always tell them you. It kinda freaked some people out once you got to be a teenager." She stops crying for a second and huffs out a half laugh. "You know exactly what to do with a baby because you've already done it with me. And barring that one near-grand jury indictment, I came out just fine."

She laughs for real now and I know I've won.

"You'd be a good father too, Ronin."

"Yeah, I really would." I kiss my sister on the head as she wipes her tears and settles down. "I'm looking forward to being a father, actually. And your new guy will be the perfect *petit garçon* to practice on."

We watch a bunch of *Vampire Diaries* shit for the next couple hours and she tells me the whole story, explaining every freaking detail of Stefan, Damon, Elena and what the fuck ever. I try to listen, but I'm too preoccupied with daydreams of baby girls who look like Rook to do more than give her an obligatory nod every once in a while.

CHAPTER EIGHTEEN

Rook

My life has gone from fast and fabulous to dead-ass boring in one week. Last week I was Rook, super naked model for Antoine Chaput and the human canvas for Spencer Shrike's amazing artwork. Now I'm a receptionist who has no idea how to subtract negative numbers and requires a paid tutor even though she is twenty fucking years old. The phone rings and I pick it up. "Good afternoon, Spencer Shrike Bikes, this is Rook, how can I help you?"

You see? This is my new life.

"Yes," I say back to the person on the line as I click through the bike production schedule on the computer. "We have a Skype conference scheduled for next Monday at ten thirty AM mountain time."

I make appointments. I pick up tailpipes from the chrome guy down in La Porte and painted frames from the body shop in Fort Collins. Sometimes, if my day is really exciting, I also swing by the upholsterer's shop in Loveland and grab a bike seat or two.

"Great, I'll call you five minutes before the meeting and we'll get your bike in production," I say enthusiastically to the guy on the other end of the phone. "Thanks!"

I hang up the phone and turn back to the shop. Ford's presence startles me because I didn't hear him walk over. "What's up?" I ask.

Ford's job here is still undefined. I'm not sure why he's on the show, let alone what his purpose is in Spencer's shop.

But no one cares what I think. I'm a fucking receptionist now, so I have to make coffee, and take sandwich orders for all these men, and when we have person-to-person meetings with important people who are gonna be on the show—we've got famous bikers coming out of the fucking walls already and we've only taped two days—it's my job to flirt with them.

"I need to go to town. Need anything?"

"Do I need anything? Yeah, you know what I need? A life, that's what I need. Can you pick one up for me?"

Ford scowls at me. "Why are you such a bitch today?"

I sigh. "I have to take a test for math by tomorrow and I'm still confused. Plus, I'd like to go see Ronin early, but fucking Spencer has some guy coming in for the show, so they want me here until six tomorrow. So how am I supposed to get to Ronin's early if I'm stuck here until six and I have to take a test after?"

"Cheat on the test and tell Spence to fuck off." He shrugs, like that's the most stupid simple answer in the world.

"Cheat? That's real nice, Ford."

"That's why I hired that tutor in the first place, Rook. I never expected you to actually *learn* the shit. When he called Monday night and said you didn't want him to take the tests for you I was appalled by your morals."

I laugh a little. "I'm not against working the system, Ford. Seriously, I'm not some high-and-mighty moral fuck who looks down on people who take shortcuts or whatever. But if I am gonna screw up my karma with underhanded tactics, I'm gonna do it for a subject that is not pre-fucking-algebra, OK? I'm gonna do it for biology or the real algebra class I have to take next semester, the one that *counts*."

"OK, I see your point for that one, but you can still tell Spencer to fuck off."

I laugh again. "What are you getting in town?"

"An apartment."

"What? Why? You're gonna move out?"

He smiles coyly as his eyes dart around the shop. "No,

not exactly. I just need a place. A place that's not here."

"Uh-huh. For that pet of yours?"

"No, I'm trying something different now."

"Get the fuck out of my reception area. I'm busy."

He walks out the front door laughing.

I shudder and try to get that image out of my head. I can't stand to think of Ford with these girls. It makes me sick. He knows this too, and I think he likes making me uncomfortable with the notion of his personal life.

Or maybe it's all in my head. Ford probably doesn't give one shit about what I think of him.

I check the clock and it's almost six, so I shut down the computer and clean up my desk so it looks presentable for the cameras. They're not here today, but they will be tomorrow because that important biker dude is taping his show. My phone buzzes just as I'm about to throw it in my purse and I read the text from Ronin.

Working late. Call you tomorrow.

I don't text back because that's the second time this week he said that and it's pissing me off.

This job sucks. The money is good, ten thousand dollars an episode, but do I really need another hundred and twenty thousand dollars?

I shrug to myself. It's a lot of money to most people. Hell, it's a lot of money to me, but it doesn't mean much when I have plenty of money these days.

I slip on my Shrike Bikes leather jacket that Spencer had custom-made for my birthday, grab my purse and backpack, and peek around the wall that separates my area from the shop. They are all busy behind the glass, laughing and joking as they work. These fucking guys love their jobs. They stay until all hours—hell, they practically live here. I push the door open and the noise of men leaks out. "Hey, I'm taking off, Spencer. I have to meet my tutor, OK?"

All of them wave but only Spencer calls out a 'goodbye.'

Yup. I'm no one special here, that's for sure.

I walk up the driveway to my Shrike truck, throw my bag and purse onto the passenger seat, and climb in. I do love this truck, though. Although I'm careful not to speed on the road into town. That deputy who busted me for speeding is always on the lookout. I think he wants to date me though, not write a ticket.

I'd rather get the ticket. So I drive the fucking speed limit all the way into Fort Collins. And let me tell you this, living thirty minutes from town sucks. I hate it. La Porte is not very far, but that place has nothing, it might as well be Bellvue. It takes even longer to get to my community college because it's all the way on the south side of FoCo, so by the time I make it to the math building, grab all my shit, and haul myself across the parking lot, my tutor Gage is already waiting for me outside.

"We gotta go somewhere else tonight, Rook. Water pipe broke and there's a massive clean-up going on in there."

Gage is kinda hot for a nerd. He doesn't have those stupid black glasses and he doesn't wear a pen protector in his pocket, but he's definitely a nerd. I know this because I asked him what he does on the weekends yesterday and he said study. He's in some special engineering department down at CU Boulder, not regular building stuff, but like robots or mechanical hearts or some shit like that.

"Well, where can we go? I'm not familiar with this area, Gage, sorry. You'll have to pick."

"There's a coffee shop with wireless down the street. We could go there."

"Great," I say as we make our way back to the parking lot. "I'll follow you."

I have a better parking spot than he does, so I reach my truck first. He eyeballs it with a weird look on his face as he walks past. Probably wondering what I'm doing with a Shrike Bikes vehicle. It's pretty conspicuous, this truck. I really need to buy a car of my own so I can blend in.

I pull the truck out and look around to see what he's

driving. There's only one car on the move and that's an old-ass light blue Camaro. He waves at me to follow and we pull out.

The coffee shop is busy and loud when we walk in, but Gage points to the back where there's doors separating a section from the main room and a sign that says, *Study Area.*

We're the only people in there, but he picks a table in the corner to get away from the noise in the other room.

"OK, here's the deal. That guy who hired me for you called earlier and said you need to take that test tonight so you can leave town tomorrow. So we're gonna pull up the test, you can do it yourself, but if you have a question, I'll be here to answer it."

"That's cheating."

"It's an online math class, Rook. Everyone is cheating. It's open book, anyway. What's the difference?"

"I just don't want help. I'd rather you check my work that I did last night and explain where I went wrong. I'll take the test tomorrow night like I planned, my boyfriend down in Denver will wait and Ford can just butt the fuck out of my life. It's none of his business, and just because he's the one who pays you doesn't mean you have to listen to him. I can pay you myself, you know. I don't need his money."

Gage is staring at me with another weird look.

"What?" I ask.

He laughs. Like loud.

"What?"

"I knew it!"

"Knew what?"

"Ford? The guy who hired me is Ford Aston, isn't it?"

"Um, well, I don't actually know his last name but—"

"Rich, pretentious asshole?"

I laugh. "Yeah, that's him."

"And you drive a Shrike Bikes truck because you're working for Spencer Shrike?"

"Yeeeahhhh…"

"Please tell me the guy you're meeting in Denver tomorrow is not Ronin Flynn. *Please.*"

"Why?" My heart starts beating super-fast at the mention of Ronin's name. "He's my boyfriend, why?"

"Are you from here?"

"No, what's that got to do with anything?"

He shakes his head as he laughs, then huffs out a long breath of air. "Well, I'm sorry to be the one to tell you this, but your friends are bad fucking news. And if I were you, I'd get as far away from them as you possibly can because they committed a high-profile murder a couple years back and walked away free and clear on a technicality."

CHAPTER NINETEEN

Rook

I blow through the doors of Best Buy on College Ave on my way home from tutoring and before the greeter guy can ask me what I need I bark out, "Laptops?" I'm already moving down the aisle he's pointing to before he can get the words out. Back in computers another kid wants to help me so I manage to say, "The best laptop you have, *now*."

Ten minutes later I'm cruising back down College, my mind racing with wild imagery of my friends committing murder. I need to do some serious research and a phone browser just isn't cutting it. Hence the laptop purchase.

I played it cool with Gage earlier. "Oh, that," I snorted. "I know the inside story, it's nothing."

I'm pretty sure he saw through me because I'm a terrible liar, but it was all I had in me. My head was spinning the whole time. I told him I'd do the test tonight on his computer if he left me alone so I wasn't tempted to cheat. I did take the test, but I definitely failed. That's because the only thing on my mind was the fucking search page I pulled up and was glancing at on and off while I was trying to subtract negative numbers.

How the fuck did I never think to Google these guys? How? After all I've been through, how the hell did I not even once get curious?

Because Gage was not lying. I found an article almost immediately, but I didn't want to leave a search history on his computer, and I don't have my own computer at Spencer's, I just use his.

So manic shopping spree through Best Buy at eight forty-five PM was in order.

I do not even know how I got myself back to Spence's house, but here I am, sitting in the idling truck in the driveway.

The outside light goes on and Spencer peeks out the door. "Hey, comin' in or what?"

I turn the truck off and grab all my shit and go inside.

"What's all that?" Spence asks as I struggle with all the bags. I got an extra power cord and a battery and pretty much everything else the salesman said I needed just so I didn't have to fight with him about it.

"Just a computer, you know I should have my own, right? I'll need it for class." I smile and make my way towards the stairs. "Well, I'm beat and we have a big day tomorrow, so I'll see you in the AM. Night, Spencer!"

"Night, Blackbird," he calls out softly to me. It's like he knows. Something's off with me.

Shit, shit, shit.

But when I get downstairs to my apartment and look back, he's not following me, so I push through the door and dump all my shit on the new couch and then start tearing into the bags. An hour later my computer's up and running and connected to the house wireless.

I wonder if they can see my browsing history remotely?

I'm a paranoid freak because of Jon. But I don't have the patience. And besides, what would they do if I found out? I mean, seriously? They have to know that I'd stumble onto it eventually.

I plug their names into the search bar and I swear my heart skips when I see what the headlines actually say.

Brutal Slaying by Local Golden Boys

Boulder Seeks Grand Jury Indictment of Aston, Flynn, and Shrike

Golden Boys Walk!

I lean back on the couch after reading more than two dozen articles and let out a long breath. "Well, Rook. You sure can pick them."

What should I do? Should I leave? Should I confront

Ronin? Should I ignore it?

I run through each one—it would be stupid to just leave. I could, I have plenty of money, but these guys have been very good to me. And Ronin's never lied about anything before. He told me all about Mardee and he admitted that they set Jon up. And I can't confront them. I'm not a confrontational person, it makes me sick, actually. I can't even imagine doing that.

So ignore it?

How? How can I ignore the fact that some millionaire businessman up in the Boulder hills was brutally killed a few years ago and my fucking boyfriend and his BFFs are the ones who were accused?

And the article says straight up the DA had the evidence but they couldn't use it in court because they obtained it illegally.

But this is Ronin, Rook. Do not overreact.

I clear my browser, cookies, and cache just in case.

Just in case what?

Shit, I'm doing it again! I'm acting like I was back in Chicago with Jon.

But I shut the computer down clean all the same, then take it in my room with me as I sit on my bed.

The bed that Ronin purchased for me, along with all the other stuff in this apartment. It's way more than ten thousand dollars' worth of stuff. The TV, the surround sound, the furniture, the kitchenette supplies.

But he did lie to the police about Jon. And he was quite convincing. They left me alone all afternoon before asking for my statement. I didn't need to lie, actually. Everything I said in my statement was true. Ronin said he saw the threatening texts on my phone, but I never saw them, and that's what I said. But then Ronin was right there next to me, saying he hid them from me so I wouldn't get scared.

The cops never even blinked at his lie.

And Ford hired Gage to help me in math and enrolled

me in college. He's been so good to me.

Actually, he hacked me into that college. Sure, I paid the fees and everything, and it's even out-of-state tuition because I haven't lived in Colorado for a year yet. But still, he cheated to get me in because I was supposed to take a test to see which classes I was eligible for, and I never did that. He faked my test scores because he's a super hacker genius or something. I'm not really one hundred percent sure what Ford is, I just know he can do that shit like Jon. Only better, because we won and Jon lost. And it was all because of Ford.

And Spencer is so nice. I've spent a lot of time with Spencer, very close and intimate time, and he was never anything but nice. I love the hell out of Spencer.

Of course, he does have guns stashed everywhere. Like *everywhere.* In the kitchen drawers, in the couch cushions, in the fucking towel cabinet in the upstairs bathroom. I found that one looking for washcloths last summer when I stayed up here on the weekends.

He's obsessed with guns. When he told me he stashes them everywhere and forgets them, he was not kidding. And he's got a huge safe down here on the other side of the basement where he says he keeps the 'good ones', whatever that means.

My phone buzzes inside my purse and I jump up to get it.

Ronin.

Sorry for being so busy this week, Gidge. I'll make it up to you tomorrow. Night, baby.

He's not a bad guy. He's not. I'd know. I mean, I was very discerning when we first met. I looked for signs and signals at every turn. I found them even when they weren't there. But still. Ronin has secrets. They all do. And I know nothing about them, really.

But what I do know is good.

This is a useless battle. I get up and run the water for a shower, then strip and get inside. I let the hot water beat the day off me and when I'm done, I feel warm and tired.

I'm gonna ignore it. I'm not gonna say anything because I have no idea if they're guilty but I do know there's no way I'm gonna ask them about it.

I do *not* want to know.

I don't. Period.

I'm ready to play dumb for a while and just let life move forward. These guys are not killers, they've done nothing but give me opportunities and love. So as long as I don't see anything weird, I'm gonna let it go.

I text Ronin back after I turn the lights out and climb into bed.

Miss you. See you tomorrow night! xxoo Rook

CHAPTER TWENTY

Ronin

The test shoots this week have been a nightmare. Total nightmare. These girls are so snooty and high-maintenance, I just want to drop-kick them.

I sigh as yet another one pouts and huffs over in the make-up salon. Elise is on hiatus with Antoine. Both of them hang around the periphery once in a while, but for the most part, Josie is in charge of the salon right now. And Josie is about to smack this girl, I can tell.

"Look," Josie snaps at the blonde with aquamarine eyes. "I might not *speak* French, you stupid bitch. But I certainly do understand it. So shut your—"

"Josie!" I call out to her just before she loses her temper. "Come here a sec, will ya?"

The model sneers as Josie walks over to me, straightening her black jacket a little. "Sorry, Ronin. But that girl—"

"I heard. Let me handle her, just start on the next one, OK? Send her over to Roger with no make-up or hair, let's see how much she enjoys that."

Josie peeks up at me through her dark bangs and smiles. "OK."

She walks away laughing and I watch the model's horrified face as she directs her hate over to me. I give the bitch a little wave of my hand and then point to a group of girls sitting at some tables near the kitchen, waiting their turns.

French blondie gets up with a breathy blow of air and makes her way towards me. *"Comment osez-vous?"*

I point to myself. "How dare I? Are you fucking kidding

me? You're pretty, you're experienced, and you're here—that's about all you have going for you right now. If you want this job you'll be nice to my family. That woman over there"—I point to Josie who is already busy with another girl—"is like a sister to me. Do not piss her off."

Aqua Eyes looks me up and down for a few seconds, then turns away.

"Oh," I say, stopping her. "And no more French. Unless your last name is Chaput, it's fucking rude. Speak English when you're dealing with us or hit the road."

I forgot what bitches these outside girls are. The regular Chaput models are all pretty nice. At the very least, they all know the rules and one of them is that I don't put up with that catty princess bullshit. I've been spoiled working with Rook, she never pulls any of that crap. She's almost always polite, except with Ford, and she's not high maintenance at all.

She's perfect.

I wish she was my Gidget instead of all these girls.

I look back over to Barbie Bitch and she's pointing at me as she spouts off to Clare in French. I shake my head as Clare looks over at me.

Clare has certainly had her moments as far as temper tantrums go, but she's been a completely different person since she came home from the treatment facility. I watch carefully to see how she handles this.

She stays perfectly still as the model complains and points to me and Josie in the salon. Clare replies in a soft voice and points to the front door.

Frenchy shoots me hate and I let out a small chuckle as I walk over to them, covering the distance in just a few paces, that's how long my pissed-off strides are. "That's it, I warned—" I stop talking just as my gaze finds the man standing at the front door. Tall, black suit, looks like the government.

I turn back to Clare. "Get rid of Aqua Bitch, OK? I've got a visitor."

Her gaze travels to the guy at the door and she looks back to me and swallows hard. "OK. Sorry, Océane, you're no longer needed. Thank you for—"

And I walk away as the bitch starts screaming in French and make my way over to the man at the door. "Can I help you?"

"Like racehorses, I guess, huh?"

"What?"

"High-strung, these girls."

We step aside as Clare pushes the girl past us and then follows her out into the stairwell and closes the door behind her. The screaming is still loud, but better than it was. "I'm sorry, let's start again. Can I help you?"

He smiles at me and I know immediately what this is.

"I'm looking for Ronin Flynn. That you?"

"And who might you be?"

"Agent Abelli, FBI." He flashes a badge, which I study quickly, then thrusts a little white card towards me, but I don't take it or even look at it.

"How can I help you, Agent Abelli?" My sincere con man voice takes over because I just punched the time clock. "I'm sort of in the middle of a model melt-down." I gesture to the door with my head then turn slightly and start walking towards Antoine's office. He follows like a good little chicken. What choice does he have? I'm walking away, he wants to talk to me, he has to follow. "So sorry about the theatrics. It's tough working with all these young women every day, right?" I give him a slimeball wink but his expression remains stoic.

I turn before the real grin pops through my facade and motion to a chair on the opposite side of Antoine's excessive desk and then I take the boss position behind the monstrosity, leaning back in my chair and kicking my feet up.

Abelli eyes the chair I pointed to and prefers to stand. "Mr. Flynn, I'd like to ask you some questions—"

"Oh, sure. I figured you guys would be around sooner or later." I stop to watch his confusion for a beat. "But I figured it'd be a lot sooner than this, to be honest. No matter, you're here now. What can I do you for, friend?"

Abelli narrows his eyes at me. I smile back at him. "Well, Mr. Flynn, I'm here on another matter, so—"

"Oh, Rook? Yeah, I've been telling her to get ready for this, ya know? She's so fragile. Testifying against Jon will be traumatic, I think. She might not make the best witness, but we gotta use what we have, am I right? Make sure that scumbag never hurts anyone else again." I stop to shake my head and look down for a moment. "What he did was so, so… so animalistic." I look up. "Ya know?"

Abelli clears his throat and tries again. "Actually, Mr. Flynn, we're here—"

"Ronin?" Clare says in a sweet voice as she belatedly knocks on the open door. "Sorry to interrupt, sir," she says, looking at Abelli. "But I need you, Ronin. Océane is gone, but there's another girl. I tried to screen them, but I think—" She stops to look at the agent.

"Go ahead, Clare, he's cool. You can say it."

"She's high, Ronin. We need to fire her, I think, and I don't want to be the one to—"

"No, I got it. One sec, sweetie." Clare leaves and I get back on my feet and walk over to the door, pause. "Well, sorry about being cut short, Agent… what was your name again? Maybe I should take a card?"

He takes a step towards me and I turn and walk back over to the front door, shaking my head at the screaming coming from the dressing room, look over my shoulder to see if Abelli is following—he is—and then pull the front door open and wait for him to catch up. He's got the little white card in his hand and I take that and put a hand on his back. "Sorry, I'm sorry you had to see this. We typically run a tight ship here, but…" I huff out a long exasperated breath. "You know, new blood always causes friction."

The screaming in the dressing room takes on a whole new level of crazy and I wince in that direction, then turn back to

Abelli. "I gotta go, man, OK? Let me know if you need any help, any help at all. We gotta put that sick fuck behind bars for a long, long time, right?"

I clap him on the back of the shoulder and walk off towards the dressing room. I turn the corner, out of Abelli's sight and then start yelling in French as Clare slips past me to go make sure Abelli is gone. Inside the dressing room Josie is throwing a fit by herself. Screaming about drugs, and dieting, and the scale, and the clothes, and fuck all else. Pretty much everything she can think of. I try to calm her loudly until Clare comes back in and closes the dressing room doors.

"He's gone."

Josie skips past me, planting a kiss on my cheek as she goes, and then calls out, "You owe me a fat bonus for that performance, *brother*."

"Is it serious?" Clare asks as soon as Josie's gone.

I let out a long slow breath. "Maybe. He never got past hello, but he'll be back."

Clare and I go back out into the studio. She does her job herding the girls for their test shoots, me hassling Roger and generally being an asshole, like they expect me to. No one mentions my visitor, no one mentions the fact that Josie threw a fit and then came back to work like nothing happened. The day just moves on.

I'm not really avoiding the FBI, just laying a foundation on which I can build. I don't call Spencer or Ford because this has absolutely nothing to do with them. If Ford were to get pulled in for hacking he'd never tell me about it. So maybe he's already been questioned, I have no idea. And Spencer really has no tangible role in this latest job, not like the others. Rook filled in for him in this case, and she's clearly the victim, so I doubt they're hassling her.

But me, I'm the face. The front man. Which means they come to me first because I'm the one who's acting all in the know, right? I'm the talker, the amicable participant, the one who answers every question without fail.

That's the only job I have. To clean the shit up after the fan throws it all over the fucking place.

I'm not one hundred percent sure why Abelli was here, but I can take a good guess.

I suddenly want a cigarette very badly. I don't really smoke, but there are times when I want to. This is one of those times.

But I don't smoke. Because that's an indicator that I'm nervous about something. And I *cannot*—can-fucking-*not*—afford to deviate from normal now.

CHAPTER TWENTY-ONE

Rook

I smile the whole way down to Ronin's. Even though I absolutely did fail that math test last night and that fucker Gage did tell me my boyfriend and two of my besties all got away with murder, it doesn't touch me today because I know in my heart that these guys would never do that. Sure, they did some illegal things, but they did those things for *me*. Not to hurt people. They stole Jon's money because he tried to steal mine. They set him up with kiddie porn because he took advantage of me as a young adult.

And even though I am ultimately responsible for my own decisions and actions, there really *was* a point in my relationship with Jon when things stopped being my fault. I need to stop feeling responsible for what happened and Jon needs to accept the fact of what he did, what he made me do, and what I became.

Because there really *was* a point where I was stripped of all my choices.

And I think that it's OK to put all the blame on Jon for those parts.

So fuck it. I love Ronin. Ford and Spencer are my friends. And that's how it's gonna stay unless I get information that requires a one-eighty.

I ease the Shrike Bikes truck off the freeway and take Park down to the stadium, then turn onto Blake and pull into our garage. Ronin is kicking back on one of his motorcycles, talking on the phone as he waits for me. He's wearing old jeans, a black t-shirt, and his favorite black biker jacket. He waves as I pull in a few spaces down and then walks over to me as he ends the call. My eyes linger on his body as he approaches and I let out a sigh. God. This man is like my smile button. He appears and I smile.

I'm smiling right now.

I giggle a little at that and throw my arms around him, taking in his scent. He smells like Sexy Man. I'm not sure what that exactly is, but if sexy man smell has a dictionary entry, the picture next to it is Ronin Flynn. "Oh, my God—I missed you so much!"

He hugs me back and hums against the tender skin on my neck. "I think we should stay in the entire weekend."

I pull back with a serious expression on my face. "And do what?"

He grabs my backpack and purse from the seat, then closes the truck door and takes my hand. "Ah, my schoolgirl needs to learn some patience, I think." We take the elevator up and then he lets go of my hand and points to the dressing room. "There's a hanger with your name on it. Meet you upstairs."

I stand there as the heat creeps up my face, just watching his ass in the moonlight as he goes up the steps. "Chop, chop, Gidget. You'll be spanked if you're late."

My chuckle comes out automatically as I make my way into the dressing room. There's just one hanger on the rack and yup, sure enough, it's got my name on it.

I peek inside and smile. Boys and their Catholic schoolgirl fantasies. He *went* to Catholic school, surely he must've gotten his fill?

I unzip the garment bag all the way and start pulling stuff out. There's a crisp white button-up blouse, a little red tie, a red-and-black tartan skirt, and some very naughty black lingerie that probably came from the GIDGET contract. The whole ensemble is completed with a pair of six-inch stilettos.

I'm already feelin' the heat down below.

I take it all over to the armless couches in the middle of the room and take off my clothes, tucking them back inside the garment bag. I line up each piece of lingerie and look it over real good. I'm not all that up on what does what, so this takes me a few minutes to figure out. I slide the black lace demi bra on and then the matching panties, garter, and stockings. I hook it all up, slip on the shoes, and check myself out in the mirror.

Not bad.

The schoolgirl stuff goes on next and by the time I'm all dressed, I'm a little sweaty and out of breath from all the anticipation.

Ronin and I do some roleplaying. Mostly that stupid cop stuff because I said I was checking to see if he was drunk when I got caught sniffing him back when we first met. It kinda stuck, and it's fun, but we both end up laughing too much to continue the fantasy. Maybe I'll try a little harder tonight.

I bite my lip as I exit the dressing room and climb the stairs to our apartment. I feel like I've been gone forever instead of just a week and my stomach gets a little flutter as I make my way down the hallway. I strain to listen for noise, but even Antoine and Elise's apartment is quiet. When I get to the door I take a deep breath and straighten my blouse a little, pulling it down a bit to reveal some of my goods.

I decide to start the roleplay with a knock. I hold my breath as the click of fancy shoes sounds behind the door and then it opens. Ronin is wearing a gray suit coat, some gray slacks, a long black tie, and no shirt.

"My, my, Mr. Flynn. You certainly look handsome tonight. I feel underdressed."

He waves me in. "If anything, Miss Corvus, you're overdressed."

I smile up at him and walk into the living room. We have no formal dining area, just a nook that connects the kitchen and the terrace sliders. But we do have a nice dark mahogany table and right now it's filled with flickering white candles. No other lights are on in the entire apartment, so the glow is soft and golden.

"Well," I say, turning to face Ronin, "there's no room on the table for food, so we must not be eating dinner."

He slides his hands around my waist and pulls my lower body tight against his, allowing my upper body to sway backwards slightly and pull the white shirt apart just the slightest bit. He peeks down and then finds my eyes. "Are you hungry for food?"

"No," I whisper as I lean forward and lay my head on his shoulder. "I'm hungry for you."

"How about dessert, then?"

"Mmmmm, maybe," I purr into his neck. "What do you have in mind?"

He leans down and kisses me softly on the lips. It's just a feather of a touch, just the slightest bare flutter of his lips against mine, just enough to create a spark of heat and then leave the cool emptiness as he pulls back. "I made a promise to you a while back and I figured it was time to make good."

"What promise?" I ask with a stupid grin, frantically racking my brain for what he might have in mind. Ronin is not an easy guy to predict, that's for sure. Whenever I think I know what he's doing, especially when it comes to the erotic photoshoots or sex, I'm almost always wrong.

I love this about him because it means he thinks about me. A lot.

Even over the summer when he was hesitant to get more adventurous with our lovemaking he always kept me on my toes with small things. A command to come before we climaxed together. A kiss in a totally unexpected place, like that dent behind my knee. Or hoisting me up against the wall of the shower, my legs wrapped tight around his middle—and then *not* fucking me, but instead talking me into an orgasm with the most amazing combination of words ever strung together in the French language.

Of course I didn't understand a single thing he said, he

could've been reciting our grocery list for all I knew, but it totally got me off.

"Want me to show you?"

A shiver runs up my back as his fingertips slip around across my jawline and caress the nape of my neck.

"Please, yes."

He grins. "I love it when you say please." His fingers leave my neck, trace down my shoulder, then my ribs, and finally grab my hand. He laces us together and pulls me with him down the hallway towards the bedroom.

"Dessert is in the bedroom?" I giggle a little.

He looks back at me with half-hooded lids and simply nods.

Our bedroom is also lit up with candles, only in here they are all on tall candelabras. Some are placed on the dressers and tables so they reach halfway up the wall, the shadow of flames caressing the ceiling. Others are on the floor and light the dark hardwood below my feet.

On the nightstand is a bowl of cherries and a bottle of champagne in an ice bucket. Two flutes are already filled with golden bubbles.

"Yes, Mr. Flynn, this is definitely dessert." I look up at him and his blue eyes are sparkling in the candlelight. "Would you like to hear how I did on my math test?"

"No, I'm not at all interested in your grades tonight, Miss Corvus."

I cock an eyebrow at him. "You're not?" I look down at my schoolgirl outfit and then back up at him. He's not smiling. "Then what's with the outfit? I thought you had something to teach me?"

"I do," he says softly, pulling me towards him. "I'm going to teach you what it means to be loved by me."

And then his mouth takes over. Both hands cup my face, pulling me into him, then one slides behind my neck while the other slides over my throat, pauses to palm it and then falls to my breast and palms that as well. My hands slip to the front of his pants and his cock comes to life as soon as I glide my fingertips over it. He groans and then his hand removes mine. "Not yet," he breathes into my mouth.

I push him, making him take a few steps back, and he ends up against the wall, but he takes a step forward before I can do anything about it. "Maybe I'd like to call the shots tonight. Did you ever think of that?"

His eyebrows shoot up. "You can try."

I almost laugh, in fact, I huff out some air before I can stop it. When I look up at him he's grinning like the devil. I push him again and this time he lets himself settle against the wall, ready to see what I'll do. I slip my hands inside his suit coat and drag my fingers across the hills and valleys of his perfect abs, then up across his chest, stopping to rub his nipple. When I look up he's got his eyes closed and his head tilted back against the wall. He likes this. I slip the suit coat down over one shoulder with one hand and drag my other hand up and around his neck, pulling on him so he will lean down enough for me to kiss him.

He refuses, simply keeps his head pressed up against the wall. "You want to be in control, right?" He opens one eye and smiles. "Control me, then."

Oh fuck. The wetness slips out between my legs and suddenly everything is throbbing. "I *can*, you know."

This time he doesn't even open his eyes. "Tell me how."

I bite my bottom lip a little and think this through in the few seconds I have before I ruin the mood. "Well," I say, a little breathless. "I could do all the predictable things." I kneel down, my hands sliding down his chest and settling on his hips as I sit back on my butt. I watch his face the entire time. He doesn't open his eyes or make any detectable shift in position. "Like bury your cock in my mouth."

This makes him let out a breath and grin, but his eyes remain closed.

"But I'm not gonna do that."

He chuckles. "Tease."

I stand back up but my hands stay between his legs. I grab him and squeeze until he moans. I leave one hand there and then take his hand and place it over the buttons on my blouse. "Undress me, but keep your eyes closed."

His other hand comes up and he works the topmost button free, but instead of unbuttoning the next one, he tugs the shirt out from my skirt and starts on the bottom ones. He releases each one until there is just a single button holding the two sides of my shirt together, the one right between my breasts.

"Do that one too," I command in a whisper.

Ronin ignores me and instead slides his hands around my hips and settles on the zipper running up my ass. His fingers linger there for a second, his eyes still closed, his breathing a little more labored now. His hands flip up my skirt and slip around the cheeks of my ass. He squeezes, slips his finger between my legs, finds the wetness, and smirks.

His eyes still closed, he says, "I think you're doing my job for me, Gidget. Stop turning yourself on." He plunges a finger inside and I gasp and my head falls back a little. Except for his hands, he remains motionless against the wall. "Are you still in control?"

"Absolutely," I say.

He laughs. "Is that right?" Before I know what's happening my skirt is unzipped and falling to the floor. I'm just coming to terms with that fact when the button of my blouse goes shooting across the room and my shirt joins my skirt. This time when I look up at his face his eyes are open.

I'm standing in my sexy lingerie while he's still got all his clothes on.

He laughs. "Good try, Gidget."

"I'm not done!"

He spins around and suddenly we've changed positions. I'm face first against the wall, my hands spread out above my head and his thigh between my legs, asking me to open for him. He presses his full erection against my ass, one hand caressing my thigh while the other plunges back into the crease between my legs. "Oh, I think you're about to come *un*done, Miss Corvus. I'm about to make sure of it." His breath is hot against my neck as the words come out and then his tongue is teasing my earlobe. The hand on my thigh presses against my skin, travels upward with the same firm pressure, and then rests on my breast. He squeezes hard now and I moan and pull away.

"Hold still now, Rook," he commands in a harsh voice as his fingers continue to probe me between my legs. His thumb finds my sweet spot and caresses tiny circles around it.

I exhale and push back against his chest because I'm having trouble getting enough air back inside my body, that's how ragged my breathing is. "Please," I whimper.

He pushes himself into me, forcing me against the wall. "Please what, babe?"

"Give me what I want."

"What do you want?" he whispers into my ear. "Tell me what you want."

"Make me come."

He pulls back, like all the way back, until he's no longer touching me. I look over my shoulder to see what he's doing.

"You're one crazy chick if you think you're gonna get off that easy."

"What do you mean?"

"'Make me come'—pfft. Gidget, I can make you come anytime I want. Tonight you're not gonna just come, babe. I'm gonna blow your fucking mind."

CHAPTER TWENTY-TWO

I swear to God, her whole body blushes pink with my words and it takes all my self-control to keep from smiling.

This fucking girl. I just want to scoop her up and devour her.

I lace our fingers together and pull her away from the wall. She's suddenly very shy, her eyes avoiding my direct gaze, her head a little bowed. I lift her chin with a fingertip and then kiss her gently on the mouth. "I love it when you watch me."

She smiles, almost tips her chin back down in embarrassment, but corrects that action before she commits. She stares back at me. "What will you do now?"

I lead her to the center of the room, drop her hand, then sit down on the bed and lean back. "Take your clothes off, Rook." I unbutton my suit trousers and slip my hand in my pants. My gaze never leaves Rook's face. She watches everything I do and when I grab myself she takes in a short quick breath, then looks me in the eyes and slides her hand down her hip until her fingertips reach the first clasp on the garter. In seconds, all those straps are hanging loose and she wiggles the thin band of lacy fabric over her curvy hips and it drops to the floor.

She steps out of the little circle and sticks one leg out in front and bends the other so she can lean over and roll her stocking down. When she gets it to the ankle she steps forward and places her foot on my thigh.

I accept her invitation and slide the stocking off with her

stiletto. They join the garter on the floor, a small pile beginning to form.

She repeats this and then my heart starts to beat wildly as she slides the straps of the sheer black teddy down her shoulders. Her nipples are bunched up and hard and her breasts push against the fabric as she wiggles it free from her body.

And then she takes my hand and places it on the string of her panties.

But I take her hand and place it between her legs. "You love it when I watch you, too."

Her fingertips start a slow circle over her slit and then push against the fabric of her panties. And I swear, I swear to fucking God, I have to reach out and make her stop or I'll lose it.

Her eyes rest on mine and she smiles.

She wins this one.

"Take them off, please," she says sweetly as she pulls the string against her hip, then releases it, making it snap against her skin.

A guttural growl escapes from my throat as I tug her panties down and let them drop to the floor. She stands naked before me. "Now what?"

I stand up and undress myself slowly. Her eyes never leave my hands. Her gaze follows my suit coat as I drape it over a chair then returns to me in time to catch me removing the tie from around my neck.

Her little Gidget tongue darts out, wets her lips, and then she takes a deep breath that makes her chest expand and lift up her breasts. My dick is so hard it's holding up the damn trousers and it takes me a second to free myself from the pants.

"Now, the shower," I finally answer her.

She tilts her head and smiles. "I thought shower sex was boring?"

"Who said anything about sex?"

She cocks an eyebrow at me. "I'm listening…"

"Follow me, Gidget." I take her across the hall to the bathroom and flick my fingers across the control panel to bring up the steam and a light drizzle. This is my favorite setting, the setting I always use when we're about to get busy in the shower. When I look back at her she's biting her lip. "What?" I ask.

"Looks pretty boring so far."

I laugh. "Is that right?" I take her inside the shower and gently push her until the backs of her knees hit the tiled bench at the far end of the stall. "Have a seat," I say in a whisper. She smirks at me, like she knows what's going on. But her expression falters when I look over my shoulder as I walk out of the shower and open a small built-in cupboard on the other side of the bathroom. I pull out a brand-new lady razor, the kind with all that soapy shit attached directly to the blade, and snap it on the handle.

"What are you doing?" Rook asks as I kneel down in front of her.

"What's it look like I'm doing?" I press against her inner thighs and open her legs up and then palm the light covering of hair between her legs and tickle her until she squirms.

She chews on her lips, trying to chase her blushing smile away. "But you told me to let it grow out after the body painting."

"I did."

"Why?"

"So I could shave it off." I grab her hair conditioner off the shelf and squirt some on the tips of my fingers and gently cover the little strip between her legs. I don't check her expression again, but I know exactly what it looks like based on her breathing. I start at the top of her hairline and use long strokes to shave her smooth. I want to rub my whole hand over the skin there, but I'm trying to keep her from coming as long as I can, and that would definitely work against me.

When I finish with the easy parts I grab her ankles and

lift them up next to her hips so her feet are flat on the bench and I have access to the hidden parts. I take a lot more time in this area and I have to stop periodically to allow her to calm down from my touches. It's inevitable that my fingers will drive her crazy. I mean, they are *my* fingers, right? I wink at her after I finish this thought. She's too busy squirming to notice.

When I'm finished she's a panting mess, her back slightly arched, her head tilting back a bit, and small whimpers escaping her mouth. I spray her gently with the shower head and then sit back and enjoy my handiwork.

She opens her eyes. "Now what?" she asks softly.

"You can come now, babe."

"Touch me, Ronin," she begs.

I shake my head. "Sorry, no can do, Gidget. But I'll let you watch as I touch myself and let's just see if that's enough to get you started." I reach down and grab my dick and start pumping. Slow and long strokes.

Her mouth falls open, then closes a little as her eyes lower to watch my hand. She bites her lip again, but this time it's not to try to maintain control. I pump a little faster and that makes her breathe out a seductively long moan and close her eyes.

"Watch me, Rook," I command. She opens her eyes but she only manages half-mast.

My plan was to make her come without touching her. I've done it before, but my tongue is far too eager to taste her newly smooth skin. She knows I'm about to cave and she wiggles a little, one foot dropping down to rest on my thigh, the other propped up on my shoulder like an invitation that I am powerless to refuse. I slide a finger inside her and pump with the same rhythm I'm using on myself. Her whole body tenses up, her back in a severe arch and her head pressing back against the tiled wall. I sink my tongue into her folds, flick against her clit, and we explode together—our moans echoing off the tiled bathroom walls.

We sit still for a few moments to enjoy the aftershocks,

but then I get to my feet and pull her up with me. "OK, I think we're ready to get started."

She laughs as I lead her out into the bathroom, shut off the shower, and then grab a fluffy white towel and pat her down. I towel myself down a little as well, and then lead her back into the bedroom. "Lie down for me."

She obeys, taking herself over to the king-size bed we share. Everything in this room is white except for the furniture and the floors. Those are both a dark mahogany wood. The soft flicker of candlelight makes her look like a goddess as she lies there, complacent and happy, wet and pink with the heat of the shower and her desire. I stand next to the bed and grab a cherry, then straddle her legs and lean down to touch the cherry to her lips. "Bite, please," I ask softly.

These cherries came straight from the fruit basket on Antoine's desk this morning. And even though it's a little late in the year for cherries, they are soft and plump because all the fruit that comes in a basket to Chaput Studios is succulent and sweet and perfect. Just like my Rook. Her teeth sink into the flesh and she pulls back, chewing.

I take the other half and bite out the pit, whoof it into the waste basket near the nightstand, and then paint the juice around her mouth. "I told you, back when we did that first photoshoot, that if I had you naked with cherries, I'd drip it all down your belly and lick it off."

Her seductive smile lets me know she's remembering our first erotic shoot together.

"But before I do that…" I eat this cherry, then grab another one and put it up to her mouth. She bites, again leaving the pit for me. I whoof it and drag the fruit around the rosy areola in the center of her breast, making her nipple bunch up tight from the cold. The cherry turns her pale skin a deep red and I almost want to explode, that's how hard this makes me. "I'm gonna do this." My mouth covers her nipple and I lick the juice, then squeeze more, and lick it again. I do it all again on her other breast and when I'm finally ready to start on her belly, she's all stained up with red juice.

I move down her abdomen, kissing her gently as I go, dragging my scratchy face along her sensitive skin, and then grab a whole handful of cherries and place them on the pristine white sheets next to me. It's gonna stain the fuck out of them, but that's the price you pay when you wanna have fun with fruit.

I bite and drip, bite and drip, then do it several more times until the little concave dip of her stomach is holding a pool of sweet nectar and her adorable belly button is overflowing. I push a fingertip into the liquid and drag it down towards her slit, stopping to let the juice collect in her folds. I repeat this until the red is diluted pink with her own wetness.

And then my tongue takes over. I eat her out like I'm starving for her sweetness, like I didn't just take her in the bathroom twenty minutes ago, like this is my last chance to ever pleasure a woman between her legs with my mouth.

She moans, she whines, she whimpers. Her whole back buckles up, cherry juice drips down her body, dirty words are coming out of her mouth, and she starts fighting to get her chance to show me what *her* mouth can do to pleasure me back.

But I don't let her up. I keep her there, at my mercy, holding her down and begging for more.

I blow her fucking mind with my tongue and fingers. I make her whimper and moan, squeal and fight when it gets too intense.

And then I fuck the shit out of her until we are exhausted and the hazy light of predawn is seeping through the blinds.

CHAPTER TWENTY-THREE

Ronin

I wish I could say we enjoyed all the hundreds of things there are to do in Colorado on Saturday. Like went up to the mountains and marveled at the fluttering golden wave created by the thousands upon thousands of aspen trees that line the cliffs. Or took advantage of an early mountain snowstorm and went skiing up at A-Basin. Or hell, stayed in town and caught an Aves game.

But we did none of those things. Because we never got out of bed.

She's still fucking trying to sleep right now and it's almost eleven on Sunday. "Gidget," I whisper into her ear. She swats me away with her hand, slapping my arm pretty good. "Gidge, we're putting clothes on today, babe. Like it or not, we're leaving the house."

"To go where?" she moans.

"The mall. Elise wants us to go baby shopping with her."

Rook grunts. "She does not. That's dumb, why would she want us to tag along?"

Damn, she's sorta cynical. And she's totally on to me because Antoine begged me to come with him so he and I can nurse some beers and watch the Broncos annihilate the Eagles while the girls shop. But I'm pretty good at faking shit, so I try it out on Rook now. "Serious, she says she wants my opinion, she knows I'm all into this baby shit. And you need some girl time, you have no girlfriends."

She turns this time, her mouth all screwed up. "Is *Clare*

gonna be there?"

"Uh, well, yeah. She's really not allowed to go anywhere alone these days. She's gotta be with one of us at all times."

"You look guilty, are you lying to me?"

"Gidget, I am nothing if not honest with you, babe. Seriously. Elise wants you to come, I swear." That's not a lie. Elise does want Rook to come. She has fully accepted the fact that I plan on marrying this girl as soon as she's ready to commit.

It takes me another hour to get Rook up and ready and by that time Clare, Elise, and Antoine are already heading out to the restaurant where we're gonna have lunch. "You look great, let's go." I jingle my truck keys at her from the front hallway, but she ignores me and just sits calmly on the couch and laces up some black work boots. Combined with her faded and ripped jeans, white t-shirt, and Shrike Bikes leather jacket, they make her look like a hot punk chick.

If we don't get out of this fucking apartment soon I might have to jump her bones.

She catches my daydream and says, "I'm sore as shit, so stop with the *I wanna fuck you* looks."

She walks over to me as she straightens out her jacket and I take her hand and lead her out the door and down the hallway. There's some commotion downstairs in the studio and when we turn the corner at the stairs, Roger is messing with a large flat package. "What's that?" I call down to him as we descend.

"That rush job for the GIDGET campaign."

It takes me a second to figure out what he's talking about and by that time it's too late. He's already ripped the brown paper off the frame and his head is tilting to the side a little as he critiques the image.

Busted.

"What the hell is *that*?" Rook asks in a huff.

She can clearly see what it is, a fucking life-sized picture of me sticking my tongue down Clare's throat, but I usher her past in a hurry. "It's an old photo the GIDGET people wanted to use for promo. We had it blown up so we can use it for the shoots this week."

Even though she's walking away from it, her eyes never leave the image. I whisk her into the stairwell and pull her out of range. "Hmmm…" is all she says.

I change the subject. "Hungry?"

"Yeah, actually I'm starving."

She chats about lunch after that. Maybe the image is still on her mind and maybe it's not, but she's dropped it for now and that's about as much as I can ask for.

The ride down to Cherry Creek Mall is uneventful beyond getting stuck in construction traffic, and by the time we make it to the sports bar at the mall, I'm starving as well. Antoine already got us a table and Elise is chowing down on fried cheese. Rook looks happy though, so maybe she's gonna let the picture drop.

It's not my fault, really. The image had to be used. I never told Rook this, but Clare was always my first pick for this contract. And we did a lot of promo stuff together to show them that I had a vision and could handle something this big on my own. That was almost a year ago now, and honestly, it never occurred to me that they'd want me to model for them. I'm the marketing manager for the campaign, I never signed anything saying I'd model. And they are certainly not paying me enough to fuck things up with Rook over some pictures. But this one was already a done deal. I had very little room since it was submitted with the project bid.

Luckily Antoine got us a table near the flat screen on the wall that's blaring the game, so he and I concentrate on that while the girls chat. I look over at Rook a few times to see how she's doing with Clare, but it doesn't seem to be an issue.

Maybe I'll get away with this fuck-up after all?

CHAPTER TWENTY-FOUR

Rook

"Adorable!" I squeal as Elise holds up a tiny blue onesie with light green sea turtles swimming across the front. It is cute but honestly, how many freaking onesies can you look at in one day and still get excited? She throws it into the waiting hands of the Gymboree sales person and continues sorting through racks of clothes. Clare is much better at this shopping stuff than I am. I'm not against shopping, I just prefer to do it online. Or have a set plan in mind when I go in. For me, shopping is more like a military exercise—get in, complete the mission, get out. Bam. Now you have the whole rest of your day to kiss your boyfriend, or eat, or watch movies.

"Hey, since we're out, you guys wanna catch that new SF flick over at the Metroplex?"

Clare sneers at me.

I hate that bitch, I swear. I'm not really a hater, I mean I can typically find the good in just about anyone. And I'm definitely not a fighter. I prefer the whole cheek-turning thing over fists any day. But I tell you what, I'd like to slap the shit out of Clare. She is the biggest fucking kiss-ass on the planet. And she blatantly flirted with Ronin all through lunch and then had the nerve to insult my choice in food.

She called me a boring date because I always get the hamburger. So I like burgers? Just because she likes weird stuff like mushroom pecan fajitas doesn't mean she's not boring. Seriously, she can't even go anywhere alone because the heroin might jump her ass and turn her back into a junkie…

OK, I went a little overboard on that one. But shit.

I huff out a long breath and busy myself shaking a baby rattle. "Hey, Elise? I'm gonna just pop over to the…" I squint out at the store across the way from Gymboree and read the sign. "Brookstone." Yeah, that's a much better store. They have cool shit in there. "I need some overpriced gadgets."

"Rook, if you're not going to help, just go back to the restaurant and watch football with the men, OK? This is a big deal for Elise."

"Rook," Elise counters, "I'm almost done, OK? Then we'll go upstairs and do grownup shopping. The guys said they'll meet us over at the baby crib store at five, so we have plenty of time."

I smile and nod. Great, crib shopping. I'm not into thinking about this baby stuff, let alone shopping for one, and it just reminds me of how different Ronin and I really are when it comes to long-term plans. I might like a kid someday, and that's a big maybe. But right now I'm all about *not* having a kid. I'm not ready for crib shopping, even if it isn't for me.

We spend the next fifteen minutes checking out and then make our way upstairs to the cool level of the mall. At least there are stores here I recognize, if only because I have clothes in my closets with these names on them. Clare heads to Lucky Jeans and I follow her in while Elise rests her feet outside the store and pokes through her bags of baby clothes.

"What size are you, Rook? I'll help you choose."

"Noneya, Clare. I'm not an infant, I can pick out my own jeans." Fuck, she is such a bitch. How can Ronin even like her as a person? And I can only imagine how unlikeable she was as an addict. I flip through some jeans laid out on a table and then decide this is stupid. "I don't need any clothes, I'm going to sit with Elise."

I walk out before she can answer and plop down next to Elise on her bench. "I'm sorry, Elise. I'm just not a shopper."

She pats my hand like a mother. "I don't care, Rook. And don't let Clare get to you. She's just high-maintenance all the time. Isn't there anything you need while we're here? You might as well pick up something."

"I could use some lotion, now that I think of it."

"Oh!" Elise squeals. "Let's hit the Crabtree & Evelyn store, it's just right over there."

Lotions I can handle. Just pick out some that smell good and pay. No need to try things on or make it match your socks—just good old-fashioned plunk-it-in-the-basket-and-pay-up-front shopping. Elise calls out to Clare as we walk past, telling her where we'll be.

"So, Rook, how are things up with Spencer and Ford? I haven't had a chance to talk to you in weeks, it seems."

"Pretty good. The job is painfully boring, you know, compared to what I was doing. But it's OK. I'm good with slipping back into regular life."

"And school?"

"Well, I don't know. I like it, and I really like the idea of going to film school. But it's a lot of work, ya know?"

She laughs. "I never went to college, so actually, I'm not a good one to ask."

"No? How'd that happened? I mean, Ronin got an excellent education, so I just figured you did as well."

"I was already grown up when I met Antoine. I did go to beauty school eventually. At first I was just Antoine's personal make-up person and he showed me what to do. But when we finally settled down in the States I had to get a license. Antoine and I wanted Ronin to have all the opportunities I never did, so we always made education a big deal."

"Maybe not everyone is cut out for a college degree?"

Elise stares hard at me as we enter the store. "Are you having doubts?"

I shrug and pick up a bottle of lotion and sniff it. "Some, maybe. It's hard. I'm not very good at it, Elise. I'm terrible at math and the science is interesting, but I have to memorize a bunch of stuff. It's just… hard."

"Everything worth getting is hard, Rook. You gotta want

it real bad, right? Like Antoine, for instance. He actually comes from a pretty wealthy family in France and they had a lot of preconceived expectations for his life. Things Antoine was not remotely interested in doing. They have a big construction business over there, major contracts all over Europe. But my Antoine decided to come to America. He had money for school but not much else, and he came here to study photography and now look at him." Elise stops to smile as she thinks about her incredible baby daddy. "He fought for his dream, Rook. My dream was to make sure Ronin turned into a good guy so that's what I fought for. And Ronin *is* a good guy, so I'm happy that I made that dream come true. Now I want my own family so I'm gonna fight for that. And if you want to get your college degree, then that's your fight."

I think about this for a few seconds as we continue to browse the lotions. "But—what if I'm fighting for the wrong thing? What if I just like the *idea* of film school and I'm not dedicated to putting in the years of hard work to make it real? What's that mean?"

"Not everyone who loves taking pictures wants to be Antoine. Not everyone who wants to putter around with a video camera needs to make blockbusters. Maybe movies are a hobby? I'm not sure, so don't take what I'm saying as gospel, OK? Because only you can figure out if it's worth it."

"Ronin wants to fight for a family too, Elise. He's so, so serious about that and I'm not sure if I feel the same way."

She sighs up at me, silent for a moment. "Not all families are bad, Rook. I did my best to make sure Ronin understood this as he grew up, but I think you need to hear it more than he ever did. Not all families are bad. Some people get stuck with bad parents, or they have a failed marriage because they ended up with the wrong partner. That's just how things shake out sometimes. But not everyone's life is like that. It took me twelve years of unconditional love from Antoine to understand this myself. So you know, if I can save you from wasting all that time doubting yourself and what you and

Ronin have together, then that's a huge win for all of us. He's moving too fast for you, I get that. But he'll wait, Rook. And if you love him and can see a future for the two of you, then let him have his dream while he waits. Because Ronin just wants to put down some roots. Even though we've called Antoine's place home for more than a decade, we've always been pretty transient. He just wants to plant himself somewhere and let out a long breath of relief that this life is permanent now."

Wow, I should've talked to Elise a long time ago about this stuff. She's like a walking reality check. "Thanks," I say as I hug her.

"Hey!" Clare calls from outside the store. "Look! It's Ronin and me!"

Elise and I are both confused for a moment, but as soon as we walk outside and direct our eyeballs across the mall where Clare is pointing, we both get it.

Because right there in the front window of the lingerie shop is a giant poster of Clare and Ronin and he has his hands all over her body and his tongue down her throat.

And this is definitely *not* the picture I saw back at the studio.

"When did you take that?" I ask.

"Oh, this one…" She stops to think.

"Last fall," Elise offers. "That was taken last fall. When Ronin was getting ready to bid on this GIDGET contract. He put together a whole fake campaign with Clare."

"Yeah, that one was a while ago, but those GIDGET people liked it so much, they had us do another shoot this week. I think the proof was getting delivered from the printer today. Did you see it when you left, Rook?"

She bats her eyelashes at me. Clearly she knows I did. "No," I answer, shaking my head. "Never saw anything." She scowls at me, not sure if I'm lying or not, not willing to push things in front of Elise. I smile back at her, playing it off.

But inside, I'm seething. That fucker. Mr. I'm-nothing-if-not-honest fucking lied to me!

CHAPTER TWENTY-FIVE

Ronin

I tug Rook into my chest and wrap my arms round her. "How about this one?" I point to the white crib with a sleigh bed shape to it. "It's sorta classic, right?" She glances over her shoulder and gives me a dirty look. I know she hates this but I can't help myself. "What? What's that face for?"

"Nothing," she replies with an annoyed growl.

Something's up but I'm just not sure what it is yet. Something happened when she went shopping with the girls but she's not acting mad. Just not happy either. I'd ask Elise, but she's way too into this crib-buying stuff. Hell, even Antoine is into it. He's all for the white cribs too, but Elise wants something dark. Apparently she has a vision of what her little boy's room should look like and nothing will deter her.

And there's no way I'm bringing Clare in because that would just make everything worse. In fact, I'm pretty fucking sure whatever did happen at the mall, Clare is the reason. I pull Rook over to the crib bedding and point down to a baseball-themed set inside the crib. "I'd pick that one."

"Yeah, that's nice."

Well, at least she didn't growl. "You wanna get out of here?"

Suddenly she's interested. "Really? But what about Elise?"

"She's got it under control. Hey, Ellie! We're taking off, see you guys later, OK?"

And that's that. I lead Rook out of the store and swing

her hand as we walk to the truck.

The drive home only takes about ten minutes, but it's ten minutes of silent hell. I know we have to talk about it, but since she's in no hurry to bring it up, well, then neither am I. I turn the truck off in the garage and then look over at her. She's fucking with her phone—doing what, I'm not sure, because the only people she really texts are me, Spencer, or Ford and I'm pretty sure she's not having some deep convo with Ford or Spencer while she sits in my truck. "OK, what's up, Rook? Obviously something is wrong and it's got my name written all over it. So let's just get it out in the open."

She flips the handle on her door and jumps out, leaving me no choice but to follow her over to the elevator. The ride up is slow and silent and never in my life have I wished for an instrumental version of *Hey Jude* to be playing in an elevator more than I do right now. Anything to break the uncomfortable silence. When the door finally opens she walks out, but instead of taking a left to head towards the stairs, she walks out into the center of the studio and stands in front of that big promo picture of Clare and me.

"OK, this is the problem?" I ask as I wave my hand towards the poster.

Rook holds up her phone and there's another picture of Clare and me on the screen. "Do you know where I took this pic, Ronin?"

I take the phone from her and look a little closer. "Shit."

"Yeah, shit. You lied to me. This picture," she says, snatching the phone back, "was the one you guys took last year and it's on display at the fucking mall. This one," she says, jacking her thumb behind her to the poster, "was a rush job shot last week. At least, that's what *Clare* tells me. So would you like to explain why you lied?"

"Well, I'm busted, what do you want me to say?"

She gasps. "Uh, how about 'sorry?' Jesus fucking Christ, Ronin. I mean, look, I'm not gonna throw a fit or some shit like that, but fuck, I hate liars. Seriously cannot fucking stand liars. OK? I like the truth, thank you. I enjoy knowing what the fuck is going on, and I thought I could trust you."

"I didn't do anything more with Clare than you did with Spencer or Billy, Rook. It was one fucking shoot. They wanted an updated image now that Clare is back to being healthy, that's all there is to it."

She walks away. Just heads to the stairs and starts hoofing it up to the apartment. I catch up with her at the top, just as she's about to turn the corner, and grab her arm. She pulls away so hard she stumbles backwards. "You're walking away again, Gidget. I'm not gonna let you do that."

She pushes past me and stops at our apartment door. "Like you can stop me?"

"So you're walking out over this lie? This one stupid, meaningless lie?"

"First of all, it's not meaningless. Maybe it's not Earth-shattering, but it's not meaningless. Because relationships are all about trust and now I'm having doubts."

"Welcome to my world."

She snorts. "Welcome to *your world*? So you're having doubts about *me*? Then just break it off if I'm not the girl you want. I'm clearly not what you're into, Ronin. I mean what the fuck was all this baby shit today?"

"This was about Elise, not us."

"No? You know I'm not ready to think about this shit and you don't even care! You have no idea how fucking confusing it is to be around Elise right now. To watch all you guys get excited over this baby and have to feel… *nothing.* I can't feel anything, OK? And all you guys are gushing about cribs and stupid outfits and baby bedding, for fuck's sake!"

Well, that's not what I was expecting. "So this isn't about the photoshoot I did with Clare last week?"

She sighs. "Yes, of course it is!"

"I'm officially confused."

"Forget it, OK? I'm not gonna throw a temper tantrum and start a huge fight over it, so just forget it. You just do your thing and don't worry about me and I'll do the same. How's that?"

She reaches over to punch the code in the door and I grab her wrist and pull it away. "Hold on," I say calmly and wait for her to look me in the eye. "I'm not even worth an argument? Really? You just want to get as far away from me as you can right now so you can avoid… what? *Dealing*?"

She laughs. "Oh, I'm not dramatic enough? Is that it? You want me to fight with you?"

"No," I say gently as I lower her hand and bring it to my waist, forcing her to touch me. "I want you to fight for *us*, Rook. You never want to fight for *us*, you just want to walk away whenever it gets hard. And dammit, this is not hard, Rook. This life we're living right now is fucking paradise. So how will you act when the shit gets out of control? Will you just leave me when I need you most? Because I'd never leave you. I hope you know that, Rook. I'd *never* walk out. I'd fight for you every single time. You'd never even have to wonder if I'd be there because I'd show the fuck up before that thought could ever cross your mind. I want you, I'd risk everything for you. I already told you I'd wait. Whatever it takes, however long it takes. I'm still gonna be here. I do want babies, I do want you as my wife, but I can live with a promise."

She swallows and looks down. I take her other hand and press it against my waist so she has to turn and face me.

"What I can't live with is you sabotaging our relationship every time you feel uncomfortable. Eventually, you're gonna have to fucking figure this shit out. Because the thought of you walking out on me just tears me up."

And then I take her purse off her shoulder and drop it on the floor so I can slip my arms around her and pull her close. "I'm sorry about the Clare shit. I'm sorry that I lied earlier. I just didn't want to talk about it right then, that's all. I was stalling for time. Of course I was gonna tell you, but it's sort of a long story and I didn't want to tell it right then."

She leans her head into me and I play with her hair a little as I talk. "Stop with the Clare jealousy, OK? I know she's irritating, I realize she's probably baiting you to piss you off, but I'm not interested in her. At all. She's living in a fantasy and I'll set her straight tonight and let you watch if you want. Because I have no problem fighting for us. None."

Rook stays silent for a few seconds and relaxes against me a little more. I sigh as she begins to speak softly. "I was pissed about the Clare thing because she knew I didn't know and it makes me feel so stupid. I felt so foolish that she knew you were keeping a secret from me. And I'm not a very confrontational person so my first reaction is always to run away. I know that. I get it. I'm just not sure how much I can do about it. When I get scared, I run. And so much about you—about us—scares me. It makes me want to just give up so I don't have to deal with it."

I tilt her chin up gently so she looks me in the eye. She fights it for a second, then relents when she realizes I'm not gonna let her get away with it. "I really don't need much, babe. Just make me feel that I'm worth something. That you'll take a risk on us, like you said on the phone the night I dropped you off at Spencer's. I just want to know that when things start to look hopeless you'll still be willing to show up and give it your best, ya know? At the very least, be willing to put in an appearance. I mean, I'd love it if you just stuck to me no matter what for everything, but seriously, I'd settle for a half-hearted try right now."

She pushes her head into my chest. "So you want me to be your Shrek?"

I can't help it, I bellow out a laugh. "What?"

"You know? When Shrek is rescuing Fiona—"

"Does it always come back to a movie with you?"

"—and he chains up that bitchy dragon named *Clare*—"

"You are too much…"

"—and breaks Fiona out of the tower. You want me to be Shrek and fight for you, get you out of that stupid tower, fine. I'll work on it."

"I'm pretty sure I'm Shrek and you're Fiona, Rook. I let you make me be Larue, but I draw the line at Fiona."

"Whatever."

I cup her face in my hands and plant a little kiss on her lips. "I love the fuck out of you, ya know that, right?"

"Now all we need is a donkey to get Clare pregnant so she'll stop braying at us. I vote for Billy."

Oh, God. I just want to squeeze her, that's how cute she is. Just squeeze her until she admits she'll never leave me. Because even if she doubts herself, I have total faith in this girl. I know she loves me. I know she'll stick. Ford was wrong, she's not gonna check out, she's in—I can feel the truth just as well as I can tell a lie. She loves me, regardless of the nightmare past that still seems to be haunting her. I lean in and kiss her again, whispering into her little Gidget mouth. "I'm sorry I lied to you and did a shoot with Clare without telling you first."

She looks up at me now, pausing to smile. "I'm sorry I threatened to run away and I'll make an effort to fight with you more."

I chuckle again. She's adorable. Everything about her squeals *perfect*. "I would like to marry you, stick you in a kitchen and get you all barefoot and pregnant. But I'll wait. I'm not in a hurry, I'm enjoying every second we spend together. I'm really not trying to pressure you with the baby talk."

Her sigh is actually a long low moan that comes off mournful. "I think you are, but it's OK. I'll learn to deal."

"Hey," I say softly as I tip her chin up. "You don't need to learn to deal with me, Rook. You got something inside that head of yours you need to get out? What's going on with the baby stuff?"

She pulls back and turns away. Not a good sign.

"I just…" She looks at me over her shoulder and then lifts her eyes to meet mine. "I'm not ready yet, OK? I told you some of what happened that last time Jon went off on me, how he found the birth control and why I felt I needed it. But there's more to it." She takes a long breath, holds it, and then lets it out slowly. "But I'm not ready to think about it yet."

Her chest expands suddenly and I know she's about to cry. I reach out and turn her around as I pull her into me. "Hey, it's OK. You don't have to talk about it." She shakes a little as she sobs and all I can do is hold her tight. "Shhh," I murmur next to her ear as she tries to stop. And then I stop trying to quiet her because there's something I've noticed about Rook over the past few months. She hardly ever cries over her past. She cries when she's frustrated about things between us and she cried pretty hard that day she found out about the missing person's report, but really, she should maybe cry a little more. She holds things in until it boils over.

So I just hug her tight and kiss her head and try to say something soft and soothing. "Don't panic, Gidget. Be still and stay calm. We'll be OK, I promise. Just keep calm and it will all work out."

And she spends the next few minutes with her face buried in my jacket letting it out in her own way.

Ford said she's got more secrets, but I figured that was about her relationship with Jon. I think this is something else, because this baby stuff is sorta coming out of nowhere and she's not making much sense. Just the few things she's told me about what that sick fuck did to her are enough, but I'm getting the feeling that as horrific as those incidents were, it's nothing compared to the secrets she's got buried inside her.

CHAPTER TWENTY-SIX

Rook

Ronin wanted to drive me back up to Fort Collins but I told him no. I need the alone time to be honest. I found out Elise was pregnant almost two months ago, so why now? I don't get it. The miscarriage is ancient history and still, I can barely even think about it without wanting to break down and cry.

I never had any counseling for that. Not even when I was living in the homeless shelter before I met Ronin. I gave the shelter people a fake name every night I stayed there, but I had to tell them about Jon just in case he came looking for me so they sorta forced that 'talking it out' shit on me. I was really paranoid for the first few weeks but Jon never showed up. And I figured if he did go looking for me he probably went to Vegas first because on paper, that's where I went. My bus ticket said Vegas. In the movies people get on a bus to Hollywood so they can make all their dreams come true, but it would've cost me another two hundred bucks to take that bus to LA and Vegas was on special when I bought my ticket.

So that's the ride I bought.

Jon went to Vegas a lot when we first started going out, but he never took me. I always wanted to go back then, but by the time I was eighteen I'd lost all interest in doing anything with Jon. He took one of the other girls instead.

And if I had answered Ford's question of how I got here more completely, that's what I would've told him—that I was heading to Vegas on a dream of being someone special. But

Ford was more concerned with the dream that landed me in Denver than the Vegas one I let drift away. After a few days on my own in Colorado I came to my senses and figured I'd just move forward here and try my best to slip back into a normal life. Denver was screaming normal, boring almost. Slow and safe. That's how I saw it back then. The complete opposite of Vegas.

And most of that stuff was pretty easy to let go. I just packed it up and put it away. Blocked it out.

But not all of it.

The baby was the only thing that still tore me up inside because you can't just grow a life inside you, allowing yourself to get used to the idea, and then turn it all off like a faucet when it's ripped away.

Every time I think of children I think of the one I lost. And even though I know it was for the best, that my life would be so much worse if I was trapped back in Illinois with this baby, and it's even possible that the baby would be in a lot of danger and we'd have very little chance of escaping together… a part of me still wishes that things would've turned out differently.

And that part of me feels so… *sick*. It makes me feel sick to want that because Jon was included in that life. And the worst part is that I can't let it go. All because of that baby. It probably means I'm really fucked up in the head. I should not want those things. But I just can't separate the two. If I love the baby then it feels like I have to love Jon, too.

I'm so fucked in the head.

It's true that I never wanted to start a family with Jon, and believe me, he threw that little fact back in my face for months after the miscarriage. He totally blamed me for the 'accident'. But once the whole pregnancy thing became real to me it changed things. I got on board, I was in, I took the vitamins, and watched what I ate, and made sure I never missed a check-up.

But in the end none of that mattered. And I can't help

but feel helpless. I always feel like it's just me against the world. How do I win that fight?

I can't.

Me against the world is not a good plan of attack in the war that is life.

I blow out a long breath of air and try to think about something else. Because it's not fair for me to take out my unresolved past on Elise, Antoine, and Ronin. They are baby people. Totally. And they are so excited. It's not fair that I disrupt their good vibes with my bad ones.

I pull into Spencer's driveway and park the truck and then grab my backpack and get out before Spence feels the need to come check on me. He's a good guy, even if he does have an unhealthy obsession with guns. I glance over at the shop and it's all dark. So that probably means Ford isn't home because it's way too early to be in bed. I go inside and drop my backpack on the floor next to the basement stairs, then go into the kitchen and look for Spencer.

"Spence?"

"Back here," he calls out from the living room.

"Whatcha doin?" I ask him as I take in the images spread out on the coffee table.

"Putting together a portfolio for you, Blackbird. So you can have a record of what we did last summer."

I plop down next to him on the couch and pick up a few of the images. "They turned out pretty good, huh?"

"Pretty good doesn't even cover it, Rook. I've sold more bikes in the last month than my old man did the entire year before I took the company over."

Spencer continues what he's doing, sorting through the images and choosing some to put into the clear pages inside the black book. "Thank you for this," I say as I watch him choose. "Which one's your favorite?"

He flips through the book to the first page. "This one," he laughs. "That's why it's first."

I take the book from his outstretched hands and look

over his choice. It's Spence and me. I'm painted up with all his tattoos on my top half, and my bottom half is a painted-on version of his ripped and faded jeans. "You know what's funny? That was my favorite outfit as well. I'm not sure why, it's just too cool that you and I had the same artwork on our bodies at the same time, ya know?"

Spencer smiles. "Yeah, that one's called *The Team*." He leans back on the couch and looks over at me. "That's what the four of us are now, you know that, right? We're a team."

And my thoughts flood back to me. The day I met Ford and we all went to dinner to celebrate our partnership at that French restaurant. That's what I thought about Ronin and me that day. That we were a team. "I'm a lucky girl, Spencer Shrike. Because this is one special team and I'm honored to be on it. I just hope I can live up to your greatness and not disappoint you."

He chuckles. "Shit, Rook, we're still floored that you put up with us at all. And Ford? You seriously deserve a fat cash bonus for mellowing that asshole out." We sit in silence as I flip the page of the book. The second picture is of cyborg sex-kitten Rook and Terminator Ronin. "That's Ronin's favorite," Spence says softly.

"I love this one too. I was so sad that day and Ford read to me and then Ronin and I had a very serious conversation about my past in the shower." I look up at Spencer to see if he knows about this, but if he does, he holds it in.

I flip the page again. This time I'm the catwoman. "That's Antoine's favorite," Spencer adds as he flips to the next page. "And this one is Ford's." The fourth image is me in the white bikini. "Because he said you started growing a backbone that day."

A laugh busts out of me unexpectedly. "Fucking Ford."

Spencer leans in and puts his arm around me, then kisses me on the head. "You know I'm here for you, whatever you need. Whenever you need it. OK?"

I look up and the tears are starting again. "Ronin called

you?"

Spence nods. "Yeah, and it's gonna be OK, Rook. I'm not sure what's going on with you or whatever. But it's gonna work out."

All the tears spill out now and I shake my head. "I'm not so sure, Spencer," I whisper. "I'm really not so sure. There's so much more about my past than I've told you guys. I have so much locked away inside."

He just lets me cry and holds me close as he continues to turn the pages of the book, commenting on each outfit until I'm calm again.

Spencer Shrike is a good guy. I feel it in my heart. He's so calm and understanding. Nothing much fazes him. Spencer Shrike screams strength.

And we're a team, he said. It doesn't have to be me against the world.

Because I'm part of the team.

CHAPTER TWENTY-SEVEN

Ronin

I pull Clare aside as Roger dismisses today's models for lunch. "I need to talk to you, Clare. Wanna have lunch with me upstairs?"

She winds her arm around mine and smiles brightly. "Absolutely!"

We walk up to my apartment together and I usher her in after I open the door. "Rook made some pasta yesterday. Want some of that? Or I have cheese and stuff."

"Rook doesn't look like the domestic type. I'm surprised she even knows how to cook pasta."

I close the fridge and turn around. "See, that's pretty much what I have to talk about. This animosity you have for Rook has to stop. I love this girl, Clare. I'm not breaking up with her, she's not breaking up with me, we're gonna get married and live out all that happily-ever-after bullshit. Because she's the one. You need to stop talking shit about her."

I expect a total capitulation, but she hands me a shrug. "I don't believe you, Ronin."

I laugh, seriously let out a total guffaw. "Which part is giving you trouble then? I'll try to be clearer."

"The part where you think Rook is sticking around. Everyone talks about her, ya know. All the Chaput models have filled me in on how things went when she got there. Even some of the photographers think she's got one foot out the door."

I can only shake my head at her brazen audacity. "Clare, listen to me very carefully, OK? Shut the fuck up about Rook. I do not give one shit what you think about my relationship with her. It's none of your goddamned business. And if I fucking even get a whiff that you're being nasty to her, or telling her shit about photoshoots, present ones or otherwise, I'll fire you from this contract so fucking fast your head will spin."

She laughs. "You couldn't fire me, Ronin. The GIDGET people want me. They'd be pissed."

"You must be under the impression that I give a fuck what those people want. I don't. I bid on this contract because it was a challenge, not because I need the fucking money. And I'll tell you something right now. I'll throw it all away, pay off every fucking model, every fucking photographer, and every fucking crew member and walk away in a second. This job is a commitment I chose to fulfill because it looked fun, and nothing else."

The shock on her face starts somewhere in the middle of my speech and by the time I'm done she looks ready to cry. "Why are you being so mean to me?"

"Mean? Fuck, girl. I've done nothing but help your ass for months. The least you can do is be fucking cordial to the woman I love."

"Ronin! I've always had your back, you know that. We've always been tight."

"We've always been friends, nothing more. So what's with all this new relationship shit?"

"I just think she's unpredictable and she's gonna end up hurting you, I can feel it."

"Well, look, Clare. I'm a big fucking boy, OK? If she does take off, you can rest assured that I can handle it. She's not gonna, by the way. She won't." My phone buzzes and I take it out of my pocket and check the message. "Someone's here to see me, so is this all clear, then?" Her look is defiant but she keeps silent as she nods her head. "Good, then let's go."

We walk back downstairs and as soon I spot my visitor near the front door I know what's up.

FBI is back.

Fuck.

I don't look at Clare but I know she knows what's up too. I just hope our little moment doesn't come back to haunt me in the form of her talking to the fucker in the black suit when I'm not looking. I straighten up my back and head over to him. "Mr…" I trail off like I forgot his name.

"Abelli," he adds to my silence. "Agent Abelli."

"Right, I knew that." I smile at him. "What can I do for you?"

"Well, Mr. Flynn, we've been noticing some discrepancies in your statement to the Denver police and we'd like you to come down to the station and take a polygraph. Do you think you could oblige us with that?"

Aaaaannnd… game starts now.

I widen my smile. "Oh, absolutely. I'd be more than happy to." I grab my leather jacket from a hook near the door and wave him out of the studio. "I'll meet you down there."

"Actually, my partner dropped me off, so if I could catch a ride with you, that'd be great."

"No problem. What'd he do, go grab some donuts?"

Abelli laughs but the tension lines on his face tell me it's forced. "No, he just needed to get back to the station and set up the machine."

"Just messing with ya, dude. I know you're not really donut eaters."

He shuts up after that and I just unlock the doors to my truck and we both slide in. The drive down to the station only takes a few minutes since it's mid-morning and traffic is light, but it feels like an eternity as we sit and listen to the radio. What the fuck could this be about? It can't be Jon. I had nothing to do with any of the hacking. And Rook would've called me if they had Ford in custody, even if Spencer wouldn't. No, it's not about Jon. I didn't even really have to lie when I gave my statement. The only thing not true was the text message. And even so, it was present and legit by the time the cops checked the phone.

No, this isn't about that asshole, but beyond that I have no other info. But I will. Because they're fishing for answers with this polygraph, which means they have to tip their hand with the questions they ask.

Well, bring it on. Because as Spencer said last summer when he was painting Rook, everyone has one God-given gift.

And mine is lying.

Actually, it's acting, but what's the difference, really? My time in India was not wasted with trips to the Taj Mahal with the tourists because there was another American artist in the hotel with us and this guy was filming a documentary about poor kids. Kinda like *Slumdog Millionaire* except it was supposed to be real. But no one wanted to talk to this guy or let their kids be manipulated into revealing how horrible their lives were, so he hired me to be his star poor kid even though I was an American living in a five-star hotel.

Turns out the guy was quite the liar himself and he set the whole thing up to be believable.

Let's just say it was an elaborate plot with parents being robbed and killed on vacation and me running for my life from the Mumbai underworld after witnessing it. He did get caught faking the documentary but he played it off like it was sort of a *Blair Witch* thing, right? And this is when I discovered I was a fucking natural liar. *Actor*. Same thing.

I saw the movie a few years later—he won some independent film award for it, even. I would cry and look desperate and beg people for money on the streets, and I told a story that had Elise uncontrollably sobbing, that's how fucking sad I made it.

But that guy never did out me. That was one of the terms in the contract Elise signed. No one would know it was me and I got a stage name. I got five thousand dollars for lying while we were in India. Which was a lot of fucking money to

Elise and me at the time.

Then the modeling gigs started coming in and they wanted me to act but not speak. So I learned to talk with my body and facial expressions.

And this is how my gift works in a nutshell. You wrap your mind around a scenario, you believe that scenario with all your heart, and then you just react—body and mind together. It's not hard at all, not really.

I never did any acting in the States because by the time we settled back down and I was in an actual school full time I was too cool for that theater shit. There is no record of Ronin Flynn ever being an actor. And if there's no record of it, it never happened.

So polygraphs? No problem. This asshole has no idea what's coming.

CHAPTER TWENTY-EIGHT

Rook

"Done yet?"

"You just fucking asked me that twenty minutes ago, Ford. No, I'm not done. I'm not quick at this shit like you are, OK? Just let me think it over." I drum my fingertips on the coffee table and try and come up with three reasons.

"Rook, the application must be in by Friday or you'll have to wait another semester to get into Boulder."

Maybe I don't want to go to Boulder, did that ever occur to him?

But I don't say that out loud because he's just trying to help me. Instead I chew on my thumbnail as I try and think of how to start. It's an application essay. I'm just a few weeks into community college writing, so yeah, I'm not that good at this shit yet. I've barely mastered the topic sentence. Ford eyeballs me as he drinks a beer in the kitchen. "It's a little early to start drinking, don't you think?"

"You *drive* me to drink, Rook. What's the hold-up? They want to know why you want to go to school. Surely you can handle *that*?"

I sneer at him and take my attention back to my laptop. The problem is I might be lazy. Now that I have all this money I don't have the same drive to push myself in this area. Would I be a waste of space at this school? I'm pretty sure there are people a lot more deserving than me who could use a shot at this education that I'm not fully appreciating.

The cushion sinks as Ford sits next to me. "What's going

on?" he asks softly. "You're not interested?"

I lean back and sigh. "I'm just not sure, Ford. This school stuff is not easy."

"I'm not following. You thought it would be easier or it's harder than you expected?"

"Both, I guess. I'm not super smart like you guys, but I'm not stupid, right?" He puts an arm around me and I almost have a heart attack. "What are you doing?"

His eyebrows go up. "Comforting you. Am I doing it wrong?"

A laugh bursts out and I just shake my head. "No, this is correct, I guess."

"Do you want to quit school, Rook?"

"Am I a failure if I do?"

"Yes," he says with zero emotion.

I laugh again. "Fuck, Ford. What the hell? I thought you were comforting me!"

"Do you want me to tell you the truth or lie?"

"Lie!"

"I'm sorry, I'm the honest one, remember? You *are* smart but you have almost no education. You should be embarrassed by that."

"What the fuck? That's enough comforting, thanks." I finagle my way out from his embrace and try to get up but he grabs me and pushes me back on the couch. "I'll do it in my room. Let me go."

"No, we're writing this essay and you're turning in the application. You have brains, you have money, you have people supporting you. A few weeks ago your dream was to go to film school so I've pointed you in that direction and you're staying on that trajectory and seeing it through until you have a damn good reason why the dream has changed. If you get in, *then* you can decide if you want to go or not. But you don't get to give up before you try just because it's *hard*. That's unacceptable. You have thirty minutes to write this essay or I'll ground you." And then he winks. "And if I was Ronin I'd spank the shit out of you and make it hurt for being such a brat."

I scoot over to the other side of the couch and kick him with my socked foot. "You're dumb."

"You're juvenile. Now give me the three main reasons you wanted to go to school."

"If it was that easy—"

"Just the top three, Rook. It's not brain surgery. Off the top of your head, right now."

"Money."

"OK, you don't really need that anymore. What else?"

"A cool job."

"You have that as well. Or you could if you wanted, but you decided to take a boring one. You have options, should you ever want a cool job again, though, right?"

"Yeah, I guess."

"So give me an internal reason. Something you can't have, something you will *feel*. Like pride. Will education make you feel proud?"

"Sure."

"What other internal things?"

"Well, respect, I guess."

"Respect from whom?"

"I'm not sure. Me? I think I am capable of more than I've been doing with my life, so getting a college degree would make me feel like I'm fulfilling my potential. Does that make sense?"

He smiles and puts his arm around me and this time I lean in. "Yes, that's a great reason. You should write that down and tell the admissions people all the reasons why you believe you have potential and what it means for you to live up to it."

"You're sneaky."

"I've been known to sneak a time or two."

I turn to my computer as Ford gets back up to grab another beer and heads out to the shop. I still, *still*, have no idea what Ford does here as far as work goes. It's like he's only here to be my friend or something.

Hmmmm…

Those sneaky fucks.

I stay and finish up the stupid college admissions application while Ford covers for me on the phones, and picturing this is so freaking funny to me that I have to get out there and actually witness it myself before I go to tutoring. I pull the door open and immediately Ford puts a hand up, like he's shushing me. Whatever. I stand patiently while he chats on the phone about this person's custom order and upcoming meeting with Spencer.

Then I sigh.

Then yawn.

"Can I help you?" Ford asks as he hangs up the phone.

"I think you're trying to replace me, actually. Since when are you polite?"

"Rook, I am nothing if not professional."

"Yeah, you're about as professional as Ronin is honest."

Ford's whole face turns white. "What did you say?"

"It was a joke, I caught him in a lie last weekend right after he fed me that same line, only it was about him being honest." Ford just stares at me for a second, then relief washes over his face. "What. The. Fuck?"

"How's your tutor? Is it time to go?"

"Oh, yeah," I say, glancing up at the clock. "I do have to go or I'll be late." I think avoiding talking to Ford about anything to do with that tutor is a good idea right about now, so I give him a wave and skip out.

I think about what Gage will say to me tonight all the way over to the college and when I finally get there and park, he's waiting for me outside again. "Wanna go to the student lounge and study instead of the math center?"

"OK." I could care less where he checks my work, as long as it gets checked and I can turn it in before midnight, because that's the deadline for this set of problems. We walk across campus to the building that contains the bookstore and the only café-type place on the small campus, order our drinks, and then find a table near the back where there are only a few other students studying. I hand my paper over to Gage and busy myself watching people as I wait.

He works on it for a little bit, then hands it back with all the wrong answers circled in red and a short note about where I went wrong.

I'm not stupid at math, I just get mixed up at what I'm supposed to do at each step. I forget how, but once Gage points it out to me, it makes sense again. So I guess if I just tried a little harder to memorize the steps I might do better. Gage busies himself grabbing some paperwork from his backpack while I work and then I hand it back.

He checks it again. "Yeah, that's good. Now just enter it into the computer and you're all set."

I do and then tick the little box that says *I promise I didn't cheat*, and press enter.

"Done! And we're early, it's only seven forty-five." I reach down to get my backpack so I can shove my shit inside and leave, but Gage slides some papers across the table at me. "What's this?"

"Printouts of your friends, Rook. I hope you thought about what I said last week. They're dangerous."

I roll my eyes at him. "Gage, I think I know them better than you. They are the farthest thing from dangerous I've ever seen in my life. Maybe you've just been really sheltered or something?" I flutter my eyelashes a little to play it down and make him back off.

"Uh-huh." He pushes the papers towards me with one finger. "Just read them, OK? Read them and then I'll never say another thing about it. Deal?"

"Whatever. I already saw them, though. I looked it all up online."

"This stuff isn't online, Rook. So just read it."

I pick up the stack of papers and read the first headline. It's not a newspaper. It's an FBI report. "What the fuck is this?"

"Just read it."

It looks like your basic FBI wanted poster you'd see on TV, except it doesn't say 'wanted,' it says 'person of interest.' And that phrase conjures up only one image since the 9/11 attacks. Terrorists. I look up at Gage and raise an eyebrow.

He pans his hands out in an innocent shrug. "Just read it."

I continue. It's all about Ronin. Height—so very, very tall. I snicker to myself. Weight—buffed the fuck out. Eye color—electrifying. Age—young. He's only nineteen in this dossier. "Well, these are his general stats which I am already very familiar with. And his picture just makes me want to kiss the photo." I look up with a smirk.

"You're laughing now, but wait."

I glare over at Gage and toss the paper back to him. "I'm just not interested. I don't care what he did in the past or why the FBI thinks he's important. It's over. He's a good guy. I love him. I'm thinking having his blue-eyed babies might be a good idea in about ten years."

"Ronin Sean Flynn, age nineteen—"

"I said I'm not interested. Besides, that was years ago if he was just nineteen."

"—picked up for human trafficking, cocaine distribution, grand larceny—"

My heart about beats out of my chest at the first charge. *Human trafficking?* "No! That's not him. He didn't do that stuff." This is some kind of joke, for the show or something? I look around wildly.

"Rook, I swear to God, OK? The fucking FBI handed me these papers not two hours ago, they wanted me to tell you so you don't get caught up in this, they would like you to talk to them—"

I grab my bag and bolt out the door, leaving Gage there with his stack of bullshit papers that might be ripping apart my whole world right now. I look around. Are they watching me? I stop in front of my truck, scanning the dark parking lot.

Nothing. No one out here at all.

I get in and take a few deep breaths. This is not my Ronin. Whatever those papers said, it's a lie. He's not involved in that kind of stuff, I know it. No man as gentle as him could possibly be involved in that stuff. I pull out of the parking lot, trying my best not to speed so I don't get pulled over, and head east towards College Ave.

Shit. Who the fuck can I ask about this?

Why don't I have any friends?

I chew on my cheek as I think. I have Elise, Spencer, Ford, Antoine, Ronin. That's it. My whole fucking circle of friends could possibly be involved.

Except one, maybe.

Veronica.

I know for a fact that Spencer is a commitment-phobe, so even if some of this stuff with them is true—and I'm not even thinking it is yet, but even if it was—I don't think Veronica would be involved. Spencer refuses to even call her his girlfriend.

I turn left on College and head up towards downtown to her tattoo shop. It's Monday night so the place might not even be open. But it's all I have right now.

Veronica, the girl who endured the agonizing pain of a bullet-induced scrape across her hip, called my ex an ass-faced bastard, and probably saved me from being dragged back to my own personal hell in Chicago, is as good as I've got as far as second opinions go.

CHAPTER TWENTY-NINE

Ronin

So this is how it works.

Listen to the question, breathe. Stop. Blink. Breathe. Recite the question back to myself so that I understand every word. Answer yes or no.

That's it.

Of course, they're trying to make you fuck up. They ask the question a few different ways. They give you throwaway questions—which, depending on the question, may be a good time to just outright lie. Like if they ask *Is your name Ronin Flynn?* And you're me? I say yes, of course, because everyone knows that's my name. But if they ask *Have you ever stolen anything?* That's a dummy question because it's an absolute—everyone has stolen something at one time or another, even if it was by accident or whatever. It's throwaway. So to that one I lie immediately and say no, but the needle stays calm, indicating I'm being truthful.

And then I sit back and smile.

Because I just did two things. I set up their machine to record that kind of response as truth and I lied to their faces but it didn't record and they know it.

A good operator will know what to do with that. They'll set me up in a pattern of repeated questions, phrased with slight variations, so that I will unconsciously lie. But I'm telling you, this is my God-given gift. Spencer paints naked girls, Ford is some evil version of Einstein, sans the bad hair and *with* the slight insanity issues, and I'm the sweet-talking bullshit liar.

That's just how it is.

I can be whatever people want me to be. You want me to be guilty? I can play that part just as well as innocent. In fact, sometimes I do play guilty when I'm being questioned. That really fucking throws them off.

And none of what I'm doing is special, not really. I'm just observant, calculating, and I spent just as much time learning to turn off my emotions as I did turning them on.

"Is your name Ronin Flynn?"

I'm all hooked up to the computer now, sitting in this slightly over-warm room that will at some point in the middle of questioning turn slightly too cold, and I'm ready.

"Yes."

"Do you live at the Chaput Studios Building in LoDo?"

"Yes." That's a lie, but I say it with confidence and the machine agrees with me. Our building is technically in Five Points, not Lower Downtown, but like I said, dummy questions.

The suits bob their heads together on that one, then regroup. "Do you live at Chaput Studios in Five Points?"

"Yes."

"Do you live in LoDo?"

"Yes." I blink and breathe to give them something to think about besides my lie. I can do this all day long.

"OK, Mr. Flynn," the older man running the machine says. "Let's get down to business. Are you aware of any human trafficking in Denver?"

"No."

"Have you ever had a conversation about human trafficking?"

"No." I blink and breathe again. What the fuck is this about?

"Do you know Rook Walsh's real name?"

Blink, breathe. "Yes."

"Is it Rook Walsh?"

"Yes." Another lie. This is a good one because they don't know if I know it or not.

"Has Mrs. Walsh ever mentioned her husband Jon Walsh?"

Ah, here we go. "Yes."

"Has Mrs. Walsh ever mentioned a safe deposit box in Las Vegas?"

I blink, breathe, and lie. "Yes." Because this is getting weird and these assholes actually get a little excited about that answer.

"Did she tell you what was in the box?" Abelli asks hurriedly.

A break in protocol from Agent Abelli is not a good sign. "Yes," I lie.

"What was it?"

I just stare at Abelli and then ask calmly, "What?"

"What's in the fucking box?"

"That's not a yes or no question. Take the straps off and we can talk normally, but I'm not answering any more questions that deviate from the standard test format."

Machine guy cuts in. "We're done here. You're free to go."

And then I'm being unstrapped and ushered out of the room and over to the elevator where I'm handed off to some bald-headed goon in the FBI uniform.

The next thing I know I'm fucking driving down Speer Boulevard towards home. I cut over on Market and then swing around the building and park the truck. "What. The. Fuck. Just. Happened?"

Human trafficking? That's what this is about?

It's bizarre, but I've been gone almost three hours so I gotta get back upstairs and check shit out with the girls and Roger. I might have to get in touch with Ford tonight and set up a meeting. Vegas. Safe deposit boxes and human trafficking. Yeah, this is not right. This is just not right. Because typically when I'm called in for a polygraph, you know, I'm being questioned about a crime I'm actually *connected* to. And I don't know anything about human trafficking or a box in Vegas that may or may not have something to do with Rook.

But I have a very bad feeling that Rook does.

I take out my phone and almost press Ford's contact, but then I come back to my senses and clear the screen.

That's what they want me to do. Call my partners and give the Feds another clue.

Fuck.

I get out of the truck and hop the stairs three at a time. Everyone is busy inside the studio. Clare is doing a shoot with Billy, the other girls are milling about in lingerie or getting fixed up in the salon, and even Elise and Antoine are hanging out in the kitchen eating fruit.

"Antoine," I say in French. "I need a minute." He follows me out onto the terrace where the roar of afternoon traffic down on 21st Street is enough to layer over our conversation if someone is getting nosy. "I just got back from the police station," I continue in French. His eyes dart back and forth, a slight panic becoming detectable by the pulsing of his carotid artery in his neck. "Don't worry, it really wasn't about me. I think it was about Rook. I think I need to go up North tonight and ask her some questions. Should I go?"

"Do you think it's safe to involve Spencer and Ford?"

I shrug. "Not sure, really. I'm not sure this is really about us, Antoine. I think it's about Rook."

He stares down at the traffic for several minutes and ponders the question. Antoine would never make a good partner in our little private business because he can't make hasty decisions. He likes to think for a while before committing to things. Most of the time this drives me up a wall but not this time. Rook might be in trouble and I only get one chance to make a move. It's worth the extra time.

"I think it's too risky, Ronin. You don't have enough information yet. Give it one more day, then one of us will go up to the shop tomorrow and see if they've heard anything. OK?" He puts a hand on my shoulder and squeezes.

"Yeah, all right."

"Just go back to work and we'll talk more later."

We go back inside and I take my place near Roger, pretending to have an opinion on the shoot Clare is doing or what the fuck ever. But really, all I can think about is Rook.

What if she's in danger again?

And what if this time I'm not around to help her?

CHAPTER THIRTY

Rook

Downtown Fort Collins is at the north end of town and even though the main drag is still College Avenue, it's not wide and busy like it is down south by the Best Buy and PetSmart. It's one of those old historic Western towns and has cute shops and lots of restaurants and bars. There's even a trolley that runs down Mountain Avenue from Old Town to City Park. And Spencer has told me numerous times that it's seriously been voted Best Place to Live in the World or some shit like that. I can see it, actually. It's got a big university smack in the center complete with veterinary hospital and research buildings, but it's still old-timey in many ways. Like parking in the middle of the street to shop in downtown. Literally. You pull into the center of the street and park between the north and southbound lanes of College Avenue.

I've passed by Veronica's downtown tattoo shop dozens of times, so I know where it is, I've just never been inside. I pull the truck into a spot a few businesses down and turn the engine off. My stomach is doing all kinds of flips.

Why? Why does everything have to be so dramatic? I know the guys have secrets, but I just assumed that the secrets were about the hacking stuff they do. Did. Do. I'm not sure if they still do that shit or not. Obviously they did it for me, but whether or not they're doing it for someone else right now, I have no idea.

But stealing from deadbeats and selling human slaves are two very different things.

It doesn't add up.

I am kicking myself for not taking those papers from Gage right now. At least then I could read the whole thing. Because last time Gage said they were accused of murdering someone and got away with it. So when you combine all the shit Ronin is being accused of human trafficking, murder, grand larceny, and selling blow.

I have no idea what this means, but I'm not buying it one bit. It's total bullshit.

I get out of the truck, wait for a few cars to pass by, then jog across the street and head up towards the tattoo place. I stop outside and look up at the sign. It says *Sick Boys Inc.* According to Spencer, Veronica Vaughn is the youngest non-Y chromosome member of the Sick Boys gang and she, her father, and all four of her brothers work at this shop. Apparently she is just one of the Boys around here, because from the sign you'd never know there was a girl inside doing ink.

It's dark out now and the lights are on, but I can't see anything because the front windows are frosted up like they belong in a bathroom. So all I can make out is a large blurry shadow and the faint buzzing of a tattoo machine.

I pull the door open and walk in, get slightly disoriented by the massive wall of tattoo photos that practically slams me in the face, and then startle at the voice to my right.

"Shrike Fucking Bikes? Roonnnnnnn-eeeeeee," the guy bellows out in a deep voice. "Spencer's Blackbird is here!"

I turn around to see someone who is probably one of the Sick Boys and look him up and down. He's huge, for one. Massive. Like over six foot two. And his tatted-up biceps are bulging out from a t-shirt that hugs every spectacular muscle on his upper body. His light hair is cropped close, military-style, and his dark eyes convey a roughness that matches the scruff on his chin. "Who the hell are you? And how do you know who I am?"

"Vic Vaughn, and your name's on the sleeve of your

jacket and the backside says Shrike Fucking Bikes. Not Shrike insert-expletive-here-because-we-are-so-cool, but actual Shrike Fucking Bikes. Like that's the name of his business. And only Spencer Shrike would put 'fuck' in the name of his business on the back of a jacket. You don't need to be Cujo to figure that one out."

I squint up at him because that just makes no sense, then look down at my jacket sleeves. One is painted up to say Blackbird and the other says Gidget. I automatically get a little protective of Spence and retaliate appropriately. "Cujo is a nasty-ass, rabies-ridden dog. You're thinking of *Columbo*. And this is a pretty hot fucking jacket if you ask me."

Vic Vaughn winks at me. "So's the girl inside, even if you didn't ask me. And I was just testing you on that Cujo thing. I heard you're a film freak. You should come by the FoCo Cinema sometime, me and the boys wouldn't mind gettin' ya in the dark for a movie."

"Shut up, Victor," Veronica says as she comes around a corner dressed like she's doing a root canal back there. She's wearing pink scrubs, a white lab coat, a pink visor with a clear plastic face shield that she flips up as she approaches, and a blue mask over her mouth. "Hey, Rook, come by for your free tat?" she says through the mask, making it puff out a little with each word.

"Uh, no." I stammer for a moment because her get-up is pretty distracting. "Actually, I was wondering if you had a minute to talk. About…" I look over at Vic, and then cover my mouth and whisper, "Spencer, Ronin, and Ford."

"Hey, Blackbird? You're like two feet away, I can still hear you. Well, Ronnie, I win this bet. I said a week and it's been"—he looks over at the calendar—"nine days."

We both ignore that remark and I change the subject and point to her clothes. "What's with the outfit, Veronica?"

She absently looks down at herself. "Blood-borne pathogens. Did you know that an ink machine can spray minute particles of blood into the air and you breathe it in if you don't protect yourself?" Veronica grabs my arm and pulls me to the back of the shop. We pass a few more rooms, each with tattoo machines buzzing—but all of the male Sick Boys look like regular ink artists with their t-shirts, jeans, and tatted-up arms.

"Come on back, Rook. I've got a guy in the chair, but he's such a pussy, he can use the distraction." She drags me into a small room that looks like a cross between a hospital surgery room with the different doctor office-type stuff lined up neatly on a long counter, and Fran the Nanny's mother's living room—because just about every single surface is covered in plastic.

You could kill someone in here, *Murder by Numbers* style, and just roll it all up in plastic and toss it in the dumpster when you were done.

I shiver.

A very large biker who has half his arm bubbling up dots of blood from the partially finished tattoo shifts in his chair and makes the plastic crinkle. "You get used to it," he says matter-of-factly, panning a hand up at the sheeting that covers the flat screen on the wall. I spy Milla Jovovich with orange hair so I'm pretty sure it's *The Fifth Element* playing, but it's hard to see through the wrinkles. "She's got a germ issue and a blood phobia."

I almost snicker as I picture her back in the Chaput parking lot freaking out about her bullet scrape. It makes more sense now.

Veronica ignores the dude and absently waves a hand at him. "Rook, this is Tiny. Tiny, Rook. Rook here needs to girl-talk with me. You don't mind, do ya, Tiny?"

The big biker smiles at me through his full beard and I force one back as well to be polite. "Nah, you girls just go right ahead."

Veronica offers me an extra face mask and visor shield, but I hold up my hand and refuse. "OK, Rook, spill it. What's up?" She slips her gloves off, washes her hands, and then snaps on a new pair, grabs her inkwell, flips down her clear plastic face shield like she's getting ready to do some welding, and the buzzing starts up again.

She is one strange chick.

"Well, it's sorta private, ya know? Like, I'm not sure I should—"

"Rook," she puffs through her mask, "we've got a pool running on how long it would take you to come by asking questions about your new roommates. It's no secret that Spence, Ford, and Ronin are knee-deep in controversy and shit. So just tell me what's on your mind."

I sigh and then try for vagueness so I don't involuntarily let out any *new* secrets. "OK, let's start with the murder charges. True or not?"

"True," Veronica says. "At least the charges part is. I have no idea if they actually did it, but everyone knows the state dropped the charges because of a procedural technicality."

OK, that I figured. Obviously, since it was in the paper and all. "How about drug-dealing?"

Veronica snorts at this one. "That's a first for me. Who says they deal drugs?"

"My math tutor had a print-out of a file the FBI is keeping on Ronin, and it said something about dealing coke, grand larceny, and..." I look around, then down at Tiny, who is all ears, just soaking up my girl gossip. "And something else that I won't repeat."

"Do you think Ronin's dealing coke? I mean, you've lived with him for a few months, right?"

"I can't see it, Veronica. I can't see any of it to be honest. He seems like a really good guy. You saw that party he gave me. And yeah, Spencer throws that danger vibe at times, but he's pretty normal as far as I can tell."

"How about Ford?"

She stops the tattoo machine and then all four of the Vaughn brothers appear in her doorway and the place is suddenly very quiet, like everyone wants to hear my answer. I shake my head nervously. "I'm not talking to an audience, guys."

Vic steps forward. He appears to be the oldest and he's definitely the biggest, so maybe he's like the family ringleader. "Hey, you came here to talk to *us*. Not the other way around."

"I came to talk to Veronica."

"Veronica is a package deal. You talk to her, you talk to us. Besides, she's been dating that fuck Spencer for years now, and I'm curious about these guys. So tell us what you think of Ford."

I guess that's fair. At any rate, I don't have a lot of room to negotiate. Either I give him what he wants so I can get their opinion on things, or I walk out. And I really need a second opinion on things, even if it is over a tattoo machine instead of coffee. "Ford's good to me and we spend a lot of time together. I like him a lot. But there's just some weird shit going down and I'm trying to figure out who to trust. I don't need to know the specifics, Veronica. I just want to know if you think they're OK."

"Well, aside from Ford, I'd say yeah. Ronin and Spencer are good guys. But Ford…" She shakes her head at me. "I'm sorry, Rook. You saw that display at your party. He keeps those girls as his pleasure slaves."

I swallow hard as Ford's words come back from the exit interview for the pilot show. *I'm not a good guy, Rook. I'm not even close to a good guy.*

This cannot be happening. Seriously cannot be happening. "Against their will? Does he keep them against their will? Or is it mutual? He took her to the party, surely it must be mutual?"

Veronica shrugs. "How should I know? You're his friend, do you think he keeps them against their will?"

I'm not sure. In fact, I have no idea whatsoever. I've never seen Ford outside our little friendship sphere. I only found out his last name because Gage blurted it out last week. "Well, that's all I needed, I guess I'll go." I get up to walk out but all four of the Vaughn brothers are still standing in the doorway. Blocking it. "Excuse me," I say nervously. The hard bodies part and I slip through. I walk quickly down the hallway, round the corner to the front reception area, and I'm just about to break through the door when a hand grabs me from behind.

"Hold on, Rook," Vic says softly as his grip loosens. "I'd like to give you my opinion."

I shake my head. "No, I've heard enough, Vic. I'm not interested."

"Well, you're gonna get it anyway. So, for what it's worth, I like Spencer. Just don't tell him that because we have this whole 'I'll kill you if you fuck over my sister' thing going." And then Vic smiles down at me and my heart slows a little at his unexpected quiet voice and gentle touch. "You know, he plays tough guy. And he's got the shit to back it up. And maybe that reputation he has is even halfway true. Maybe he did kill that guy? I have no idea. But I let him take my sister out, so you know, I think he's OK."

Vic releases my arm and I push through the door, mumbling out a 'thank you' as I slip into the darkness.

Maybe Spencer *killed* that guy? That's even a possibility?

Holy fucking shit. I'm sure Vic thought his words would make me feel better, but they don't. Because I never, not for one moment, really believed these guys actually *murdered* someone.

Until now.

Just when I think my day could not get any worse it starts to rain.

I walk hastily down the sidewalk, look both ways, wait for a car to pass, and then head towards my truck. I fish my keys out of my pocket, look up, and then stop dead in the middle of the southbound lane of College Avenue.

Wade fucking Minix is standing six feet away.

CHAPTER THIRTY-ONE

Rook

A set of headlights flash, then a horn honks but I can't drag my eyes away from the man standing before me. *Where the hell did he come from?*

Then Wade has me by the waist and he throws me down on the wet ground near the back tire of my truck. My breath comes out with a loud oomph with the impact and then my head slams back onto the concrete, temporarily stunning me. "Jesus fucking Christ, Rook! You almost got flattened by a goddamn van!"

He lies there on top of me, breathing heavy, staring into my eyes, and I'm paralyzed. He comes back to his senses before I do and stands up, extending his hand.

I process what he's doing but nothing moves. I'm just frozen. "What the hell are you doing here?"

He reaches down, grabs my arm, and hoists me to my feet. I lean back against the truck and realize he never answered me. "I said—"

"I heard you, Rook," he says so softly I can barely make out his words over the constant stream of traffic flowing through the little downtown. "Let's sit in your truck. Can we sit and talk in your truck?"

I'm too stunned to even answer. I haven't talked to this guy in five years. The last time we had a conversation I was a kid, about to be thrown back into the foster care system because his mom wanted to keep us apart. Wade takes the keys from my hand, unlocks the door, and pushes me to get in the driver's seat. I watch him walk around the front of the truck, then get in next to me, setting a backpack down on the floor in front of him.

"Rook—" he starts. But I put up a hand.

"Don't. I don't even know why I let you in this truck. Give me the keys." I hold my hand out and he drops them into my palm. I shove the key in the ignition and start the truck. "Leave. I have nothing to say to you, Wade. If I wanted to talk to you I would've done it up in Sturgis."

He shakes his head at me and I take him in. Like, really take him in for the first time since that horrible day that changed my life forever. His blond hair is wet and plastered against his face and even though I know he's got gorgeous green eyes, I can't really make out the color in the dark. He's a lot bigger than I remember him, maybe because we were just kids back then. Five years can mean a lot of changes to a teen boy's body.

"Rook, listen to me, OK? I just want to talk to you, that's it. I just want a chance to talk to you."

"Why? What could you possibly have to say to me that hasn't already been said?"

"I'm sorry." His eyes search my face, almost as if they're pleading.

"Sorry?" I shake my head. Un-fucking-believable. "You're sorry? You're sorry for what, Wade?"

"For what happened." I just stare at him. "What happened after… you know, after my mom kicked you out and you ended up with that Jon guy."

"*What?*" I ask, stunned.

"I know what happened, Rook."

"You don't know shit. Get the fuck out of my truck."

"I know everything, Rook." And then he reaches down into the backpack and removes a folder and thrusts it at me.

I just stare at it. And I'm not sure how I know, but I know—"I do not want that."

"I don't care," he says in a low voice. "You're taking it.

They've been trying to reach you through your math tutor but you just won't listen."

I look around wildly. They *are* following me! "Who sent you with this?"

"The FBI, Rook. You're in so damn deep, baby, they just—"

"Do not fucking call me baby, OK? I'm not your fucking baby."

"Sorry," he says, raising his hands in an *I surrender* motion. "Sorry, I just need to talk to you and then I'll leave if you want."

"I'm not talking about Ronin, Wade. I'm not sure what's going on, but that paper Gage showed me was utter bullshit. He's not any of those things they say he is and I don't care what kind of so-called proof those guys have, I'm not buying it."

"This isn't about Ronin, Rook. It's about Jon, and those things he was doing back in Illinois. The things he made you participate in, the things—"

"What the fuck are you talking about?" My heart is racing so fast I might pass out, that's how rattled I am right now. "Who sent you?"

"I told you—"

"No, who specifically. I want a name, right fucking now, or I'm calling the police and reporting you for stalking."

He hesitates for a second and then gives it up. "Agent Abelli, he's out of the Chicago FBI field office. He's been hunting Jon down for years and they were very close to busting him when you took off to Vegas last spring. Jon disappeared after that and then, of course, he resurfaced here."

I've never heard that name. Who the fuck? "So? Why do they want to talk to *me*?"

"They think you have something of Jon's. Something you got in Vegas. Did you get something of Jon's in Vegas, Rook?"

My entire body is buzzing with anxiety right now. What

the hell is all this about? I want to say I never went to Vegas and I have nothing of Jon's, not a damn thing. But I'm just not sure I should play that card so soon. "What if I did?"

Wade breathes out a sigh of relief. "Oh, fuck, thank God. You need to hand that over, Rook. These people are not fucking around, OK? They want that information and if you saw any of it, you better pretend you didn't." He stops and grabs my shoulders with both hands. "Did you read any of it?"

I shake my head, far too frightened to actually form words right now.

"Where is it?" His eyes race around my face like he's too amped up to concentrate on one point for more than a millisecond.

"I never saw it," I say, backpedaling. I know Jon went to Vegas on business sometimes, but I have no idea what he did there. "I lied, I never saw it. I never went to Vegas, Wade, I came straight here, to Denver. You can check, I was in a homeless shelter, then I had a house-cleaning job—"

"So you never went to Vegas? Do you know if he had a security box there?"

I nod my head, because he is freaking me the fuck out and I need to give up something. "But I don't know anything else about it. Not where it is or how to get into it, nothing."

"Well, they checked the box, Rook. And it's empty." He sorta laughs here, but it's one of those I'm-about-to-go-insane laughs and my heart rate jacks up about a thousand notches. "So that means someone has the stuff." He shakes his head. It's a jerky motion that definitely tells me he's about to lose it and then he turns, his head down a little so his eyes are peeking up at me though a curtain of wet hair and dark lashes. He whispers, "Do you have the stuff?"

I swallow down the fear and say calmly, "I have no stuff, Wade. I don't have anything of Jon's."

"Rook, listen to me, OK? You and those guys you're with are the only ones who've had access to Jon, OK? So one of you has the shit they're looking for. And let me just tell you, these people are not fucking around, OK?"

Each time he says 'OK,' the pitch of his voice raises, making him sound even more crazy, and my whole body begins to tremble, because I might not get out of this. Wade is not acting right.

"If you have it, Rook, you gotta tell me. Because they've got my mom, Rook. They've got my mom locked up on some fake-ass charges and they'll send her to prison if I don't figure out where this shit is. Do you understand?"

This snaps me back from the edge of fear and puts me on the offense immediately. "Am I supposed to give a shit about your *mother*?" I laugh. "Really? Let them lock her up! After what she did to me!"

"I'm sorry about that. I tried to stop her, you know that. I tried to stop her from sending you back to the State. She just wouldn't listen and she threatened to cut me off. I needed her help to race."

"You were a grown-ass man, Wade. You were eighteen years old. You could've helped me if you cared one shit about what was happening."

"Yeah, and you were underage, Rook. It's called statutory rape, sexual predator-type stuff—it was a huge risk."

He's serious. This asshole thinks that saving me from living on the streets, from those crack-houses the fucking foster care people sent me to… *saving* me was a *risk*? "You're pathetic. You have no idea what it means to take a risk for someone you love. To put it all on the line for them. None. You're nothing but one pathetic, selfish, fucking asshole."

"What was I supposed to do, go to jail for you? That would've helped how? How would throwing my life away help you?"

"Oh, you poor, poor baby. And for your information, Jon was twenty-one when he found me. And he sure the fuck found a way to keep me."

"Yeah, and look what that sick fuck was doing!"

"And you know who I blame for all those years, Wade?

Just take one educated guess." I stop to glare at him, the full depth of my hatred for everyone who ever met me as a child coming out, seeping through my pores like some hot sticky mess left over from all that sex I had with Jon as a teenager. All that filthy fucking sex that was not anything close to love. That entire relationship made me feel dirty, and unwanted, and useless, and… and… and *insignificant.*

"You, that's who," I say in a whisper. "I blame you for all the terrible, horrific things that happened to me back in that house. All of it. It's one hundred percent *your* fault. Because I was just a girl, you were a man. I asked you for help. You said you loved me, for fuck's sake. And then you just walked out. You are nothing but a selfish fucking piece-of-shit coward! You left me to live on the streets, to be picked up by that predator, to be held under his thumb for years."

"That wasn't me, Rook. I had nothing to do with that. That wasn't—"

"You are the darkness, Wade. You are nothing but my dark, disgusting past trying to suck me back in to a life of shame."

"I just want to say I'm sorry, Rook. And please, just listen to me about this FBI stuff, OK? I need you to—"

"Get out!"

My scream is echoing though my head when someone knocks on my window and scares the fuck out of me. I take a deep breath and realize it's Vic Vaughn. I roll it down and look up at him.

"Everything OK in here, Blackbird?"

I shake my head. "No, he's bothering me. I want him to leave."

Vic reaches into the truck and presses the unlock button. The other three Vaughn brothers appear, open the passenger side door and pull Wade out.

"Rook, listen to what I said, OK? Read those papers. They took my mom and they'll take someone from you too. They will, Rook, you'll see!"

Vic and I watch as the Vaughn brothers drag Wade across the street and throw him on the ground in front of a candle shop that's closed for the night. "You want some help, Rook? Want me to drive you home? My brothers can follow us, make sure everything's cool."

My first instinct is to say, 'no, thank you.' But I stop the words and nod up at Vic. "I would really appreciate that, thank you."

"Scoot over, Gidget," he says with a smile as he pushes me into the passenger seat. "And I swear, you'd think one odd name was enough, but woman, you seem to have a collection of them. Hey, Vinn!" he calls out the window. "I'm driving Rook over to Spencer's, you guys follow to keep an eye out for any more psychos." And then he gets in the truck and I breathe out a huge sigh of relief.

Until I pick up the papers and see exactly what they say. I scan the stack quickly. All bad stuff. All the same stuff Gage was trying to tell me.

All stuff that can't be true.

But maybe it is?

And then the fear comes back and it takes all my willpower not to collapse right there in the front seat.

CHAPTER THIRTY-TWO

Rook

I stuff the papers into my backpack and listen as Vic calls Spencer, telling him we're on our way. He gives a few curt responses to whatever Spencer's saying, then holds the phone out towards me.

I turn my head and stare out the window, ignoring the phone, and Vic tells Spencer we'll see him in thirty minutes. I have no idea what to think right now. I just need time to process all this information, make sense of it. Vic talks to me constantly as we drive down the dark and deserted road. I hate this road at night. It's curvy and when it's wet, like it is now, you can't see the lines painted on the road. One side is the damn river and the other side is just forest. It creeps me the fuck out.

I catch Vic eyeballing the rear-view the entire way there, but the only other headlights behind us are his brothers. When we pull into the driveway Spencer and Ford are already outside waiting in the carport to stay out of the rain. Ford opens my door and pulls me out as Spencer talks to Vic.

"What happened?" Ford asks.

I'm not sure I should reveal all the FBI stuff, so I just say, "Wade."

"Oh." That's all Ford says.

"Did you know who he is?"

"I know, Rook. I saw him hanging around up in Sturgis and Spencer filled me in on the missing pieces. Did you talk to him?"

I nod. "Yes, but I never want to talk to him again. *Ever.*" I push Ford away and go inside, wanting very badly to hide away in my room, but there's no chance of that until I talk to them, so I just grab a beer from the fridge and sit on the couch. They come in a few minutes later and I catch the crunch of gravel as the Vaughn brothers leave. They must think I'm crazy. And they probably told Spencer I was just at their shop asking questions about him and Ford.

Great.

Ford sits down next to me and Spencer flips off the TV, taking the chair across from the couch. "So what's up, Rook? You got something to tell us?"

I shake my head. "Nope, nothing. Wade showed up, I sorta lost it, end of story. I don't want to see him again." I stop to look up at Spencer. "Ever. I'm going to call the police if he comes near me again."

"I thought this guy was your old flame or something?" Spencer asks in a low voice. "You sorta sounded like you'd like to see him again when we talked about it."

"I was just depressed that day, reliving the past. Thinking about the good things when the only ones that count are the bad. I'm over it. I want the past to go away and stop fucking up my new life."

"Rook, I'm not sure you're telling us the whole story. Let's start from the beginning, OK?"

"Fuck the beginning, Ford. The beginning starts with my life back in Illinois, and I'm not reliving that shit with you, no matter what. I'm done talking about it, I'm done thinking about it, I'm done answering questions, I'm done with secrets, and fucking Jon, and everything else." I stand up. "I'm done." I step over Ford's legs to get past when Spencer's phone rings.

"Antoine. Hmmm, wonder what the fuck this is about? Yeah," Spence barks into the phone.

I stop in the middle of the living room and listen to the frantic French that is almost fully audible even though the phone's not on speaker, that's how loud Antoine is talking.

"What? What is it?" Spencer ignores me, just listens and shakes his head. When I look down at Ford he's wincing. "What happened?"

Spence ends the call and looks over at me. "Ronin just got arrested. They're booking him into Denver County right now on felony obstruction charges."

I collapse back into another chair near the hallway. "Why?" But as soon as the word leaves my mouth I know why. Wade. And that FBI shit. And Gage. They did just what Wade said. They took someone I love. I lean over and prop my head in my hands and then Ford and Spencer each have me by an arm and they're dragging me outside. "What the fuck?"

Ford leans down into my ear and says, "Shut it, Rook. Just shut up for once and do as you're told." He jerks on my arm a little to make his point and I'm powerless to fight.

Spencer leads us across the backyard and towards the woods and then I really start to freak out. "Why are we going in the woods?" I struggle but they hold tighter, say nothing, and by the time we make the tree line they're dragging me through the mud. I start kicking and screaming, but Ford's hand clamps over my mouth and I have to use all my energy just to breathe. They drag me down towards the river and I swear, I am so fucking stupid for trusting these guys. They're gonna kill me and throw my body in the river.

"Rook," Spencer says this time. "Just calm the fuck down. We need to get away from the house to have this conversation, OK? Just relax." We stop next to the river and he pushes me to sit on a rock.

"Are you gonna be quiet and listen?" Ford asks in his most businesslike voice. "Because I'm not in the mood to baby you tonight, got it? We need to talk."

I nod, but my body is trembling badly, the adrenaline still rushing through my bloodstream. Ford removes his hand. "I've tried to tell you this several times but…" He stops and runs his fingers through his hair and looks away. "But you never wanted to hear it, so I let it go. But you need to know now, because this shit with Ronin is big time, got it? We're playing in the majors right now, Rook. This is real fucking shit, serious shit, and you have to follow the rules now because you're on the team. Do you understand this?"

I look over at Spencer. "The team?"

Spence nods. "It's got a lot of perks, Blackbird. But it's got a lot of rules too. So you need to know the rules. Because it's gonna get ugly and the only way we all stay out of jail is by following the rules."

Ford kneels down next to me and Spencer sits on the rock, squishing his body into mine. "First of all, you know what I do on the team, right?"

"Computer stuff," I say in a small voice.

"Yes. And Spencer here is our logistics guy, OK? But he's also the muscle. So if we need someone roughed up, that's Spencer's job."

I look up at Spence and he shrugs. "Can't help it, Blackbird. I'm the biggest guy here, I got the job by default."

"Did you guys murder that businessman, like all the papers say?"

"Rook." Ford pulls my attention back to him before Spencer can answer. "Look, we don't go looking for trouble and we're not violent. You shot Jon, not us. We had no intention of physically hurting him. But as you saw firsthand, things don't always go as planned. Veronica showed up and as good as that was for you, it almost got her killed, right? Even though we never intended for her to be involved, let alone get hurt, or God fucking forbid, killed. Sometimes shit happens and the plans just disintegrate."

"Did you guys murder that businessman?" I ask again.

"Well," Spencer says. "Look, it wasn't meant to happen. It was not meant for him to die, all right? I did what I had to do to prevent him from involving another innocent party."

"I need to hear this whole story. Like now. I never signed up for this, Ford. I never wanted to be a part of this shit."

Ford opens his mouth to speak, but Spencer's words are the ones that come out.

"I killed him, Rook. We were stealing his money, money he used to fund too many dirty things to even list off the top of my head. Shit like drugs, embezzlement from non-profits, porn. Just filthy shit. And we needed to get inside the house for some codes and it just all went down wrong."

"How did you find that out? The bad stuff he was doing?"

"His daughter told us," Ford says. "Told Ronin, actually. She never knew we were involved until after and the papers got a hold of the story. But this isn't what you need to know. We're telling you about that because you're already in and we need you to trust us, to cooperate, and to understand what it means that Ronin is in jail."

I have a very bad feeling about this.

"You see, what I do has risk. I hack into very secure databases and networks. Some of them very high-level. I'm risking a lot of prison time, possibly even a treason charge when I do some of this. Do you understand?"

"OK."

"And Spencer's job has risk. He killed that man. He's guilty as fuck, Rook. He's got a murder charge all over him. Do you understand this? Spencer's job has risk."

I nod but I'm not liking how often he's repeating the word *risk* one bit.

"Ronin's job also has a risk. Ronin's job is to be the front man, the face of the operation, to clean up the mess. Lie to the police, take the heat, and get the rest of us off. Ronin's job is to lie, Rook. He's a very, *very* gifted liar when he's working."

"Oh, God," I moan. My boyfriend is a professional liar!

"Ronin is the only one of us allowed to talk to the police. He's the only one allowed to give a statement. If Spencer and I are brought in or questioned for any reason—for *anything*—we are to exercise our right to remain silent. And if we ever get to court, we are to plead the Fifth and not testify. We are not allowed to be involved, Rook. We cannot in any way make a statement in favor of or against ourselves or each other. Only Ronin is allowed to talk. Do you understand this?"

"No. I don't get it."

"Oh, I think you do," Ford says in a cold voice. "You get it, because you're not stupid. But I'll spell it out for you anyway. Ronin is the *fall guy*, Rook. If Ronin gets picked up and we don't, we do not help him. His job is to get himself off. And we won't be getting involved in this mess right now, either. I've got no idea what he's in for—it reeks of that Boulder job, but it's got Jon written all over it as well. So we can't take any chances. We will stay up here, shut our faces, and sit tight. Do you understand?"

I nod, because what choice do I have? I've got a psycho hacker on one side and an admitted murderer on the other. I'm out-gangstered on both ends. But as we walk back to the house, the guys still holding on to my arms—I'd like to think to prevent me from falling in the moonless dark, but that's wishful thinking—the only thought running through my head is that I need to grab my shit and go.

CHAPTER THIRTY-THREE

Rook

"Sit." Ford's words come out as a command. My training kicks in and I sit the fuck down in the nearest chair and keep my mouth shut. Spencer takes the couch and Ford stands in front of the TV. "Who's hungry?"

Who's hungry? I roll my eyes at him but I ask permission before I get up. "May I go downstairs and take a shower? You guys dragged me though the fucking mud."

Spence mumbles out a, "Sure, go ahead."

"I'll go with you, Rook. Spencer, you sweep the place and lock us up." Ford grabs my arm and pulls on me until I stand. "Come on. I don't like the basement, I don't want you down there. There's no escape except for the window well in the bedroom."

"You know what I don't like?" He doesn't answer, just walks me through the kitchen and waves a hand at the stairs. "Well, I'll tell you anyway, since you've suddenly found your mute button. I hate being treated like I'm weak and stupid. If you'd told me to follow you outside I would've gone, you didn't need to try and suffocate me as I was being pulled through the mud."

"Well, Rook," he says as we enter my little apartment. "You are pretty weak and you do a lot of very stupid things. So"—he stops to look me in the eyes—"you can expect to be treated like a liability until we know what part you'll play and where your loyalties lie."

"Ha! Where my loyalties lie?" Oh, I am so angry. "That

really pisses me off, you know that? I trusted you, I—"

The hand clamps over my mouth again. "No talking. Just get in the shower and I'll wait here." His hand is still firmly pressed against my mouth as he stares at me. "I expect an answer, Rook. So nod, or give me the sign language version of a *yes, sir.*"

I nod, but what I really want to do is bite his hand.

He releases me, huffs out a long breath of air, plops down on my couch and turns on a hockey game.

I go into my room and throw open my closet door, grab a clean pair of jeans, a long-sleeve white thermal, and a Shrike Rook t-shirt.

The backpack is calling my name before I even get the shirt off the hanger. I peek out my bedroom door and listen. Ford is still watching hockey and the announcer is screaming "Goal!" so I figure he's pretty wrapped up in it. I turn the shower on and then go back to my closet.

This backpack is the only thing besides my Converse shoes that I have left from my other life.

I can't help it, I fall to my knees and slide the drawstring cord to open it up, then check the little side pocket for the key. I took it from Jon's office before I left. The other stuff inside is everything I need to make a quick escape. I packed it up the day I shot Jon in the knee because I figured even if I wasn't arrested, I might still get in trouble. Maybe not from the cops, but eventually *someone* would come looking for me. It was a given.

And I was right. All those someones are breathing down my neck right fucking now.

Inside the bag I have twenty thousand in cash. I take the money out and flip the bills like you see people do in the movies. Twenty grand doesn't look like much when they're all hundreds. You'd be surprised how small it actually is when they are wrapped up in two little bundles. I've also got one change of clothes and some basic toiletries and the fake ID Jon made me use when we went places before I turned eighteen.

I stuff the backpack under the hanging t-shirts and go take my shower. When I get out I put clothes on and when I walk out in the living room Ford gives me a dirty look.

"What are you wearing?"

I roll my eyes. "Clearly you can see what I'm wearing."

"Are you going somewhere?"

"No, Ford. I just like being fully clothed when I think something bad might happen. There's nothing worse than running for your life through the woods wearing a nightie with a crazed boyfriend on your tail. Believe me, I know from experience. I'm wearing clothes, so shut the fuck up about it."

"Whatever. Let's go upstairs."

He gets up and I follow. I guess my sympathy card with Ford has been played, because that last remark didn't even get an eyebrow raise. I might as well settle in and be nice, that'll make my night go a little easier.

"Find anything, Spence?" Ford asks.

"No, I swept the downstairs at least. We'll just stay in here. But"—Spencer looks over at me—"no talking," he says, putting a finger to his lips. "We need to go outside if you feel the need to *talk*, and to be honest, we should just wait and see what happens tomorrow at Ronin's arraignment. So it's no use anyway."

Ronin is in jail.

It hits me hard and I sink down onto the couch and scrub my face with my hands, trying to stave off a headache. I'm pretty pissed that I didn't figure out these guys had a past. *I mean, fuck, Rook. How stupid can you be? How gullible? How naive?* And now I'm right back where I was when I showed up at Antoine's.

Confused.

Is Ronin a good guy?

Fucking Ford admits *he's* not a good guy. That shit came right out of his own mouth at my birthday party. In fact, he brought that woman on purpose, to show me specifically that he's got serious issues. The kind of issues I am very familiar with.

And Spencer admitted to killing a guy.

And they're all responsible for at least two illegal jobs that I know of. How many more are there?

"Rook," Spencer says as he takes a seat next to me. "I'm the same guy I was last night when you cried on my shoulder. I'm the same guy who painted your body all summer, remember?"

I sigh. "I know, Spencer." He does know *me* awful well, doesn't he? Practically reads my mind now.

"And even though Ford is an asshole when he's working, he's still the same guy he was this morning when he took you running. Right?"

I look over at Ford and he's glaring at me. "What's with that look?"

"Blackbird," Spence says, pulling my attention back to him. "He's still the same guy. You've just never met the asshole version we all know and hate. And right now we *all* have to morph into that other version of ourselves. Because we gotta get out of this, Rook. No one's coming to help us. So please, we just all need to do our jobs."

"But what's my job, Spencer?"

"Be quiet and do what you're told. Just let us handle this one, OK? Just let us take care of it."

"But you said you're not gonna help Ronin, right?"

"Ronin will help himself. He's good at what he does, he's smart, he's devious and sneaky and all those things you hate about men and certainly don't want to hear are your boyfriend's God-given gifts. But he'll figure something out. It just might take some time, that's all."

I avoid Ford's penetrating stare as I mull all this over. Because I don't want to know these versions of my friends.

I want Ford to stay the guy I trust to point me in the right direction and force me to do things that are good for me even though I hate it.

I want Spencer to stay the guy who makes me laugh, paints me pretty biker jackets, and makes scrapbooks of our body art so I'll be happy.

And I want Ronin to be the guy I spend forever with. I want to sleep next to him, and go on long vacations with him, and take beastly sexy showers with him.

But as long as this shit is hanging over us, nothing will ever be like that again.

So I just curl up on the end of the couch and close my eyes. I'm tired and I'm gonna grab some shuteye while I can. Because I will be one busy girl in a few hours.

CHAPTER THIRTY-FOUR

Ronin

This is how I get through jail. Because this isn't the first time I've been under suspicion, nor will it probably be the last, considering the wake of crime spraying out behind me from all our previous jobs. But this is what I do.

One. Embrace the orange jumpsuit. You cannot fight it. It's dirty, it smells like that cheap-ass soap they use, and it's had more hands on it than you want to think about. But unless you want to go naked—and you don't, trust me, the mattresses are revolting enough to make you want to sleep on the floor, even with the sheets and orange jumpsuit—just learn to love it.

Two. Do not eat more than once a day. No matter what. They really are trying to poison you.

Three. Do not think about what you might be guilty of. That just makes you vulnerable to questioning.

Four. Embrace your alone time. No people to talk to means fewer ways to screw yourself over.

Five. Try your hardest not to think about the girl on the outside and what she may be thinking of you right now.

Rook has got to be out of her mind. And the really fucked-up part about all this is that I have no idea what I'm being held for. They said felony obstruction, but that could pertain to just about anything I've done over the past five years. I've had a long career of justice obstruction.

But I'm not supposed to think about that shit, or Rook, or Spencer, or Ford, or Elise.

Elise is gonna kill me.

I am so fucking dead when I get out of jail. She's gonna want answers, she's gonna want promises, she's gonna want all kinds of shit I might not be able to tell her.

Damn, this jumpsuit is itchy. And I could really go for some fresh fruit.

A loud buzzer sounds and my door clicks open. A guard appears with his hand on his weapon. "Flynn, you've got a visitor."

"Awesome, finally someone to talk to in this shithole."

Did I mention rule six? Don't fool yourself into thinking you can stick to these rules. Because jail, and especially county jail, sucks ass. And you will have no choice but to wish for company, think about the shitty clothes, the poisonous food, your crime—real or imaginary—and your girl, who probably left your ass as soon as she heard you were incarcerated.

I pass by the guard and then follow the hallway until I get to a door. This visitor can only be one of two people. Elise—and I'm so hoping not, because she's gonna cry and shit and that's just not good for the baby—or Rook. Because our partnership rules state that Spencer and Ford are not allowed to come visit.

They buzz me into the visiting area where a few guys are already talking to their friends or family, and then the guard barks out, "Last stall."

I can't see my visitor as I walk down the aisle because they have cinder block walls between each visiting station. Thick Plexiglas separates the prisoner and the visitor, so there is no hope of any contact at all. And a phone hangs on a holder affixed to the wall. I try not to notice a dude crying his eyes out to his pregnant significant other, another guy pressing his hand up against the plastic as his little girl presses back on the other side, and some kid who doesn't even look like he's old enough to be in the county lockup as he tries to comfort a woman who might be his mother.

I am fully expecting Rook to be my visitor, but it's not

Rook.

It's Clare.

I stop and do not approach the bench where I'm supposed to sit and talk. I look her in the eye and mouth the words, *What the fuck are you doing?*

She picks up her phone, then taps it on the Plexiglas, indicating I should sit down.

I do. I pick up the phone and all I hear is her breathing.

"What the fuck are you doing, Clare?"

"She ran, Ronin."

"Who?" I ask, even though I know who.

"Rook, she's missing. She left sometime in the middle of the night, she—"

I don't catch the rest because I hang up the phone and walk away.

So much for rule number five. I go to the door, wait for the buzzer, and then exit back into the hallway. There's no guard this time. That fuck Abelli is waiting for me.

"Mr. Flynn, we'd like to speak to you, if you don't mind."

"I do mind actually, I'm still waiting on my lawyer."

A guard grabs my arm and escorts me the opposite direction from where I came from, then Abelli opens a door and waves me inside. "No need for lawyers, Flynn. Just an informal chat about your missing girlfriend."

I take a deep breath. *Games, Ronin. Keep cool, they're baiting you,* Spencer's voice says in my head. *Just games, dude.*

Right. *Shut the hell up, Spencer.*

This is what a little bit of alone time in a cell does to you, so yeah, rule number four creates condition number one. Two-way conversations with people who are not, in fact, present.

"Sit," Abelli commands.

I sit, because I might as well play a little, pass the time, right? I'm in no hurry to get back to my cell, that's for sure.

"We know where your girlfriend is. Would you like to know?"

"OK, sure," I answer. "Tell me."

"Well, see, we were hoping you'd do a little information exchange with us if we give you that info."

And this, little grasshoppers, is what I like to call the no-lose situation. Pay close attention, because here's how it goes down.

"OK, you go first, tell me what you know. Where's Rook?"

"Bahahaha, Mr. Flynn, not so fast. We deserve an answer to one of our questions first, don't you think? Since we're the ones with the information you need?"

Just agree at this point. The correct answer would be, 'uh, fuck no,' but you want to keep them rolling. "Sure. Shoot, how can I help you folks?"

"What do you know about the contents of the security box in Las Vegas?"

Ah, Vegas box again. So this *is* about Rook. See, grasshoppers, this is all I needed. I am free to move about the cabin because I already got what I want from Abelli. He's got nothing on Rook's whereabouts because obviously she would know more about said Vegas box than I would. So, Clare's right. Rook left. Which means Rook's *doing* something. Which means this guy wants to know *what* she's doing. As do I, but I'm not gonna get that info from Abelli.

In addition, I also found out this is not about my illustrious obstruction of justice career, but about this guy and his obsession with this stupid box in Vegas. And this, in combination with the slip-up during my polygraph, means this is personal for him.

His ass is on the line. Somehow, some way, Abelli is in deep.

"I'm done here."

He eyes me cautiously. "You didn't answer my question."

"No, but you just answered *all* of mine. So I'm done here." I fold my hands over my chest and wait him out.

He talks, he screams into my face, flinging his spit all over my cheek, he stomps around like a baby, he sends in the good-cop partner and that guys flips out when I start humming a pretty dead-on balls accurate rendition of *Bohemian Rhapsody*—the *Wayne's World* version complete with head bang and air drums—and then finally, some fat higher-up comes in and says they need the room back.

I am escorted to my cell to wait it out alone, ready to put all the rules back into practice.

CHAPTER THIRTY-FIVE

Rook

Spencer drifts off some time after two AM. I know because I wake up around midnight, hoping they'll be asleep already, but no such luck. Ford, on the other hand, lasts until almost four. And say what you will about Ford, but he takes his sentry duty very seriously. He sits in a chair in the pitch dark, no lights on in the house, no lights on outside the house, staring out the window for hours.

When he finally does drift off I creep downstairs, grab my backpack, and slip out the bedroom window. I only own one mode of transportation, my Shrike Rook. So I push it down the road so I can start it up without being heard and take off.

Because this whole thing is bullshit. And I'm tired of it.

Once I get back into FoCo I head east on the highway until I hit Sterling, then catch the 76 up to Julesburg and get on I-80.

And this road will take me straight to Illinois where I will stop running for good.

I'm so tired of waiting for things to go bad, for things to fall apart, for that stupid fucking rug to be pulled out from under me. I mean, they're doing a pretty good job right now, right? Ronin's in jail, the FBI has Wade tracking me down, and I just learned that my best friends are killers and maybe even traitors. I'm not sure what that remark was from Ford—I'm hoping a generic *I hack into secret databases* type of treason—because one needs to draw the line somewhere and betraying my country is pretty much where the Crayola comes out.

And a motorcycle is definitely not the best way to travel a thousand miles, but I've got no choice. I have the money to charter a jet—wouldn't that've been awesome? But there's the whole TSA thing and I can't risk them knowing where I'm going until I get what I need.

Lincoln, Nebraska is about halfway to Chicago, so I pull into a Holiday Inn Express. I know from commercials that they have a free breakfast in the morning with one of those do-it-yourself waffle makers. Why this makes a difference to me when I have twenty thousand dollars in my backpack, I have no idea. It just does. I park the bike in the check-in carport, then duck into the restroom so I can shuffle out a few hundred-dollar bills. My gaze catches my reflection in the mirror and I wince.

Damn, I look tore up. There are dark circles under my eyes from riding the last eight hours, my hair is a rat's nest even though I braided it before I left, and my face is pale white. I splash some cold water on my cheeks and then rub them with a scratchy paper towel to force some color back.

It almost works.

I get my money out and then go to the front desk.

"Can ah help ya?" the girl behind the desk says in a friendly Midwest accent.

"I just need a single room, no reservation."

"OK, I can do tha-at." Her drawl makes her words slower than normal and it's almost comforting. "But check-in isn't until three, so I'll set it up and you can come back in then, will that be okaaaay?"

"Sure," I mumble. Like I have a choice. "Is there an electronics store around here?"

"Ye-as, just down on Superior. Would you like me to print you out directions?"

"Yes, please. That'd be great." And ten minutes later I've got my room reserved, a key card that will activate at three PM, and I'm on my way to the Super Wal-Mart. When I get there I wait around for a near front parking space because I suddenly have a bout of paranoia that someone will steal my bike. It is a custom Shrike, and those can't be common around here.

I head right to the electronics section and pick up a pre-paid iPhone and some minutes, pay cash at the counter, then go get some cheap clothes and snacks to hold me over until I get back home.

Home. I shake my head at that internal slip. That place is not my home anymore and it repulses me to think of it like that.

I pay up front for the rest of my stuff, then sit in the attached Subway drinking a soda while I deal with my phone activation and by the time that's taken care of, it's almost three. I shove my purchases into my backpack and head over to the hotel and find my room.

It's a room. King-sized bed, ugly-ass comforter that I remove immediately, a nightstand, a desk, microwave, and a table. I take a shower and watch TV from bed.

How long has it been since I was really alone somewhere? When I got to Denver I was pretty lost, but I found the homeless shelter. God, I don't know how I did all that by myself. I was such a mess. I'd never been in a homeless shelter before so I had no idea that you had to get in line for a bed. I spent the first night at the bus station because there were no beds available. And that was so fucking scary and cold. It was late March and it snowed that night and even though the bus station had heat, the doors were constantly opening and closing, so it was never warm.

I learned my lesson. I got to the shelter early the next day, got a number for a bed, and was once again on the streets that night because I didn't know you had to get there right at six PM to line up with your number or they'd give your bed away to someone else.

I think I cried the whole night. And one night in the bus station is forgiven by the Denver PD, but not two.

Two is a habit, the cop told me. But he let me stay because

I was so upset. In fact, he almost called social services thinking I was a runaway. But I showed him my ID and told him a little bit of my story, so he never ran my name. He even bought me a cup of coffee from the vending machine.

By day three I had learned the ropes. I got my bed number, I got in line early, and I finally got the pleasure of sleeping on a cot in a smelly room filled with drunks, addicts, and criminals. And a couple weeks later I was still there, being robbed of all my clothes and trying my best not to get raped.

Just after I got robbed of my clothes, I met Ronin wearing my thrift store equivalent replacements and my whole life changed.

What if I had never met him? What if I hadn't spent that last ten dollars on a ridiculous coffee at Starbucks? What if those models hadn't sat next to me and what if I hadn't been so upset and desperate that taking a chance on a test shoot with Antoine Chaput seemed reasonable?

It makes me so sick to think about that. How horrible my life would be if Ronin wasn't in it. And not because of the money and the jobs, but because of *him*. I've never known love until him. He's everything to me now. Everything. I do not care what he did in the past, and I know that's probably wrong in all kinds of ways, but I can't even muster up some righteous indignation to feel bad about it. Because life is not some cakewalk through the land of the straight and narrow. Life is a crazy, crooked, fucked-up road that sometimes requires a bit of cheating.

Sure, you gotta do your best to prepare for your luck to arrive, and you have to be ready for the opportunities, but in the end it always takes more than luck. And sometimes, skill isn't enough either.

So if something is important—I'm not talking pre-algebra important, OK? I'm talking real life-or-death important shit—well, then you do what you gotta do.

When you want to win no matter what, you just get the job done and say fuck the straight-and-narrow. Karma can kiss my ass for this one, I earned it.

Life is not always fair, but it does present you with choices. I could've taken my ten bucks and bought food. I could've ignored that card and called myself delusional for even thinking I could be worthy of that kind of job. I could've walked out when I heard what the TRAGIC contract really was and I could've told Spencer Shrike no when he asked to paint my body.

Fate is fragile. Deviate from it just a tiny fraction and you end up somewhere else. And as scary as that sounds, what it really means is that I'm the one in control. I've always been the one in control, I just never saw it clearly before. *I* control my reactions to the things life throws at me, so *I* control my fate.

Ronin might not be perfect, but he's close enough for me.

I want him, I love him, and he's mine.

That's why I'm on the road right now. I know Ford and Spencer are probably going crazy—and if I turned my phone on I'd have dozens of messages telling me how pissed off they are—but I do not care.

Ronin might be required to take the fall for them, but he will *not* take a fall for me.

No way.

I'd rather go down fighting than give up and slink away like a coward. I can fix this, I know what that FBI guy wants, and I'm gonna go chase it down and get Ronin out of that jail cell if it's the last thing I do.

CHAPTER THIRTY-SIX

Rook

The drive to the village where my life with Jon made my dark childhood look like a bright Easter morning sunrise is long, filled with dread, and scary as fuck. I have all that time to just replay all the terrible things that happened inside that house.

Wayne, Illinois is not the kind of place where horrors happen. Wayne is the type of place where little girls join the Pony Club, boys get Porsches for their eighteenth birthdays, and parents stay together because there's too much money at stake to split up. At least that's how it is now. But a hundred years ago it was just another farm town known for breeding draft horses.

Our property butts up against a pretty forest preserve and I pull into a parking lot about half a mile from the house. The park is deserted this time of year unless there's a classroom of little kids on a field trip, and today there isn't. So no one notices when I ride the bike into the woods, weaving my way between trees, until I get far enough away from the lot to hide it behind a thicket of shrubbery. This way I can walk up to the house from the back and make sure no one's waiting for me. It also gives me a nice hidden getaway route and all that fucking running with Ford is gonna pay off big if I have to make a break for it.

The house Jon and I lived in is at least a hundred years old and when it comes into view through the heavily wooded trees, I get the same creepy feeling I did that first day we came to look at it after his uncle died.

Picture the house in *Night of the Living Dead*. Not that pussy remake where the house is some beautiful, sprawling Victorian-ish thing. But the original *Night of the Living Dead*, the black and white one from the Sixties that has that two-story farmhouse sitting off in the distance in a large field, white siding, half-ass porch, and those tall, skinny windows that just scream horror movie.

That's my house in Wayne, Illinois.

The first time Jon and I came to look at it I refused to get out of the car. I was so creeped out he didn't even push the issue, simply left me there in the passenger seat while he went inside and looked around. He only stayed about fifteen minutes and when he came back all he said was, *I'll clean it up and remodel the kitchen*. I just stared at him. Because it was so out of character for him to give a shit about what I thought that I couldn't even process it. I have no idea what he saw that day but I can take a good guess. Because his uncle was psycho. Psycho as in *I keep my quadruple amputee mother under the bed on wheels, X-Files style.*

I'm not exaggerating. Uncle Pete was caught with body parts in his basement and died while on trial.

I almost forget to breathe as little by little the house comes into view. It looks small on the outside but inside it's one of those old places with huge rooms. It's dumpy because the outside never got any attention. The siding is still a dingy grayish white, the tall hedges that line the far side of the property are all overgrown and bushy, the unattached garage roof is slightly sagging, and the yard grass is knee-high. But if you include the third-floor attic and the basement, it's almost three thousand square feet of dump.

I never once set foot upstairs. Not even the second floor. It was off limits to me and even though it was kinda cramped only living in that little bit of space, I had absolutely no problem with that. I gladly made do.

Money did not make a shit of difference in my life once I

got with Jon. When I was out on the streets, hungry, cold, and desperate, I thought for sure money was the answer. That's the whole reason I went home with Jon in the first place. He had it all. He was cute, he had the job, the college degree, the Lincoln Park condo, the car, the clothes. He had everything I thought I wanted.

Just like Ronin, right? Ronin had all that too. And he wonders why it took me so long to get on board with him. It was a *fool me twice* kinda thing.

And seriously, if you were me back then and you suddenly had an established, nice-looking guy interested in taking care of you, you'd go for it too. What girl on the streets would say no to that? Who?

No one, that's who. But I know better now.

Yeah, everything I did with Antoine and Spencer was for money, but it was *my* money. Not someone else's. There's a big, big difference. After I left Jon I wasn't looking for the things money could buy, I was looking for the freedom to walk away any time I wanted.

That's what money really gives you. Walking privileges.

I hesitate at the edge of the woods. I don't see anyone but I stay hidden and stalk around the perimeter as best I can before setting foot out on what's left of the lawn. Both of our cars are still there. He must've picked mine up from where I left it the day I ran. I peek in the window as I walk past and catch sight of the crystal glass hanging from the rear-view. I open the door impulsively and snatch it until the nylon string breaks, and then close the door gently.

It glitters in the sun and makes my stomach turn. Jon gave me this early in our relationship. I huck it out into the grass because it needs to be forgotten, just like all the rest of the stuff in this place. I continue on to Jon's car and peek in his windows too. Mine's an old Toyota Camry, but Jon drove a late-model Mustang. There's nothing in there, not even a scrap of paper from a straw wrapper.

Jon is a neat freak.

I suppose he left his car here because it would be stupid to disappear in your own car. I don't open his door, just continue walking up to the back stoop. No railing, just five concrete steps leading up to a door. I stop and lift up the roof of an empty birdfeeder off to the side and take out the spare key taped to the top. The back door doesn't function. Nailed shut courtesy of Psycho Uncle Pete. Too close to the basement, I always figured. So I creep around to the front of the house and listen for signs that someone might be inside.

I wait a few minutes and then hop up the identical stoop in front, push the key in the lock, and twist the door knob.

It swings open with a creak and I hesitate for a second, but I'm more afraid of someone pulling into the driveway and catching me here than I am of crossing the threshold.

So I step inside, close the door, and remind myself it's just a place. It's not alive, it's not evil, it's just a *place.*

But it's a place that has been tossed from ceiling to floor. The leather couch is standing on end, the lining underneath split open. Every cushion as well. Stuffing coats the floor and it looks like it snowed in here. The end table drawers are upside down on the coffee table, their meager contents—Jon never did tolerate a junk drawer—spilled out. All the pictures are strewn about, their canvases split open, like we were hiding secret documents under the paintings.

When I look to the right the kitchen is in the same state. I walk in there. Jon did live up to his promise. My kitchen has granite countertops, maple cabinets, travertine tiles on the floor, and stainless steel appliances. All of which are dented now with what looks to be booted footprints. The French doors of the fridge are open, as is the lower freezer drawer, the contents inside long past spoiled. All the cupboards are open and the remains of the dishes are scattered around on the floor, my boots crunching in the debris as I back out and wind my way through the strewn-about furniture, towards the first floor bedrooms.

I want to stop myself. I want to scream at myself, tell the

inner Rook not to go there. Nothing good can come of it. Just turn back and get what you came for.

But I can't.

I can't leave here without looking at it one more time.

All the doors are open as I pass. Our bedroom is ransacked, the guest room is ransacked, the hall bathroom is ransacked, and the office is also ransacked.

But one door remains closed and this alone makes me want to cry. I walk slowly to the last door on the left at the end of the hallway and open it.

My baby's room is not a mess. In fact, it's almost neat and tidy—the bedding in the crib is in a heap, the mattress ripped down the side, but it's all there. When I pull open a drawer all the tiny clothes are messed up, but they are all still there. Proof that whoever the searcher was, they must've either taken their time to look through things properly or they fixed everything after they were done.

I wonder what kind of thug does that?

The crib is white and the bedding is blue. All the bottles are lined up near the bottle warmer on the changing table. The Diaper Genie is still standing at attention in the corner, its askew top the only clue that it was searched by the thugs who trashed my house.

I suck in a breath as my eyes wash over the picture frame on the dresser.

It's me. Eight months pregnant.

I'm wearing a fluffy peach dress, I'm barefoot, I'm huge, and I'm standing outside in front of the blooming purple lilac bush on the east side of the house.

I'm also smiling. Because even though my world would fall apart very soon after this picture was taken, I was happy that day. I was hopeful that Jon was changing, that this baby was a good idea after all, that he'd be better, happier, satisfied—if he just had a son.

I didn't miscarry at six weeks like most girls. I carried that baby to term.

I went to all those check-ups, heard the heartbeat, saw the ultrasound, had a name picked out, had a room, a car seat, a crib, breast pump, baby swing, the cute bedding, the adorable onesies, the rocking chair by the window, and a baby bag packed and ready for the hospital—I had *everything*.

I slip the photo out of the frame real fast and stuff it inside my jacket. I didn't want it when I left because I thought I could just forget it ever happened. Just put it behind me and move on.

But I can't move on. I never had the chance to properly grieve because as soon as I came home from the hospital, Jon was even worse than ever. He blamed me. And I never had a chance to feel the sadness. I had to push it away so I could survive.

I don't have time to feel anything right now either, but some day. Someday soon, I will look good and hard at that picture and figure it out. Let it all out and really say goodbye like I should've when it happened.

I take one last look at what I almost had and then I back out of the room and pull the door closed behind me.

Let that one room remain sweet and hidden away from the ugliness out here.

I walk briskly down the hallway, picking my way through the various pieces of broken things, and go through the kitchen to the back of the house. The basement is where I need to be. That's where everything is. All the horror, all the tears, all the beatings, all the death, all the sickness, all the filth, all the bad, bad things that happened in this house took place in this basement.

When I get to the top of the stairs I stop and replay it all in my mind.

His hand on my shoulder.

The smack across the back of my head that turned into a push.

The fall.

The blood.

The hours it took for Jon to decide that I really did need to go to the hospital.

The look on the doctor's face when he told me it was too late.

The screaming as they strapped me to a gurney and rolled me down the hallway so they could medically induce me into giving birth to a dead baby.

And then waking up in a hospital bed to the man who caused it all, handing me balloons.

Balloons.

And a card.

The anger and hate I felt that day washes over me again. But I let it flow like wind and then it dissipates. Because I came here for a reason and this memory lane shit needs to be over now.

I walk slowly down the steps and let the baby go so the other horrors can fill in the space. The basement is tossed too, and while it does make me a little sad to see all my things trashed upstairs, down here nothing belonged to me. Down here I was a piece of property. Down here I was *his* piece of property and I spent most of the months after the baby down here being punished for some reason or another.

Jon likes the kinky stuff. And I'm not talking the fun kinky stuff. I'm not talking about cute pink cheeks from an erotic spanking, or teasing a girl so she wants to come, but can't. Or any of that play stuff.

I'm talking painful, 'I never signed up for this, there is no word that will keep me safe, I don't want this, it does not feel good, please, for fuck's sake, stop' kind of kinky stuff.

Ford likes the kinky stuff too, so he hints. And Ronin *thinks* he likes the kinky stuff.

But I'm doubting either of them have ever hog-tied a teenager and hung her up from the ceiling with a ball gag in her mouth and then proceeded to sexually torture her and called it fun.

I eye the ceiling hook as I step onto the cobblestones that

line the basement floor and let out an uncontrollable shiver before taking my attention to the room around me. Most of the walls are made of some sort of gray rock. The floors are these old-ass bricks in some places, and crumbling concrete in others.

I head to the laundry room where the floor is crumbling concrete and try not to look at the shattered pieces of the St. Andrew's cross as I pick my way past. This is a long room, but it's pretty much bare of anything except the laundry stuff. Washer, drier, ironing board, folding table.

And one secret.

There is only single small basement window on the far side near the utility sink. The late afternoon light seeps in and blasts about six feet of air with illuminated floating dust particles. Across from that is the massive coal-powered furnace left over from when the house was first built. I used to hide behind it sometimes, but Jon always found me. He *always* found me.

I bend down and pick up the crowbar that's mostly hidden underneath the washer, then insert it into the large drain grate in the crumbling floor. It lifts up so I set it aside and I lie down so I can peek in, straining to see if what I'm looking for is still there.

It is and the tips of my fingers just barely graze across the metal safe when a car door slams outside.

Fuck!

I get up and run to the little window which looks out to the front walkway.

Men's voices.

And one of those voices belongs to Jon.

CHAPTER THIRTY-SEVEN

Rook

How? How is this even possible? He's supposed to be in jail!

I'm so stunned I stand there gazing up at three sets of feet as they walk up the front steps. I waste any time I might've had to get out of this basement. The front door slams closed and I panic. What the fuck?

I look around frantically for a hiding place. The coal furnace calls to me, I could crawl behind that, but what if Jon knows I'm here somehow? He'll definitely look there first because that's where I always went. Hard footsteps thud over my head as the men walk across the living room floor. My gaze travels past the coal chute and I rush over, swing the door up, and I'm just about ready to climb in and crawl up to the side yard when I realize the footsteps are crossing into the kitchen.

They're coming down here.

I give up on the coal chute—I'll be caught for sure—and I refocus on the drain where we hide the secret shit. I'm not as skinny as I was when Jon made me climb in here, dig out a hole around the sewer pipes, and shove that fire-proof box in a little nook down there. But I wiggle as the first thuds on the basement stairs pound in my head, then slip through and pull the grate over the top.

Fuck, I left the crowbar. The footsteps are louder now, but not down yet. I slide the grate, grab the crowbar, slip back inside the hole, and slide the grate again.

"We're tired of playing, Jon," a voice says. "We know it's

here and the only way you're getting out of here alive is if you give it to us. So let's make this easy."

I scoot away from the light filtering through the grate and push my back against the dirt wall as the men continue to talk near the stairs. I fish out my new iPhone and start the video camera and set it on a pipe on the other side of the hole, pointing up at the grate.

"Where is it?" another man says.

I'm so busted if he tells them because I'm sitting right next to the very thing they're looking for.

"I told you," Jon says. "I gave it to friends to hold for me. You kill me, they release it to the public. We walk out of here together or we don't. But if I go down, so do you."

A loud crack and a thud as someone falls to the ground almost makes me gasp. "You want to threaten me?"

There's more shuffling and then the men are headed my way. I hold my breath.

"It's in this basement, we know it is. One of your buddies gave you up."

"That right?" Jon says, then spits on the floor, swallows hard, like he's swallowing blood, and then coughs. "Then why don't you tell me where it is, since you seem to know so much."

They hit him again and this time he falls to the floor and his cheek lands right on the grate above me.

I suck in a long breath.

His eyes shift downward.

At first I think he can't see me. And then his expression morphs though several different phases. Shock. Grimace. Anger.

And then nothing.

We open our mouths at the same time, but only he speaks. "I'll never tell," he says, looking me straight in the eye.

What? Is he talking to me?

One of the guys kicks him in the ribs and he spits out more blood. This time it clings to the rusty grate and drips down.

Please, God, I pray. *Please don't let me be caught here with these men.*

"I won't tell," he says in a low voice. "I won't tell."

"You'll tell, asshole. Because we're gonna beat the living shit out of you if you don't," one of the other guys says.

"They ransacked the baby's room, but I cleaned it up as best I could," he chokes out. And then he whispers so softly I almost miss it. "I swear it was an accident. I swear to God, *it was an accident.*"

He *is* talking to me. I sink back against the wall and try to hold my tears in.

"Yeah, yeah, your dead baby's room. We've already heard about it. Now you either tell us where the shit is, Jon, or we'll go get that little raven of yours next. And if she thinks what you did to her was bad, she's in for a surprise. I have a guy in Columbia who'll pay a half a million for a girl like her. I can pick her up and have her sold before anyone knows she's gone. We've got her boyfriend in jail, and she's on the run from the other two, just like we planned. Hell, they might not even miss her. Might just figure she moved on and found a new place to hide."

Jon coughs again and more blood comes up. "I'm so sorry," he breathes, again so low it almost doesn't exist. He stops for a moment, his eyes still looking down at me. "I'm sorry. You'll just have to kill me, boys." And then his gaze finds the iPhone in a hazy beam of light that slips past his body and hits it in just such a way as to create a glint. He smiles for a moment, the blood spilling out of his mouth, and I quickly reach out and move the phone slightly just as Jon rolls himself over.

"It's not here, Agent Abelli," he says loudly. Plenty loud for the phone camera to pick up the name. "I gave it to the media, so just do what you want, I've got nothing to give you. Nothing at all."

I close my eyes and put my fingers in my ears after that.

They beat him, they kick him, they lift up his head and crack it against the grate so hard pieces of blood and bone from his cheek spray down on me.

His screams fill the basement and then, gradually, they turn to moans.

And even though I spent years wishing I could make him writhe in pain like that, it brings me no comfort.

I hate this. I hate everything about this. It makes me sick.

But I'm forced to listen for what seems like an eternity as they pummel him, knock him unconscious, bring him back, and then do it again. Until finally, he's unable to be brought back and there is a moment of heavy silence when everyone realizes it's over.

"Shoot him to make sure he's dead then burn this place down. I'll be in the car," the Abelli voice says as he walks away. "If he's hidden anything here, it'll all go up in flames."

That Abelli guy doesn't even make it to the basement stairs before the gunshot rings out and pieces of Jon splatter down into the hole.

I clamp my hand over my mouth and close my eyes tight as the smell of gasoline fills the basement.

I wait for the whoosh of flame and then the heavy footsteps of the other man going back upstairs. I frantically push against the grate so I can climb out, but Jon's body is in the way.

My breath starts coming in ragged gasps as the smoke fills the basement and I start to panic, my chest hitching as I try to take in air and push against Jon's body. I'm ready to give up when I think of Ronin's words the last time I saw him. *Don't panic, Gidget.*

Calm down, Rook, and push for fuck's sake!

I get to my feet, still crouched down, and push my shoulder up against the grate.

It moves, barely, but it moves. So I do it again and Jon's body rolls a little. I do it again and again and again.

And finally the grate flips on its side.

I reach up, push the grate across the floor, and then shove Jon's body until he's clear of the hole in the floor. I'm so filled with adrenaline and fear trying to make my escape, I almost forget the phone and everything I came for. I grab the key from my pocket and try my best to steady my shaking hand as I insert it into the lock. For a second it refuses to engage and I swear to God, I almost have a panic attack. My whole plan flashes before my eyes and I feel the crush of defeat.

Keep calm, Gidget. Don't panic. Ronin's voice in my head soothes me and I take a deep breath, push the key in farther and feel it click into place. I turn it and swing the metal door of the safe open.

I scan the contents then stuff all of it inside my jacket pocket and pull myself back up into the basement. The smoke is so thick I can't even see the stairs and the flames are too high that way to even consider escaping. I panic again.

No, be still.

"How will I get out?" I ask Ronin's voice in my head. I look over at the window, already coughing and gasping as the thick smoke penetrates into my lungs. But it's just one of those small basement windows. And this house is too old to have a window well as a fire escape. My eyes dart around, panic starting to consume me again, when I spy the coal chute. And then I'm lifting up the metal door and shoving myself inside.

The negative pressure from outside sucks the fire in my direction and the flames are nipping at my boots before I'm even halfway up.

I scream from the heat and then the outside chute opens, forcing the flames to lick up against my legs even higher. Two hands reach down to grab my wrists. It never even occurred to me that those bad guys might still be around, but it's too late now.

The hands pull me up with force and then the fresh air rushes into my lungs and the heat on my legs is replaced with cool autumn air.

I land in a heap at the feet of some biker boots.

And when I look up Spencer Shrike is shaking his head at me. "I'm gonna tell Ronin what you did and he's gonna spank the shit out of you for this."

I pat my jacket as he lifts me up and pulls me back towards the woods. "I have so much proof," I cough out as I half-limp, half-run from the burning pain in my lower legs as Spence and I make our way through the nature preserve.

And when I look back at the burning house I realize something…

All my old demons are going up in flames with that piece-of-shit place.

I'm finally free to fight another battle.

And I've got a team to help me.

CHAPTER THIRTY-EIGHT

Rook

Spencer and I trek all the way back through the woods, me coughing so hard I keep looking around to make sure no one is gonna come kill us because I can't be quiet.

"Don't worry, Rook, Ford's just up ahead with the van. He's got your bike loaded and I saw those assholes back there leave, we're cool."

"How'd you know where I was?"

He chuckles and grabs my arm hard, saving me from a nasty fall that could've made the pain in my burned legs unbearable after I trip over a tree root. "I put a tracker on your bike and your jacket. You're not gonna get away from us that easy, chick. We're a team, remember?"

"But you're not allowed to help."

He glares down at me for a moment and then the hard expression in his eyes softens a little. "We have rules for a reason, Rook. You could've really fucked things up. You could've been killed, you could've—"

"OK, I get it. But Spencer—" I stop and pull on his leather jacket to make him stop with me. "If you knew what I got out of that house you wouldn't be angry with me."

"You're wrong. If they knew you were there they would've killed you, you almost got burned alive. You got lucky, Rook. And we're all pretty attached to you. Ronin will get himself out of this eventually. And when he does, the last thing he wants to hear is that the girl he's gonna marry died doing something stupid."

I stay quiet and just limp along after that. We exit the forest a few hundred yards down from where I went in and there's a large white van waiting for us. Ford gets out of the driver's seat with a gun in his hand, not even trying to hide it. Spencer and I are walking casually across the parking lot when Ford's expression rests on me.

I stop dead in my tracks, making Spence stumble. "He's mad at me."

"Damn right he's mad at you. And you deserve it." Spencer pulls on me hard and hands me off to Ford, then walks over to the driver's side and gets in.

I look up at Ford and try a pouty frown.

"Save that shit for Ronin. It won't work on me. I am not talking to you. You scared the fuck out of us, you made me drive a thousand miles in a van alone with *Spencer*. You missed your university application deadline, and most of all, you didn't trust me enough to help you."

Ford takes my arm and pushes me over to the van, opens the door, and barks, "Get in. Sit on the floor between Spencer and me, there's only room for two up front and I don't even trust you enough to stay out of trouble locked in back with the bike right now."

I do what I'm told. They did come get me after all. And my skin might be falling off from the burns instead of screaming at me from the pain if Spence hadn't pulled me up out of the coal chute. There's a small space behind the two front seats and a few sleeping bags lying longways on the floor, so I just lie down, stretch out, and let out a long breath. "I might need to go to the hospital. My legs really hurt."

Spencer has already started rolling and Ford is just getting settled when this comes out. The van stops short and they both look down at me. "What do you mean?" Spencer asks, so I scoot around so I can prop my leg up on Ford's thigh.

"I'm burned from the fire." They both look down at my jeans, charred and with a few holes in them, and then Ford lifts up my pant leg and winces.

"Shit, Rook."

"Is it bad?" I ask. "It hurts."

"Drive, Spencer. I'll check it out." Ford lifts up my pant leg and unties my boot and slips it off, then asks for the other leg. "Take off your pants, Rook. Spencer, we need to find a drug store."

"Is it bad?" I ask again as I wiggle out of my jeans, trying my best not to cry out as the rough fabric rubs against my red skin. Ford doesn't even glance down at my goods, just lifts my foot back up. And why should he look? He's seen me naked so often it hardly matters.

"No, I don't think so," he says, patting the skin on my calf gently, but not gentle enough to keep me from wincing. "It's like a really bad sunburn, but if we find a drug store I know what will make it feel better." And then he smiles and I lie back and relax.

I'm forgiven. His worry about me outweighs his anger.

I reach into my jacket pocket and pull out the contents of the basement box and my new iPhone and hand it up to him. "Here, Ford. I think this will help us get Ronin out."

One eyebrow raises. "Is that why you ran?"

"I didn't *run,* I just… left. To go get this stuff. And I did trust you, Ford. I trusted that you guys were telling the truth when you said you weren't gonna help Ronin. So I'm sorry. But I know what these people want. Jon was into some really bad shit and he made me help him hide a whole bunch of evidence in case his partners ever turned on him. It implicates a lot of very important people in the buying and selling of girls to rich clients all over the world. That FBI guy in the house with Jon was involved—"

"What?" they both say together.

"Jon?" Ford asks.

"FBI guy?" Spencer adds.

I gulp some air and swallow, not quite ready to talk about what just happened but knowing I have to anyway. "Some guy named Abelli was the one in charge here and somehow he got

Jon out of jail so he could make him give up the evidence. I was hiding in the floor grate, that's where Jon and I made a safe place a couple years ago and put that stuff." I nod at the flash drives in Ford's hand. "Jon's dead now though. They beat him until he was unconscious because he wouldn't tell them where it was hidden. And then they shot him and set the house on fire to cover it up." I leave out the part about Jon apologizing and saving my life. I'm not sure how to process that just yet.

Ford looks down at the drives I handed him and then grabs a bag on the floor near his feet and fishes out his laptop. He looks at me for a second as he pushes the flash drive in a USB port and waits for the files to appear. He studies it as Spence and I wait in silence. I'm not sure I want to know what's on that drive and Spencer is navigating his way through a nearby town looking for a drugstore, so we sit quietly.

"What's on the iPhone?" Ford asks after Spencer parks and gets out to go buy me some aloe vera sunburn spray.

"A video of that Abelli guy admitting he was gonna kidnap me and sell me to a guy in Columbia for half a million dollars."

Ford's eyes squint down into killer asshole mode.

"And Jon getting the life beat out of him and getting shot in the head."

His eyes soften at this. "Did you see it?"

I nod.

"I'm sorry," he whispers. "No one should have to see that." He watches me struggle with the tears and then leans down a little. "It's OK to feel bad about it, Rook. Even if he was evil. It's still OK to feel bad."

"Jon saved me at the end. He saw me hiding down in the grate hole. He pretended like he was talking to those guys, but he was really talking to me. He apologized."

Ford stares at me for several silent seconds and then shakes his head and lets out a long breath. "Is it over? Can you let go now?"

I nod. "Even though he's not here to witness it, I've decided to accept his apology." I shrug my shoulders and start to cry. "I don't want to hang on to that stuff anymore, Ford."

Ford scoots around to the edge of the seat and pulls my head into his lap. "You're allowed to do that, you know. It's OK to forgive him and let it go."

Spencer opens the door and jumps in the van, handing Ford the bag of spray. "You OK, Blackbird?"

"No, not yet," I say as I sniffle my nose back under control. "But I will be if we can use that stuff to get Ronin out."

"Lie back, Rook," Ford says quietly as he opens the bag.

"I got you some shorts, too, Rook. Just cheap drugstore leftovers from summer, but it' s better than sitting in your panties." He winks down at me. "Not that we mind, you know, but I'm sure Ronin would not appreciate us driving you all over the Midwest in your panties."

Ford hands me the shorts as Spencer takes us back on the road. I wiggle into them, which is not easy considering I'm sitting on the floor of a van behind some seats and my legs are burning like hell, but I manage after several embarrassing seconds of Ford watching.

"Put your foot up here," he says, pointing to his lap.

I do.

He shakes the can of aloe vera and I wince as the fine mist hits my skin and then the cold spray settles and relief washes over me. "Ohhhhhhh," I moan. 'That feels so much better I can't even tell you."

Ford smiles and lifts my leg up to spray the underside. "Give me the other foot, Rook."

We repeat the whole procedure and I moan again. "Thank you, Ford. You're a genius."

He shrugs and then he and Spencer exchange a conspiratorial look.

I've seen that look before. Back when they started thinking about taking Jon out.

"What are you guys doing? You have a plan I need to know about or something?"

"Rook—" Spencer talks this time. Which means this is a delicate subject. I know them all pretty well by now. And whenever they need to give or get information to or from me, they take turns based on what kind of conversation it needs to be. When bluntness is needed, Ford takes the lead. When the talk involves personal things it's supposed to be Ronin. And when someone needs to keep things light because I might freak out, that's Spencer's cue to do the talking.

But Ronin's not here, so I guess Spencer is the personal guy now too.

"—we really need to know the whole story before we can do anything with this information, OK?"

I just lie down on the puffy sleeping bags, enjoying the relief from the spray and the coolness of the synthetic fabric. "What exactly do you need to know?"

"Everything," he says. "We need for you to start at the beginning. Like Rook's story, day one. And we especially need to know why your ex-husband had this shit in his possession, what his role was…" He hesitates and lets out a long breath. "What *your* role was. And how all these people are connected. *If* we get Ronin out, you have to understand, we're missing a pretty important part of the team, OK? He's the cleanup, he's the whole reason we get away with this stuff. Yeah, I make good plans, and yeah, Ford's good at covering his tracks. But this is the FBI, Rook. They do not take kindly to being fucked with and they ask a shitload of fucking questions, no matter how good the plan is. A shitload of questions. And our front man is incarcerated. You understand this?"

I swallow hard. "I do, Spencer."

"So, here's what we're gonna do." He stops to look at Ford and Ford nods at him to continue. I guess Spencer really is the logistics guy. "We're gonna go to Ogallala, Nebraska, lie low and get your story from beginning to end, and then figure it out. Sound good?"

"What's in Nebraska?" I ask.

"The safe house. And we definitely need it because these guys will pick us up as soon as we go home. We talked to Clare before we left and she said the guy who came to talk to Ronin twice before he was arrested was named Abelli. This Abelli guy is our main problem, because it looks like he was involved in this trafficking stuff and this means he's desperate to keep his name out of things. Desperate men are very dangerous."

I wait for him to finish it, but the seconds tick off and he keeps silent, so I have to ask. "What do you mean by that?"

He lets out another long breath. "We could all end up in prison or dead, Rook. Those are the facts we're dealing with now."

I stretch my legs out on the sleeping bags and close my eyes. "I'm not gonna think about that, Spencer. Ronin's in jail because of me and I told him I'd fight for us. So that's what I'm gonna do. I'm done running, these people are all guilty, there are dozens of women I know of personally who are wrapped up in this trafficking stuff. And I talked myself into leaving without them the first time. I rationalized it. I'm just one single tragic girl, what can I do? And that was probably the right decision back then because I was all alone."

I stop for a moment and Ford turns to look at me.

"But now I'm on the team, so I'm out of excuses."

CHAPTER THIRTY-NINE

Rook

Ford and Spence take turns driving through the night and by mid-morning the next day we're at Lake McConaughy in Nebraska pulling into a campground.

"The safe house is in a campground?" I ask Spencer as I strain to see out the window. It's pretty boring sitting in the makeshift back of a van on the floor, not even able to gaze out at the passing countryside.

"Not just any campground, Rook. My campground." He swings the van around a circular driveway that allows him to pull up next to the main office and parks the van. "Wait here."

I jump up into Spencer's seat so I can at least sit in a real chair for a few minutes. "Spencer sure does own a lot of businesses."

"Yeah," Ford replies. "He's not into holding onto money. He spends it as fast as he makes it." And then he stops to look up at me. "He likes to own property and businesses. Some grand scheme of his." Then he absently looks out at the campground. "He tried to get me to come deer-hunting with him out here a few years back." I try to picture Ford deer-hunting and then we both burst out laughing. "It's like he had a mental breakdown that day. I dunno." And then he looks at me again and gets serious. "I do not *hunt*."

"I figured. Me either. I won't be joining that party."

Spencer returns and pushes me out of his seat. "We got the Eagle's Nest cabin. Sleeps ten, but at least it has a bathroom."

We stop off at the campground market to pick up provisions, then head out to our new digs. It's a pretty place—very Daniel Boone.

Inside the cabin is just like a three-bedroom house, complete with wi-fi and satellite TV. Spencer starts the grill to make burgers, Ford is still messing around on his computer, and I just sit and watch them from the dining room table, thinking about home. "Maybe we should call Elise or Antoine and see if there's any news of Ronin."

"Negative," Spencer says. "Those FBI assholes are just waiting for us to show ourselves."

When lunch is ready we all grab some food and eat in silence and then when we're done, Spencer hands everyone a beer and brings a bottle of Jack and three shot glasses out to the living room, beckoning us to take a seat. I take a large overstuffed chair, Ford sits opposite me in a wingback, and Spencer stretches out on the couch. "OK, Rook. Spill it. Start from the beginning and end with climbing up a coal chute yesterday."

So I do.

And it feels good to finally get it all out. I tell them about my mom overdosing when I was just a kid, all my various foster homes, and how I ended up with Wade. Spencer's heard this part before, but Ford hasn't. They lean in a little as my story progresses into the time after Wade. "I was in my last foster home and the father"—I stop to snort—"tried to come into my bedroom and touch me a few times. And believe it or not, even after all those foster homes, the crack ones, the single moms with scummy boyfriends, the ones who collected foster kids just so they could make the mortgage every month, this was the first time one of the grownup guys tried anything. And I figured I'd had enough. I was sixteen, I already took my GED, so I never went to school, and I was just done being someone's problem. So I left and lived on the streets for a while with a girl I knew from a previous foster home. Then she got busted for drugs and I was all alone. And then Jon found me in a diner, scarfing down a sandwich that I bought with my beg money.

"And he had everything, you guys. And he was handsome. He was just like Ronin. He had a college degree, he had an apartment in Lincoln Park. It was small, and not all that nice, but it was still an apartment in Lincoln Park. He had a job and a car and food." I shrug my shoulders and look between Ford and Spencer to see what they think of this but they just nod, like they get it.

"So I stayed with him. He never touched me at first. Not for a long time actually. I was only sixteen and he waited months before even kissing me. It lulled me into a false sense of security. Like he was a gentleman or something.

"But he wasn't. He was a predator who knew exactly what he was doing because I wasn't the first girl he took in and I definitely wasn't the last one either. He liked the kinky sex, that *Fifty Shades* shit. Except… not sweet." I stop and look directly at Ford. "He liked it rough and mean."

Ford's jaw clenches and he downs his shot and pours himself another one. We all stop to drink. Me because I know what comes next, them because they can take a good guess.

"So one day, before we even slept together, he came to me with this piece of paper. It was a sex slave contract. And even though I realize now that it wasn't legal, I really thought it was back then. I feel so stupid, but I just didn't know any better. And he said this was what he needed from me in order to allow me to stay with him, so I signed it."

"You couldn't have known, Rook," Ford says. "It's not something a child should ever know about. It's not your fault."

"I know, Ford. But I just accepted it. I was so dumb. So after that he started having sex with me and it started out bad right away. I was a virgin and the things he was doing to me… they were just *weird.* I was so confused, and it was just too much for me. I—*God*, I'm so fucking embarrassed to tell you guys this."

"Rook," Spencer says, "we're not judging, OK? We just

need to understand how we got to this day, you know? We need to know so we can make the right decisions going forward."

I get that part, but it's still so embarrassing. I take a deep breath and continue. "Well, to cut to the chase, even though he tried his hardest to make me… come"—I look away and blush as I say the word—"I just, it just… it never felt good. You know?" I look up and they're both nodding at me, somber frowns on their faces. "And this made Jon very angry. And one night he took me to his BDSM club to do a scene and I didn't… get off. And his friends there realized he wasn't able to get me ready, and they all talked about their girls and how they should trade us off, see if that might improve our… responsiveness."

"Oh, fuck, Rook," Spencer says.

"No, Jon didn't agree. He was possessive of me. But he did agree to help those guys with their girls. By this time we had already moved out to the country in the serial killer house, that's what I called it. So these girls would come stay with us and he… *trained* them in the basement. He liked them a lot better than me, to be honest. He stopped fucking me so much after that. I sorta just became the house slave. Which I could definitely live with, but he got more and more violent.

"And then, I'm not sure how it happened, but somehow he became involved in like, matchmaking. Selling, I guess, since there was money exchanged. They had auctions in our barn, I kid you not. Girls showed up, willing, money was exchanged, and at first I'm pretty sure the girls were the ones getting the money wired to offshore bank accounts. Their contracts had expiration dates. Six months, a year, that sort of stuff. But later, those girls were not there because they wanted to be. They were kidnapped."

I look over at Ford and he's slumped over, his elbows on his knees, his head in his hands. Spencer's got his hand over his eyes, like he's picturing the scene and wants it to go away.

"Jon came to me one night soon after this started. I'd just

found out I was pregnant."

"Pregnant?" Spencer and Ford say at the same time.

"Yeah, I had just found out I was pregnant and things sorta got better. Jon seemed happy about it, and by this time we were already married, so in a rare moment of trust, he came to me and asked me to help him hide some stuff. In case these partners of his ever decided they wanted to get rid of him or turn him in for what he was doing. He told me it was in my best interest since I was his accomplice. So we went down to the basement where his uncle had already made the hidey-hole underneath the laundry room drain grate. Jon knew about it but he was too big to do anything with it, he needed me to squeeze down there, dig it out and make a safe spot where he could keep me and the important things he had in case anyone ever came to mess with him. I would be his ace in the hole, he said."

"What happened to the baby?" Ford asks quietly. He's still got his head in his hands.

"I lost it. Miscarriage." I continue quickly before they start asking too many questions about my son. "Things got pretty bad after that happened. Jon was angry and I mean constantly. He started beating me. Violently, much worse than any of the stuff he ever did sexually. And then he almost killed me. And that's when I ran away and ended up in Denver."

We sit in the silence for a few minutes and I take the opportunity to down my beer and take a shot.

Spencer is still pinching the bridge of his nose and covering his eyes at the same time.

It's killing me to know what they think of me right now.

"Rook." Spencer blows out a long breath of air and then opens his eyes and stares straight at me. "You are the bravest fucking chick I've ever met."

I realize I was holding my breath and I let it escape in a rush.

And then Ford straightens up, leans back in his chair and starts talking. "Those drives contain the names of everyone involved in that little trafficking ring Jon was part of. There are seven FBI agents, twelve Chicago cops, a mayor of a small Illinois town, a state senator, two US House members, and a shitload of well-off businessmen. One of whom"—Ford raises his eyebrows at Spencer for this—"is our friend Cooperson Smyth from Boulder."

Spencer sits up for this bit of news. "No."

"Yes," Ford says. "He was part of it so you know what, Spencer? You can stop with your own guilt about that now. He was even dirtier than we could ever have imagined. I never heard about this, did you?"

"No, I knew about the money crimes and what his daughter told Ronin about him…" Spencer trails off as he looks over at me.

"His name is all over these documents. And it makes you wonder, right?" Ford looks over at me now, shaking his head and huffing out a breath of incredulity before continuing. "If this was fate after all."

Our conversation all those months ago at Coors Field floods back. When I told Ford that I got off the bus because of the film department at CU Boulder. 'Fate,' he'd said. 'Weird,' I'd replied.

But maybe he was right.

These guys have always been my future.

"That's just the US people. We have several dozen international men as well. Including one particularly nasty cartel head from Columbia. We have signatures, wire-taps, which are probably not admissible in court, video, which probably is admissible, phone records, bank account numbers and transaction records, passwords, and a complete list of girls—both the ones who were traded by mutual agreement and those who were kidnapped and sold. Jon kept very, very thorough records."

"Great, so we're good, right? We can use that to bargain for Ronin, can't we?"

"Well, Blackbird," Spencer says from the couch. "Yeah,

it's damn good stuff. Almost airtight, in fact. But the problem is, we might be killed for exposing it. This is high-level shit. People will not take kindly to us barging in on their well-planned crime ring, guns a-blazing, making demands."

"So what do we do?"

Spencer blows out a long breath of air and pinches the bridge of his nose with his fingers, staving off a headache or trying to beat one back down into submission. "Take them all down at once, knock them out before they see it coming. But we're down a team member. We need a front man, and it's gotta be you. Because Ford and I do not, let me make this clear, we *do not* get involved in the public side of things. We've got too much history, Rook. We can't do it. Ronin is like a brother, but we can't risk being the face of these crimes. And just so you know, you're a nobody now. Next year, if we never get involved in this, you'll be a minor curiosity with the show and the modeling.

"But if you do this you'll be famous whether you want to or not. People will dig up your past, smear your name, probably send you hate mail and stand outside wherever you live with giant signs telling you you're going to hell.

"They'll call you a whore, find every last foster home and get them to talk shit about you, and you'll never be invisible again. Say goodbye to grocery shopping and say hello to your own Wikipedia page complete with editors fighting over how to portray you publicly for years to come. Your children will grow up knowing you were a sex slave for a sadistic man and watched human beings being auctioned off in your barn. And that's just for starters, God only knows what could happen. So, Blackbird…" He sighs deeply. "It's your call. You lead, we follow."

I chew on my nail a little, thinking it over. I'm so ashamed that I was part of what happened back in Illinois. And if I'm honest with myself, that's why I always want to run from things. I have no guts. I'm so weak. Ford was right. And I have done so many stupid, stupid things that I'm not sure I can even make up for it.

But I can try.

Even though it will be difficult and I'll have to admit all these things to the cops and reporters, and God only knows who else—shit, maybe they'll even put me on trial for not turning them in sooner—I still have to try.

I look over at Spencer and swallow down the fear. "Can you come up with a plan that will make sure the cops believe me? Might they just blow me off? Maybe the person we tell is involved? I mean, I know how far-fetched that is, but there are a lot of names on that list, Spencer. What if that's not all of them?"

"That's your risk, Blackbird. This is most definitely not all of them. You can bet that Jon's whole part in this scheme was small, it's international. Even if we get all the names on this list, this is probably a small fraction of the people involved."

"Will they come after me?"

He shrugs. "Maybe. Look, we're not gonna just leave you to deal with it alone, OK? We'll be here behind the scenes, but we won't be fielding questions in front of cameras. You're the one connected to these people through Jon. Ford and I will just make it more complicated. They'll start looking into our pasts, they might even try to pin it on us."

"I might throw up."

"I already have a plan buzzing around in my head and we'll just kick back here for a few days and figure it all out. I'm certain I can set it up so at the very least Ronin will get out of jail for the comments about getting him arrested. And we can probably get some of the people on this list arrested, but beyond that, Rook..." He throws out his hands. "I have no idea. They could all walk in the end. That's just how the system works."

CHAPTER FORTY

Ronin

On day three, rule one and I are no longer on friendly terms. Maybe because orange is not my color or maybe because this shit is like wearing burlap, or maybe because it smells like it was washed in armpits.

I'm not quite sure, all I know is that I'm done embracing the orange jumpsuit.

On day four condition number one is out in full force. Only now I'm talking to Ford in my head, practically begging him to find Rook and figure this shit out.

On day five I break down and call Antoine collect to ask about her. He denies the charges like he's supposed to and saves my ass.

One day six I stop eating. All I do is think about her. Where is she? Did they find her? Is she safe? Hurt? *Fuck, fuck, fuck!*

On day seven I'm getting ready to admit to everything because I'm not very good at obeying rule three right now.

But my lawyer stood me up today, so luckily, my temporary insanity cures itself and I come back to my senses.

And this is just about the time I admit I suck at this jail shit. One week without Rook and I'm insane. I know now for sure—not that I ever doubted it, but now I have proof—I am addicted to Rook and this is my withdrawal.

It fucking hurts.

I let out a long sigh just as my door buzzes signaling someone's on the other side and wants me to come out.

"Finally, fucking lawyer shows up."

But when the door opens it's not my lawyer. It's a big black dude in a suit. "Flynn, come with me," he says, waving me out of the cell.

Gladly, I think to myself. But now that I'm working I'm all business, so that shit stays tucked. We walk past the door to the visitors' hallway. We walk past the door to the rec area, which I hardly ever see since I'm in solitary. Another door buzzes and then we enter a large room filled with more guards. "What's this, beat-the-shit-out-of-Flynn night?"

"It's ten AM, Flynn."

"Oh, well, no windows in the cell, how am I supposed to know?"

"You're not, now just shut up and watch the fucking TV. Hit play, Lenny."

And just as Lenny hits play I glance up at the screen and see Rook standing at a podium with a shit-ton of microphones in front of her. "What the—"

"Just watch," black suit guy says.

She looks a little nervous as she begins, swiping at a stray piece of hair that whips across her face in the Denver wind. The crawl at the bottom of the screen says Denver County Courthouse. I listen as she tells her story. Mostly calm, mostly strong, but a few moments of hesitation and eye-wiping to thwart off the tears. She describes what she's been doing for the past week. The trip to Chicago, Jon, the secret stash, the fire, the rescue.

She tells of corruption in the FBI, calls that bitch Abelli out by name as being one of them, then rattles off a list of people that has the crowd gasping, time… after time… after time. She ends with a name everyone who lived on the Front Range three years ago recognizes.

Davis Cooperson Smyth. The guy we killed in that last job.

Only that's not how Rook tells it.

Because this guy's name is on record as being part of the major human trafficking ring Rook just blew up with her statement. And Jon, the guy who tried to "kill" us last summer, was part of this whole thing from the beginning. She uses the word *assassin* as she holds up thumb drives and an iPhone that contains a video of Abelli—the network shows this video in-screen as Rook talks—beating the shit out of Jon and then ordering him shot and the house set on fire.

Rook's house in the Chicago burbs. While she was inside. Trying to save people and put the bad guys behind bars.

She even flashes a bit of leg to show what's left of her burns and the cameras can't zoom in on her skin fast enough.

Yeah, she's gorgeous, you assholes, and she's mine, so back the fuck off.

And then Rook goes in for the kill shot.

"The FBI set up Ronin Flynn and his friends as the murderers of the wealthy Boulder businessman, Davis Cooperson Smyth, because they found out he was part of this disgusting crime ring and the other men involved wanted to neutralize the threat. Ronin Flynn, Spencer Shrike, and Ford Aston tried to stop the buying and selling of women and girls years ago, and they almost went to prison for their troubles. They've been badgered repeatedly by these criminals and the general public, constantly threatened and shunned in the community. And this past summer these bad men sent my abusive ex-husband to assassinate us. But he failed and I shot him in self-defense."

Ho. Leee. Shit.

Rook just flipped that whole case on its head.

I laugh and when I look around every one of these guys laughs with me. The suit pokes me with his elbow. "She's good, man. We know she's full of shit, you know she's full of shit, but hey, she's still damn good. And I guess no one cares that one less sadist who was buying and selling humans in the hills above Boulder is dead. Your lawyer's here too, by the way. This presser was outside the courthouse because the charges were just dropped and you're gonna walk out of here just as soon as we process the paperwork."

The guards let me hang out in their break room for the duration of my stay. They even give me back my clothes and feed me donuts and coffee.

And I can't stop fucking smiling.

My little Gidget just saved my ass.

Shit, who am I kidding. My little Gidget just saved a whole bunch of people's asses. Women and girls who were kidnapped and those who might've been in the future. She blew open a crime ring that spanned more than a hundred and fifty people.

Even after Rook leaves the podium we all sit and watch as the different news personalities discuss what just happened and run down the timeline.

At seven AM Eastern this morning the State Department was tipped off that a private jet traced to a Columbian drug cartel had landed at the Fort Collins airport with a known representative on board. At the same time, bank records from an account attached to Agent Abelli were also mysteriously forwarded to the same authorities, documenting a transaction the night before out of the Cayman Islands.

A half a million dollars was transferred from the drug lord to Abelli and that little money move has Ford written all over it. He set that sale up with the cartel guy and Abelli probably had no clue it was even going down.

The screen switches to the video Rook talked about in her statement. The one where Abelli tells Jon he plans on selling Rook to a Columbian drug lord for half a million dollars.

All three of the women sitting on the news panel on screen do a collective "mmm-hmm," complete with neck roll, because Abelli is guilty as sin in their eyes.

Enter the court of public opinion.

Abelli has been tried and sentenced. And we're only an hour into the bust.

On top of that, the network states that sources inside the State Department confirm that Abelli's Cayman account can also be directly tied back to the money stolen from "that dirty bastard"—the woman anchor talking actually calls him this on camera—Davis Cooperson Smyth when he was killed three years ago.

Enter nice tidy noose hanging Agent Abelli by his own FBI-issued tie.

I can barely hold down a snicker because this little move proves that Spencer really is a genius. According to Rook, Abelli killed Cooperson Smyth for reasons unknown, but presumably related to this whole crime ring, looted his bank accounts, and stuffed it into a Cayman Island bank. Then used that account to accept money from a Columbian drug cartel so he could sell Rook Corvus into a life of sexual slavery.

One by one, people are arrested on live TV. The state senator in Illinois, the two US House members right out of their DC offices, several high-ranking FBI members including Abelli here in Denver, and on and on. Even the Columbian drug rep is held.

After the specifics are dissected the news people talk book deals and then the personal stuff comes out. A Japanese erotica cover flashes on the screen and they discuss Rook's recent stint as a body-painting model on a post-production reality TV show.

I think Spencer Shrike is negotiating a new contract with the Biker Channel right fucking now.

They leave the Japanese book cover up on screen as they talk and this makes me smile. Because it's the sweet one in the pink dress where she looks like Gidget, not the one with my hand between her legs where I look like the devil.

The whole country goes wild over Rook.

The mayors of Denver and Fort Collins almost come to blows trying to claim her when they do an impromptu news conference.

And every major news channel has a van outside the jail waiting to get a peek at us when they set me free. The tragic girl who swoops in against all odds to save a local golden boy from being the fall guy for an international crime ring.

When they say that shit, I really do laugh.

It takes DPD almost all day to process me out and at the end of it all black suit guy, whose name is actually Detective Carl Murphy, is riding down the elevator to the garage with me. I'm so ready to see my Rook I'm actually nervous.

She's waiting where they keep the cop cars in order to foil the reporters. The elevator doors open and I hold my breath until she comes into view. She's stopped mid-stride, like she was pacing. And then she is nothing but blurry motion as she runs toward me and flings herself at my chest. I catch her and pull her tight, cupping her ass and copping a feel at the same time.

Life beyond Rook's face ceases to exist.

I kiss her. Not hard and desperate, no. I kiss her softly. I kiss her like the precious thing she is. I kiss her gently. And passionately. And carefully.

And when our tongues are tired of the kiss and we need to come up for air, I dip my mouth into her neck and whisper, "What did you do?"

She leans back in my arms, but her legs are still wrapped around my middle and my hands are still cupped under her ass. "Fiona, it's me, Shrek. I rescued you from your tower to prove I'll fight for us. I'll fight for us every single time. You'll never even have to wonder if I'll be there, because I'll show the fuck up before that thought can even cross your mind. I want you, Ronin, and I'll risk everything for you. I will never walk out on you."

I squeeze her. I just want to make her part of me, pull her so close that we merge together and become one soul. "I love the fuck out of you, ya know."

She smiles and then gets a little more serious. "I hope you still have it," she says.

"Have what, babe?"

"My heart. Because it's the only one I got and I don't want to lose it."

I pat my chest. "I put it right here, Gidget, right next to mine. I'm gonna hold on to it for you. Keep it safe forever."

Antoine throws us a huge party. Everyone shows up.

And relief washes over me for the first time in a long time. Relief that says things are gonna be OK now.

Rook didn't drink even one beer tonight. Not even one. I noticed this early so I stopped drinking too. She's perceptive, but so am I. It's part of my training. Usually I watch so I can imitate later, bring those feelings and emotions out in modeling or lying to the fucking cops during an interrogation. But with Rook I watch because I want to learn more. I want to find her secrets and uncover her soul.

What she said at the press conference revealed a lot about her, but I know there's more. And if she's getting ready to tell me tonight, the last thing I want to be is drunk when she finally gets enough courage to say it.

I'm already in bed, waiting for her to come out of the bathroom. The water shuts off as she finishes brushing her teeth, then the door handle jiggles and she appears wearing some lacy pink boy shorts and a white tank top.

Just Rook.

But she's got something in her hand when she gets in bed and I know this is it.

"I have something to show you, Ronin."

I look at the paper clenched in her fist and then up at her eyes. Tears are already flowing down her face. "What is it, babe?"

She wipes them away and then thrusts the crumpled paper towards me. I take it and realize it's a picture.

My world stops.

When she'd told me she'd lost a baby, I'd figured it was early in the pregnancy. But in this picture she is very pregnant.

And she looks young in that peach dress. Her expression says she's happy, her hair is pulled back, and her bare feet and ankles are so swollen I almost start to worry about pregnant Rook. When I look up she's got her hands over her mouth, trying to stifle the sobs. I hug her close and we sink down into the covers a little more. "What happened?" I ask in a soft voice.

She opens her mouth to speak, then stops and shrugs her shoulders. "It was an accident." She nods her head and says it again. "A terrible accident and I lost the baby. I do want kids, Ronin, but this"—she taps the picture with her finger—"this feels like it happened *today*, that's how bad it still hurts. I almost had him, Ronin. My son was two weeks away from being born." And then she breaks and rivers pour down her cheeks. "I'm sorry I'm so emotional and indecisive, but I'm just not over it yet." Her eyes peer up to me, her dark lashes heavy with tears. "That baby…" She stops and chokes on a sob and my chest is suddenly filled with sadness. An aching that pours into me and makes me hold her tighter. "I was gonna name him Jake." She looks away and takes a deep breath. "And his crib was white."

"Rook, I'm so sorry, babe." I feel like total shit dragging her to that baby store.

"It's not your fault, Ronin. I tried to forget about it, to pretend it never happened." She looks up at me again. "But it did happen. And I can't be over it yet because I never took the time to just… experience it. But I'm gonna do that now. I'm gonna make an appointment with a counselor. And one day…" She stops to sniff and wipe her face, taking her time until every last tear is dry and her breathing is slow and calm. She turns those bright blue eyes up at me and nods. "One day, I'll be ready."

At that same moment I give her what she needs, I tell her what she wants to hear and what I need her to understand. "I'll be here waiting. I will wait forever. If that's what it takes. I'll wait for you until the end of time."

She takes the picture and places it gently on her bedside table and then snuggles down into my chest. "You saved me, Ronin."

"And you saved me, Rook."

"So I guess we're even."

"I guess we are."

"And I'm still Shrek because I'm the one who thought of it."

I laugh and kiss her on the head.

My world will never be the same. This girl blew in like the spring wind and whipped me around like a hurricane. She took over my life, she got Spencer to commit to her, and she made Ford feel things. Antoine and Elise love her so much they want us to be godparents and she got an entire city to cheer for her and set me free.

She is a force.

And she's not done yet, I can feel it.

Hurricane Rook is just picking up speed.

EPILOGUE

Ford

The Chaput New Year's Eve party is famous in Denver. I'm not a party person and for me New Year's Eve is a time to be alone, so I've only ever been once besides this year. I wouldn't even be here tonight if we weren't filming for the season finale of Shrike Bikes, but Rook disappeared almost the entire month of December with Ronin. First the GIDGET runway show in LA, then a week in Cancun, then Christmas.

So, here I am, trying to pin her ass down and get this over with.

I'd rather be anywhere but here. I'd rather talk to anyone but her.

The entire studio has been cleared of equipment and replaced with tables and a dance floor. The band is playing, the lighting is moody and atmospheric, and there are almost three hundred people here all dressed in black. I've finished the exit interviews for everyone except Rook, but she's conveniently made herself scarce.

A waitress walks by with a tray and I tap her on the shoulder as she passes. "Have you seen Miss Corvus?" I ask politely. I creep her out, I can tell, because she immediately pulls away from me and then points wordlessly over the crowd to Antoine's office.

She's gone before I can thank her.

It's quite difficult to be polite and when I'm handed rudeness in return, it makes me want to morph back into the old me.

I drop that thought as I make my way through the throngs of people and spy Rook standing just inside the door with Veronica. They are thick as thieves these days. If I were Spencer I'd watch out. They will be into trouble soon, if they're not already.

Ronnie is wearing a short black dress with very high heels. Her look says she takes her fun seriously.

Rook, on the other hand, is dressed like a dark princess. Her dress is not a dress. It's a gown. A long midnight-blue gown that breaks the black only rule, but no one cares because she is stunning. The dress has a tight strapless bodice and elaborate skirts that touch the ground. Her hair is flowing down her back in long waves and atop her head is a shiny blue cardboard tiara.

Just as she turns and spies me, the light catches the blue of her eyes and her crown at the same time. It's like a flashbulb and my mind takes a picture.

"Rook," I say loudly and with a smile. She winces and it's official. She's been avoiding me. "It's your turn, let's go." Veronica pats her on the shoulder like she needs her sympathy and that makes me angry. But I strike through that emotion and beckon my friend with a finger.

"Ford," she starts. "I'm not in the mood. I'm tired of talking. I'm sorta drunk. I'm not ready for this. I'm—"

She goes on and on like that but she follows like a good girl and I just tune it out. We exit the studio and walk down the hallway to the room where I've set up the camera. When I wave her through the doorway she's still talking about waiting guests and Ronin missing her if she stays too long.

I nod. *Yes, yes, yes, I get it*, that nod says. I motion for her to sit. She sits. She always does as she's told when I'm the one asking.

It should make me feel good, that I have this control over her. But it doesn't.

I sit across from her and sigh.

And it's only then that she notices. I'm surprised it took her so long, her skills at reading body language are astute.

"What?" she asks. "What's going on? Did something happen?"

"I'm not going to tape an exit interview of you, Rook. We have so much footage of you from the news, there's no need."

She smiles and the knife slips in. She gathers her dress in her fingertips and rises out of the chair. "Good, then I'm not needed here and I'll just be going," she says, twisting the knife just a little.

"I'm leaving," I say quickly.

"What?" she asks, halting her fleeing feet mid-stride. "But it's not midnight yet."

"I just want you to know I did it all for you," I say, ignoring her statement. "And I'd do it again if that's what makes you happy. I only ever wanted what's best for you."

Her whole body softens at my words. "Ford…"

"And I understand why you wanted to stay in community college and finish your general ed classes and not transfer into Boulder just yet. Online classes are better. The weirdoes and haters are thinning, but they're still out there, so that keeps you safe. I'm proud of you, I want you to know that. Whatever makes you happy makes me happy."

She sits back down, rests her elbows on her knees and props her chin up in her hands. Surely she knew this would have to end eventually.

"If it were anyone else, anyone but you who wanted me to give them so much for so little in return, I would've walked away and never looked back a long time ago. But you make it so, *so* difficult to turn away. And I couldn't let the sadness and pain touch you. It drives me mad when you're unhappy. I lie awake at night wishing I could bring Jon back to life and torture him myself. I wanted to kill that Abelli asshole for even entertaining the thought of selling you. I want to pull you into my chest right now and keep you for myself. Because, Rook, I just want you." I stop to study the shock on her face for a moment before continuing.

"I. Fucking. Want. You," I say, my voice a deep rumble in my throat. "If I'd found you first instead of Ronin, you'd be mine right now. And I'd never let you go. I know what you think of me, of the girls I have, of my"—I look away for a fraction of a second, then drag my heated stare back to her slumped shoulders and sad face—"idiosyncrasies. But I am nothing like Jon. I have never been anything like those men on that list."

"I know that, Ford," she says softly as she reaches out to touch my arm.

"Don't." I pull away before she makes contact with my suit coat. "You can*not* touch me. If you touch me…" I shake my head, unable to continue.

"If I touch you what?" she asks with an air of challenge.

My own mother hasn't even touched me as many times as Rook has, so this probably does deserve an explanation. "If you touch me I'll touch you back. I'll cup your face and kiss your mouth. I'll hold you close and make you choose me." I stop and swallow hard and then lean into her space and whisper, "I'll ruin everything if you touch me. I'll ruin us. I'll ruin this. I'll ruin you, just like you said. I'll ruin you and I'll ruin your life. And I love you too much to ruin you. So I'm leaving."

Her shoulders slump a little more. "I don't want you to leave, Ford. I'm not sure life without you is possible."

"And I'm not sure life with you is possible. I can't watch you with him, Rook. I'm seething with jealousy. It infuriates me that time and time again he gets what he wants. Ronin pulls love towards him like he's gravity." I stop to laugh. "He only has to ask and love appears in his life. And me? I beg for it. I want love more than anything, yet everyone thinks I'm insufferable." I kneel down in front of her and shake my head. "Everyone but you, Rook. You are the only person on this entire Earth I care about. And you belong to someone else. And if it were anyone but him I'd just take you and say fuck the consequences. But you chose one of two people who will stand by me no matter what I do. And even though these days I count Ronin as a friend, and I would never betray him, I'm so fucking jealous. His life since Antoine has been one long string of lucky breaks. And every day I ask myself, why? Why does he get you? Why does he deserve this luck and I'm always left with nothing?"

I shrug and stand up and her eyes follow me, making her head tilt.

It takes every ounce of willpower not to slip my hand across the milky white skin on her throat, grasp the back of her neck, pull her towards me, and claim her mouth. "This isn't even me talking right now. I don't feel these things, Rook. Ever. When did I become capable of jealousy?" I huff out some air. "Well, it's not really a mystery. It was the day I met you, that's when. You've changed me, Rook. You make me weak, you make me stumble, you make me fall, and even though I know you'll pick me up if I ask you to, it's not enough. I want you to make me stronger, just like I made you. I want it all or I want nothing. And since I can't have it all, I'll take nothing."

She stares up at me in silence, the shock of my words displayed on her face.

I can't stand to see the hurt in her eyes. I can't stand to see her fear and sadness as the realization of what's happening finally sinks in.

So I do what I have to do. I make it worse.

So she's left with no more doubts about what kind of man I am. So she will release her hold on me. So she will stop looking at me like she cares.

So I can let go and move on.

I turn away.

I walk out.

And I never look back.

Books four and five in this series are called Ford and Spencer, respectively. Book Four is about Ford and Book five is about Spencer and Veronica.

Spencer is the complete ending of the story arc of Rook, Ronin, Ford, Spencer, and Veronica. And a few new characters too—Ashleigh, Sasha, James, and Merc. All of whom intersect in the book called The Company and standalones called Meet Me In The Dark and Wasted Lust.

So if you're looking to enter a WORLD. If you're looking to meet characters so real, you feel like you know them. If you're looking to go on the ride of your life with Rook and her friends, keep reading, bitches.

I got you.

Julie
JA Huss

About The Author

JA Huss never wanted to be a writer and she still dreams of that elusive career as an astronaut. She originally went to school to become an equine veterinarian but soon figured out they keep horrible hours and decided to go to grad school instead. That Ph.D wasn't all it was cracked up to be (and she really sucked at the whole scientist thing), so she dropped out and got a M.S. in forensic toxicology just to get the whole thing over with as soon as possible.

After graduation she got a job with the state of Colorado as their one and only hog farm inspector and spent her days wandering the Eastern Plains shooting the shit with farmers.

After a few years of that, she got bored. And since she was a homeschool mom and actually does love science, she decided to write science textbooks and make online classes for other homeschool moms.

She wrote more than two hundred of those workbooks and was the number one publisher at the online homeschool store many times, but eventually she covered every science topic she could think of and ran out of shit to say.

So in 2012 she decided to write fiction instead. That year she released her first three books and started a career that would make her a New York Times bestseller and land her on the USA Today Bestseller's List eighteen times in the next three years.

Her books have sold millions of copies all over the world, the audio version of her semi-autobiographical book,

Eighteen, was nominated for an Audie award in 2016, her book Mr. Perfect was nominated for a Voice Arts Award in 2017 and her book Taking Turns was nominated for an Audie award in 2018.

She also writes book and screenplays with her friend, actor and writer, Johnathan McClain. Their first book, Sin With Me, will release on March 6, 2018. And they are currently working with MGM as producing partners to turn their adaption of her series, The Company, into a TV series.

She lives on a ranch in Central Colorado with her family, two donkeys, four dogs, three birds, and two cats.

If you'd like to learn more about JA Huss or get a look at her schedule of upcoming appearances, visit her website at www.JAHuss.com or www.HussMcClain.com to keep updated on her projects with Johnathan. You can also join her fan group, Shrike Bikes, on Facebook, www.facebook.com/groups/shrikebikes and follow her Twitter handle, @jahuss.

www.ingramcontent.com/pod-product-compliance
Lightning Source LLC
Chambersburg PA
CBHW020344310726
48979CB00015B/2502/J
* 9 7 8 1 9 5 0 2 3 2 3 4 5 *